THE
WOMEN
AND
LANGUAGE
DEBATE

THE WOMEN AND LANGUAGE DEBATE

a sourcebook

edited by

CAMILLE   ROMAN

SUZANNE   JUHASZ

CRISTANNE   MILLER

rutgers university press • *new brunswick, new jersey*

Library of Congress Cataloging-in-Publication Data

The Women and language debate : a sourcebook / edited by Camille
  Roman, Suzanne Juhasz, Cristanne Miller.
      p.   cm.
    Includes bibliographical references and index.
    ISBN 0-8135-2011-8—ISBN 0-8135-2012-6 (pbk.)
    1. Women—Language.   2. Language and languages—Sex differences.
  3. Feminism.   I. Roman, Camille   II. Juhasz, Suzanne.
  III. Miller, Cristanne.
  P120.W66W63   1994
    306.4' 4' 082—dc20   *93-7642*
                                                                                  CIP

British Cataloging-in-Publication information available

to our families

CONTENTS

PART THREE   Cristanne Miller

ACKNOWLEDGMENTS

The Women and Language Debate: A Sourcebook would not have been possible without the collective enterprise of the thinkers included in this volume; to them, we all owe an immeasurable debt. As we acknowledge in our general introductory essay, we are indebted as well to countless scholars and researchers whom we have not been able to cite fully. To all of these colleagues from whom we have learned about language and gender, we express our deepest appreciation.

Among our many advisers and colleagues, the following were of special help in the development and completion of this project. Camille Roman wishes to thank Paula Bennett, Mutlu Blasing, Walter Davis, Coppélia Kahn, William Keach, Elizabeth Kirk, George Monteiro, Susanne Woods, Patricia Yaeger, and the participants in the 1991–1992 seminar at the Pembroke Center for Teaching and Research on Women for their contributions to the general development of Part One, "Female Sexual Drives, Subjectivity, and Language: The Dialogue with/beyond Freud and Lacan." Part Three of this volume, "Who Says What to Whom: Empirical Studies on Language and Gender," benefitted from Nancy Henley's generous sharing of her expertise in this area, and from the valuable advice of Susan Gal. Deborah Burke provided helpful comments on a draft of Cristanne Miller's introductory essay.

For financial and staff support, we wish to thank Pomona College, Brown University, and Washington State University. In addition, Camille Roman expresses appreciation for funding from the Jean Starr Untermeyer Fellowship, Department of English, Brown University, and a research completion grant, the Division of Humanities and Social Sciences, the Office of Dean John Pierce, Washington State University. She also thanks Alex Hammond, acting chair, Department of English, Washington State University, for timely and invaluable research assistance and grant support, and the Humanities Research Center.

To Leslie Mitchner, our editor at Rutgers, we express deep appreciation for her invaluable role in the development of this project; and we especially thank her for her enthusiam, her counsel, and her professionalism. We are grateful as well to the rest of the staff at the Press for their dedication and support, especially Marilyn Campbell, Stephen Maikowski, Bonnie Kaplan, Kate Harrie, John Romer, Tricia Politi, Lisa Woodley, and Ann Cham, and to our copy editor, Susan Thornton.

Finally, we wish to thank each other.

THE
WOMEN
AND
LANGUAGE
DEBATE

INTRODUCTION

Do women talk like ladies—that is, differently from men? Is language patriarchal—because some thinkers say it is acquired during the oedipal period of gender and sexual identification with the father? Or do infants develop language with their mothers in the preoedipal period? Is language comprehended and used differently by women and men? These are some of the questions that have consistently recurred in the fields of psychoanalysis, anthropology, linguistics, and literary criticism and theory since the turn of the century. With the international revival of feminist politics and research in the last few decades, such questions have become increasingly important. This book, which gathers together for the first time under one cover influential essays that have sparked the various historical moments in the debate, provides a history of language and gender study to help pursue these questions. This history is crucial to an understanding of the theory and politics that inform the various stances toward language and gender and the current questions in this debate.

Our sourcebook provides an overview of the issues of the debate in the 1990s as well as an outline of the history behind them. A brief explanation of the terms in our title—*The Women and Language Debate*—may help to clarify the relationship between that history and the terms which dominate in the discourse about women's speech. Until relatively recently in popular and academic discussions, men's speech has been perceived as standard or normative, and hence has been used as the yardstick against which women's speech has been measured. Questions about language and *gender* have been articulated almost solely in terms of women's relation to language, while examinations of *language* have traditionally concerned themselves with men's speech and conceptions. One studied either "language"—the norm—or "women's language"—the speech that deviated. Studies focusing on women's relation to language provided the basis for differentiating between men's and women's speech. Within this perspective, both women and men were seen in monolithic or universal and ahistorical terms, so that one could speak of "woman" and "man" as representative of the group—of all women and all men. Over the last few decades, the assumption that "men's language" constitutes a norm and hence contains no gendered elements has been effectively overthrown. As a consequence, most theoretical discussion has begun to shift away from the exclusive focus on women and language and toward the examination of gender and language, although much work that explores questions of language and gender continues to take women's relation to language as its focus. However, now such work typically regards men's relationship to language as equally marked by gender and tends moreover to acknowledge the impact of other social and cultural factors in the individual's environment.

The general critical recognition that gender is not synonymous with female, however, has not put an end to debate about what the terms "gender," "women," and "language" mean. As the authors presented in this volume indicate, these three terms are arguable. While some regard gender as an essentialist entity based on biology, others believe that gender is a social-linguistic-cultural construction. Still others refuse to accept the binary split between culture and biology and insist that gender—and "women"—come into being through both culture and biology. Other theorists stress the plural form of "women" in order to emphasize the movement away from theorizing about an ahistorical, universal entity "woman" and toward inquiring about culturally specific "women." These writers investigate language in the context of specific communities, defined as broadly as race, class, ethnicity, and sexual orientation, or as narrowly as neighborhood. Lastly, "language" is also a term defined and discussed variously. How does it develop? When does it develop? Is there a distinction between "language" and "babbling"? How is language comprehended? What is the relation of language to status or power? How do learned speech patterns affect psychological development, self-esteem, access to power—or even to justice? Is there any such thing as normative or hegemonic language, or does this change with every speaking context and group of speakers? The essays in this book offer a wide range of approaches for formulating and considering such questions.

The essays here are in great demand in research and teaching and come from more than one field of inquiry. They are gathered from a wide scattering of periodicals and collections so diverse that anyone in the past aiming to explore these issues has had to resort to endless xeroxing or the use of review essays and summaries. They are presented here as much as possible in their original and uncut versions. Yet, despite their importance as representations of arguments in the past or the current debate, the selections are not meant to stand as complete statements about any line of inquiry. We wish to present diverse "voices" in the debate rather than a prescriptive canon in the hope that juxtaposing them will generate a spirited exchange between and within the three major fields of language and gender study.

All three of us editing this volume are literary critics, informing our own studies of gender, language, and literary texts through the interdisciplinary perspectives represented here. Inevitably our introductions, selections, and organization of material are related to our primary professional preoccupations. Yet, while we share a single disciplinary position, we believe that the uses of this text are not limited to a focus on literary study. Moreover, our own academic interests and training within the field of literary study are widely divergent, and the essays we have chosen to reprint in our sections reflect that divergence. Additionally, the status of these three areas of focus varies in the discourses of the literary community and in other fields interested in questions of language and gender. Camille Roman's introductory essay begins with French theory grounded in Freudian-Lacanian psychoanalytic thinking and then moves to its interrogation from class and race perspectives. While this line of inquiry on gender and language is the most influential and conspicuous in literary studies, its influence does not extend very far into social science and psychological investigations. To bring this theory to a wider audience, her section focuses on summarizing and elucidating its various positions and counter-positions. Suzanne Juhasz, to the contrary, is working with a psychological tradition that has been little utilized for language study and gender issues. Consequently, her essay and section are more hortatory in nature, developing an argument about gender and language that challenges many of the major conclusions of the Freudian and French-influenced theorists. In turn, Cristanne Miller's essay introduces empirical studies in language and gender to literary critics and others who have typically made little use of this field's findings and reviews the epistemology of empirical research for readers in the social sciences, linguistics, and psychology most likely already familiar with such material. In doing so, she not only interprets the premises of this research so that it may be more broadly understood and utilized but also challenges assumptions held by key theorists in the earlier two sections. Taken as a whole, then, the three introductory essays offer a range of ways of presenting and interpreting the rich body of material that is contained in this volume.

Part One, "Female Sexual Drives, Subjectivity and Language: The Dialogue with/beyond Freud and Lacan," begins with Sigmund Freud and the French Freudian interpreter Jacques Lacan. Freud and Lacan define the original psychoanalytic theories of gender and of language: namely, that language development is connected to the child's identification with the father during the oedipal period. For the daughter, this means that she must turn her sexual drives from her mother to her father as she acquires subjectivity and language. Thus her transformation into a person with language is based on her heterosexual orientation toward her father, at the same time her sexual differentiation from him is structured by and in language. This section then presents a series of feminist responses and theories by Julia Kristéva, Hortense Spillers, Hélène Cixous, Luce Irigaray, and Gayatri Spivak to explore heterogeneous approaches to women's access to language. These later essays not only consider the role of female sexuality but begin to explore such equally vital salient features of female subjectivity and women's relationship to language as class, race, and ethnicity. These writers, especially Spillers and Spivak, rewrite the terms of the debate, stressing the urgency of theorizing within a range of specific cultural and social contexts.

Part Two, "Object Relations and Women's Use of Language: Readings from British and American Psychology," begins with a history of object relations in psychoanalytic theory. The focus on object relations, rather than instinctual drives, for generating human development disputes the pivotal role of the father for initiating identity formation and language use. The influence of the mother during the preoedipal period assumes centrality, even as development is understood to be interpersonal in nature, self-identity to be implicated in relationship with others. These premises have important repercussions for theories about the practice and significance of language in culture. The discussion of object-relations theory is followed first by feminist interpretations of this material, which add the issue of gender to developmental paradigms, and then by explorations of language acquisition and functioning, which focus on ways in which language evolves in the mother-child relationship. A selection from the writings of D. W. Winnicott represents object-relations theory. Feminist analyses of gender and development by Nancy Chodorow, Judith Jordan, and Jessica Benjamin are included, along with studies of language and development by Daniel Stern,

Colwyn Trevarthen, John Dore, and Jean Berko Gleason. Part Two concludes with a discussion of some very recent multicultural and non-heterosexual studies of development based in object-relations theory by Cynthia Garcia Coll and Wendy Rosen, which further expand the implications of associating earliest developmental patterns with language use.

Part Three, "Who Says What To Whom? Empirical Studies on Language and Gender," provides a brief survey of empirical linguistic, psychological, and anthropological studies related to language. It then moves quickly from the field's early focus on women's language as deviant from a male "norm" to current research perspectives that acknowledge multiple constructions of gender, hence both displacing male language as normative and framing questions of gender within intersecting constructions of race, class, and other cultural and social features of modern society. This section offers contemporary essays on a variety of subjects within this broad field. The studies by Mykol Hamilton, Barbara Hunter, and Shannon Stuart-Smith, and Marianne LaFrance and Eugene Hahn focus on how sexist speech patterns or gender-based interpretations of speech in the English language may affect the comprehension and, in dramatic cases, the lives of those hearing or described by such language. Penelope Brown and Marjorie Harness Goodwin examine speech patterns of particular groups of girls or women in particular cultural and social circumstances, while Candace West investigates sexual difference in initiating topics in conversations between women and men. Nancy Henley and Cheris Kramarae as well as Susan Gal question in broadly theoretical terms how gender-based cultural structures and assumptions interact with types of language use in affecting or revealing power relationships, while Penelope Eckert and Sally McConnell-Ginet emphasize the importance of acknowledging an individual's shifting position among several local linguistic communities. All three of these essays argue that both interdisciplinary and multicultural or crosscultural perspectives are crucial to a full understanding of the operations and structures of language, and that such perspectives place important constraints on the "universalizing" tendencies of theory.

By and large, exchange among the scholars in these broadly defined fields of research on the women and language debate is rare. These fields have typically dismissed each other's positions rather than built upon them. When philosophers talk about gender and language, they do so without recourse to information available in empirical studies. And vice versa. When Freudian psychoanalytic theorists talk about gender and language, they do so without recourse to the data of developmental psychology's empirical studies. And vice versa. Similarly, empirical research in the sciences and social sciences rarely takes into account the symbolic and psychological thinking in either Freudian-related or object-relations theory.

Yet, as the essays in this volume attest, there are promising signs of a growing dialogue across the fields of study on gender and language as well as increased recognition of the need for more such work. We hope that the juxtaposition of studies from these different fields in a single volume will allow for and encourage a dialogue among them by removing some of the practical barriers that presently exist for studying women and language in a complex and interdisciplinary way. Because of this sourcebook, those interested in linguistics will also have easy access to essays revealing the linguistic basis of French theories on language and gender. Psychoanalytic thinkers will have easy access to empirical studies that may critique their directions and findings, as well as to key essays in their own field. Object-relations-based psychologists may see more clearly the relationship of their own research to language and gender studies in the other two fields.

While we believe that our collection contributes uniquely to the ongoing debate about language and gender by bringing together an array of perspectives, we wish to pay tribute to a few crucial collections of essays that have maintained and popularized previous work in this area, thus encouraging the sophistication and range of developments to which we call attention here. *Women and Language in Literature and Society* (1980) edited by Sally McConnell-Ginet, Ruth Borkar, and Nelly Furman is a pathbreaking interdisciplinary collection offering essays from the 1970s that juxtapose "discussions of language in literature with discussions of language in ordinary life" (xiii). Barrie Thorne and Nancy Henley have edited, with Cheris Kramarae, *Language, Gender, and Society* (1983), which contains comprehensive annotated bibliographies that are invaluable to scholars of language and gender in all areas and fields—theoretical and descriptive as well as empirical. Deborah Cameron's *The Feminist Critique of Language: A Reader* (1990) has contributed vitally to work on gender and language with recent essays in literary criticism and linguistics. Her valuable earlier edited collection with Jennifer Coates, entitled *Women in Their Speech Communities: New Perspectives on Language and Sex* (1988), studies British and British post-colonial discourses and speech communities. Joyce Penfield has edited *Women and Language in Transition* (1987), an important collection of empirical and analytical essays, which includes practical suggestions on how to eliminate sex bias in language. Finally, David Graddol and Joan Swann offer a vital examination of language and sex difference in *Gender Voices* (1989). In addition, we wish to recognize the many excellent single-author book-length studies, as well as articles, reviews, and course offerings, that have contributed to the debate. This sourcebook would not have been possible without this collective enterprise. Readers are invited to begin exploring this research through the suggestions for further reading at the end of each introductory essay; they are presented to encourage readers to consider the gender and language debate from crossdisciplinary and multidisciplinary perspectives.

Just as this work collects essays from several fields of study, we envision our audience as a heterogeneous group of scholars of literature, psychology, anthropology, linguistics, women's studies, and other disciplines, as well as many kinds of readers inside and outside the classroom. We hope this sourcebook will be used as a portable interdisciplinary library of readings on the debate that will enable readers to participate in today's conversations about gender and language.

C.R., S.J., C.M.

SELECTED BIBLIOGRAPHY

CAMERON, DEBORAH. *The Feminist Critique of Language: A Reader.* London/New York: Routledge, 1990.

———— AND JENNIFER COATES. *Women in Their Speech Communities: New Perspectives on Language and Sex.* London and New York: Longman, 1988.

GRADDOLL, DAVID, AND JOAN SWANN. *Gender Voices*. New York: Basil Blackwell, 1989.

McCONNELL-GINET, SALLY, RUTH BORKER, AND NELLY FURMAN, EDS. *Women and Language in Literature and Society*. New York: Praeger, 1980.

PENFIELD, JOYCE. *Women and Language in Transition*. Albany: SUNY Press, 1987.

THORNE, BARRIE, CHERIS KRAMARAE, AND NANCY HENLEY, EDS. *Language, Gender, and Society*. Rowley, Mass.: Newbury House, 1983.

part one

FEMALE SEXUAL DRIVES, SUBJECTIVITY, AND LANGUAGE

The Dialogue with/beyond Freud and Lacan

O ur Introduction asks, "Is language patriarchal—because some thinkers say it is acquired during the oedipal period of gender and sexual identification with the father?" To this question we might add, "If language is patriarchal—and therefore gendered—how do women and men acquire language? What roles do their sexual drives play?" In exploring questions like these, many scholars, especially in literary studies, have found it useful to turn to the psychoanalytic-based theories about the nature of language and the process of language acquisition presented in this section. The original psychoanalytic theory, to which these scholars respond, is grounded in Sigmund Freud's revolutionary thinking about human sexuality and subjectivity in the early part of this century and Jacques Lacan's pioneering work in language acquisition. According to the Freudian-Lacanian psychoanalytic model, children develop subjectivity and language in connection with their sexual and gender identification during the oedipal period. This means that both male and female children must turn their instinctual sexual drives from their mothers to their fathers in order to become persons with language; at the same time their sexual difference is structured and represented by and in language. Since the introduction of this language acquisition paradigm, the intertwining of sexuality and gender with subjectivity and language has been a central topic of debate.

Beginning with the French linguist and psychoanalyst Julia Kristéva's classic critique of the patriarchal bias in this model of subjectivity and language and her formulation in the 1970s of a bisexual model of language to include the role of the mother, two major lines of inquiry on the sexed and gendered nature of language and of language acquisition have developed. Some scholars, like Kristéva and Hortense Spillers, have focused on exploring mothering in culture and language as well as language development for both male and female speakers. Others, like Hélène Cixous, Luce Irigaray, and Gayatri Spivak, have been more concerned with the problem of women's access to and manipulation of language—and the sexual and symbolic locations of language sources specifically for women. During the 1980s, this major field's research on gender and language as a whole was transformed by these writers, especially Spillers and Spivak, who stress the importance of theorizing within culturally and socially specific contexts that consider the social and cultural features of class, race, and ethnicity in the construction of heterogeneous female sexualities and subjectivities—and relationships to language. By the end of the 1980s, the original terms of this debate had been effectively rewritten.

Before turning to a brief overview of these topics of investigation on gender and language, we need to understand more about the work of Freud and Lacan in order to become adequately acquainted with the original psychoanalytic theory of language. The historical starting point for this theory is Freud's work analyzing the development of masculinity and femininity on the basis of sexual drives during the oedipal period oriented toward the father. Freud's essay "Femininity," presented here, contains his now famous definitions of masculinity and femininity in which his notion of the proper "norm"—male sexual anatomy and drive—is used as the model for female development. Three basic premises in his theory of female development are important for discussions on gender and sexuality's relationship to language. First, female subjectivity, like male subjectivity, is rooted in a sexuality defined in relation to the father. Second, women are different from and unequal to men, because they lack the penis, and therefore desire men in order to obtain a penis. Third, the definition of "normative" or "feminine" woman depends upon heterosexual desire. In sum, female heterosexuality is compulsory for a normative female identity and hence relationship to language.

Freud's definition of "woman" based on a male "norm" informs the entire essay. When Freud discusses how boys and girls arrive at the oedipal phase or the stage of identification with their fathers, for example, he insists on using the male as the model of behavior and observes that "the little girl is a little man" (146). She, like the boy with his "small penis," is interested during the pre-oedipal period in sexuality and attempts to derive sexual pleasure from her "still smaller clitoris." In other words, the clitoris is a "penis-equivalent" in the pre-oedipal phase, which is tied to the mother.

Because Freud's project is phallocentric, with the penis at the center of desire either because boys have it or little girls wish to have it, he insists that the girl must relinquish this "penis-equivalent" in order to interact with the penis she lacks. In order for the "little girl" to develop into a "normal" woman, he argues that her pleasure in her clitoris must be eradicated and replaced by the "truly feminine" or heterosexual organ, the vagina. The girl's love-object then must change from the mother to the father as she passes "from her masculine phase" identified with clitoral pleasure to the feminine one associated with the vagina "to which she is biologically destined" (147).

But this biological destiny does not necessarily come easily, according to Freud. The girl's transformation of her desire for her mother into a desire for her father is troublesome, because her phase with her mother is "so rich in content and so long-lasting" (148). Indeed, Freud states that the pre-oedipal attachment to the mother must be understood in order to account for the change to the oedipal father which he attributes to the castration complex. He bases her complex on the idea that "anatomical distinction [between the sexes] must express itself in psychical consequences" (154). Girls hold their mothers responsible for not giving them a penis and develop "penis-envy." They desire their fathers, because of his penis, and desire his child as a penis-substitute. These desires are termed "par excellence . . . feminine," suggesting a link between female sexuality and gender. The absence of a penis results in a sexual desire coded as a "feminine" gender trait.

This intertwining infers that female heterosexuality must be at the base of both women's sexual and gender (social role) development and therefore subjectivity, even though Freud indicates that the girl's turn to the father may not mean the total absence of desire for the mother. He states that studies of psychosexual development do not indicate that sexuality is fixed and static. As he observes, each person is bisexual: "the proportion in which masculine and feminine are mixed in an individual is subject to quite considerable fluctuations" (141). Yet in the case of women, he seems to indicate that women's heterosexuality must always be predominant, suggesting the need to regulate the clitoris.

Objections to Freud's construction of "woman" are numerous, as one might expect in such a richly complex theory. The major criticisms are worth considering here, because his views are fundamental premises for the work on gender and language in this section. His formulation of "woman" has been attacked because of its overtly phallocentric bias, which displays itself most prominently, perhaps, in his insistence that heterosexuality be the condition for "normative woman" and that "woman" be defined in relation to a male model.

Proponents of Freud, however, believe that the advantages of Freud's interpretation outweigh these problems. They find it helpful to draw upon his exposure of the inner workings of phallocentric culture because it provides a theory of the intersections between gender and power. The relationship between gender and power in furthering the interests of male dominance, for example, is blatantly revealed in his derivation of "woman" from the male, rather than from extensive observations of women, and in his insistence that female sexuality must be oriented toward men. Moreover, Freud offers an understanding of how binary categorization serves male domination or the asymmetrical power arrangements between male and female. In the formulation of a binary, one term is contrasted unfavorably with another, and circular thinking may be substituted for logic. For example, female is female because she lacks the male penis. The colonized is colonized because it lacks the attributes of the colonizer. One term is placed "above" or "below" the other, connoting both a power positioning and a sexual positioning. As Jacqueline Rose has pointed out, "the force of psychoanalysis is . . . precisely that it gives an account of patriarchal culture as a transhistorical and cross-cultural force. It therefore conforms to a feminist demand for a theory that can explain women's subordination across specific cultures and different historical moments" (90).

As the work on gender and language here attests, Freud has contributed significantly to it. His intimation that the daughter's bond to the pre-oedipal mother is powerful enough to delay, disrupt, or repudiate the father's primacy in the daughter's life has led to the theorizing about the oedipal language model found not only in the work of thinkers like Kristéva and Spillers in this section, but in the major field of object relations in the section that follows. His explanation of the necessary suppression of the clitoris because it does not serve heterosexuality and reproduction has been a point of departure for theorizing and critiquing by Cixous, Irigaray, and Spivak as well as lesbian theorists like Judith Roof.

While these thinkers draw heavily on Freudian thinking, they also draw upon the highly suggestive and imaginative work of Lacan, which is based on his reading of both Freudian psychoanalysis and Saussurean linguistics. Offering an examination of the inner workings of the intersections among selfhood, sexuality, and language, he asserts that all speakers of language must locate themselves in relationship to the phallus, as occurs in Freud's oedipal stage, and must separate themselves from the pre-oedipal mother in order to have the power to speak and to become subjects recognized by culture. Thus he articulates an oedipal theory of language by grafting the acquisition of language onto Freud's oedipal theory of sexuality and subjectivity.

In his influential essay "The Signification of the Phallus" (1958) from *Écrits* included here, Lacan appropriates Freud's work to explain the basis of Saussurean linguistics, which works from the notion that human societies tend to create symbolic systems such as language. He opens the essay by discussing Freud's idea of the unconscious castration complex. For him, the Freudian theory of castration and desire, which forms the basis for human social development, explains the laws of language embodied in the Saussurean theory of the signified and signifier. In Saussure's work the single word or *sign* is the inseparable union of *signifier*, the speech sounds or written marks designating the *sign*, and *signified*, the conceptual meaning of the *sign* or single word. But in Lacan's melding of Saussure and Freud, these terms develop sexuality: "the signifier has an active [masculine] function in determining certain effects in which the signifiable appears as submitting to its mark, by becoming through that passion the signified" (284). Throughout the essay, statements like this continue as the following excerpt indicates: "It can be said that this signifier [phallus] is chosen because it is the most tangible element in the real of sexual copulation, and also the most symbolic in the literal (typographical) sense of the term . . ." (287).

The unconscious, for Lacan, is the site of sexual drives—and the "other scene," which is structured like a language. It reminds speakers of the reorientation of their sexual drives from their mothers to the fathers: of the "splitting" that occurs when speakers enter language through submission to the phallus, which is a signifier, and separate from the pre-oedipal mother, who represents the "jouissance" the "split" speakers desire. As Lacan states, "man cannot aim at being whole . . . while ever the play of displacement and condensation to which he is doomed in the exercise of his functions marks his relation as a subject to the signifier [phallus]" (287). No speaker is a whole or unified subject or ego. Crucial to the Lacanian conception of subjectivity and language here is the fact that the difference between sexes is structured by language, not biology. The "splitting" occurs upon entry into language, which structures the differences between male and female.

As the speaker submits to the phallus, the phallus becomes the symbol of the loss of the mother's body. The child begins its perpetual search through the phallus, or symbolic order, for the desired missing relationship with the pre-oedipal mother. The castration complex and the incest taboo introduced by the father in the oedipal stage prevent the child from returning to the mother's body. Thus the phallus becomes a signifier of law and order in culture by regulating the child's relationship to the mother.

While sons in this theory of language acquisition are not assured that they will gain the phallus with which to speak, daughters are placed in a much more severely disadvantaged position for they can only desire the phallus. As Lacan states, "it is in order to be the phallus, that is to say, the signifier of the desire of the Other, that a woman will reject an essential part of femininity, namely, all her attributes in the masquerade. It is for that which she is not that she wishes to be desired as well as loved. But she finds the signifier of her own desire in the body of him to whom she addresses her demand for love" (290). This suggests that, while a daughter can be represented or spoken of in language by the phallus because of her desire, she cannot represent or speak herself.

While Lacan's work is highly controversial, as thinkers like Kristéva readily point out, his paradigm has been richly mined for the gender and language debate. Lacanian followers, exemplified by Jacqueline Rose in her text *Sexuality in the Field of Vision* (1986), believe that de-essentializing gender, by severing it from biology or the unconscious sexual drives described by Freud and relocating it to culture and language, exposes the regulatory power of male dominance over women. Women are not excluded from language and culture because of their bodies; they are left out because of male dominance. As Rose explains throughout her text, Lacan offers a theory of women's disadvantaged positions in language which is ahistorical and therefore capable of explaining paternal power regardless of culturally and historically specific moments.

Both Kristéva and Spillers contribute significantly to the gender and language debate by countering the Freudian-Lacanian terms for defining the position of women and language in culture and the role of sexual drives in language development for both male and female speakers. Each locates a more powerful position for women through women's reproductive or uterine sexual system, either by embracing mothering fully or by manipulating paternal culture's control over it. Moreover, they insist upon the need to acknowledge the pre-oedipal drives of the child, because they believe either that they are encoded in language for their speakers or that their speakers are deprived of this encoding.

Kristéva counters women's exclusion from language and culture, whether because of their bodies or male dominance or both, by claiming that language includes pre-oedipal drives in relation to the maternal body. This calls into question the primacy of the father's role in language acquisition. Building upon Lacan's work as well as Freud's observations on the powerful pre-oedipal tie between child and mother, she creates a complex theory about subjectivity and language which is arguably a more accurate grafting of the language process onto the Freudian model of human subjectivity. Kristéva's most important contribution to date in the gender and language debate may be this pioneering articulation of the gendered features in language.

She offers a definition of language that states that the imprint of woman's maternal body is inherent in language itself. In *The Revolution in Poetic Language* (1984), she rewrites Lacan's "phallus" model of language and subjectivity, treating the acquisition of both language and subjecthood as a dynamic that begins between mother and both male and female children in the pre-oedipal period and continues beyond the oedipal stage. She takes Chomsky's linguistic theory that all languages ultimately share one universal structure, dictated by the human mind, and maps it onto the pre-oedipal/oedipal binary structure of the mind developed by Freud in order to isolate universal linguistic elements that derive from the pre-oedipal and oedipal stages, respectively. Even more revolutionary is her concept of an interplay between the maternal semiotic and paternal symbolic in the development of subjectivity which builds upon the Freudian observation that the masculine and feminine are in flux within the individual. In this schema of subjectivity and language, neither the maternal nor the paternal is primary.

Kristéva's major goal is the articulation of a feminine (maternal) position in language that is accessible to both women and men. The feminine in language is related to the reexperience of the *jouissance* or physical pleasures of infancy in the pre-oedipal period, which is repressed according to Freud and Lacan in the turn to the father and makes itself heard in language through rhythm, intonation, gaps, meaninglessness, and other forms of cultural, syntactical, and textual disruption.

For chapters 1 and 2 of "The Semiotic and the Symbolic" section in *Revolution in Poetic Language* presented here, an explanation of two terms may be helpful. Semiotic "chora" refers to the mobile, uncertain, and indeterminant non-expressive articulation formed by pre-oedipal bodily/psychical drives or pulsations and rhythms in relation to the nourishing and maternal body. The Symbolic refers to Lacan's formulation of the Symbolic, but Kristéva revises it to indicate that it both depends upon and represses the semiotic "chora" aligned with the mother. Language, then, is indebted both to the phallic signifier of the symbolic, which is associated with the oedipal stage of development, and to the mother of the pre-oedipal period.

Spillers, like Kristéva, is interested in the role of the maternal and paternal in subjectivity and language. Drawing upon Freud and Lacan, she pursues the relationships among sexuality, subjectivity, and language when cultural specificity is considered and hence suggests that their model is culturally and socially marked as well as gendered. She positions psychoanalytic discourse within a culturally and historically specific African-American discourse, asserting that African-American men and women are deprived of the benefits of the mothering and fathering that this model of language assumes. The American "master" language or discourse and culture, in the interest of ethnic hegemony, is grounded on the subjugated black maternal body, but this body has the power to disrupt this "master" language. This "captive and mutilated" object reveals the horror of maternal objectification in the name of Western phallocentrism.

In the essay here entitled "Mama's Baby, Papa's Maybe: An American Grammar Book" (1987), Spillers traces the objectification of both male and female black bodies begun in the texts and trade of captors and recorded in slave narratives. The "reproduction of mothering" in this historic instance, says Spillers, "carries few of the benefits of a *patriarchilized* female gender, which, from one point of view, is the only female gender there is" (73). Further, she reveals that African-American offspring of captive African-American mothers, because of the intervention of slavery and the subsequent questionable access of parents to them, do not necessarily experience the same subjectivity and language process that Freud and Lacan discuss. The pre-oedipal bonding with the mother, which takes place through the child's instinctual drives, and the oedipal turning to the father cannot occur under the material conditions of slavery, which provides for no personal relation between mother and infant nor father and infant.

As Spillers stresses, the very conditions of mothering and fathering assumed by the oedipal model of language do not exist in every culture, or in every historical period. She calls into question, then, the foundational premises underlying this model, which assumes an ahistorical universal "mother," "father," "woman," and "man." Does this mean, then, that African-American men and women have no position from which to speak? Spillers finds in her "mother and mother-dispossessed" female *in the flesh* outside the traditional symbolics of female gender a radically different female social subject whose power lies in her ability to break into the phallocentric chain of paternity and legitimacy. Thus the very phallocentric language that would claim her as reproductive object becomes marked by her presence from outside the "Law of the Father." Her account of African-American oppressive relationships to language reveals the liberatory potential for acquiring a language position outside the phallic Symbolic from which to speak.

While scholars like Spillers and Kristéva have pursued the relationship of sexual drives, mothering, and acquisition of language for male and female speakers in order to position women more favorably in language and culture, Cixous, Irigaray, and Spivak have investigated possible feminine-specific linguistic sources in both reproductive (uterine) and nonreproductive (sometimes referred to as clitoral) systems of women's sexuality. They are concerned primarily with giving primacy to female sexuality rather than male sexuality in the gender and language discussion.

The French philosopher Cixous's feminine-specific psychosexual model of women's future linguistic expression draws generally upon women's bodily pleasures as a source of subjectivity and language which bypasses the oedipal phallus. In her influential essay "The Laugh of the Medusa" (1975) presented here, she moves from considering the problems of language acquisition for one universal subject to plural subjects, observing, "There is, at this time, no general women, no one typical woman. . . . You can't talk about a female sexuality, uniform, homogeneous, classifiable into codes. . . ." (875–876). In her theory, women have access to language based on "a systematic experimentation with the bodily functions, a passionate and precise interrogation of her erotogeneity" which includes the pre-oedipal erotic pleasures of female masturbation, thus suggesting that this offers a way for women to "write women . . . in female-sexed texts" (876–877). She links this bodily pleasure directly to the unconscious, indicating that the road to the suppressed feminine unconscious on which culture and language depend is through the linguistic release of women's eroticism. Only then can women hear themselves, just as men hear themselves, through language and break out of their phallocentrically defined domain of silence in language. Women have this ability, she claims, because "woman is never far from 'mother'" (879). As we have seen in Kristéva's theory of language, the mother is the generative source of language power even as she is repressed or given "non-name" in contrast to the Lacanian "name of the Father." But what Cixous has in mind here is not a phallocentrically-regulated maternity to serve the reproductive interests of heterosexism, but a deregulated maternity: "Let us dematerpaternalize . . . in an effort to avoid the cooptation of procreation" (889).

Cixous declares as well, though, that woman can have this linguistic prowess because of her libido, because she "arrives, vibrant, over and again" (880), in contrast to men, who, one might say, arrive in one ejaculation. This libido intersects with several histories: "personal history blends together with the history of all women, as well as national and world history" (880–881). Men, meanwhile, participate in a "unifying, regulating history that homogenizes" (880). Defining a feminine language, or *écriture féminine*, is thus impossible, according to Cixous, because phallocentric language and history cannot imagine them, not because they cannot exist, thereby betraying the arbitrariness of phallocentric language and history. Language and culture are regulatory fictions rather than fact or truth capable of adapting to new discoveries and evidence.

Like Cixous, the philosopher Irigaray focuses on women's sexual drives as a power source for acquiring a language for women in her widely read 1977 essay "This Sex Which Is Not One" from *This Sex Which Is Not One* chosen for this section. She moves the most radically into a gynocentric mapping of language and subjectivity in which the female body and mind displace phallocentric mapping with its focus on the male body and mind. She focuses specifically on the bisexuality of women's bodies. Irigaray takes the definition of "bisexuality" which Freud introduces and uses it as a strategy to focus on the bisexual within women which does not need the penis in the same way that men require the vagina. She writes: "her sex is composed of two lips, which embrace continually. Thus, within herself she is already two—but not divisible into ones—who stimulate each other" (24).

For Irigaray this lack of dependence upon heterosexual coitus for pleasure resists the phallocentric fiction of regulation by classification, for "woman is neither one nor two" and therefore defies the binary process of phallocentric definitions. In fact, she states, "her sexuality, always at least double, is in fact *plural*. . . . Woman's pleasure does not have to choose between clitoral activity and vaginal passivity, for example. . . . [W]oman has sex organs just about everywhere" (26).

Both female desire and language are multiple in Irigaray's language model for women. They resist the ready-made grids of phallocentric thinking, which defines female desire in terms of "penis-desire" and the reproductive maternal imaginary, and of phallocentric discourse, which perpetuates male domination through its demands for meaning that coincides with what men desire. Thus women must seek their language elsewhere outside a phallic language which uses them as social objects or commodities, be it psychoanalytic discourse, Marxist discourse, or capitalist discourse. With this move into social commodification, Irigaray begins to raise the issue of intersections of women's oppression with class. She writes, "women are not, strictly speaking, a class and their dispersion in several classes makes their political struggle complex and their demands sometimes contradictory" (29).

Spivak roots the beginning of a female-specific or gynocentric theoretical model giving women a language to cross boundaries of difference like class in the discourse of the clitoris, but an "effaced clitoris" rather than a "celebratory clitoris." In "French Feminism in an International Frame" (1981) she speaks from a multiculturalism drawn from her position at the professional intersections of French, American, and Third World feminisms and at the personal boundaries of several cultures. The excerpt from the essay's conclusion included here explores the possibility of a "common yet history-specific" discourse for the "historically discontinuous yet common 'object-'ification of the sexed subject as woman" and brings to the feminist critique of phallic language a heterogeneous theoretical practice in which psychoanalytic discourse is part of a larger discursive dialogue that encompasses the French deconstructionist Derrida and others.

She imagines a discourse on the effacement of the clitoris which escapes its present reproductive framing in phallocentric language and culture. She points out in her analysis that "in legally defining woman as object of exchange, passage, or possession in terms of reproduction, it is not only the womb that is literally 'appropriated'; it is the clitoris as the signifier of the sexed subject that is effaced" (181). This discourse would situate the uterine social or reproductive organization of phallocentric culture and language in terms of the exclusion of clitoral social organization. While it will not resolve issues around sexuality, race, class, and First World feminism's colonialism toward the Third by itself, Spivak believes that such a discourse can help to promote fruitful dialogue across these differences. Of crucial importance to the gender and language debate is her focus on the ways in which discussions about the clitoris, like discussions about mothering, are culturally and socially marked and thus in need of continual contextualization.

Cixous's, Irigaray's, and Spivak's thinking on the clitoris has generated a growing body of very recent work among writers who wish to take the clitoris centrally, rather than peripherally, into account in discussions of gender and language. Landmark work appears in Jane Gallop's *Thinking Through the Body* (1988), Barbara Johnson's "Is Female to Male as Ground Is to Figure?" (1989), Judith Roof's "The Match in the Crocus: Representations of Lesbian Sexuality" (1989), and Paula Bennett's "Critical Clitoridectomy: Female Sexual Imagery and Feminist Psychoanalytic Theory" (1993). As Roof explains, women need to find a way of discussing the primacy of the clitoris which does not derive from Freud's definition of it as "surplus" because it did not fit into the binary phallus-vagina model by which sexual difference and sexuality are represented and understood—and by which male dominance is perpetuated (115).

All of the scholars presented here offer a variety of ways of thinking about the questions posed in the opening of this essay. Their heterogeneous positionings indicate the extent to which this major field of study on gender and language has undergone and continues to undergo major reconstruction. While these writers share an interest in the intertwining of sexuality and gender with subjectivity and language, there is no monolithic discourse to be found here. Instead, there are three major theoretical positions that pursue questions about the gendered and sexed nature of language and of the language acquisition process: the original Freudian-Lacanian language model; the Kristévan and Spillers paradigms for male and female speakers; and the Cixous-Irigaray-Spivak investigations of feminine-specific discourses for women.

Camille Roman

SELECTED BIBLIOGRAPHY

ABEL, ELIZABETH. "Race, Class, and Psychoanalysis? Opening Questions." *Conflicts in Feminism*. Eds. Marianne Hirsch and Evelyn Fox Keller. New York and London: Routledge, 1990.

———. ED. *Writing and Sexual Difference*. Special Issue of *Critical Inquiry* (Winter 1981).

——— AND EMILY, EDS. *The Signs Reader: Women, Gender, and Scholarship*. Chicago: The University of Chicago Press, 1983.

BENNETT, PAULA. "Critical Clitoridectomy: Female Sexual Imagery and Feminist Psychoanalytic Theory." *Signs* 18.2 (1993): 235–259.

CIXOUS, HÉLÈNE. "The Laugh of the Medusa." *Signs* 1.4 (1975): 875–893.

——— AND CATHERINE CLEMENT. *The Newly Born Woman*. Trans. Betsy Wing. Minneapolis: Minnesota University Press, 1986.

DE LAURETIS, TERESA. *Alice Doesn't: Feminism, Semiotics, Cinema*. Bloomington: Indiana University Press, 1984.

FREUD, SIGMUND. "Femininity." *New Introductory Lectures on Psycho-Analysis.* Trans. James Strachey. New York: W. W. Norton, 1965. 139–167.

———. *The Standard Edition of the Complete Psychological Works of Sigmund Freud.* Trans. James Strachey et al., ed. James Strachey. London: Hogarth, 1974; rpt. 1986.

GALLOP, JANE. *Feminism and Psychoanalysis: The Daughter's Seduction.* Ithaca: Cornell University Press, 1982.

———. *Thinking Through the Body.* New York: Columbia University Press, 1988.

GROSZ, ELIZABETH. *Jacques Lacan: A Feminist Introduction.* London and New York: Routledge, 1990.

IRIGARAY, LUCE. *This Sex Which Is Not One.* Trans. Catherine Porter with Carolyn Burke. Ithaca: Cornell University Press, 1985.

———. *Speculum of the Other Woman.* Trans. Gillian C. Gill. Ithaca: Cornell University Press, 1985.

JOHNSON, BARBARA. "Is Female to Male as Ground Is to Figure?" *Feminism and Psychoanalysis.* Eds. Richard Feldstein and Judith Roof. Ithaca: Cornell University Press, 1989. 255–268.

KRISTÉVA, JULIA. *About Chinese Women.* Trans. Anita Barrows. New York: Urizen, 1977.

———. *Desire in Language.* Ed. Leon Roudiez. Trans. Thomas Gora, Alice Jardine, and Leon Roudiez. New York: Columbia University Press, 1980.

———. *The Kristéva Reader.* Ed. Toril Moi. New York: Columbia University Press, 1986.

———. *The Revolution in Poetic Language.* Trans. Margaret Waller. New York: Columbia University Press, 1984.

LACAN, JACQUES. *Écrits: A Selection.* Trans. Alan Sheridan. New York: W. W. Norton, 1977.

LEMAIRE, ANIKA. *Jacques Lacan.* New York: Routledge Chapman and Hall, 1977.

MARKS, ELAINE AND ISABELLE DE COURTIVRON, EDS. *New French Feminisms.* Amherst: University of Massachusetts Press, 1980.

MITCHELL, JULIET. *Psychoanalysis and Feminism.* New York: Pantheon, 1974.

MOI, TORIL. *Sexual/Textual Politics: Feminist Literary Theory.* London: Methuen, 1985.

ROOF, JUDITH. "The Match in the Crocus: Representations of Lesbian Sexuality." *Discontented Discourses: Feminism/Textual Intervention/Psychoanalysis.* Eds. Marlene S. Barr and Richard Feldstein. Urbana and Chicago: The University of Illinois Press, 1989. 100–116.

ROSE, JACQUELINE. *Sexuality in the Field of Vision.* London: Verso, 1986.

SPILLERS, HORTENSE. "Interstices: A Small Drama of Words." *Pleasure and Danger.* Ed. Carol Vance. Boston: Routledge and Kegan Paul, 1984.

———. "Mama's Baby, Papa's Maybe: An American Grammar Book." *Diacritics* 17.2 (1987): 65–81.

———. "'The Permanent Obliquity of an In[pha]llibly Straight': In the Time of the Daughters and the Fathers." *Daughters and Fathers.* Ed. Lynda E. Boose and Betty S. Flowers. Baltimore: Johns Hopkins University Press, 1989.

SPIVAK, GAYATRI CHAKRAVORTY. "French Feminism in an International Frame." *Yale French Studies* 62 (1981): 154–184.

———. *In Other Worlds: Essays in Cultural Politics.* New York and London: Methuen, 1987.

WHITFORD, MARGARET. *Luce Irigaray: Philosophy in the Feminine.* New York: Routledge, 1991.

sigmund freud

FEMININITY

Ladies and Gentlemen,—All the while I am preparing to talk to you I am struggling with an internal difficulty. I feel uncertain, so to speak, of the extent of my license. It is true that in the course of fifteen years of work psycho-analysis has changed and grown richer; but, in spite of that, an introduction to psycho-analysis might have been left without alteration or supplement. It is constantly in my mind that these lectures are without a *raison d'être*. For analysts I am saying too little and nothing at all that is new; but for you I am saying too much and saying things which you are not equipped to understand and which are not in your province. I have looked around for excuses and I have tried to justify each separate lecture on different grounds. The first one, on the theory of dreams, was supposed to put you back again at one blow into the analytic atmosphere and to show you how durable our views have turned out to be. I was led on to the second one, which followed the paths from dreams to what is called occultism, by the opportunity of speaking my mind without constraint on a department of work in which prejudiced expectations are fighting to-day against passionate resistances, and I could hope that your judgement, educated to tolerance on the example of psychoanalysis, would not refuse to accompany me on the excursion. The third lecture, on the dissection of the personality, certainly made the hardest demands upon you with its unfamiliar subject-matter; but it was impossible for me to keep this first beginning of an ego-psychology back from you, and if we had possessed it fifteen years ago I should have had to mention it to you then. My last lecture, finally, which you were probably able to follow only by great exertions, brought forward necessary corrections—fresh attempts at solving the most important conundrums; and my introduction would have been leading you astray if I had been silent about them. As you see, when one starts making excuses it turns out in the end that it was an inevitable, all the work of destiny. I submit to it, and I beg you to do the same.

To-day's lecture, too, should have no place in an introduction; but it may serve to give you an example of a detailed piece of analytic work, and I can say two things to recommend it. It brings forward nothing but observed facts, almost without any speculative additions, and it deals with a subject which has a claim on your interest second almost to no other. Throughout history people have knocked their heads against the riddle of the nature of femininity—

> *Häupter in Hieroglyphenmützen,*
> *Häupter in Turban und schwarzem Barett,*

From New Introductory Lectures on Psycho-Analysis, *trans. and ed. James Strachey. Reprinted by permission of W. W. Norton & Company, Inc. Copyright © 1965, 1964 by James Strachey. Copyright © 1933 by Sigmund Freud. Copyright renewed 1961 by W.J.H. Sprott.*

Perückenhäupter und tausend andre
Arme, schwitzende Menschenhäupter. . . .[1]

Nor will *you* have escaped worrying over this problem—those of you who are men; to those of you who are women this will not apply—you are yourselves the problem. When you meet a human being, the first distinction you make is 'male or female?' and you are accustomed to make the distinction with unhesitating certainty. Anatomical science shares your certainty at one point and not much further. The male sexual product, the spermatozoon, and its vehicle are male; the ovum and the organism that harbours it are female. In both sexes organs have been formed which serve exclusively for the sexual functions; they were probably developed from the same [innate] disposition into two different forms. Besides this, in both sexes the other organs, the bodily shapes and tissues, show the influence of the individual's sex, but this is inconstant and its amount variable; these are what are known as the secondary sexual characters. Science next tells you something that runs counter to your expectations and is probably calculated to confuse your feelings. It draws your attention to the fact that portions of the male sexual apparatus also appear in women's bodies, though in an atrophied state, and vice versa in the alternative case. It regards their occurrence as indications of *bisexuality*,[2] as though an individual is not a man or a woman but always both—merely a certain amount more the one than the other. You will then be asked to make yourselves familiar with the idea that the proportion in which masculine and feminine are mixed in an individual is subject to quite considerable fluctuations. Since, however, apart from the very rarest cases, only one kind of sexual product—ova or semen—is nevertheless present in one person, you are bound to have doubts as to the decisive significance of those elements and must conclude that what constitutes masculinity or femininity is an unknown characteristic which anatomy cannot lay hold of.

Can psychology do so perhaps? We are accustomed to employ 'masculine' and 'feminine' as mental qualities as well, and have in the same way transferred the notion of bisexuality to mental life. Thus we speak of a person, whether male or female, as behaving in a masculine way in one connection and in a feminine way in another. But you will soon perceive that this is only giving way to anatomy or to convention. You cannot give the concepts of 'masculine' and 'feminine' *any* new connotation. The distinction is not a psychological one; when you say 'masculine', you usually mean 'active', and when you say 'feminine', you usually mean 'passive'. Now it is true that a relation of the kind exists. The male sex-cell is actively mobile and searches out the female one, and the latter, the ovum, is immobile and waits passively. This behaviour of the elementary sexual organisms is indeed a model for the conduct of sexual individuals during intercourse. The male pursues the female for the purpose of sexual union, seizes hold of her and penetrates into her. But by this you have precisely reduced the characteristic of masculinity to the factor of aggressiveness so far as psychology is concerned. You may well doubt whether you have gained any real advantage from this when you reflect that in some classes of animals the females are the stronger and more aggressive and the male is active only in the single act of sexual union. This is so, for instance, with the spiders. Even the functions of rearing and caring for the young, which strike us as feminine *par excellence,* are not invariably attached to the female sex in animals. In quite high species we find that the sexes share the task of caring for the young between them or even that the male alone devotes himself to it. Even in the sphere of human sexual life you soon see how inadequate it is to make masculine behaviour coincide with activity and feminine with passivity. A mother is active in every sense towards her child; the act of lactation itself may equally be described as the mother suckling the baby or as her being sucked by it. The further you go from the narrow sexual sphere the more obvious will the 'error of superimposition'[3] become. Women can display great activity in various directions, men are not able to live in company with their own kind unless they develop a large amount of passive adaptability. If you now tell me that these facts go to prove precisely that both men and women are bisexual in the psychological sense, I shall conclude that you have decided in your own minds to make 'active' coincide with 'masculine' and 'passive' with 'feminine'. But I advise you against it. It seems to me to serve no useful purpose and adds nothing to our knowledge.[4]

One might consider characterizing femininity psychologically as giving preference to passive aims. This is not, of course, the same thing as passivity; to achieve a passive aim may call for a large amount of activity. It is perhaps the case that in a woman, on the basis of her share in the sexual function, a preference for passive behaviour and passive aims is carried over into her life to a greater or lesser extent, in proportion to the limits, restricted or far-reaching, within which her sexual life thus serves as a model. But we must beware in this of underestimating the influence of social customs, which similarly force women into passive situations. All this is still far from being cleared up. There is one particularly constant relation between femininity and instinctual life which we do not want to overlook. The suppression of women's aggressiveness which is prescribed for them constitutionally and imposed on them socially favours the development of powerful masochistic impulses, which succeed, as we know, in binding erotically the destructive trends which have been diverted inwards. Thus masochism, as people say, is truly feminine. But if, as happens so often, you meet with masochism in men, what is left to you but to say that these men exhibit very plain feminine traits?

And now you are already prepared to hear that psychology too is unable to solve the riddle of femininity. The explanation must no doubt come from elsewhere, and cannot come till we have learnt how in general the differentiation of living organisms into two sexes came about. We know nothing about it, yet the existence of two sexes is a most striking characteristic of organic life which distinguishes it sharply from inanimate nature. However, we find enough to study in those human individuals who, through the possession of female genitals, are characterized as manifestly or predominantly feminine. In conformity with its peculiar nature, psycho-analysis does not try to describe what a woman is—that would be a task it could scarcely perform—but sets about enquiring how she comes into being, how a woman develops out of a child with a bisexual disposition. In recent times we have begun to learn a little about this, thanks to the circumstance that several of our excellent women colleagues in analysis have begun to work at the question. The discussion of this has gained special attractiveness from the distinction between the sexes. For the ladies, whenever some comparison seemed to turn out unfavourable to their sex, were able to utter a suspicion that we, the male analysts, had been unable to overcome certain deeply-rooted prejudices against what was feminine, and that this was being paid for in the partiality of our researches. We, on the other hand, standing on the ground of bisexuality, had no difficulty in avoiding impoliteness. We had only to say: 'This doesn't apply to *you*. You're the exception; on this point you're more masculine than feminine.'

We approach the investigation of the sexual development of women with two expectations. The first is that here once more the constitution will not adapt itself to its function without a struggle. The second is that the decisive turning-points will already have been prepared for or completed before puberty. Both expectations are promptly confirmed. Furthermore, a comparison with what happens with boys tell us that the development of a little girl into a normal woman is more difficult and more complicated, since it includes two extra tasks, to which there is nothing corresponding in the development of a man. Let us follow the parallel lines from their beginning. Undoubtedly the material is different to start with in boys and girls: it did not need psycho-analysis to establish that. The difference in the structure of the genitals is accompanied by other bodily differences which are too well known to call for mention. Differences emerge too in the instinctual disposition which give a glimpse of the later nature of women. A little girl is as a rule less aggressive, defiant and self-sufficient; she seems to have a greater need for being shown affection and on that account to be more dependent and pliant. It is probably only as a result of this pliancy that she can be taught more easily and quicker to control her excretions: urine and faeces are the first gifts that children make to those who look after them, and controlling them is the first concession to which the instinctual life of children can be induced. One gets an impression, too, that little girls are more intelligent and livelier than boys of the same age; they go out more to meet the external world and at the same time form stronger object-cathexes. I cannot say whether this lead in development has been confirmed by exact observations, but in any case there is no question that girls cannot be described as intellectually backward. These sexual differences are not, however, of great consequence: they can be outweighed by individual variations. For our immediate purposes they can be disregarded.

Both sexes seem to pass through the early phases of libidinal development in the same manner. It might have been expected that in girls there would already have been some lag in aggressiveness in the sadistic-anal phase, but such is not the case. Analysis of children's play has shown our women analysts that the aggressive impulses of little girls leave nothing to be desired in the way of abundance and violence. With their entry into the phallic phase the differences between the sexes are completely eclipsed by their agreements. We are now obliged to recognize that the little girl is a little man. In boys, as we know, this phase is marked by the fact that they have learnt how to derive pleasurable sensations from their small penis and connect its excited state with their ideas of sexual intercourse. Little girls do the same thing with their still smaller clitoris. It seems that with them all their masturbatory acts are carried out on this penis-equivalent, and that the truly feminine vagina is still undiscovered by both sexes. It is true that there are a few isolated reports of early vaginal sensations as well, but it could not be easy to distinguish these from sensations in the anus or vestibulum; in any case they cannot play a great part. We are entitled to keep to our view that in the phallic phase of girls the clitoris is the leading erotogenic zone. But it is not, of course, going to remain so. With the change to femininity the clitoris should wholly or in part hand over its sensitivity, and at the same time its importance, to the vagina. This would be one of the two tasks which a woman has to perform in the course of her development, whereas the more fortunate man has only to continue at the time of his sexual maturity the activity that he has previously carried out at the period of the early efflorescence of his sexuality.

We shall return to the part played by the clitoris; let us now turn to the second task with which a girl's development is burdened. A boy's mother is the first object of his love, and she remains so too during the formation of his Oedipus complex and, in essence, all through his life. For a girl too her first object must be her mother (and the figures of wet-nurses and foster-mothers that merge into her). The first object-cathexes occur in attachment to the satisfaction of the major and simple vital needs,[5] and the circumstances of the care of children are the same for both sexes. But in the Oedipus situation the girl's father has become her love-object, and we expect that in the normal course of development she will find her way from this paternal object to her final choice of an object. In the course of time, therefore, a girl has to change her erotogenic zone and her object—both of which a boy retains. The question then arises of how this happens: in particular, how does a girl pass from her mother to an attachment to her father? or, in other words, how does she pass from her masculine phase to the feminine one to which she is biologically destined?

It would be a solution of ideal simplicity if we could suppose that from a particular age onwards the elementary influence of the mutual attraction between the sexes makes itself felt and impels the small woman towards men, while the same law allows the boy to continue with his mother. We might suppose in addition that in this the children are following the pointer given them by the sexual preference of their parents. But we are not going to find things so easy; we scarcely know whether we are to believe seriously in the power of which poets talk so much and with such enthusiasm but which cannot be further dissected analytically. We have found an answer of quite another sort by means of laborious investigations, the material for which at least was easy to arrive at. For you must know that the number of women who remain till a late age tenderly dependent on a paternal object, or indeed on their real father, is very great. We have established some surprising facts about these women with an intense attachment of long duration to their father. We knew, of course, that there had been a preliminary stage of attachment to the mother, but we did not know that it could be so rich in content and so long-lasting, and could leave behind so many opportunities for fixations and dispositions. During this time the girl's father is only a troublesome rival; in some cases the attachment to her mother lasts beyond the fourth year of life. Almost everything that we find later in her relation to her father was already present in this earlier attachment and has been transferred subsequently on to her father. In short, we get an impression that we cannot understand women unless we appreciate this phase of their pre-Oedipus attachment to their mother.

We shall be glad, then, to know the nature of the girl's libidinal relations to her mother. The answer is that they are of very many different kinds. Since they persist through all three phases of infantile sexuality, they also take on the characteristics of the different phases and express themselves by oral, sadistic-anal and phallic wishes. These wishes represent active as well as passive impulses; if we relate them to the differentiation of the sexes which is to appear later—though we should avoid doing so as far as possible—we may call them masculine and feminine. Besides this, they are completely ambivalent, both affectionate and of a hostile and aggressive nature. The latter often only come to light after being changed into anxiety ideas. It is not always easy to point to a formulation of these early sexual wishes; what is most clearly expressed is a wish to get the mother with child and the corresponding wish to bear her a child—both belonging to the phallic period and sufficiently surprising, but established beyond doubt by analytic observation. The attractiveness of these investigations lies in the surprising detailed findings which they bring us. Thus, for instance, we discover the fear of being murdered or poisoned, which may later form the core of a paranoic illness, already present in this pre-Oedipus period, in relation to the mother. Or another case: you will recall an interesting episode in the history of analytic research which caused me many distressing hours. In the period in which the main interest was directed to discovering infantile sexual traumas, almost all my women patients told me that they had been seduced by their father. I was driven to recognize in the end that these reports were untrue and so came to understand that hysterical symptoms are derived from phantasies and not from real occurrences. It was only later that I was able to recognize in this phantasy of being seduced by the father the expression of the typical Oedipus complex in women. And now we find the phantasy of seduction once more in the pre-Oedipus prehistory of girls; but the seducer is regularly the mother. Here, however, the phantasy touches the ground of reality, for it was really the mother who by her activities over the child's bodily hygiene inevitably stimulated, and perhaps even roused for the first time, pleasurable sensations in her genitals.[6]

I have no doubt you are ready to suspect that this portrayal of the abundance and strength of a little girl's sexual relations with her mother is very much overdrawn. After all, one has opportunities of seeing little girls and notices nothing of the sort. But the objection is not to the point. Enough can be seen in the children if one knows how to look. And besides, you should consider how little of its sexual wishes a child can bring to preconscious expression or communicate at all. Accordingly we are only within our rights if we study the residues and consequences of this emotional world in retrospect, in people in whom these processes of development had attained a specially clear and even excessive degree of expansion. Pathology has always done us the service of making discernible by isolation and exaggeration conditions which would remain concealed in a normal state. And since our investigations have been carried out on people who were by no means seriously abnormal, I think we should regard their outcome as deserving belief.

We will now turn our interest on to the single question of what it is that brings this powerful attachment of the girl to her mother to an end. This, as we know, is its usual fate: it is destined to make room for an attachment to her father. Here we come upon a fact which is a pointer to our further advance. This step in development does not involve only a simple change of object. The turning away from the mother is accompanied by hostility; the attachment to the mother ends in hate. A hate of that kind may become very striking and last all through life; it may be carefully overcompensated later on; as a rule one part of it is overcome while another part persists. Events of later years naturally influence this greatly. We will restrict ourselves, however, to studying it at the time at which the girl turns to her father and to enquiring into the motives for it. We are then given a long list of accusations and grievances against the mother which are supposed to justify the child's hostile feelings; they are of varying validity which we shall not fail to examine. A number of them are obvious rationalizations and the true sources of enmity remain to be found. I hope you will be interested if on this occasion I take you through all the details of a psycho-analytic investigation.

The reproach against the mother which goes back furthest is that she gave the child too little milk—which is construed against her as lack of love. Now there is some justification for this reproach in our families. Mothers often have insufficient nourishment to give their children and are content to suckle them for a few months, for half or three-quarters of a year. Among primitive peoples children are fed at their mother's breast for two or three years. The figure of the wet-nurse who suckles the child is as a rule merged into the mother; when this has not happened, the reproach is turned into another one—that the nurse, who fed the child so willingly, was sent away by the mother too early. But whatever the true state of affairs may have been, it is impossible that the child's reproach can be justified as often as it is met with. It seems, rather, that the child's avidity for its earliest nourishment is altogether insatiable, that it never gets over the pain of losing its mother's breast. I should not be surprised if the analysis of a primitive child, who could still suck at its mother's breast when it was already able to run about and talk, were to bring the same reproach to light. The fear of being poisoned is also probably connected with the withdrawal of the breast. Poison is nourishment that makes one ill. Perhaps children trace back their early illnesses too to this frustration. A fair amount of intellectual education is a prerequisite for believing in chance; primitive people and uneducated ones, and no doubt children as well, are able to assign a ground for everything that happens. Perhaps originally it was a reason on animistic lines. Even to-day in some strata of our population no one can die without having been killed by someone else—preferably by the doctor. And the regular reaction of a neurotic to the death of someone closely connected with him is to put the blame on himself for having caused the death.

The next accusation against the child's mother flares up when the next baby appears in the nursery. If possible the connection with oral frustration is preserved: the mother could not or would not give the child any more milk because she needed the nourishment for the new arrival. In cases in which the two children are so close in age that lactation is prejudiced by the second pregnancy, this reproach acquires a real basis, and it is a remarkable fact that a child, even with an age difference of only 11 months, is not too young to take notice of what is happening. But what the child grudges the unwanted intruder and rival is not only the suckling but all the other signs of maternal care. It feels that it has been dethroned, despoiled, prejudiced in its rights; it casts a jealous hatred upon the new baby and develops a grievance against the faithless mother which often finds expression in a disagreeable change in its behaviour. It becomes 'naughty', perhaps, irritable and disobedient and goes back on the advances it has made towards controlling its excretions. All of this has been very long familiar and is accepted as self-evident; but we rarely form a correct idea of the strength of these jealous impulses, of the tenacity with which they persist and of the magnitude of their influence on later development. Especially as this jealousy is constantly receiving fresh nourishment in the later years of childhood and the whole shock is repeated with the birth of each new brother or sister. Nor does it make much difference if the child happens to remain the mother's preferred favourite. A child's demands for love are immoderate, they make exclusive claims and tolerate no sharing.

An abundant source of a child's hostility to its mother is provided by its multifarious sexual wishes, which alter according to the phase of the libido and which cannot for the most part be satisfied. The strongest of these frustrations occur at the phallic period, if the mother forbids pleasurable activity with the genitals—often with severe threats and every sign of displeasure—activity to which, after all, she herself had introduced the child. One would think these were reasons enough to account for a girl's turning away from her mother. One would judge, if so, that the estrangement follows inevitably from the nature of children's sexuality, from the immoderate character of their demand for love and the impossibility of fulfilling their sexual wishes. It might be thought indeed that this first love-relation of the child's is doomed to dissolution for the very reason that it is the first, for these early object-cathexes are regularly ambivalent to a high degree. A powerful tendency to aggressiveness is always present beside a powerful love, and the more passionately a child loves its object the more sensitive does it become to disappointments and frustrations from that object; and in the end the love must succumb to the accumulated hostility. Or the idea that there is an original ambivalence such as this in erotic cathexes may be rejected, and it may be pointed out that it is the special nature of the mother-child relation that leads, with equal inevitability, to the destruction of the child's love; for even the mildest upbringing cannot avoid using compulsion and introducing restrictions, and any such intervention in the child's liberty must provoke as a reaction an inclination to rebelliousness and aggressiveness. A discussion of these possibilities might, I think, be most interesting; but an objection suddenly emerges which forces our interest in another direction. All these factors—the slights, the disappointments in love, the jealousy, the seduction followed by prohibition—are, after all, also in operation in the relation of a *boy* to his mother and are yet unable to alienate him from the maternal object. Unless we can find something that is specific for girls and is not present or not in the same way present in boys, we shall not have explained the termination of the attachment of girls to their mother.

I believe we have found this specific factor, and indeed where we expected to find it, even though in a surprising form. Where we expected to find it, I say, for it lies in the castration complex. After all, the anatomical distinction [between the sexes] must express itself in psychical consequences. It was, however, a surprise to learn from analyses that girls hold their mother responsible for their lack of a penis and do not forgive her for their being thus put at a disadvantage.

As you hear, then, we ascribe a castration complex to women as well. And for good reasons, though its content cannot be the same as with boys. In the latter the castration complex arises after they have learnt from the sight of the female genitals that the organ which they value so highly need not necessarily accompany the body. At this the boy recalls to mind the threats he brought on himself by his doings with that organ, he begins to give credence to them and falls under the influence of fear of castration, which will be the most powerful motive force in his subsequent development. The castration complex of girls is also started by the sight of the genitals of the other sex. They at once notice the difference and, it must be admitted, its significance too. They feel seriously wronged, often declare that they want to 'have something like it too', and fall a victim to 'envy for the penis', which will leave ineradicable traces on their development and the formation of their character and which will not be surmounted in even the most favourable cases without a severe expenditure of physical energy. The girl's recognition of the fact of her being without a penis does not by any means imply that she submits to the fact easily. On the contrary, she continues to hold on for a long time to the wish to get something like it herself and she believes in that possibility for improbably long years; and analysis can show that, at a period when knowledge of reality has long since rejected the fulfilment of the wish as unattainable, it persists in the unconscious and retains a considerable cathexis of energy. The wish to get the longed-for penis eventually in spite of everything may contribute to the motives that drive a mature woman to analysis, and what she may reasonably expect from analysis—a capacity, for instance, to carry on an intellectual profession—may often be recognized as a sublimated modification of this repressed wish.

One cannot very well doubt the importance of envy for the penis. You may take it as an instance of male injustice if I assert that envy and jealousy play an even greater part in the mental life of women than of men. It is not that I think these characteristics are absent in men or that I think they have no other roots in women than envy for the penis; but I am inclined to attribute their greater amount in women to this latter influence. Some analysts, however, have shown an inclination to depreciate the importance of this first installment of penis-envy in the phallic phase. They are of opinion that what we find of this attitude in women is in the main a secondary structure which has come about on the occasion of later conflicts by regression to this early infantile impulse. This, however, is a general problem of depth psychology. In many pathological—or even unusual—instinctual attitudes (for instance, in all sexual perversions) the question arises of how much of their strength is to be attributed to early infantile fixations and how much to the influence of later experiences and developments. In such cases it is almost always a matter of complemental series such as we put forward in our discussion of the aetiology of the neuroses.[7] Both factors play a part in varying amounts in the causation; a less on the one side is balanced by a more on the other. The infantile factor sets the pattern in all cases but does not always determine the issue, though it often does. Precisely in the case of penis-envy I should argue decidedly in favour of the preponderance of the infantile factor.

The discovery that she is castrated is a turning-point in a girl's growth. Three possible lines of development start from it: one leads to sexual inhibition or to neurosis, the second to change of character in the sense of a masculinity complex, the third, finally, to normal femininity. We have learnt a fair amount, though not everything, about all three.

The essential content of the first is as follows: the little girl has hitherto lived in a masculine way, has been able to get pleasure by the excitation of her clitoris and has brought this activity into relation with her sexual wishes directed towards her mother, which are often active ones; now, owing to the influence of her penis-envy, she loses her enjoyment in her phallic sexuality. Her self-love is mortified by the comparison with the boy's far superior equipment and in consequence she renounces her masturbatory satisfaction from her clitoris, repudiates her love for her mother and at the same time not infrequently represses a good part of her sexual trends in general. No doubt her turning away from her mother does not occur all at once, for to begin with the girl regards her castration as an individual misfortune, and only gradually extends it to other females and finally to her mother as well. Her love was directed to her *phallic* mother; with the discovery that her mother is castrated it becomes possible to drop her as an object, so that the motives for hostility, which have long been accumulating, gain the upper hand. This means, therefore, that as a result of the discovery of women's lack of a penis they are debased in value for girls just as they are for boys and later perhaps for men.

You all know the immense aetiological importance attributed by our neurotic patients to their masturbation. They make it responsible for all their troubles and we have the greatest difficulty in persuading them that they are mistaken. In fact, however, we ought to admit to them that they are right, for masturbation is the executive agent of infantile sexuality, from the faulty development of which they are indeed suffering. But what neurotics mostly blame is the masturbation of the period of puberty; they have mostly forgotten that of early infancy, which is what is really in question. I wish I might have an opportunity some time of explaining to you at length how important all the factual details of early masturbation become for the individual's subsequent neurosis or character: whether or not it was discovered, how the parents struggled against it or permitted it, or whether he succeeded in suppressing it himself. All of this leaves permanent traces on his development. But I am on the whole glad that I need not do this. It would be a hard and tedious task and at the end of it you would put me in an embarrassing situation by quite certainly asking me to give you some practical advice as to how a parent or educator should deal with the masturbation of small children.[8] From the development of girls, which is what my present lecture is concerned with, I can give you the example of a child herself trying to get free from masturbating. She does not always succeed in this. If envy for the penis has provoked a powerful impulse against clitoridal masturbation but this nevertheless refuses to give way, a violent struggle for liberation ensues in which the girl, as it were, herself takes over the role of her deposed mother and gives expression to her entire dissatisfaction with her inferior clitoris in her efforts against obtaining satisfaction from it. Many years later, when her masturbatory activity has long since been suppressed, an interest still persists which we must interpret as a defence against a temptation that is still dreaded. It manifests itself in the emergence of sympathy for those to whom similar difficulties are attributed, it plays a part as a motive in contracting a marriage and, indeed, it may determine the choice of a husband or lover. Disposing of early infantile masturbation is truly no easy or indifferent business.

Along with the abandonment of clitoridal masturbation a certain amount of activity is renounced. Passivity now has the upper hand, and the girl's turning to her father is accomplished principally with the help of passive instinctual impulses. You can see that a wave of development like this, which clears the phallic activity out of the way, smooths the ground for femininity. If too much is not lost in the course of it through repression, this femininity may turn out to be normal. The wish with which the girl turns to her father is no doubt originally the wish for the penis which her mother has refused her and which she now expects from her father. The feminine situation is only established, however, if the wish for a penis is replaced by one for a baby, if, that is, a baby takes the place of a penis in accordance with an ancient symbolic equivalence. It has not escaped us that the girl has wished for a baby earlier, in the undisturbed phallic phase: that, of course, was the meaning of her playing with dolls. But that play was not in fact an expression of her femininity; it served as an identification with her mother with the intention of substituting activity for passivity. *She* was playing the part of her mother and the doll was herself: now she could do with the baby everything that her mother used to do with her. Not until the emergence of the wish for a penis does the doll-baby become a baby from the girl's father, and thereafter the aim of the most powerful feminine wish. Her happiness is great if later on this wish for a baby finds fulfilment in reality, and quite especially so if the baby is a little boy who brings the longed-for penis with him.[9] Often enough in her combined picture of 'a baby from her father' the emphasis is laid on the baby and her father left unstressed. In this way the ancient masculine wish for the possession of a penis is still faintly visible through the femininity now achieved. But perhaps we ought rather to recognize this wish for a penis as being *par excellence* a feminine one.

With the transference of the wish for a penis-baby on to her father, the girl has entered the situation of the Oedipus complex. Her hostility to her mother, which did not need to be freshly created, is now greatly intensified, for she becomes the girl's rival, who received from her father everything that she desires from him. For a long time the girl's Oedipus complex concealed her pre-Oedipus attachment to her mother from our view, though it is nevertheless so important and leaves such lasting fixations behind it. For girls the Oedipus situation is the outcome of a long and difficult development; it is a kind of preliminary solution, a position of rest which is not soon abandoned, especially as the beginning of the latency period is not far distant. And we are now struck by a difference between the two sexes, which is probably momentous, in regard to the relation of the Oedipus complex to the castration complex. In a boy the Oedipus complex, in which he desires his mother and would like to get rid of his father as being a rival, develops naturally from the phase of his phallic sexuality. The threat of castration compels him, however, to give up that attitude. Under the impression of the danger of losing his penis, the Oedipus complex is abandoned, repressed and, in the most normal cases, entirely destroyed, and a severe super-ego is set up as its heir. What happens with a girl is almost the opposite. The castration complex prepares for the Oedipus complex instead of destroying it; the girl is driven out of her attachment to her mother through the influence of her envy for the penis and she enters the Oedipus situation as though into a haven of refuge. In the absence of fear of castration the chief motive is lacking which leads boys to surmount the Oedipus complex. Girls remain in it for an indeterminate length of time; they demolish it late and, even so, incompletely. In these circumstances the formation of the super-ego must suffer; it cannot attain the strength and independence which give it its cultural significance, and feminists are not pleased when we point out to them the effects of this factor upon the average feminine character.

To go back a little. We mentioned [p. 28] as the second possible reaction to the discovery of female castration the development of a powerful masculinity complex. By this we mean that the girl refuses, as it were, to recognize the unwelcome fact and, defiantly rebellious, even exaggerates her previous masculinity, clings to her clitoridal activity and takes refuge in an identification with her phallic mother or her father. What can it be that decides in favour of this outcome? We can only suppose that it is a constitutional factor, a greater amount of activity, such as is ordinarily characteristic of a male. However that may be, the essence of this process is that at this point in development the wave of passivity is avoided which opens the way to the turn towards femininity. The extreme achievement of such a masculinity complex would appear to be the influencing of the choice of an object in the sense of manifest homosexuality. Analytic experience teaches us, to be sure, that female homosexuality is seldom or never a direct continuation of infantile masculinity. Even for a girl of this kind it seems necessary that she should take her father as an object for some time and enter the Oedipus situation. But afterwards, as a result of her inevitable disappointments from her father, she is driven to regress into her early masculinity complex. The significance of these disappointments must not be exaggerated; a girl who is destined to become feminine is not spared them, though they do not have the same effect. The predominance of the constitutional factor seems indisputable; but the two phases in the development of female homosexuality are well mirrored in the practices of homosexuals, who play the parts of mother and baby with each other as often and as clearly as those of husband and wife.

What I have been telling you here may be described as the prehistory of women. It is a product of the very last few years and may have been of interest to you as an example of detailed analytic work. Since its subject is woman, I will venture on this occasion to mention by name a few of the women who have made valuable contributions to this investigation. Dr. Ruth Mack Brunswick (1928) was the first to describe a case of neurosis which went back to a fixation in the pre-Oedipus stage and had never reached the Oedipus situation at all. The case took the form of jealous paranoia and proved accessible to therapy. Dr. Jeanne Lampl-de Groot (1927) has established the incredible phallic activity of girls towards their mother by some assured observations, and Dr. Helene Deutsch (1932) has shown that the erotic actions of homosexual women reproduce the relations between mother and baby.

It is not my intention to pursue the further behaviour of femininity through puberty to the period of maturity. Our knowledge, moreover, would be insufficient for the purpose. But I will bring a few features together in what follows. Taking its prehistory as a starting-point, I will only emphasize here that the development of femininity remains exposed to disturbance by the residual phenomena of the early masculine period. Regressions to the fixations of the pre-Oedipus phases very frequently occur; in the course of some women's lives there is a repeated alternation between periods in which masculinity or femininity gains the upper hand. Some portion of what we men call 'the enigma of women' may perhaps be derived from this expression of bisexuality in women's lives. But another question seems to have become ripe for judgement in the course of these researches. We have called the motive force of sexual life 'the libido'. Sexual life is dominated by the polarity of masculine-feminine; thus the notion suggests itself of considering the relation of the libido to this antithesis. It would not be surprising if it were to turn out that each sexuality had its own special libido appropriated to it, so that one sort of libido would pursue the aims of a masculine sexual life and another sort those of a feminine one. But nothing of the kind is true. There is only one libido, which serves both the masculine and the feminine sexual functions. To it itself we cannot assign any sex; if, following the conventional equation of activity and masculinity, we are inclined to describe it as masculine, we must not forget that it also covers trends with a passive aim. Nevertheless the juxtaposition 'feminine libido' is without any justification. Furthermore, it is our impression that more constraint has been applied to the libido when it is pressed into the service of the feminine function, and that—to speak teleologically—Nature takes less careful account of its [that function's] demands than in the case of masculinity. And the reason for this may lie—thinking once again teleologically—in the fact that the accomplishment of the aim of biology has been entrusted to the aggressiveness of men and has been made to some extent independent of women's consent.

The sexual frigidity of women, the frequency of which appears to confirm this disregard, is a phenomenon that is still insufficiently understood. Sometimes it is psychogenic and in that case accessible to influence; but in other cases it suggests the hypothesis of its being constitutionally determined and even of there being a contributory anatomical factor.

I have promised to tell you of a few more psychical peculiarities of mature femininity, as we come across them in analytic observation. We do not lay claim to more than an average validity for these assertions; nor is it always easy to distinguish what should be ascribed to the influence of the sexual function and what to social breeding. Thus, we attribute a larger amount of narcissism to femininity, which also affects women's choice of object, so that to be loved is a stronger need for them than to love. The effect of penis-envy has a share, further, in the physical vanity of women, since they are bound to value their charms more highly as a late compensation for their original sexual inferiority.[10] Shame, which is considered to be a feminine characteristic *par excellence* but is far more a matter of convention than might be supposed, has as its purpose, we believe, concealment of genital deficiency. We are not forgetting that at a later time shame takes on other functions. It seems that women have made few contributions to the discoveries and inventions in the history of civilization; there is, however, one technique which they may have invented—that of plaiting and weaving. If that is so, we should be tempted to guess the unconscious motive for the achievement. Nature herself would seem to have given the model which this achievement imitates by causing the growth at maturity of the pubic hair that conceals the genitals. The step that remained to be taken lay in making the threads adhere to one another, while on the body they stick into the skin and are only matted together. If you reject this idea as fantastic and regard my belief in the influence of lack of a penis on the configuration of femininity as an *idée fixe*, I am of course defenceless.

The determinants of women's choice of an object are often made unrecognizable by social conditions. Where the choice is able to show itself freely, it is often made in accordance with the narcissistic ideal of the man whom the girl had wished to become. If the girl has remained in her attachment to her father—that is, in the Oedipus complex—her choice is made according to the paternal type. Since, when she turned from her mother to her father, the hostility of her ambivalent relation remained with her mother, a choice of this kind should guarantee a happy marriage. But very often the outcome is of a kind that presents a general threat to such a settlement of the conflict due to ambivalence. The hostility that has been left behind follows in the train of the positive attachment and spreads over on to the new object. The woman's husband, who to begin with inherited from her father, becomes after a time her mother's heir as well. So it may easily happen that the second half of a woman's life may be filled by the struggle against her husband, just as the shorter first half was filled by her rebellion against her mother. When this reaction has been lived through, a second marriage may easily turn out very much more satisfying.[11] Another alteration in a woman's nature, for which lovers are unprepared, may occur in a marriage after the first child is born. Under the influence of a woman's becoming a mother herself, an identification with her own mother may be revived, against which she had striven up till the time of her marriage, and this may attract all the available libido to itself, so that the compulsion to repeat reproduces an unhappy marriage between her parents. The difference in a mother's reaction to the birth of a son or a daughter shows that the old factor of lack of a penis has even now not lost its strength. A mother is only brought unlimited satisfaction by her relation to a son; this is altogether the most perfect, the most free from ambivalence of all human relationships.[12] A mother can transfer to her son the ambition which she has been obliged to suppress in herself, and she can expect from him the satisfaction of all that has been left over in her of her masculinity complex. Even a marriage is not made secure until the wife has succeeded in making her husband her child as well and in acting as a mother to him.

A woman's identification with her mother allows us to distinguish two strata: the pre-Oedipus one which rests on her affectionate attachment to her mother and takes her as a model, and the later one from the Oedipus complex which seeks to get rid of her mother and take her place with her father. We are no doubt justified in saying that much of both of them is left over for the future and that neither of them is adequately surmounted in the course of development. But the phase of the affectionate pre-Oedipus attachment is the decisive one for a woman's future: during it preparation are made for the acquisition of the characteristics with which she will later fulfil her role in the sexual function and perform her invaluable social tasks. It is in this identification too that she acquires her attractiveness to a man, whose Oedipus attachment to his mother it kindles into passion. How often it happens, however, that it is only his son who obtains what he himself aspired to! One gets an impression that a man's love and a woman's are a phase apart psychologically.

The fact that women must be regarded as having little sense of justice is no doubt related to the predominance of envy in their mental life; for the demand for justice is a modification of envy and lays down the condition subject to which one can put envy aside. We also regard women as weaker in their social interests and as having less capacity for sublimating their instincts than men. The former is no doubt derived from the dissocial quality which unquestionably characterizes all sexual relations. Lovers find sufficiency in each other, and families too resist inclusion in more comprehensive associations.[13] The aptitude for sublimation is subject to the greatest individual variations. On the other hand I cannot help mentioning an impression that we are constantly receiving during analytic practice. A man of about thirty strikes us as a youthful, somewhat unformed individual, whom we expect to make powerful use of the possibilities for development opened up to him by analysis. A woman of the same age, however, often frightens us by her psychical rigidity and unchangeability. Her libido has taken up final positions and seems incapable of exchanging them for others. There are no paths open to further development; it is as though the whole process had already run its course and remains thenceforward insusceptible to influence—as though, indeed, the difficult development to femininity had exhausted the possibilities of the person concerned. As therapists we lament this state of things, even if we succeed in putting an end to our patient's ailment by doing away with her neurotic conflict.

That is all I had to say to you about femininity. It is certainly incomplete and fragmentary and does not always sound friendly. But do not forget that I have only been describing women in so far as their nature is determined by their sexual function. It is true that that influence extends very far; but we do not overlook the fact that an individual woman may be a human being in other respects as well. If you want to know more about femininity, enquire from your own experiences of life, or turn to the poets, or wait until science can give you deeper and more coherent information.

NOTES

This lecture is mainly based on two earlier papers: "Some Psychical Consequences of the Anatomical Distinction between the Sexes" (1925) and "Female Sexuality" (1931). The last section, however, dealing with women in adult life, contains new material. Freud returned to the subject once again in chapter VII of the posthumous *Outline of Psycho-Analysis* (1904 [1938]).

1. Heads in hieroglyphic bonnets, / Heads in turbans and black birettas, / Heads in wigs and thousand other / Wretched, sweating heads of humans. . . . (Heine, *Nordsee* [Second Cycle, VII, 'Fragen']).

2. Bisexuality was discussed by Freud in the first edition of his *Three Essays on the Theory of Sexuality* (1905). The passage includes a long footnote to which he made additions in later issues of the work.

3. I.e., mistaking two different things for a single one. The term was explained in *Introductory Lectures on Psycho-Analysis*, XX.

4. The difficulty of finding a psychological meaning for 'masculine' and 'feminine' was discussed in a long footnote added in 1915 to section 4 of the third of his *Three Essays on the Theory of Sexuality* (1905), and again at the beginning of a still longer footnote at the end of chapter IV of *Civilization and Its Discontents* (1930).

5. Cf. *Introductory Lectures on Psycho-Analysis*, XXI.

6. In his early discussions of the aetiology of hysteria Freud often mentioned seduction by adults as among its commonest causes (see, for instance, section I of "Further Remarks on the Neuro-Psychoses of Defence (1896) and section II(*b*) of "The Aetiology of Hysteria" (1896). But nowhere in these early publications did he specifically inculpate the girl's father. Indeed, in some additional footnotes written in 1924 for the *Gesammelte Schriften* reprint of *Studies on Hysteria*, he admitted to having on two occasions suppressed the fact of the father's responsibility. He made this quite clear, however, in the letter to Fliess of September 21, 1897 ("Extracts from the Fliess Papers," letter 69), in which he first expressed his scepticism about these stories told by his patients. His first published admission of his mistake was given several years later in a hint in the second of the *Three Essays on the Theory of Sexuality* (1905), but a much fuller account of the position followed in his contribution on the aetiology of the neuroses to a volume by Löwenfeld (1906). Later on he gave two accounts of the effects that this discovery of his mistake had on his own mind—in his "History of the Psycho-Analytic Movement" (1914), and in his *Autobiographical Study* (1925). The further discovery which is described in the present paragraph of the text had already been indicated in the paper "Female Sexuality" (1931).

7. See *Introductory Lectures on Psycho-Analysis*, XXII and XXIII.

8. Freud's fullest discussion of masturbation was in his "Contributions to a Discussion on Masturbation," in the Vienna Psycho-Analytical Society (1912).

9. See p. 33.

10. Cf. section II of "On Narcissism: An Introduction" (1914).

11. This had already been remarked upon earlier, in "The Taboo of Virginity" (1918).

12. This point seems to have been made by Freud first in a footnote to chapter VI of *Group Psychology and the Analysis of the Ego* (1921). He repeated it in the *Introductory Lectures on Psycho-Analysis*, XII and in chapter V of *Civilization and Its Discontents* (1930). Exceptions may occur.

13. Cf. some remarks on this in chapter XII (D) of *Group Psychology and the Analysis of the Ego* (1921).

SELECTED BIBLIOGRAPHY

BRUNSWICK, RUTH MACK. "The Analysis of a Case of Paranoia." 1928. *The Journal of Nervous Mental Disorder* 70 (1929): 177.

DEUTSCH, HELENE. "Homosexuality in Women." 1932. *International Journal of Psycho-Analysis.* 14 (1933): 34–56.

FREUD, SIGMUND. *Autobiographical Study.* New York: W. W. Norton, 1963.

———. *The Standard Edition of the Complete Psychological Works of Sigmund Freud.* 24 vols. Trans. James Strachey et al. Ed. James Strachey. London: Hogarth Press, 1974; rpt. 1986. (The initials *SE* are used to refer to this edition in subsequent entries.)

———. "The Aetiology of Hysteria." 1896. *SE* 3: 187–221.

———. *Civilization and Its Discontents.* 1930. *SE* 21: 57–145.

———. "Contributions to a Discussion on Masturbation." 1912. *SE* 12: 243–254.

———. "Female Sexuality." 1931. *SE* 21: 221–243.

———. "Further Remarks on the Neuro-Psychoses of Defence." 1896. *SE* 3: 162–185.

———. *Group Psychology and the Analysis of the Ego.* 1921. *SE* 18: 65–144.

———. *Introductory Lectures on Psycho-Analysis.* 1929. *SE* 15–16.

———. "My Views on the Part Played by Sexuality in the Aetiology of the Neuroses." 1906. *SE* 7: 271–279.

———. "On the History of the Psycho-Analytic Movement." 1914. *SE* 14: 7–66.

———. "On Narcissism: An introduction." 1914. *SE* 14: 73–102.

————. "Extracts from the Fliess Papers." *The Origins of Psycho-Analysis*. 1950. *SE* 1: 175–279.

————. *Outline of Psycho-Analysis*. 1940. *SE* 23: 139–208.

————. "Some Psychical Consequences of the Anatomical Distinction between the Sexes." 1925. *SE* 19: 241–258.

————. "The Taboo of Virginity." 1918. *SE* 11: 191–208.

————. *Three Essays on the Theory of Sexuality*. 1905. *SE* 7: 125–245.

LAMPL-DE GROOT, JEANNE. "The Evolution of the Oedipus Complex in Women." 1927. *International Journal of Psycho-Analysis* 9 (1928): 332–345.

jacques lacan

THE SIGNIFICATION OF
THE PHALLUS

The following is the original, unaltered text of a lecture that I delivered in German on 9 May, 1958, at the Max-Planck Institute, Mu-
nich, where Professor Paul Matussek had invited me to speak. If one
has any notion of the state of mind then prevalent in even the least
unaware circles, one will appreciate the effect that my use of such
terms as, for example, 'the other scene', which I was the first to extract from Freud's work, must have had. If 'deferred action' (*Nach-
trag*), to rescue another of these terms from the facility into which
they have since fallen, renders this effort impracticable, it should be
known that they were unheard of at that time.

We know that the unconscious castration complex has the function of a knot:

(1)   in the dynamic structuring of symptoms in the analytic sense of the term, that
        is to say, in that which is analysable in the neuroses, perversions, and psychoses;
(2)   in a regulation of the development that gives its *ratio* to this first role: namely,
        the installation in the subject of an unconscious position without which he would
        be unable to identify himself with the ideal type of his sex, or to respond with-
        out grave risk to the needs of his partner in the sexual relation, or even to accept
        in a satisfactory way the needs of the child who may be produced by this
        relation.

There is an antinomy, here, that is internal to the assumption by man (*Mensch*)
of his sex: why must he assume the attributes of that sex only through a
threat—the threat, indeed, of their privation? In 'Civilization and Its Discontents' Freud, as we know, went so far as to suggest a disturbance of human
sexuality, not of a contingent, but of an essential kind, and one of his last articles
concerns the irreducibility in any finite (*endliche*) analysis of the sequellae resulting from the castration complex in the masculine unconscious and from *penisneid*
in the unconscious of women.

This is not the only aporia, but it is the first that the Freudian experience and
the metapsychology that resulted from it introduced into our experience of man.
It is insoluble by any reduction to biological givens: the very necessity of the
myth subjacent to the structuring of the Oedipus complex demonstrates this
sufficiently.

It would be mere trickery to invoke in this case some hereditary amnesic trait,

From Écrits, A Selection, *trans. Alan Sheridan. Reprinted by permission of W. W. Norton & Company, Inc. Copyright © 1977 by Tavistock Publications Limited.*

not only because such a trait is in itself debatable, but because it leaves the problem unsolved: namely, what is the link between the murder of the father and the pact of the primordial law, if it is included in that law that castration should be the punishment for incest?

It is only on the basis of the clinical facts that any discussion can be fruitful. These facts reveal a relation of the subject to the phallus that is established without regard to the anatomical difference of the sexes, and which, by this very fact, makes any interpretation of this relation especially difficult in the case of women. This problem may be treated under the following four headings:

(1)   from this 'why', the little girl considers herself, if only momentarily, as castrated, in the sense of deprived of the phallus, by someone, in the first instance by her mother, an important point, and then by her father, but in such a way that one must recognize in it a transference in the analytic sense of the term;

(2)   from this 'why', in a more primordial sense, the mother is considered, by both sexes, as possessing the phallus, as the phallic mother;

(3)   from this 'why', correlatively, the signification of castration in fact takes on its (clinically manifest) full weight as far as the formation of symptoms is concerned, only on the basis of its discovery as castration of the mother;

(4)   these three problems lead, finally, to the question of the reason, in development, for the phallic stage. We know that in this term Freud specifies the first genital maturation: on the one hand, it would seem to be characterized by the imaginary dominance of the phallic attribute and by masturbatory *jouissance* and, on the other, it localizes this *jouissance* for the woman in the clitoris, which is thus raised to the function of the phallus. It therefore seems to exclude in both sexes, until the end of this stage, that is, to the decline of the Oedipal stage, all instinctual mapping of the vagina as locus of genital penetration.

This ignorance is suspiciously like *méconnaissance* in the technical sense of the term—all the more so in that it is sometimes quite false. Does this not bear out the fable in which Longus shows us the initiation of Daphnis and Chloe subordinated to the explanations of an old woman?

Thus certain authors have been led to regard the phallic stage as the effect of a repression, and the function assumed in it by the phallic object as a symptom. The difficulty begins when one asks, *what* symptom? Phobia, says one, perversion, says another, both says a third. It seems in the last case that nothing more can be said: not that interesting transmutations of the object of a phobia into a fetish do not occur, but if they are interesting it is precisely on account of the difference of their place in the structure. It would be pointless to demand of these authors that they formulate this difference from the perspectives currently in favour, that is to say, in terms of the object relation. Indeed, there is no other reference on the subject than the approximate notion of part-object, which—unfortunately, in view of the convenient uses to which it is being put in our time, has never been subjected to criticism since Karl Abraham introduced it.

The fact remains that the now abandoned discussion of the phallic stage, to be found in the surviving texts of the years 1928–32, is refreshing for the example it sets us of a devotion to doctrine—to which the degradation of psychoanalysis consequent on its American transplantation adds a note of nostalgia.

Merely to summarize the debate would be to distort the authentic diversity of the positions taken up by a Helene Deutsch, a Karen Horney, and an Ernest Jones, to mention only the most eminent.

The series of three articles devoted by Jones to the subject are especially fruitful—if only for the development of the notion of *aphanisis*, a term that he himself had coined.[1] For, in positing so correctly the problem of the relation between castration and desire, he demonstrates his inability to recognize what he nevertheless grasped so clearly that the term that earlier provided us with the key to it seems to emerge from his very failure.

Particularly amusing is the way in which he manages to extract from a letter by Freud himself a position that is strictly contrary to it: an excellent model in a difficult *genre*.

Yet the matter refuses to rest there, Jones appearing to contradict his own case for a re-establishment of the equality of natural rights (does he not win the day with the Biblical 'God created them man and woman' with which his plea concludes?). In fact, what has he gained in normalizing the function of the phallus as a part-object if he has to invoke its presence in the mother's body as an internal object, which term is a function of the phantasies revealed by Melanie Klein, and if he cannot separate himself from Klein's view that these phantasies originate as far back as in early childhood, during Oedipal formation?

It might be a good idea to re-examine the question by asking what could have necessitated for Freud the evident paradox of his position. For one has to admit that he was better guided than anyone in his recognition of the order of unconscious phenomena, of which he was the inventor, and that, failing an adequate articulation of the nature of these phenomena, his followers were doomed to lose their way to a greater or lesser degree.

It is on the basis of the following bet—which I lay down as the principle of a commentary of Freud's work that I have pursued during the past seven years—that I have been led to certain results: essentially, to promulgate as necessary to any articulation of analytic phenomena the notion of the signifier, as opposed to that of the signified, in modern linguistic analysis. Freud could not take this notion, which postdates him, into account, but I would claim that Freud's discovery stands out precisely because, although it set out from a domain in which one could not expect to recognize its reign, it could not fail to anticipate its formulas. Conversely, it is Freud's discovery that gives to the signifier/signified opposition the full extent of its implications: namely, that the signifier has an active function in determining certain effects in which the signifiable appears as submitting to its mark, by becoming through that passion the signified.

This passion of the signifier now becomes a new dimension of the human condition in that it is not only man who speaks, but that in man and through man *it* speaks (*ça parle*), that his nature is woven by effects in which is to be found the structure of language, of which he becomes the material, and that therefore there resounds in him, beyond what could be conceived of by a psychology of ideas, the relation of speech.

In this sense one can say that the consequences of the discovery of the unconscious have not yet been so much as glimpsed in theory, although its effects have been felt in praxis to a greater degree than perhaps we are aware of, if only in the form of effects of retreat.

It should be made clear that this advocacy of man's relation to the signifier as such has nothing to do with a 'culturalist' position in the ordinary sense of the term, the position in which Karen Horney, for example, was anticipated in the dispute concerning the phallus by a position described by Freud himself as a feminist one. It is not a question of the relation between man and language as a social phenomenon, there being no question even of something resembling the ideological psychogenesis with which we are familiar, and which is not super-seded by peremptory recourse to the quite metaphysical notion, which lurks beneath its question-begging appeal to the concrete, conveyed so pitifully by the term 'affect'.

It is a question of rediscovering in the laws that govern that other scene (*ein andere Schauplatz*), which Freud, on the subject of dreams, designates as being that of the unconscious, the effects that are discovered at the level of the chain of materially unstable elements that constitutes language: effects determined by the double play of combination and substitution in the signifier, according to the two aspects that generate the signified, metonymy and metaphor; determining effects for the institution of the subject. From this test, a topology, in the mathe-matical sense of the term, appears, without which one soon realizes that it is impossible simply to note the structure of a symptom in the analytic sense of the term.

It speaks in the Other, I say, designating by the Other the very locus evoked by the recourse to speech in any relation in which the Other intervenes. If *it* speaks in the Other, whether or not the subject hears it with his ear, it is because it is there that the subject, by means of a logic anterior to any awakening of the signified, finds its signifying place. The discovery of what it articulates in that place, that is to say, in the unconscious, enables us to grasp at the price of what splitting (*Spaltung*) it has thus been constituted.

The phallus reveals its function here. In Freudian doctrine, the phallus is not a phantasy, if by that we mean an imaginary effect. Nor is it as such an object (part-, internal, good, bad, etc.) in the sense that this term tends to accentuate the reality pertaining in a relation. It is even less the organ, penis or clitoris, that it symbolizes. And it is not without reason that Freud used the reference to the simulacrum that it represented for the Ancients.

For the phallus is a signifier, a signifier whose function, in the intrasubjective economy of the analysis, lifts the veil perhaps from the function it performed in the mysteries. For it is the signifier intended to designate as a whole the effects of the signified, in that the signifier conditions them by its presence as a signifier.

Let us now examine the effects of this presence. In the first instance, they proceed from a deviation of man's needs from the fact that he speaks, in the sense that in so far as his needs are subjected to demand, they return to him alienated. This is not the effect of his real dependence (one should not expect to find here the parasitic conception represented by the notion of dependence in the theory of neurosis), but rather the turning into signifying form as such, from the fact that it is from the locus of the Other that its message is emitted.

That which is thus alienated in needs constitutes an *Urverdrängung* (primal repression), an inability, it is supposed, to be articulated in demand, but it re-appears in something it gives rise to that presents itself in man as desire (*das Begehren*). The phenomenology that emerges from analytic experience is cer-tainly of a kind to demonstrate in desire the paradoxical, deviant, erratic, eccentric, even scandalous character by which it is distinguished from need. This fact has been too often affirmed not to have been always obvious to moralists worthy of the name. The Freudianism of earlier days seemed to owe its status to this fact. Paradoxically, however, psychoanalysis is to be found at the head of an ever-present obscurantism that is still more boring when it denies the fact in an ideal of theoretical and practical reduction of desire to need.

This is why we must articulate this status here, beginning with *demand*, whose proper characteristics are eluded in the notion of frustration (which Freud never used).

Demand in itself bears on something other than the satisfactions it calls for. It is demand of a presence or of an absence—which is what is manifested in the primordial relation to the mother, pregnant with that Other to be situated *within* the needs that it can satisfy. Demand constitutes the Other as already possessing the 'privilege' of satisfying needs, that it is to say, the power of depriving them of that alone by which they are satisfied. This privilege of the Other thus outlines the radical form of the gift of that which the Other does not have, namely, its love.

In this way, demand annuls (*aufhebt*) the particularity of everything that can be granted by transmuting it into a proof of love, and the very satisfactions that it obtains for need are reduced (*sich erniedrigt*) to the level of being no more than the crushing of the demand for love (all of which is perfectly apparent in the psychology of child-rearing, to which our analyst-nurses are so attached).

It is necessary, then, that the particularity thus abolished should reappear *beyond* demand. It does, in fact, reappear there, but preserving the structure contained in the unconditional element of the demand for love. By a reversal that is not simply a negation of the negation, the power of pure loss emerges from the residue of an obliteration. For the unconditional element of demand, desire substitutes the 'absolute' condition: this condition unties the knot of that element in the proof of love that is resistant to the satisfaction of a need. Thus desire is neither the appetite for satisfaction, nor the demand for love, but the difference that results from the subtraction of the first from the second, the phenomenon of their splitting (*Spaltung*).

One can see how the sexual relation occupies this closed field of desire, in which it will play out its fate. This is because it is the field made for the production of the enigma that this relation arouses in the subject by doubly 'signifying' it to him: the return of the demand that it gives rise to, as a demand on the subject of the need—an ambiguity made present on to the Other in question in the proof of love demanded. The gap in this enigma betrays what determines it, namely, to put it in the simplest possible way, that for both partners in the relation, both the subject and the Other, it is not enough to be subjects of need, or objects of love, but that they must stand for the cause of desire.

This truth lies at the heart of all the distortions that have appeared in the field of psychoanalysis on the subject of the sexual life. It also constitutes the condition of the happiness of the subject: and to disguise the gap it creates by leaving it to the virtue of the 'genital' to resolve it through the maturation of tenderness (that is to say, solely by recourse to the Other as reality), however well intentioned, is fraudulent nonetheless. It has to be said here that the French analysts, with their hypocritical notion of genital oblativity, opened the way to the moralizing tendency, which, to the accompaniment of its Salvationist choirs, is now to be found everywhere.

In any case, man cannot aim at being whole (the 'total personality' is another of the deviant premises of modern psychotherapy), while ever the play of displacement and condensation to which he is doomed in the exercise of his functions marks his relation as a subject to the signifier.

The phallus is the privileged signifier of that mark in which the role of the logos is joined with the advent of desire.

It can be said that this signifier is chosen because it is the most tangible element in the real of sexual copulation, and also the most symbolic in the literal (typographical) sense of the term, since it is equivalent there to the (logical) copula. It might also be said that, by virtue of its turgidity, it is the image of the vital flow as it is transmitted in generation.

All these propositions merely conceal the fact that it can play its role only when veiled, that is to say, as itself a sign of the latency with which any signifiable is struck, when it is raised (*aufgehoben*) to the function of signifier.

The phallus is the signifier of this *Aufhebung* itself, which it inaugurates (initiates) by its disappearance. That is why the demon of Αἰδώς (*Scham*, shame) arises at the very moment when, in the ancient mysteries, the phallus is unveiled (cf. the famous painting in the Villa di Pompei).

It then becomes the bar which, at the hands of this demon, strikes the signified, marking it as the bastard offspring of this signifying concatenation.

Thus a condition of complementarity is produced in the establishment of the subject by the signifier—which explains the *Spaltung* in the subject and the movement of intervention in which that 'splitting' is completed.

Namely:

(1)   that the subject designates his being only by barring everything he signifies, as it appears in the fact that he wants to be loved for himself, a mirage that cannot be dismissed as merely grammatical (since it abolishes discourse);

(2)   that the living part of that being in the *urverdrängt* (primally repressed) finds its signifier by receiving the mark of the *Verdrängung* (repression) of the phallus (by virtue of which the unconscious is language).

The phallus as signifier gives the ratio of desire (in the sense in which the term is used in music in the 'mean and extreme ratio' of harmonic division).

I shall also be using the phallus as an algorithm, so if I am to help you to grasp this use of the term I shall have to rely on the echoes of the experience that we share—otherwise, my account of the problem could go on indefinitely.

The fact that the phallus is a signifier means that it is in the place of the Other that the subject has access to it. But since this signifier is only veiled, as ratio of the Other's desire, it is this desire of the Other as such that the subject must recognize, that is to say, the other in so far as he is himself a subject divided by the signifying *Spaltung*.

The emergences that appear in psychological genesis confirm this signifying function of the phallus.

Thus, to begin with, the Kleinian fact that the child apprehends from the outset that the mother 'contains' the phallus may be formulated more correctly.

But it is in the dialectic of the demand for love and the test of desire that development is ordered.

The demand for love can only suffer from a desire whose signifier is alien to it. If the desire of the mother *is* the phallus, the child wishes to be the phallus in order to satisfy that desire. Thus the division immanent in desire is already felt to be experienced in the desire of the Other, in that it is already opposed to the fact that the subject is content to present to the Other what in reality he may *have* that corresponds to this phallus, for what he has is worth no more than what he does not have, as far as his demand for love is concerned because that demand requires that he be the phallus.

Clinical experience has shown us that this test of the desire of the Other is decisive not in the sense that the subject learns by it whether or not he has a real phallus, but in the sense that he learns that the mother does not have it. This is the moment of the experience without which no symptomatic consequence (phobia) or structural consequence (*Penisneid*) relating to the castration complex can take effect. Here is signed the conjunction of desire, in that the phallic signifier is its mark, with the threat or nostalgia of lacking it.

Of course, its future depends on the law introduced by the father into this sequence.

But one may, simply by reference to the function of the phallus, indicate the structures that will govern the relations between the sexes.

Let us say that these relations will turn around a 'to be' and a 'to have', which, by referring to a signifier, the phallus, have the opposed effect, on the one hand, of giving reality to the subject in this signifier, and, on the other, of derealizing the relations to be signified.

This is brought about by the intervention of a 'to seem' that replaces the 'to have', in order to protect it on the one side, and to mask its lack in the other, and which has the effect of projecting in their entirety the ideal or typical manifestations of the behaviour of each sex, including the act of copulation itself, into the comedy.

These ideals take on new vigour from the demand that they are capable of satisfying, which is always a demand for love, with its complement of the reduction of desire to demand.

Paradoxical as this formulation may seem, I am saying that it is in order to be the phallus, that is to say, the signifier of the desire of the Other, that a woman will reject an essential part of femininity, namely, all her attributes in the masquerade. It is for that which she is not that she wishes to be desired as well as loved. But she finds the signifier of her own desire in the body of him to whom she addresses her demand for love. Perhaps it should not be forgotten that the organ that assumes this signifying function takes on the value of a fetish. But the result for the woman remains that an experience of love, which, as such (cf. above), deprives her ideally of that which the object gives, and a desire which finds its signifier in this object, converge on the same object. That is why one can observe that a lack in the satisfaction proper to sexual need, in other words, frigidity, is relatively well tolerated in women, whereas the *Verdrängung* (repression) inherent in desire is less present in women than in men.

In the case of men, on the other hand, the dialectic of demand and desire engenders the effects—and one must once more admire the sureness with which

Freud situated them at the precise articulations on which they depended—of a specific depreciation (*Erniedrigung*) of love.

If, in effect, the man finds satisfaction for his demand for love in the relation with the woman, in as much as the signifier of the phallus constitutes her as giving in love what she does not have—conversely, his own desire for the phallus will make its signifier emerge in its persistent divergence towards 'another woman' who may signify this phallus in various ways, either as a virgin or as a prostitute. There results from this a centrifugal tendency of the genital drive in love life, which makes impotence much more difficult to bear for him, while the *Verdrängung* inherent in desire is more important.

Yet it should not be thought that the sort of infidelity that would appear to be constitutive of the male function is proper to it. For if one looks more closely, the same redoubling is to be found in the woman, except that the Other of Love as such, that is to say, in so far as he is deprived of what he gives, finds it difficult to see himself in the retreat in which he is substituted for the being of the very man whose attributes she cherishes.

One might add here that male homosexuality, in accordance with the phallic mark that constitutes desire, is constituted on the side of desire, while female homosexuality, on the other hand, as observation shows, is oriented on a disappointment that reinforces the side of the demand for love. These remarks should really be examined in greater detail, from the point of view of a return to the function of the mask in so far as it dominates the identifications in which refusals of demand are resolved.

The fact that femininity finds its refuge in this mask, by virtue of the fact of the *Verdrängung* inherent in the phallic mark of desire, has the curious consequence of making virile display in the human being itself seem feminine.

Correlatively, one can glimpse the reason for a characteristic that had never before been elucidated, and which shows once again the depth of Freud's intuition: namely, why he advances the view that there is only one *libido*, his text showing that he conceives it as masculine in nature. The function of the phallic signifier touches here on its most profound relation: that in which the Ancients embodied the Νοῦς and the Λογὸς.

NOTE

1. *Aphanisis*, the disappearance of sexual desire. This Greek term was introduced into psychoanalysis by Jones in 'Early Development of Female Sexuality' (1927), in *Papers on Psycho-analysis*, 5th edn., London, 1950. For Jones, the fear of aphanisis exists, in both boys and girls, at a deeper level than the castration complex [Tr.].

julia kristéva

THE SEMIOTIC AND
THE SYMBOLIC

THE PHENOMENOLOGICAL SUBJECT
OF ENUNCIATION

We must specify, first and foremost, what we mean by the *signifying process* vis-à-vis general theories of meaning, theories of language, and theories of the subject.

Despite their variations, all modern linguistic theories consider language a strictly "formal" object—one that involves syntax or mathematicization. Within this perspective, such theories generally accept the following notion of language. For Zellig Harris, language is defined by: (1) the arbitrary relation between signifier and signified, (2) the acceptance of the sign as a substitute for the extra-linguistic, (3) its discrete elements, and (4) its denumerable, or even finite, nature.[1] But with the development of Chomskyan generative grammar and the logico-semantic research that was articulated around and in response to it, problems arose that were generally believed to fall within the province of "semantics" or even "pragmatics," and raised the awkward question of the *extra-linguistic*. But language [*langage*]—modern linguistics' self-assigned object[2]—lacks a subject or tolerates one only as a *transcendental ego* (in Husserl's sense or in Benveniste's more specifically linguistic sense),[3] and defers any interrogation of its (always already dialectical because trans-linguistic) "externality."

Two trends in current linguistic research do attend to this "externality" in the belief that failure to elucidate it will hinder the development of linguistic theory itself. Although such a lacuna poses problems (which we will later specify) for "formal" linguistics, it has always been a particular problem for semiotics, which is concerned with specifying the functioning of signifying practices such as art, poetry, and myth that are irreducible to the "language" object.

1. The first of these two trends addresses the question of the so-called "arbitrary" relation between signifier and signified by examining signifying systems in which this relation is presented as "motivated." It seeks the principle of this motivation in the Freudian notion of the unconscious insofar as the theories of drives [*pulsions*] and primary processes (displacement and condensation) can connect "empty signifiers" to psychosomatic functionings, or can at least link them in a sequence of metaphors and metonymies; though undecidable, such a sequence replaces "arbitrariness" with "articulation." The discourse of analysands, language "pathologies," and artistic, particularly poetic, systems are especially suited to such an exploration.[4] Formal linguistic relations are thus connected to an "externality" in the psychosomatic realm, which is ultimately

Excerpts from Revolution in Poetic Language, Julia Kristéva, © *1984, Columbia University Press, New York. Reprinted with the permission of the publisher.*

reduced to a fragmented substance [*substance morcelée*] (the body divided into erogenous zones) and articulated by the developing ego's connections to the three points of the family triangle. Such a linguistic theory, clearly indebted to the positions of the psychoanalytic school of London and Melanie Klein in particular, restores to formal linguistic relations the dimensions (instinctual drives) and operations (displacement, condensation, vocalic and intonational differentiation) that formalistic theory excludes. Yet for want of a dialectical notion of the *signifying process* as a whole, in which signifiance puts the subject in process/on trial [*en procès*], such considerations, no matter how astute, fail to take into account the syntactico-semantic functioning of language. Although they rehabilitate the notion of the fragmented body—pre-Oedipal but always already invested with semiosis—these linguistic theories fail to articulate its transitional link to the post-Oedipal subject and his always symbolic and/or syntactic language. (We shall return to this point.)

2. The second trend, more recent and widespread, introduces within theory's own formalism a "layer" of *semiosis*, which had been strictly relegated to pragmatics and semantics. By positing a *subject of enunciation* (in the sense of Benveniste, Culioli, etc.), this theory places logical modal relations, relations of presupposition, and other relations between interlocutors within the speech act, in a very deep "deep structure." This *subject of enunciation*, which comes directly from Husserl and Benveniste (see n. 3), introduces, through categorial intuition, both *semantic fields* and *logical*—but also *intersubjective*—*relations*, which prove to be both intra- and trans-linguistic.[5]

To the extent it is assumed by a subject who "means" (*bedeuten*), language has "deep structures" that articulate *categories*. These categories are semantic (as in the semantic fields introduced by recent developments in generative grammar), logical (modality relations, etc.), and intercommunicational (those which Searle called "speech acts" seen as bestowers of meaning).[6] But they may also be related to historical linguistic changes, thereby joining diachrony with synchrony.[7] In this way, through the subject who "means," linguistics is opened up to all possible categories and thus to philosophy, which linguistics had thought it would be able to escape.

In a similar perspective, certain linguists, interested in explaining semantic constraints, distinguish between different types of *styles* depending on the speaking subject's position vis-à-vis the utterance. Even when such research thereby introduces stylistics into semantics, its aim is to study the workings of signification, taking into account the subject of enunciation, which always proves to be the phenomenological subject.[8] Some linguistic research goes even further: starting from the subject of enunciation/transcendental ego, and prompted by the opening of linguistics onto semantics and logic, it views signification as an ideological and therefore historical production.[9]

We shall not be able to discuss the various advantages and drawbacks of this second trend in modern linguistics except to say that it is still evolving, and that although its conclusions are only tentative, its epistemological bases lead us to the heart of the debate on phenomenology which we can only touch on here—and only insofar as the specific research we are presently undertaking allows.[10]

To summarize briefly what we shall elucidate later, the two trends just mentioned designate *two modalities* of what is, for us, the same signifying process. We shall call the first *"the semiotic"* and the second *"the symbolic."* These two modalities are inseparable within the *signifying process* that constitutes language, and the dialectic between them determines the type of discourse (narrative, metalanguage, theory, poetry, etc.) involved; in other words, so-called "natural" language allows for different modes of articulation of the semiotic and the symbolic. On the other hand, there are nonverbal signifying systems that are constructed exclusively on the basis of the semiotic (music, for example). But, as we shall see, this exclusivity is relative, precisely because of the necessary dialectic between the two modalities of the signifying process, which is constitutive of the subject. Because the subject is always *both* semiotic *and* symbolic, no signifying system he produces can be either "exclusively" semiotic or "exclusively" symbolic, and is instead necessarily marked by an indebtedness to both.

THE SEMIOTIC *CHORA* ORDERING THE DRIVES

We understand the term "semiotic" in its Greek sense: σημεῖον = distinctive mark, trace, index, precursory sign, proof, engraved or written sign, imprint, trace, figuration. This etymological reminder would be a mere archaeological embellishment (and an unconvincing one at that, since the term ultimately encompasses such disparate meanings), were it not for the fact that the preponderant etymological use of the word, the one that implies a *distinctiveness*, allows us to connect it to a precise modality in the signifying process. This modality is the one Freudian psychoanalysis points to in postulating not only the *facilitation* and the structuring *disposition* of drives, but also the so-called *primary processes* which displace and condense both energies and their inscription. Discrete quantities of energy move through the body of the subject who is not yet constituted as such and, in the course of his development, they are arranged according to the various constraints imposed on this body—always already involved in a semiotic process—by family and social structures. In this way the drives, which are "energy" charges as well as "psychical" marks, articulate what we call a *chora*: a nonexpressive totality formed by the drives and their stases in a motility that is as full of movement as it is regulated.

We borrow the term *chora* [11] from Plato's *Timaeus* to denote an essentially mobile and extremely provisional articulation constituted by movements and their ephemeral stases. We differentiate this uncertain and indeterminate *articulation* from a *disposition* that already depends on representation, lends itself to phenomenological, spatial intuition, and gives rise to a geometry. Although our theoretical description of the *chora* is itself part of the discourse of representation that offers it as evidence, the *chora*, as rupture and articulations (rhythm), precedes evidence, verisimilitude, spatiality, and temporality. Our discourse—all discourse—moves with and against the *chora* in the sense that it simultaneously depends upon and refuses it. Although the *chora* can be designated and regulated, it can never be definitively posited: as a result, one can situate the *chora* and, if necessary, lend it a topology, but one can never give it axiomatic form. [12]

The *chora* is not yet a position that represents something for someone (i.e., it is not a sign); nor is it a *position* that represents someone for another position (i.e., it is not yet a signifier either); it is, however, generated in order to attain to this signifying position. Neither model nor copy, the *chora* precedes and under- lies figuration and thus specularization, and is analogous only to vocal or kinetic rhythm. We must restore this motility's gestural and vocal play (to mention only the aspect relevant to language) on the level of the socialized body in order to remove motility from ontology and amorphousness[13] where Plato confines it in an apparent attempt to conceal it from Democritean rhythm. The theory of the subject proposed by the theory of the unconscious will allow us to read in this rhythmic space, which has no thesis and no position, the process by which sig- nificance is constituted. Plato himself leads us to such a process when he calls this receptacle or *chora* nourishing and maternal,[14] not yet unified in an ordered whole because deity is absent from it. Though deprived of unity, identity, or deity, the *chora* is nevertheless subject to a regulating process [*réglementation*], which is different from that of symbolic law but nevertheless effectuates discon- tinuities by temporarily articulating them and then starting over, again and again.

The *chora* is a modality of significance in which the linguistic sign is not yet articulated as the absence of an object and as the distinction between real and symbolic. We emphasize the regulated aspect of the *chora:* its vocal and gestural organization is subject to what we shall call an objective *ordering* [*ordonnance- ment*], which is dictated by natural or socio-historical constraints such as the bio- logical difference between the sexes or family structure. We may therefore posit that social organization, always already symbolic, imprints its constraint in a me- diated form which organizes the *chora* not according to a *law* (a term we reserve for the symbolic) but through an *ordering*.[15] What is this mediation?

According to a number of psycholinguists, "concrete operations" precede the acquisition of language, and organize preverbal semiotic space according to logi- cal categories, which are thereby shown to precede or transcend language. From their research we shall retain not the principle of an operational state[16] but that of a preverbal functional state that governs the connections between the body (in the process of constituting itself as a body proper), objects, and the protago- nists of family structure.[17] But we shall distinguish this functioning from symbolic operations that depend on language as a sign system—whether the language [*langue*] is vocalized or gestural (as with deaf-mutes). The kinetic functional stage of the *semiotic* precedes the establishment of the sign; it is not, therefore, cognitive in the sense of being assumed by a knowing, already constituted sub- ject. The genesis of the *functions*[18] organizing the semiotic process can be accu- rately elucidated only within a theory of the subject that does not reduce the subject to one of understanding, but instead opens up within the subject this other scene of pre-symbolic functions. The Kleinian theory expanding upon Freud's positions on the drives will momentarily serve as a guide.

Drives involve pre-Oedipal semiotic functions and energy discharges that con- nect and orient the body to the mother. We must emphasize that "drives" are always already ambiguous, simultaneously assimilating and destructive; this du- alism, which has been represented as a tetrad[19] or as a double helix, as in the configuration of the DNA and RNA molecule,[20] makes the semiotized body a place of permanent scission. The oral and anal drives, both of which are oriented and structured around the mother's body,[21] dominate this sensorimotor organization. The mother's body is therefore what mediates the symbolic law organizing social relations and becomes the ordering principle of the semiotic *chora*,[22] which is on the path of destruction, aggressivity, and death. For although drives have been described as disunited or contradictory structures, simultaneously "positive" and "negative," this doubling is said to generate a dominant "destructive wave" that is drive's most characteristic trait: Freud notes that the most instinctual drive is the death drive.[23] In this way, the term "drive" denotes waves of attack against stases, which are themselves constituted by the repetition of these charges; together, charges and stases lead to no identity (not even that of the "body proper") that could be seen as a result of their functioning. This is to say that the semiotic *chora* is no more than the place where the subject is both generated and negated, the place where his unity succumbs before the process of charges and stases that produce him. We shall call this process of charges and stases a *negativity* to distinguish it from negation, which is the act of a judging subject.

Checked by the constraints of biological and social structures, the drive charge thus undergoes stases. Drive facilitation, temporarily arrested, marks *discontinuities* in what may be called the various material supports [*matériaux*] susceptible to semiotization: voice, gesture, colors. Phonic (later phonemic), kinetic, or chromatic units and differences are the marks of these stases in the drives. Connections or *functions* are thereby established between these discrete marks which are based on drives and articulated according to their resemblance or opposition, either by slippage or by condensation. Here we find the principles of metonymy and metaphor indissociable from the drive economy underlying them.

Although we recognize the vital role played by the processes of displacement and condensation in the organization of the semiotic, we must also add to these processes the relations (eventually representable as topological spaces) that connect the zones of the fragmented body to each other and also to "external" "objects" and "subjects," which are not yet constituted as such. This type of relation makes it possible to specify the *semiotic* as a psychosomatic modality of the signifying process; in other words, not a symbolic modality but one articulating (in the largest sense of the word) a continuum: the connections between the (glottal and anal) sphincters in (rhythmic and intonational) vocal modulations, or those between the sphincters and family protagonists, for example.

All these various processes and relations, anterior to sign and syntax, have just been identified from a genetic perspective as previous and necessary to the acquisition of language, but not identical to language. Theory can "situate" such processes and relations diachronically within the process of the constitution of the subject precisely because *they function synchronically within the signifying process of the subject himself,* i.e., the subject of *cogitatio.* Only in *dream* logic, however, have they attracted attention, and only in certain signifying practices, such as the *text,* do they dominate the signifying process.

It may be hypothesized that certain semiotic articulations are transmitted through the biological code or physiological "memory" and thus form the inborn bases of the symbolic function. Indeed, one branch of generative linguistics asserts the principle of innate language universals. As it will become apparent in what follows, however, the *symbolic*—and therefore syntax and all linguistic categories—is a social effect of the relation to the other, established through the objective constraints of biological (including sexual) differences and concrete, historical family structures. Genetic programmings are necessarily semiotic: they include the primary processes such as displacement and condensation, absorption and repulsion, rejection and stasis, all of which function as innate preconditions, "memorizable" by the species, for language acquisition.

Mallarmé calls attention to the semiotic rhythm within language when he speaks of "The Mystery in Literature" ["Le Mystère dans les lettres"]. Indifferent to language, enigmatic and feminine, this space underlying the written is rhythmic, unfettered, irreducible to its intelligible verbal translation; it is musical, anterior to judgment, but restrained by a single guarantee: syntax. As evidence, we could cite "The Mystery in Literature" in its entirety.[24] For now, however, we shall quote only those passages that ally the functioning of that "air or song beneath the text" with woman:

> And the instrument of Darkness, whom they have designated, will not set down a word from then on except to deny that she must have been the enigma; lest she settle matters with a wisk of her skirts: 'I don't get it!'"
>
> . . . .
>
> —They [the critics] play their parts disinterestedly or for a minor gain: leaving our Lady and Patroness exposed to show her dehiscence or lacuna, with respect to certain dreams, as though this were the standard to which everything is reduced.[25]

To these passages we add others that point to the "mysterious" functioning of literature as a rhythm made intelligible by syntax: "Following the instinct for rhythms that has chosen him, the poet does not deny seeing a lack of proportion between the means let loose and the result." "I know that there are those who would restrict Mystery to Music's domain; when writing aspires to it."[26]

> What pivot is there, I mean within these contrasts, for intelligibility? a guarantee is needed—
>   Syntax—
>   . . . an extraordinary appropriation of structure, limpid, to the primitive lightning bolts of logic. A stammering, what the sentence seems, here repressed [. . .]
>
> . . . .
>
> The debate—whether necessary average clarity deviates in a detail—remains one for grammarians.[27]

Our positing of the semiotic is obviously inseparable from a theory of the subject that takes into account the Freudian positing of the unconscious. We view the subject in language as decentering the transcendental ego, cutting through it, and opening it up to a dialectic in which its syntactic and categorical understanding is merely the liminary moment of the process, which is itself always acted upon by the relation to the other dominated by the death drive and its productive reiteration of the "signifier." We will be attempting to formulate the distinction between *semiotic* and *symbolic* within this perspective, which was

introduced by Lacanian analysis, but also within the constraints of a practice—the *text*—which is only of secondary interest to psychoanalysis.

NOTES

1. See Zellig Harris, *Mathematical Structures of Language* (New York: Interscience Publishers, 1968). See also Maurice Gross and André Lentin, *Introduction to Formal Grammars*,
M. Salkoff, tr. (Berlin: Springer-Verlag, 1970). M.-C. Barbault and I.-P. Desclés, *Transformations formelles et théories linguistiques*, Documents de linguistique quantitative, no. 11
(Paris: Dunod, 1972).

2. On this "object" see *Langages* (December 1971), vol. 24, and, for a didactic, popularized account, see Julia Kristeva, *Le Langage cet inconnu* (Paris: Seuil, 1981).

3. Edmund Husserl, in *Ideas: General Introduction to Pure Phenomenology*, W. R. Boyce
Gibson, tr. (London: Allen & Unwin, 1969), posits this subject as a subject of intuition,
sure of this universally valid unity [of consciousness], a unity that is provided in *categories*
itself, since transcendence is precisely the immanence of this "Ego," which is an expansion of the Cartesian *cogito*. "We shall consider conscious experiences," Husserl writes,
"*in the concrete fullness and entirety* with which they figure in their concrete context—the
stream of experience—and to which they are closely attached through their own proper essence. It then becomes evident that every experience in the stream which our reflexion
can lay hold on has *its own essence open to intuition*, a 'content' which can be considered in
its *singularity in and for itself*. We shall be concerned to grasp this individual content of the
cogitatio in its *pure* singularity, and to describe it in its general features, excluding everything which is not to be found in the *cogitatio* as it is in itself. We must likewise describe
the *unity of consciousness* which is demanded *by the intrinsic nature of the cogitationes*, and so
necessarily demanded that they could not be without this unity" (p. 116). From a similar
perspective, Benveniste emphasizes language's dialogical character, as well as its role in
Freud's discovery. Discussing the I/you polarity, he writes: "This polarity does not mean
either equality or symmetry 'ego' always has a position of transcendence with regard to
you." In Benveniste, "Subjectivity in Language," *Problems in General Linguistics*, Miami
Linguistics Series, no. 8, Mary Elizabeth Meek, tr. (Coral Gables, Fla.: University of
Miami Press, 1971), p. 225. In Chomsky, the subject-bearer of syntactic synthesis is
clearly shown to stem from the Cartesian *cogito*. See his *Cartesian Linguistics: A Chapter in
the History of Rationalist Thought* (New York: Harper & Row, 1966). Despite the difference
between this Cartesian-Chomskyan subject and the transcendental ego outlined by Benveniste and others in a more clearly phenomenological sense, both these notions of the act
of understanding (or the linguistic act) rest on a common metaphysical foundation: consciousness as a synthesizing unity and the sole guarantee of Being. Moreover, several
scholars—without renouncing the Cartesian principles that governed the first syntactic
descriptions—have recently pointed out that Husserlian phenomenology is a more explicit
and more rigorously detailed basis for such description than the Cartesian method. See
Roman Jakobson, who recalls Husserl's role in the establishment of modern linguistics.
"Linguistics in Relation to Other Sciences," in *Selected Writings*, 2 vols. (The Hague:
Mouton, 1971), 2.655–696, and S.-Y. Kuroda, "The Categorical and the Thetic Judgment: Evidence from Japanese Syntax," *Foundations of Language* (November 1972), 9(2):
153–185.

4. See the work of Ivan Fónagy, particularly "Bases pulsionnelles de la phontation,"
Revue Française de Psychanalyse (January 1970), 34(1): 101–136, and (July 1971), 35(4):
543–591.

5. On the "subject of enunciation," see Tzvetan Todorov, spec. ed. *Langages* (March
1970), vol. 17. Formulated in linguistics by Benveniste ("The Correlations of Tense in

the French Verb" and "Subjectivity in Language," in *Problems*, pp. 205–216 and 223–230), the notion is used by many linguists, notably Antoine Culioli. "A propos d'opérations intervenant dans le traitement formel des langues naturelles," *Mathématiques et Sciences Humaines* (Summer 1971), 9(34): 7–15; and Oswald Ducrot, "Les Indéfinis et l'énonciation," *Langages* (March 1970), 5(17): 91–111. Chomsky's "extended standard theory" makes use of categorial intuition but does not refer to the subject of enunciation, even though the latter has been implicit in his theory ever since *Cartesian Linguistics* (1966); see his *Studies on Semantics in Generative Grammar*, Janua Linguarum, series minor, no. 107 (The Hague: Mouton, 1972).

6.   See John R. Searle, *Speech Acts: An Essay on the Philosophy of Language* (London: Cambridge University Press, 1969).

7.   See Robert D. King, *Historical Linguistics and Generative Grammar* (Englewood Cliffs, N.J.: Prentice-Hall, 1969); Paul Kiparsky, "Linguistic Universals and Linguistic Change," in *Universals of Linguistic Theory*, Emmon Bach and Robert T. Harms, eds. (New York: Holt, Rinehart and Winston, 1968), pp. 170–202; and Kiparsky, "How Abstract Is Phonology?" mimeograph reproduced by Indiana University Linguistics Club, October 1968.

8.   S.-Y. Kuroda distinguishes between two styles, "reportive" and "non-reportive." "Reportive" includes first-person narratives as well as those in the second and third person in which the narrator is "effaced"; "non-reportive" involves an omniscient narrator or "multi-consciousness." This distinction explains certain anomalies in the distribution of the adjective and verb of sensation in Japanese. (Common usage requires that the adjective be used with the first person but it can also refer to the third person. When it does, this agrammaticality signals another "grammatical style": an omniscient narrator is speaking in the name of a character, or the utterance expresses a character's point of view.) No matter what its subject of enunciation, the utterance, Kuroda writes, is described as representing that subject's *"Erlebnis"* ("experience"), in the sense Husserl uses the term in *Ideas*. See Kuroda, "Where Epistemology, Style, and Grammar Meet," mimeographed, University of California, San Diego, 1971.

9.   Even the categories of dialectical materialism introduced to designate a discourse's conditions of production as essential bestowers of its signification are based on a "subject-bearer" whose logical positing is no different from that found in Husserl (see above, n. 3). For example, Cl. Haroche, P. Henry, and Michel Pêcheux stress "the importance of linguistic studies on the relation between utterance and enunciation, by which the 'speaking subject' situates himself with respect to the representations he *bears*—representations that are put together by means of the linguistically analyzable 'pre-constructed.'" They conclude that "it is undoubtedly on this point—together with that of the syntagmatization of the characteristic substitutions of a discursive formation—that the contribution of the theory of discourse to the study of ideological formation (and the theory of ideologies) can now be most fruitfully developed." "La Sémantique et la coupure saussurienne: Langue, langage, discours," *Langages* (December 1971), 24: 106. This notion of the subject as always already there on the basis of a "pre-constructed" language (but how is it constructed? and what about the subject *who constructs* before *bearing* what has been constructed?) has even been preserved under a Freudian cover. As a case in point, Michel Tort questions the relation between psychoanalysis and historical materialism by placing a subject-bearer between "ideological agency" and "unconscious formations." He defines this subject-bearer as "the biological specificity of individuals (individuality as a biological concept), inasmuch as it is the material basis upon which individuals are called to function by social relations." "La Psychanalyse dans le matérialisme historique," *Nouvelle Revue de Psychoanalyse* (Spring 1970), 1: 154. But this theory provides only a hazy view of how this subject-bearer is produced through the unconscious and within the "ideological" signifier, and does not allow us to see this production's investment in ideological representations

themselves. From this perspective, the only thing one can say about "arts" or "religions," for example, is that they are "relics." On language and history, see also Jean-Claude Chevalier, "Langage et histoire," *Langue Française* (September 1972), 15: 3–17.

10. On the phenomenological bases of modern linguistics, see Kristéva, "Les Epistémologies de la linguistique," *Langages* (December 1971), 24: 11; and especially: Jacques Derrida, "The Supplement of Copula: Philosophy Before Linguistics," Josué V. Harari, tr., *Textual Strategies*, Josué V. Harari, ed. (Ithaca, N.Y.: Cornell University Press, 1979), pp. 82–120; *Of Grammatology*, Gayatri Chakravorty Spivak, tr. (Baltimore: Johns Hopkins University Press, 1976), pp. 27–73; and *Speech and Phenomena, and Other Essays on Husserl's Theory of Signs*, David B. Allison, introd. and tr. (Evanston, Ill.: Northwestern University Press, 1973).

11. The term *"chora"* has recently been criticized for its ontological essence by Jacques Derrida, *Positions*, Alan Bass, annotator and tr. (Chicago: University of Chicago Press, 1981), pp. 75 and 106, n. 39.

12. Plato emphasizes that the receptacle (ὑποδχεῖον), which is also called space (χώρα) vis-à-vis reason, is necessary—but not divine since it is unstable, uncertain, ever changing and becoming; it is even unnameable, improbable, bastard: "Space, which is everlasting, not admitting destruction; providing a situation for all things that come into being, but itself apprehended without the senses by a sort of bastard reasoning, and hardly an object of belief. This, indeed, is that which we look upon as in a dream and say that anything that is must needs be in some place and occupy some room. . ." (*Timaeus*, Francis M. Cornford, tr., 52a–52b). Is the receptacle a "thing" or a mode of language? Plato's hesitation between the two gives the receptacle an even more uncertain status. It is one of the elements that antedate not only the *universe* but also *names* and even *syllables:* "We speak . . . positing them as original principles, elements (as it were, letters) of the universe, whereas one who has ever so little intelligence should not rank them in this analogy even so low as syllables" (*ibid.*, 48b). "It is hard to say, with respect to any one of these, which we ought to call really water rather than fire, or indeed which we should call by any given name rather than by all the names together or by each severally, so as to use language in a sound and trustworthy way. . . . Since, then, in this way no one of these things ever makes its appearance as the *same* thing, which of them can we steadfastly affirm to be *this*—whatever it may be—and not something else, without blushing for ourselves? It cannot be done" (*ibid.*, 49b–d).

13. There is a fundamental ambiguity: on the one hand, the receptacle is mobile and even contradictory, without unity, separable and divisible: pre-syllable, pre-word. Yet, on the other hand, because this separability and divisibility antecede numbers and forms, the space or receptacle is called *amorphous;* thus its suggested rhythmicity will in a certain sense be erased, for how can one think an articulation of what is not yet singular but is nevertheless necessary? All we may say of it, then, to make it intelligible, is that it is amorphous but that it "is of such and such a quality," not even an index or something in particular ("this" or "that"). Once named, it immediately becomes a container that takes the place of infinitely repeatable separability. This amounts to saying that this repeated separability is "ontologized" the moment a *name* or a *word* replaces it, making it intelligible. "Are we talking idly whenever we say that there is such a thing as an intelligible Form of anything? Is this nothing more than a word?" (*ibid.*, 51c). Is the Platonic *chora* the "nominability" of rhythm (of repeated separation)?

Why then borrow an ontologized term in order to designate an articulation that antecedes positing? First, the Platonic term makes explicit an insurmountable problem for discourse, once it has been named, that functioning, even if it is pre-symbolic, is brought back into a symbolic position. All discourse can do is differentiate, by means of a "bastard reasoning," the receptacle from the motility, which, by contrast, is not posited as being "a *certain* something" ["une *telle*"]. Second, this motility is the precondition for symbolicity, heterogeneous to it, yet indispensable. Therefore what needs to be done is to try and differentiate, always through a "bastard reasoning," the specific arrangements of this motility, without seeing them as recipients of accidental singularities, or a *Being* always posited in itself, or a projection of the *One*. Moreover, Plato invites us to differentiate in this fashion when he describes this motility, while gathering it into the receiving membrane: "But because it was filled with powers that were neither alike nor evenly balanced, there was no equipoise in any region of it; but it was everywhere swayed unevenly and shaken by these things, and by its motion shook them in turn. And they, being thus moved, were perpetually being separated and carried in different directions; just as when things are shaken and winnowed by means of winnowing baskets and other instruments for cleaning corn . . . it separated the most unlike kinds farthest apart from one another, and thrust the most alike closest together; whereby the different kinds came to have different regions, even before the ordered whole consisting of them came to be . . . but were altogether in such a condition as we should expect for anything when deity is absent from it" (*ibid.*, 52d–53b). Indefinite "conjunctions" and "disjunctions" (functioning, devoid of Meaning), the *chora* is governed by a necessity that is not God's law.

14. The Platonic space or receptacle is a mother and wet nurse: "Indeed we may fittingly compare the Recipient to a mother, the model to a father, and the nature that arises between them to their offspring" (*ibid.*, 50d); "Now the wet nurse of Becoming was made watery and fiery, received the characters of earth and air, and was qualified by all the other affections that go with these. . ." *Ibid.*, 52d; translation modified.

15. "Law," which derives etymologically from *lex*, necessarily implies the act of judgment whose role in safeguarding society was first developed by the Roman law courts. "Ordering," on the other hand, is closer to the series "rule," "norm" (from the Greek γνώμων, meaning "discerning" [adj.], "carpenter's square" [noun]), etc., which implies a numerical or geometrical necessity. On normativity in linguistics, see Alain Rey, "Usages, jugements et prescriptions linquistiques," *Langue Française* (December 1972), 16: 5. But the temporary ordering of the *chora* is not yet even a *rule:* the arsenal of geometry is posterior to the *chora*'s motility; it fixes the *chora* in place and reduces it.

16. Operations are, rather, an act of the subject of understanding (Hans G. Furth, in *Piaget and Knowledge: Theoretical Foundations* (Englewood Cliffs, N.J.: Prentice-Hall, 1969), offers the following definition of "concrete operations": "Characteristic of the first stage of operational intelligence. A concrete operation implies underlying general systems or 'groupings' such as classification, seriation, number. Its applicability is limited to objects considered as real (concrete)" (p. 260)—Trans.]

17. Piaget stresses that the roots of sensorimotor operations precede language and that the acquisition of thought is due to the symbolic function, which, for him, is a notion separate from that of language per se. See Jean Piaget, "Language and Symbolic Operations," in *Piaget and Knowledge*, pp. 121–130.

18. By "function" we mean a dependent variable determined each time the independent variables with which it is associated are determined. For our purposes, a function is what links stases within the process of semiotic facilitation.

19. Such a position has been formulated by Lipot Szondi, *Experimental Diagnostic of Drives*, Gertrude Aull, tr. (New York: Grune & Stratton, 1952).

20. See James D. Watson, *The Double Helix: A Personal Account of the Discovery of the Structure of DNA* (London: Weidenfeld & Nicholson, 1968).

21. Throughout her writings, Melanie Klein emphasizes the "pre-Oedipal" phase, i.e., a period of the subject's development that precedes the "discovery" of castration and the positing of the superego, which itself is subject to (paternal) Law. The processes she describes for this phase correspond, *but on a genetic level*, to what we call the semiotic, as opposed to the symbolic, which underlies and conditions the semiotic. Significantly, these pre-Oedipal processes are organized through projection onto the mother's body, for girls

as well as for boys: "at this stage of development children of both sexes believe that it is the body of their mother which contains all that is desirable, especially their father's penis." *The Psycho-analysis of Children*, Alix Strachey, tr. (London: Hogarth Press, 1932), p. 269. Our own view of this stage is as follows: Without "believing" or "desiring" any "object" whatsoever, the subject is in the process of constituting himself vis-à-vis a non-object. He is in the process of separating from this non-object so as to make that non-object "one" and posit himself as "other": the mother's body is the not-yet-one that the believing and desiring subject will imagine as a "receptacle."

22. As for what situates the mother in symbolic space, we find the phallus again (see Jacques Lacan, "La Relation d'objet et les structures freudiennes," *Bulletin de Psychologie*, April 1957, pp. 426–430), represented by the mother's father, i.e., the subject's maternal grandfather (see Marie-Claire Boons, "Le Meurtre du Père chez Freud," *L'Inconscient*, January–March 1968, 5: 101–129).

23. Though disputed and inconsistent, the Freudian theory of drives is of interest here because of the predominance Freud gives to the death drive in both "living matter" and the "human being." The death drive is transversal to identity and tends to disperse "narcissisms" whose constitution ensures the link between structures and, by extension, life. But at the same time and conversely, narcissism and pleasure are only temporary positions from which the death drive blazes new paths [*se fraye de nouveaux passages*]. Narcissism and pleasure are therefore inveiglings and realizations of the death drive. The semiotic *chora*, converting drive discharges into stases, can be thought of both as a delaying of the death drive and as a possible realization of this drive, which tends to return to a homeostatic state. This hypothesis is consistent with the following remark: "at the beginning of mental life," writes Freud, "the struggle for pleasure was far more intense than later but not so unrestricted: it had to submit to frequent interruptions." *Beyond the Pleasure Principle*, in *The Standard Edition of the Works of Sigmund Freud*, James Strachey, ed. (London: Hogarth Press and the Institute of Psychoanalysis, 1953), 18: 63.

24. Mallarmé, *Œuvres complètes* (Paris: Gallimard, 1945), pp. 382–387.

25. *Ibid.*, p. 383.

26. *Ibid.*, pp. 383 and 385.

27. *Ibid.*, pp. 385–386.

hortense j. spillers

MAMA'S BABY, PAPA'S MAYBE

An American Grammar Book

Let's face it. I am a marked woman, but not everybody knows my name. "Peaches" and "Brown Sugar," "Sapphire" and "Earth Mother," "Aunty," "Granny," God's "Holy Fool," a "Miss Ebony First," or "Black Woman at the Podium": I describe a locus of confounded identities, a meeting ground of investments and privations in the national treasury of rhetorical wealth. My country needs me, and if I were not here, I would have to be invented.

W.E.B. DuBois predicted as early as 1903 that the twentieth century would be the century of the "color line." We could add to this spatiotemporal configuration another thematic of analogously terrible weight: if the "black woman" can be seen as a particular figuration of the split subject that psychoanalytic theory posits, then this century marks the site of "its" profoundest revelation. The problem before us is deceptively simple: the terms enclosed in quotation marks in the preceding paragraph isolate overdetermined nominative properties. Embedded in bizarre axiological ground, they demonstrate a sort of telegraphic coding; they are markers so loaded with mythical prepossession that there is no easy way for the agents buried beneath them to come clean. In that regard, the names by which I am called in the public place render an example of signifying property *plus*. In order for me to speak a truer word concerning myself, I must strip down through layers of attenuated meanings, made an excess in time, over time, assigned by a particular historical order, and there await whatever marvels of my own inventiveness. The personal pronouns are offered in the service of a collective function.

In certain human societies, a child's identity is determined through the line of the Mother, but the United States, from at least one author's point of view, is not one of them: "In essence, the Negro community has been forced into a matriarchal structure which, because it is so far out of line with the *rest of American society*, seriously retards the progress of the group as a whole, and imposes a crushing burden on the Negro male and, in consequence, on a great many Negro women as well" [Moynihan 75; emphasis mine].

The notorious bastard, from Vico's banished Roman mothers of such sons, to Caliban, to Heathcliff, and Joe Christmas, has no official female equivalent. Because the traditional rites and laws of inheritance rarely pertain to the female child, bastard status signals to those who need to know which son of the Father's

From Diacritics *17, no. 2 (1987). Reprinted by permission of the author and The Johns Hopkins University Press.*

is the legitimate heir and which one the impostor. For that reason, property seems wholly the business of the male. A "she" cannot, therefore, qualify for bastard, or "natural son" status, and that she cannot provides further insight into the coils and recoils of patriarchal wealth and fortune. According to Daniel Patrick Moynihan's celebrated "Report" of the late sixties, the "Negro Family" has no Father to speak of—his Name, his Law, his Symbolic function mark the impressive missing agencies in the essential life of the black community, the "Report" maintains, and it is, surprisingly, the fault of the Daughter, or the female line. This stunning reversal of the castration thematic, displacing the Name and the Law of the Father to the territory of the Mother and Daughter, becomes an aspect of the African-American female's misnaming. We attempt to undo this misnaming in order to reclaim the relationship between Fathers and Daughters within this social matrix for a quite different structure of cultural fictions. For Daughters and Fathers are here made to manifest the very same *rhetorical* symptoms of absence and denial, to embody the double and contrastive agencies of a *prescribed* internecine degradation. "Sapphire" enacts her "Old Man" in drag, just as her "Old Man" becomes "Sapphire" in outrageous caricature.

In other words, in the historic outline of dominance, the respective subject-positions of "female" and "male" adhere to no symbolic integrity. At a time when current critical discourses appear to compel us more and more decidedly toward gender "undecidability," it would appear reactionary, if not dumb, to insist on the integrity of female/male gender. But undressing these conflations of meaning, as they appear under the rule of dominance, would restore, as figurative possibility, not only Power to the Female (for Maternity), but also Power to the Male (for Paternity). We would gain, in short, the *potential* for gender differentiation as it might express itself along a range of stress points, including human biology in its intersection with the project of culture.

Though among the most readily available "whipping boys" of fairly recent public discourse concerning African-Americans and national policy, "The Moynihan Report" is by no means unprecedented in its conclusions; it belongs, rather, to a class of symbolic paradigms that 1) inscribe "ethnicity" as a scene of negation and 2) confirm the human body as a metonymic figure for an entire repertoire of human and social arrangements. In that regard, the "Report" pursues a behavioral rule of public documentary. Under the Moynihan rule, "ethnicity" itself identifies a total objectification of human and cultural motives—the "white" family, by implication, and the "Negro Family," by outright assertion, in a constant opposition of binary meanings. Apparently spontaneous, these "actants" are *wholly* generated, with neither past nor future, as tribal currents moving out of time. Moynihan's "Families" are pure present and always tense. "Ethnicity" in this case freezes in meaning, takes on constancy, assumes the look and the affects of the Eternal. We could say, then, that in its powerful stillness, "ethnicity," from the point of view of the "Report," embodies nothing more than a mode of memorial time, as Roland Barthes outlines the dynamics of myth [see "Myth Today" 109–59; esp. 122–23]. As a signifier that has no movement in the field of signification, the use of "ethnicity" for the living becomes purely appreciative, although one would be unwise not to concede its dangerous and fatal effects.

"Ethnicity" perceived as mythical time enables a writer to perform a variety of conceptual moves all at once. Under its hegemony, the human body becomes a defenseless target for rape and veneration, and the body, in its material and abstract phase, a resource for metaphor. For example, Moynihan's "tangle of pathology" provides the descriptive strategy for the work's fourth chapter, which suggests that "underachievement" in black males of the lower classes is primarily the fault of black females, who achieve out of all proportion, both to their numbers in the community and to the paradigmatic example before the nation: "Ours is a society which presumes male leadership in private and public affairs. . . . A subculture, such as that of the Negro American, in which this is not the pattern, is placed at a distinct disadvantage" [75]. Between charts and diagrams, we are asked to consider the impact of qualitative measure on the black male's performance on standardized examinations, matriculation in schools of higher and professional training, etc. Even though Moynihan sounds a critique on his own argument here, he quickly withdraws from its possibilities, suggesting that black males should reign because that is the way the majority culture carries things out: "It is clearly a disadvantage for a minority group to be operating under one principle, while the great majority of the population . . . is operating on another" [75]. Those persons living according to the perceived "matriarchal" pattern are, therefore, caught in a state of social "pathology."

Even though Daughters have their own agenda with reference to this order of Fathers (imagining for the moment that Moynihan's fiction—and others like it—does not represent an adequate one and that there *is*, once we dis-cover him, a Father here), my contention that these social and cultural subjects make doubles, unstable in their respective identities, in effect transports us to a common historical ground, the socio-political order of the New World. That order, with its human sequence written in blood, *represents* for its African and indigenous peoples a scene of *actual* mutilation, dismemberment, and exile. First of all, their New-World, diasporic plight marked a *theft of the body*—a willful and violent (and unimaginable from this distance) severing of the captive body from its motive will, its active desire. Under these conditions, we lose at least *gender* difference *in the outcome,* and the female body and the male body become a territory of cultural and political maneuver, not at all gender-related, gender-specific. But this body, at least from the point of view of the captive community, focuses a private and particular space, at which point of convergence biological, sexual, social, cultural, linguistic, ritualistic, and psychological fortunes join. This profound intimacy of interlocking detail is disrupted, however, by externally imposed meanings and uses: 1) the captive body becomes the source of an irresistible, destructive sensuality; 2) at the same time—in stunning contradiction—the captive body reduces to a thing, becoming *being for* the captor; 3) in this absence *from* a subject position, the captured sexualities provide a physical and biological expression of "otherness"; 4) as a category of "otherness," the captive body translates into a potential for pornotroping and embodies sheer physical powerlessness that slides into a more general "powerlessness," resonating through various centers of human and social meaning.

But I would make a distinction in this case between "body" and "flesh" and impose that distinction as the central one between captive and liberated subject-positions. In that sense, before the "body" there is the "flesh," that zero degree of social conceptualization that does not escape concealment under the brush of discourse, or the reflexes of iconography. Even though the European hegemonies stole bodies—some of them female—out of West African communities in concert with the African "middleman," we regard this human and social irreparability as high crimes against the *flesh,* as the person of African females and African males registered the wounding. If we think of the "flesh" as a primary narrative, then we mean its seared, divided, ripped-apartness, riveted to the ship's hole, fallen, or "escaped" overboard.

One of the most poignant aspects of William Goodell's contemporaneous study of the North American slave codes gives precise expression to the tortures and instruments of captivity. Reporting an instance of Jonathan Edwards's observations on the tortures of enslavement, Goodell narrates: "The smack of the whip is all day long in the ears of those who are on the plantation, or in the vicinity; and it is used with such dexterity and severity as not only to lacerate the skin, but to tear out small portions of the flesh at almost every stake" [221]. The anatomical specifications of rupture, of altered human tissue, take on the objective description of laboratory prose—eyes beaten out, arms, backs, skulls branded, a left jaw, a right ankle, punctured; teeth missing, as the calculated work of iron, whips, chains, knives, the canine patrol, the bullet.

These undecipherable markings on the captive body render a kind of hieroglyphics of the flesh whose severe disjunctures come to be hidden to the cultural seeing by skin color. We might well ask if this phenomenon of marking and branding actually "transfers" from one generation to another, finding its various *symbolic substitutions* in an efficacy of meanings that repeat the initiating moments? As Elaine Scarry describes the mechanisms of torture [Scarry 27–59], these lacerations, woundings, fissures, tears, scars, openings, ruptures, lesions, rendings, punctures of the flesh create the distance between what I would designate a cultural *vestibularity* and the *culture,* whose state apparatus, including judges, attorneys, "owners," "soul drivers," "overseers," and "men of God," apparently colludes with a protocol of "search and destroy." This body whose flesh carries the female and the male to the frontiers of survival bears in person the marks of a cultural text whose inside has been turned outside.

The flesh is the concentration of "ethnicity" that contemporary critical discourses neither acknowledge nor discourse away. It is this "flesh and blood" entity, in the vestibule (or "pre-view") of a colonized North America, that is essentially ejected from "The Female Body in Western Culture" [see Suleiman, ed.], but it makes good theory, or commemorative "herstory" to want to "forget," or to have failed to realize, that the African female subject, under these historic conditions, is not only the target of rape—in one sense, an interiorized violation of body and mind—but also the topic of specifically *externalized* acts of torture and prostration that we imagine as the peculiar province of *male* brutality and torture inflicted by other males. A female body strung from a tree limb, or bleeding from the breast on any given day of field work because the "overseer," standing the length of a whip, has popped her flesh open, adds a lexical and living dimension to the narratives of women in culture and society [Davis 9]. This materialized scene of unprotected female flesh—of female flesh "ungendered"—offers a praxis and a theory, a text for living and for dying, and a method for reading both through their diverse mediations.

Among the myriad uses to which the enslaved community was put, Goodell identifies its value for medical research: "Assortments of diseased, *damaged,* and disabled Negroes, deemed incurable and otherwise worthless are *bought up,* it seems . . . by medical institutions, to be experimented and operated upon, for purposes of 'medical education' and the interest of medical science" [86–87; Goodell's emphasis]. From the *Charleston Mercury* for October 12, 1838, Goodell notes this advertisement:

> 'To planters and others.—Wanted, fifty Negroes, any person, having sick Negroes, considered incurable by their respective physicians, and wishing to dispose of them, Dr. S. will pay *cash* for Negroes affected with scrofula, or king's evil, confirmed hypochrondriasm, apoplexy, diseases of the liver, kidneys, spleen, stomach and intestines, bladder and its appendages, diarrhea, dysentery, etc. The *highest cash price will be paid,* on application as above.' at No. 110 Church Street, Charleston. [87, Goodell's emphasis]

This profitable "atomizing" of the captive body provides another angle on the divided flesh: we lose any hint or suggestion of a dimension of ethics, of relatedness between human personality and its anatomical features, between one human personality and another, between human personality and cultural institutions. To that extent, the procedures adopted for the captive flesh demarcate a total objectification, as the entire captive community becomes a living laboratory.

The captive body, then, brings into focus a gathering of social realities as well as a metaphor for *value* so thoroughly interwoven in their literal and figurative emphases that distinctions between them are virtually useless. Even though the captive flesh/body has been "liberated," and no one need pretend that even the quotation marks do not *matter,* dominant symbolic activity, the ruling episteme that releases the dynamics of naming and valuation, remains grounded in the originating metaphors of captivity and mutilation so that it is as if neither time nor history, nor historiography and its topics, shows movement, as the human subject is "murdered" over and over again by the passions of a bloodless and anonymous archaism, showing itself in endless disguise. Faulkner's young Chick Mallison in *The Mansion* calls "it" by other names—"the ancient subterrene atavistic fear . . ." [227]. And I would call it the Great Long National Shame. But people do not talk like that anymore—it is "embarrassing," just as the retrieval of mutilated female bodies will likely be "backward" for some people. Neither the shameface of the embarrassed, nor the not-looking-back of the self-assured is of much interest to us, and will not help at all if rigor is our dream. We might concede, at the very least, that sticks and bricks *might* break our bones, but words will most certainly *kill* us.

The symbolic order that I wish to trace in this writing, calling it an "American grammar," begins at the "beginning," which is really a rupture and a radically different kind of cultural continuation. The massive demographic shifts, the violent formation of a modern African consciousness, that take place on the subsaharan Continent during the initiative strikes which open the Atlantic Slave Trade in the fifteenth century of our Christ, interrupted hundreds of years of black African culture. We write and think, then, about an outcome of aspects of African-American life in the United States under the pressure of those events. I might as well add that the familiarity of this narrative does nothing to appease the hunger of recorded memory, nor does the persistence of the repeated rob these well-known, oft-told events of their power, even now, to startle. In a very real sense, every writing as revision makes the "discovery" all over again.

2

The narratives by African peoples and their descendants, though not as numerous from those early centuries of the "execrable trade" as the researcher would wish, suggest, in their rare occurrence, that the visual shock waves touched off when African and European "met" reverberated on both sides of the encounter. The narrative of the "Life of Olaudah Equiano, or Gustavus Vassa, the African. Written by Himself," first published in London in 1789, makes it quite clear that the first Europeans Equiano observed on what is now Nigerian soil were as unreal for him as he and others must have been for the European captors. The cruelty of "these white men with horrible looks, red faces, and long hair," of these "spirits," as the narrator would have it, occupies several pages of Equiano's attention, alongside a firsthand account of Nigerian interior life [27 ff.]. We are justified in regarding the outcome of Equiano's experience in the same light as he himself might have—as a "fall," as a veritable descent into the loss of communicative force.

If, as Todorov points out, the Mayan and Aztec peoples "lost control of communication" [61] in light of Spanish intervention, we could observe, similarly, that Vassa falls among men whose language is not only strange to him, but whose habits and practices strike him as "astonishing":

> [The sea, the slave ship] filled me with astonishment, which was soon converted into terror, when I was carried on board. I was immediately handled, and tossed up to see if I were sound, by some of the crew; and I was now persuaded that I had gotten into a world of bad spirits, and that they were going to kill me. Their complexions, too, differing so much from ours, their long hair, and the language they spoke (which was different from any I had ever heard), united to confirm me in this belief. [Equiano 27]

The captivating party does not only "earn" the right to dispose of the captive body as it sees fit, but gains, consequently, the right to name and "name" it: Equiano, for instance, identifies at least three different names that he is given in numerous passages between his Benin homeland and the Virginia colony, the latter and England—"Michael," "Jacob," "Gustavus Vassa" [35; 36].

The nicknames by which African-American women have been called, or regarded, or imagined on the New World scene—the opening lines of this essay provide examples—demonstrate the powers of distortion that the dominant community seizes as its unlawful prerogative. Moynihan's "Negro Family," then, borrows its narrative energies from the grid of associations, from the semantic and iconic folds buried deep in the collective past, that come to surround and signify the captive person. Though there is no absolute point of chronological initiation, we might repeat certain familiar impression points that lend shape to the business of dehumanized naming. Expecting to find direct and amplified reference to African women during the opening years of the Trade, the observer is disappointed time and again that this cultural subject is concealed beneath the mighty debris of the itemized account, between the lines of the massive logs of commercial enterprise that overrun the sense of clarity we believed we had gained concerning this collective humiliation. Elizabeth Donnan's enormous, four-volume documentation becomes a case in point.

Turning directly to this source, we discover what we had not expected to find—that this aspect of the search is rendered problematic and that observations of a field of manners and its related sociometries are an outgrowth of the industry of the "exterior other" [Todorov 3], called "anthropology" later on. The European males who laded and captained these galleys and who policed and corralled these human beings, in hundreds of vessels from Liverpool to Elmina, to Jamaica; from the Cayenne Islands, to the ports at Charleston and Salem, and for three centuries of human life, were not curious about this "cargo" that bled, packed like so many live sardines among the immovable objects. Such inveterate obscene blindness might be denied, point blank, as a possibility for *anyone*, except that we know it happened.

Donnan's first volume covers three centuries of European "discovery" and "conquest," beginning 50 years before pious Cristobal, Christum Ferens, the bearer of Christ, laid claim to what he thought was the "Indies." From Gomes Eannes de Azurara's "Chronicle of the Discovery and Conquest of Guinea, 1441–1448" [Donnan 1 : 18–41], we learn that the Portuguese probably gain the dubious distinction of having introduced black Africans to the European market of servitude. We are also reminded that "Geography" is not a divine gift. Quite to the contrary, its boundaries were shifted during the European "Age of Conquest" in giddy desperation, according to the dictates of conquering armies, the edicts of prelates, the peculiar myopia of the medieval Christian mind. Looking for the "Nile River," for example, according to the fifteenth-century Portuguese notion, is someone's joke. For all that the pre-Columbian "explorers" knew about the sciences of navigation and geography, we are surprised that more parties of them did not end up "discovering" Europe. Perhaps, from a certain angle, that is precisely all that they found—an alternative reading of ego. The Portuguese, having little idea where the Nile ran, at least understood right away that there were men and women darker-skinned than themselves, but they were not specifically knowledgeable, or ingenious, about the various families and groupings represented by them. De Azurara records encounters with "Moors," "Mooresses," "Mulattoes," and people "black as Ethiops" [1 : 28], but it seems that the "Land of Guinea," or of "Black Men," or of "The Negroes" [1 : 35] was located anywhere southeast of Cape Verde, the Canaries, and the River Senegal, looking at an eighteenth-century European version of the subsaharan Continent along the West African coast [1 : frontispiece].

Three genetic distinctions are available to the Portuguese eye, all along the riffs of melanin in the skin: in a field of captives, some of the observed are "white enough, fair to look upon, and well-proportioned." Others are less "white like mulattoes," and still others "black as Ethiops, and so ugly, both in features and in body, as almost to appear (to those who saw them) the images of a lower hemisphere" [1 : 28]. By implication, this "third man," standing for the most aberrant phenotype to the observing eye, embodies the linguistic community most unknown to the European. Arabic translators among the Europeans could at least "talk" to the "Moors" and instruct them to ransom themselves, or else. . . .

Typically, there is in this grammar of description the perspective of "declension," not of simultaneity, and its point of initiation is solipsistic—it begins with a narrative self, in an apparent unity of feeling, and unlike Equiano, who also saw "ugly" when he looked out, this collective self uncovers the means by which to subjugate the "foreign code of conscience," whose most easily remarkable and irremediable difference is perceived in skin color. By the time of De Azurara's mid-fifteenth century narrative and a century and a half before Shakespeare's "old black ram" of an Othello "tups" that "white ewe" of a Desdemona, the magic of skin color is already installed as a decisive factor in human dealings.

In De Azurara's narrative, we observe males looking at other males, as "female" is subsumed here under the general category of estrangement. Few places in these excerpts carve out a distinct female space, though there are moments of portrayal that perceive female captives in the implications of socio-cultural function. When the field of captives (referred to above) is divided among the spoilers, no heed is paid to relations, as fathers are separated from sons, husbands from wives, brothers from sisters and brothers, mothers from children—male and female. It seems clear that the political program of European Christianity promotes this hierarchical view among *males*, although it remains puzzling to us exactly how this version of Christianity transforms the "pagan" also into the "ugly." It appears that human beings came up with degrees of "fair" and then the "hideous," in its overtones of bestiality, as the opposite of "fair," all by themselves, without stage direction, even though there is the curious and blazing exception of Nietzsche's Socrates, who was Athens's ugliest and wisest and best citizen. The intimate choreography that the Portuguese narrator sets going between the "faithless" and the "ugly" transforms a partnership of dancers into a single figure. Once the "faithless," indiscriminate of the three stops of Portuguese skin color, are transported to Europe, they become an *altered* human factor:

> And so their lot was now quite contrary to what it had been, since before they had lived in perdition of soul and body; of their souls, in that they were yet pagans, without the clearness and the light of the Holy Faith; and of their bodies, in that they lived like beasts, without any custom of reasonable beings—for they had no knowledge of bread and wine, and they were without covering of clothes, or the lodgment of houses; and worse than all, through the great ignorance that was in them, in that they had no understanding of good, but only knew how to live in bestial sloth. [1:30]

The altered human factor renders an alterity of European ego, an invention, or "discovery" as decisive in the full range of its social implications as the birth of a newborn. According to the semantic alignments of the excerpted passage, personhood, for this European observer, locates an immediately outward and superficial determination, gauged by quite arbitrarily opposed and *specular* categories: that these "pagans" did not have "bread" and "wine" did not mean that they were feastless, as Equiano observes about the Benin diet, c. 1745, in the province of Essaka:

> Our manner of living is entirely plain; for as yet the natives are unacquainted
> with those refinements in cookery which debauch the taste; bullocks, goats,
> and poultry supply the greatest part of their food. (These constitute likewise
> the principal wealth of the country, and the chief articles of its commerce.)
> The flesh is usually stewed in a pan; to make it savory we sometimes use
> pepper, and other spices, and we have salt made of wood ashes. Our vege-
> tables are mostly plaintains, eadas, yams, beans and Indian corn. The head
> of the family usually eats alone; his wives and slaves have also their separate
> tables. . . . [Equiano 8]

Just as fufu serves the Ghanaian diet today as a starch-and-bread-substitute,
palm wine (an item by the same name in the eighteenth-century palate of the
Benin community) need not be Heitz Cellars Martha's Vineyard and vice-versa
in order for a guest, say, to imagine that she has enjoyed. That African hous-
ing arrangements of the fifteenth century did not resemble those familiar to
De Azurara's narrator need not have meant that the African communities he en-
countered were without dwellings. Again, Equiano's narrative suggests that by
the middle of the eighteenth century, at least, African living patterns were not
only quite distinct in their sociometrical implications, but that also their architec-
tonics accurately reflected the climate and availability of resources in the local
circumstance: "These houses never exceed one story in height; they are always
built of wood, or stakes driven into the ground, crossed with wattles, and neatly
plastered within and without" [9]. Hierarchical impulse in *both* De Azurara's and
Equiano's narratives translates all *perceived* difference as a fundamental degradation *or* transcendence, but at least in Equiano's case, cultural practices are not
observed in any intimate connection with skin color. For all intents and purposes,
the politics of melanin, not isolated in its strange powers from the imperatives of
a mercantile and competitive economics of European nation-states, will make of
"transcendence" and "degradation" the basis of a historic violence that will rewrite the histories of modern Europe and black Africa. These mutually exclusive
nominative elements come to rest on the same governing semantics—the ahistorical, or symptoms of the "sacred."

By August 1518, the Spanish king, Francisco de Los Covos, under the aegis
of a powerful negation, could order "4000 negro slaves both male and female,
provided they be Christians" to be taken to the Caribbean, "the islands and the
mainland of the ocean sea already discovered or to be discovered" [Donnan
1:42]. Though the notorious "Middle Passage" appears to the investigator as a
vast background without boundaries in time and space, we see it related in Donnan's accounts to the opening up of the entire Western hemisphere for the specific purposes of enslavement and colonization. De Azurara's narrative belongs,
then, to a discourse of appropriation whose strategies will prove fatal to communities along the coastline of West Africa, stretching, according to Olaudah
Equiano, "3400 miles, from Senegal to Angola, and [will include] a variety of
kingdoms" [Equiano 5].

The conditions of "Middle Passage" are among the most incredible narratives available to the student, as it remains not easily imaginable. Late in the
chronicles of the Atlantic Slave Trade, Britain's Parliament entertained discussions concerning possible "regulations" for slave vessels. A Captain Perry visited
the Liverpool port, and among the ships that he inspected was "The Brookes,"

probably the most well-known image of the slave galley with its representative *personae* etched into the drawing like so many cartoon figures. Elizabeth Donnan's second volume carries the "Brookes Plan," along with an elaborate delineation of its dimensions from the investigative reporting of Perry himself: "Let it now be supposed . . . further, that every man slave is to be allowed six feet by one foot four inches for room, every woman five feet ten by one foot four, every boy five feet by one foot two, and every girl four feet six by one foot. . ." [2:592, n]. The owner of "The Brookes," James Jones, had recommended that "five females be reckoned as four males, and three boys or girls as equal to two grown persons" [2:592].

These scaled inequalities complement the commanding terms of the dehumanizing, ungendering, and defacing project of African persons that De Azurara's narrator might have recognized. It has been pointed out to me that these measurements do reveal the application of the gender rule to the material conditions of passage, but I would suggest that "gendering" takes place within the confines of the domestic, an essential metaphor that then spreads its tentacles for male and female subject over a wider ground of human and social purposes. Domesticity appears to gain its power by way of a common origin of cultural fictions that are grounded in the specificity of proper names, more exactly, a patronymic, which, in turn, situates those persons it "covers" in a particular place. Contrarily, the cargo of a ship might not be regarded as elements of the domestic, even though the vessel that carries it is sometimes romantically (ironically?) personified as "she." The human cargo of a slave vessel—in the fundamental effacement and remission of African family and proper names—offers a *counter*-narrative to notions of the domestic.

Those African persons in "Middle Passage" were literally suspended in the "oceanic," if we think of the latter in its Freudian orientation as an analogy for undifferentiated identity: removed from the indigenous land and culture, and not-yet "American" either, these captive persons, without names that their captors would recognize, were in movement across the Atlantic, but they were also *nowhere* at all. Inasmuch as, on any given day, we might imagine, the captive personality did not know where s/he was, we could say that they were the culturally "unmade," thrown in the midst of a figurative darkness that "exposed" their destinies to an unknown course. Often enough for the captains of these galleys, navigational science of the day was not sufficient to guarantee the intended destination. We might say that the slave ship, its crew, and its human-as-cargo stand for a wild and unclaimed richness of *possibility* that is not interrupted, not "counted"/"accounted," or differentiated, until its movement gains the land thousands of miles away from the point of departure. Under these conditions, one is neither female, nor male, as both subjects are taken into "account" as *quantities*. The female in "Middle Passage," as the apparently smaller physical mass, occupies "less room" in a directly translatable money economy. But she is, nevertheless, quantifiable by the same rules of accounting as her male counterpart.

It is not only difficult for the student to find "female" in "Middle Passage," but also, as Herbert S. Klein observes, "African women did not enter the Atlantic slave trade in anything like the numbers of African men. At all ages, men outnumbered women on the slave ships bound for America from Africa" [Klein

29]. Though this observation does not change the reality of African women's captivity and servitude in New World communities, it does provide a perspective from which to contemplate the *internal* African slave trade, which, according to Africanists, remained a predominantly *female* market. Klein nevertheless affirms that those females forced into the trade were segregated "from men for policing purposes" ["African Women" 35]. He claims that both "were allotted the same space between decks . . . and both were fed the same food" [35]. It is not altogether clear from Klein's observations *for whom* the "police" kept vigil. It is certainly known from evidence presented in Donnan's third volume ("New England and the Middle Colonies") that insurrection was both frequent and feared in passage, and we have not yet found a great deal of evidence to support a thesis that female captives participated in insurrectionary activity [see White 63–64]. Because it was the rule, however—not the exception—that the African female, in both indigenous African cultures and in what becomes her "home," performed tasks of hard physical labor—so much so that the quintessential "slave" is *not* a male, but a female—we wonder at the seeming docility of the subject, granting her a "feminization" that enslavement kept at bay. Indeed, across the spate of discourse that I examined for this writing, the acts of enslavement and responses to it comprise a more or less agonistic engagement of confrontational hostilities among males. The visual and historical evidence betrays the dominant discourse on the matter as incomplete, but *counter*-evidence is inadequate as well: the sexual violation of captive females and their own express rage against their oppressors did not constitute events that captains and their crews rushed to record in letters to their sponsoring companies, or sons on board in letters home to their New England mamas.

One suspects that there are several ways to snare a mockingbird, so that insurrection might have involved, from time to time, rather more subtle means than mutiny on the "Felicity," for instance. At any rate, we get very little notion in the written record of the life of women, children, and infants in "Middle Passage," and no idea of the fate of the pregnant female captive and the unborn, which startling thematic Bell Hooks addresses in the opening chapter of her pathfinding work [see Hooks 15–49]. From Hooks's lead, however, we might guess that the "reproduction of mothering" in this historic instance carries few of the benefits of a *patriarchilized* female gender, which, from one point of view, is the *only* female gender there is.

The relative silence of the record on this point constitutes a portion of the disquieting lacunae that feminist investigation seeks to fill. Such silence is the nickname of distortion, of the unknown human factor that a revised public discourse would both undo *and* reveal. This cultural subject is inscribed historically as anonymity/anomie in various public documents of European-American mal(e) venture, from Portuguese De Azurara in the middle of the fifteenth century, to South Carolina's Henry Laurens in the eighteenth.

What confuses and enriches the picture is precisely the sameness of anonymous portrayal that adheres tenaciously across the division of gender. In the vertical columns of accounts and ledgers that comprise Donnan's work, the terms "Negroes" and "Slaves" denote a common status. For instance, entries in one account, from September 1700 through September 1702, are specifically descriptive of the names of ships and the private traders in Barbados who will receive the stipulated goods, but "No. Negroes" and "Sum sold for per head" are so exactly arithmetical that it is as if these additions and multiplications belong to the other side of an equation [Donnan 2:25]. One is struck by the detail and precision that characterize these accounts, as a narrative, or story, is always implied by a man or woman's *name:* "Wm. Webster," "John Dunn," "Thos. Brownbill," "Robt. Knowles." But the "other" side of the page, as it were, equally precise, throws no *face* in view. It seems that nothing breaks the uniformity in this guise. If in no other way, the destruction of the African name, of kin, of linguistic, and ritual connections is so obvious in the vital stats sheet that we tend to overlook it. Quite naturally, the trader is not interested, in any *semantic* sense, in this "baggage" that he must deliver, but that he is not is all the more reason to search out the metaphorical implications of *naming* as one of the key sources of a bitter Americanizing for African persons.

The loss of the indigenous name/land provides a metaphor of displacement for other human and cultural features and relations, including the displacement of the genitalia, the female's and the male's desire that engenders future. The fact that the enslaved person's access to the issue of his/her own body is not entirely clear in this historic period throws in crisis all aspects of the blood relations, as captors apparently felt no obligation to acknowledge them. Actually trying to understand how the confusions of consanguinity worked becomes the project, because the outcome goes far to explain the rule of gender and its application to the African female in captivity.

3

Even though the essays in Claire C. Robertson's and Martin A. Klein's *Women and Slavery in Africa* have specifically to do with aspects of the internal African slave trade, some of their observations shed light on the captivities of the Diaspora. At least these observations have the benefit of altering the kind of questions we might ask of these silent chapters. For example, Robertson's essay, which opens the volume, discusses the term "slavery" in a wide variety of relationships. The enslaved person as *property* identifies the most familiar element of a most startling proposition. But to overlap *kinlessness* on the requirements of property might enlarge our view of the conditions of enslavement. Looking specifically at documents from the West African societies of Songhay and Dahomey, Claude Meillassoux elaborates several features of the property/kinless constellation that are highly suggestive for our own quite different purposes.

Meillassoux argues that "slavery creates an economic and social agent whose virtue lies in being outside the kinship system" ["Female Slavery," Robertson and Klein 50]. Because the Atlantic trade involved heterogeneous social and ethnic formations in an explicit power relationship, we certainly cannot mean "kinship system" in precisely the same way that Meillassoux observes at work within the intricate calculus of descent among West African societies. However, the idea becomes useful as a point of contemplation when we try to sharpen our own sense of the African female's reproductive uses within the diasporic enterprise of enslavement and the genetic reproduction of the enslaved. In effect, under conditions of captivity, the offspring of the female does not "belong" to the Mother, nor is s/he "related" to the "owner," though the latter "possesses" it, and in the

African-American instance, often fathered it, *and,* as often, without whatever benefit of patrimony. In the social outline that Meillassoux is pursuing, the off-spring of the enslaved, "being unrelated both to their begetters and to their owners. . . , find themselves in the situation of being orphans" [50].

In the context of the United States, we could not say that the enslaved off-spring was "orphaned," but the child does become, under the press of a patro-nymic, patrifocal, patrilineal, and patriarchal order, the man/woman on the boundary, whose human and familial status, by the very nature of the case, had yet to be defined. I would call this enforced state of breach another instance of vestibular cultural formation where "kinship" loses meaning, *since it can be invaded at any given and arbitrary moment by the property relations.* I certainly do not mean to say that African peoples in the New World did not maintain the powerful ties of sympathy that bind blood-relations in a network of feeling, of continuity. It is precisely *that* relationship—not customarily recognized by the code of slav-ery—that historians have long identified as the inviolable "Black Family" and further suggest that this structure remains one of the supreme social achieve-ments of African-Americans under conditions of enslavement [see John Blassin-game 79 ff.].

Indeed, the *revised* "Black Family" of enslavement has engendered an older tradition of historiographical and sociological writings than we usually think. Ironically enough, E. Franklin Frazier's *Negro Family in the United States* likely provides the closest *contemporary* narrative of conceptualization for the "Moy-nihan Report." Originally published in 1939, Frazier's work underwent two redactions in 1948 and 1966. Even though Frazier's outlook on this familial con-figuration remains basically sanguine, I would support Angela Davis's skeptical reading of Frazier's "Black Matriarchate" [Davis 14]. "*Except where the master's will was concerned,*" Frazier contends, this matriarchal figure "developed a spirit of independence and a keen sense of her personal rights" [1966: 47; emphasis mine]. The "exception" in this instance tends to be overwhelming, as the African-American female's "dominance" and "strength" come to be interpreted by later generations—both black and white, oddly enough—as a "pathology," as an instrument of castration. Frazier's larger point, we might suppose, is that African-Americans developed such resourcefulness under conditions of captivity that "family" must be conceded as one of their redoubtable social attainments. This line of interpretation is pursued by Blassingame and Eugene Genovese [*Roll, Jordan, Roll* 70–75], among other U.S. historians, and indeed assumes a centrality of focus in our own thinking about the impact and outcome of captivity.

It seems clear, however, that "Family," as we practice and understand it "in the West"—the *vertical* transfer of a bloodline, of a patronymic, of titles and entitlements, of real estate and the prerogatives of "cold cash," from *fathers* to *sons* and in the supposedly free exchange of affectional ties between a male and a female of *his* choice—becomes the mythically revered privilege of a free and freed community. In that sense, African peoples in the historic Diaspora had nothing to prove, *if* the point had been that they were not capable of "family" (read "civilization"), since it is stunningly evident, in Equiano's narrative, for instance, that Africans were not only capable of the concept and the practice of "family," including "slaves," but in modes of elaboration and naming that were at least as complex as those of the "nuclear family" "in the West."

Whether or not we decide that the support systems that African-Americans derived under conditions of captivity should be called "family," or something else, strikes me as supremely impertinent. The point remains that captive persons were *forced* into patterns of *dispersal*, beginning with the Trade itself, into the *horizontal* relatedness of language groups, discourse formations, bloodlines, names, and properties by the legal arrangements of enslavement. It is true that the most "well-meaning" of "masters" (and there must have been some) *could not, did not* alter the *ideological* and hegemonic mandates of dominance. It must be conceded that African-Americans, under the press of a hostile and compulsory patriarchal order, bound and determined to destroy them, or to preserve them only in the service and at the behest of the "master" class, exercised a degree of courage and will to survive that startles the imagination even now. Although it makes good revisionist history to read this tale *liberally*, it is probably truer than we know at this distance (and truer than contemporary social practice in the community would suggest on occasion) that the captive person developed, time and again, certain ethical and sentimental features that tied her and him, *across* the landscape to others, often sold from hand to hand, of the same and different blood in a common fabric of memory and inspiration.

We might choose to call this connectedness "family," or "support structure," but that is a rather different case from the moves of a dominant symbolic order, pledged to maintain the supremacy of race. It is that order that forces "family" to modify itself when it does not mean family of the "master," or dominant enclave. It is this rhetorical and symbolic move that declares primacy over any other human and social claim, and in that political order of things, "kin," just as gender formation, has no decisive legal or social efficacy.

We return frequently to Frederick Douglass's careful elaborations of the arrangements of captivity, and we are astonished each reading by two dispersed, yet poignantly related, familial enactments that suggest a connection between "kinship" and "property." Douglass tells us early in the opening chapter of the 1845 *Narrative* that he was separated in infancy from his mother: "For what this separation is [sic] done, I do not know, unless it be to hinder the development of the child's affection toward its mother, and to blunt and destroy the natural affection of the mother for the child. This is the inevitable result" [22].

Perhaps one of the assertions that Meillassoux advances concerning indigenous African formations of enslavement might be turned as a question, against the perspective of Douglass's witness: is the genetic reproduction of the slave and the recognition of the rights of the slave to his or her offspring a check on the *profitability* of slavery? And how so, if so? We see vaguely the route to framing a response, especially to the question's second half and perhaps to the first: the enslaved must not be permitted to perceive that he or she has any human rights that matter. Certainly if "kinship" were possible, the property relations would be undermined, since the offspring would then "belong" to a mother and a father. In the system that Douglass articulates, genetic reproduction becomes, then, not an elaboration of the life-principle in its cultural overlap, but an extension of the boundaries of proliferating properties. Meillassoux goes so far as to argue that "slavery exists where the slave class is reproduced through institutional apparatus: war and market" [50]. Since, in the United States, the market of slavery identified the chief institutional means for maintaining a class of enforced servile labor, it seems that the biological reproduction of the enslaved was not alone sufficient to reenforce the *estate* of slavery. If, as Meillassoux contends, "femininity loses its sacredness in slavery" [64], then so does "motherhood" as female blood-rite/right. To that extent, the captive female body locates precisely a moment of converging political and social vectors that mark the flesh as a prime commodity of exchange. While this proposition is open to further exploration, suffice it to say now that this open exchange of female bodies in the raw offers a kind of Ur-text to the dynamics of signification and representation that the gendered female would unravel.

For Douglass, the loss of his mother eventuates in alienation from his brother and sisters, who live in the same house with him: "The early separation of us from our mother had well nigh blotted the fact of our relationship from our memories" [45]. What could this mean? The *physical* proximity of the siblings survives the mother's death. They grasp their connection in the physical sense, but Douglass appears to mean a *psychological* bonding whose success mandates the *mother's* presence. Could we say, then, that the *feeling* of kinship is *not* inevitable? That it describes a relationship that appears "natural," but must be "cultivated" under actual material conditions? If the child's humanity is mirrored initially in the eyes of its mother, or the maternal function, then we might be able to guess that the social subject grasps the whole dynamic of resemblance and kinship by way of the same source.

There is an amazing thematic synonymity on this point between aspects of Douglass's *Narrative* and Malcolm El-Hajj Malik El Shabazz's *Autobiography of Malcolm X* [21 ff.]. Through the loss of the mother, in the latter contemporary instance, to the institution of "insanity" and the state—a full century after Douglass's writing and under social conditions that might be designated a post-emancipation neo-enslavement—Malcolm and his siblings, robbed of their activist father in a kkk-like ambush, are not only widely dispersed across a makeshift social terrain, but also show symptoms of estrangement and "disremembering" that require many years to heal, and even then, only by way of Malcolm's prison ordeal turned, eventually, into a redemptive occurrence.

The destructive loss of the natural mother, whose biological/genetic relationship to the child remains unique and unambiguous, opens the enslaved young to social ambiguity and chaos: the ambiguity of his/her fatherhood and to a structure of other relational elements, now threatened, that would declare the young's connection to a genetic and historic future by way of their own siblings. That the father in Douglass's case was most likely the "master," not by any means special to Douglass, involves a hideous paradox. Fatherhood, at best a supreme cultural courtesy, attenuates here on the one hand into a monstrous accumulation of power on the other. One has been "made" and "bought" by disparate currencies, linking back to a common origin of exchange and domination. The denied genetic link becomes the chief strategy of an undenied ownership, as if the interrogation into the father's identity—the blank space where his proper name will fit—were answered by the fact, *de jure* of a material possession. "And this is done," Douglass asserts, "too obviously to administer to the [masters'] own lusts, and make a gratification of their wicked desires profitable as well as pleasurable" [23].

Whether or not the captive female and/or her sexual oppressor derived "pleasure" from their seductions and couplings is not a question we can politely ask.

Whether or not "pleasure" is possible at all under conditions that I would aver as non-freedom for both or either of the parties has not been settled. Indeed, we could go so far as to entertain the very real possibility that "sexuality," as a term of implied relationship and desire, is dubiously appropriate, manageable, or accurate to *any* of the familial arrangements under a system of enslavement, from the master's family to the captive enclave. Under these arrangements, the customary lexis of sexuality, including "reproduction," "motherhood," "pleasure," and "desire" are thrown into unrelieved crisis.

If the testimony of Linda Brent/Harriet Jacobs is to be believed, the official mistresses of slavery's "masters" constitute a privileged class of the tormented, if such contradiction can be entertained [Brent 29–35]. Linda Brent/Harriet Jacobs recounts in the course of her narrative scenes from a "psychodrama," opposing herself and "Mrs. Flint," in what we have come to consider the classic alignment between captive woman and free. Suspecting that her husband, Dr. Flint, has sexual designs on the young Linda (and the doctor is nearly humorously incompetent at it, according to the story line), Mrs. Flint assumes the role of a perambulatory nightmare who visits the captive woman in the spirit of a veiled seduction. Mrs. Flint imitates the incubus who "rides" its victim in order to exact confession, expiation, and anything else that the immaterial power might want. (Gayle Jones's *Corregidora* [1975] weaves a contemporary fictional situation around the historic motif of entangled female sexualities.) This narrative scene from Brent's work, dictated to Lydia Maria Child, provides an instance of a repeated sequence, purportedly based on "real" life. But the scene in question appears to so commingle its signals with the fictive, with casebook narratives from psychoanalysis, that we are certain that the narrator has her hands on an explosive moment of New-World/U.S. history that feminist investigation is beginning to unravel. The narrator recalls:

> Sometimes I woke up, and found her bending over me. At other times she whispered in my ear, as though it were her husband who was speaking to me, and listened to hear what I would answer. If she startled me, on such occasion, she would glide stealthily away; and the next morning she would tell me I had been talking in my sleep, and ask who I was talking to. At last, I began to be fearful for my life. . . . [Brent 33]

The "jealous mistress" here (but "jealous" for whom?) forms an analogy with the "master" to the extent that male dominative modes give the male the material means to fully act out what the female might only *wish*. The mistress in the case of Brent's narrative becomes a metaphor for *his* madness that arises in the ecstasy of unchecked power. Mrs. Flint enacts a male alibi and prosthetic motion that is mobilized *at night*, at the material place of the dream work. In both male and female instances, the subject attempts to *inculcate* his or her will into the vulnerable, supine body. Though this is barely hinted on the surface of the text, we might say that Brent, between the lines of her narrative, demarcates a sexuality that is neuter-bound, inasmuch as it represents an open vulnerability to a gigantic sexualized repertoire that may be alternately expressed as male/female. Since the gendered female *exists for* the male, we might suggest that the ungendered female—in an amazing stroke of pansexual potential—might be invaded/ raided by another *woman* or man.

If *Incidents in the Life of a Slave Girl* were a novel, and not the memoirs of an escaped female captive, then we might say that "Mrs. Flint" is also the narrator's projection, her creation, so that for all her pious and correct umbrage toward the outrage of her captivity, some aspect of Linda Brent is released in a manifold repetition crisis that the doctor's wife comes to stand in for. In the case of both an imagined fiction and the narrative we have from Brent/Jacobs/Child, published only four years before the official proclamations of Freedom, we could say that African-American women's community and Anglo-American women's community, under certain shared cultural conditions, were the twin actants on a common psychic landscape, were subject to the same fabric of dread and humiliation. Neither could claim her body and its various productions—for quite different reasons, albeit—as her own, and in the case of the doctor's wife, *she* appears not to have wanted *her* body at all, but to desire to enter someone else's, specifically, Linda Brent's, in an apparently classic instance of sexual "jealousy" and appropriation. In fact, from one point of view, we cannot unravel one female's narrative from the other's, cannot decipher one without tripping over the other. In that sense, these "threads cable-strong" of an incestuous, interracial genealogy uncover slavery in the United States as one of the richest displays of the psychoanalytic dimensions of culture before the science of European psychoanalysis takes hold.

4

But just as we duly regard similarities between life conditions of American women—captive and free—we must observe those undeniable contrasts and differences so decisive that the African-American female's historic claims to the territory of womanhood and "femininity" still tends to rest too solidly on the subtle and shifting calibrations of a liberal ideology. Valerie Smith's reading of the tale of Linda Brent as a tale of "garreting" enables our notion that female gender for captive women's community is the tale writ between the lines and in the not-quite spaces of an American domesticity. It is this tale that we try to make clearer, or, keeping with the metaphor, "bring on line."

If the point is that the historic conditions of African-American women might be read as an unprecedented occasion in the national context, then gender and the arrangements of gender are both crucial and evasive. Holding, however, to a specialized reading of female gender as an *outcome* of a certain political, sociocultural empowerment within the context of the United States, we would regard dispossession as the *loss* of gender, or one of the chief elements in an altered reading of gender: "Women are considered of no value, *unless* they continually increase their owner's stock. They were put on par with animals" [Brent 49; emphasis mine]. Linda Brent's witness appears to contradict the point I would make, but I am suggesting that even though the enslaved female reproduced other enslaved persons, we do not read "birth" in this instance as a reproduction of mothering precisely because the female, like the male, has been robbed of the parental right, the parental function. One treads dangerous ground in suggesting an equation between female gender and mothering; in fact, feminist inquiry/praxis and the actual day-to-day living of numberless American women—black and white—have gone far to break the enthrallment of a female subject-position to the theoretical and actual situation of maternity. Our task here would be lightened considerably if we could simply slide over the powerful "No," the significant *exception*. In the historic formation to which I point, however, motherhood and female gendering/ungendering appear so intimately aligned that they *seem* to speak the same language. At least it is plausible to say that motherhood, while it does not exhaust the problematics of female gender, offers one prominent line of approach to it. I would go farther: Because African-American women experienced uncertainty regarding their infants' lives in the historic situation, gendering, in its coeval reference to African-American women, *insinuates* an implicit and unresolved puzzle both within current feminist discourse *and* within those discursive communities that investigate the entire problematics of culture. Are we mistaken to suspect that history—at least in this instance—repeats itself yet again?

Every feature of social and human differentiation disappears in public discourses regarding the African-American person, as we encounter, in the juridical codes of slavery, personality reified. William Goodell's study not only demonstrates the rhetorical and moral passions of the abolitionist project, but also lends insight into the corpus of law that underwrites enslavement. If "slave" is perceived as the essence of stillness (an early version of "ethnicity"), or of an undynamic human state, fixed in time and space, then the law articulates this impossibility as its inherent feature: "Slaves will be deemed, sold, taken, reputed and adjudged in law to be *chattels personal*, in the hands of their owners and possessors, and their executors, administrators, and assigns, to all intents, constructions, and purposes whatsoever" [23; Goodell emphasis].

Even though we tend to parody and simplify matters to behave as if the various civil codes of the slave-holding United States were monolithically informed, unified, and executed in their application, or that the "code" itself is spontaneously generated in an undivided historic moment, we read it nevertheless as exactly this—the *peak points*, the salient and characteristic features of a human and social procedure that evolves over a natural historical sequence and represents, consequently, the narrative *shorthand* of a transaction that is riddled, *in practice*, with contradictions, accident, and surprise. We could suppose that the legal encodations of enslavement stand for the statistically average case, that the legal code provides the *topics* of a project increasingly threatened and self-conscious. It is, perhaps, not by chance that the laws regarding slavery appear to crystallize in the precise moment when agitation against the arrangement becomes articulate in certain European and New-World communities. In that regard, the slave codes that Goodell describes are themselves an instance of the counter and isolated text that seeks to silence the contradictions and antitheses engendered by it. For example, aspects of Article 461 of the South Carolina Civil Code call attention to just the sort of uneasy oxymoronic character that the "peculiar institution" attempts to sustain in transforming *personality* into *property*.

1) The "slave" is movable by nature, but "immovable by the operation of law" [Goodell 24]. As I read this, law itself is compelled to a point of saturation, or a reverse zero degree, beyond which it cannot move in the behalf of the enslaved *or* the free. We recall, too, that the "master," under these perversions of judicial power, is impelled to *treat* the enslaved as property, and not as person. These laws stand for the kind of social formulation that armed forces will help

excise from a living context in the campaigns of civil war. They also embody the untenable human relationship that Henry David Thoreau believed occasioned acts of "civil disobedience," the moral philosophy to which Martin Luther King, Jr. would subscribe in the latter half of the twentieth century.

2) Slaves shall be *reputed* and *considered* real estate, "subject to be mortgaged, according to the rules prescribed by law" [Goodell 24]. I emphasize "reputed" and "considered" as predicate adjectives that invite attention because they denote a *contrivance*, not an intransitive "is," or the transfer of nominative property from one syntactic point to another by way of a weakened copulative. The status of the "reputed" can change, as it will significantly before the nineteenth century closes. The mood here—the "shall be"—is pointedly subjunctive, or the situation devoutly to be wished. That the slave-holding class is forced, in time, to think and do something else is the narrative of violence that enslavement itself has been preparing for a couple of centuries.

Louisiana's and South Carolina's written codes offer a paradigm for praxis in those instances where a *written* text is missing. In that case, the "chattel principle has . . . been affirmed and maintained by the courts, and involved in legislative acts" [Goodell 25]. In Maryland, a legislative enactment of 1798 shows so forceful a synonymity of motives between branches of comparable governance that a line between "judicial" and "legislative" functions is useless to draw: "In case the personal property of a ward shall consist of specific articles, such as slaves, working beasts, animals of any kind, stock, furniture, plates, books, and so forth, the Court if it shall deem it advantageous to the ward, may at any time, pass an order for the sale thereof" [56]. This inanimate and corporate ownership—the voting district of a ward—is here spoken for, or might be, as a single slave-holding male in determinations concerning property.

The eye pauses, however, not so much at the provisions of this enactment as at the details of its delineation. Everywhere in the descriptive document, we are stunned by the simultaneity of disparate items in a grammatical series: "Slave" appears in the same context with beasts of burden, *all* and *any* animal(s), various livestock, and a virtually endless profusion of domestic content from the culinary item to the book. Unlike the taxonomy of Borges's "Certain Chinese encyclopedia," whose contemplation opens Foucault's *Order of Things*, these items from a certain American encyclopedia do not sustain discrete and localized "powers of contagion," nor has the ground of their concatenation been desiccated beneath them. That imposed uniformity comprises the shock, that somehow this mix of named things, live and inanimate, collapsed by contiguity to the same text of "realism," carries a disturbingly prominent item of misplacement. To that extent, the project of liberation for African-Americans has found urgency in two passionate motivations that are twinned—1) to break apart, to rupture violently the laws of American behavior that make such *syntax* possible; 2) to introduce a new *semantic* field/fold more appropriate to his/her own historic movement. I regard this twin compulsion as distinct, though related, moments of the very same narrative process that might appear as a concentration or a dispersal. The narratives of Linda Brent, Frederick Douglass, and Malcolm El-Hajj Malik El-Shabazz (aspects of which are examined in this essay) each represent both narrative ambitions as they occur under the auspices of "author."

Relatedly, we might interpret the whole career of African-Americans, a decisive factor in national political life since the mid-seventeenth century, in light of the *intervening, intruding* tale, or the tale—like Brent's "garret" space— "between the lines," which are already inscribed, as a *metaphor* of social and cultural management. According to this reading, gender, or sex-role assignation, or the clear differentiation of sexual stuff, sustained elsewhere in the culture, does not emerge for the African-American female in this historic instance, except indirectly, except as a way to reenforce through the process of birthing, "the reproduction of the relations of production" that involves "the reproduction of the values and behavior patterns necessary to maintain the system of hierarchy in its various aspects of gender, class, and race or ethnicity" [Margaret Strobel, "Slavery and Reproductive Labor in Mombasa," Robertson and Klein 121]. Following Strobel's lead, I would suggest that the foregoing identifies one of the three categories of reproductive labor that African-American females carry out under the regime of captivity. But this replication of ideology is never simple in the case of female subject-positions, and it appears to acquire a thickened layer of motives in the case of African-American females.

If we can account for an originary narrative and judicial principle that might have engendered a "Moynihan Report," many years into the twentieth century, we cannot do much better than look at Goodell's reading of the *partus sequitur ventrem:* the condition of the slave mother is "forever entailed on all her remotest posterity." This maxim of civil law, in Goodell's view, the "genuine and degrading principle of slavery, inasmuch as it places the slave upon a level with brute animals, prevails universally in the slave-holding states" [Goodell 27]. But what is the "condition" of the mother? Is it the "condition" of enslavement the writer means, or does he mean the "mark" and the "knowledge" of the *mother* upon the child that here translates into the culturally forbidden and impure? In an elision of terms, "mother" and "enslavement" are indistinct categories of the illegitimate inasmuch as each of these synonymous elements defines, in effect, a cultural situation that is *father-lacking.* Goodell, who does not only report this maxim of law as an aspect of his own factuality, but also regards it, as does Douglass, as a fundamental degradation, supposes descent and identity through the female line as comparable to a brute animality. Knowing already that there are human communities that align social reproductive procedure according to the line of the mother, and Goodell himself might have known it some years later, we can only conclude that the provisions of patriarchy, here exacerbated by the preponderant powers of an enslaving class, declare Mother Right, by definition, a negating feature of human community.

Even though we are not even talking about *any* of the matriarchal features of social projection/reproduction—matrifocality, matrilinearity, matriarchy—when we speak of the enslaved person, we perceive that the dominant culture, in a fatal misunderstanding, assigns a matriachist value where it does not belong; actually *misnames* the power of the female regarding the enslaved community. Such naming is false because the female could not, in fact, claim her child, and false, once again, because "motherhood" is not perceived in the prevailing social climate as a legitimate procedure of cultural inheritance.

The African-American male has been touched, therefore, by the *mother,* *handed* by her in ways that he cannot escape, and in ways that the white American male is allowed to temporize by a fatherly reprieve. This human and historic development—the text that has been inscribed on the benighted heart of the continent—takes us to the center of an inexorable difference in the depths of American women's community: the African-American woman, the mother, the daughter, becomes historically the powerful and shadowy evocation of a cultural synthesis long evaporated—the law of the Mother—only and precisely because legal enslavement removed the African-American male not so much from sight as from *mimetic* view as a partner in the prevailing social fiction of the Father's name, the Father's law.

Therefore, the female, in this order of things, breaks in upon the imagination with a forcefulness that marks both a denial and an "illegitimacy." Because of this peculiar American denial, the black American male embodies the *only* American community of males which has had the specific occasion to learn *who* the female is within itself, the infant child who bears the life against the could-be fateful gamble, against the odds of pulverization and murder, including her own. It is the heritage of the *mother* that the African-American male must regain as an aspect of his own personhood—the power of "yes" to the "female" within.

This different cultural text actually reconfigures, in historically ordained discourse, certain *representational* potentialities for African-Americans: 1) motherhood as female blood-rite is outraged, is denied, at the *very same time* that it becomes the founding term of a human and social enactment; 2) a dual fatherhood is set in motion, comprised of the African father's *banished* name and body and the captor father's mocking presence. In this play of paradox, only the female stands *in the flesh*, both mother and mother-dispossessed. This problematizing of gender places her, in my view, *out* of the traditional symbolics of female gender, and it is our task to make a place for this different social subject. In doing so, we are less interested in joining the ranks of gendered femaleness than gaining the *insurgent* ground as female social subject. Actually *claiming* the monstrosity (of a female with the potential to "name"), which her culture imposes in blindness, "Sapphire" might rewrite after all a radically different text for a female empowerment.

SELECTED BIBLIOGRAPHY

BARTHES, ROLAND. *Mythologies.* Trans. Annette Lavers. New York: Hill and Wang, 1972.

BLASSINGAME, JOHN. *The Slave Community: Plantation Life in the Antebellum South.* New York: Oxford UP, 1972.

BRENT, LINDA. *Incidents in the Life of a Slave Girl.* Ed. L. Maria Child. Introduced by Walter Teller. Rpt. New York: Harvest/HBJ Book, 1973.

DAVIS, ANGELA Y. *Women, Race, and Class.* New York: Random House, 1981.

DE AZURARA, GOMES EANNES. *The Chronicle of the Discovery and Conquest of Guinea.* Trans. C. Raymond Beazley and Edgar Prestage. London: Hakluyt Society, 1896, 1897, in Elizabeth Donnan, *Documents Illustrative of the History of the Slave Trade to America.* Washington, D.C.: Carnegie Institution of Washington, 1932, 1:18–41.

DONNAN, ELIZABETH. *Documents Illustrative of the History of the Slave Trade to America;* 4 vols. Washington, D.C.: The Carnegie Institution of Washington, 1932.

DOUGLASS, FREDERICK. *Narrative of the Life of Frederick Douglass An American Slave, Written by Himself.* Rpt. New York: Signet Books, 1968.

EL-SHABAZZ, MALCOLM EL-HAJJ MALIK. *Autobiography of Malcolm X.* With Alex Haley. Introduced by M. S. Handler. New York: Grove Press, 1966.

EQUIANO, OLAUDAH. "The Life of Olaudah Equiano, or Gustavus Vassa, The African, Written by Himself," in *Great Slave Narratives*. Introduced and selected by Arna Bontemps. Boston: Beacon Press, 1969. 1–192.

FAULKNER, WILLIAM. *The Mansion*. New York: Vintage Books, 1965.

FRAZIER, E. FRANKLIN. *The Negro Family in the United States*. Rev. with foreword by Nathan Glazer. Chicago: The U of Chicago P, 1966.

GENOVESE, EUGENE. *Roll, Jordan, Roll: The World the Slaves Made*. New York: Pantheon Books, 1974.

GOODELL, WILLIAM. *The American Slave Code in Theory and Practice Shown By Its Statutes, Judicial Decisions, and Illustrative Facts;* 3rd ed. New York: American and Foreign Anti-Slavery Society, 1853.

HOOKS, BELL. *Ain't I a Woman: Black Women and Feminism*. Boston: South End Press, 1981.

KLEIN, HERBERT S. "African Women in the Atlantic Slave Trade." Robertson and Klein 29–39.

MEILLASSOUX, CLAUDE. "Female Slavery." Robertson and Klein 49–67.

MOYNIHAN, DANIEL P. "The Moynihan Report" [*The Negro Family: The Case for National Action*. Washington, D.C.: U.S. Department of Labor, 1965]. *The Moynihan Report and the Politics of Controversy: A Transaction Social Science and Public Policy Report*. Ed. Lee Rainwater and William L. Yancey. Cambridge: MIT Press, 1967. 47–94.

ROBERTSON, CLAIRE C., AND MARTIN A. KLEIN, EDS. *Women and Slavery in Africa*. Madison: U of Wisconsin P, 1983.

SCARRY, ELAINE. *The Body in Pain: The Making and Unmaking of the World*. New York: Oxford UP, 1985.

SMITH, VALERIE. "Loopholes of Retreat: Architecture and Ideology in Harriet Jacobs's *Incidents in the Life of a Slave Girl*." Paper presented at the 1985 American Studies Association Meeting, San Diego. Cited in Henry Louis Gates, Jr. "What's Love Got to Do With It?" *New Literary History* 18.2 (Winter 1987): 360.

STROBEL, MARGARET. "Slavery and Reproductive Labor in Mombasa." Robertson and Klein 111–30.

SULEIMAN, SUSAN RUBIN, ED. *The Female Body in Western Culture*. Cambridge: Harvard UP, 1986.

TODOROV, TZVETAN. *The Conquest of America: The Question of the Other*. Trans. Richard Howard. New York: Harper Colophon Books, 1984.

WHITE, DEBORAH GREY. *Ar'n't I A Woman? Female Slaves in the Plantation South*. New York: Norton, 1985.

hélène cixous

THE LAUGH OF THE MEDUSA

I shall speak about women's writing: about *what it will do*. Woman must write her self: must write about women and bring women to writing, from which they have been driven away as violently as from their bodies—for the same reasons, by the same law, with the same fatal goal. Woman must put herself into the text—as into the world and into history—by her own movement.

The future must no longer be determined by the past. I do not deny that the effects of the past are still with us. But I refuse to strengthen them by repeating them, to confer upon them an irremovability the equivalent of destiny, to confuse the biological and the cultural. Anticipation is imperative.

Since these reflections are taking shape in an area just on the point of being discovered, they necessarily bear the mark of our time—a time during which the new breaks away from the old, and, more precisely, the (feminine) new from the old (*la nouvelle de l'ancien*). Thus, as there are no grounds for establishing a discourse, but rather an arid millennial ground to break, what I say has at least two sides and two aims: to break up, to destroy; and to foresee the unforeseeable, to project.

I write this as a woman, toward women. When I say "woman," I'm speaking of woman in her inevitable struggle against conventional man; and of a universal woman subject who must bring women to their senses and to their meaning in history. But first it must be said that in spite of the enormity of the repression that has kept them in the "dark"—that dark which people have been trying to make them accept as their attribute—there is, at this time, no general woman, no one typical woman. What they have *in common* I will say. But what strikes me is the infinite richness of their individual constitutions: you can't talk about *a* female sexuality, uniform, homogeneous, classifiable into codes—any more than you can talk about one unconscious resembling another. Women's imaginary is inexhaustible, like music, painting, writing: their stream of phantasms is incredible.

I have been amazed more than once by a description a woman gave me of a world all her own which she had been secretly haunting since early childhood. A world of searching, the elaboration of knowledge, on the basis of a systematic experimentation with the bodily functions, a passionate and precise interrogation of her erotogeneity. This practice, extraordinarily rich and inventive, in particular as concerns masturbation, is prolonged or accompanied by a production of forms, a veritable aesthetic activity, each stage of rapture inscribing a resonant vision, a composition, something beautiful. Beauty will no longer be forbidden.

I wished that that woman would write and proclaim this unique empire so that

From Signs 1, no. 4 (1976): 875–894. Copyright © by the University of Chicago Press.

other women, other unacknowledged sovereigns, might exclaim: I, too, over-flow; my desire has invented new desires, my body knows unheard-of songs. Time and again I, too, have felt so full of luminous torrents that I could burst—burst with forms much more beautiful than those which are put up in frames and sold for a stinking fortune. And I, too, said nothing, showed nothing; I didn't open my mouth, I didn't repaint my half of the world. I was ashamed. I was afraid, and I swallowed my shame and my fear. I said to myself: You are mad! What's the meaning of these waves, these floods, these outbursts? Where is the ebullient, infinite woman who, immersed as she was in her naïveté, kept in the dark about herself, led into self-disdain by the great arm of parental-conjugal phallocentrism, hasn't been ashamed of her strength? Who, surprised and horri-fied by the fantastic tumult of her drives (for she was made to believe that a well-adjusted normal woman has a . . . divine composure), hasn't accused herself of being a monster? Who, feeling a funny desire stirring inside her (to sing, to write, to dare to speak, in short, to bring out something new), hasn't thought she was sick? Well, her shameful sickness is that she resists death, that she makes trouble.

And why don't you write? Write! Writing is for you, you are for you; your body is yours, take it. I know why you haven't written. (And why I didn't write before the age of twenty-seven.) Because writing is at once too high, too great for you, it's reserved for the great—that is for "great men"; and it's "silly." Besides, you've written a little, but in secret. And it wasn't good, because it was in secret, and because you punished yourself for writing, because you didn't go all the way, or because you wrote, irresistibly, as when we would masturbate in secret, not to go further, but to attenuate the tension a bit, just enough to take the edge off. And then as soon as we come, we go and make ourselves feel guilty—so as to be forgiven; or to forget, to bury it until next time.

Write, let no one hold you back, let nothing stop you: not man; not the im-becilic capitalist machinery, in which publishing houses are the crafty, obsequi-ous relayers of imperatives handed down by an economy that works against us and off our backs; and not *yourself*. Smug-faced readers, managing editors, and big bosses don't like the true texts of women—female-sexed texts. That kind scares them.

I write woman: woman must write woman. And man, man. So only an oblique consideration will be found here of man; it's up to him to say where his mascu-linity and femininity are at: this will concern us once men have opened their eyes and seen themselves clearly.[1]

Now women return from afar, from always: from "without," from the heath where witches are kept alive; from below, from beyond "culture"; from their childhood which men have been trying desperately to make them forget, con-demning it to "eternal rest." The little girls and their "ill-mannered" bodies immured, well-preserved, intact unto themselves, in the mirror. Frigidified. But are they ever seething underneath! What an effort it takes—there's no end to it—for the sex cops to bar their threatening return. Such a display of forces on both sides that the struggle has for centuries been immobilized in the trembling equilibrium of a deadlock.

Here they are, returning, arriving over and again, because the unconscious is impregnable. They have wandered around in circles, confined to the narrow room in which they've been given a deadly brainwashing. You can incarcerate them, slow them down, get away with the old Apartheid routine, but for a time only. As soon as they begin to speak, at the same time as they're taught their name, they can be taught that their territory is black: because you are Africa, you are black. Your continent is dark. Dark is dangerous. You can't see anything in the dark, you're afraid. Don't move, you might fall. Most of all, don't go into the forest. And so we have internalized this horror of the dark.

Men have committed the greatest crime against women. Insidiously, violently, they have led them to hate women, to be their own enemies, to mobilize their immense strength against themselves, to be the executants of their virile needs. They have made for women an antinarcissism! A narcissism which loves itself only to be loved for what women haven't got! They have constructed the infamous logic of antilove.

We the precocious, we the repressed of culture, our lovely mouths gagged with pollen, our wind knocked out of us, we the labyrinths, the ladders, the trampled spaces, the bevies—we are black and we are beautiful.

We're stormy, and that which is ours breaks loose from us without our fearing any debilitation. Our glances, our smiles, are spent; laughs exude from all our mouths; our blood flows and we extend ourselves without ever reaching an end; we never hold back our thoughts, our signs, our writing; and we're not afraid of lacking.

What happiness for us who are omitted, brushed aside at the scene of inheritances; we inspire ourselves and we expire without running out of breath, we are everywhere!

From now on, who, if we say so, can say no to us? We've come back from always.

It is time to liberate the New Woman from the Old by coming to know her—by loving her for getting by, for getting beyond the Old without delay, by going out ahead of what the New Woman will be, as an arrow quits the bow with a movement that gathers and separates the vibrations musically, in order to be more than her self.

I say that we must, for, with a few rare exceptions, there has not yet been any writing that inscribes femininity; exceptions so rare, in fact, that, after plowing through literature across languages, cultures, and ages,[2] one can only be startled at this vain scouting mission. It is well known that the number of women writers (while having increased very slightly from the nineteenth century on) has always been ridiculously small. This is a useless and deceptive fact unless from their species of female writers we do not first deduct the immense majority whose workmanship is in no way different from male writing, and which either obscures women or reproduces the classic representations of women (as sensitive—intuitive—dreamy, etc.).[3]

Let me insert here a parenthetical remark. I mean it when I speak of male writing. I maintain unequivocally that there is such a thing as *marked* writing; that, until now, far more extensively and repressively than is ever suspected or admitted, writing has been run by a libidinal and cultural—hence political, typically masculine—economy; that this is a locus where the repression of women has been perpetuated, over and over, more or less consciously, and in a manner that's frightening since it's often hidden or adorned with the mystifying charms of fiction; that this locus has grossly exaggerated all the signs of sexual opposition (and not sexual difference), where woman has never *her* turn to speak—this being all the more serious and unpardonable in that writing is precisely *the very possibility of change*, the space that can serve as a springboard for subversive thought, the precursory movement of a transformation of social and cultural structures.

Nearly the entire history of writing is confounded with the history of reason, of which it is at once the effect, the support, and one of the privileged alibis. It has been one with the phallocentric tradition. It is indeed that same self-admiring, self-stimulating, self-congratulatory phallocentrism.

With some exceptions, for there have been failures—and if it weren't for them, I wouldn't be writing (I-woman, escapee)—in that enormous machine that has been operating and turning out its "truth" for centuries. There have been poets who would go to any lengths to slip something by at odds with tradition—men capable of loving love and hence capable of loving others and of wanting them, of imagining the woman who would hold out against oppression and constitute herself as a superb, equal, hence "impossible" subject, untenable in a real social framework. Such a woman the poet could desire only by breaking the codes that negate her. Her appearance would necessarily bring on, if not revolution—for the bastion was supposed to be immutable—at least harrowing explosions. At times it is in the fissure caused by an earthquake, through that radical mutation of things brought on by a material upheaval when every structure is for a moment thrown off balance and an ephemeral wildness sweeps order away, that the poet slips something by, for a brief span, of woman. Thus did Kliest expend himself in his yearning for the existence of sister-lovers, maternal daughters, mother-sisters, who never hung their heads in shame. Once the palace of magistrates is restored, it's time to pay: immediate bloody death to the uncontrollable elements.

But only the poets—not the novelists, allies of representationalism. Because poetry involves gaining strength through the unconscious and because the unconscious, that other limitless country, is the place where the repressed manage to survive: women, or as Hoffman would say, fairies.

She must write her self, because this is the invention of a *new insurgent* writing which, when the moment of her liberation has come, will allow her to carry out the indispensable ruptures and transformations in her history, first at two levels that cannot be separated.

a) Individually. By writing her self, woman will return to the body which has been more than confiscated from her, which has been turned into the uncanny stranger on display—the ailing or dead figure, which so often turns out to be the nasty companion, the cause and location of inhibitions. Censor the body and you censor breath and speech at the same time.

Write your self. Your body must be heard. Only then will the immense resources of the unconscious spring forth. Our naphtha will spread, throughout the world, without dollars—black or gold—nonassessed values that will change the rules of the old game.

To write. An act which will not only "realize" the decensored relation of woman to her sexuality, to her womanly being, giving her access to her native strength; it will give her back her goods, her pleasures, her organs, her immense bodily territories which have been kept under seal; it will tear her away from the superegoized structure in which she has always occupied the place reserved for the guilty (guilty of everything, guilty at every turn: for having desires, for not having any; for being frigid, for being "too hot"; for not being both at once; for being too motherly and not enough; for having children and for not having any; for nursing and for not nursing . . .)—tear her away by means of this research, this job of analysis and illumination, this emancipation of the marvelous text of her self that she must urgently learn to speak. A woman without a body, dumb, blind, can't possibly be a good fighter. She is reduced to being the servant of the militant male, his shadow. We must kill the false woman who is preventing the live one from breathing. Inscribe the breath of the whole woman.

b) An act that will also be marked by woman's *seizing* the occasion to *speak*, hence her shattering entry into history, which has always been based *on her suppression*. To write and thus to forge for herself the antilogos weapon. To become *at will* the taker and initiator, for her own right, in every symbolic system, in every political process.

It is time for women to start scoring their feats in written and oral language.

Every woman has known the torment of getting up to speak. Her heart racing, at times entirely lost for words, ground and language slipping away—that's how daring a feat, how great a transgression it is for a woman to speak—even just open her mouth—in public. A double distress, for even if she transgresses, her words fall almost always upon the deaf male ear, which hears in language only that which speaks in the masculine.

It is by writing, from and toward women, and by taking up the challenge of speech which has been governed by the phallus, that women will confirm women in a place other than that which is reserved in and by the symbolic, that is, in a place other than silence. Women should break out of the snare of silence. They shouldn't be conned into accepting a domain which is the margin or the harem.

Listen to a woman speak at a public gathering (if she hasn't painfully lost her wind). She doesn't "speak," she throws her trembling body forward; she lets go of herself, she flies; all of her passes into her voice, and it's with her body that she vitally supports the "logic" of her speech. Her flesh speaks true. She lays herself bare. In fact, she physically materializes what she's thinking; she signifies it with her body. In a certain way she *inscribes* what she's saying, because she doesn't deny her drives the intractable and impassioned part they have in speaking. Her speech, even when "theoretical" or political, is never simple or linear or "objectified," generalized: she draws her story into history.

There is not that scission, that division made by the common man between the logic of oral speech and the logic of the text, bound as he is by his antiquated relation—servile, calculating—to mastery. From which proceeds the niggardly lip service which engages only the tiniest part of the body, plus the mask.

In women's speech, as in their writing, that element which never stops resonating, which, once we've been permeated by it, profoundly and imperceptibly touched by it, retains the power of moving us—that element is the song: first music from the first voice of love which is alive in every woman. Why this privileged relationship with the voice? Because no woman stockpiles as many defenses for countering the drives as does a man. You don't build walls around yourself, you don't forego pleasure as "wisely" as he. Even if phallic mystification has generally contaminated good relationships, a woman is never far from "mother" (I mean outside her role functions: the "mother" as nonname and as source of goods). There is always within her at least a little of that good mother's milk. She writes in white ink.

Woman for women.—There always remains in woman that force which produces/is produced by the other—in particular, the other woman. *In* her, matrix, cradler; herself giver as her mother and child; she is her own sister-daughter. You might object, "What about she who is the hysterical offspring of a bad mother?" Everything will be changed once woman gives woman to the other woman. There is hidden and always ready in woman the source; the locus for the other. The mother, too, is a metaphor. It is necessary and sufficient that the best of herself be given to woman by another woman for her to be able to love herself and return in love the body that was "born" to her. Touch me, caress me, you the living no-name, give me my self as myself. The relation to the "mother," in terms of intense pleasure and violence, is curtailed no more than the relation to childhood (the child that she was, that she is, that she makes, remakes, undoes, there at the point where, the same, she mothers herself). Text: my body—shot through with streams of song; I don't mean the overbearing, clutchy "mother" but, rather, what touches you, the equivoice that affects you, fills your breast with an urge to come to language and launches your force; the rhythm that laughs you; the intimate recipient who makes all metaphors possible and desirable; body (body? bodies?), no more describable than god, the soul, or the Other; that part of you that leaves a space between yourself and urges you to inscribe in language your woman's style. In women there is always more or less of the mother who makes everything all right, who nourishes, and who stands up against separation; a force that will not be cut off but will knock the wind out of the codes. We will rethink womankind beginning with every form and every period of her body. The Americans remind us, "We are all Lesbians"; that is, don't denigrate woman, don't make of her what men have made of you.

Because the "economy" of her drives is prodigious, she cannot fail, in seizing the occasion to speak, to transform directly and indirectly *all* systems of exchange based on masculine thrift. Her libido will produce far more radical effects of political and social change than some might like to think.

Because she arrives, vibrant, over and again, we are at the beginning of a new history, or rather of a process of becoming in which several histories intersect with one another. As subject for history, woman always occurs simultaneously in several places. Woman un-thinks[4] the unifying, regulating history that homogenizes and channels forces, herding contradictions into a single battlefield. In woman, personal history blends together with the history of all women, as well as national and world history. As a militant, she is an integral part of all liberations. She must be farsighted, not limited to blow-by-blow interaction. She foresees that her liberation will do more than modify power relations or toss the ball over to the other camp; she will bring about a mutation in human relations, in thought, in all praxis: hers is not simply a class struggle, which she carries forward into a much vaster movement. Not that in order to be a woman-in-struggle(s) you have to leave the class struggle or repudiate it; but you have to split it open, spread it out, push it forward, fill it with the fundamental struggle so as to prevent the class struggle, or any other struggle for the liberation of a class of people, from operating as a form of repression, pretext for postponing the inevitable, the staggering alteration in power relations and in the production of individuals. This alteration is already upon us—in the United States, for example, where millions of night crawlers are in the process of undermining the family and disintegrating the whole of American sociality.

The new history is coming; it's not a dream, though it does extend beyond men's imagination, and for good reason. It's going to deprive them of their conceptual orthopedics, beginning with the destruction of their enticement machine.

It is impossible to *define* a feminine practice of writing, and this is an impossibility that will remain, for this practice can never be theorized, enclosed, coded—which doesn't mean that it doesn't exist. But it will always surpass the discourse that regulates the phallocentric system; it does and will take place in areas other than those subordinated to philosophico-theoretical domination. It will be conceived of only by subjects who are breakers of automatisms, by peripheral figures that no authority can ever subjugate.

Hence the necessity to affirm the flourishes of this writing, to give form to its movement, its near and distant byways. Bear in mind to begin with (1) that sexual opposition, which has always worked for man's profit to the point of reducing writing, too, to his laws, is only a historico-cultural limit. There is, there will be more and more rapidly pervasive now, a fiction that produces irreducible effects of femininity. (2) That it is through ignorance that most readers, critics, and writers of both sexes hesitate to admit or deny outright the possibility or the pertinence of a distinction between feminine and masculine writing. It will usually be said, thus disposing of sexual difference: either that all writing, to the extent that it materializes, is feminine; or, inversely—but it comes to the same thing—that the act of writing is equivalent to masculine masturbation (and so the woman who writes cuts herself out a paper penis); or that writing is bisexual, hence neuter, which again does away with differentiation. To admit that writing is precisely working (in) the in-between, inspecting the process of the same and of the other without which nothing can live, undoing the work of death—to admit this is first to want the two, as well as both, the ensemble of the one and the other, not fixed in sequences of struggle and expulsion or some other form of death but infinitely dynamized by an incessant process of exchange from one subject to another. A process of different subjects knowing one another and beginning one another anew only from the living boundaries of the other: a multiple and inexhaustible course with millions of encounters and transformations of the same into the other and into the in-between, from which woman takes her forms (and man, in his turn, but that's his other history).

In saying "bisexual, hence neuter," I am referred to the classic conception of bisexuality, which, squashed under the emblem of castration fear and along with the fantasy of a "total" being (though composed of two halves), would do away with the difference experienced as an operation incurring loss, as the mark of dreaded sectility.

To this self-effacing, merger-type bisexuality, which would conjure away castration (the writer who puts up his sign: "bisexual written here, come and see," when the odds are good that it's neither one nor the other), I oppose the *other bisexuality* on which every subject not enclosed in the false theater of phallocentric representationalism has founded his/her erotic universe. Bisexuality: that is, each one's location in self (*repérage en soi*) of the presence—variously manifest and insistent according to each person, male or female—of both sexes, nonexclusion either of the difference or of one sex, and, from this "self-permission," multiplication of the effects of the inscription of desire, over all parts of my body and the other body.

Now it happens that at present, for historico-cultural reasons, it is women who are opening up to and benefiting from this vatic bisexuality which doesn't annul differences but stirs them up, pursues them, increases their number. In a certain way, "woman is bisexual"; man—it's a secret to no one—being poised to keep glorious phallic monosexuality in view. By virtue of affirming the primacy of the phallus and of bringing it into play, phallocratic ideology has claimed more than one victim. As a woman, I've been clouded over by the great shadow of the scepter and been told: idolize it, that which you cannot brandish. But at the same time, man has been handed that grotesque and scarcely enviable destiny (just imagine) of being reduced to a single idol with clay balls. And consumed, as Freud and his followers note, by a fear of being a woman! For, if psychoanalysis was constituted from woman, to repress femininity (and not so successful a repression at that—men have made it clear), its account of masculine sexuality is now hardly refutable: as with all the "human" sciences, it reproduces the masculine view, of which it is one of the effects.

Here we encounter the inevitable man-with-rock, standing erect in his old Freudian realm, in the way that, to take the figure back to the point where linguistics is conceptualizing it "anew," Lacan preserves it in the sanctuary of the phallos (ϕ) "sheltered" from *castration's lack!* Their "symbolic" exists, it holds power—we, the sowers of disorder, know it only too well. But we are in no way obliged to deposit our lives in their banks of lack, to consider the constitution of the subject in terms of a drama manglingly restaged, to reinstate again and again the religion of the father. Because we don't want that. We don't fawn around the supreme hole. We have no womanly reason to pledge allegiance to the negative. The feminine (as the poets suspected) affirms: ". . . And yes," says Molly, carrying *Ulysses* off beyond any book and toward the new writing: "I said yes, I will Yes."

The Dark Continent is neither dark nor unexplorable.—It is still unexplored only because we've been made to believe that it was too dark to be explorable. And because they want to make us believe that what interests us is the white continent, with its monuments to Lack. And we believed. They riveted us between two horrifying myths: between the Medusa and the abyss. That would be enough to set half the world laughing, except that it's still going on. For the phallologocentric sublation is with us, and it's militant, regenerating[5] the old patterns, anchored in the dogma of castration. They haven't changed a thing: they've theorized their desire for reality! Let the priests tremble, we're going to show them our sexts!

Too bad for them if they fall apart upon discovering that women aren't men, or that the mother doesn't have one. But isn't this fear convenient for them? Wouldn't the worst be, isn't the worst, in truth, that women aren't castrated, that they have only to stop listening to the Sirens (for the Sirens were men) for history to change its meaning? You only have to look at the Medusa straight on to see her. And she's not deadly. She's beautiful and she's laughing.

Men say that there are two unrepresentable things: death and the feminine sex. That's because they need femininity to be associated with death; it's the jitters that give them a hard-on! for themselves! They need to be afraid of us. Look at the trembling Perseuses moving backward toward us, clad in apotropes. What lovely backs! Not another minute to lose. Let's get out of her.

Let's hurry: the continent is not impenetrably dark. I've been there often. I was overjoyed one day to run into Jean Genet. It was in *Pompes funèbres*.[6] He had come there led by his Jean. There are some men (all too few) who aren't afraid of femininity.

Almost everything is yet to be written by women about femininity: about their sexuality, that is, its infinite and mobile complexity, about their eroticization, sudden turn-ons of a certain miniscule-immense area of their bodies; not about destiny, but about the adventure of such and such a drive, about trips, crossings, trudges, abrupt and gradual awakenings, discoveries of a zone at one time timorous and soon to be forthright. A woman's body, with its thousand and one thresholds of ardor—once, by smashing yokes and censors, she lets it articulate the profusion of meanings that run through it in every direction—will make the old single-grooved mother tongue reverberate with more than one language.

We've been turned away from our bodies, shamefully taught to ignore them, to strike them with that stupid sexual modesty; we've been made victims of the old fool's game: each one will love the other sex. I'll give you your body and you'll give me mine. But who are the men who give women the body that women blindly yield to them? Why so few texts? Because so few women have as yet won back their body. Women must write through their bodies, they must invent the impregnable language that will wreck partitions, classes, and rhetorics, regulations and codes, they must submerge, cut through, get beyond the ultimate reserve-discourse, including the one that laughs at the very idea of pronouncing the word "silence," the one that, aiming for the impossible, stops short before the word "impossible" and writes it as "the end."

Such is the strength of women that, sweeping away syntax, breaking that famous thread (just a tiny little thread, they say) which acts for men as a surrogate umbilical cord, assuring them—otherwise they couldn't come—that the old lady is always right behind them, watching them make phallus, women will go right up to the impossible.

When the "repressed" of their culture and their society returns, it's an explosive, *utterly* destructive, staggering return, with a force never yet unleashed and equal to the most forbidding of suppressions. For when the Phallic period comes to an end, women will have been either annihilated or borne up to the highest and most violent incandescence. Muffled throughout their history, they have lived in dreams, in bodies (though muted), in silences, in aphonic revolts.

And with such force in their fragility; a fragility, a vulnerability, equal to their incomparable intensity. Fortunately, they haven't sublimated; they've saved their skin, their energy. They haven't worked at liquidating the impasse of lives without futures. They have furiously inhabited these sumptuous bodies: admirable hysterics who made Freud succumb to many voluptuous moments impossible to confess, bombarding his Mosaic statue with their carnal and passionate body words, haunting him with their inaudible and thundering denunciations, dazzling, more than naked underneath the seven veils of modesty. Those who, with a single word of the body, have inscribed the vertiginous immensity of a history which is sprung like an arrow from the whole history of men and from biblicocapitalist society, are the women, the supplicants of yesterday, who come as forebears of the new women, after whom no intersubjective relation will ever be the same. You, Dora, you the indomitable, the poetic body, you are the true "mistress" of the Signifier. Before long your efficacity will be seen at work when your speech is no longer suppressed, its point turned in against your breast, but written out over against the other.

In body.—More so than men who are coaxed toward social success, toward sublimation, women are body. More body, hence more writing. For a long time it has been in body that women have responded to persecution, to the familial-conjugal enterprise of domestication, to the repeated attempts at castrating them. Those who have turned their tongues 10,000 times seven times before not speaking are either dead from it or more familiar with their tongues and their mouths than anyone else. No, I-woman am going to blow up the Law: an explosion henceforth possible and ineluctable; let it be done, right now, *in* language.

Let us not be trapped by an analysis still encumbered with the old automatisms. It's not to be feared that language conceals an invincible adversary, because it's the language of men and their grammar. We mustn't leave them a single place that's any more theirs alone than we are.

If woman has always functioned "within" the discourse of man, a signifier that has always referred back to the opposite signifier which annihilates its specific energy and diminishes or stifles its very different sounds, it is time for her to dislocate this "within," to explode it, turn it around, and seize it; to make it hers, containing it, taking it in her own mouth, biting that tongue with her very own teeth to invent for herself a language to get inside of. And you'll see with what ease she will spring forth from that "within"—the "within" where once she so drowsily crouched—to overflow at the lips she will cover the foam.

Nor is the point to appropriate their instruments, their concepts, their places, or to begrudge them their position of mastery. Just because there's a risk of identification doesn't mean that we'll succumb. Let's leave it to the worriers, to masculine anxiety and its obsession with how to dominate the way things work—knowing "how it works" in order to "make it work." For us the point is not to take possession in order to internalize or manipulate, but rather to dash through and to "fly." [7]

Flying is woman's gesture—flying in language and make it fly. We have all learned the art of flying and its numerous techniques; for centuries we've been able to possess anything only by flying; we've lived in flight, stealing away, finding, when desired, narrow passageways, hidden crossovers. It's no accident that *voler* has a double meaning, that it plays on each of them and thus throws off the agents of sense. It's no accident: women take after birds and robbers just as robbers take after women and birds. They (*illes*) [8] go by, fly the coop, take pleasure in jumbling the order of space, in disorienting it, in changing around the furniture, dislocating things and values, breaking them all up, emptying structures, and turning propriety upside down.

What woman hasn't flown/stolen? Who hasn't felt, dreamt, performed the gesture that jams sociality? Who hasn't crumbled, held up to ridicule, the bar of separation? Who hasn't inscribed with her body the differential, punctured the system of couples and opposition? Who, by some act of transgression, hasn't overthrown successiveness, connection, the wall of circumfusion?

A feminine text cannot fail to be more than subversive. It is volcanic; as it is written it brings about an upheaval of the old property crust, carrier of masculine investments; there's no other way. There's no room for her if she's not a he. If she's a her-she, it's in order to smash everything, to shatter the framework of institutions, to blow up the law, to break up the "truth" with laughter.

For once she blazes *her* trail in the symbolic, she cannot fail to make of it the chaosmos of the "personal"—in her pronouns, her nouns, and her clique of referents. And for good reason. There will have been the long history of gynocide. This is known by the colonized peoples of yesterday, the workers, the nations, the species off whose backs the history of men has made its gold; those who have known the ignominy of persecution derive from it an obstinate future desire for grandeur; those who are locked up know better than their jailers the taste of free air. Thanks to their history, women today know (how to do and want) what men will be able to conceive of only much later. I say woman overturns the "personal," for if, by means of laws, lies, blackmail, and marriage, her right to herself has been extorted at the same time as her name, she has been able, through the very movement of mortal alienation, to see more closely the inanity of "propriety," the reductive stinginess of the masculine-conjugal subjective economy, which she doubly resists. On the one hand she has constituted herself necessarily as that "person" capable of losing a part of herself without losing her integrity. But secretly, silently, deep down inside, she grows and multiplies, for, on the other hand, she knows far more about living and about the relation between the economy of the drives and the management of the ego than any man. Unlike man, who holds so dearly to his title and his titles, his pouches of value, his cap, crown, and everything connected with his head, woman couldn't care less about the fear of decapitation (or castration), adventuring, without the masculine temerity, into anonymity, which she can merge with, without annihilating herself: because she's a giver.

I shall have a great deal to say about the whole deceptive problematic of the gift. Woman is obviously not that woman Nietzsche dreamed of who gives only in order to.[9] Who could ever think of the gift as a gift-that-takes? Who else but man, precisely the one who would like to take everything?

If there is a "propriety of woman," it is paradoxically her capacity to depropriate unselfishly, body without end, without appendage, without principle "parts." If she is a whole, it's a whole composed of parts that are wholes, not simple partial objects but a moving, limitlessly changing ensemble, a cosmos carelessly traversed by Eros, an immense astral space not organized around any one sun that's any more of a star than the others.

This doesn't mean that she's an undifferentiated magma, but that she doesn't lord it over her body or her desire. Though masculine sexuality gravitates around the penis, engendering that centralized body (in political anatomy) under the dictatorship of its parts, woman does not bring about the same regionalization which serves the couple head/genitals and which is inscribed only within boundaries. Her libido is cosmic, just as her unconscious is worldwide. Her writing can only keep going, without ever inscribing or discerning contours, daring to make these vertiginous crossings of the other(s) ephemeral and passionate sojourns in him, her, them, whom she inhabits long enough to look at from the point closest to their unconscious from the moment they awaken, to love them at the point closest to their drives; and then further, impregnated through and through with these brief, identificatory embraces, she goes and passes into infinity. She alone dares and wishes to know from within, where she, the outcast, has never ceased to hear the resonance of fore-language. She lets the other language speak—the language of 1,000 tongues which knows neither enclosure nor death. To life she refuses nothing. Her language does not contain, it carries; it does not hold back, it makes possible. When id is ambiguously uttered—the wonder of being several—she doesn't defend herself against these unknown women whom she's surprised at becoming, but derives pleasure from this gift of alterability. I am spacious, singing flesh, on which is grafted no one knows which I, more or less human, but alive because of transformation.

Write! and your self-seeking text will know itself better than flesh and blood, rising, insurrectionary dough kneading itself, with sonorous, perfumed ingredients, a lively combination of flying colors, leaves, and rivers plunging into the sea we feed. "Ah, there's her sea," he will say as he holds out to me a basin full of water from the little phallic mother from whom he's inseparable. But look, our seas are what we make of them, full of fish or not, opaque or transparent, red or black, high or smooth, narrow or bankless; and we are ourselves sea, sand, coral, seaweed, beaches, tides, swimmers, children, waves. . . . More or less wavily sea, earth, sky—what matter would rebuff us? We know how to speak them all.

Heterogeneous, yes. For her joyous benefits she is erogenous; she is the erotogeneity of the heterogeneous; airborne swimmer, in flight, she does not cling to herself; she is dispersible, prodigious, stunning, desirous and capable of others, of the other woman that she will be, of the other woman she isn't, of him, of you.

Woman, be unafraid of any other place, of any same, or any other. My eyes, my tongue, my ears, my nose, my skin, my mouth, my body-for-(the)-other—not that I long for it in order to fill up a hole, to provide against some defect of mine, or because, as fate would have it, I'm spurred on by feminine "jealousy"; not because I've been dragged into the whole chain of substitutions that brings that which is substituted back to its ultimate object. That sort of thing you would expect to come straight out of "Tom Thumb," out of the *Penisneid* whispered to us by old grandmother ogresses, servants to their father-sons. If they believe, in order to muster up some self-importance, if they really need to believe that we're dying of desire, that we are this hole fringed with desire for their penis—that's their immemorial business. Undeniably (we verify it at our own expenses—but also to our amusement), it's their business to let us know they're getting a hardon, so that we'll assure them (we the maternal mistresses of their little pocket signifier) that they still can, that it's still there—that men structure themselves only by being fitted with a feather. In the child it's not the penis that the woman desires, it's not that famous bit of skin around which every man gravitates. Pregnancy cannot be traced back, except within the historical limits of the ancients, to some form of fate, to those mechanical substitutions brought about by the unconscious of some eternal "jealous woman"; not to penis envies; and not to narcissism or to some sort of homosexuality linked to the ever-present mother!

Begetting a child doesn't mean that the woman or the man must fall ineluctably into patterns or must recharge the circuit of reproduction. If there's a risk there's not an inevitable trap: may women be spared the pressure, under the guise of consciousness-raising, of a supplement of interdictions. Either you want a kid or you don't—*that's your business*. Let nobody threaten you; in satisfying your desire, let not the fear of becoming the accomplice to a sociality succeed the oldtime fear of being "taken." And man, are you still going to bank on everyone's blindness and passivity, afraid lest the child make a father and, consequently, that in having a kid the woman land herself more than one bad deal by engendering all at once child—mother—father—family? No; it's up to you to break the old circuits. It will be up to man and woman to render obsolete the former relationship and all its consequences, to consider the launching of a brand-new subject, alive, with defamilialization. Let us demater-paternalize rather than deny woman, in an effort to avoid the cooptation of procreation, a thrilling era of the body. Let us defetishize. Let's get away from the dialectic which has it that the only good father is a dead one, or that the child is the death of his parents. The child is the other, but the other without violence, bypassing loss, struggle. We're fed up with the reuniting of bonds forever to be severed, with the litany of castration that's handed down and genealogized. We won't advance backward anymore; we're not going to repress something so simple as the desire for life. Oral drive, anal drive, vocal drive—all these drives are our strengths, and among them is the gestation drive—just like the desire to write: a desire to live self from within, a desire for the swollen belly, for language, for blood. We are not going to refuse, if it should happen to strike our fancy, the unsurpassed pleasures of pregnancy which have actually been always exaggerated or conjured away—or cursed—in the classic texts. For if there's one thing that's been repressed, here's just the place to find it: in the taboo of the pregnant woman. This says a lot about the power she seems invested with at the time, because it has always been suspected, that, when pregnant, the woman not only doubles her market value, but—what's more important—takes on intrinsic value as a woman in her own eyes and, undeniably, acquires body and sex.

There are thousands of ways of living one's pregnancy; to have or not to have with that still invisible other a relationship of another intensity. And if you don't have that particular yearning, it doesn't mean that you're in any way lacking. Each body distributes in its own special way, without model or norm, the nonfinite and changing totality of its desires. Decide for yourself on your position in the arena of contradictions, where pleasure and reality embrace. Bring the other to life. Women know how to live detachment; giving birth is neither losing nor increasing. It's adding to life an other. Am I dreaming? Am I misrecognizing? You, the defenders of "theory," the sacrosanct yes-men of Concept, enthroners of the phallus (but not the penis):

Once more you'll say that all this smacks of "idealism," or what's worse, you'll splutter that I'm a "mystic."

And what about the libido? Haven't I read the "Signification of the Phallus"? And what about separation, what about that bit of self for which, to be born, you undergo an ablation—an ablation, so they say, to be forever commemorated by your desire?

Besides, isn't it evident that the penis gets around in my texts, that I give it a place and appeal? Of course I do. I want all. I want all of me with all of him. Why should I deprive myself of a part of us? I want all of us. Woman of course has a desire for a "loving desire" and not a jealous one. But not because she is gelded; not because she's deprived and needs to be filled out, like some wounded person who wants to console herself or seek vengeance. I don't want a penis to decorate my body with. But I do desire the other for the other, whole and entire, male or female; because living means wanting everything that is, everything that lives, and wanting it alive. Castration? Let others toy with it. What's a desire originating from a lack? A pretty meager desire.

The woman who still allows herself to be threatened by the big dick, who's still impressed by the commotion of the phallic stance, who still leads a loyal master to the beat of the drum: that's the woman of yesterday. They still exist, easy and numerous victims of the oldest of farces: either they're cast in the original silent versions in which, as titanesses lying under the mountains they make with their quivering, they never see erected that theoretic monument to the golden phallus looming, in the old manner, over their bodies. Or, coming today out of their *infans* period and into the second, enlightened" version of their virtuous debasement, they see themselves suddenly assaulted by the builders of the analytic empire and, as soon as they've begun to formulate the new desire, naked, nameless, so happy at making an appearance, they're taken in their bath by the new old men, and then, whoops! Luring them with flashy signifiers, the demon of interpretation—oblique, decked out in modernity—sells them the same old handcuffs, baubles, and chains. Which castration do you prefer? Whose degrading do you like better, the father's or the mother's? Oh, what pwetty eyes, you pwetty little girl. Here, buy my glasses and you'll see the Truth-Me-Myself tell you everything you should know. Put them on your nose and take a fetishist's look (you are me, the other analyst—that's what I'm telling you) at your body and the body of the other. You see? No? Wait, you'll have everything explained to you, and you'll know at last which sort of neurosis you're related to. Hold still, we're going to do your portrait, so that you can begin looking like it right away.

Yes, the naïves to the first and second degree are still legion. If the New Women, arriving now, dare to create outside the theoretical, they're called in by the cops of the signifier, fingerprinted, remonstrated, and brought into the line of order that they are supposed to know; assigned by force of trickery to a precise place in the chain that's always formed for the benefit of a privileged signifier. We are pieced back to the string which leads back, if not to the Name-of-the-Father, then, for a new twist, to the place of the phallic-mother.

Beware, my friend, of the signifier that would take you back to the authority of a signified! Beware of diagnosis that would reduce your generative powers. "Common" nouns are also proper nouns that disparage your singularity by classifying it into species. Break out of the circles; don't remain within the psychoanalytic closure. Take a look around, then cut through!

And if we are legion, it's because the war of liberation has only made as yet a tiny breakthrough. But women are thronging to it. I've seen them, those who will be neither dupe nor domestic, those who will not fear the risk of being a woman; will not fear any risk, any desire, any space still unexplored in themselves, among themselves and others or anywhere else. They do not fetishize, they do not deny, they do not hate. They observe, they approach, they try to see the other woman, the child, the lover—not to strengthen their own narcissim or verify the solidity or weakness of the master, but to make love better, to invent.

Other love.—In the beginning are our differences. The new love dares for the other, wants the other, makes dizzying, precipitous flights between knowledge and invention. The woman arriving over and over again does not stand still; she's everywhere, she exchanges, she is the desire-that-gives. (Not enclosed in the paradox of the gift that takes nor under the illusion of unitary fusion. We're past that.) She comes in, comes-in-between herself me and you, between the other me where one is always infinitely more than one and more than me, without the fear of ever reaching a limit; she thrills in our becoming. And we'll keep on becoming! She cuts through defensive loves, motherages, and devourations: beyond selfish narcissism, in the moving, open, transitional space, she runs her risks. Beyond the struggle-to-the-death that's been removed to the bed, beyond the love-battle that claims to represent exchange, she scorns at an Eros dynamic that would be fed by hatred. Hatred: a heritage, again, a reminder, a duping subservience to the phallus. To love, to watch-think-seek the other in the other, to despecularize, to unhoard. Does this seem difficult? It's not impossible, and this is what nourishes life—a love that has no commerce with the apprehensive desire that provides against the lack and stultifies the strange; a love that rejoices in the exchange that multiplies. Wherever history still unfolds as the history of death, she does not tread. Opposition, hierarchizing exchange, the struggle for mastery which can end only in at least one death (one master—one slave, or two nonmasters ≠ two dead)—all that comes from a period in time governed by phallocentric values. The fact that this period extends into the present doesn't prevent woman from starting the history of life somewhere else. Elsewhere, she gives. She doesn't "know" what she's giving, she doesn't measure it; she gives, though, neither a counterfeit impression nor something she hasn't got. She gives more, with no assurance that she'll get back even some unexpected profit from what she puts out. She gives that there may be life, thought, transformation. This is an "economy" that can no longer be put in economic terms. Wherever she loves, all the old concepts of management are left behind. At the end of a more or less conscious computation, she finds not her sum but her differences. I am for you what you want me to be at the moment you look at me in a way you've never seen me before: at every instant. When I write, it's everything that we don't know we can be that is written out of me, without exclusions, without stipulation, and everything we will be calls us to the unflagging, intoxicating, unappeasable search for love. In one another we will never be lacking.

TRANSLATED BY KEITH COHEN AND PAULA COHEN

NOTES

1. Men still have everything to say about their sexuality, and everything to write. For what they have said so far, for the most part, stems from the opposition activity/passivity from the power relation between a fantasized obligatory virility meant to invade, to colonize, and the consequential phantasm of woman as a "dark continent" to penetrate and to "pacify." (We know what "pacify" means in terms of scotomizing the other and misrecog-

nizing the self.) Conquering her, they've made haste to depart from her borders, to get out of sight, out of body. The way man has of getting out of himself and into her whom he takes not for the other but for his own, deprives him, he knows, of his own bodily territory. One can understand how man, confusing himself with his penis and rushing in for the attack, might feel resentment and fear of being "taken" by the woman, of being lost in her, absorbed or alone.

2. I am speaking here only of the place "reserved" for women by the Western world.

3. Which works, then, might be called feminine? I'll just point out some examples: one would have to give them full readings to bring out what is pervasively feminine in their significance. Which I shall do elsewhere. In France (have you noted our infinite poverty in this field?—the Anglo-Saxon countries have shown resources of distinctly greater consequence), leafing through what's come out of the twentieth century—and it's not much—the only inscriptions of femininity that I have seen were by Colette, Marguerite Duras, . . . and Jean Genet.

4. *Dé-pense*, a neologism formed on the verb *penser*, hence "unthinks," but also "spends" (from *dépenser*).—Tr.

5. Standard English terms for the Hegelian *Aufhebung*, the French *la relève*.

6. Jean Genet, *Pompes funèbres* (Paris, 1948), p. 185 (privately published).

7. Also, "to steal." Both meanings of the verb *voler* are played on, as the text itself explains in the following paragraph.—Tr.

8. *Illes* is a fusion of the masculine pronoun *ils*, which refers back to birds and robbers, with the feminine pronoun *elles*, which refers to women.—Tr.

9. Reread Derrida's text, "Le style de la femme," in *Nietzsche aujourd'hui* (Union Générale d'Editions, Coll. 10/18), where the philosopher can be seen operating an *Aufhebung* of all philosophy in its systematic reducing of woman to the place of seduction: she appears as the one who is taken for; the bait in person, all veils unfurled, the one who doesn't give but who gives only in order to (take).

luce irigaray

THIS SEX WHICH IS NOT ONE

Female sexuality has always been conceptualized on the basis of masculine pa-rameters. Thus the opposition between "masculine" clitoral activity and "femi-nine" vaginal passivity, an opposition which Freud—and many others—saw as stages, or alternatives in the development of a sexually "normal" woman, seems rather too clearly required by the practice of male sexuality. For the clitoris is conceived as a little penis pleasant to masturbate so long as castration anxiety does not exist (for the boy child), and the vagina is valued for the "lodging" it offers the male organ when the forbidden hand has to find a replacement for pleasure-giving.

In these terms, woman's erogenous zones never amount to anything but a clitoris-sex that is not comparable to the noble phallic organ, or a hole-envelope that serves to sheathe and massage the penis in intercourse: a non-sex, or a mas-culine organ turned back upon itself, self-embracing.

About woman and her pleasure, this view of the sexual relation has nothing to say. Her lot is that of "lack," "atrophy" (of the sexual organ), and "penis envy," the penis being the only sexual organ of recognized value. Thus she attempts by every means available to appropriate that organ for herself: through her some-what servile love of the father-husband capable of giving her one, through her desire for a child-penis, preferably a boy, through access to the cultural values still reserved by right to males alone and therefore always masculine, and so on. Woman lives her own desire only as the expectation that she may at least come to possess an equivalent of the male organ.

Yet all this appears quite foreign to her own pleasure, unless it remains within the dominant phallic economy. Thus, for example, woman's autoeroticism is very different from man's. In order to touch himself, man needs an instrument: his hand, a woman's body, language. . . . And this self-caressing requires at least a minimum of activity. As for woman, she touches herself in and of herself without any need for mediation, and before there is any way to distinguish activity from passivity. Woman "touches herself" all the time, and moreover no one can forbid her to do so, for her genitals are formed of two lips in continuous contact. Thus, with herself, she is already two—but not divisible into one(s)—that caress each other.

From This Sex Which Is Not One, *pp. 23–33. Trans. Catherine Porter with Carolyn Burke. Copy-right © 1985 by Cornell University. Used by permission of the publisher, Cornell University Press. This text was originally published as "Ce Sexe qui n'en est pas un," in* Cahiers du Grif, *no. 5. English translation: "This Sex Which Is Not One," trans. Claudia Reeder, in* New French Feminisms, *ed. Elaine Marks and Isabelle de Courtivron (New York, 1981), pp. 99–106.*

This autoeroticism is disrupted by a violent break-in: the brutal separation of the two lips by a violating penis, an intrusion that distracts and deflects the woman from this "self-caressing" she needs if she is not to incur the disappearance of her own pleasure in sexual relations. If the vagina is to serve *also*, but *not only*, to take over the little boy's hand in order to assure an articulation between autoeroticism and heteroeroticism in intercourse (the encounter with the totally other always signifying death), how, in the classic representation of sexuality, can the perpetuation of autoeroticism for woman be managed? Will woman not be left with the impossible alternative between a defensive virginity, fiercely turned in upon itself, and a body open to penetration that no longer knows, in this "hole" that constitutes its sex, the pleasure of its own touch? The more or less exclusive—and highly anxious—attention paid to erection in Western sexuality proves to what extent the imaginary that governs it is foreign to the feminine. For the most part, this sexuality offers nothing but imperatives dictated by male rivalry: the "strongest" being the one who has the best "hard-on," the longest, the biggest, the stiffest penis, or even the one who "pees the farthest" (as in little boys' contests). Or else one finds imperatives dictated by the enactment of sadomasochistic fantasies, these in turn governed by man's relation to his mother: the desire to force entry, to penetrate, to appropriate for himself the mystery of this womb where he has been conceived, the secret of his begetting, of his "origin." Desire/need, also to make blood flow again in order to revive a very old relationship—intrauterine, to be sure, but also prehistoric—to the maternal.

Woman, in this sexual imaginary, is only a more or less obliging prop for the enactment of man's fantasies. That she may find pleasure there in that role, by proxy, is possible, even certain. But such pleasure is above all a masochistic prostitution of her body to a desire that is not her own, and it leaves her in a familiar state of dependency upon man. Not knowing what she wants, ready for anything, even asking for more, so long as he will "take" her as his "object" when he seeks his own pleasure. Thus she will not say what she herself wants; moreover, she does not know, or no longer knows, what she wants. As Freud admits, the beginnings of the sexual life of a girl child are so "obscure," so "faded with time," that one would have to dig down very deep indeed to discover beneath the traces of this civilization, of this history, the vestiges of a more archaic civilization that might give some clue to woman's sexuality. That extremely ancient civilization would undoubtedly have a different alphabet, a different language. . . . Woman's desire would not be expected to speak the same language as man's; woman's desire has doubtless been submerged by the logic that has dominated the West since the time of the Greeks.

Within this logic, the predominance of the visual, and of the discrimination and individualization of form, is particularly foreign to female eroticism. Woman takes pleasure more from touching than from looking, and her entry into a dominant scopic economy signifies, again, her consignment to passivity: she is to be the beautiful object of contemplation. While her body finds itself thus eroticized, and called to a double movement of exhibition and of chaste retreat in order to stimulate the drives of the "subject," her sexual organ represents *the horror of nothing to see*. A defect in this systematics of representation and desire. A "hole" in its scoptophilic lens. It is already evident in Greek statuary that this nothing-to-see has to be excluded, rejected, from such a scene of representation. Woman's genitals are simply absent, masked, sewn back up inside their "crack."

This organ which has nothing to show for itself also lacks a form of its own. And if woman takes pleasure precisely from this incompleteness of form which allows her organ to touch itself over and over again, indefinitely, by itself, that pleasure is denied by a civilization that privileges phallomorphism. The value granted to the only definable form excludes the one that is in play in female autoeroticism. The *one* of form, of the individual, of the (male) sexual organ, of the proper name, of the proper meaning . . . supplants, while separating and dividing, that contact of *at least two* (lips) which keeps woman in touch with herself, but without any possibility of distinguishing what is touching from what is touched.

Whence the mystery that woman represents in a culture claiming to count everything, to number everything by units, to inventory everything as individualities. *She is neither one nor two.* Rigorously speaking, she cannot be identified either as one person, or as two. She resists all adequate definition. Further, she has no "proper" name. And her sexual organ, which is not *one* organ, is counted as *none.* The negative, the underside, the reverse of the only visible and morphologically designatable organ (even in the passage from erection to detumescence does pose some problems): the penis.

But the "thickness" of that "form," the layering of its volume, its expansions and contractions and even the spacing of the moments in which it produces itself as form—all this the feminine keeps secret. Without knowing it. And if woman is asked to sustain, to revive, man's desire, the request neglects to spell out what it implies as to the value of her own desire. A desire of which she is not aware, moreover, at least not explicitly. But one whose force and continuity are capable of nurturing repeatedly and at length all the masquerades of "femininity" that are expected from her.

It is true that she still has the child, in relation to whom her appetite for touch, for contact, has free rein, unless it is already lost, alienated by the taboo against touching of a highly obsessive civilization. Otherwise her pleasure will find, in the child, compensations for and diversion from the frustrations that she too often encounters in sexual relations per se. Thus maternity fills the gaps in a repressed female sexuality. Perhaps man and woman no longer caress each other except through that mediation between them that the child—preferably a boy—represents? Man, identified with his son, rediscovers the pleasure of maternal fondling; woman touches herself again by caressing that part of her body: her baby-penis-clitoris.

What this entails for the amorous trio is well known. But the Oedipal interdiction seems to be a somewhat categorical and factitious law—although it does provide the means for perpetuating the authoritarian discourse of fathers—when it is promulgated in a culture in which sexual relations are impracticable because man's desire and woman's are strangers to each other. And in which the two desires have to try to meet through indirect means, whether the archaic one of a sense-relation to the mother's body, or the present one of active or passive extension of the law of the father. These are regressive emotional behaviors, exchanges of words too detached from the sexual arena not to constitute an exile with respect to it: "mother" and "father" dominate the interactions of the couple, but as social roles. The division of labor prevents them from making love. They produce or reproduce. Without quite knowing how to use their leisure. Such little as they have, such little indeed as they wish to have. For what are they to do with leisure? What substitute for amorous resource are they to invent? Still . . .

Perhaps it is time to return to that repressed entity, the female imaginary. So woman does not have a sex organ? She has at least two of them, but they are not identifiable as ones. Indeed, she has many more. Her sexuality, always at least double, goes even further: it is *plural*. Is this the way culture is seeking to characterize itself now? Is this the way texts write themselves/are written now? Without quite knowing what censorship they are evading? Indeed, woman's pleasure does not have to choose between clitoral activity and vaginal passivity, for example. The pleasure of the vaginal caress does not have to be substituted for that of the clitoral caress. They each contribute, irreplaceably, to woman's pleasure. Among other caresses. . . . Fondling the breasts, touching the vulva, spreading lips, stroking the posterior wall of the vagina, brushing against the mouth of the uterus, and so on. To evoke only a few of the most specifically female pleasures. Pleasures which are somewhat misunderstood in sexual difference as it is imagined—or not imagined, the other sex being only the indispensable complement to the only sex.

But *woman has sex organs more or less everywhere.* She finds pleasure almost anywhere. Even if we refrain from invoking the hystericization of her entire body, the geography of her pleasure is far more diversified, more multiple in its differences, more complex, more subtle, than is commonly imagined—in an imaginary rather too narrowly focused on sameness.

"She" is indefinitely other in herself. This is doubtless why she is said to be whimsical, incomprehensible, agitated, capricious . . . not to mention her language, in which "she" sets off in all directions leaving "him" unable to discern the coherence of any meaning. Hers are contradictory words, somewhat mad from the standpoint of reason, inaudible for whoever listens to them with ready-made grids, with a fully elaborated code in hand. For in what she says, too, at least when she dares, woman is constantly touching herself. She steps ever so slightly aside from herself with a murmur, an exclamation, a whisper, a sentence left unfinished. . . . When she returns, it is to set off again from elsewhere. From another point of pleasure, or of pain. One would have to listen with another ear, as if hearing *an "other meaning" always in the process of weaving itself, of embracing itself with words, but also of getting rid of words in order not to become fixed, congealed in them.* For if "she" says something, it is not, it is already no longer, identical with what she means. What she says is never identical with anything, moreover; rather, it is contiguous. *It touches* (*upon*). And when it strays too far from that proximity, she breaks off and starts over at "zero": her body-sex.

It is useless, then, to trap women in the exact definition of what they mean, to make them repeat (themselves) so that it will be clear; they are already elsewhere in that discursive machinery where you expected to surprise them. They have returned within themselves. Which must not be understood in the same way as within yourself. They do not have the interiority that you have, the one you perhaps suppose they have. Within themselves means *within the intimacy of that silent, multiple, diffuse touch.* And if you ask them insistently what they are thinking about, they can only reply: Nothing. Everything.

Thus what they desire is precisely nothing, and at the same time everything. Always something more and something else besides that *one*—sexual organ, for example—that you give them, attribute to them. Their desire is often interpreted, and feared, as a sort of insatiable hunger, a voracity that will swallow you whole. Whereas it really involves a different economy more than anything else, one that upsets the linearity of a project, undermines the goal-object of desire, diffuses the polarization toward a single pleasure, disconcerts fidelity to a single discourse. . . .

Must this multiplicity of female desire and female language be understood as shards, scattered remnants of a violated sexuality? A sexuality denied? The question has no simple answer. The rejection, the exclusion of a female imaginary certainly puts woman in the position of experiencing herself only fragmentarily, in the little-structured margins of a dominant ideology, as waste, or excess, what is left of a mirror invested by the (masculine) "subject" to reflect himself, to copy himself. Moreover, the role of "femininity" is prescribed by this masculine specula(riza)tion and corresponds scarcely at all to woman's desire, which may be recovered only in secret, in hiding, with anxiety and guilt.

But if the female imaginary were to deploy itself, if it could bring itself into play otherwise than as scraps, uncollected debris, would it represent itself, even so, in the form of *one* universe? Would it even be volume instead of surface? No. Not unless it were understood, yet again, as a privileging of the maternal over the feminine. Of a phallic maternal, at that. Closed in upon the jealous possession of its valued product. Rivaling man in his esteem for productive excess. In such a race for power, woman loses the uniqueness of her pleasure. By closing herself off as volume, she renounces the pleasure that she gets from the *nonsuture of her lips:* she is undoubtedly a mother, but a virgin mother; the role was assigned to her by mythologies long ago. Granting her a certain social power to the extent that she is reduced, with her own complicity, to sexual impotence.

(Re-)discovering herself, for a woman, thus could only signify the possibility of sacrificing no one of her pleasures to another, of identifying herself with none of them in particular, *of never being simply one.* A sort of expanding universe to which no limits could be fixed and which would not be incoherence nonetheless—nor that polymorphous perversion of the child in which the erogenous zones would lie waiting to be regrouped under the primacy of the phallus.

Woman always remains several, but she is kept from dispersion because the other is already within her and is autoerotically familiar to her. Which is not to say that she appropriates the other for herself, that she reduces it to her own property. Ownership and property are doubtless quite foreign to the feminine. At least sexually. But not *nearness.* Nearness so pronounced that it makes all discrimination of identity, and thus all forms of property, impossible. Woman derives pleasure from what is *so near that she cannot have it, nor have herself.* She herself enters into a ceaseless exchange of herself with the other without any possibility of identifying either. This puts into question all prevailing economies: their calculations are irremediably stymied by woman's pleasure, as it increases indefinitely from its passage in and through the other.

However, in order for woman to reach the place where she takes pleasure as a woman, a long detour by way of the analysis of the various systems of oppression brought to bear upon her is assuredly necessary. And claiming to fall back on the single solution of pleasure risks making her miss the process of going back through a social practice that *her* enjoyment requires.

For woman is traditionally a use-value for man, an exchange value among men; in other words, a commodity. As such, she remains the guardian of material substance, whose price will be established, in terms of the standard of their work and of their need/desire, by "subjects": workers, merchants, consumers. Women are marked phallically by their fathers, husbands, procurers. And this branding determines their value in sexual commerce. Woman is never anything but the locus of a more or less competitive exchange between two men, including the competition for the possession of mother earth.

How can this object of transaction claim a right to pleasure without removing her/itself from established commerce? With respect to other merchandise in the marketplace, how could this commodity maintain a relationship other than one of aggressive jealousy? How could material substance enjoy her/itself without provoking the consumer's anxiety over the disappearance of his nurturing ground? How could that exchange—which can in no way be defined in terms "proper" to woman's desire—appear as anything but a pure mirage, more foolishness, all too readily obscured by a more sensible discourse and by a system of apparently more tangible values?

A woman's development, however radical it may seek to be, would thus not suffice to liberate woman's desire. And to date no political theory or political practice has resolved, or sufficiently taken into consideration this historical problem, even though Marxism has proclaimed its importance. But women do not constitute, strictly speaking, a class, and their dispersion among several classes makes their political struggle complex, their demands sometimes contradictory.

There remains, however, the condition of underdevelopment arising from women's submission by and to a culture that oppresses them, uses them, makes of them a medium of exchange, with very little profit to them. Except in the quasi-monopolies of masochistic pleasure, the domestic labor force, and reproduction. The power of slaves? Which are not negligible powers, moreover. For where pleasure is concerned, the master is not necessarily well served. Thus to reverse the relation, especially in the economy of sexuality, does not seem a desirable objective.

But if women are to preserve and expand their autoeroticism, their homosexuality, might not the renunciation of heterosexual pleasure correspond once again to the disconnection from power that is traditionally theirs? Would it not involve a new prison, a new cloister, built of their own accord? For women to undertake tactical strikes, to keep themselves apart from men long enough to learn to defend their desire, especially through speech, to discover the love of other women while sheltered from men's imperious choices that put them in the position of rival commodities, to forge for themselves a social status that compels recognition, to earn their living in order to escape from the condition of prostitute . . . these are certainly indispensable stages in the escape from their proletarization on the exchange market. But if their aim were simply to reverse the order of things, even supposing this to be possible, history would repeat itself in the long run, would revert to sameness: to phallocratism. It would leave room neither for women's sexuality, nor for women's imaginary, nor for women's language to take (their) place.

gayatri chakravorty spivak

FRENCH FEMINISM IN AN
INTERNATIONAL FRAME

"One of the areas of greatest verbal concentration among French feminists is the description of women's pleasure." [1] Paradoxically enough, it is in this seemingly esoteric area of concern that I find a way of re-affirming the historically discontinuous yet common "object"-ification of the sexed subject as woman.

If it is indeed true that the best of French feminism encourages us to think of a double effort (*against* sexism and *for* feminism, with the lines forever shifting), that double vision is needed in the consideration of women's reproductive freedom as well. For to see women's liberation as identical with reproductive liberation is to make counter-sexism an end in itself, to see the establishment of women's subject-status as an unquestioned good and indeed not to heed the best lessons of French anti-humanism, which discloses the historical dangers of a subjectivist normativity; and it is also to legitimate the view of culture as general exchange of women, constitutive of kinship structures where women's object-status is clearly seen as identified with her reproductive function. [2]

The double vision that would affirm feminism as well as undo sexism suspects a pre-comprehended move *before* the reproductive coupling of man and woman, *before* the closing of the circle whose only productive excess is the child, and whose "outside" is the man's "active" life in society. It recognizes that "nature had programmed female sexual pleasure independently from the needs of production." [3]

Male and female sexuality are asymmetrical. Male orgasmic pleasure "normally" entails the male reproductive act—semination. Female orgasmic pleasure (it is not, of course, the "same" pleasure, only called by the same name) does not entail any one component of the heterogeneous female reproductive scenario: ovulation, fertilization, conception, gestation, birthing. The clitoris escapes reproductive framing. In legally defining woman as object of exchange, passage, or possession in terms of reproduction, it is not only the womb that is literally "appropriated"; it is the clitoris as the signifier of the sexed subject that is effaced. All historical and theoretical investigation into the definition of woman as legal *object*—in or out of marriage; or as politico-economic passageway for property and legitimacy would fall within the investigation of the varieties of the effacement of the clitoris.

Psychological investigation in this area cannot only confine itself to the effect of clitoridectomy on women. It would also ask why and show how, since an at least symbolic clitoridectomy has always been the "normal" accession to womanhood and the unacknowledged name of motherhood, it might be necessary to

Conclusion from "French Feminism in an International Frame," Yale French Studies *62 (1981): 180–184. Reprinted by permission of* Yale French Studies.

plot out the entire geography of female sexuality in terms of the imagined possibility of the dismemberment of the phallus. The arena of research here is not merely remote and primitive societies; the (sex) objectification of women by the elaborate attention to their skin and façade as represented by the immense complexity of the cosmetics, underwear, clothes, advertisement, women's magazine, and pornography networks, the double standard in the criteria of men's and women's aging; the public versus private dimensions of menopause as opposed to impotence, are all questions within this circuit. The pre-comprehended suppression or effacement of the clitoris relates to every move to define woman as sex object, or as means or agent of reproduction—with no recourse to a subject-function except in terms of those definitions or as "imitators" of men.

The woman's voice as Mother or Lover or Androgyne has sometimes been caught by great male writers. The theme of woman's *norm* as clitorally ex-centric from the reproductive orbit is being developed at present in our esoteric French group and in the literature of the gay movement. There is a certain melancholy exhilaration in working out the patriarchal intricacy of Tiresias's standing as a prophet—master of ceremonies at the Oedipal scene—in terms of the theme of the feminine norm as the suppression of the clitoris: "Being asked by Zeus and Hera to settle a dispute as to which sex had more pleasure of love, he decided for the female; Hera was angry and blinded him, but Zeus recompensed him by giving him long life and power of prophecy" (*Oxford Classical Dictionary*).[4]

Although French feminism has not elaborated these possibilities, there is some sense of them in women as unlike as Irigaray and the *Questions féministes* group. Irigaray: "In order for woman to arrive at the point where she can enjoy her pleasure as a woman, a long detour by the analysis of the various systems of oppression which affect her is certainly necessary. By claiming to resort to pleasure alone as the solution to her problem, she runs the risk of missing the reconsideration of a social practice upon which *her* pleasure depends."[5] *Questions féministes:* "What we must answer is—not the false problem . . . which consists in measuring the 'role' of biological factors and the 'role' of social factors in the behavior of sexed individuals—but rather the following questions: (1) in what way is the biological political? In other words, what is the political function of the biological?"[6]

If an analysis of the suppression of the clitoris in general as the suppression of woman-in-excess is lifted from the limitations of the "French" context and pursued in all its "historical," "political," and "social" dimensions, then *Questions féministes* would not need to make a binary opposition such as the following: "It is legitimate to expose the oppression, the mutilation, the 'functionalization' and the 'objectivation' of the female body, but it is also dangerous to put the female body at the center of a search for female identity."[7] It would be possible to suggest that, the typology of the subtraction or excision of the clitoris in order to determine a biologico-political female identity is opposed, in discontinuous and indefinitely context-determined ways, by both the points of view above. It would also not be necessary, in order to share a detailed and ecstatic analysis of motherhood as "ultimate guarantee of sociality," to attack feminist collective commitments virulently: A true feminine innovation . . . is not possible before maternity is clarified. . . . To bring that about, however, we must stop making feminism a new religion, an enterprise or a sect."[8]

The double vision is not merely to work against sexism and for feminism. It is also to recognize that, even as we reclaim the excess of the clitoris, we cannot fully escape the symmetry of the reproductive definition. One cannot write off what may be called a uterine social organization (the arrangement of the world in terms of the reproduction of future generations, where the uterus is the chief agent and means of production) *in favor of* a clitoral. The uterine social organization should, rather, be "situated" through the understanding that it has so far been established by excluding a clitoral social organization. (The restoration of a continuous bond between mother and daughter even *after* the "facts" of gestation, birthing, and suckling is, indeed, of great importance as a persistent effort against the sexism of millenia, an effort of repairing psychological damage through questioning norms that are supposedly self-evident and descriptive. Yet, for the sake of an affirmative feminism, this too should be "situated": to establish *historical* continuity by sublating a *natural* or *physiological* link as an end in itself is the idealistic subtext of the patriarchal project.) Investigation of the effacement of the clitoris—where clitoridectomy is a metonym for women's definition as "legal object as subject of reproduction"—would persistently seek to de-normalize uterine social organization. At the moment, the fact that the entire complex network of advanced capitalist economy hinges on home-buying, and that the philosophy of home-ownership is intimately linked to the sanctity of the nuclear family, shows how encompassingly the uterine norm of womanhood supports the phallic norm of capitalism. At the other end of the spectrum, it is this ideologico-material repression of the clitoris as the signifier of the sexed subject that operates the specific oppression of women, as the lowest level of the cheap labor that the multi-national corporations employ by remote control in the extraction of absolute surplus-value in the less developed countries. Whether the "social relations of patriarchy can be mapped into the social relations characteristic of a mode of production" or whether it is a "relatively autonomous structure written into family relations"; whether the family is a place of the production of socialization or the constitution of the subject of ideology; what such a heterogeneous sex-analysis would disclose is that the repression of the clitoris in the general or the narrow sense (the difference cannot be absolute) is presupposed by both patriarchy and family.[9]

I emphasize discontinuity, heterogeneity, and typology as I speak of such a sex-analysis, because this work cannot by itself obliterate the problems of race and class. It will not necessarily escape the inbuilt colonialism of First World feminism toward the Third. It might, one hopes, promote a sense of our common yet history-specific lot. It ties together the terrified child held down by her grandmother as the blood runs down her groin and the "liberated" heterosexual woman who, in spite of Mary Jane Sherfey and the famous page 53 of *Our Bodies, Ourselves*, in bed with a casual lover—engaged, in other words, in the "freest" of "free" activities—confronts, at worst, the "shame" of admitting to the "abnormality" of her orgasm: at best, the acceptance of such a "special" need; and the radical feminist who, setting herself apart from the circle of reproduction, systematically discloses the beauty of the lesbian body; the dowried bride—a body for burning—and the female wage-slave—a body for maximum exploitation.[10] There can be other lists; and each one will straddle and undo the ideological-material opposition. For me it is the best gift of French feminism, that it cannot itself fully acknowledge, and that we must work at; here is a theme that can liberate my colleague from Sudan, and a theme the old washerwomen by the river would understand.

NOTES

1. Elaine Marks and Isabelle de Courtivron, eds., *New French Feminisms* (Amherst: The University of Massachusetts Press, 1980), p. 37.

2. Claude Lévi-Strauss, "Structural Study of Myth," in *Myth: A Symposium*, ed. Thomas A. Sebeok (Bloomington: Indiana University Press, 1958), p. 103. The classic defense, to be found in *Structuralist Anthropology*, trans. Claire Jacobson Brooke Grundfest-Schoepf (New York: Basic Books, 1963), vol. 1, pp. 61–62, against the feminist realization that this was yet another elaboration of the objectification of women, seems curiously disingenuous. For if women had indeed been symbolized, on that level of generality, as *users* of signs rather than as signs, the binary opposition of exchanger and exchanged, founding structures of kinship, would collapse.

3. *New French Feminisms*, p. 155.

4. For further ironies of the prohibitions associated with Hera's pleasure, see C. Kerényi, *Zeus and Hera: Archetypal Image of Father, Husband, and Wife*, trans. Christopher Holme (Princeton: Princeton University Press, 1975), pp. 97, 113.

5. *New French Feminisms*, p. 105.

6. *New French Feminisms*, p. 227.

7. *New French Feminisms*, p. 218.

8. "Un nouveau type d'intellectuel: le dissident," *Tel Quel* 74 (Winter 1977), 71.

9. *Feminism and Materialism: Women and Modes of Production*, ed. Annette Kuhn and Ann Marie Wolpe (London: Routledge and Kegan Paul, 1978), pp. 49, 51. For an eloquent reverie on the ethic of penetration as it denies the clitoris see Irigaray, *New French Feminisms*, p. 100. In "Displacement and the Discourse of Woman," in Mark Krupnick, eds., *Displacement: Derrida and After* (Bloomington: Indiana University Press, 1983), pp. 169–195, I suggest that such a gesture of penetrative appropriation is not absent from Derrida's reach for the "name of women."

10. Sherfey, *The Nature and Evolution of Female Sexuality* (New York: Vintage, 1973); *Our Bodies, Ourselves: A Book by and for Women* (New York: Simon and Schuster, 2nd ed., 1971).

part two

OBJECT RELATIONS AND WOMEN'S USE OF LANGUAGE

Readings from British and American Psychology

Theories about what language does and how it is used are influenced by underlying concepts about the nature of development and self-identity. British and American psychoanalytic theories of object relations challenge many assumptions of Freudian-Lacanian theory about language and gender, because they view human development as interpersonal; self-identity as implicated in relationship with others. The focus on object relations as central to the beginnings of infant development—the influence of the mother during the preoedipal period—shifts attention away from the importance of the Oedipal crisis and the necessity of the father for initiating identity-formation and language practice. Further, the pivotal role of drives in Freud's and his followers' theories is mitigated or replaced by the centrality of relationship. As Jay R. Greenberg and Stephen Mitchell put it, "The most significant tension in the history of psychoanalytic ideas has been the dialectic between the original Freudian model, which takes as its starting point the instinctual drives, and an alternative comprehensive model in the work of Fairbairn and Sullivan, which evolves structure solely from the individual's relations with other people" (*Object Relations in Psychoanalytic Theory*, 20). This distinction is of the utmost importance, because if human activity is motivated by drives, the individual is basically a closed system; on the other hand, if such activity finds its impulse in the need to relate to other "objects" (persons), then a person must be understood as fundamentally social in nature. When W.D.R. Fairbairn opposed Freud on this matter in 1943, he suggested that the object, not gratification, is the ultimate aim of libidinal striving ("The Repression and Return of Bad Objects . . ." in *An Object Relations Theory of the Personality*).

The centrality to human development and identity formation given by object relations psychology to the mother has wide-reaching implications. Freud saw the Oedipus complex as the crucial drama of childhood, its resolution involving rejection of the primacy of the mother, fidelity to the power of the father. The concepts of father, culture, super-ego—once installed as protection against the dangerous urge for connection with the mother—inaugurate *difference* and *separateness* as the necessary prerequisites for successful human functioning. Whether the person is a boy, who identifies with his father in order to prevent the castration that their rivalry would produce, or a girl, who comes to understand her mother's inadequacy (she has no penis!) and so cleaves to her father to get one via the substitutory act of having "his" baby, distancing oneself from the mother is de rigeur and may be understood as the founding principle of identity. "Union" or "merger" with the mother, as the condition of the preoedipal period is consistently described, is therefore understood as lack of identity, a kind of living death. Lacanian ideas about language, for example, stress its importance in maintaining that life-giving gap between signifier and signified, desire and satisfaction, culture and non-culture, child and mother.

But what if development is already well under way by time of the toddler period of the Oedipus complex? What if the child has already begun to form an identity, a process initiated and negotiated by relationship with the mother? What if the dreaded symbiotic merger is something more like interaction, inter-subjectivity, the give and take of mutual affiliation, empathy, and need? More like a procedure in which both differentiation and likeness are important, because both are necessary for identity to ensue. What if the libidinal desire for sexual intercourse—for incest—may be understood as an anxious translation of something at once more salutary and more basic—the desire for love? Then the early relationship with the mother looks quite different from the Freudian picture—a modality not to be avoided at all costs but a way of psychodynamic life. Then language, which is learned by a child during the preoedipal period, might well function not to keep the mother at bay so much as to maintain and expand the principles of intersubjectivity and affiliation so central to the primary relationship with her.

The readings in this section ask and answer some of these questions. They trace in abbreviated form a history of object relations in psychoanalytic theory that leads both to feminist interpretations of this material and to exploration of language acquisition and functioning. Object–relations theory is not per se an approach directly focused on either gender or language. It is an analysis of human psychodynamic development that works to describe both normal patterns and psychopathologic conditions arising from developmental deficiencies or distortions. It concentrates on clinical issues and treatment. Consequently, this section, after describing the premises of object–relations theory, seeks to indicate its relevance to theories of gender and of language. It is designed to suggest how object–relations theory is both germane and necessary to the study of women and language. For to begin with the revisionary idea that the object, not gratification, is the ultimate aim of libidinal striving is to set into motion a chain of psychological investigation that has powerful implications for our understanding of women and language.

If the Oedipus complex initiates a process that forces and emphasizes the cultural construct of gender, if it concomitantly privileges one version of gender over another and dichotomizes the designated distinctions between them, then language can become a powerful agent for formalizing cultural norms that likewise promote the institutionalization of difference and the hegemony of values. On the other hand, it is important to see how properties and qualities assigned to the feminine and accordingly devalued in a patriarchal society might continue to have both significance and agency. When the modality of the "feminine" is associated both with the preoedipal relationship to the mother and with the development of language between mother and child during this period, then its propensities for relationality and intersubjectivity might influence a language practice that opens a new domain of relatedness, a new field for "being with" experiences, in Daniel Stern's terms (*The Interpersonal World of the Infant*, 162). Language can institute what Stern calls "we-meanings," making it possible for the infant "to negotiate shared meaning with another about personal knowledge" (171, 165).

Variable functions for language seem to be possible, so that speakers and writers can use language in the service of preoedipal or Oedipal values and constructs. Cultural and historical circumstances and situations, especially as demarcated by gender, race, and class, will influence these choices and inclinations and their ultimate consequences. However, to suggest that language as a symbolic formulation might possess structures and features organized in accordance with modes that are alternative to masculinist principles means that such modes are available to speakers in ways that do not demand tactics of radical reconstruction from within the boundaries of language itself. Thus, women's relationship to language may depend less on the nature of language itself (as argued by Lacan and the influential French feminists) and more on cultural conditions for speaking and writing. These cultural conditions are internalized as well as external, so that gender as well as other circumstances, with their attendant power arrangements, function as powerful mandates for inequality, exclusion, oppression, and abuse. Nonetheless, it is important to maintain, as object–relations theory does, that the maternal and all that it signifies are part and not pre-conditions of culture.

Object relations in psychoanalytic theory were first conceptualized in Britain and America in the early twentieth century. Major initiators of these ideas are Melanie Klein, D. W. Winnicott, W.R.D. Fairbairn, Margaret Mahler, and Harry Stack Sullivan. Klein can be called the "mother" of the object relations perspective. Her work in psychoanalyzing children rather than adults, beginning in the mid-1920s in England, led her to emphasize the child's focus on the mother and to place the onset of Oedipal feelings and fantasies earlier and earlier in the infant's life. Later in the 1940s in America, Margaret Mahler, also working directly with children, stressed the environmental (object relational) conditions of the preoedipal period and the interpersonal experience central to it. Mahler writes: "I believe it is from the symbiotic phase of the mother-infant dual unity that those experiential precursors of individual beginnings are derived which, together with inborn constitutional factors, determine every human individual's unique somatic and psychological makeup" (*Psychoanalytic Study of the Child*, 307). Mahler's insistence on a developmental line from symbiosis to separation-individuation has been both accepted and questioned: "The problem with this formulation," writes Jessica Benjamin in the essay included in this volume, "is the idea of separation from oneness; it contains the implicit assumption that we grow *out of* relationships rather than becoming more active and sovereign *within* them, that we start in a state of dual oneness and wind up in a state of singular oneness" (*The Bonds of Love*, 18). Nonetheless, Mahler's theory is so important, in Benjamin's words, "because she formulated more completely the actual interaction between parent and child, admitting the importance of interpersonal dynamics without denying inner unconscious reality" (18).

Harry Stack Sullivan's "interpersonal" theory of psychiatry more vigorously yet asserted the centrality of object relations: "The field of Psychiatry is the field of interpersonal relations—a personality can never be isolated from the complex of interpersonal relations in which the person lives and has his being" (*Conceptions of Modern Psychiatry*, 10). Sullivan developed his theories in America while doing clinical work with schizophrenics in the 1920s. As Greenberg and Mitchell write, "the infant in Sullivan's system has no psychological existence prior to his or her embeddedness in interactions with the caretakers and discovers him- or herself as well as the 'object' through a complex developmental process" (95); in Sullivan's words, "everything that can be found in the human mind has been put there by interpersonal relations, excepting only the capabilities to receive *and elaborate* the relevant experiences. This statement is also intended to be the antithesis of any doctrine of human instincts" (*The Fusion of Psychiatry and Social Science*, 302). The emphasis on cultural contributions to personality set Sullivan apart from the British school of object-relations theory, but these approaches are clearly related.

British object–relations theory is most notably represented by D. W. Winnicott and W. R. D. Fairbairn, the Scottish psychoanalyst whose work in the 1940s challenged Freud's drive theory in a powerful way by his suggestion that human experience and behavior derive fundamentally from the search for and maintenance of contacts with others and that the "universal endopsychic situation" is established in the earliest relation with the mother. The tripartite splitting of the ego with its corresponding objects results from the child's earliest struggles to maintain good relations with the mother and persists throughout life. When parents are fully or partially unavailable, the child establishes internal objects within himself or herself, as substitutes and solutions for unsatisfying relationships with real external objects. It is not sexual gratification that fuels the desire for others but contact and nurturance: "It is not the libidinal attitude which determines object-relationship, but the object-relationship which determines the libidinal attitude" (*An Object-Relations Theory of the Personality*, 340).

I have chosen a selection from the writings of D. W. Winnicott to represent the formative work in object–relations theory. Winnicott, psychoanalyst and pediatrician, student of Melanie Klein, was innovative and profoundly influential in his description of early ego-development in the facilitating or holding environment of the mother-infant matrix. "The Theory of the Parent-Infant Relationship," 1960 (in *The Maturational Processes and the Facilitating Environment*), concentrates on the earliest phase of development, the establishment of the holding environment. The developmental process "depends on being seen" (*Playing and Reality*, 114). It depends on the mother's recognition of the infant as someone who is there: "The mother is looking at the baby and *what she looks like is related to what she sees there*" (*Playing and Reality*, 110). Maternal empathy is prerequisite and leads to the mother's ability to provide a facilitating environment, a condition of maximum dependence in which the infant can develop a personal existence or continuity of being. "The infant and the maternal care together form a unit" (39).

Maternal empathy promotes proper care; its obverse opens up profound anxiety about annihilation. The organization of a false self in defense of the threatened true self is introduced here and given closer analysis in much of Winnicott's writing, such as "Ego Distortion in Terms of True and False Self" (1960), where he makes the distinction between the "good-enough mother" and the "not good-enough mother" on the basis of the mother's ability to "meet the infant gesture . . . and make sense of it." This is what the good-enough mother does, but the mother who is not good enough "repeatedly fails to meet the infant gesture; instead she substitutes her own gesture which is to be given sense by the compliance of the infant" (*The Maturational Processes and the Facilitating Environment*, 145). Whereas much of Winnicott's work develops the model of a healthy development, his concept of the false self, which defends the true self against annihilation through compliance and imitation, lets us see some of the consequences of deficient maternal care.

Winnicott's concept of the transitional object and of transitional space posits a necessary next stage in development. Much of his work is devoted to an exploration of the intermediate area between dependence and differentiation; between "the subjective and that which is objectively perceived"—between "me-extensions" and the "not-me" (*Playing and Reality*, 3, 100). Transitional objects occupy a crucial space in the developmental process, in that they are at once not part of the infant's body and yet not fully recognized as belonging to external reality. As the infant grows from a belief that she has created the object—that is, the mother—to an understanding that the mother has a reality external to and independent of the baby's identity, transitional objects, which "stand for the breasts, or the object of the first relationship" (9), permit the tricky negotiation between internality and externality.

The completed maturational process in Winnicott's theory allows for both a self and an external world, a society. "Maturity of the human being," he writes, "is a term that implies not only growth but socialization." His ideas about the adult self in relation to society are essentially an expansion of his picture of the child's relationship to the mother: "the adult is able to identify with society without too great a sacrifice of personal spontaneity; or, the other way around, the adult is able to attend to his or her personal needs without being anti-social, and indeed, without a failure to take some responsibility for the maintenance or for the modification of society as it is found" (*The Maturational Processes and the Facilitating Environment*, 83). Taken as a whole, Winnicott's complex body of work provides a rich analysis of the earliest developmental processes, linking them emphatically and resonantly with the preoedipal mother and her primary relationship to the newborn child.

Feminist psychoanalytic theory and empirical research into infant psychology have subsequently amplified object–relations premises to address more directly the relationship between early development and gender, on the one hand, and early development and language, on the other. Feminist theory has gendered a process which has traditionally been left neutral, particularly as it relates to the infant. Whereas the caretaker is almost always "the mother" (in accordance with child-rearing practices in most cultures), the child is not gendered. Feminist theory, on the contrary, problematizes and explores the relation between gender and identity, and a large body of work examines how the "infant" becomes the "girl" or the "boy," as well as what the gender of the "mother" means to infant development.

These writers point out that the child is not free from genderization before the Oedipal crisis, although many would agree that the introduction of the third "object" or "term" makes a serious difference in terms of the significance and function of gender as a cultural construct. Additionally, the premise of object–relations theory that self-development is initiated in a maternal or feminized environment is examined. What does it mean that the qualities needed by a primary caretaker—whether she be the biological mother or another woman, or indeed, even if "she" is a man taking this role—are those assigned to women in Western culture? In object–relations theory, the concern and capacity for intimacy, devotion, empathy, relationality, and nurture—all associated with women—become central rather than peripheral to ideas about the nature of human development.

On the other hand, women, gendered female, also can possess attributes that hinder good mothering. Passivity, insecurity, tentativeness, self-hatred, indeed, lack of self-definition or self-identity itself, often result from the process of genderization. Yet it takes a well-developed sense of self-identity to *be* good-enough as a mother! There is a reason why psychoanalytic theories of maternal nurture were evolved by clinicians whose work focused on the treatment of deficiencies and abuses in preoedipal mothering. The good-enough mother is an idealized construct. Too often gender socialization brings with it attitudes and characteristics that impede rather than assist the process of nurture. The implications of gender for mothering, and the possibilities and problematics of the mother-infant bond, have become the province of feminist study.

Nancy Chodorow's groundbreaking study, *The Reproduction of Mothering: Psychoanalysis and the Sociology of Gender* (1978), brings attention both to the issues of gender in Freudian theory and to the relevance of object–relations theory to issues of gender and development. Chodorow's emphasis on the role of the mother and mothering in psychosexual development and identity formation in terms of its different implications for girls and boys rests squarely on her reading in object–relations psychology. Included here is chapter 6, "Gender Differences in the Preoedipal Period," which argues that the nature of the girl's preoedipal attachment to her mother is different from the boy's, and that this difference has implications for Freud's all-important resolution of the Oedipus complex in girls—that is, that the attachment to the mother is not given up so much as it is extended or expanded, and that this "relational complexity" is normal, not pathological—central to gendered identity for women in our society. Noting that marked gender differentiation is set in place during the Oedipal period, Chodorow discusses gender differences in the nature and quality of the preoedipal mother-child relationship. There is analytic agreement that the preoedipal period is of different length for boys and girls (longer for girls); evidence appears fuzzier for what constitutes those differences in "nature and quality," but Chodorow concludes by stating that, because of differences in maternal treatment, "girls . . . seem to become and experience themselves as the self of the mother's fantasy, whereas boys become the other" (103). Differences in the experiencing and resolution of the Oedipal crisis are clearer. Especially, "relational capacities that are curtailed in boys as a result of the masculine oedipus complex are sustained in girls," so that "girls come to define themselves more in relation to others" (93). This point has proved a veritable springboard for contemporary feminist thinking about gender difference. One notable example is Carol Gilligan's *In a Different Voice: Psychological Theory and Women's Development* (1982).

Ideas about relationality as a positive, empowering source of mature social functioning are at the heart of the theories about female development and the resultant clinical work undertaken by the members of the Stone Center for Developmental Services and Study at Wellesley College. Judith Jordan's essay "Empathy and Self Boundaries" is included here. Empathy becomes an important concept in the discussion of relationality and its implications for healthy female development. "Empathy," writes Jordan, "is central to an understanding of that aspect of the self which involves we-ness. . . . Without empathy, there is no intimacy, no real attainment of an appreciation of the paradox of separateness within connection" (*Women's Growth in Connection*, 68–69). Jordan's examination of empathy in relation to ideas about self-identity shows it to be less a regressive merging, a total loss of self-boundaries, than a matter of using both differences and similarities to arrive at an understanding of another's inner state. Jordan writes to establish empathy as a mature, rather than a primitive or regressive, phenomenon; to show how its link with female gendered activity is positive rather than negative; and to suggest the concept of "self-empathy" as a means whereby women might use this skill on behalf of self-representation and understanding. In later work, such as her paper "The Meaning of Mutuality," she extends the concept of empathy into an investigation of mutuality and, especially, "mutual intersubjectivity"—empathy as an agency for mutual growth and impact. "When empathy and concern flow both ways, there is an intense affirmation of the self and, paradoxically, a transcendence of the self, a sense of the self as part of a larger relational unity" (82).

Jessica Benjamin's *The Bonds of Love: Psychoanalysis, Feminism, and the Problem of Domination* (1988) extends the concepts of empathy and mutuality to show how the inability to sustain the paradox in such interaction (the idea that recognition of self from another can come only from an other who is recognized as a self in his or her own right) can convert the exchange of recognition into domination and submission (12). In chapter 1, "The First Bond," included here, she develops a theory of intersubjectivity that focuses on the process of mutual recognition, "the necessity of recognizing as well as being recognized by another," which implies among other things the infant's need to see the mother, too, as an independent subject, not simply as the "external world" or as the adjunct to her or his ego (23). Benjamin notes that "no psychological theory has adequately articulated the mother's independent existence," and yet "the real mother is not simply an object for her child's demands; she is, in fact, another subject whose independent center must be outside her child if she is to grant him the recognition he seeks" (23, 24). In this way she extends the introduction of gender into object–relations theory to identify the primary caretaker as a person who is a woman who is a mother. This person possesses a human subjectivity that extends beyond although it encompasses her nurturing role; that very subjectivity, gendered though it may be, is essential to good-enough mothering.

Benjamin also explores how the paradox of recognition might bring about a struggle for control, as the process goes awry and the self resorts to asserting omnipotence (either its own or the other's). Mutual recognition cannot be achieved through obedience, through identification with the other's power, or through repression. The stage is set for domination: "one side is devalued, the other idealized" (50). Thus Benjamin's theory of a powerful preoedipal model shows us as well its (negative) alternative: the Oedipal model.

In their examination of interactive and reciprocal modes, Benjamin and Jordan utilize the important work of Daniel Stern in *The Interpersonal World of the Infant: A View from Psychoanalysis and Developmental Psychology* (1985), because as he combines psychoanalytic theory with infant research "to imagine what an infant might experience" (4), Stern offers a compelling depiction of mutuality and intersubjectivity in action. Stern's study of the interpersonal world of the infant and her or his caregiver, or mother, challenges the idea of a developmental trajectory from symbiosis to independence by showing an infant "capable of having—in fact, likely to have—an integrated sense of self and others." Although Stern's work complements Winnicott's, he also calls into question Winnicott's assumptions about the period of primary identification and dependence: "These new findings support the view that the infant's first order of business, in creating an interpersonal world, is to form the sense of a core self and core others. The evidence also supports the notion that this task is largely accomplished during the period between two and seven months. Further, it suggests that the capacity to have merger or fusion-like experiences as described in psychoanalysis is secondary to and dependent upon an already existing sense of self and other" (70).

Stern stresses the presence from the beginning of both discreteness and connection: "When one watches infants play their role in these mutual regulations, it is difficult not to conclude that they sense the presence of a separate other and sense their capacity to alter the behavior of the other as well as their own experience" (75). He distinguishes between relationship and merger, showing how the connection between a self-regulating other and the self which reacts to and needs that other does not create a loss of the ability to distinguish between self and other as much as it creates a sense that self-experience both occurs in response to and affects the behavior of an other.

Included in this volume is chapter 8, "The Sense of a Verbal Self," which predicates an idea about language formation and language use that follows directly from the notion of a self that is always in relationship, inherently social. Stern points out that although "the acquisition of language has traditionally been seen as a major step in the achievement of separation and individuation, next only to acquiring locomotion, [the] present view asserts that the opposite is equally true, that the acquisition of language is potent in the service of union and togetherness" (172). Language can thus open a new domain of relatedness; on the other hand, it creates at the same time a problem for the integration of self-experience and self-other experience, as it "moves relatedness onto the impersonal, abstract level . . . and away from the personal, immediate level intrinsic to other domains of relatedness" (163). (Surely gender identity is related to language's double functions, but Stern does not explore this issue.)

Two papers on children's language acquisition by Colwyn Trevarthen and John Dore describe research that demonstrates this "intersubjective" or "dialogic" function of language, processes based squarely in the preoedipal mother-infant relationship. Colwyn Trevarthen's "Communication and Cooperation in Early Infancy: A Description of Primary Intersubjectivity," 1979 (in Margaret Bullowa, ed., *Before Speech: The Beginning of Interpersonal Communication*), focuses on the period of pre-speech, during ages two to three months. It describes a "protoconversational" process of communication between infant and caretaker that he terms "primary intersubjectivity." This is a "complex form of mutual understanding" (346) in which there is innovation of meaning by *both* infant and mother, with the mother adapting to the baby's expressions and gestures, even as the baby both responds to and influences the mother's utterances—a "reciprocal exchange" that shows "the close integration of subjective emotional states with interpersonal communication. . . . On this base learning will later permit the infant to achieve much more elaborate expressions and more subtle recognition of the mother, adding strength and content to their growing affectional and communicative attachment" (334, 335).

John Dore's "Feeling, Form, and Intention in the Baby's Transition to Language," 1983 (in Roberta Michnick Golinkoff, ed., *The Transition from Prelinguis-*

tic to Linguistic Communication), looks at the transitional period between words and babbling, usually occurring near the end of the first year, describing the dialogue between infant and caregiver and proposing that first words emerge in the infant "as consequences of dialogic functions of affective expressions across members of an intimate dyad" (168). He argues that "apart from any cognitive invention and social discovery, the origin of words occurs in the immediate context of affective conflict, arising as solutions to maintain and negotiate relationship through dialogue" (168). He shows how the mother matches the baby's expressed affect, "analoging," "complementing," or "imitating" so that the baby can observe a form of her or his affects, transforming the baby's expressions into intents to express those affect-states. Most importantly, Dore proposes that the baby's change from expressing to intending is motivated by desire to maintain some intimate state of connection with the mother. "Being able to express his state intentionally allows the baby to invite a match of positive affect and to deny negative matches. It allows him to *test the state of their relationship.* The intent to express becomes the first cognitive tool for communicating about their relative states in their dialogue with one another. Because the same affect can be differentiated into two forms and communicated cross-modally, partnership in dialogue emerges. *But the analog of affect is the foundation of dialogue*" (169, 170).

These psychologists describe language as both emerging from and intrinsically related to the intimacy of the first relationship. They relate their results to psycholinguistic debates about the origin of language that posit mind *or* environment as primary source of development, not to Lacanian theories of language and gender. Nonetheless, their conclusions are directly relevant to the women and language debate. If the facts that the mother possesses language, that an aspect of her relationship to the child is the production of language for the child, make of her an agent of acculturation, then the significance of acculturation itself changes dramatically from its role in the theories of Lacan and the French feminists. The mother can no longer be understood as that-which-is-not-culture; nor, I would argue, can culture be understood as only the domain of the father (that-which-is-not-mother). No matter how powerful the ethics, norms, institutions associated with the father (what we call the patriarchy), modes of behavior and thought associated with the preoedipal maternal experience (of both mother and child) belong as well to culture. They may be devalued, outlawed, censured, repressed, but exist they must. Exist in culture and in language, in that language is indeed an instrument of culture—and language is as well an agent, an aspect of the preoedipal mother-infant bond.

Very recent object relations-based psychological studies from multi-cultural and non-heterosexual perspectives underlines both the centrality of the primary caregiver to the development of identity and her complex role in relation to dominant cultural values and modes of social interaction. As Cynthia Garcia Coll points out in "Cultural Diversity: Implications for Theory and Practice" (1992), in the same way that "there are some universal aspects of development that may vary only in timing, content, or expression in different cultures, there are some aspects of human development that are more specific to some cultural contexts than to others" (3). For example, despite wide variations in child-rearing techniques around the world, most human beings show remarkable consistency in some developmental patterns, such as the formation of primary attachments that will powerfully influence later interpersonal relationships. "What may differ from one culture to another," suggests Coll, "is how you express affection, how you foster growth within the relationship, or how much you value separation and individuation" (3).

Both positive and negative aspects of maternal care reflect the mother's immeshment in—rather than separation from—culture. For example, in a study of lesbians and their mothers, Wendy Rosen discusses how three central features of relational development for women that typically find their source in the mother-daughter relationship—mutual empathy, relationship authenticity, and relationship differentiation—can be "derailed" because of the mother's participation in the cultural value system of heterosexism ("On the Integration of Sexuality: Lesbians and Their Mothers," 1992, 5). This current work reinforces my position that the maternal is a modality that is part and parcel of culture, even though many (but not all) of its elements may work against the cultural grain. The specifics of the preoedipal experience depend on the culture as well as the gender; but the experience is not acultural. Mothers, like language, exist in culture; and mothers are the primary source for children's language acquisition.

The assumption that the mother is the primary caretaker has an historical and cultural basis. Mothers not only give birth to babies; they are usually the persons primarily responsible for the early care of those infants. If not biological mothers then women—for whether the culture or subculture in question assumes that the biological mother might not be the primary caregiver (as in the case, for example, of wetnurses, nannies, ayahs, mammies—or grandmothers, aunts, or sisters), that caregiver is male only under unusual circumstances. What would or does happen if a person gendered and socialized as male becomes the primary caregiver? Does the role determine the qualities eschewed—or does gender-identity affect the role? That is, do caregivers who are male act in a traditionally "feminine" manner toward infants; or do they carry their traditional gender attributes with them? This is an important issue as we question not only the validity of traditional roles but the essentialism of gender and gender-assigned qualities and attributes.

The final essay in this section, "Sex Differences in Parent-Child Interaction," by Jean Berko Gleason, 1987 (in Philips, Steele, and Tanz, eds., *Language, Gender, and Sex in Comparative Perspective*), is a preliminary attempt to map out some of the issues involved when gender differences among caretakers are taken into account. In these studies, the fathers are not necessarily the primary caretakers, but the assumptions are both that language is learned from fathers, too, and that language is a form of socialization—a process which includes assumption of gender identity. Beginning with the available research on what is termed input language, or child directed speech (CDS), which shows that caretakers have a special way of speaking to young children, Gleason and her colleagues tried to see whether variation in this separate style or register occurred along gender lines: in terms of both the gender of the child and the gender of the adult speaker. In both laboratory and home settings they studied differences between mothers' and fathers' speech to children, regardless of the child's gender; differences in parents' speech to girls and to boys; and emerging gender-associated differences in the speech of children. Many differences were indicated by these exploratory studies. In home studies, they found that mothers were better able to understand what their child was saying than fathers and misunderstood less often than fathers did. Fathers used more direct imperatives in speech to children; they also used "rarer vocabulary" (i.e., "construction site"), disparaging terms of address with sons, and threats. In laboratory studies, fathers again used more complex vocabulary; mothers were more polite; fathers interrupted their children more than mothers did, and both fathers and mothers interrupted little girls more than they interrupted little boys; mothers were more likely to use question forms, and fathers' speech had a higher proportion of both direct imperatives and implied direct forms. All of these differences suggest that language learning and language use are gender-influenced.

Object–relations theory and the developments in feminist theory and language study that have basis in its tenets have important implications for the study of language practice, be it writing or speaking. Emphasis on language as a form of relationship, as a way of perpetuating and enacting forms of we-experience as initiated in the preoedipal mother-child relationship, gives us new ideas about ways in which gender affects language, and vice versa. Emphasis on the mother as central to the development of both identity and language is also immensely suggestive for the study of gender and language, particularly because the mother is understood as a participant in culture rather than a force beyond or before or outside it. We can, for example, look at the relationship between women and language not as an issue concerning the influences or tensions or battles between non-culture and culture but as a matter of how gender functions as an aspect of culture in the acquisition and usage of language. Consequently, object–relations psychoanalytic theory calls into question some of the more important assumptions of Freudian and French theory, offering different and parallel insights that must be, at the very least, debated.

Suzanne Juhasz

SELECTED BIBLIOGRAPHY

BENJAMIN, JESSICA. *The Bonds of Love: Psychoanalysis, Feminism, and the Problem of Domination.* New York: Pantheon Books, 1988.

BULLOWA, MARGARET, ED. *Before Speech: The Beginning of Interpersonal Communication.* New York: Cambridge University Press, 1980.

BUCKLEY, PETER, ED. *Essential Papers on Object Relations.* New York: New York University Press, 1986.

CHODOROW, NANCY. *Feminism and Psychoanalytic Theory.* New Haven: Yale University Press, 1989.

———. *The Reproduction of Mothering: Psychoanalysis and the Sociology of Gender.* Berkeley: University of California Press, 1978.

COLL, CYNTHIA GARCIA. "Cultural Diversity: Implications for Theory and Practice." *Works in Progress.* Wellesley, Mass.: The Stone Center, 1992.

DORE, JOHN. "Holophrases Revisited, Dialogically." *Children's Single Word Speech.* Ed. M. Barrett. London: Wiley, 1985.

FAIRBAIRN, W.D.R. *An Object Relations Theory of the Personality.* New York: Basic Books, 1952.

GILLIGAN, CAROL. *In a Different Voice: Psychological Theory and Women's Development.* Cambridge: Harvard University Press, 1982.

GOLINKOFF, ROBERTA MICHNICK, ED. *The Transition from Prelinguistic to Linguistic Communication.* Hillsdale, N.J.: Lawrence Erlbaum Associates, 1983.

GREENBERG, JAY R. AND STEPHEN A. MITCHELL. *Object Relations in Psychoanalytic Theory.* Cambridge: Harvard University Press, 1983.

JORDAN, JUDITH, ALEXANDRA G. KAPLAN, JEAN BAKER MILLER, IRENE P. STIVER, AND JANET L. SURREY. *Women's Growth in Connection: Writings from the Stone Center.* New York: Guilford Press, 1991.

KLEIN, MELANIE. *Contributions to Psychoanalysis 1921–1945.* New York: McGraw-Hill, 1964.

MAHLER, MARGARET. *Psychoanalytic Study of the Child* 18 (1963): 307–324.

———, FRED PINE, AND ANNI BERGMAN. *The Psychological Birth of the Human Infant.* New York: Basic Books, 1975.

PHILIPS, SUSAN U., SUSAN STEELE, AND CHRISTINE TANZ, EDS. *Language, Gender, and Sex in Comparative Perspective.* Cambridge: Cambridge University Press, 1987.

ROSEN, WENDY. "On the Integration of Sexuality: Lesbians and Their Mothers." *Works in Progress.* Wellesley, Mass.: The Stone Center, 1992.

STERN, DANIEL. *The Interpersonal World of the Infant: A View from Psychoanalysis and Development Psychology.* New York: Basic Books, 1985.

SULLIVAN, HARRY STACK. *Conceptions of Modern Psychiatry.* New York: Norton, 1940.

———. *The Fusion of Psychiatry and Social Science.* New York: Norton, 1964.

———. *The Interpersonal Theory of Psychiatry.* New York: Norton, 1953.

TREVARTHEN, COLWYN. "The Foundation of Intersubjectivity: Development of Interpersonal and Cooperative Understanding in Infants." *The Social Foundation of Language and Thought: Essays in Honor of Jerome Bruner.* Ed. D. R. Olson. New York: Norton, 1980.

WINNICOTT, D. W. *Collected Papers: Through Paediatrics to Psychoanalysis.* New York: Basic Books, 1958.

———. *The Maturational Processes and the Facilitating Environment.* New York: International Universities Press, 1965.

———. *Playing and Reality.* London and New York: Tavistock Publications, 1982.

d. w. winnicott

THE THEORY OF THE
PARENT-INFANT RELATIONSHIP

The main point of this paper can perhaps best be brought out through a comparison of the study of infancy with the study of the psycho-analytic transference.[1] It cannot be too strongly emphasized that my statement is about infancy, and not primarily about psycho-analysis. The reason why this must be understood reaches to the root of the matter. If this paper does not contribute constructively, then it can only add to the existing confusion about the relative importance of personal and environmental influences in the development of the individual.

In psycho-analysis as we know it there is no trauma that is outside the individual's omnipotence. Everything eventually comes under ego-control, and thus becomes related to secondary processes. The patient is not helped if the analyst says: 'Your mother was not good enough' . . . 'your father really seduced you' . . . 'your aunt dropped you.' Changes come in an analysis when the traumatic factors enter the psycho-analytic material in the patient's own way, and within the patient's omnipotence. The interpretations that are alterative are those that can be made in terms of projection. The same applies to the benign factors, factors that led to satisfaction. Everything is interpreted in terms of the individual's love and ambivalence. The analyst is prepared to wait a long time to be in a position to do exactly this kind of work.

In infancy, however, good and bad things happen to the infant that are quite outside the infant's range. In fact infancy is the period in which the capacity for gathering external factors into the area of the infant's omnipotence is in process of formation. The ego-support of the maternal care enables the infant to live and develop in spite of his being not yet able to control, or to feel responsible for, what is good and bad in the environment.

The events of these earliest stages cannot be thought of as lost through what we know as the mechanisms of repression, and therefore analysts cannot expect to find them appearing as a result of work which lessens the forces of repression. It is possible that Freud was trying to allow for these phenomena when he used the term primary repression, but this is open to argument. What is fairly certain is that the matters under discussion here have had to be taken for granted in much of the psycho-analytic literature.[2]

Returning to psycho-analysis, I have said that the analyst is prepared to wait till the patient becomes able to present the environmental factors in terms that allow of their interpretation as projections. In the well-chosen case this result comes from the patient's capacity for confidence, which is rediscovered in the reliability of the analyst and the professional setting. Sometimes the analyst

From The Maturational Processes and the Facilitating Environment: Studies in the Theory of Emotional Development *(Madison, Conn.: International Universities Press, 1965), pp. 37–55.*

needs to wait a very long time; and in the case that is *badly* chosen for classical psycho-analysis it is likely that the reliability of the analyst is the most important factor (or more important than the interpretations) because the patient did not experience such reliability in the maternal care of infancy, and if the patient is to make use of such reliability he will need to find it for the first time in the analyst's behaviour. This would seem to be the basis for research into the problem of what a psycho-analyst can do in the treatment of schizophrenia and other psychoses.

In borderline cases the analyst does not always wait in vain; in the course of time the patient becomes able to make use of the psycho-analytic interpretations of the original traumata as projections. It may even happen that he is able to accept what is good in the environment as a projection of the simple and stable going-on-being elements that derive from his own inherited potential.

The paradox is that what is good and bad in the infant's environment is not in fact a projection, but in spite of this it is necessary, if the individual infant is to develop healthily, that everything shall seem to him to be a projection. Here we find omnipotence and the pleasure principle in operation, as they certainly are in earliest infancy; and to this observation we can add that the recognition of a true 'not-me' is a matter of the intellect; it belongs to extreme sophistication and to the maturity of the individual.

In the writings of Freud most of the formulations concerning infancy derive from a study of adults in analysis. There are some childhood observations ('Cotton reel' material (1920)), and there is the analysis of Little Hans (1909). At first sight it would seem that a great deal of psycho-analytic theory is about early childhood and infancy, but in one sense Freud can be said to have neglected infancy as a state. This is brought out by a footnote in *Formulations on the Two Principles of Mental Functioning* (1911, p. 220) in which he shows that he knows he is taking for granted the very things that are under discussion in this paper. In the text he traces the development from the pleasure-principle to the reality-principle, following his usual course of reconstructing the infancy of his adult patients. The note runs as follows:

> It will rightly be objected that an organization which was a slave to the pleasure-principle and neglected the reality of the external world could not maintain itself alive for the shortest time, so that it could not have come into existence at all. The employment of a fiction like this is, however, justified when one considers that the infant—provided one includes with it the care it receives from its mother—does almost realize a physical system of this kind.

Here Freud paid full tribute to the function of maternal care, and it must be assumed that he left this subject alone only because he was not ready to discuss its implications. The note continues:

> It probably hallucinates the fulfilment of its internal needs; it betrays its unpleasure, when there is an increase of stimulus and an absence of satisfaction, by the motor discharge of screaming and beating about with its arms and legs, and it then experiences the satisfaction it has hallucinated. Later, as an older child, it learns to employ these manifestations of discharge inten-

tionally as methods of expressing its feelings. Since the later care of children is modelled on the care of infants, the dominance of the pleasure-principle can really come to an end only when a child has achieved complete psychical detachment from its parents.

The words: 'provided one includes with it the care it receives from its mother' have great importance in the context of this study. The infant and the maternal care together form a unit.[3] Certainly if one is to study the theory of the parent-infant relationship one must come to a decision about these matters, which concern the real meaning of the word dependence. It is not enough that it is acknowledged that the environment is important. If there is to be a discussion of the theory of the parent-infant relationship, then we are divided into two if there are some who do not allow that at the earliest stages the infant and the maternal care belong to each other and cannot be disentangled. These two things, the infant and the maternal care, disentangle and dissociate themselves in health; and health, which means so many things, to some extent means a disentanglement of maternal care from something which we then call the infant or the beginnings of a growing child. This idea is covered by Freud's words at the end of the footnote: 'the dominance of the pleasure-principle can really come to an end only when a child has achieved complete psychical detachment from its parents'. (The middle part of this footnote will be discussed in a later section, where it will be suggested that Freud's words here are inadequate and misleading in certain respects, if taken to refer to the earliest stage.)

THE WORD 'INFANT'

In this paper the word infant will be taken to refer to the very young child. It is necessary to say this because in Freud's writings the word sometimes seems to include the child up to the age of the passing of the Oedipus complex. Actually the word infant implies 'not talking' (*infans*), and it is not un-useful to think of infancy as the phase prior to word presentation and the use of word symbols. The corollary is that it refers to a phase in which the infant depends on maternal care that is based on maternal empathy rather than on understanding of what is or could be verbally expressed.

This is essentially a period of ego development, and integration is the main feature of such development. The id-forces clamour for attention. At first they are external to the infant. In health the id becomes gathered into the service of the ego, and the ego masters the id, so that id-satisfactions become ego-strengtheners. This, however, is an achievement of healthy development and in infancy there are many variants dependent on relative failure of this achievement. In the ill-health of infancy achievements of this kind are minimally reached, or may be won and lost. In infantile psychosis (or schizophrenia) the id remains relatively or totally 'external' to the ego, and id-satisfactions remain physical, and have the effect of threatening the ego structure, that is, until defences of psychotic quality are organized.[4]

I am here supporting the view that the main reason why in infant development the infant usually becomes able to master, and the ego to include, the id, is the fact of the maternal care, the maternal ego implementing the infant ego and so making it powerful and stable. How this takes place will need to be examined, and also how the infant ego eventually becomes free of the mother's ego-support, so that the infant achieves mental detachment from the mother, that is, differentiation into a separate personal self.

In order to examine the parent-infant relationship it is necessary first to attempt a brief statement of the theory of infant emotional development.

HISTORICAL

In psycho-analytic theory as it grew up the early hypothesis concerned the id and the ego mechanisms of defence. It was understood that the id arrived on the scene very early indeed, and Freud's discovery and description of pregenital sexuality, based on his observations of the regressive elements found in genital fantasy and in play and in dreams, are main features of clinical psychology.

Ego mechanisms of defence were gradually formulated.[5] These mechanisms were assumed to be organized in relation to anxiety which derived either from instinct tension or from object loss. This part of psycho-analytic theory presupposes a separateness of the self and a structuring of the ego, perhaps a personal body scheme. At the level of the main part of this paper this state of affairs cannot yet be assumed. The discussion centres round the establishment of precisely this state of affairs, namely the structuring of the ego which makes anxiety from instinct tension or object loss possible. Anxiety at this early stage is not castration anxiety or separation anxiety; it relates to quite other things, and is, in fact, anxiety about annihilation (cf. the aphanisis of Jones).

In psycho-analytic theory ego mechanisms of defence largely belong to the idea of a child that has an independence, a truly personal defence organization. On this borderline the researches of Klein add to Freudian theory by clarifying the interplay of primitive anxieties and defence mechanisms. This work of Klein concerns earliest infancy, and draws attention to the importance of aggressive and destructive impulses that are more deeply rooted than those that are reactive to frustration and related to hate and anger; also in Klein's work there is a dissection of early defences against primitive anxieties, anxieties that belong to the first stages of the mental organization (splitting, projection, and introjection).

What is described in Melanie Klein's work clearly belongs to the life of the infant in its earliest phases, and to the period of dependence with which this paper is concerned. Melanie Klein made it clear that she recognized that the environment was important at this period, and in various ways at all stages.[6] I suggest, however, that her work and that of her co-workers leaves open for further consideration the development of the theme of full dependence, that which appears in Freud's phrase: '. . . the infant, provided one includes with it the care it receives from its mother . . .' There is nothing in Klein's work that contradicts the idea of absolute dependence, but there seems to me to be no specific reference to a stage at which the infant exists only because of the maternal care, together with which it forms a unit.

What I am bringing forward for consideration here is the difference between the analyst's acceptance of the reality of dependence, and his working with it in the transference.[7]

It would seem that the study of ego-defences takes the investigator back to pregenital id-manifestations, whereas the study of ego psychology takes him back to dependence, to the maternal-care–infant unit.

One half of the theory of the parent-infant relationship concerns the infant, and is the theory of the infant's journey from absolute dependence, through relative dependence, to independence, and, in parallel, the infant's journey from the pleasure principle to the reality principle, and from autoerotism to object relationships. The other half of the theory of the parent-infant relationship concerns maternal care, that is to say the qualities and changes in the mother that meet the specific and developing needs of the infant towards whom she orientates.

THE INFANT

The key word in this part of the study is *dependence*. Human infants cannot start to *be* except under certain conditions. These conditions are studied below, but they are part of the psychology of the infant. Infants come into *being* differently according to whether the conditions are favourable or unfavourable. At the same time conditions do not determine the infant's potential. This is inherited, and it is legitimate to study this inherited potential of the individual as a separate issue, *provided always that it is accepted that the inherited potential of an infant cannot become an infant unless linked to maternal care.*

The inherited potential includes a tendency towards growth and development. All stages of emotional growth can be roughly dated. Presumably all developmental stages have a date in each individual child. Nevertheless, not only do these dates vary from child to child, but also, *even if they were known in advance* in the case of a given child, they could not be used in predicting the child's actual development because of the other factor, maternal care. If such dates could be used in prediction at all, it would be on the basis of assuming a maternal care that is adequate in the important respects. (This obviously does not mean adequate only in the physical sense; the meaning of adequacy and inadequacy in this context is discussed below.)

THE INHERITED POTENTIAL AND ITS FATE

It is necessary here to attempt to state briefly what happens to the inherited potential if this is to develop into an infant, and thereafter into a child, a child reaching towards independent existence. Because of the complexities of the subject such a statement must be made on the assumption of satisfactory maternal care, which means parental care. Satisfactory parental care can be classified roughly into three overlapping stages:

(*a*)   Holding.
(*b*)   Mother and infant living together. Here the father's function (of dealing with the environment for the mother) is not known to the infant.
(*c*)   Father, mother, and infant, all three living together.

The term 'holding' is used here to denote not only the actual physical holding of the infant, but also the total environmental provision prior to the concept of *living with.* In other words, it refers to a three-dimensional or space relationship with time gradually added. This overlaps with, but is initiated prior to, instinctual experiences that in time would determine object relationships. It includes the management of experiences that are inherent in existence, such as the *completion* (and therefore the *non-completion*) of processes, processes which from the outside may seem to be purely physiological but which belong to infant psychology and take place in a complex psychological field, determined by the awareness and the empathy of the mother. (This concept of holding is further discussed below.)

The term 'living with' implies object relationships, and the emergence of the infant from the state of being merged with the mother, or his perception of objects as external to the self.

This study is especially concerned with the 'holding' stage of maternal care, and with the complex events in infants' psychological development that are related to this holding phase. It should be remembered, however, that a division of one phase from another is artificial, and merely a matter of convenience, adopted for the purpose of clearer definition.

Infant Development During the Holding Phase

In the light of this some characteristics of infant development during this phase can be enumerated. It is at this stage that

> primary process
> primary identification
> auto-erotism
> primary narcissism

are living realities.

In this phase the ego changes over from an unintegrated state to a structured integration, and so the infant becomes able to experience anxiety associated with disintegration. The word disintegration begins to have a meaning which it did not possess before ego integration became a fact. In healthy development at this stage the infant retains the capacity for re-experiencing unintegrated states, but this depends on the continuation of reliable maternal care or on the build-up in the infant of memories of maternal care beginning gradually to be perceived as such. The result of healthy progress in the infant's development during this stage is that he attains to what might be called 'unit status'. The infant becomes a person, an individual in his own right.

Associated with this attainment is the infant's psychosomatic existence, which begins to take on a personal pattern; I have referred to this as the psyche indwelling in the soma.[8] The basis for this indwelling is a linkage of motor and sensory and functional experiences with the infant's new state of being a person. As a further development there comes into existence what might be called a limiting membrane, which to some extent (in health) is equated with the surface of the skin, and has a position between the infant's 'me' and his 'not-me'. So the infant comes to have an inside and an outside, and a body-scheme. In this way meaning comes to the function of intake and output; moreover, it gradually becomes meaningful to postulate a personal or inner psychic reality for the infant.[9]

During the holding phase other processes are initiated; the most important is the dawn of intelligence and the beginning of a mind as something distinct from the psyche. From this follows the whole story of the secondary processes and of symbolic functioning, and of the organization of a personal psychic content, which forms a basis for dreaming and for living relationships.

At the same time there starts in the infant a joining up of two roots of impulsive behaviour. The term 'fusion' indicates the positive process whereby diffuse elements that belong to movement and to muscle erotism become (in health) fused with the orgiastic functioning of the erotogenic zones. This concept is more familiar as the reverse process of defusion, which is a complicated defence in which aggression becomes separated out from erotic experience after a period in which a degree of fusion has been achieved. All these developments belong to the environmental condition of *holding*, and without a good enough holding these stages cannot be attained, or once attained cannot become established.

A further development is in the capacity for object relationships. Here the infant changes from a relationship to a subjectively conceived object to a relationship to an object objectively perceived. This change is closely bound up with the infant's change from being merged with the mother to being separate from her, or to relating to her as separate and 'not-me'. This development is not specifically related to the holding, but is related to the phase of 'living with'.

Dependence

In the holding phase the infant is maximally dependent. One can classify dependence thus:

(i)   *Absolute Dependence.* In this state the infant has no means of knowing about the maternal care, which is largely a matter of prophylaxis. He cannot gain control over what is well and what is badly done, but is only in a position to gain profit or to suffer disturbance.

(ii)   *Relative Dependence.* Here the infant can become aware of the need for the details of maternal care, and can to a growing extent relate them to personal impulse, and then later, in a psycho-analytic treatment, can reproduce them in the transference.

(iii)   *Towards Independence.* The infant develops means for doing without actual care. This is accomplished through the accumulation of memories of care, the projection of personal needs and the introjection of care details, with the development of confidence in the environment. Here must be added the element of intellectual understanding with its tremendous implications.

Isolation of the Individual

Another phenomenon that needs consideration at this phase is the hiding of the core of the personality. Let us examine the concept of a central or true self. The central self could be said to be the inherited potential which is experiencing a continuity of being, and acquiring in its own way and at its own speed a personal psychic reality and a personal body-scheme.[10] It seems necessary to allow for the concept of the isolation of this central self as a characteristic of health. Any threat to this isolation of the true self constitutes a major anxiety at this early stage, and defences of earliest infancy appear in relation to failures on the part of the mother (or in maternal care) to ward off impingements which might disturb this isolation.

Impingements may be met and dealt with by the ego organization, gathered into the infant's omnipotence and sensed as projections.[11] On the other hand they may get through this defence in spite of the ego-support which maternal care provides. Then the central core of the ego is affected, and this is the very nature of psychotic anxiety. In health the individual soon becomes invulnerable in this respect, and if external factors impinge there is merely a new degree and quality in the hiding of the central self. In this respect the best defence is the organization of a false self. Instinctual satisfactions and object relationships themselves constitute a threat to the individual's personal going-on-being. *Example:* a baby is feeding at the breast and obtains satisfaction. This fact by itself does not indicate whether he is having an ego-syntonic id experience or, on the contrary, is suffering the trauma of a seduction, a threat to personal ego continuity, a threat by an id experience which is not ego-syntonic, and with which the ego is not equipped to deal.

In health object relationships can be developed on the basis of a compromise, one which involves the individual in what later would be called cheating and dishonesty, whereas a direct relationship is possible only on the basis of regression to a state of being merged with the mother.

Annihilation

Anxiety in these early stages of the parent-infant relationship relates to the threat of annihilation,[12] and it is necessary to explain what is meant by this term.

In this place which is characterized by the essential existence of a holding environment, the 'inherited potential' is becoming itself a 'continuity of being'. The alternative to being is reacting, and reacting interrupts being and annihilates. Being and annihilation are the two alternatives. The holding environment therefore has as its main function the reduction to a minimum of impingements to which the infant must react with resultant annihilation of personal being. Under favourable conditions the infant establishes a continuity of existence and then begins to develop the sophistications which make it possible for impingements to be gathered into the area of omnipotence. At this stage the word death has no possible application, and this makes the term death instinct unacceptable in describing the root of destructiveness. Death has no meaning until the arrival of hate and of the concept of the whole human person. When a whole human person can be hated, death has meaning, and close on this follows that which can be called maiming; the whole hated and loved person is kept alive by being castrated or otherwise maimed instead of killed. These ideas belong to a phase later than that characterized by dependence on the holding environment.

Freud's Footnote Re-examined

At this point it is necessary to look again at Freud's statement quoted earlier. He writes: 'Probably it (the baby) hallucinates the fulfilment of its inner needs; it betrays its pain due to increase of stimulation and delay of satisfaction by the motor discharge of crying and struggling, and then experiences the hallucinated satisfaction.' The theory indicated in this part of the statement fails to cover the requirements of the earliest phase. Already by these words reference is being made to object relationships, and the validity of this part of Freud's statement depends on his taking for granted the earlier aspects of maternal care, those which are here described as belonging to the holding phase. On the other hand, this sentence of Freud fits exactly the requirements in the *next* phase, that which is characterized by a relationship between infant and mother in which object relationships and instinctual or erotogenic-zone satisfactions hold sway; that is, when development proceeds well.

THE ROLE OF THE MATERNAL CARE

I shall now attempt to describe some aspects of maternal care, and especially holding. In this paper the concept of holding is important, and a further development of the idea is necessary. The word is here used to introduce a full development of the theme contained in Freud's phrase '. . . when one considers that the infant—provided one includes with it the care it receives from its mother—does almost realize a psychical system of this kind'. I refer to the actual state of the infant-mother relationship at the beginning when the infant has not separated out a self from the maternal care on which there exists absolute dependence in a psychological sense.[13]

At this stage the infant needs and in fact usually gets an environmental provision which has certain characteristics:

> It meets physiological needs. Here physiology and psychology have not yet become distinct, or are only in the process of doing so; and
> It is reliable. But the environmental provision is not mechanically reliable. It is reliable in a way that implies the mother's empathy.

Holding:

> Protects from physiological insult.
> Takes account of the infant's skin sensitivity—touch, temperature, auditory sensitivity, visual sensitivity, sensitivity to falling (action of gravity) and of the infant's lack of knowledge of the existence of anything other than the self.
> It includes the whole routine of care throughout the day and night, and it is not the same with any two infants because it is part of the infant, and no two infants are alike.
> Also it follows the minute day-to-day changes belonging to the infant's growth and development, both physical and psychological.

It should be noted that mothers who have it in them to provide good-enough care can be enabled to do better by being cared for themselves in a way that acknowledges the essential nature of their task. Mothers who do not have it in them to provide good-enough care cannot be made good enough by mere instruction.

Holding includes especially the physical holding of the infant, which is a form of loving. It is perhaps the only way in which a mother can show the infant her love. There are those who can hold an infant and those who cannot; the latter quickly produce in the infant a sense of insecurity, and distressed crying.

All this leads right up to, includes, and co-exists with the establishment of the infant's first object relationships and his first experiences of instinctual gratification.[14]

It would be wrong to put the instinctual gratification (feeding etc.) or object relationships (relation to the breast) before the matter of ego organization (i.e. infant ego reinforced by maternal ego). The basis for instinctual satisfaction and for object relationships is the handling and the general management and the care of the infant, which is only too easily taken for granted when all goes well.

The mental health of the individual, in the sense of freedom from psychosis or liability to psychosis (schizophrenia), is laid down by this maternal care, which when it goes well is scarcely noticed, and is a continuation of the physiological provision that characterizes the prenatal state. This environmental provision is also a continuation of the tissue aliveness and the functional health which (for the infant) provides silent but vitally important ego-support. In this way schizophrenia or infantile psychosis or a liability to psychosis at a later date is related to a failure of environmental provision. This is not to say, however, that the ill-effects of such failure cannot be described in terms of ego distortion and of the defences against primitive anxieties, that is to say in terms of the individual. It will be seen, therefore, that the work of Klein on the splitting defence mechanisms and on projections and introjections and so on, is an attempt to state the effects of failure of environmental provision in terms of the individual. This work on primitive mechanisms gives the clue to only one part of the story, and a reconstruction of the environment and of its failures provides the other part. This other part cannot appear in the transference because of the patient's lack of knowledge of the maternal care, either in its good or in its failing aspects, as it existed in the original infantile setting.

EXAMINATION OF ONE DETAIL OF MATERNAL CARE

I will give an example to illustrate subtlety in infant care. An infant is merged with the mother, and while this remains true the nearer the mother can come to an exact understanding of the infant's needs the better. A change, however, comes with the end of merging, and this end is not necessarily gradual. As soon as mother and infant are separate, from the infant's point of view, then it will be noted that the mother tends to change in her attitude. It is as if she now realizes that the infant no longer expects the condition in which there is an almost magical understanding of need. The mother seems to know that the infant has a new capacity, that of giving a signal so that she can be guided towards meeting the infant's needs. It could be said that if now she knows too well what the infant needs, this is magic and forms no basis for an object relationship. Here we get to Freud's words: 'It (the infant) probably hallucinates the fulfilment of its internal needs; it betrays its unpleasure, when there is an increase of stimulus and an absence of satisfaction, by the motor discharge of screaming and beating about with its arms and legs, and it then experiences the satisfaction it has hallucinated.' In other words, at the end of merging, when the child has become separate from the environment, an important feature is that the infant has to give a signal.[15] We find this subtlety appearing clearly in the transference in our analytic work. It is very important, except when the patient is regressed to earliest infancy and to a state of merging, that the analyst shall *not* know the answers except in so far as the patient gives the clues. The analyst gathers the clues and makes the interpretations, and it often happens that patients fail to give the clues, making certain thereby that the analyst can do nothing. This limitation of the analyst's power is important to the patient, just as the analyst's power is important, represented by the interpretation that is right and that is made at the right moment, and that is based on the clues and the unconscious co-operation of the patient who is supplying the material which builds up and justifies the interpretation. In this way the student analyst sometimes does better analysis than he will do in a few years' time when he knows more. When he has had several patients he begins to find it irksome to go as slowly as the patient is going, and he begins to make interpretations based not on material supplied on that particular day by the patient but on his own accumulated knowledge or his adherence for the time being to a particular group of ideas. This is of no use to the patient. The analyst may appear to be very clever, and the patient may express admiration, but in the end the correct interpretation is a trauma, which the patient has to reject, because it is not his. He complains that the analyst attempts to hypnotize him, that is to say, that the analyst is inviting a severe regression to dependence, pulling the patient back to a merging in with the analyst.

The same thing can be observed with the mothers of infants; mothers who have had several children begin to be so good at the technique of mothering that they do all the right things at the right moments, and then the infant who has begun to become separate from the mother has no means of gaining control of all the good things that are going on. The creative gesture, the cry, the protest, all the little signs that are supposed to produce what the mother does, all these things are missing, because the mother has already met the need just as if the infant were still merged with her and she with the infant. In this way the mother, by being a seemingly good mother, does something worse than castrate the infant. The latter is left with two alternatives: either being in a permanent state of regression and of being merged with the mother, or else staging a total rejection of the mother, even of the seemingly good mother.

We see therefore that in infancy and in the management of infants there is a very subtle distinction between the mother's understanding of her infant's need based on empathy, and her change over to an understanding based on something in the infant or small child that indicates need. This is particularly difficult for mothers because of the fact that children vacillate between one state and the other; one minute they are merged with their mothers and require empathy, while the next they are separate from her, and then if she knows their needs in advance she is dangerous, a witch. It is a very strange thing that mothers who are quite uninstructed adapt to these changes in their developing infants satisfactorily and without any knowledge of the theory. This detail is reproduced in psycho-analytic work with borderline cases, and in all cases at certain moments of great importance when dependence in transference is maximal.

UNAWARENESS OF SATISFACTORY MATERNAL CARE

It is axiomatic in these matters of maternal care of the holding variety that when things go well the infant has no means of knowing what is being properly provided and what is being prevented. On the other hand it is when things do not go well that the infant becomes aware, not of the failure of maternal care, but of the results, whatever they may be, of that failure; that is to say, the infant becomes aware of reacting to some impingement. As a result of success in maternal care there is built up in the infant a continuity of being which is the basis of ego-strength; whereas the result of each failure in maternal care is that the continuity of being is interrupted by reactions to the consequences of that failure, with resultant ego-weakening.[16] Such interruptions constitute annihilation, and are evidently associated with pain of psychotic quality and intensity. In the extreme case the infant exists only on the basis of a continuity of reactions to impingement and of recoveries from such reactions. This is in great contrast to the continuity of being which is my conception of ego-strength.

THE CHANGES IN THE MOTHER

It is important in this context to examine the changes that occur in women who are about to have a baby or who have just had one. These changes are at first almost physiological, and they start with the physical holding of the baby in the womb. Something would be missing, however, if a phrase such as 'maternal instinct' were used in description. The fact is that in health women change in their orientation to themselves and to the world, but however deeply rooted in physiology such changes may be, they can be distorted by mental ill-health in the woman. It is necessary to think of these changes in psychological terms and this in spite of the fact that there may be endocrinological factors which can be affected by medication.

No doubt the physiological changes sensitize the woman to the more subtle psychological changes that follow.

Soon after conception, or when conception is known to be possible, the woman begins to alter in her orientation, and to be concerned with the changes that are taking place within her. In various ways she is encouraged by her own body to be interested in herself.[17] The mother shifts some of her sense of self on to the baby that is growing within her. The important thing is that there comes into existence a state of affairs that merits description and the theory of which needs to be worked out.

The analyst who is meeting the needs of a patient who is reliving these very early stages in the transference undergoes similar changes of orientation; and the analyst, unlike the mother, needs to be aware of the sensitivity which develops in him or her in response to the patient's immaturity and dependence. This could be thought of as an extension of Freud's description of the analyst as being in a voluntary state of attentiveness.

A detailed description of the changes in orientation in a woman who is becoming or who has just become a mother would be out of place here, and I have made an attempt elsewhere to describe these changes in popular or non-technical language (Winnicott, 1949a).

There is a psycho-pathology of these changes in orientation, and the extremes of abnormality are the concern of those who study the psychology of puerperal insanity. No doubt there are many variations in quality which do not constitute abnormality. It is the degree of distortion that constitutes abnormality.

By and large mothers do in one way or another identify themselves with the baby that is growing within them, and in this way they achieve a very powerful sense of what the baby needs. This is a projective identification. This identification with the baby lasts for a certain length of time after parturition, and then gradually loses significance.

In the ordinary case the mother's special orientation to the infant carries over beyond the birth process. The mother who is not distorted in these matters is ready to let go of her identification with the infant as the infant needs to become separate. It is possible to provide good initial care, but to fail to complete the process through an inability to let it come to an end, so that the mother tends to remain merged with her infant and to delay the infant's separation from her. It is in any case a difficult thing for a mother to separate from her infant at the same speed at which the infant needs to become separate from her.[18]

The important thing, in my view, is that the mother through identification of herself with her infant knows what the infant feels like and so is able to provide almost exactly what the infant needs in the way of holding and in the provision of an environment generally. Without such an identification I consider that she is not able to provide what the infant needs at the beginning, which is *a live adaptation to the infant's needs*. The main thing is the physical holding, and this is the basis of all the more complex aspects of holding, and of environmental provision in general.

It is true that a mother may have a baby who is very different from herself so that she miscalculates. The baby may be quicker or slower than she is, and so on. In this way there may be times when what she feels the baby needs is not in fact correct. However, it seems to be usual that mothers who are not distorted by ill-health or by present-day environmental stress do tend on the whole to know accurately enough what their infants need, and further, they like to provide what is needed. This is the essence of maternal care.

With 'the care that it receives from its mother' each infant is able to have a personal existence, and so begins to build up what might be called *a continuity of being*. On the basis of this continuity of being the inherited potential gradually develops into an individual infant. If maternal care is not good enough then the infant does not really come into existence, since there is no continuity of being; instead the personality becomes built on the basis of reactions to environmental impingement.

All this has significance for the analyst. Indeed it is not from direct observation of infants so much as from the study of the transference in the analytic setting that it is possible to gain a clear view of what takes place in infancy itself. This work on infantile dependence derives from the study of the transference and counter-transference phenomena that belong to the psycho-analyst's involvement with the borderline case. In my opinion this involvement is a legitimate extension of psycho-analysis, the only real alteration being in the diagnosis of the illness of the patient, the etiology of whose illness goes back behind the Oedipus complex, and involves a distortion at the time of absolute dependence.

Freud was able to discover infantile sexuality in a new way because he reconstructed it from his analytic work with psycho-neurotic patients. In extending his work to cover the treatment of the borderline psychotic patient it is possible for us to reconstruct the dynamics of infancy and of infantile dependence, and the maternal care that meets this dependence.

SUMMARY

(i)   An examination is made of infancy; this is not the same as an examination of primitive mental mechanisms.

(ii)   The main feature of infancy is dependence; this is discussed in terms of the holding environment.

(iii)   Any study of infancy must be divided into two parts:
        (*a*) Infant development facilitated by good-enough maternal care;
        (*b*) Infant development distorted by maternal care that is not good enough.

(iv)   The infant ego can be said to be weak, but in fact it is strong because of the ego support of maternal care. Where maternal care fails the weakness of the infant ego becomes apparent.

(v)   Processes in the mother (and in the father) bring about, in health, a special state in which the parent is orientated to the infant, and is thus in a position to meet the infant's dependence. There is a pathology of these processes.

(vi)   Attention is drawn to the various ways in which these conditions inherent in what is here termed the holding[19] environment can or cannot appear in the transference if at a later date the infant should come into analysis.

NOTES

This paper, together with one by Dr. Phyllis Greenacre on the same theme, was the subject of a discussion at the 22nd International Psycho-Analytical Congress at Edinburgh, 1961. It was first published in *International Journal of Psycho-Analysis* 1960 41 (1900): 585–595.

1. I have discussed this from a more detailed clinical angle in *Primitive Emotional Development* (1945).

2. I have reported (1954) some aspects of this problem, as met with in the case of a female patient while she was in deep regression.

3. I once said: 'There is no such thing as an infant', meaning, of course, that whenever one finds an infant one finds maternal care, and without maternal care there would be no infant. (Discussion at a Scientific Meeting of the British Psycho-Analytical Society, *circa* 1940.) Was I influenced, without knowing it, by this footnote of Freud's?

4. I have tried to show the application of this hypothesis to an understanding of psychosis in my paper, 'Psychoses and Child Care' (Winnicott, 1952).

5. Researches into defence mechanisms which followed Anna Freud's *The Ego and the Mechanisms of Defence* (1936) have from a different route arrived at a re-evaluation of the role of mothering in infant care and early infant development. Anna Freud (1953) has reassessed her views on the matter. Willi Hoffer (1955) also has made observations relating to this area of development. My emphasis in this paper, however, is on the importance of an understanding of the role of the early parental environment in infant development, and on the way this becomes of clinical significance for us in our handling of certain types of cases with affective and character disorders.

6. I have given a detailed account of my understanding of Melanie Klein's work in this area in two papers (Winnicott, 1954b, and Winnicott, 1965, chapter 1). See Klein (1946, p. 297).

7. For a clinical example see my paper, 'Withdrawal and Regression' (1954).

8. For an earlier statement by me on this issue see my paper, 'Mind and Its Relation to the Psyche-Soma' (1949b).

9. Here the work on primitive fantasy, with whose richness and complexity we are familiar through the teachings of Melanie Klein, becomes applicable and appropriate.

10. In chapter 2 of Winnicott (1965) I have tried to discuss another aspect of this developmental phase as we see it in adult health. Cf. Greenacre (1958).

11. I am using the term 'projections' here in its descriptive and dynamic and not in its full metapsychological sense. The function of primitive psychic mechanisms, such as introjection, projection, and splitting, falls beyond the scope of this paper.

12. I have described clinical varieties of this type of anxiety from a slightly different aspect in a previous paper (1949a).

13. Reminder: to be sure of separating this off from object relationships and instinct-gratification I must *artificially* confine my attention to the body needs of a general kind. A patient said to me: 'A good analytic hour in which the right interpretation is given at the right time *is* a good feed.'

14. For further discussion of this aspect of the developmental processes see my paper, 'Transitional Objects and Transitional Phenomena' (1951).

15. Freud's later (1926) theory of anxiety as a signal to the ego.

16. In character cases it is this ego-weakening and the individual's various attempts to deal with it that presents itself for immediate attention, and yet only a true view of the etiology can make possible a sorting out of the defence aspect of this presenting symptom from its origin in environmental failure. I have referred to one specific aspect of this in the diagnosis of the antisocial tendency as the basic problem behind the Delinquency Syndrome (19).

17. For a more detailed statement on this point see 'Primary Maternal Preoccupation' (1956).

18. Case-material to illustrate one type of problem that is met with clinically and relates to this group of ideas is presented in an earlier paper (1948).

SELECTED BIBLIOGRAPHY

FREUD, S. (1909). 'The Analysis of a Phobia in a Five-Year-Old Boy,' *Standard Edition*.
———. (1911). 'Formulations on the Two Principles of Mental Functioning.' *Standard Edition*.
———. (1920). *Beyond the Pleasure Principle. Standard Edition*.
———. (1926). *Inhibitions, Symptoms and Anxiety. Standard Edition*.
GREENACRE, P. (1958). 'Early Physical Determinants in the Development of the Sense of Identity.' *J. Amer. Psychoanal. Assoc.*
KLEIN, M. (1946). 'Notes on Some Schizoid Mechanisms.' In: *Developments in Psycho-Analysis*, ed. J. Riviere. (London: Hogarth)
WINNICOTT, C. (1954). 'Casework Techniques in the Child Care Services.' *Child Care and Social Work*. (Codicote Press, 1964)
WINNICOTT, D. W. (1945). 'Primitive Emotional Development.' *ibid.*
———. (1947). 'Hate in the Counter-Transference.' *ibid.*
———. (1948). 'Reparation in Respect of Mother's Organized Defence against Depression.' *ibid.*
———. (1949b). 'Birth Memories, Birth Trauma, and Anxiety.' *Collected Papers.*
———. (1949c). 'Mind and its Relation to the Psyche-Soma.' *ibid.*
———. (1951). 'Transitional Objects and Transitional Phenomena.' *ibid.*
———. (1952). 'Psychoses and Child Care.' *ibid.*
———. (1954a). 'Withdrawal and Regression.' *ibid.*
———. (1956a). 'Primary Maternal Preoccupation.' *ibid.*
———. (1965). *Maturational Processes and the Facilitating Environment: Studies in the Theory of Emotional Development*. (Madison, Conn.: Int. Univ. Press)

nancy chodorow

GENDER DIFFERENCES IN THE PREOEDIPAL PERIOD

> We knew, of course, that there had been a preliminary stage of attachment to the mother, but we did not know that it could be so rich in content and so long-lasting, and could leave behind so many opportunities for fixations and dispositions. During this time the girl's father is only a troublesome rival; in some cases the attachment to her mother lasts beyond the fourth year of life. Almost everything that we find later in her relation to her father was already present in this earlier attachment and has been transferred subsequently on to her father. In short, we get an impression that we cannot understand women unless we appreciate this phase of their pre-Oedipus attachment to their mother.
>
> FREUD,
"Femininity"

> Our insight into this early pre-Oedipus phase in girls comes to us as a surprise, like the discovery, in another field, of the Minoan-Mycenaen civilization behind the civilization of Greece.
>
> FREUD,
"Female Sexuality"

Family structure produces crucial differentiating experiences between the sexes in oedipal object-relations and in the way these are psychologically appropriated, internalized, and transformed. Mothers are and have been the child's primary caretaker, socializer, and inner object: fathers are secondary objects for boys and girls. My interpretation of the oedipus complex, from a perspective centered on object-relations, shows that these basic features of family structure entail varied modes of differentiation for the ego and its internalized object-relations and lead to the development of different relational capacities for girls and boys.

The feminine oedipus complex is not simply a transfer of affection from mother to father and a giving up of mother. Rather, psychoanalytic research demonstrates the continued importance of a girl's external and internal relation to her mother, and the way her relation to her father is added to this. This process entails a relational complexity in feminine self-definition and personality which is not characteristic of masculine self-definition or personality. Relational capacities that are curtailed in boys as a result of the masculine oedipus complex are sustained in girls.

Because of their mothering by women, girls come to experience themselves as less separate than boys, as having more permeable ego boundaries. Girls come to define themselves more in relation to others. Their internalized object-relational structure becomes more complex, with more ongoing issues. These personality features are reflected in superego development.

My investigation, then, does not focus on issues at the center of the traditional psychoanalytic account of the oedipus complex—superego formation, gender identity, the attainment of gender role expectations, differential valuations of the sexes, and the genesis of sexual orientation. It takes other issues as equally central. I will be concerned with traditional issues only insofar as my analysis of oedipal object-relations of boys and girls sheds new insight on the different nature of male and female heterosexual object-relations.

My interpretation of the feminine oedipus complex relies for the most part on the early psychoanalytic account of female development. Aspects of this account of female psychology, sexuality, and development have been criticized and shown to be inaccurate or limited.[1] However, those elements of it which I emphasize—the clinically derived description and interpretation of experienced female object-relations in a nuclear family in which women mother and fathers are more remote figures to the children—have not been subjected to substantial revision within the psychoanalytic tradition nor criticism from without, and remain valid.[2]

EARLY PSYCHOANALYTIC FORMULATIONS

Freud's account of the boy's oedipus complex is relatively simple and straightforward.[3] In response to, or in collaboration with, his heterosexual mother, a boy's preoedipal attachment to her becomes charged with phallic/sexual overtones. He comes to see his father as a rival for his mother's love and wishes to replace him. He fantasizes taking his father's penis, murdering or castrating him. He fears retaliation, and specifically castration, by his father for these wishes; thus he experiences a conflict between his self-love (narcissistic interest in his penis and body integrity) and his love for his mother (libidinal cathexis). As a result, he gives up his heterosexual attachment to his mother, radically repressing and denying his feelings toward her. (These feelings are not only repressed, but also are partly expressed in "aim-inhibited" modes, in affectionate feelings and sublimated activities.) At the same time, a "successful" resolution of his oedipus complex requires that he remain heterosexual. Therefore, he is supposed to detach his heterosexual orientation from his mother, so that when he grows up he can reattach it to some other woman.

He receives a reward for his self-sacrifice, in addition to his avoidance of punishment. The carrot of the masculine oedipus complex is identification with his father, and the superiority of masculine identification and prerogatives over feminine (if the threat of castration is the stick). A new psychic integration appears in place of the oedipus complex, as the boy's ego is modified and transformed through the incorporation of paternal prohibitions to form his superego, and as he substitutes a general sexual orientation for the specific attachment to his mother (this attachment is composed of both the remainders of his infantile love and his newer sexualized and genitalized attachment).

Freud originally believed that the object-relational configurations of the feminine and masculine oedipus complexes were completely symmetrical. According to this view, little girls at around age three, and as genital component drives become important, discover that they do not have a penis.[4] They automatically think they are castrated and inferior, and experience their lack as a wound to their self-esteem (a narcissistic wound). As Freud says, they "fall a victim to envy for the penis."[5] They also develop contempt for others, like their mother, who do not have penises and at the same time blame her for their own atrophied state. This contempt, plus their anger at her, leads them to turn away in anger and hostility from their mother, who has been their first love object. They turn to their father, who has a penis and might provide them with this much desired appendage. They give up a previously active sexuality for passive sexuality in relation to him. Finally, they change from wanting a penis from their father to wanting a child from him, through an unconscious symbolic equation of penis and child.

At the same time, their mother becomes a rival because she has sexual access to and possession of their father. The female oedipus complex appears only when the mother has become a rival and the father a desired object. It consists in love for the father and rivalry with the mother, and is symmetrically opposed to the male oedipus complex. Heterosexual orientation is thus an oedipal outcome for girls as well as for boys. (Freud also speaks to differences in oedipal outcome—the girl does not need to give up her oedipus stance in the same manner as the boy, since she no longer has castration to fear.[6])

THE DISCOVERY OF THE PREOEDIPAL MOTHER-DAUGHTER RELATIONSHIP

Jeanne Lampl-de Groot described two clinical examples of a "negative oedipus complex" in girls, in which they cathected their mothers and saw their fathers as rivals.[7] This fundamentally disrupted Freud's original postulation of oedipal symmetry. Analysts continued to hold to much of Freud's original account, but Lampl-de Groot's discovery also substantially modified views of feminine oedipal object-relations, and turned attention to the unique qualities of the preoedipal mother-daughter relationship.

In Freud's original view, a daughter sees her mother only as someone who deprives her first of milk, then of sexual gratification, finally of a penis. A mother is seen as initiating only rivalry and hostility. In the light of Lampl-de Groot's finding, Freud reviewed his own clinical experience. He came to agree with her that the preoedipal phase was central in feminine development, that daughters, just as sons, begin life attached exclusively to their mothers.[8] Children were not originally bisexual, though they were potentially so. They were, rather, gynesexual, or matrisexual.

The discovery of the preoedipal mother-daughter relationship required a general reformulation of psychoanalytic theory and its understanding of the development of object-relations. Freud has claimed that the oedipus complex was the nucleus of neurosis and the basis of personality formation, and he was now led to revise radically this claim.[9] Freud compares his new insight into the preoedipal phase of feminine development to a similarly layered historical discovery. Just as the Minoan-Mycenaean civilization underlies and explains the origins and form of classical Greece, so the preoedipal phase in girls underlies and explains the origins and form of the feminine oedipus complex.

Freud points to three major features of a girl's preoedipal phase and her relationship to her mother during this phase. First, her preoedipal attachment to her mother lasts through all three periods of infantile sexuality, often well into her fourth or fifth year. Second, this attachment is dramatically intense and ambivalent. Finally, Freud reports a surprising finding from his analysis of women with a strong attachment to their father: This strong attachment has been preceded by an equally strong and passionate attachment to their mother. More generally, he finds that a woman's preoedipal attachment to her mother largely determines both her subsequent oedipal attachment to her father and her later relationship to men in general.

A girl's preoedipal relationship to her mother and her entrance into the oedipus situation contrast to those of a boy. Freud and Brunswick claim that a boy's phase of preoedipal mother-attachment is much shorter than a girl's, that he moves earlier into an oedipal attachment.[10] What this means is not immediately apparent. If a girl retains a long preoedipal attachment to her mother, and if a boy's oedipal attachment is to his mother, then both boy and girl remain attached to their mother throughout the period of childhood sexuality. Brunswick suggests further that both boy and girl pass from a period of "passive" attachment to their mother to one of "active" attachment to her. On one level, then, it looks as though both boy and girl maintain similar attachments to their mother, their first love object, throughout most of their early years.

On another level, however, these attachments to the mother are very different—the retention of dichotomous formulations is necessary. On the basis of Freud's account and a later more extended discussion by Helene Deutsch in the *Psychology of Women*,[11] one can argue that the *nature* of the attachment is different. A boy's relation to his mother soon becomes focused on competitive issues of possession and phallic-sexual oppositeness (or complementarity) to her. The relation becomes embedded in triangular conflict as a boy becomes preoccupied with his father as a rival. A girl, by contrast, remains preoccupied for a long time with her mother alone. She experiences a continuation of the two-person relationship of infancy. Playing with dolls during this period, for instance, not only expresses "the *active* side of [the girl's] femininity" but also "is probably evidence of the exclusiveness of her attachment to her mother, with complete neglect of her father-object."[12]

The issue here is the father as an internal object, or object of conflict and ambivalence. As we saw in the previous chapters, fathers often become external attachment figures for children of both genders during their preoedipal years. But the intensity and exclusivity of the relationship is much less than with a mother, and fathers are from the outset separate people and "special." As a result, representations of the father relationship do not becomes so internalized and subject to ambivalence, repression, and splitting of good and bad aspects, nor so determining of the person's identity and sense of self, as do representations of the relationship to a mother. As a boy moves into oedipal attachment and phallic-possessive competition, and as he tries to consolidate his masculine identity, his father does become an object of his ambivalence. At this time, the girl's intense ambivalent attachment remains with her mother.

The content of a girl's attachment to her mother differs from a boy's precisely in that it is not at this time oedipal (sexualized, focused on possession, which means focused on someone clearly different and opposite). The preoedipal attachment of daughter to mother continues to be concerned with early mother-infant relational issues. It sustains the mother-infant exclusivity and the intensity, ambivalence, and boundary confusion of the child still preoccupied with issues of dependence and individuation. By contrast, the boy's "active attachment" to his mother expresses his sense of difference from and masculine oppositeness to her, in addition to being embedded in the oedipal triangle. It helps him to differentiate himself from his mother, and his mother from his father.

The use of two different concepts for the early relationship between mother and daughter (mother-infant relationship, with reference to issues of development; preoedipal, with reference to the girl's relation to her mother) obscures the convergence of the two processes. The terminological distinction is an artifact of the emergence of different aspects of psychoanalytic theory at different times ("preoedipal" emerged early in investigating the feminine oedipus complex; "mother-infant relationship" emerged later, as research focused on the early developmental stage as a distinct period).

There is analytic agreement that the preoedipal period is of different length in girls and boys. There is also an agreed on, if undeveloped, formulation concerning those gender differences in the nature and quality of the preoedipal mother-child relationship I have been discussing. This claim stands as an empirical finding with substantial descriptive and interpretive clinical support. The implications of these early developmental tendencies for psychological gender differences also stand on their own (Freud's claim that the early attachment to her mother affects a girl's attachment to her father and men, for instance). But Freud and his colleagues do not explain how such differences come about.

The different length and quality of the preoedipal period in boys and girls are rooted in women's mothering, specifically in the fact that a mother is of the same gender as her daughter and of a different gender from her son. This leads to her experiencing and treating them differently. I do not mean this as a biological claim. I am using *gender* here to stand for the mother's particular psychic structure and relational sense, for her (probable) heterosexuality, and for her conscious and unconscious acceptance of the ideology, meanings, and expectations that go into being a gendered member of our society and understanding what gender means. Being a grown woman and mother also means having been the daughter of a mother, which affects the nature of her motherliness and quality of her mothering.

It is not easy to prove that mothers treat and experience differently preoedipal boys and girls. Maccoby and Jacklin, in the currently definitive review of the observational and experimental literature of psychology on sex differences,[13] claim that the behavioral evidence—based on interviews of parents and observations of social science researchers—indicates little differential treatment.[14] They report that most studies of children in the first four or five years concerning parent-child interaction, parental warmth, reaction to dependence or independence, and amount of praise and positive feedback show no difference according to the gender of the child.[15] They also report no gender difference in proximity-seeking, touching, and resistance to separation from parents or caretakers in young children.[16] These studies measure observable behaviors, which can be coded, counted and replicated, and they take for proof of gender difference only statistically significant findings.

Yet a report summarizing the proceedings of a panel on the psychology of women at the annual meeting of the American Psychoanalytic Association in 1976 claims that "there is increasing evidence of distinction between the mother's basic attitudes and handling of her boy and girl children starting from the earliest days and continuing thereafter."[17] This surprising contradiction suggests that academic psychologists and psychoanalysts must be looking at quite different things. The kinds of differences I am postulating (and that psychoanalysts are beginning to find) are differences of nuance, tone, quality. These differences are revealed in a small range of analytic clinical case material as well as in some cultural research.[18] These cases give us insight into the subtleties of mothers' differential treatment and experiencing of sons and daughters and of the differential development that results.[19]

PREOEDIPAL MOTHER-DAUGHTER RELATIONSHIPS: THE CLINICAL PICTURE

Many psychoanalysts report cases[20] of particular kinds of mother-infant relationships which throw light on differences in the preoedipal mother-daughter and mother-son relationship.[21] Fliess presents the psychopathological extreme and also the most numerous examples, unintentionally showing the way a certain sort of psychotic mother inflicts her pathology predominantly on daughters.[22] The mothers of his patients carried to an extreme that which is considered to be, or is described as, "normal" in the preoedipal mother-infant relationship. His account is significant because, having chosen to focus on a certain kind of neurotic patient and accompanying early patient-mother relationship, it turns out that an overwhelmingly large percentage (almost eight times as many) of his case illustrations are women. His explanation for this disproportion is that "the picture is more easily recognized in the female because of the naturally longer duration of the preoedipal phase."[23] This explanation is tautological, because he is talking about precisely those features of maternal behavior which in a less extreme but similar form create and maintain a preoedipal relationship in the normal case.

The mothers that Fliess describes were "asymbiotic" during the period when their child needed symbiosis and experienced oneness with them. They were unable to participate empathetically in a relationship to their child. However, from the time that these daughters began to differentiate themselves mentally from their mothers and to practice physical separation, these mothers became "hypersymbiotic." Having denied their daughters the stability and security of a confident early symbiosis, they turned around and refused to allow them any leeway for separateness or individuation. Instead, they now treated their daughters and cathected them as narcissistic physical and mental extensions of themselves, attributing their own body feelings to them. The mothers took control over their daughters' sexuality and used their daughters for their own autoerotic gratification. As Fliess puts it, "The mother employs the 'transitivism' of the psychotic"—"I am you and you are me"[24]—in her experiencing and treatment of her daughter. The result, in Fliess's patients, was that these daughters, as neurotics, duplicated many features of their mothers' psychotic symptoms, and retained severe ego and body-ego distortions. Their ego and body-ego retained an undifferentiated connection to their mother. Their relation to reality was, like an infant's, mediated by their mother as external ego.

Thus, these mothers maintained their daughters in a nonindividuated state through behavior which grew out of their own ego and body-ego boundary blurring and their perception of their daughters as one with, and interchangeable with, themselves. If we are to believe Fliess's account, this particular pathology—the psychotic distortion and prolongation of the normal preoedipal relationship—is predominantly a mother-daughter phenomenon.[25]

Olden, Enid Balint, and Angel provide further examples of the tendencies Fliess describes. Balint describes a state she calls "being empty of oneself"—a feeling of lack of self, or emptiness.[26] This happens especially when a person who has this feeling is with others who read the social and emotional setting differently but do not recognize this, nor recognize that the person herself is in a different world.

Balint claims that women are more likely to experience themselves this way. Women who feel empty of themselves feel that they are not being accorded a separate reality nor the agency to interpret the world in their own way. This feeling has its origins in the early mother-daughter relationship. Balint provides a case example to illustrate. She claims that the "empathy" of the patient's mother was a false empathy, that from the outset it was probably a distorted projection of what the mother thought her infant daughter's needs should be. As her daughter grew, and was able to express wants and needs, the mother systematically ignored these expressions and gave feedback not to her actual behavior but rather to what she had in the first place projected onto her child. Balint describes the results of this false empathy: "Because of this lack of feed-back, Sarah felt that she was unrecognized, that she was empty of herself, that she had to live in a void."[27] This mother-infant interaction began in earliest infancy, but certainly continued throughout the patient's childhood. It is useful to quote Balint at length to indicate the quality of this mother-daughter interaction:

(*i*)   [Although she] on the surface developed satisfactorily, there was apparently a vitally important area where there was no reliable understanding between mother and daughter.

(*ii*)   Although the mother tried her best, she responded more to her own preconceived ideas as to what a baby ought to feel than to what her baby actually felt. . . . Probably Sarah's mother could not bear unhappiness or violence or fear in her child, did not respond to it, and tried to manipulate her so that everything wrong was either put right at once or denied.

(*iii*)   What was missing, therefore, was the acceptance that there might be bad things, or even good ones, which must be recognized; that

> it is not sufficient merely to put things right; moreover, that the
> child was neither identical with her mother, nor with what the
> mother wanted her to be. . . .
>   Sarah's mother was impervious to any communication which was different
> from the picture she had of her daughter, and, in consequence, Sarah could
> not understand her mother's communications and felt that her mother never
> saw her as she was; neither found an echo in the other; and consequently
> only a spurious interaction between the growing child and the environment
> could develop.[28]

Olden describes a disruption in mother-child empathy that occurs when mothers who had originally formed (or seem to have formed) an appropriate unity
with their infant were then unable to give it up.[29] She is describing "a specific
psychic immaturity that will keep a mother from sensing her child's needs, from
following his pace and understanding his infantile world; and in turn keep the
child from developing ego capacities." [30] Olden does not note that both cases she
recounts are mother-daughter cases (one in which the daughter—a child—was
in analysis, the other from an analysis of the mother). Both mothers felt unreal
and were depressed. Olden described characteristics that both Balint and Fliess
describe. The mothers lacked real empathy but had pseudo-empathy which kept
the daughters from forming their own identity, either through identifying and
feeling like someone or through contrasting themselves to someone (this was
more true for the daughter who had less relationship to her father). The mothers
attained instinctual gratification through their daughters, not through directly
using their daughters for autoerotic gratification, but by identifying vicariously
with their sexuality and sex lives.

The Olden cases move even further from pathology than Balint, and further
toward the norm that the direction of pathology implies. These mothers felt real
closeness to their daughters, unlike the Balint and Fliess examples.[31] Olden
describes

> two very immature mothers who shared and, as it were, acted out the chil-
> dren's wishes yet were unable to perceive their children's real needs. These
> mothers and their children were extremely attached to each other; some of
> their friends characterized the relationship as "overidentification." Despite
> this emotional closeness, or perhaps on account of it, the mothers were un-
> able to empathize with their children; the goal and function of this "close-
> ness" was exclusively narcissistic.[32]

> These mothers had maintained the primitive narcissistic mother-infant fu-
> sion with their children. This enabled them vicariously to gratify their own
> frustrated instinctual needs by virtue of projecting themselves onto the
> child.[33]

Angel provides further examples, this time by contrasting adult patients rather
than by discussing the mother-infant relationship itself.[34] He is contrasting "symbiosis and pseudosymbiosis"—two versions of fantasies and wishes of merging
in adult patients.

In (real) symbiosis, according to Angel, there is an extreme fear of merging as
well as a wish to merge, because there is no firm sense of individuation in the

first place. In pseudosymbiosis, there need not be and is not such fear, because the distinction between self and object is firm, and the wish to (re)merge is only a defensive one, usually against feelings of aggression toward the object:

1. In symbiosis, merging fantasies are a true reflection of the state of the ego; the self and object representations are merged.
2. In pseudosymbiosis, merging fantasies are defensive formations, and the self and object representations are more or less distinct.
3. In adults with true symbiotic object relations, the scale is weighted heavily on the side of fixation to the infantile symbiotic phase. In pseudosymbiosis, the element of fixation is minimal or absent, and the scale is weighted heavily on the side of defensive regression.[35]

Between symbiosis and pseudosymbiosis is a middle syndrome, which arises through fixation to the period when separateness is being established but still fluctuates and is in doubt. Like Olden, Angel does not tie his distinction to gender differences. His case examples of true symbiosis and in-between syndrome are women, however, and his case examples of pseudosymbiosis is a man. This points again to gender differences in issues of separateness and sense of self.

The choices of examples of Fliess, Olden, Angel, and Balint are not accidental. The patterns of fusion, projection, narcissistic extension, and denial of separateness they describe are more likely to happen in early mother-daughter relationships than in those of mothers and sons. The same personality characteristics in mothers certainly produce problematic mother-son relationships, but of a different kind. In all these cases, the mother does not recognize or denies the existence of the daughter as a separate person, and the daughter herself then comes not to recognize, or to have difficulty recognizing, herself as a separate person. She experiences herself, rather, as a continuation or extension of (or, in the Balint case, a subsumption within) her mother in particular, and later of the world in general.

In the next two examples, my interpretation is less secure. Both authors give examples of mothers and daughters and mothers and sons to demonstrate a larger issue—as Burlingham phrases it, "empathy between infant and mother,"[36] and as Sperling puts it, "children's interpretations and reaction to the unconscious of their mother."[37] It is my impression that although there was certainly understanding or empathy between mothers and children of both genders, and ways in which children of both genders lived out their mother's preoccupations or fantasies, the quality of the child's empathy and its reaction to the mother's unconscious differed according to gender.[38] With one possible exception,[39] Burlingham and Sperling describe girls who act *as extensions of* their mothers, who act out the aggression which their mothers feel but do not allow themselves to recognize or act on. They describe boys, by contrast, who equally intuitively *react to* their mothers' feelings and wishes as if they were the *objects* of their mothers' fantasies rather than the subjects.[40] Girls, then, seem to become and experience themselves as the self of the mother's fantasy, whereas boys become the other.

Neither Burlingham nor Sperling links her insights to gender differences.

However, Burlingham mentions that when she and her children were in analysis at the same time, and an issue preoccupying her would arise in the analysis of her children, appearing "our of context . . . as if it were a foreign body,"[41] these links were more obvious with sons than daughters. Burlingham does not have an explanation. If my interpretation is right, then the explanation is that her daughter's preoccupations, as continuations of her, might appear more ego syntonic—seeming to emerge out of her daughter's ego—and thus be less identifiable than issues which emphasized her sons as acted-on objects.

These accounts indicate the significance of gender differences, despite the lack of attention paid to these differences. With the exception of Balint, who says that being empty of oneself is found more often in women, the authors claim simply to focus on a certain kind of person and certain kind of early mother-infant relationship, and then either use predominantly mother-*daughter* examples or mother-daughter and mother-son examples which reflect gender-linked variations in the processes they discuss, as in the cases of Angel, Burlingham, and Sperling. All these accounts indicate, in different ways, that prolonged symbiosis and narcissistic overidentification are particularly characteristic of early relationships between mothers and daughters.

PREOEDIPAL MOTHER-SON RELATIONSHIPS: THE CLINICAL PICTURE

Both the absence of mother-son examples in some discussions, and their character in others, indicate how early mother-daughter relationships contrast to those between a mother and son. In Burlingham and Sperling, sons are objects for their mothers, even while they maintain symbiotic bonds of empathy and oneness of identification. In the Angel case, a man pretends symbiosis when boundaries are in fact established.

Psychoanalytic and anthropological clinical accounts further illuminate specific tendencies in early mother-son relationships.[42] Bibring argues that the decline of the husband's presence in the home has resulted in a wife "as much in need of a husband as the son is of a father."[43] This wife is likely to turn her affection and interest to the next obvious male—her son—and to become particularly seductive toward him. Just as the father is often not enough present to prevent or break up the mother-daughter boundary confusion, he is also not available to prevent either his wife's seductiveness or his son's growing reciprocated incestuous impulses. A mother, here, is again experiencing her son as a definite other—an opposite-gendered and -sexed other. Her emotional investments and conflicts, given her socialization around issues of gender and sex and membership in a sexist society, make this experience of him particularly strong. The son's solution, moreover, emphasizes differentiation buttressed by heavy emotional investment. He projects his own fears and desires onto his mother, whose behavior he then gives that much more significance and weight.

Slater's account of Greek mother-son relationships in the Classical period,[44] read into his later work on contemporary American society, gives us further insight into the dynamics Bibring discusses.[45] Greek marriages, Slater suggests, were characterized by a weak marital bond, and the society was ridden with sex antagonism and masculine fear and devaluation of mature women. Wives were isolated in their marital homes with children. In reaction, mothers reproduced in their own sons the same masculine fears and behaviors that their husbands and the men in their society had. They produced in these sons a precarious and vulnerable masculinity and sense of differentiation by alternating sexual praise and seductive behavior with hostile deflation, ridicule, and intrusive definitions of their sons' intrapsychic situation. Like the maternal treatment Bibring discusses, this treatment kept sons dependent on their mothers for a sense of self-sufficiency and self-esteem. At the same time, it emphasized these sons' sexuality and sexual difference, and encouraged participation in a heavily sexualized relationship in boys who had not resolved early issues of individuation and the establishment of ego boundaries.[46]

Bibring's and Slater's work implies that in societies like ours, which are male-dominated but have relatively father-absent families and little paternal participation in family life and child care, masculinity and sexual difference ("oedipal" issues) become intertwined with separation-individuation ("preoedipal") issues almost from the beginning of a boy's life.[47] This conclusion receives confirmation from Whiting's cross-cultural analyses of patrilocal societies with sleeping arrangements in which children sleep exclusively with their mothers during their first two years (and husband/fathers sleep elsewhere) and postpartum sex taboos.[48] Such societies are usually characterized by a general pattern of sex segregation and sex antagonism—again, a (perhaps) extreme form of the sex-gender arrangements in modern society.

Such arrangements create difficulties for the development of a sense of masculinity in boys. Although their account is allegedly about feminine role identification, Whiting and his colleagues are in fact talking about the period of early infancy. In some formulations of the problem, it is clear that they are concerned with fundamental feelings of dependence, overwhelming attachment, and merging with the mother, developed by a son during the intense and exclusive early years, that he feels he must overcome in order to attain independence and a masculine self-identification.[49] They suggest further that an explicitly sexual relationship between mother and son may exist. Citing "clinical evidence from women in our own society suggesting that nursing is sexually gratifying to some women at least,"[50] and informant reports in one society with postpartum sex taboo and mother-infant sleeping arrangements that mothers had no desire for sex as long as they were nursing, they suggest that "it is possible that the mother obtains some substitute sexual gratification from nursing and caring for her infant."[51]

Cross-cultural accounts of father-absence and mother-infant sleeping arrangements do not mention the effects of extreme father-absence and antagonism between the sexes on mother-daughter relationships or on female development.[52] It may well be that the kind of mother-daughter boundary confusion and overidentification I have discussed here is the answer. Slater suggests that it is not simply sleeping arrangements but maternal ambivalence and inconsistent behavior toward sons which lead to the results Whiting describes. Without this ambivalence and seductiveness, mother-infant sleeping arrangements may not produce conflict and dependency. Alternatively, it may be that dependency in girls is not, in the patriarchal cultural case, an obstacle to the successful attainment of femininity.

I conclude, from the evidence in Bibring's, Slater's and Whiting's accounts, that a mother, of a different gender from her son and deprived of adult emotional, social, and physical contact with men (and often without any supportive adult contact at all), may push her son out of his preoedipal relationship to her into an oedipally toned relationship defined by its sexuality and gender distinction. Her son's maleness and oppositeness as a sexual other become important, even while his being an infant remains important as well. Because of this, sons (men) come to have different kinds of preoedipally engendered problems than daughters (women). Greenacre points to these in her discussion of the genesis of "perversions" and especially of fetishism, which, according to psychoanalysts, are predominantly masculine phenomena.[53]

Greenacre suggests that fetishes,[54] and other perversions as well, serve to deny (on an unconscious level usually) that women do not have penises: "The phallic woman [is a] ubiquitous fantasy in perversions."[55] The reason the fetishist needs to deny the existence of different genitalia than his own is that his sense of his own genital body identity is not firm. Being presented with different genitalia, therefore, he feels threatened and potentially castrated himself. Greenacre argues that fetishism is a result of conflict centering on issues of separation and individuation in the early years. It results from boundary confusion and a lack of sense of self firmly distinguished from his mother, leading him to experience (again, all this is probably not conscious) as his own what he takes to be the castration of first his mother and then women in general.

Greenacre's account points to gender differences surrounding early issues of differentiation and individuation. Even while primary separateness is being established in boys, issues of masculinity and conflicts around genital differences are important. Her account also leads me to conclude that the early period is sexualized for boys in a way that it is not for girls, that phallic-masculine issues become intertwined with supposedly nongender-differentiated object-relational and ego issues concerning of a sense of separate self.

According to Greenacre and Herman Roiphe, children of both genders go through a phase during their second year when their genitals become important as part of their developing body self and their developing gender identity.[56] Conflictual object-relations concerning these issues can lead a child to focus anxiety and emotion on genital difference—to develop castration anxiety or penis envy. Greenacre's account indicates, however, that this aspect of individuation is more important and conflictual for men. That the early mother-son relationship is likely to emphasize phallic oedipal issues along with preoedipal individuation issues explains this difference. It is another instance in which a supposedly nongender-differentiated process has different meanings for boys and girls.[57]

In a society like ours, in which mothers have exclusive care for infants and are isolated from other adults, in which there is physical and social separation of men/fathers from women/mothers and children, and institutionalized male dominance, a mother may impose her reactions to this situation on her son, and confuse her relationship to him as an infant with a sexualized relationship to him as a male.[58] It is precisely such a situation which accounts for the early entrance into the oedipus situation on the part of boys in our society.

CONCLUSIONS

The clinical and cultural examples I have discussed all point to the conclusion that preoedipal experiences of girls and boys differ. The girl's preoedipal mother-love and preoccupation with preoedipal issues are prolonged in a way that they are not for the boy. With the exception of Whiting's cross-cultural analysis, all the examples I cite are cases which their authors have taken to be noteworthy for their "abnormality" or "pathology." However, the extent of such pathology varies (from preoccupation to mild neurosis to psychosis). More important, there is systematic variation in the form it takes depending on whether a person is female or male—on whether we are talking about mother-daughter or mother-son relationships. In all cases the pathology reflects, in exaggerated form, differences in what are in fact normal tendencies. The cases give us, as Freud suggests about neurosis in general, insight into what we would otherwise miss just because it is subtle, typical, and familiar. These cases, then, point to typical gender differences in the preoedipal period, differences that are a product of the asymmetrical organization of parenting which founds our family structure.

Because they are the same gender as their daughters and have been girls, mothers of daughters tend not to experience these infant daughters as separate from them in the same way as do mothers of infant sons. In both cases, a mother is likely to experience a sense of oneness and continuity with her infant. However, this sense is stronger and lasts longer, vìs-à-vis daughters. Primary identification and symbiosis with daughters tend to be stronger and cathexis of daughters is more likely to retain and emphasize narcissistic elements, that is, to be based on experiencing a daughter as an extension or double of a mother herself, with cathexis of the daughter as a sexual other usually remaining a weaker, less significant theme.

Other accounts also suggest that mothers normally identify more with daughters and experience them as less separate. Signe Hammer's book, *Daughters and Mothers: Mothers and Daughters,* based on interviews with over seventy-five mothers, daughters, and grandmothers, describes how issues of primary identification, oneness, and separateness follow mother-daughter pairs from a daughter's earliest infancy until she is well into being a mother or even grandmother herself:

> Most of the daughters in this book have received enough support from their mothers to emerge from the stage of complete symbiosis in early infancy. But for the vast majority of mothers and daughters, this emergence remains only partial. At some level mothers and daughters tend to remain emotionally bound up with each other in what might be called a semisymbiotic relationship, in which neither ever quite sees herself or the other as a separate person.[59]

Hammer's study is certainly confirmed by my own discussions with a number of mothers of daughters and sons, first in a women's group devoted to the discussion and analysis of mother-daughter relationships in particular and family relation-ships in general, and later with individual acquaintances. Finally, the resurfacing and prevalence of preoedipal mother-daughter issues in adolescence (anxiety, intense and exclusive attachment, orality and food, maternal control of a daugh-ter's body, primary identification) provide clinical verification of the claim that elements of the preoedipal mother-daughter relationship are maintained and pro-longed in both maternal and filial psyche.[60]

Because they are of different gender than their sons, by contrast, mothers experience their sons as a male opposite. Their cathexis of sons is more likely to consist from early on in an object cathexis of a sexual other, perhaps in addition to narcissistic components. Sons tend to be experienced as differentiated from their mothers, and mothers push this differentiation (even while retaining, in some cases, a kind of intrusive controlling power over their sons). Maternal be-havior, at the same time, tends to help propel sons into a sexualized, genitally toned relationship, which in its turn draws the son into triangular conflicts.

Early psychoanalytic findings about the special importance of the preoedipal mother-daughter relationship describe the first stage of a general process in which separation and individuation remain particularly female developmental issues. The cases I describe suggest that there is a tendency in women toward boundary confusion and a lack of sense of separateness from the world. Most women do develop ego boundaries and a sense of separate self. However, wom-en's ego and object-relational issues are concerned with this tendency on one level (of potential conflict, of experience of object-relations), even as on another level (in the formation of ego boundaries and the development of a separate identity) the issues are resolved.

That these issues become more important for girls than for boys is a product of children of both genders growing up in families where women, who have a greater sense of sameness with daughters than sons, perform primary parenting functions.[61] As long as women mother, we can expect that a girl's preoedipal period will be longer than that of a boy and that women, more than men, will be more open to and preoccupied with those very relational issues that go into moth-ering—feelings of primary identification, lack of separateness or differentiation, ego and body-ego boundary issues and primary love not under the sway of the reality principle. A girl does not simply identify with her mother or want to be like her mother. Rather, mother and daughter maintain elements of their primary relationship which means they will feel alike in fundamental ways. Object-relations and conflicts in the oedipal period build upon this preoedipal base.

NOTES

1. See, for example, Roy Schafer, 1974, "Problems in Freud's Psychology of Women," *Journal of the American Psychoanalytic Association,* 22, #3, pp. 459–485; Wil-liam H. Masters and Virginia E. Johnson, 1966, *Human Sexual Response;* Mary Jane Sher-fey, 1966, "The Evolution and Nature of Female Sexuality in Relation to Psychoanalytic Theory," *Journal of the American Psychoanalytic Association,* 14, #1, pp. 28–128.

2. My reading of this account, however, as a description and interpretation of family structure and its effects in male-dominant industrial capitalist society would not be ac-cepted by all psychoanalysts.

3. Freud, 1924, "The Dissolution of the Oedipus Complex," *SE,* vol. 19, pp. 172–179; Freud, 1933, *New Introductory Lectures on Psychoanalysis.*

4. Freud, 1925, "Some Psychical Consequences."

5. Ibid., p. 252.

6. Freud is especially interested in the implication of this difference for feminine superego formation, but his account is not directly relevant here. Further on I examine the biases inherent in his formulation and some of its logical and clinical contradictions.

7. Jeanne Lampl-de Groot, 1927, "The Evolution of the Oeidpus Complex in Women," in Fliess, ed., *The Psychoanalytic Reader,* pp. 180–194.

8. Freud, 1931, "Female Sexuality," *SE,* vol. 21, pp. 223–243; see also Freud, 1933, *New Introductory Lectures.*

9. Since that time, major contributions to the theory of development have been concerned much more with the preoedipal years—the early mother-infant relationship and early infantile development. Few analysts now hold that the oedipus complex is the *nucleus* of neurosis, though they might say it contributes to its final *form.*

10. Freud, 1933, *New Introductory Lectures,* and Brunswick, 1940, "The Preoedipal Phase."

11. Helene Deutsch, 1944, *Psychology of Women.*

12. Freud, 1933, *New Introductory Lectures,* p. 237.

13. Rather, the studies they report produce such inconsistent findings that one could support almost any hypothesis about gender differences in treatment by selective references.

14. Maccoby and Jacklin, 1974, *The Psychology of Sex Differences.*

15. On many measures, however, they find that where studies do report a gender difference, it tends to be in the same direction. For instance, where mothers do talk more to children of one gender, it turns out to be to girls; where they touch, hold, or spend more time feeding, it tends to be boys.

16. The arousal of gross motor behavior, punishment, and pressure against what is thought to be gender-inappropriate behavior all tend to happen more to boys. I am wary of this seemingly scientific investigation. The message of Maccoby and Jacklin's book is that one cannot find any consistent gender differences anywhere if one looks at the "hard scientific facts." As support against biological arguments for gender differences, these findings may do the trick. But I was left feeling a little as if a magic disappearing trick had been performed. All the experiences of being manipulated, channeled, and restricted which women and men have been commenting on, and which they have felt deeply and continuously, were suddenly figments of our imagination.

17. Eleanor Galenson, 1976, "Scientific Proceedings—Panel Reports," Panels on the Psychology of Women, Annual Meeting of the American Psychoanalytic Association, 1974. *Journal of the American Psychoanalytic Association,* 24, #1, p. 159.

18. Not to give up on the academic psychology findings completely, we know that some forms of similar maternal behavior may produce different effects on sons and daughters. For instance, Kagan and Freeman and Crandall report that maternal criticism and lack of nurturance correlate with intellectual achievement in girls but the opposite behavior does in boys. Maternal overprotection and affection predict later conformity in boys, whereas conformity in girls is predicted by excessive severity of discipline and restrictiveness. Therefore, the similarity in maternal behavior which Maccoby and Jacklin report may not have similar effects on feminine and masculine development.

19. Jerome Kagan and Marion Freeman, 1963, "Relation of Childhood Intelligence, Maternal Behaviors and Social Class to Behavior During Adolescence," *Child Development,* 36, pp. 899–911, and Virginia C. Crandall, 1972, "The Fels Study; Some Contributions to Personality Development and Achievement in Childhood and Adulthood," *Seminars in Psychiatry,* 4, 4, pp. 383–397.

20. In what follows, I rely on extensive accounting and quoting. This is necessary because a simple assertion of the distinctions that I wish to demonstrate would not be persuasive without the clinical illustrations.

21. Robert Fliess, 1961, *Ego and Body Ego;* Klaus Angel, 1967, "On Symbiosis and Pseudosymbiosis," *Journal of the American Psychoanalytic Association*, 15, #2, pp. 294–316; Enid Balint, 1963, "On Being Empty of Oneself," *International Journal of Psycho-Analysis*, 44, #4, pp. 470–480; Melitta Sperling, 1950, "Children's Interpretation and Reaction to the Unconscious of Their Mothers," *International Journal of Psycho-Analysis*, 31, pp. 36–41; C. Olden, 1958, "Notes on Empathy"; and Dorothy Burlingham, 1967, "Empathy Between Infant and Mother," *Journal of the American Psychoanalytic Association*, 15, pp. 764–780.

22. Robert Fliess, 1961, *Ego and Body Ego*.

23. Ibid., p. 49.

24. Ibid., p. 48.

25. For a more accessible example of what Fliess describes—again, a mother-daughter case—see Flora Schreiber, 1973, *Sybil*.

26. Enid Balint, 1963, "On Being Empty."

27. Ibid., p. 478.

28. Ibid., p. 476.

29. Christine Olden, 1958, "Notes on Empathy."

30. Ibid., p. 505.

31. The mothers were, in Fliess's terms, hypersymbiotic but not asymbiotic.

32. Ibid.

33. Ibid., p. 512.

34. Klaus Angel, 1967, "On Symbiosis."

35. Ibid., p. 315.

36. Dorothy Burlingham, 1967, "Empathy Between Infant."

37. Melitta Sperling, 1950, "Children's Interpretation."

38. It is hard to substantiate this impression without repeating all of the cases involved. I report them, however, because there are few such cases in the literature. I encourage the most committed (or skeptical) to read them.

39. Ann, described by Sperling.

40. In one case, for instance, a son (Paul, described by Sperling) has become a substitute for the mother's brother, toward whom she had and continues to have very complicated feelings.

41. Dorothy Burlingham, 1967, "Empathy Between Infant," p. 779.

42. Grete Bibring, 1953, "On the 'Passing of the Oedipus Complex' in a Matriarchal Family Setting," in R. M. Loewenstein, ed., *Drives, Affects, and Behavior: Essays in Honor of Marie Bonaparte*, pp. 278–284; Philip E. Slater, 1968, *The Glory of Hera;* John W. M. Whiting, 1959, "Sorcery, Sin and the Superego: A Cross-Cultural Study of Some Mechanisms of Social Control," in Clellan S. Ford, ed., *Cross-Cultural Approaches: Readings in Comparative Research*, pp. 147–168; 1960, "Totem and Taboo—A Re-evaluation," in Jules H. Masserman, ed., *Psychoanalysis and Human Values;* Whiting et al., 1958, "The Function of Male Initiation"; Roger V. Burton and Whiting, 1961, "The Absent Father"; and Phyllis Greenacre, 1968, "Perversions: General Considerations Regarding Their Genetic and Dynamic Background," *Psychoanalytic Study of the Child*, 23, pp. 47–62.

43. Grete Bibring, 1953, "On the 'Passing of the Oedipus Complex,'" p. 281.

44. Philip E. Slater, 1968, *The Glory of Hera*, 1970, *The Pursuit of Loneliness*, 1974, *Earthwalk*.

45. Slater discusses the psychic outcome of structural features of the family and the organization and ideology of gender not unique to Greek society but very much present in our own. His later works do not present his analysis in such full detail, though they

assume that it is very much applicable to American society. Therefore, I rely in what follows on the analysis of Greece to shed light on our contemporary situation.

46. This combination of the blurring of generational boundaries between mother and son, and the elevation of the son to a role as masculine partner, or opposite, to the mother, replicates Lidz's description of schizophrenogenic family structure and practice for boys. (Theodore Lidz, Stephen Fieck, and Alice R. Cornelison, 1965, *Schizophrenia and the Family*). Slater in fact suggests that maternal treatment of sons in Greece was schizophren- ogenic. He points out that we have no record of the actual incidence of madness in ancient Greek society, but that Greek culture was dominated by maternally caused madness: "No other mythology with which I am familiar contains so many explicitly designated instances of madness. . . . The most striking fact is that of all the clear instances of madness delib- erately produced in one being by another, none can be said to be caused by a truly mas- culine or paternal agent. Most are afflicted by goddesses, and the remainder by the effeminate Dionysus, himself a previous victim at the hands of Hera. . . . Nor is the relationship between the sex of an agent and the sex of a victim a random one: in the overwhelming majority of cases madness is induced in persons of the opposite sex" (Philip E. Slater, 1968, *The Glory of Hera*).

47. Slater does not restrict his discussion to the period of the early mother-son rela- tionship. But all the relational and ego problems he discusses, and his use of the label "oral-narcissistic dilemma" to summarize these, point to early mother-infant issues: myths concerned with birth, with maternal attacks on the infant in the womb or on the neonate, with oral reincorporation by the mother; or with the maternal lack of reality principle vis- à-vis her son.

48. See John Whiting, 1959, "Sorcery, Sin," and 1960, "Totem and Taboo"; Whiting et al., 1958, "The Function of Male Initiation"; and Burton and Whiting, 1961, "The Absent Father."

49. For example, Whiting et al., 1958, "The Function of Male Initiation."

50. Ibid., p. 362.

51. John Whiting, 1959, "Sorcery, Sin," p. 150.

52. In fact, their omission provided the original impetus for my study here.

53. Phyllis Greenacre, 1968, "Perversions."

54. I realize that this kind of claim verges on the incredible to those unpersuaded by psychoanalytic theory. It is certainly the area in psychoanalytic theory in which I feel least comfortable, but in this case Greenacre's account is persuasive and illuminating.

55. Ibid., p. 47.

56. Ibid., and Herman Roiphe, 1968, "On an Early Genital Phase: With an Adden- dum on Genesis," *Psychoanalytic Study of the Child*, 23, pp. 348–365.

57. As noted previously, children of both genders go through a symbiotic phase of unity, primary identification, and mutual empathy with their mother, and then go through a period of differentiation from her—but these issues remain more central for women.

58. Barbara Deck (personal communication) suggests that whether the boy is a child or an adult makes a big difference to his mother. As a little man with a penis, he excites her; however, in order for her fondling and sexualized treatment not to produce conscious guilt, he must remain a neuter baby. This ambivalence does not arise in the case of a girl baby, who is "just a baby" or at most a "baby mother/self." She is not an *other*, like a "baby husband" or a "baby father."

59. Signe Hammer, 1975, *Daughters and Mothers: Mothers and Daughters*.

60. See Peter Blos, 1957, *On Adolescence: A Psychoanalytic Interpretation;* Deutsch, 1944, *Psychology of Women;* Kata Levy, 1960, "Simultaneous Analysis of a Mother and Her Ado- lescent Daughter: The Mother's Contribution to the Loosening of the Infantile Object Tie," *Psychoanalytic Study of the Child*, 15, pp. 378–391; Marjorie P. Sprince, 1962, "The

Development of a Preoedipal Partnership Between an Adolescent Girl and Her Mother," *Psychoanalytic Study of the Child*, 17, pp. 418–450.

61. I must admit to fudging here about the contributory effect in all of this of a mother's sexual orientation—whether she is heterosexual or lesbian. Given a female gender identity, she is "the same as" her daughter and "different from" her son, but part of what I am talking about also presumes a different kind of cathexis of daughter and son deriving from her heterosexuality.

SELECTED BIBLIOGRAPHY

ANGEL, KLAUS, 1967, "On Symbiosis and Pseudosymbiosis," *Journal of the American Psychoanalytic Association*, 15, #2, pp. 294–316.

BALINT, ENID, 1963, "On Being Empty of Oneself," *International Journal of Psycho-Analysis*, 44, #4, 470–480.

BIBRING, GRETE, 1953, "On the 'Passing of the Oedipus Complex' in a Matriarchal Family Setting," pp. 278–284 in Rudolph M. Loewenstein, ed., *Drives, Affects, and Behavior: Essays in Honor of Marie Bonaparte*. New York, International Universities Press.

BLOS, PETER, 1957, "Preoedipal Factors in the Etiology of Female Delinquency," *Psychoanalytic Study of the Child*, 12, pp. 229–249.

BURLINGHAM, DOROTHY, 1967, "Empathy Between Infant and Mother," *Journal of the American Psychoanalytic Association*, 15, pp. 764–780.

BURTON, ROGER V., AND JOHN W. M. WHITING, 1961, "The Absent Father and Cross-Sex Identity," *Merrill-Palmer Quarterly of Behavior and Development*, 7, #2, 1961, pp. 85–95.

CRANDALL, VIRGINIA C., 1972, "The Fels Study: Some Contributions to Personality Development and Achievement in Childhood and Adulthood," *Seminars in Psychiatry*, 4, #4, pp. 383–397.

DEUTSCH, HELENE, 1944 and 1945, *Psychology of Women*, vols. 1 and 2. New York, Grune & Stratton.

FLIESS, ROBERT, 1961, *Ego and Body Ego: Contributions to Their Psychoanalytic Psychology*. New York, International Universities Press, 1970.

FREUD, SIGMUND, 1924, "The Dissolution of the Oedipus Complex," *SE*, vol. 19, pp. 172–179.

———. 1925, "Some Psychical Consequences of the Anatomical Distinction Between the Sexes," *SE*, vol. 19, pp. 243–258.

———. 1931, "Female Sexuality," *SE*, vol. 21, pp. 223–243.

———. 1933, *New Introductory Lectures on Psychoanalysis, SE*, vol. 22, pp. 3–182.

GALENSON, ELEANOR, 1976, "Scientific Proceedings—Panel Reports," Panels on the Psychology of Women, Annual Meeting of the American Psychoanalytic Association, 1974. *Journal of the American Psychoanalytic Association*, 24, #1, pp. 141–160.

GREENACRE, PHYLLIS, 1968, "Perversions: General Considerations Regarding Their Genetic and Dynamic Background," *Psychoanalytic Study of the Child*, 23, pp. 47–62.

HAMMER, SIGNE, 1975, *Daughters and Mothers: Mothers and Daughters*. New York, Quadrangle, New York Times Book Co.

KAGAN, JEROME, AND MARION FREEMAN, 1963, "Relation of Childhood Intelligence, Maternal Behaviors, and Social Class to Behavior During Adolescence," *Child Development*, 36, pp. 899–911.

LAMPL-DE GROOT, JEANNE, 1927, "The Evolution of the Oedipus Complex in Women," pp. 180–194 in Robert Fliess, ed., 1969, *The Psychoanalytic Reader: An Anthology of Essential Papers with Critical Introductions*. New York, International Universities Press.

LEVY, KATA, 1960, "Simultaneous Analysis of a Mother and Her Adolescent Daughter: The Mother's Contribution to the Loosening of the Infantile Object Tie," *Psychoanalytic Study of the Child*, 15, pp. 378–391.

LIDZ, THEODORE, STEPHEN FLECK, AND ALICE R. CORNELISON, 1965, *Schizophrenia and the Family*. New York, International Universities Press.

MACCOBY, ELEANOR, AND CAROL JACKLIN, 1974, *The Psychology of Sex Differences*. Stanford, Stanford University Press.

MASTERS, WILLIAM H., AND VIRGINIA E. JOHNSON, 1966, *Human Sexual Response*. Boston, Little, Brown.

OLDEN, CHRISTINE, 1958, "Notes on the Development of Empathy," *Psychoanalytic Study of the Child*, 13, pp. 505–518.

ROIPHE, HERMAN, 1968, "On an Early Genital Phase: With an Addendum on Genesis," *Psychoanalytic Study of the Child*, 23, pp. 348–365.

SCHAFER, ROY, 1974, "Problems in Freud's Psychology of Women," *Journal of the American Psychoanalytic Association*, 22, #3, pp. 459–485.

SCHREIBER, FLORA RHETA, 1973, *Sybil*. New York, Warner Books.

SHERFEY, MARY JANE, 1966, "The Evolution and Nature of Female Sexuality in Relation to Psychoanalytic Theory," *Journal of the American Psychoanalytic Association*, 14, #1, pp. 28–128.

SLATER, PHILIP E., 1968, *The Glory of Hera: Greek Mythology and the Greek Family*. Boston, Beacon Press.

——. 1970, *The Pursuit of Loneliness*. Boston, Beacon Press.

SPERLING, MELITTA, 1950, "Children's Interpretation and Reaction to the Unconscious of Their Mothers," *International Journal of Psycho-Analysis*, 31, pp. 36–41.

SPRINCE, MARJORIE P., 1962, "The Development of a Preoedipal Partnership Between an Adolescent Girl and Her Mother," *Psychoanalytic Study of the Child*, 17, pp. 418–450.

WHITING, JOHN W. M., 1959, "Sorcery, Sin and the Superego: A Cross-Cultural Study of Some Mechanisms of Social Control," pp. 147–168 in Clellan S. Ford, ed., 1967, *Cross-Cultural Approaches: Readings in Comparative Research*, New Haven, Human Relations Area Files.

——. 1960, "Totem and Taboo—A Re-evaluation," in Jules H. Masserman, ed., *Psychoanalysis and Human Values*. New York, Grune and Stratton.

WHITING, JOHN W. M., RICHARD KLUCKHOHN, AND ALBERT ANTHONY, 1958, "The Function of Male Initiation Rites at Puberty," in Eleanor E. Maccoby, T. M. Newcomb, and E. L. Hartley, eds., *Readings in Social Psychology*. New York, Holt.

judith v. jordan

EMPATHY AND SELF BOUNDARIES

Developmental and clinical theory have generally emphasized the growth of the autonomous, individuated self in such a way that early developmental milestones are typically characterized by greater separation from mother, increasing sense of boundedness, self-control, self as origin of action and intention, and increasing use of logical, abstract thought. This particular bias, if we can call it that, likely derives from several influences: (1) The modeling of psychology as a science on Newtonian physics, which emphasized notions of discrete, separate entities acting on each other in measurable ways; (2) the emphasis in Western, democratic countries on the sanctity and freedom of the individual; (3) a culture that perceives its task as a weaning of the helpless, dependent infant toward greater self-sufficiency and independence (unlike Japanese culture, which views the infant as initially independent, in need of shaping toward dependency); and (4) a study of the psyche that grew from an understanding of pathology in which the ego was seen as needing to protect itself from assaults by both internal impulses and external demands. Freud commented that "protection against stimuli is an almost more important function for the living organism than reception of stimuli" (Freud, S., 1920, p. 27). In traditional psychoanalytic theory, the individual is seen as growing from an undifferentiated, then embedded and symbiotic phase into an individuated, separate state. Mahler's (Mahler, Pine, & Bergman, 1975) theory of separation-individuation details the hypothetical normal development of an increasingly individuated and separate self. Early studies of schizophrenia (Freeman, Cameron, & McKhie, 1958), which emphasized the pathological disruption of boundaries between self and other in psychotic decompensations, reinforced the notion that healthier, more mature modes of functioning were predicated on greater separation of self and other. Landis points out in his review of ego boundary research that "in most discussion in the literature, firmer boundaries, even extremely impermeable ones, are seen as positive and adaptive, and 'open,' 'weak' boundaries are usually viewed as indications of serious defect" (Landis, 1970, p 17).

George Klein (1976) was one of the first analytic theorists to point to an imbalance in much of self theory. He posited two major lines of development of the self: "One is an autonomous unit, distinct from others as a locus of action and decision. The second aspect is one's self construed as a necessary part of a unit transcending one's autonomous actions. 'We' identities are also part of the self. Like any biological 'organ' or 'part,' the organism is . . . and must feel itself to be . . . both separate and a part of an entity beyond itself" (Klein, 1976, p. 178). More recently, systems theorists have applied the ideas of "a set of interacting units with relationships among them" to development (Miller, 1978, p. 16). Stern (1980) has referred to the "self with the other," Stechler and Kaplan (1980) have written about the coexistence of affiliative and autonomous tendencies, Pollack (1982) has studied "we-ness" in children and their parents, Kohut (1982), Miller (1976), and Surrey (1983) have posited the special importance of what might be called a "relational self" in women. Concomitantly, Newtonian physics has given way to the "new physics" and quantum theory, which emphasizes flow, waves, and interconnections. Instead of emphasis on static structure and discrete, bounded objects existing separately in space, then, we are seeing a growing appreciation of process, relationship, and interaction. In developmental and clinical theory, this is mirrored in growing emphasis on the development of interpersonal connection and relationship rather than on the self as developing away from, or independent of, relationship. Too often, however, relational issues have been phrased in regressive terms, such as *merged, symbiotic,* or *undifferentiated,* suggesting that intense interpersonal connection involves a movement into more primitive functioning. If there is not appreciation for the development of more complex, differentiated patterns of connection and intimacy, then the relational aspect of the definition of self will continue to be inadequately understood and devalued.

It is against this backdrop of developmental bias that I find the study of empathy most stimulating and relevant. Empathy is central to an understanding of that aspect of the self which involves we-ness, transcendence of the separate, disconnected self. It is, in fact, the process through which one's experienced sense of basic connection and similarity to other humans is established. Heinz Kohut has described empathy as "a fundamental mode of human relatedness, the recognition of the self in the other; it is the accepting, confirming and understanding human echo" (Kohut, 1978, pp. 704–705). Without empathy, there is no intimacy, no real attainment of an appreciation of the paradox of separateness within connection.

Perhaps in part because of the tendency to see less autonomous functioning as regressive, or merely because of the relative lack of attention to the developmental line of the relational self, empathy has often been construed as a mysterious, contagion-like, and primitive phenomenon or dismissed as a vague and unknowable subjective state. Empathy, however, is a complex process, relying on a high level of ego development and ego strength and, in fact, may provide a good index of both of these. Kohut (1959) has referred to empathy as "vicarious introspection," and Schafer has spoken of generative empathy as "the inner experience of sharing in and comprehending the momentary psychological state of another person" (Schafer, 1959, p. 345). Schafer emphasizes the point that this knowing is approximate, "based to a great extent on remembered, corresponding, affective states of one's own" (1959, p. 347). Again, this points to the affective-cognitive integration. Greenson (1960, p. 418) refers to "emotional knowing," and Fliess (1942, p. 213) writes of "trial identification."

There are actually several components to empathy as I understand it. In order to empathize, one must have a well-differentiated sense of self in addition to an appreciation of and sensitivity to the differentness as well as sameness of the other. Empathy always involves surrender to feelings and active cognitive structuring; in order for empathy to occur, self boundaries must be flexible. Experientially, empathy begins with some general motivation for interpersonal relatedness that allows the perception of the other's affective cues (both verbal and nonverbal) followed by surrender to affective arousal in oneself. This involves temporary identification with the other's state, during which one is aware that the source of the affect is in the other. In the final resolution period, the affect subsides and one's self feels more separate; therapeutically, the final step involves making use of this experience to help the patient understand his or her inner world better.

For empathy to be effective, there must be a balance of affective and cognitive, subjective and objective, active and passive. Self boundary flexibility is important, since there is an "as if," trying-out quality to the experience, whereby one places one's self in the other's shoes or looks through the other's eyes. There is a momentary overlap between self and other representations as distinctions between self and other blur experientially.

Piaget's (1952) principles of assimilation and accommodation may provide one way to conceptualize what happens in the empathic process. In empathy there is likely a rapid oscillation of accommodation of images of the self to images of the other, and assimilation of the images of the other to the images of the self. As in Piaget's model, these two processes move toward equilibrium, which is never reached in a static, final way. There is a shifting balance, with momentary overlaps or congruence of self and other representations which then differentiate. When assimilation predominates, the self boundaries may be too rigid to allow the other's affective state to have any real impact, leading to lack of understanding of the other's inner state or projection of one's own affects onto the other. On the other hand, if self-representations are fluid or poorly articulated, the imbalance will be in the direction of overreliance on accommodation, in which case one could become lost in the other's experience, possibly causing difficulty in accurately observing or structuring the experience. Without an adequately articulated and relatively constant set of self-representations or self-images, any temporary identification might become a threat to the constancy of the self. On the other hand, self-images that do not allow for a sense of "we-ness" or affective joining with another would also contribute to a sense of self as endangered by the empathic process; for example, empathy would be experienced as a regressive loss of self-distinctiveness.

Because self-representations are not global, but cohere around specific affective experiences, it is possible that self boundaries vis-a-vis certain affects might be more rigid or loose than with others. Similarly, then, empathic attunement can be more highly developed with regard to certain experiences than others. When there is dissociation of affects or less richly developed affective awareness, there is less likelihood of development of both vicarious affective arousal and cognitive appreciation of certain affects in others. Thus empathy cannot be accurately spoken of as a global function. While there may be general factors that influence empathic attunement (e.g., certain interpersonal motivational dispositions, comfort with a wide range of affective arousal, self boundary flexibility), individuals will differ in their empathic responsiveness to different internal states of another. For example, one woman I see in treatment is tremendously empathic vis-a-vis most of her husband's psychological states. She is someone, however, who has never been allowed to know her own anger, using reaction formation to keep it from awareness. Similarly, when her husband is angry, even when not at her, she is relatively unresponsive, lacking in understanding and distant from his inner state. It is as if a generally empathic approach was lost in this area because of the defense against aggressive impulses that this woman has developed. In my work with couples, it is not an atypical complaint that when the wife gets tearful or particularly affectively charged, the husband either gets uncomfortable and wants to do something to change the situation, or wants to get his wife to do something, while the wife simply wants him to acknowledge her affect and to be with her while she experiences it. It may be that the husband's intolerance of his own tearfulness or sad affect makes it difficult for him to empathize with these feelings in his wife.

An interesting question in the study of the developmental line of empathy arises in the context of the above examples. In part, we may be concerned with the increasing complexity and differentiation of emotional attunement as the individual matures, but it may also be that certain aspects of empathic responsiveness are constricted or lost as the individual develops. McLean (1958) has suggested there is a neural basis in the limbic system for primitive empathic responses. Simner (1971) and Sagi and Hoffman (1976) have demonstrated that 1-to-2-day-old infants cry in response to the distress cry of another infant, clearly not something we could call empathy as we understand it, but a possible precursor to real empathy. According to Hoffman (1978), by 2 or 3 years of age, children are developing a sense that others may have inner states differing from their own and can recognize certain affects in others. Piaget (1928) suggests that conceptual role taking and the decline in egocentrism occur more clearly around 7 to 8 years of age. A study by Dymond, Hughes, and Raabe found that empathy, both social insight and ability to take the role of the other, increases from age 7 to 11; it was also suggested that older children "become more aware of which feelings are 'safe' to recognize and admit and which need 'defenses'" (Dymond, Hughes, & Raabe, 1952, p. 206). It is likely that this is where the sex differences found in empathic ability become salient as well; Hoffman's (1977) review of these studies indicates that males and females tend to be equally able to recognize and label the affective experiences of another person (cognitive awareness) but that females demonstrate generally more vicarious affective responsiveness to another's affect. Women tend to imagine themselves in the other's place more; this does not involve self-other diffusion, since females are as capable of knowing another's inner state even when it is different from their own. It is likely that this sex difference, already present in school-aged children, is augmented in adolescence, as males are taught to act or master rather than "merely feel" in response to affective arousal, while there is more latitude for affective arousal, particularly in the area of distress or vulnerable feelings, for females. A study by Lenrow (1965) found that children who express distress with tears are more apt to respond empathetically to others in distress than brave, noncrying children. Again, this suggests that the broader the range of affective arousal and tolerance of feelings in oneself, the more potential empathic responsiveness may occur to the other. As there is a narrowing of which affects are appropriate for the self, there also may be a curtailment of empathic responsiveness, a loss of the immediate, pressing reactivity to another's inner state.

When we think in terms of self-representations instead of "the self," it becomes clear that to think of self boundaries as a unitary phenomenon may also be misleading. Thus to speak of empathy as a regressive merging suggests that the empathizing individual undergoes a widespread loss of distinctness of self that runs counter to ordinary functioning in which the self is experienced as separate, contained. Even the modification that this is a "temporary identification" (Schafer, 1959) suggests a momentary total surrender; or, as Olden comments, in empathy "the subject temporarily gives up his own ego for that of the object" (Olden, 1953, pp. 112–113). While this points to the temporally limited and reversible quality of empathy, it also perpetuates the error in the sense of seeing the self as *either* distinct and autonomous *or* merged and embedded. It is not possible to experience a sense of feeling connected and affectively joined and at the same time cognitively appreciate one's separateness (Kaplan, 1983)? Different self-representations coexist and can rapidly be activated, each contributing specially to the overall shape of the self, if you will. Klein points to the organizational function of the self as providing continuity, coherence, and integrity. For the 3-year-old dealing with separation as a physical act where one either steps toward or away from the mother, autonomous and affiliative motivations may appear mutually exclusive. To contain both motives, then, might threaten the sense of continuity, coherence, and integrity of the self. And even in adults, there may be occasions when these two functions are incompatible, leading to conflict. However, the two can and do coexist. Self-representations characterized by clear boundaries and appreciation of differentness from important others can exist alongside self-representations in which there is much self and other overlap. Self-representations are schemata that form through the processes of accommodation and assimilation. As such, they have a responsive, self-modifying quality as well as an active, shaping function. There is an ever-changing balance between separation and inclusion. We can look at one side or the other, but it is the overall process that best captures the ongoing nature of self-definition and awareness.

Just as it has been suggested that one is either connected or separate, merged or autonomous, there has been a tendency to view affective arousal as involving loss of effective cognitive functioning, that is, one is either emotional or rational. Empathy, as an affective experience of joining with the other, then, has been thought of as a more primitive mode of functioning or knowing the other. Several concrete examples of empathy elucidate some of the complexity of the empathic process. The first example involves a comparison of two mothers feeding a 1½-year-old child. The first mother is watching TV as she sits by her child and mixes the cereal. She more or less shovels the food in, with little eye contact or attention to the child. Sometimes the baby's mouth is still full when the next spoonful comes at him; sometimes he has already swallowed. There is very little affective response to the baby's reactions on the mother's part. There is little or no accommodation of the mother to the infant, virtually no empathic involvement. The second mother sits across from her baby, with good eye contact and occasional physical contact. As she moves the spoon toward the baby's mouth, one can see her own head begin to lift slightly and her mouth will open in anticipation, often as the child's mouth opens, but sometimes before. If some of the food dribbles out, the mother lifts the food back toward the child's mouth and opens her own mouth again. It is possible that what we are seeing is motor mimicry, in which the mother unconsciously imitates the child's facial movements, or a complicated interactional process in which the mother actually provides cues to the baby to engage in a mirroring interaction. The mother is perfectly aware she is not eating, but she is also experiencing some identification with the eating child; she is cognitively, affectively, and motorically aroused and interacting with the child at a level that involves some overlap of boundaries. She is simultaneously aware of separateness and joined with her child. Her identification with the child in part allows greater accommodation to the special needs of the child. In this case, then, greater overlap of self-other representations and identification lead to a clearer and sharper appreciation of the separate state of the other. This is the paradox of empathy; in the joining process one develops a more articulated and differentiated image of the other and hence responds in a more accurate and specific way, quite the opposite of what regressive merging would lead to.

A detailed examination of an empathic moment in a therapy session might shed further light on the quality of affect and self-other representations during this process. A patient is describing to me getting ready for her first prom; as she tells me about her preparations, I find myself feeling, with her, anticipation and excitement . . . a little anxiety. I am listening to the details of her experience, what her dress looks like, her date's name, but the images of her adolescent excitement are blurring now with memories of wearing my first pair of high heels, my first lipstick. In my mind, I see her walk down the stairs I walked down in my high-heeled shoes. There is an oscillation back and forth; she is now in her pink dress, now in my green one. As this occurs, I am also observing my affective state, aware of the process. I am not cognitively confused about who is who, but I feel deeply present and sharing, knowing what she is feeling. I do not get lost in my own reverie, and the images that I examine are a shifting mix of my own memories and the images I have built up over time in working with this patient. I am sensitive to the glow in her face, the expectancy in her posture. Again, using a Piagetian model, I am engaged in a process of assimilating the patient's story into my own memories and constructions, but I am constantly alert to the places where her images and affect become distorted by my own associations and I adjust, or accommodate, my affect and thought to match hers more clearly. It is important that I attend to my affect as well as my thoughts in this process. In an informal survey, therapists indicated they were aware of empathic moments most keenly in therapy because of their own compelling affective arousal ("I found myself feeling like crying," "I felt an urge to yell 'stop it' to the abusive parent being described to me"). To assume that affective arousal necessarily leads to cognitive confusion is to underestimate the capacity for integrated functioning; similarly, to assume that an experience of "we-ness," to borrow George Klein's term, necessarily disrupts the experience of "I-ness," is to fall into polarities of functioning that may not be accurate. Such dichotomizing suggests an overly concrete and rigid definition of boundaries rather than an appreciation of the ongoing adjustments and tensions inherent in the experience of self.

We have already touched on the possibility that the capacity for empathic functioning may be somewhat specific to the affective experience involved; for example, someone might be quite empathically attuned to sadness but not to anger, to self-pride but not to shame. Realizing that empathic attunement is a relative rather than absolute potential, let us look at some broad problems that can arise in empathic capacity. In the renewed interest in empathy in the last decade we have tended to look primarily at the empathic ability of the therapist or at empathy as the psychoanalytic mode of understanding (Kohut, 1959). It is also very important, however, to address the quality of empathy in the people we see in treatment. Here, again, attention to the self boundaries enriches the picture of empathy.

Mr. R. is a 35-year-old architect who came to treatment at the urging of his wife; his rather vague complaint was that he was unhappy in his marriage and in his job. At first glance he is a very attractive, well-built man with finely chiseled features. But Mr. R's boyish good looks have little aliveness. Eye contact is rare, and there is little modulation in his voice; he ruminates a good deal with little affect. Mr. R. was the only child of elderly parents; mother was depressed and father quite obsessive. He grew up in an isolated, constricted household in which feelings were rarely shown and never discussed. Mr. R. has never felt close to anyone. He did not feel angry or sad when he came to therapy; he simply did not feel. In talking about people in his world, Mr. R. rarely appreciated the inner experience of others. In fact, at times he was puzzled greatly by his wife's emotional reactions. Mr. R. clearly lacked a rich affective repertoire, so that when others discussed feelings with him he often had no internal referent for comprehending their experience. Further, he had developed rigid self-definitions. In family therapy, which he attended in addition to individual therapy, he spent much of his time pointing out the ways he differed from others, particularly if they expressed strong feelings. In his marriage he frequently faced the complaint that his wife felt she had no impact on him. In the beginning of treatment Mr. R. was not overly unhappy about his isolation, but in his second year he has begun to speak of a deep sense of loneliness. On occasion he has cried about the sadness of his childhood; and he has expressed some understanding of others' feeling states; and eye contact has increased. His family therapist reports that although his difficulty in listening is still a source of frustration for other family members, Mr. R. is more tuned in to others and more accurate in his reading of their feeling states. In this man we can see the overly rigid self boundaries and the poor tolerance of affect of isolated individuals. Classically lacking in empathy, these individuals cannot relax self boundaries enough to allow the affective flow necessary for empathic connection.

Another source of empathic failure may be the individual who becomes overly stimulated by another's affect. For these individuals the self boundaries may be excessively permeable, and responsiveness to the other's affect may in fact diminish the sense of a separate self. Ms. S. is a 30-year-old housewife who came to therapy because she was in the midst of a divorce and was feeling increasingly depressed and anxious. Complicating the divorce was the fact that her husband was romantically involved with her best friend of the last 10 years. Earlier she had supported her husband's availability to this friend following the death of the friend's fiance, because she "felt so much for her pain and loneliness." Although very upset about the loss of both her husband and her best friend, Ms. S. began to recognize that she had become more aware of herself and her needs since her husband had left home. She notes that now when her husband returns to visit their children, she can identify what probably had been happening in the relationship all along:

"I get smaller and smaller when he's around. It's like his needs and feelings fill up the room. All I know is how he thinks about everything. He gets bigger and bigger and I start feeling his feelings and thoughts; I lose myself and get smaller. I can't hold on to myself or my feelings. The same with her [the friend] when she's around; it's always her thoughts or feelings that I notice. They're both so selfish and I can't even figure out what I feel or think. My whole life has been taking care of other people's feelings so I don't even know my own."

This is not a disturbed woman describing grossly impaired ego boundaries; this is a relatively well-functioning woman whose self boundaries at times may be too permeable in the sense of being too sensitive to the distress of others in such a way that she ceases to act in her own best interest. While Mr. R. initially could not, even with great cognitive elaboration, develop an appreciation of another's inner states so that he might feel less isolated, Ms. S. was unable to prevent herself from responding strongly to distressing affective cues in others. She was unable to maintain a sense of boundedness, and her language paints a vivid picture of the shrinking of the sense of self as she experienced a strong vulnerability to the other's affective state. In both cases we have what might be called faulty empathy related to self boundaries; with Mr. R. we see that overly rigid boundaries and fear of influence by the outside world interferes with empathic attunement, while in Ms. S.'s case self boundaries did not adequately protect her in the sense of helping her act on her own behalf. While at times the permeability of self boundaries was not adaptive for Ms. S. and in therapy she developed more control over her responsiveness to others' affective distress, it should also be noted that this woman had a vital, warm sensitivity to people and a genuine concern and involvement with others. She was someone to whom many friends turned when they sought understanding and astute advice. One change for her in therapy might be construed as an increase in empathy directed toward the self.

Self-empathy is a construct that many find troublesome. Schafer has referred to "intrapsychic empathy" (Schafer, 1964, p. 294). Kohut speaks of the "ability of empathizing with ourselves, i.e., with our own past mental organizations" (1959, p. 467), and Blanck and Blanck speak of "retrospective self-empathy" (1974, p. 251). If one takes Schafer's (1968) tripartite definition of self as "agent" (knower, doer), "object," and "locus," or if one thinks of the conventional division of ego into observing and experiencing ego, this construct may be of some use. The observing, often judging, self can then make empathic contact with some aspect of the self as object. This could occur in the form of having a memory of oneself in which the inner state at that time has not been fully integrated because it was not acceptable. To be able to observe and tolerate the affect of that state in a context of understanding becomes a kind of intrapsychic empathy that actually can lead to lasting structural change in self-representations. Unlike empathy with another, where the self boundaries undergo more temporary alteration and the final accommodation may be slight, with intrapsychic empathy there is more opportunity for enduring change in both the representation of self taken as object and in the observing self. The motivational and attitudinal state of nonjudgment and openness, taking an experience seriously, readiness to experience affect and the cognitive understanding may contribute to important shifts in the inner experience of troublesome self-images. As a therapist, I have often been moved by seeing this experience of self-empathy.

One patient, who was quite identified with her critical, punitive father and spoke of herself in very derogatory terms, one day was giving an extremely unfavorable description of herself as she went off for her first day of school. Every comment seemed to come from the rejecting paternal introject: "I was such an obnoxious little kid. I wanted everyone to pay attention. No wonder my father got so mad." A therapeutic intervention indicating that of course she wanted to feel special as she went out into this new, maybe even scary, part of the world at first did not seem to have any impact. The self-condemnations rolled forth like armored tanks. Later in treatment, when we were looking at the same incident, however, this woman burst into tears and said, "Suddenly I saw myself as the little girl, so scared and uncertain. My heart just went out to her. I could see myself, that little girl, and really see what was happening inside. I feel it now for her . . . the pain. I feel it now for me. I couldn't feel it then. But I understand why I was acting that way." It was not simply that she became more accepting and less punitive vis-a-vis certain self-representations, although that was an important part of it. But she also actually connected with the affect that had been split off in the memory: both the self as object and the experiencing self as modified by this exchange. And the identification with the critical father was altered in the direction of being less punitive and harsh in her self-judgments. As Schafer points out, this is "an aspect of benevolent or loving superego function as well as attentive ego function" (Schafer, 1964, 294).

Another woman I see is in many ways characterized by a richly developed empathy. She came to therapy because of depression, fear of leaving her house, and lack of confidence in social situations. She was somewhat constricted in presenting herself at first and felt she had little of interest to say to anyone. As we explored her relationships, however, it became clear that she was actually quite close to many friends and to her husband. The descriptions of her interactions with her husband in particular suggested that she was very attuned to his inner world, listening in an accepting, nonjudgmental way to his thoughts and feelings and understanding a good deal about his feelings. She demonstrated the same responsiveness with her friends, who appeared to appreciate deeply her ability to listen, understand, and provide insight. The capacity to apply these skills (if we can call them that) to herself, however, was quite lacking. Until the therapy, she did not seem able to take her own inner experience as a serious object for interest and attention; she also was plagued by punitive introjects, so that rather than understanding certain affective experiences, she condemned them in herself. She later described the difference in the attitude she extended to others and the one she extended to herself by noting: "I care for others sometimes like a sheepherder. I watch and notice and pay attention to their distress. It isn't that I'm just totally accepting because sometimes I point out if I think they're off the mark or something, but I put myself in their place and I understand. With myself, though, I used to be like a lion tamer with a bull whip." In the course of therapy she experienced major shifts such that she could bring her very rich skills for empathy to bear on herself as well as on her friends; her depression has shifted dramatically. She has gone back to graduate school, and people have remarked on her confidence and social ease.

This resonates with some of the research and theory building Carol Gilligan has done in which she points to the morality of responsibility and of caretaking among women (Gilligan, 1982); a crucial, sometimes difficult component of this is the ability to bring the sense of responsibility and caring to bear on the self as well as on others. It involves a balance of autoplastic and alloplastic modification in which at times the self-representations are altered in the direction of accommodating to the demands of external reality, including other people, but at other times finding a way to assimilate the external to fit existing schema.

The relative paucity of research on empathy is troubling, although recent developmental studies by Sander (1980), Hoffman (1977, 1978), Demos (1982), and Stern (1980), among others, are beginning to provide us with a far more complex picture of early mother-infant interaction than we had envisioned before. Concurrently, Kohut's emphasis on empathy in the analytic situation has spurred a renewed interest in this topic among clinicians. Recent infant research has dispelled the old image of the infant as existing in a confused, disorganized state, the passive recipient of impinging internal and external stimuli (Stern, 1980; Sander, 1980). And clinical observations of patients and "normal" adults have suggested that the old notion of the autonomous, separate self may exist in epigenetic charts but not in reality. Thus in the infant we see autonomous, active structuring of experience from an early age and early evidence of differentiation, while in the adult we see ongoing need for selfobjects and definition of self in terms of "we-ness" as well as "I-ness." We are, then, beginning to construct new models of self that can encompass both the sense of coherent separateness and meaningful connection as emergent structures throughout the life span. The old lines of movement from fusion to separateness, from domination by drive to secondary process, and from undifferentiation to differentiation are presently being questioned. A major flaw in existing theory has been the lack of elaboration of the developmental lines of connection and relationship; there has been a tendency to resort to either the now questionable model of the fused mother–infant pair or heterosexual genital union to conceptualize intimacy and self–other connectedness. Clearly, a vast and rich array of what Stern would call "self with other" experiences are lost in this model. It has been noted, particularly in understanding female development, that this model is sadly lacking and even distorting; I think as we begin carefully to explore empathy and relational development we will see that the model misrepresents self-experiences of both males and females. We have further juxtaposed connection versus separateness as if they were mutually incompatible, and we have failed to trace the complicated evolution of autonomous functioning in the context of self in relationship. The study of empathy, depending on the balance of cognitive and affective processes, involving overlapping self–other representations, is crucial to the delineation of a developmental model that encompasses the self as separated and the self as part of a relationship structure.

Basch has noted that "reality lies in relationships, not in the elements that make the relationships possible"; "man is best studied as an activity, one delineated at any given time by the relationships in which he is active" (1983, pp. 52–53). Both researchers and clinicians must direct increased attention to the complexities of the self in relationship; this will necessarily involve a better understanding of how self boundaries are formed, maintained, and altered. Empathy, which Kohut called "the resonance of essential human alikeness" (Kohut, 1978, p. 713), is central to the growth of the emergent self as a structure of coherent separateness and meaningful connection.

In summary, this chapter points to the need for new models of self in which the developmental lines of connection and relationship are explored. Empathy, here described as a complex cognitive and affective process, is central to an understanding of the paradox of separateness within connection. Using Piaget's model of assimilation-accommodation, the importance of self boundary flexibility to empathic attunement is discussed. Self-representations, involving overlap of self–other images, are rarely characterized by absolute separations of self and other. In addition to a developmental outline of self boundaries and empathy, patients' problems with empathy are traced to overly rigid self boundaries or excessively permeable boundaries. Self-empathy is introduced as a useful therapeutic construct.

NOTE

This paper was presented at a Stone Center Colloquium in January 1984.

SELECTED BIBLIOGRAPHY

BLANCK, G. & R. (1979). *Ego psychology II: Psychoanalytic developmental psychology.* New York: Columbia University Press.

DYMOND, R., HUGHES, A., & RAABE, V. (1952), Measurable changes in empathy with age. *Journal of Consulting Psychology, 16,* 202–206.

FLIESS, R. (1942). The metapsychology of the analyst. *Psychoanalytic Quarterly, 11,* 211–227.

FREEMAN, T., CAMERON, J., & McGHIE, A. (1958). *Chronic schizophrenia.* New York: International Universities Press.

FREUD, S. (1920). Beyond the pleasure principle. *The Standard Edition, 18.* London: Hogarth.

GILLIGAN, C. (1982). *In a different voice: Psychological theory and women's development.* Cambridge: Harvard University Press.

GREENSON, R. (1960). Empathy and its vicissitudes. *International Journal of Psychoanalysis, 41,* 418–424.

HOFFMAN, M. (1977). Sex differences in empathy and related behaviors. *Psychological Bulletin, 84(4),* 712–722.

———. (1978). Toward a theory of empathic arousal and development. In M. Lewis & L. Rosenblum (Eds.), *The development of affect.* New York: Plenum Press.

KLEIN, G. (1976). *Psychoanalytic theory: An explanation of essentials.* New York: International Universities Press.

KOHUT, H. (1959). Introspection, empathy and psychoanalysis. *Journal of the American Psychoanalytic Association, 7,* 459–483.

———. (1978). The psychoanalyst in the community of scholars. In P. Ornstein (Ed.), *The search for the self: Selected writings of Heinz Kohut,* Vol. 2 (pp. 685–724). New York: International Universities Press.

———. (1983). Selected problems of self psychological theory. In J. Lichtenberg & S. Kaplan (Eds.), *Reflections on self psychology.* Hillsdale, NJ: Analytic Press.

LANDIS, B. (1970). *Ego boundaries.* New York: International Universities Press.

LENROW, P. (1965). Studies of sympathy. In S. S. Tomkins & C. E. Isard (Eds.), *Affect, cognition and personality.* New York: Springer Publishing Co.

MACLEAN, P. (1958). The limbic system with respect to self-preservation and the preservation of the species. *Journal of Nervous and Mental Diseases, 127,* 1–11.

MAHLER, M., PINE, F., & BERMAN, A. (1975). *The psychological birth of the human infant: Symbiosis and individuation.* New York: Basic Books.

MILLER, J. (1978). *Living systems.* New York: McGraw-Hill.

MILLER, J. B. (1976). *Toward a new psychology of women.* Boston: Beacon Press.

OLDEN, C. (1972). On adult empathy with children. *Psychoanalytic Study of the Child, 8,* 11–126.

PIAGET, J. (1928). *Judgment and measuring in the child.* New York: Harcourt Brace.

———. (1952). *The origins of intelligence in children.* New York: W. W. Norton.

POLLACK, S., & GILLIGAN, C. (1982). Images of violence in Thematic Apperception Test stories. *Journal of Personality and Social Psychology, 42*(1), 159–167.

SAGI, A., & HOFFMAN, M. L. (1976). Empathic distress in newborns. *Developmental Psychology, 12,* 175–176.

SANDER, L. (1980). Investigation of the infant and its caretaking environment as a biological system. In S. Greenspan & G. Pollock (Eds.), *The course of life: Vol. I.* Washington, DC: US Government Printing Office.

SCHAFER, R. (1959). Generative empathy in the treatment situation. *Psychoanalytic Quarterly, 28(3),* 342–373.

———. (1964). The clinical analysis of affects. *Journal of the American Psychoanalytic Association, 12,* 275–299.

———. (1968). *Aspects of internalization.* New York: International Universities Press.

STECHLER, G. & KAPLAN, S. (1980). The development of the self: A psychoanalytic perspective. *Psychoanalytic Study of the Child, 35,* 85–106.

STERN, D. (1980, October). The early differentiation of self and other. In *Reflections on self psychology.* Symposium at the Boston Psychoanalytic Society, Boston, Massachusetts.

SURREY, J. (1982). *Survey of eating patterns at Wellesley College.* Unpublished research report, Wellesley College.

jessica benjamin

THE FIRST BOND

Psychoanalysis has shifted its focus since Freud, aiming its sights toward ever earlier phases of development in childhood and infancy. This reorientation has had many repercussions: it has given the mother-child dyad an importance in psychic development rivaling the oedipal triangle, and consequently, it has stimulated a new theoretical construction of individual development. This shift from oedipal to preoedipal—that is, from father to mother—can actually be said to have changed the entire frame of psychoanalytic thinking. Where formerly the psyche was conceived as a force field of drives and defenses, now it became an inner drama of ego and objects (as psychoanalysis terms the mental representation of others). Inevitably, the focus on the ego and its inner object relationships led to an increased interest in the idea of the self, and more generally, in the relationship between self and other. The last twenty-five years have seen a flowering of psychoanalytic theories about the early growth of the self in the relationship with the other.[1]

In this chapter I will show how domination originates in a transformation of the relationship between self and other. Briefly stated, domination and submission result from a breakdown of the necessary tension between self-assertion and mutual recognition that allows self and other to meet as sovereign equals.

Assertion and recognition constitute the poles of a delicate balance. This balance is integral to what is called "differentiation": the individual's development as a self that is aware of its distinctness from others. Yet this balance, and with it the differentiation of self and other, is difficult to sustain.[2] In particular, the need for recognition gives rise to a paradox. Recognition is that response from the other which makes meaningful the feelings, intentions, and actions of the self. It allows the self to realize its agency and authorship in a tangible way. But such recognition can only come from an other whom we, in turn, recognize as a person in his or her own right. This struggle to be recognized by an other, and thus confirm our selves, was shown by Hegel to form the core of relationships of domination. But what Hegel formulated at the level of philosophical abstraction can also be discussed in terms of what we now know about the psychological development of the infant. In this chapter we will follow the course of recognition in the earliest encounters of the self with the nurturing other (or others), and see how the inability to sustain paradox in that interaction can, and often does, convert the exchange of recognition into domination and submission.

THE BEGINNING OF RECOGNITION

As she cradles her newborn child and looks into its eyes, the first-time mother says, "I believe she knows me. You do know me, don't you? Yes, you do." As she croons to her baby in that soft, high-pitched repetitive voice (the "infantized" speech that scientists confirm is the universal baby talk), she attributes to her infant a knowledge beyond ordinary knowing. To the skeptical observer this knowledge may appear to be no more than projection. For the mother, this peaceful moment after a feeding—often after a mounting storm of cries and body convulsions, the somewhat clumsy effort to get baby's mouth connected to the nipple, the gradual relaxation as baby begins to suck and milk begins to flow, and finally baby's alert, attentive, yet enigmatic look—this moment is indeed one of recognition. She says to her baby, "Hey, stranger, are you really the one I carried around inside of me? Do you know me?" Unlike the observer, she would not be surprised to hear that rigorous experiments show that her baby can already distinguish her from other people, that newborns already prefer the sight, sound, and smell of their mothers.[3]

The mother who feels recognized by her baby is not simply projecting her own feelings into her child—which she assuredly does. She is also linking the newborn's past, inside her, with his future, outside of her, as a separate person.[4] The baby is a stranger to her, she is not yet sure who this baby is, although she is certain that he or she is already someone, a unique person with his or her own destiny.[5] Although the baby is wholly dependent upon her—and not only on her, but perhaps equally on a father or others—never for a moment does she doubt that this baby brings his own self, his unique personality, to bear on their common life. And she is already grateful for the baby's cooperation and activity—his willingness to be soothed, his acceptance of frustration, his devotion to her milk, his focusing on her face. Later, as baby is able to demonstrate ever more clearly that he does know and prefer her to all others, she will accept this glimmer of recognition as a sign of the mutuality that persists in spite of the tremendous inequality of the parent-child relationship. But perhaps never will she feel more strongly, than in those first days of her baby's life, the intense mixture of his being part of herself, utterly familiar and yet utterly new, unknown, and other.

It may be hard for a mother to accept this paradox, the fact that this baby has come from her and yet is so unknown to her. She may feel frustrated that her child cannot yet tell her who he is, what he knows or doesn't know. Certainly, a new mother has a complex range of feelings, many of which are dismissed or utterly denied by the common sentimentality surrounding motherhood. She may feel bored, unsure of what she should be doing to quiet or please baby, exhausted, anxious about herself and her body, angry that baby demands so much from her, dismayed at the lack of visible gratitude or response, impatient for baby to reveal himself, afraid that her baby is not normal, that he is going to stay like this forever.

Despite such doubts and difficulties, however, most first-time mothers are able to sustain a powerful connection to a newborn child. Naturally, some of a mother's ability to mother reflects the nurturance her own parents gave her and the support she receives from other adults. But what sustains her from moment to moment is the relationship she is forming with her infant, the gratification she feels when baby, with all that raw intensity, responds to her.[6] In this early inter- action, the mother can already identify the first signs of mutual recognition: "I recognize *you* as my baby who recognizes *me*."

To experience recognition in the fullest, most joyful way, entails the paradox that "you" who are "mine" are also different, new, outside of me. It thus in- cludes the sense of loss that you are no longer inside me, no longer simply my fantasy of you, that we are no longer physically and psychically one, and I can no longer take care of you simply by taking care of myself. I may find it prefer- able to put this side of reality out of my consciousness—for example, by declar- ing you the most wonderful baby who ever lived, far superior to all other babies, so that you are my dream child, and taking care of you is as easy as taking care of myself and fulfills my deepest wishes for glory. This is a temptation to which many new parents succumb in some measure.

Still, the process of recognition, charted here through the experience of the new mother, always includes this paradoxical mixture of otherness and togeth- erness: You belong to me, yet you are not (any longer) part of me. The joy I take in your existence must include *both* my connection to you *and* your independent existence—I recognize that you are real.

INTERSUBJECTIVITY

Recognition is so central to human existence as to often escape notice; or, rather, it appears to us in so many guises that it is seldom grasped as one overarching concept. There are any number of near-synonyms for it: to recognize is to affirm, validate, acknowledge, know, accept, understand, empathize, take in, tolerate, appreciate, see, identify with, find familiar, . . . love. Even the sober expositions of research on infancy, which detail the exchange of infant and caregiver, are full of the language of recognition. What I call *mutual recognition* includes a number of experiences commonly described in the research on mother-infant interaction: emotional attunement, mutual influence, affective mutuality, sharing states of mind. The idea of mutual recognition seems to me an ever more crucial category of early experience. Increasingly, research reveals infants to be active partici- pants who help shape the responses of their environment, and "create" their own objects. Through its focus on interaction, infancy research has gradually widened psychology's angle of observation to include infant *and* parent, the si- multaneous presence of two living subjects.[7]

While this may seem rather obvious, psychoanalysis has traditionally ex- pounded theories of infancy that present a far less active exchange between mothers and infants. Until very recently, most psychoanalytic discussions of in- fancy, early ego development, and early mothering depicted the infant as a pas- sive, withdrawn, even "autistic" creature. This view followed Freud, for whom the ego's initial relation to the outside world was hostile, rejecting its impinge- ment. In Freud's reconstruction, the first relationship (i.e., with mother) was based on oral drive—a physiological dependency, a nonspecific need for some- one to reduce tension by providing satisfaction. The caregiver merely appeared as the object of the baby's need, rather than as a specific person with an indepen- dent existence. In other words, the baby's relationship to the world was only shaped by the need for food and comfort, as represented by the breast; it did not include any of the curiosity and responsiveness to sight and sound, face and voice, that are incipiently social.[8] Those elements of psychic life that demand a living, responsive other had little place in psychoanalytic thought.

Much of the impetus for change came from research based on nonpsychoanalytic models of development. Piaget's developmental psychology, which saw the infant as active and stimulus-seeking, as constructing its environment by action and interaction, eventually led to a wave of research and theory that challenged the psychoanalytic view of infantile passivity.[9] Equally important was the influence of ethological research that studied animal and human infants in their natural environments, and so identified the growth of attachment, the social connection to others—especially the mother—that we have been describing.[10] From knowing and preferring its mother, the infant proceeds to form a relationship with her that involves a wide range of activities and emotions, many of which are independent of feeding and caregiving.

Basing their work largely on infant observation, the "attachment theorists"—preeminently the British psychoanalyst John Bowlby—argued that sociability was a primary rather than a secondary phenomenon. In the late 1950s, Bowlby explicitly contested the earlier psychoanalytic view that saw the infant's tie to the mother exclusively in terms of his oral investment in her. Bowlby drew on extensive research which showed that separation from parents and deprivation of contact with other adults catastrophically undermined infant emotional and social development.[11] Social stimulation, warmth, and affective interchange, he concluded, are indispensable to human growth from the beginning of life. Research with infants who were securely embedded in a relationship confirmed that attachment to specific persons (not only mothers but fathers, siblings, and caregivers as well) was a crucial milestone of the second six months of life.[12] Bowlby's work coincided with an influential tendency in British psychoanalysis called object relations theory, which put new emphasis on the child's early relationship with others. Together they offered psychoanalysis a new foundation: the assumption that we are fundamentally social beings.[13]

The idea that the infant's capacity and desire to relate to the world is incipiently present at birth and develops all along has important consequences. It obviously demands a revision of Freud's original view of the human subject as a monadic energy system, in favor of a self that is active and requires other selves. But it also contests the view of early infancy in the dominant American psychoanalytic paradigm, ego psychology. Ego psychology's most important theory of infant development, formulated by the child analyst and observer Margaret Mahler in the late 1960s, describes the child's gradual separation and individuation from an initial symbiotic unity with the mother.[14] The problem with this formulation is the idea of separation from oneness; it contains the implicit assumption that we grow *out of* relationships rather than becoming more active and sovereign *within* them, that we start in a state of dual oneness and wind up in a state of singular oneness.

Mahler's work on separation-individuation was, nevertheless, a landmark in the theory of the self. It offered a genealogy of the anxiety and conflict associated with becoming independent, and thus profoundly changed the focus of both clinical practice and psychoanalytic theory. Separation-individuation theory influenced psychoanalytic thinking in its drift toward the object relations approach; it also formulated more concretely the actual interaction between parent and child, admitting the importance of interpersonal dynamics without denying inner unconscious reality. In separation-individuation theory, the self-other relationship almost has its day. However, its theoretical construction of early infancy reiterates the old view of the baby who never looks up from the breast. This baby, who "hatches" like a bird from the egg of symbiosis, is then brought to the world by its mother's ministrations, just as Freud thought the ego was brought into being by the pressure of the outside world.[15]

It was, therefore, a radical challenge to the contemporary American psychoanalytic paradigm of infancy as well as to the classical Freudian view, when psychoanalyst and infancy researcher Daniel Stern contended in the 1980s that the infant is never totally undifferentiated (symbiotic) from the mother, but is primed from the beginning to be interested in an to distinguish itself from the world of others.[16] Once we accept the idea that infants do not begin life as part of an undifferentiated unity, the issue is not only how we separate from oneness, but also how we connect to and recognize other; the issue is not how we become free of the other, but how we actively engage and make ourselves known in relationship to the other.

This view of the self emerged not only from the observation of infants, but also in the consulting rooms where psychoanalysts began to discern the infant cry in the adult voice. The desperate anguish of those who feel dead and empty, unable to connect to themselves or to others, led to the question, What makes a person feel authentic? a question which also led back to the infant. In the words of the British psychoanalyst D. W. Winnicott, the question is, What kind of relationship "enables the infant to begin to exist, to build a personal ego, to ride instincts, and to meet with all the difficulties inherent in life?"[17] This question motivated the "backward" shift of psychoanalytic interest: away from neurosis, oedipal conflicts, and sexual repression, toward the preoedipal conflicts of the ego, disturbances in the sense of self, and the feeling of acute loneliness and emptiness. What psychoanalysts began to look at was how a sense of self is consolidated or disrupted. Their focus was no longer on just the wish that is gratified or repressed, but on the self that is affected by the other's denial or fulfillment of that wish. Each denial or fulfillment could make a child feel either confirmed or thwarted in his sense of agency and self-esteem. The issue of the self's attitude to itself (self-love, self-cohesion, self-esteem) gave rise to the psychoanalytic preoccupation with narcissism as a clinical and a theoretical issue. In the 1970s, Heinz Kohut founded a new direction in American psychoanalysis called self psychology, which reinterpreted psychic development in terms of the self's need to find cohesion and mirroring in the other.[18]

From the study of the self who suffers the lack of recognition, as well as the new perception of the active, social infant who can respond to and differentiate others, emerges what I call the *intersubjective view*.[19] The intersubjective view maintains that the individual grows in and through the relationship to other subjects. Most important, this perspective observes that the other whom the self meets is also a self, a subject in his or her own right. It assumes that we are able and need to recognize that other subject as different and yet alike, as an other who is capable of sharing similar mental experience. Thus the idea of intersubjectivity reorients the conception of the psychic world from a subject's relations to its object toward a subject meeting another subject.[20]

The intersubjective view, as distinguished from the intrapsychic, refers to what happens in the field of self and other. Whereas the intrapsychic perspective conceives of the person as a discrete unit with a complex internal structure, intersubjective theory describes capacities that emerge in the interaction between self and others. Thus intersubjective theory, even when describing the self alone, sees its aloneness as a particular point in the spectrum of relationships rather than as the original, "natural state" of the individual. The crucial area we uncover with intrapsychic theory is the unconscious; the crucial element we explore with intersubjective theory is the representation of self and other as distinct but interrelated beings.

I suggest that intrapsychic and intersubjective theory should not be seen in opposition to each other (as they usually are) but as complementary ways of understanding the psyche.[21] To recognize the intersubjective self is not to deny the importance of the intrapsychic: the inner world of fantasy, wish, anxiety, and defense; of bodily symbols and images whose connections defy the ordinary rules of logic and language. In the inner world, the subject incorporates and expels, identifies with and repudiates the other, not as a real being, but as a mental object. Freud discovered these processes, which constitute the dynamic unconscious, largely by screening out the real relations with others and focusing on the individual mind.[22] By my point here is not to reverse Freud's decision for the inner world by choosing the outside world; it is, rather, to grasp both realities.[23] Without the intrapsychic concept of the unconscious, intersubjective theory becomes one-dimensional, for it is only against the background of the mind's private space that the *real* other stands out in relief.

In my view, the concept that unifies intersubjective theories of self development is the need for recognition. A person comes to feel that "I am the doer who does, I am the author of my acts," by being with another person who recognizes her acts, her feelings, her intentions, her existence, her independence. Recognition is the essential response, the constant companion of assertion. The subject declares, "I am, I do," and then waits for the response, "You are, you have done." Recognition is, thus, reflexive; it includes not only the other's confirming response, but also how we find ourselves in that response. We recognize ourselves in the other, and we even recognize ourselves in inanimate things: for the baby, the ability to recognize what she has seen before is as Stern says, "self-affirming as well as world-affirming," enhancing her sense of effective agency: "My mental representation works!"[24]

Psychologists speak of contingent responsiveness—this refers to the baby's pleasure in things that respond directly to the baby's own acts, the mobile that moves when baby jerks the cord tied to her wrist, the bells that ring when she kicks her feet. Contingent responses confirm the baby's activity and effectiveness, and therein lies the pleasure: the baby becomes more involved in making an impact (the kicking has results!) than in the particular sight or sound of the thing.[25] And soon the pleasure derives from both the effect on the object and the reaction of the other subject who applauds. The nine-month-old already looks to the parent's face for the shared delight in a sound. The two-year-old says, "I did it!" showing the peg she has hammered and waiting for the affirmation that she has learned something new, that she has exercised her agency.

Of course not all actions are undertaken in direct relation to a recognizing other. The child runs down the hill and feels the pleasure of her body in motion. She is simply aware of herself and her own action, absorbed in herself and the moment. This experience, like the play with objects, may be based on pleasure in mastery as well as self-expression. Yet we know that such pleasure in one's own assertion requires and is associated with a supportive social context. We know that serious impairment of the sense of mastery and the capacity for pleasure results when the self-other matrix is disrupted, when the life-giving exchange with others is blocked. The ten-month-old may hesitate to crawl away and explore the new toys in the corner if he senses that the mother will withdraw her attention the moment he is not absorbed in her, or if the mother's doubtful look suggests it is not all right to go.[26] As life evolves, assertion and recognition become the vital moves in the dialogue between self and other.

Recognition is not a sequence of events, like the phases of maturation and development, but a constant element through all events and phases. Recognition might be compared to that essential element in photosynthesis, sunlight, which provides the energy for the plant's constant transformation of substance. It includes the diverse responses and activities of the mother that are taken for granted as the background in all discussions of development—beginning with the mother's ability to identify and respond to her infant's physical needs, her "knowing her baby," when he wants to sleep, eat, play alone, or play together. Indeed, within a few months after birth, this so-called background becomes the foreground, the raison d'être, the meaning and the goal of being with others. As we trace the development of the infant, we can see how recognition becomes increasingly an end in itself—first an achievement of harmony, and then an arena of conflict between self and other.

But the need for *mutual* recognition, the necessity of recognizing as well as being recognized by the other—this is what so many theories of the self have missed. The idea of mutual recognition is crucial to the intersubjective view; it implies that we actually have a need to recognize the other as a separate person who is like us yet distinct. This means that the child has a need to see the mother, too, as an independent subject, not simply as the "external world" or an adjunct of his ego.

It must be acknowledged that we have only just begun to think about the mother as a subject in her own right, principally because of contemporary feminism, which made us aware of the disastrous results for women of being reduced to the mere extension of a two-month-old.[27] Psychology in general and psychoanalysis in particular too often partake of this distorted view of the mother, which is so deeply embedded in the culture as a whole.[28] No psychological theory has adequately articulated the mother's independent existence. Thus even the accounts of the mother-infant relationship which do consider parental responsiveness always revert to a view of the mother as the baby's vehicle for growth, an object of the baby's needs.[29] The mother is the baby's first object of attachment, and later, the object of desire. She is provider, interlocutor, caregiver, contingent reinforcer, significant other, empathic understander, mirror. She is also a secure presence to walk away from, a setter of limits, an optimal frustrator, a shockingly real outside otherness. She is external reality—but she is rarely regarded as another subject with a purpose apart from her existence for her child. Often enough, abetted by the image of mothering in childrearing literature and by the real conditions of life with baby, mothers themselves feel they are so confined. Yet the real mother is not simply an object for her child's demands; she is, in fact, another subject whose independent center must be outside her child if she is to grant him the recognition he seeks.[30]

This is no simple enterprise. It is too often assumed that a mother will be able to give her child faith in tackling the world even if she can no longer muster it for herself. And although mothers ordinarily aspire to more for their children than for themselves, there are limits to this trick: a mother who is too depressed by her own isolation cannot get excited about her child learning to walk or talk; a mother who is afraid of people cannot feel relaxed about her child's association with other children; a mother who stifles her own longings, ambitions, and frustrations cannot tune in empathically to her child's joys and failures. The recognition a child seeks is something the mother is able to give only by virtue of her independent identity. Thus self psychology is misleading when it understands the mother's recognition of the child's feelings and accomplishments as maternal mirroring. The mother cannot (and should not) be a mirror; she must not merely reflect back what the child asserts; she must embody something of the not-me; she must be an independent other who responds in her different way.[31] Indeed, as the child increasingly establishes his own independent center of existence, her recognition will be meaningful only to the extent that it reflects her own equally separate subjectivity.

In this sense, notwithstanding the inequality between parent and child, recognition must be mutual and allow for the assertion of each self. Thus I stress that mutual recognition, including the child's ability to recognize the mother as a person in her own right, is as significant a developmental goal as separation. Hence the need for a theory that understands how the capacity for mutuality evolves, a theory based on the premise that from the beginning there are always (at least) two subjects.

MUTUALITY: THE ESSENTIAL TENSION

So far I have tried to convey the idea that differentiation requires, ideally, the reciprocity of self and other, the balance of assertion and recognition. While this may seem obvious, it has not been easy to conceptualize psychological development in terms of mutuality. Most theories of development have emphasized the goal of autonomy more than relatedness to others, leaving unexplored the territory in which subjects meet. Indeed, it is hard to locate the intersubjective dimension through the lens of such theories. Let us look more closely at the dominant psychoanalytic paradigm, ego psychology, and at its most important expression, Mahler's separation-individuation theory, to see the difference intersubjectivity makes.

Mahler's theory, it will be remembered, conceptualized a unilinear trajectory that leads from oneness to separateness, rather than a continual, dynamic, evolving balance of the two.[32] Moving along this unilinear trajectory, the subject presumably extricates himself from the original oneness, the primary narcissism, in which he began. Although Mahler acknowledges that the child grows into a fuller appreciation of the other's independence, her emphasis is on how the self separates, how the baby comes to feel not-one with the mother. Seen in this light, relationship is the ground and separation is the figure;[33] recognition appears as a fuzzy background and individual activity thrusts forward out of it. This has seemed plausible to so many people for many reasons, but especially because of our culture's high valuation of individualism. And, of course, it corresponds to our subjective feeling of being "the center of our own universe" and to our struggle to enhance the intensity of that feeling.

Interestingly enough, when we do succeed in reaching that enhanced state of self-awareness, it is often in a context of sharpened awareness of others—of their unique particularity and independent existence. The reciprocal relationship between self and other can be compared with the optical illusion in which the figure and ground are constantly changing their relation even as their outlines remain clearly distinct—as in Escher's birds, which appear to fly in both directions. What makes his drawings visually difficult is a parallel to what makes the idea of self-other reciprocity conceptually difficult: the drawing asks us to look two ways simultaneously, quite in opposition to our usual sequential orientation. Since it is more difficult to think in terms of simultaneity than in terms of sequence, we begin to conceptualize the movement in terms of a directional trajectory. Then we must try to correct this inaccurate rendering of what we have seen by putting the parts back together in a conceptual whole which encompasses both directions. Although this requires a rather laborious intellectual reconstruction, intuitively, the paradoxical tension of this way and that way "feels right."

In the last fifteen years, infancy research has developed a new model for early experiences of emotional intensity and exchange which emphasizes reciprocity as opposed to instinctual gratification or separation. Already at three to four months, the infant has the capacity to interact in sophisticated facial play whose main motive is social interest. At this age, the baby can already initiate play. She can elicit parental response by laughing and smiling; she can transform a diaper change into a play session. In this play, the reciprocity that two subjects can create, or subvert, is crucial.[34] True, the moving ducks on the mobile respond to the kick of the infant's foot and so "recognize" her, providing her with the vital experience of contingent response that fosters a sense of mastery and agency. But the mother's response is both more attuned (it "matches" the infant) and more unpredictable than the ducks'. The child enjoys a dose of otherness. Let mother not coo in a constant rhythm, let her vary her voice and gestures, mixing novelty with repetition, and the baby will focus longer on her face and show pleasure in return. The combination of resonance and difference that the mother offers can open the way to a recognition that transcends mastery and mechanical response, to a recognition that is based on *mutuality*.

Frame-by-frame analysis of films of mothers and babies interacting reveals the minute adaptation of each partner's facial and gestural response to the other: mutual influence.[35] The mother addresses the baby with the coordinated action of her voice, face, and hands. The infant responds with his whole body, wriggling or alert, mouth agape or smiling broadly. Then they may begin a dance of interaction in which the partners are so attuned that they move together in unison.[36] This early experience of unison is probably the first emotional basis for later feelings of oneness that characterize group activities such as music or dance. Reciprocal attunement to one another's gestures prefigures adult erotic play as well. Play interaction can be as primary a source of the feeling of oneness as nursing or being held. Thus the ultimate gratification of being in attunement with another person can be framed not—or not only—in terms of instinctual satisfaction, but of cooperation and recognition.

The study of early play interaction also reveals that the baby's principal means of regulating her own feelings, her inner state of mind, is to act on her partner outside. Being able to make herself feel better is directly dependent on being able to make the other act in attunement with her feelings. As Stern points out, "The issue at stake is momentous. The infant requires the integrative experience [that her action] successfully restructures the external world"—that what she does changes the other. Since these acts are also charged with emotion, with pleasure or pain, acting on the world also means being able to change one's own feelings "in the desired direction."[37] In the interaction situation, when stimulation becomes too intense, the infant regulates her own arousal by turning her head away. If the partner reads this correctly as a message to lay back, the baby experiences relief of tension without losing the connection and dropping out of the exchange. The baby can control her own level of excitement by directing the other. Now she is able to feel both that the world is responsive and that she is effective. If the baby is not successful, she feels a simultaneous loss of inner and outer control.

We also observe how mutual regulation breaks down and attunement fails: when baby is tired and fussy, when mother is bored and depressed, or when baby is unresponsive and this makes mother anxious. Then we will see not just the absence of play, but a kind of anti-play in which the frustration of the search for recognition is painfully apparent. The unsuccessful interaction is sometimes almost as finely tuned as the pleasurable one. With each effort of the baby to withdraw from the mother's stimulation, to avert his gaze, turn his head, pull his body away, the mother responds by "chasing" after the baby.[38] It is as if the mother anticipates her baby's withdrawal with split-second accuracy and can only read his message to give space as a frustration of her own efforts to be recognized. Just as the baby's positive response can make the mother feel affirmed in her being, the baby's unresponsiveness can amount to a terrible destruction of her self-confidence as a mother. The mother who jiggles, pokes, looms, and shouts "look at me" to her unresponsive baby creates a negative cycle of recognition out of her own despair at not being recognized. Here in the earliest social interaction we see how the search for recognition can become a power struggle: how assertion becomes aggression.

If we take this unsuccessful interaction as a model, we can see how the fine balance of mutual recognition goes awry. The child loses the opportunity for feeling united and attuned, as well as the opportunity for appreciating (knowing) his mother. He is never able to fully engage in or fully disentangle himself from this kind of sticky, frustrating interaction. Neither separateness nor union is possible. Even as he is retreating he has to carefully monitor his mother's actions to get away from them: even withdrawal is not simple.[39] Thus the child can never lose sight of the other, yet never see her clearly; never shut her out and never let her in. In the ideal balance, a person is able to be fully self-absorbed or fully receptive to the other, he is able to be alone or together. In a negative cycle of recognition, a person feels that aloneness is only possible by obliterating the intrusive other, that attunement is only possible by surrendering to the other.

While the failure of early mutuality seems to promote a premature formation of the defensive boundary between inside and outside, the positive experience of attunement allows the individual to maintain a more permeable boundary and enter more readily into states in which there is a momentary suspension of felt boundaries between inside and outside. The capacity to enter into states in which distinctness and union are reconciled underlies the most intense experience of adult erotic life. In erotic union we can experience that form of mutual recognition in which both partners lose themselves in each other without loss of self; they lose self-consciousness without loss of awareness. Thus early experiences of mutual recognition already prefigure the dynamics of erotic life.

This description of the intersubjective foundation of erotic life offers a different perspective than the Freudian construction of psychosexual phases, for it emphasizes the tension *between interacting individuals* rather than that *within the individual*. Yet, as I have said above, these rival perspectives seem to me not so much mutually exclusive as concerned simply with different issues. The inner psychic world of object representations—the intrapsychic life with which classical psychoanalysis is concerned—does not yet exist at four months; indeed, it awaits the development of the capacity to symbolize in the second year of life. The distinction between inner and outer is only beginning to be developed; inner and outer regulation still overlap. This does not mean that the infant is unable to differentiate self and other in actual practice or to represent them mentally. It means that the infant represents self and other concretely, not through the mediation of symbols that later characterize mental representation.[40]

The mental organization of self and other enters a new phase, Stern theorizes, when the infant begins to be aware of the existence of "other minds." While the infant of four months can participate in a complex social interaction, she does not do so self-consciously. But at seven to nine months, she takes a great leap forward to the discovery that different minds can share the same feelings or intentions. This is where Stern introduces the term *intersubjectivity* proper, to designate the moment at which we know that others exist who feel and think as we do. In my view, however, intersubjective development is best understood as a spectrum, and this moment marks a decisive point along that spectrum at which the infant more consciously recognizes the other as like and different.[41]

Now, when the infant reaches excitedly for a toy, he looks up to see if mother is sharing his excitement; he gets the meaning when she says, "Wow!" The mother shows that she is feeling the same, not by imitating the infant's gesture (he shakes the rattle), but by matching his level of intensity in a different mode (she whoops). This translation into a different form of expression more clearly demonstrates the congruence of *inner* experience than simple, behavioral imitation.[42] Technically the mother is not feeling the exact same feeling as her child: she is not excited by the rattle itself; but she is excited by his excitement, and she wants to communicate that fact. When mother and child play "peekaboo" (a game based on the tension between shared expectancy and surprise), the mother takes similar pleasure in contacting her child's mind. The conscious pleasure in sharing a feeling introduces a new level of mutuality—a sense that inner experience can be joined, that two minds can cooperate in one intention. This conception of emerging intersubjectivity emphasizes how the awareness of the separate other enhances the felt connection with him: this *other* mind can share *my* feeling.

The development toward increasingly mutual and self-conscious recognition,

Stern argues, contrasts sharply with Mahler's theory of separation-individuation.[43] That theory focuses on the infant's sense of separateness, but does not show how this sense of separateness simultaneously enhances the capacity for sharing with and appreciating the other. According to Mahler, the infant of ten months is primarily involved in the pleasure of expressing his separate mind by exploring the world. The infant's psychological well-being depends on whether he can use the mother to refuel for his forays into the world, whether he can maintain a certain amount of contact while venturing off on his own, and whether the mother can give her infant the push from the nest rather than responding anxiously to his new independence.[44]

But, as I see it, intersubjective theory expands and complements (without negating) this picture, by focusing on the affective content of the mother-child exchange. The baby who looks back as he crawls off toward the toys in the corner is not merely refueling or checking to see that mother is still there, but is wondering whether mother is *sharing* the feeling of his adventure—the fear, the excitement, or that ambiguous "scarey-wonderful" feeling.[45] The sense of shared feeling about the undertaking is not only a reassurance, but is, itself, a source of pleasurable connection. For the separation-individuation perspective, such emotional attunement may be part of the landscape, but it is absent at the level of theory; the concepts grasp only how mother protects the child's ego from anxiety so that it can separate. Intersubjective theory introduces attunement, or the lack of it, as an important concept.[46] In so doing, it reintroduces the idea of *pleasure*, pleasure in being with the other, which had gotten lost in the transition from drive theory to ego psychology—but redefines it as pleasure in being with the other.

At the same time, the awareness of separate minds and the desire for attunement raises the possibility of a new kind of conflict. Already at one year the infant can experience the conflict between the wish to fulfill his own desire (say, to push the buttons on the stereo), and the wish to remain in accord with his parents' will.[47] Given such inevitable conflict, the desire to remain attuned can be converted into submission to the other's will. At each phase of development, the core conflict between assertion and recognition is recast in terms of the new level at which the child experiences his own agency and the distinctness of the other.

THE PARADOX OF RECOGNITION

The conflict between assertion of self and need for the other was articulated long before modern psychology began to explore the development of self. Hegel analyzed the core of this problem in his discussion of the struggle between "the independence and dependence of self-consciousness" and its culmination in the master-slave relationship.[48] He showed how the self's wish for absolute independence clashes with the self's need for recognition. In Hegel's discussion two hypothetical selves (self-consciousness and the other, who is another self-consciousness) meet. The movement between them is the movement of recognition; each exists only by existing for the other, that is, by being recognized. But for Hegel, it is simply a given that this mutuality, the tension between asserting the self and recognizing the other, *must* break down; it is fated to produce an insoluble conflict. The breakdown of this tension is what leads to domination.[49]

The need of the self for the other is paradoxical, because the self is trying to establish himself as an absolute, an independent entity, yet he must recognize the other as like himself in order to *be* recognized by him. He must be able to find himself in the other. The self can only be known by his acts—and only if his acts have meaning for the other do they have meaning for him. Yet each time he acts he negates the other, which is to say that if the other is affected then he is no longer *identical* with who he was before. To preserve his identity, the other resists instead of recognizing the self's acts ("Nothing you do or say can affect me, I am who I am").

Hegel creates a conceptual representation of the two-sided interplay of opposites. As each subject attempts to establish his reality, he must take account of the other, who is trying to do the same: "they recognize themselves as mutually recognizing one another."[50] But almost immediately Hegel observes that this abstract reciprocity is not really how the subject experiences things. Rather, the subject, first of all, experiences himself as an absolute, and then searches for affirmation of self through the other. The mutuality that is implied by the concept of recognition is a problem for the subject, whose goal is only to be certain of himself. This absoluteness, the sense of being one ("My identity is entirely independent and consistent") and alone ("There is nothing outside of me that I do not control"), is the basis for domination—and the master-slave relationship.[51]

Now we can see how Hegel's notion of the conflict between independence and dependence meshes with the psychoanalytic view. Hegel posits a self that has no intrinsic need for the other, but uses the other only as a vehicle for self-certainty. This monadic, self-interested ego is essentially the one posited in classical psychoanalytic theory. For Hegel, as for classical psychoanalysis, the self begins in a state of "omnipotence" (Everything is an extension of me and my power), which it wants to affirm in its encounter with the other, who, it now sees, is like itself. But it cannot do so, for to affirm itself it must acknowledge the other, and to acknowledge the other would be to deny the absoluteness of the self. The need for recognition entails this fundamental paradox: at the very moment of realizing our own independence, we are dependent upon another to recognize it. At the very moment we come to understand the meaning of "I, myself," we are forced to see the limitations of that self. At the moment when we understand that separate minds can share the same state, we also realize that these minds can disagree.

To see just how close this conceptual picture comes to the psychoanalytic one, let us again look at Mahler's theory of separation-individuation. According to Mahler, the infant moves through subphases: differentiation,[52] practicing, and rapprochement. From the first hatching in the differentiation phase (six to eight months), we follow the infant, who is able to move around, and so maintain distance and closeness to mother, into the practicing phase (ten to thirteen months). The practicing phase is an elated, euphoric phase of discovery in which the infant is delighted with the world and himself, discovering his own agency as well as the fascinating outside. It has been called "a love affair with the world."[53] The screech of delight at moving about is the hallmark of practicing. But in this phase of new self-assertion the infant still takes himself for granted, and his mother as well. He does not realize that it is mother, not himself, who insures that he does not fall when he stands on the chair to reach for something interesting on the table. He is too excited by *what* he is doing to reflect on the relation of his will and ability to his sovereignty.

But soon this Eden of blissful ignorance comes to an end. At fourteen months or so the infant enters rapprochement, a phase of conflict in which he must begin to reconcile his grandiose aspirations and euphoria with the perceived reality of his limitations and dependency. Although he is now able to do more, the toddler will insist that mother (or father) share everything, validate his new discoveries and independence. He will insist that mother participate in all his deeds. He will tyranically enforce these demands if he can, in order to assert—and have mother affirm—his will. The toddler is confronting the increased awareness of separateness and, consequently, of vulnerability: he can move away from mother, but mother can also move away from him.[54] To the child, it now appears that his freedom consists in absolute control over his mother. He is ready to be the master in Hegel's account, to be party to a relationship in which the mutuality breaks down into two opposing elements, the one who is recognized and the one whose identity is negated. He is ready, in his innocence, to go for complete control, to insist on his omnipotence.[55]

What is life like for the mother of a toddler who manifests the constant willfulness, the clinging or the tyrannical demands typical of rapprochement? Depending, in part, on how imperious or clinging the child is, the mother may feel extremely put upon ("Her reactions are tinged with feelings of annoyance," Mahler reports).[56] Suddenly the child's demands no longer appear to be merely the logical results of needs that ought to be met with good grace, but, rather, as irrational and willful. The issue is no longer what the child needs, but what he *wants*. Here, of course, is where many a mother-child pair come to grief. A variety of feelings well up in the mother: the distance from her no-longer-perfect child, the wish to retaliate, the temptation to take the easier path of giving in, the fear or resentment of her child's will. What the mother feels during rapprochement and how she works this out will be colored by her ability to deal straightforwardly with aggression and dependence, her sense of herself as entitled to a separate existence, and her confidence in her child's wholeness and ability to survive conflict, loss, and imperfection.

As Freud reminds us, the parents' abandoned expectations of their own perfection are recalled to life in their child, "His Majesty the Baby."[57] The rapprochement crisis is thus also a crisis of parenting. By identifying with her child's disillusionment, and by knowing that he will survive it, the parent is able to respond appropriately; in doing so she has to accept that she cannot make a perfect world for her child (where he can get everything he wants)—and this is the blow to her own narcissism. The self-obliteration of the permissive parent who cannot face this blow does not bring happiness to the child who gets everything he demands. The parent has ceased to function as an other who sets a boundary to the child's will, and the child experiences this as abandonment; the parent co-opts all the child's intentions by agreement, pushing him back into an illusory oneness where he has no agency of his own. The child will rebel against this oneness by insisting on having his way even more absolutely. The child who feels that others are extensions of himself must constantly fear the emptiness and loss of connection that result from his fearful power. Only he exists; the other is effaced, has nothing real to give him. The painful result of success in the battle for omnipotence is that to win is to win nothing: the result is negation, emptiness, isolation.

Alternatively, the parent who cannot tolerate the child's attempt to do things independently will make the child feel that the price of freedom is aloneness, or even, that freedom is not possible. Thus if the child does not want to do without approval, she must give up her will. This usually results in the "choice" to stay close to home and remain compliant. Not only is she constantly in need of a parent's protection and confirmation in lieu of her own agency, but the parent remains omnipotent in her mind.

In both cases the sense of omnipotence survives, projected onto the other or assumed by the self; in neither case can we say that the other is recognized, or, more modestly (given the child's age), that the process of recognition has begun. The ideal "resolution" of the paradox of recognition is for it to continue as a *constant tension*, but this is not envisaged by Hegel, nor is it given much place in psychoanalysis. Mahler, for example, views the resolution of rapprochement as the moment when the child takes the mother inside himself, can separate from her or be angry at her and still know her to be there—as a "constant object." [58] But this does not tell us how the toddler comes to terms with the difficulty that his own freedom depends on the other's freedom, that recognition of independence must be mutual.

The decisive problem remains *recognizing the other*. Establishing *my*self (Hegel's "being for itself") means winning the recognition of the other, and this, in turn, means I must finally acknowledge the other as existing for *him*self and not just for me. The process we call differentiation proceeds through the movement of recognition, its flow from subject to subject, from self to other and back. The nature of this movement is necessarily contradictory, paradoxical. Only by deepening our understanding of this paradox can we broaden our picture of human development to include not only the separation but also the meeting of minds—a picture in which the bird's flight is always in two directions.

DISCOVERING THE OTHER

Even if we assume that life begins with an emergent awareness of self and other, we know that many things will conspire to prevent full attainment of that consciousness. The problem of recognizing the other was addressed directly by Winnicott, and his original, innovative perceptions point the way out of the paradox of recognition. Winnicott, as we have noted, was concerned with what makes a person feel unreal to himself, with the deadness and despair that accompany the sense of unreality, with what he called "the false self." [59] He concluded that one of the most important elements in feeling authentic was the recognition of an outside reality that is not one's own projection, the experience of contacting other minds.

In his essay, "The Use of an Object," [60] which is, in many ways, a modern echo of Hegel's reflections on recognition, Winnicott presents the idea that in order to be able to "use" the object we first have to "destroy" it. He distinguishes between two dimensions of experience: *relating* to the object and *using* the object. (These terms can be troublesome, for Winnicott uses them in quite the opposite sense than we might in ordinary speech: "using" here does not mean instrumentalizing or demeaning, but being able to creatively benefit from another person; it refers to the experience of "shared reality" in which "the object's independent existence" is vital. "Relating" refers to the experience of "the subject as an isolate," in which the object is merely a "phenomenon of the subject.")[61]

At first, Winnicott says, an object is "related" to, it is part of the subject's mind and not necessarily experienced as real, external, or independent. But there comes a point in the subject's development where this kind of relatedness must give way to an appreciation of the object as an outside entity, not merely something in one's mind. This ability to enter into exchange with the outside object is what Winnicott calls "using" the object. And here he finds "the most irksome of all the early failures that come for mending." When the subject fails to make the transition from "relating" to "using," it means that he has not been able to place the object outside himself, to distinguish it from his mental experience of omnipotent control. He can only "use" the object when he perceives it "as an external phenomenon, not as a projective entity," when he recognizes it *"as an entity in its own right"*[62] (italics added).

Winnicott explains that the recognition of the other involves a paradoxical process in which the object is *in fantasy* always being destroyed.[63] The idea that to place the other outside, in reality, always involves destruction has often been a source of puzzlement. Intuitively, though, one senses that it is quite simple. Winnicott is saying that the object must be destroyed *inside* in order that we know it to have survived *outside;* thus we can recognize it as not subject to our mental control. This relation of destruction and survival is a reformulation of and solution to Hegel's paradox: in the struggle for recognition each subject must stake his life, must struggle to negate the other—and woe if he succeeds. For if I completely negate the other, he does not exist; and if he does not survive, he is *not there* to recognize me. But to find this out, I must *try* to exert this control, *try* to negate his independence. To find out that he exists, I must wish myself absolute and all alone—then, as it were, upon opening my eyes, I may discover that the other is still there.

Destruction, in other words, is an effort to differentiate. In childhood, if things go well, destruction results simply in survival; in adulthood, destruction includes the intention *to discover* if the other will survive. Winnicott's conception of destruction is innocent; it is best understood as a refusal, a negation, the mental experience of "You do not exist for me," whose favorable outcome is pleasure in the other's survival.[64] When I act upon the other it is vital that he be affected, so that I know that I exist—but not completely destroyed, so that I know he also exists.

Winnicott's description of what destruction means in the analytic context is also evocative of early childhood experiences.

> The subject [patient] says to the object [analyst]: "I destroyed you," and the object is there to receive the communication. From now on the subject says: "Hullo object!" "I destroyed you." "I love you." "You have value for me

because of your survival of my destruction of you." "While I am loving you
I am all the time destroying you in (unconscious) *fantasy.*" [65]

Perhaps this tension between denial and affirmation is another of the many
meanings of that favorite toddler game "Peekaboo" or of Freud's observations of
the toddler making the spool disappear and reappear (the famous "*fort-da,*" or
gone-there, game). Probably destruction in fantasy also underlies the joy in the
young toddler's constant repetition of "Hi!" It has something to do with constantly rediscovering that *you* are there.

The wish for absolute assertion of oneself, the demand to have one's way, the
negation of the outside—all that Freud understood as aggression and omnipotence—must sometime crash against the reality of an other who reflects back the
intransigent assertion that the self displays. The paradox of recognition, the need
for acknowledgment that turns us back to dependence on the other, brings about
a struggle for control. This struggle can result in the realization that if we fully
negate the other, that is, if we assume complete control over him and destroy his
identity and will, then we have negated ourselves as well. For then there is no
one there to recognize us, no one there for us to desire.

The experience of rapprochement might be reframed in light of Winnicott's
understanding of destruction: If I completely destroy the other, she ceases to
exist for me; and if she completely destroys me, I cease to exist—that is, I cease
to be an autonomous being. So if the mother sets no limits for the child, if she
obliterates herself and her own interests and allows herself to be wholly controlled, then she ceases to be a viable other for him. She is destroyed, and not
just in fantasy. If she retaliates, attempting to break his will, believing that any
compromise will "spoil" him, she will also inculcate the idea that there is room
for only one ego in any relationship—he must obliterate his for now, and hope
to get it back, with a vengeance, later. Only through the other's survival can the
subject move beyond the realm of submission and retaliation to a realm of mutual
respect.

Elsa First, a child psychoanalyst influenced by Winnicott, has offered a picture of how the rapprochement struggle for control may yield to mutual respect.
Observing toddlers, she suggests how the post-rapprochement child may begin
to apprehend mutuality in relation to the mother's leaving. The toddler's initial
role-playing imitation of the departing mother is characterized by the spirit of
pure retaliation and reversal—"I'll do to you what you do to me." But gradually
the child begins to identify with the mother's subjective experience and realizes
that "I could miss you as you miss me," and, therefore, that "I know that you
could wish to have your own life as I wish to have mine." First shows how, by
recognizing such shared experience, the toddler actually moves from a retaliatory
world of control to a world of mutual understanding and shared feeling. From
the intersubjective standpoint, this movement is crucial. By accepting the other's
independence, the child gains something that replaces control—a renewed sense
of connection with the other. [66]

Mutual recognition cannot be achieved through obedience, through identification with the other's power, or through repression. It requires, finally, contact
with the other. The meaning of destruction is that the subject can engage in an

all-out collision with the other, can hurtle himself against the barriers of otherness in order to feel the shock of the fresh, cold outside.[67] And he can experience this collision as hurtful neither to the other nor to himself, as occasioning neither withdrawal nor retaliation. Thus Winnicott advises parents:

> It is a healthy thing for a baby to get to know the full extent of his rage. . . .
> If he really is determined he can hold his breath and go blue in the face, and
> even have a fit. For a few minutes he really intends to destroy or at least to
> spoil everyone and everything, and he does not even mind if he destroys
> himself in the process. Naturally you do what you can to get the child out of
> this state. It can be said, however, that if a baby cries in a state of rage and
> feels as if he has destroyed everyone and everything, and yet the people
> round him remain calm and unhurt, this experience greatly strengthens his
> ability to see that what he feels to be true is not necessarily real. . . .[68]

Winnicott's theory of destruction also implies a revision in the psychoanalytic idea of reality—it suggests a "reality principle" that is a positive source of pleasure, the pleasure of connecting with the outside, and not just a brake on narcissism or aggression. Beyond the sensible ego's bowing to reality is the joy in the other's survival and the recognition of shared reality. Reality is thus *discovered*, rather than *imposed;* and authentic selfhood is not absorbed from without but discovered within. Reality neither wholly creates the self (as the pressure of the external world creates Freud's ego) nor is it wholly created by the self.

Winnicott's view of reality echoes the themes of his earlier work on "transitional objects," things like teddy bears, blankets, even special ways of humming or stroking. The child both creates and discovers these things, without ever having to decide which: "The baby creates the object, but the object was there waiting to be created. . . . We will never challenge the baby to elicit an answer to the question: Did you create that or did you find it?"[69] The object existed objectively, waiting to be found, and yet the infant has created it subjectively, as if it emerged from herself. This paradox is crucial to the evolving sense of reality.

The transitional object is literally a means of passage toward the awareness of otherness, toward establishing a boundary between inside and outside. But it is precisely an intermediate experience in which that boundary has not yet hardened. Out of this initial conception Winnicott created the broader notion of a transitional *realm* in which the child can play and create as if the outside were as malleable as his own fantasy. One could say the baby experiences something like this: "Reality recognizes me so I recognize it—wholly, with faith and trust, with no grudge or self-constraint." Thus the transitional realm allows "the enjoyment and love of reality," and not merely adaptation to it.[70]

The infancy researcher Louis Sander has conceptualized a very early form of transitional experience that he calls "open space."[71] Open space occurs in the first month of life when the mother and infant have achieved sufficient equilibrium to allow for moments of relaxation from internal pressure or external stimulation. In these moments of optimal disengagement, the infant can explore himself and his surroundings, can experience his own initiative and distinguish it from the other's action, for example, by putting thumb into mouth. The baby might lie on his side and move his hands slowly in front of his face, watching them intently—an activity one baby's parents aptly called "doing Tai Chi." In the balance between self and other, disengagement (open space) is as important as engagement. Indeed, as we saw in the antagonistic anti-play between mother and infant, disengagement and engagement form a crucial balance: the opportunity to disengage is the condition of freely engaging, its counterpoint.

What disengagement means here is not simple detachment, but what Winnicott called "being alone in the presence of the other,"[72] that is, in the safety that a nonintrusive other provides. Prior to self-consciousness, this experience will appear to the child as that of the self alone; but later it will be understood as a particular way of being with the other. In these moments of relaxation, Winnicott proposed, when there is no need to react to external stimuli, an impulse can arise from within and feel real. Here begins the sense of authorship, the conviction that one's act originates *inside* and reflects one's own intention. Here, too, begins the capacity for full receptivity and attention to what is outside, the freedom to be interested in the object independent of the pressure of need or anxiety. In this sense, the earliest transitional experience forms a continuum with the most developed capacities for contemplation and creativity, for discovering the outside as an object existing in its own right.[73]

BEYOND INTERNALIZATION

The discovery of the object as a real, external being distinguishes the intersubjective view of differentiation from the more conventional ego psychology of separation-individuation theory. In ego psychology, development occurs through separation and identification—by taking something in from the object, by assimilating the other to the self.[74] Most of psychoanalytic theory has been formulated in terms of the isolated subject and his internalization of what is outside to develop what is inside. Internalization implies that the other is consumed, incorporated, digested by the subject self. That which is not consumed, what we do not get and cannot take away from others by consumption, seems to elude the concept of internalization. The joy of discovering the other, the agency of the self, and the outsideness of the other—these are at best only fuzzily apprehended by internalization theory. When it defines differentiation as separating oneself from the other rather than as coming together with him, internalization theory describes an instrumental relationship. It implies an autonomous individual defined by his ability to do without the "need-satisfying object." The other seems more and more like a cocoon or a husk that must gradually be shed—one has got what one needs, and now, goodbye.

Let us consider how ego psychology thinks about the matter Winnicott called destruction, the matter of the infant's aggression and the mother's survival. Ego psychology conceives of the establishment of a constant internal object that survives frustration and absences, so that the mother is not internally destroyed when the infant is angry or when she goes away. In this conception, the infant can separate and yet be internally connected, be angry and yet still reclaim his love.[75] This is both an accurate and a useful statement of what is going on from the intrapsychic point of view. What it does not capture, however—and what

Winnicott's theory includes—is the intersubjective aspect of destruction, the recognition of the other, the joy and urgency of discovering the external, independent reality of another person.

A similar difference appears when we look at how ego psychology understands the phenomenon Winnicott identified as transitional experience.[76] In ego psychology's terms, the infant uses the transitional object (the favorite bear or the beloved blanket) to soothe and comfort himself, as a substitute for the mother's function in regulating tension. He *internalizes* the soothing function of the mother, and this represents a shift "from passivity to increasing activity," doing to himself what was previously done to him by the mother. By means of such internalization, the child progresses toward autonomy; he frees himself "from exclusive dependence on the need-satisfying object." Accordingly, the ego psychologist Marie Tolpin argues that Winnicott was wrong to say that the transitional object is not internalized. In her view, it goes inside just as the mother does, as mental structure.[77] And in the process of clinical work with adults, one can see how this framing of the problem occurs. One sees the way in which certain persons are unable to soothe themselves or regulate their own self-esteem. They act as if the internal "good mother," or her structural equivalent, were missing.

But Winnicott's transitional realm was primarily about creativity and play, about fantasy and reality, not about soothing. And even in regard to soothing, his concepts were getting at something beside internalization, something which is implied by his use of terms like "the holding environment" and "the facilitating environment." I think he was trying to define the area in which the child is able to develop his innate capacities because the people around him facilitate such development.[78] The ability to soothe oneself is not generated by internalizing the other's function; it is a capacity of the self which the other's response helps to activate. Infants are born with this capacity in more or less developed forms; some are quite adept from the first day, while others need someone to comfort them in order to fall asleep or stay awake without feeling uncomfortable. Within a few months an infant can also regulate himself through interaction—for example, when he looks away to reduce stimulation.[79] The activation of innate capacities is a very different developmental process from internalization; it presupposes at all times the presence of *two* interacting subjects who each contribute, rather than *one* subject who incorporates the action of the object.

Internalization theory and intersubjective theory are not mutually exclusive. But they are radically different ways of looking at development. Intersubjective theory is concerned not with how we take in enough from the other to be able to go away, but how the other gives us the opportunity to do it ourselves to begin with. This theory attributes all agency neither to the subject with his innate capacities or impulses, nor to the object which stamps the blank slate of the psyche with its imprint. It argues that the other plays an active part in the struggle of the individual to creatively discover and accept reality.

Intersubjective theory also permits us to distinguish two subjects recognizing each other from one subject regulating another. Stern has argued that we should not conflate instances where our main experience is of *being with* the other person with those in which the other simply helps to regulate our physiological tension. He suggests that although psychoanalysis has traditionally seen only certain moments of need gratification as "the cardinal 'magic moments' against which most all else in early infancy is background,"[80] these only represent one kind of relationship to the other. Nursing and going blissfully to sleep, says Stern, is an instance of having one's self dramatically transformed by the other's ministrations. It is quite different from facial play where the essential experience is *with* the other.[81]

Of course, the experiences of need gratification and soothing are an indispensable part of gaining a sense of the reliability and responsiveness of the external world—what Erikson called basic trust, and what Stern calls core relatedness. Such experiences contribute in a major way to faith in the other and a sense of one's own agency. But the experience of *being with* the other cannot be reduced to the experience of *being regulated* by an other. Indeed, the model of drive satisfaction has left an entire dimension unaccounted for; and that model has been greatly expanded since Freud. American ego psychology added to it by focusing on the relationship in which regulation occurs, and how that relationship is internalized. Object relations theory modified it by pointing out that the ultimate need is for the whole object, not simply the satisfaction of a drive.[82] But these elaborations still did not conceptualize the elements of activity, reciprocity, and mutual exchange that we now see when we study infants and their interaction with adults. The intrapsychic model thus missed what I consider the essence of differentiation: the paradoxical balance between recognition of the other and assertion of self. It also missed the fact that we have to get beyond internalization theory if we are to break out of the solipsistic omnipotence of the single psyche.

The classic psychoanalytic viewpoint did not see differentiation as a balance, but as a process of disentanglement. Thus it cast experiences of union, merger, and self-other harmony as regressive opposites to differentiation and self-other distinction. Merging was a dangerous form of undifferentiation, a sinking back into the sea of oneness—the "oceanic feeling" that Freud told Romain Rolland he frankly couldn't relate to.[83] The original sense of oneness was seen as absolute, as "limitless narcissm," and, therefore, regression to it would impede development and prevent separation. In its most extreme version, this view of differentiation pathologized the sensation of love: relaxing the boundaries of the self in communion with others threatened the identity of the isolate self. Yet this oneness was also seen as the ultimate pleasure, eclipsing the pleasure of difference. Oneness was not seen as a state that could coexist with (enhance and be enhanced by) the sense of separateness.[84]

One of the most important insights of intersubjective theory is that sameness and difference exist simultaneously in mutual recognition. This insight allows us to counter the argument that human beings fundamentally desire the impossible absolutes of "oneness" and perfection with the more moderate view that things don't have to be perfect, that, in fact, it is *better* if they are not. It reminds us that in every experience of similarity and subjective sharing, there must be enough difference to create the feeling of reality, that a degree of imperfection "ratifies" the existence of the world.[85]

Experiences of "being with" are predicated on a continually evolving awareness of difference, on a sense of intimacy felt as occurring between "the *two* of us." The fact that self and other are not merged is precisely what makes experiences of merging have such high emotional impact. The externality of the other makes one feel one is truly being "fed," getting nourishment from the outside, rather than supplying everything for oneself.

As infancy research informs us, the intense high feeling of union occurs as much in the active exchange *with* the other as in experiences of being regulated or transformed *by* the other. But psychoanalysis has seen only those interactions in which the infant's state of tension is regulated—feeding and holding—as the prototypical merging experiences. Above all, psychoanalysis has stressed complementarity in interaction over mutuality. The other is represented as the answer, and the self as the need; the other is the breast, and the self is the hunger; or the other is actively holding, and the self is passively being held.[86] This complementarity of activity and passivity forms a dual unity which can be internalized and reversed ("Now I'm the Mommy and you're the baby"). The dual unity form has within it this tendency to remain constant even in reversal, never to equalize but simply invert itself within relationships of dependency. The complementary dual unity is the basic structure of domination. And while it is certainly one of the structures of the psyche, it is not the only one. To see it as such is to leave no space for equality.

To transcend the experience of duality, so that both partners are equal, requires a notion of mutuality and sharing. In the intersubjective interaction both partners are active; it is not a reversible union of opposites (a doer and a done-to). The identification with the other person occurs through the sharing of similar states, rather than through reversal. "Being with" breaks down the oppositions between powerful and helpless, active and passive; it counteracts the tendency to objectify and deny recognition to those weaker or different—to the other. It forms the basis of compassion, what Milan Kundera calls "co-feeling,"[87] the ability to share feelings and intentions without demanding control, to experience sameness without obliterating difference.

The intersubjective view certainly doesn't negate all that we have learned from Freud, nor does it erase the many grounds he saw for pessimism. Often enough we see evidence of the striving for omnipotent control, and the hostility to otherness. The intersubjective view, however, suggests that there are aspects of the self, missing from the Freudian account, that can oppose (and help to explain) these tendencies. Perhaps Freud had them in mind when he referred to the instinctual force of Eros, the life force that aims at creating unities, but he never gave Eros a place in psychic structure.[88] It is this missing dimension of the psyche that finally enables us to confront the painful aspect of external reality—its uncontrollable, tenacious otherness—as a condition of freedom rather than of domination.

NOTES

1. There are different currents involved in the psychoanalytic shift toward interest in object relations; some emphasize the internal relationship to the object, while others include the real external object. These currents have fared quite differently in England and America, although both are considered to be about object relations. The British object relations tendency began with Melanie Klein's work on the earliest phases of the mother-child relationship (see, for example, *Envy and Gratitude*) in the thirties

and forties, and then took a turn away from instinct theory with the works of Ronald Fairbairn (see *Psychoanalytic Studies of the Personality*), D. W. Winnicott (see *The Maturational Process and the Facilitating Environment*), and Michael Balint, whose work on primary love was the first to clearly posit a social origin to the infant's relationships. (Balint is sometimes treated separately, as part of the Hungarian School; see *The Basic Fault.*) A summary of the development of and differences among object relations theorists, with special emphasis on Fairbairn, can be found in Harry Guntrip, *Personality Structure and Human Interaction*.

In America, object relations theory was eclipsed by ego psychology, the position of mainstream theorists in the post-war period. This school of thought did not focus until significantly later on the inner world of objects; a landmark in this evolution of position was Edith Jacobson's *The Self and the Object World* (1964). The work of Margaret Mahler et al. on separation-individuation in infancy (*The Psychological Birth of the Human Infant*) also moved ego psychology significantly in the direction of object relations. And important American psychoanalysts have contributed to the development of object relations theory, for example Hans Loewald (e.g., "The Therapeutic Action of Psychoanalysis") and Arnold Modell (*Object Love and Reality*). Some of the criticisms of instinct theory made by the British object relations theorists were made in this country by Heinz Kohut, who founded self psychology in the seventies (see *The Restoration of the Self*). Harry Stack Sullivan (see *The Interpersonal Theory of Psychiatry*), who concurred with the British School's focus on relationships, did influence, despite his official separation from and rejection by Freudian psychoanalysts in the post-war period, clinical practitioners to pay greater attention to external reality, especially in psychosis. The relations between these different developments is discussed by Jay Greenberg and Stephen Mitchell in *Object Relations in Psychoanalytic Theory*.

2. The focus on differentiation in infancy does not mean that infancy determines later experiences, but that it establishes certain issues and patterns that reappear later, sometimes in other forms.

3. The amount of research being done on neonatal abilities is enormous. Experiments designed to document the infant's early identification of its own mother are becoming increasingly more common. See T. B. Brazelton on the infant's preference for its mother's face and voice in the first week of life in "Neonatal Assessment"; J. McFarlane's discussion of infant preference for maternal milk in "Olfaction in the Development of Social Preferences in the Human Neonate"; G. Carpenter on two-week-old infants' preference for the mother's face in "Mother's Face and the Newborn"; and A. DeCasper and W. Fifer, "Of Human Bonding: Newborns Prefer Their Mother's Voices."

4. Although I use the word "carried" and refer to research on mother-infant pairs in which the infant was the biological offspring of this mother, I am not suggesting that the experience is radically different in adoption. Adoptive mothers, like biological ones, hold their baby inside their minds before birth, and identify with their own mothers who carried them. It is this mental holding, and the shift to a relationship with a real—outside—baby that I am referring to here.

5. Since there is no graceful solution to the problem of what gender pronoun to use for the infant, I shall alternate between masculine and feminine. In those paragraphs where I refer to the mother as "she," I will generally avoid confusion by calling the infant "he." In those paragraphs where I refer to the infant alone and therefore the referent for the pronoun is clear, the infant will generally be "she." Although I write about the mother, I mean simply the significant adult, which could equally be a father or any other caregiver well known to the child. But since it is quite relevant to my argument that the principal caregiver in our culture is usually (or is assumed to be) "the mother," this ambiguity will have to remain.

6. Infancy researchers stress that the infant is an active partner in the relationship.

They speak of the "competent" infant who can elicit the kind of behavior from adult caregivers that is optimal for emotional security and development; that is, the infant gives readable cues and is responsive and actively interested in parental stimulation. See S. Goldberg, "Social Competence in Infancy"; M. D. S. Ainsworth and S. Bell, "Mother-Infant Interaction and the Development of Competence"; R. Q. Bell, "The Contribution of Human Infants to Caregiving and Social Interaction"; and Lewis and Rosenblum, eds., *The Effect of the Infant on Its Caregiver.*

7. The idea of infant and parent each mutually influencing the other become prominent especially as a result of the observation of play interaction. My reading of this interaction has been most influenced by the work of Beatrice Beebe (see "Mother-Infant Mutual Influence and Precursors of Self and Object Representations") and Daniel Stern. For an introduction to this research, see Daniel Stern, *The First Relationship.*

8. The drive's indiscriminateness toward the object and the ego's indifference, or hostility, toward the outside world were discussed by Freud in "Formulations on the Two Principles in Mental Functioning" and "Instincts and Their Vicissitudes." Freud's position was criticized by two early influential exponents of the infant's activity and curiosity, Ernst Schachtel (*Metamorphosis*) and R. W. White ("Motivation Reconsidered: The Concept of Competence"). They address the problem of Freud's theory of primary narcissism, which was also critiqued by Balint. Yet another wave of criticism of Freud's view developed later, in response to Mahler's notion of infant autism (*The Psychological Birth of the Human Infant*), and is well summed up by Emanuel Peterfreund ("Some Critical Comments on Psychoanalytic Conceptualizations of Infancy") and Stern (*The Interpersonal World of the Infant*).

9. See Piaget and Inhelder (*The Psychology of the Child*) and Piaget (*The Construction of Reality in the Child*). Psychologists were, of course, influenced by many nonpsychoanalytic trends—not only Piaget, but also G. H. Meade (*Mind, Self, and Society*) and C. H. Cooley (*Human Nature and the Social Order*), whose theories of social psychology asserted the central place of the relationship to the other in the genesis of the self.

10. John Bowlby made use of ethological research on animals as well as children to formulate his highly influential theory of the primacy of attachment. In a study written for the World Health Organization, *Maternal Care and Mental Health*, Bowlby formulated the basic themes of attachment theory. Bowlby's point was that, whereas Freudian theory makes attachment a secondary phenomenon and defines it as "anaclitic" (dependent on the drive for oral gratification), attachment can be observed as a behavior independent of such needs (see Bowlby, "The Nature of the Child's Tie to His Mother," and Ainsworth, "Object Relations, Dependency and Attachment").

11. Bowlby (*Attachment*) describes how those infants who were separated from their parents but placed in a setting that afforded considerable social interaction were able to form a normal attachment to their parents within two weeks of their return, whereas those who were in a hospital setting without such interaction required eight weeks or more to develop the same attachment. See also H. R. Schaffer, *The Growth of Sociability.*

12. Ainsworth and Bell ("Attachment, Exploration, and Separation") developed an important research technique, the observation of infants in a strange situation, to evaluate a child's attachment to its mother. The test makes use of the infant's anxiety reaction to strangers that develops in the second six months of life, and presumes that normally attached infants cling to the mother when anxious. Ainsworth observed how well the child was able to reunite with the mother after separation and gain reassurance from her presence.

13. Guntrip (*Personality Structure and Human Interaction*) especially emphasized Fairbairn's idea (*Psychoanalytic Studies of the Personality*) that when the drive is directed primarily to one psychosexual aspect rather than the whole object this represents a deterioration of the relationship.

14. Mahler et al., *The Psychological Birth of the Human Infant.*

15. Mahler's idea of hatching has also been challenged by those researchers who have found infant responsiveness and interaction to be a cumulative process. See note 5.

16. Stern, "The Early Development of Schemas of Self, of Other, and of Various Experiences of 'Self with Other.'" See also *The Interpersonal World of the Infant.* Stern, a pioneer in infancy research, argues that emergent structures or capacities are built into the infant and have only to enter into interaction with other people to unfold. For example, since the infant can discriminate between constant and intermittent reinforcement of behavior, this means it quickly learns to discriminate between what it does (voice resonates in chest) and the other does (answer).

17. Winnicott, "Primary Maternal Preoccupation," p. 304.

18. Kohut, *The Restoration of the Self.* Self psychology argues that we need to use other people as "selfobjects" in the service of self-esteem and cohesion throughout life, and criticizes what it sees as psychoanalysis's erroneous inflation of independence as the goal of maturity. As Greenberg and Mitchell point out (*Object Relations*), this critique exaggerates the psychoanalytic disparagement of dependency. It also fails to distinguish between using others as "selfobjects" and recognizing the other as an outside subject, missing the key point of the intersubjective view.

19. The concept of intersubjectivity has its origins in the social theory of Jürgen Habermas (1970), who used the expression "the intersubjectivity of mutual understanding" to designate an individual capacity and a social domain. I have taken the concept as theoretical standpoint from which to criticize the exclusively intrapsychic conception of the individual in psychoanalysis. The term was first brought from Habermas's theory to infant psychology by Colwyn Trevarthen, who documented a "period of primary intersubjectivity, when sharing of intention with others becomes an effective psychological activity." More recently, Daniel Stern has outlined the psychological development of intersubjectivity in infancy, locating intersubjective relatedness as a crucial point in self development when the infant is able to share subjective (especially emotional) experiences. Because intersubjectivity refers both to a capacity and to a theoretical standpoint, I will generally call the capacity recognition, and the theory intersubjectivity.

20. See Habermas, "A Theory of Communicative Competence"; Trevarthen, "Communication and Cooperation in Early Infancy: A Description of Primary Intersubjectivity"; and Stern, *The Interpersonal World of the Infant.* Meade's (*Mind, Self, and Society*) theorizing about the creation of shared meaning prefigured Habermas's remarks on intersubjectivity, and his discussion of gestures is relevant to a social theory perspective on infant development. Arnold Modell's distinction (*Psychoanalysis in a New Context*) between one-person psychology and two-person psychology is essentially similar to that I am making between intersubjective and intrapsychic. Lichtenberg's account of intersubjectivity (*Psychoanalysis and Infant Research*) locates it in terms of self-consciousness of doing, in the second year of life, much later than Stern and Trevarthen locate it.

21. The idea of complementarity is useful here, as Michael Eigen has shown in his discussion of Winnicott ("The Area of Faith in Winnicott, Lacan and Bion"). Modell (*Psychoanalysis in New Context*) also argues that we ought to see them as complementary approaches, and that it is premature to think of synthesizing them.

22. As Emmanuel Ghent points out ("Credo: The Dialectic of One-Person and Two-Person Psychologies"), it is not necessary to make the choice between external and inner reality that Freud posed when he switched from the seduction theory to the idea that his patients were not really seduced but fantasizing.

23. Unfortunately it is beyond the scope of this discussion to propose a scheme for synthesizing the two approaches. The problem is that each focuses on different aspects of psychic experience which are too interdependent to be simply severed from one another. I am emphasizing intersubjectivity over intrapsychic theory because the latter is better

developed and usually overshadows the former, not because I think one ought to preclude the other.

24. Stern, *The Interpersonal World of the Infant,* pp. 92–93.

25. See J. S. Watson, "Smiling, Cooing, and 'The Game.'" See also M. Lewis and S. Goldberg, "Perceptual-Cognitive Development in Infancy."

26. This phenomenon of checking back with the mother has been documented by Emde and his colleagues in an experiment using the "visual cliff," in which the illusion of a drop is created and the infant either proceeds or stops, depending on maternal response—doubt or encouragement. See Klinnert et al., "Emotions as Behavior Regulators: Social Referencing in Infancy"; and Emde and Sorce, "The Rewards of Infancy: Emotional Availability and Maternal Referencing."

27. On the necessity of the child's recognition of the mother as a subject in her own right, see Dinnerstein *The Mermaid and the Minotaur,* Chodorow, "Gender, Relation and Difference in Psychoanalytic Perspective" and Keller, *Reflections on Gender and Science.*

28. See Chodorow, *The Reproduction of Mothering;* Chodorow and Contratto, "The Fantasy of the Perfect Mother"; and Dinnerstein, *The Mermaid and the Minotaur.*

29. Recognizing the infant as an active, social being who relates to the mother as a person does not entirely remove the problem of psychology's infant-centered perspective, which views the parent as merely the facilitator of the child's development. This perspective tends to make development competence an end in itself and has somewhat devalued the emotional relationship of the infant with the parents (perhaps because it ignores the intrapsychic). Some of this emphasis on infant activity and competence, especially on early cognitive abilities, stems more from the dominant tendency to stress performance than from an interest in sociability (see Adrienne Harris, "The Rationalization of Infancy").

30. Chodorow (*The Reproduction of Mothering*) points out that psychoanalysts, with a few important exceptions, ignore the discrepancy between the total nature of the infant's love and the partial nature of the mother's. What psychoanalysis stresses is appropriate to the clinical situation but not to the theoretical one, the child's view, the view of inner, not outer, reality.

31. The use of the concept of maternal mirroring is a common, but problematic, one in psychoanalysis. (See Winnicott on "The Mirror Role of Mother and Family in Child Development" and Kohut's idea of the mirroring object in *The Restoration of the Self.*) The mirror metaphor has been criticized from a feminist viewpoint by Gilligan ("Remapping the Moral Domain") and from the standpoint of infancy research by Stern (*The Interpersonal World of the Infant*).

32. The criticism of separateness as a goal has been made by several feminists, especially the group around Jean Baker Miller (see the *Works in Progress* of the Stone Center), Chodorow, "Gender, Relation and Difference," and Gilligan, "Remapping the Moral Domain."

33. These terms, the figure and the ground, were used somewhat differently by Fred Pine in his illuminating contribution to the debate about the nature of differentiation ("In the Beginning"). Pine, who co-authored the major statement of separation-individuation theory with Mahler and Bergmann (*The Psychological Birth of the Human Infant*), tried to correct the difficulties that arose from the idea of the infant's initial autism. However, he still maintains that play and interaction are the background while drive satisfaction and merging experiences are the intense "magic moments" that form the figure. Thus moments of distress constitute the alternate element in the symbiotic phase to the intensity of merging blissfully in nursing. Stern ("The Early Development of Schemas of Self") criticized Pine's formulation on the grounds that self-other differentiation is a continual process and is not really undone by the intense physical intimacy called merging. Further-

more, exuberant active play in which differentiation is clearly a feature constitutes as intense a high point as merger experiences.

34. Early work on mother-infant interaction in the seventies focused on the structure of reciprocity and how play can be seen as a model of interaction. Research on mother-infant facial play was conducted by several groups, who reached similar conclusions (see Brazelton, Koslowski, and Main, "The Origins of Reciprocity"; Tronick, Als, and Adamson, "Structure of Early Face-to-Face Communicative Interactions"; and Tronick, Als, and Brazelton, "Mutuality in Mother-Infant Interaction"; see also Stern's "The Goal and Structure of Mother-Infant Play," "Mother and Infant at Play: The Dyadic Interaction Involving Facial, Vocal and Gaze Behavior," and *The First Relationship;* and Stern, Beebe, Jaffe, and Bennett, "The Infant's Stimulus World During Social Interaction"; see also Trevarthen, "Descriptive Analyses of Infant Communicative Behavior" and "The Foundations of Intersubjectivity."

35. Beebe, "Mother-Infant Mutual Influence and Precursors of Self and Object Representations."

36. Stern, *The First Relationship*, and Beebe, Stern, and Jaffe, "The Kinesic Rhythm of Mother-Infant Interactions."

37. Stern, *The First Relationship*, p. 116. Stern's formulations emphasize that this is not an instrumental kind of learning; it is bound up with having fun, with excitement, and pleasure.

38. Discussions of "chase and dodge" interactions can be found in Beebe and Stern, "Engagement-Disengagement"; Stern, *The First Relationship;* and Stern, "A Microanalysis of Mother-Infant Interaction."

39. Beebe and Stern, "Engagement-Disengagement."

40. The dynamic patterns of interpersonal interaction coincide with the determinants of inner regulation at this point. The separate sphere—the symbolic unconscious—where the psyche reconstructs and elaborates what has taken place in the exchange with the outside does not yet exist. But representation is already beginning in an earlier form, as Beebe suggests ("Mother-Infant Mutual Influence"), in the interiorization of interaction patterns between self and other, which are the precursors of later representations. She argues that "the very process of reciprocal adjustments, as these create expected patterns," will form early "'interactive representations.'"

41. Stern (*The Interpersonal World of the Infant*) defines earlier relatedness not as intersubjectivity but as core relatedness; although he agrees with Trevarthen that intersubjectivity is an innate, emergent human capacity, he argues that it does not exist at three to four months. In my view, intersubjectivity is best used as a theoretical construct encompassing the trajectory of experiences building up to the recognition of separate minds sharing the same state. If this awareness takes a leap forward in attunement at age seven to nine months, then we might say that intersubjectivity takes its first step toward being self-conscious, "intersubjectivity for itself."

42. Stern, *The Interpersonal World of the Infant*, pp. 138–42.

43. Ibid., p. 127.

44. Mahler et al., *The Psychological Birth of the Human Infant*. See the discussion of refueling, pp. 65–75. Mahler et al. note that children take their first unaided steps away from, not toward, the mother (p. 73). Attachment theory, as formulated by Ainsworth ("Object Relations, Dependency and Attachment"), also sees the main events of development this way, but emphasizes the balance between attachment and exploration. This construction of the tension within the self has begun to influence the proponents of separation-individuation theory. In a response to Stern's critique of Mahler, her research associate Louise Kaplan ("Symposium on *The Interpersonal World of the Infant*") argues for the balance between individuation and attachment, claiming that Stern exaggerates the one-sidedness of separation-individuation theory when he says: "For Mahler, connected-

ness is the result of a failure in differentiation; for us it is a success of psychic function" (*The Interpersonal World of the Infant*, p. 241). Elsewhere in the book Stern writes—more evenhandedly—that the point is not to reverse the order of development, but that "both separation/individuation and new forms of experiencing union (or being-with) emerge equally out of the same experience of intersubjectivity" (p. 127).

45. As Stern emphasizes, the sharing of affective states is the baseline of intersubjectivity (see *The Interpersonal World of the Infant*).

46. See Modell (*Psychoanalysis in a New Context*), who contends that affects are the central aspect of two-person psychology.

47. See Stechler and Kaplan, "The Development of the Self: A Psychoanalytic Perspective."

48. Hegel, *Phänomenologie des Geistes;* my translation.

49. The reader may ask, Why does this tension have to break down? The answer is, for Hegel every tension between oppositional elements carries the seeds of its own destruction and transcendence (*Aufhebung*) into another form. That is how life is. Without this process of contradiction and dissolution, there would be no movement, change, or history. We do not need to accept this conclusion in order to draw on Hegel's understanding of this process; but if we wish to argue that tension can be sustained, it behooves us to show how that is possible.

50. "It is for [consciousness], that it is and is not immediately the other consciousness; and even so, that this other is only for itself, in that it transcends itself as existing for itself; only in existing for the other is it for itself. Each is the medium for the other, through which each is mediated and united with itself; and each is for itself and the other an immediate being, existing for itself, which simultaneously is only for itself by virtue of this mediation. They *recognize* themselves as *mutually recognizing one another.*" *Phänomenologie*, p. 143.

51. As Hegel continues to elucidate the relationship of the two consciousnesses, he explains that each person must try to prove the certainty of himself or herself in the life-and-death struggle that we all face with one another. This struggle to the death culminates in the master-slave relationship, as one gives in and the other establishes himself over the other. This outcome, rather than mutual recognition, Hegel views as the origin of domination.

52. This subphase, differentiation, is not to be confused with the larger process of establishing the awareness of self as distinct from the other, which is also called differentiation.

53. Mahler et al., *The Psychological Birth of the Human Infant*, pp. 65–75.

54. Ibid., pp. 76–108.

55. Classical psychoanalysis, like Hegel, starts with the individual in a state of omnipotence. Thus Mahler uses omnipotence to characterize the feelings of the child, in the symbiotic union of earliest infancy, who experiences the other's support as an extension of the self. She also uses it in her discussion of the rapprochement toddler who clamors "for omnipotent control." The idea of omnipotence has been criticized with reference to both phases (e.g., Peterfreund, "Some Critical Comments on Psychoanalytic Conceptualizations of Infancy") for projecting an adult state (the belief that you can control others) onto infancy. To this, Mahler's colleague Pine ("In the Beginning") has replied that omnipotence is not about making "impossible demands," but describes an infant's feelings when he or she believes that their cries have "magically" made the mother come to nurse the infant. But one could argue that the infant's subjective feeling when mother answers his cry is probably not one of omnipotence, but simply of effectiveness. The idea of omnipotence, I believe, can only appear in the context of impotence and helplessness. The toddler in rapprochement who encounters the limits of his effectiveness seems to me a better illustration of the idea of omnipotence than the infant who can make no distinc-

tion between real and magical accomplishments. Omnipotence is a meaningful idea not as the original state, but as a fantasy that children construct in the face of disappointment, a reaction to loss—indeed, it is usually derived from a perception of the parent's power. It is the sense or threat of loss that leads to "impossible demands," the attempt to get back what we never had but imagine we did. Omnipotence describes a defensive wish, buried in every psyche, that one will have a perfect world, will prevail over time, death, and the other—and that coercion can succeed.

56. Mahler et al., *The Psychological Birth of the Human Infant*, p. 96.

57. Freud, "On Narcissism."

58. Object constancy is ego psychology's term for the ability to maintain a representation of the other as present and good even when the other is absent or there is conflict. Important as this internalization may arguably be, it is not the same as recognizing the other's independence. By conceptualizing the resolution of rapprochement in terms of object constancy, the developmental issue of separation is reduced to being able to tolerate absence or aggression; this leaves out actually appreciating or enjoying the other's separateness, as a mother is supposed to do with her child.

59. Winnicott, "Ego Distortion in Terms of True and False Self."

60. Winnicott, *Playing and Reality*.

61. Ibid., pp. 103–4.

62. Ibid., p. 105.

63. Ibid., p. 106.

64. André Green, "Potential Space in Psychoanalysis: The Object in the Setting."

65. Winnicott, *Playing and Reality*, p. 106.

66. Elsa First, "The Leaving Game: I'll Play You and You Play Me."

67. Eigen, "The Area of Faith in Winnicott, Lacan and Bion."

68. Winnicott, *The Child, the Family and the Outside World*, p. 62.

69. Winnicott, "Transitional Objects and Transitional Phenomena," in *Playing and Reality*.

70. Susan Deri, "Transitional Phenomena: Vicissitudes of Symbolization and Creativity." She explains that when the mother adapts herself to the baby's needs, giving in response to his hungry call, the baby has the "illusion" that he has actually created the breast with his need, that his need is creative; Winnicott called this "the creative illusion."

71. Sander, "Polarity, Paradox, and the Organizing Process in Development."

72. Sander cites Winnicott's article on "The Capacity to Be Alone": "'. . . the basis of the capacity to be alone is a paradox; it is the experience of being alone while someone else is present.'" And further, "'it is only when alone (that is to say, in the presence of someone) that the infant can discover his own personal life. The pathological alternative is a false life built on reactions to external stimuli.'" (Sander, "Polarity, Paradox, and the Organizing Process in Development," p. 322; Winnicott, "The Capacity to Be Alone," p. 34.)

73. Schachtel's *Metamorphosis* contains one of the earliest descriptions of how the object comes into full view, into focal attention, when there is no pressure from need or anxiety. He writes of the absorption—of becoming lost in contemplation of the object—that can occur in this state when the subject no longer injects himself into the thing. This is obviously the counterpoint to being free from intrusion or impingement by the other.

74. The theory of identification has been central to psychoanalysis since Freud's development of ego psychology in the 1920s. The Oedipus complex now resulted not only the resolution of the conflict between wish and defense, but also in the consolidation of the tripartite structure of id, ego, and superego. The ego and superego developed through identification with the parental objects. Since those formulations, the theory has been greatly expanded to include the internalization of a whole world of objects.

75. Freud's theory that the ego is the precipitate of abandoned objects has been the basis of ego psychology. Its beginning is usually dated to publication of Freud's "Mourning and Melancholia," and its major formulation was in *The Ego and the Id.* The development of ego psychology continued in the thirties, with Anna Freud's *The Ego and Its Mechanisms of Defense* (1936) and Heinz Hartmann's *Ego Psychology and the Problem of Adaptation* (1939).

76. Marie Tolpin, "On the Beginnings of the Cohesive Self."

77. In this way Tolpin sees the idea of the transitional object as another step in Freud's notion of ego formation s the "precipitate of abandoned object-cathexes." Tolpin here anticipated the thinking of self psychology, of which she later became an important exponent, which views psychic structure as created by "transmuting internalizations."

78. Thus the analytic situation itself has come to be understood as a potential transitional space, creating the conditions for the growth of authentic agency through play, rather than merely a context for interpretation, in which the analyst "changes" the patient. See André Green, "The Analyst, Symbolization and Absence in the Analytic Setting."

79. T. Field, "Infant Gaze Aversion and Heart Rate During Face-to-Face Interactions." Beebe (in discussion) has suggested a perspective of development in which the infant refines its own capacities for regulation through exercising them, that is, in interaction.

80. Here Stern ("The Early Developmental of Schemas of Self") is arguing with Pine ("In the Beginning"), who has described the "magic moments" of gratification, like nursing, as the moments of real union. Pine wants to privilege these intense moments of oneness as the figure while still giving importance to the everyday background of distinguishing self from other. Schachtel first introduced this distinction, in a slightly different form.

81. I would add that the nursing experience itself has legitimately been understood quite variously: in terms of oral sexual pleasure, reduction of tension, the sense of efficacy resulting from the caregiver's responsiveness, an intense merging or oneness, the "creative illusion" that one has made the breast appear. One might distinguish the element of soothing and relief of hunger from the element of emotional attunement and facial mirroring that follow or accompany relief. Within a few weeks of birth, the infant has sufficient control over physiological tension that hunger may be less pressing than his interest in mother's face. Thus nursing, as a primary metaphor of infancy, encompasses all three kinds of relationships to the other that, according to Stern, "The Early Development of Schemas of Self," appear in psychoanalytic thinking: being transformed by another (as in tension relief), complementarity (as in being held), and mental sharing (as in mutual gaze). The power of the breast metaphor, I believe, has always lain in the multiplicity of meanings it evoked.

82. For example, see Fairbairn, "Steps in the Development of an Object-Relations Theory of the Personality."

83. Freud, *Civilization and Its Discontents.*

84. Keller (*Reflections on Gender and Science*), noting the derogation of oneness in Freudian theory, gives a very good account of a different kind of union that does allow the simultaneous sense of distinctness and of losing self in the other in her discussion of Schachtel and dynamic objectivity.

85. We can trace the desire for difference back to the infant's early interest in the novel, the discrepant, and even the disjunctive. Bahrick and Watson ("Detection of Intermodal and Proprioceptive Visual Contingency") demonstrated that infants preferred looking at a delayed over a simultaneous (mirroring) video playback of their motions. Recognizing the difference as the complement to sameness or oneness is a major point that distinguishes intersubjective theory from self psychology.

86. Following Stern's taxonomy (in "The Early Development of Schemas of Self") we can say that both having one's state transformed by the other, as in drive theory, and the

complementarity of being held, as in object-relations theory, focus on the individually conceived subject and his complementary relationship to the object. Both stand in contrast to the mutuality posited by intersubjective theory.

87. Kundera, *The Unbearable Lightness of Being.*
88. Freud, *Civilization and Its Discontents.*

SELECTED BIBLIOGRAPHY

AINSWORTH, M. D. S. "Object Relations, Dependency, and Attachment: A Theoretical Overview of the Infant-Mother Relationship." *Child Development* 40 (1969): 969–1025.

AINSWORTH, M. D. S., AND S. BELL. "Attachment, Exploration, and Separation Illustrated by the Behavior of One-Year-Olds in a Strange Situation." *Child Development* 41 (1970): 49–67.

BAHRICK, LORRAINE, AND JOHN WATSON. "Detection of Intermodal and Proprioceptive Visual Contingency as a Basis of Self-Perception in Infancy." *Developmental Psychology* 21 (1985): 963–73.

BALINT, MICHAEL. *The Basic Fault.* London: Tavistock Publications, 1968.

BEEBE, BEATRICE. "Mother-Infant Mutual Influence and Precursors of Self and Object Representations." In J. Massling, ed., *Empirical Studies of Psychoanalytic Theories,* vol. 2. Hillsdale, N.J.: Lawrence Erlbaum, 1985.

BEEBE, BEATRICE, AND DANIEL STERN. "Engagement-Disengagement and Early Object Experiences." In N. Freedman and S. Frand, eds., *Communicative Structures and Psychic Structures.* New York: Plenum Press, 1977.

BEEBE, BEATRICE, DANIEL STERN, AND JOSEPH JAFFE. "The Kinesic Rhythm of Mother-Infant Interactions." In A. W. Siegman and S. Felstein, eds., *Of Speech and Time: Temporal Patterns in Interpersonal Contexts.* Hillsdale, N.J.: Lawrence Erlbaum, 1979.

BELL, R. Q. "The Contribution of Human Infants to Caregiving and Social Interaction." In Lewis and Rosenblum, eds., *The Effect of the Infant on Its Caregiver.* New York: John Wiley, 1974.

BOWLBY, JOHN. *Maternal Care and Mental Health.* (1951) New York: Schocken, 1966.

———. "The Nature of the Child's Tie to His Mother." *International Journal of Psychoanalysis* 39 (1958): 350–73.

———. *Attachment.* London: Penguin Books, 1971.

BRAZELTON, T. B. "Neonatal Assessment." In S. I. Greenspan and G. H. Pollock, eds., *The Course of Life: Psychoanalytic Contributions Toward Understanding Personality Development.* Vol. I. *Infancy and Early Childhood.* Rockville, Md.: NIMH, 1980.

BRAZELTON, T. B., B. KOSLOWSKI, AND M. MAIN. "The Origins of Reciprocity." In M. Lewis and L. R. Rosenblum, eds., *The Effect of the Infant on Its Caregiver.* New York: Wiley, 1974.

CARPENTER, G. "Mother's Face and the Newborn." *New Scientist* 61 (1974): 742–46.

CHODOROW, NANCY. *The Reproduction of Mothering: Psychoanalysis and the Sociology of Gender.* Berkeley: University of California Press, 1978.

———. "Gender, Relation, and Difference in Psychoanalytic Perspective." In Hester Eisenstein and Alice Jardine, eds., *The Future of Difference.* Boston: G. K. Hall, 1980.

COOLEY, C. H. *Human Nature and the Social Order.* (1902) New York: Schocken, 1970.

DECASPER, A., AND W. FIFER. "Of Human Bonding: Newborns Prefer Their Mother's Voices." *Science* 208 (1980): 1174–76.

DERI, SUSAN. "Transitional Phenomena: Vicissitudes of Symbolization and Creativity." In Simon Grolnick and Leonard Barkin, eds., *Between Reality and Fantasy.* New York: Jason Aronson, 1978.

EIGEN, MICHAEL. "The Area of Faith in Winnicott, Lacan and Bion." *International Journal of Psycho-analysis* 62 (1981): 413–33.

EMDE, R. N., AND J. E. SORCE. "The Rewards of Infancy: Emotional Availability and Maternal Referencing." In J. D. Call, E. Galenson, and R. Tyson, eds., *Frontiers of Infant Psychiatry*, vol. 2. New York: Basic Books, 1983.

FAIRBAIRN, RONALD. *Psychoanalytic Studies of the Personality.* London: Routledge and Kegan Paul, 1952.

———. "Steps in the Development of an Object-Relations Theory of the Personality." In *Psychoanalytic Studies of the Personality.*

FIELD, TIFFANY. "Infant Gaze Aversion and Heart Rate During Face-to-Face Interactions." *Infant Behavior and Development* 4 (1981): 307–15.

FIRST, ELSA. "The Leaving Game: I'll Play You and You Play Me: The Emergence of the Capacity for Dramatic Role Play in Two-Year-Olds." In Arieta Slade and Denny Wolfe, eds., *Modes of Meaning: Clinical and Developmental Approaches to Symbolic Play.* New York: Oxford University Press, 1988.

FREUD, ANNA. *The Ego and Its Mechanisms of Defense.* (1936) New York: International Universities Press, 1954.

FREUD, SIGMUND. "Formulations on the Two Principles in Mental Functioning." (1911) SE 12: 213–26.

———. "On Narcissism: An Introduction." (1914) SE 14: 67–102.

———. "Instincts and Their Vicissitudes." (1915) SE 14: 11–140.

———. "Mourning and Melancholia." (1917) SE 14: 239–58.

———. *The Ego and the Id.* (1923) SE 19: 1–66.

———. *Civilization and Its Discontents.* (1930) SE 21: 57–146.

GHENT, EMMANUEL. "Credo: The Dialectics of One-Person and Two-Person Psychologies," Colloquium, New York University Postdoctoral Psychology Program, 1986.

Gilligan, Carol. "Remapping the Moral Domain: New Images of the Self in Relationship." In Thomas Heller, Morton Sosna, and David Wellbery, eds., *Reconstructing Individualism: Autonomy, Individuality, and the Self in Western Thought.* Stanford, Calif.: Stanford University Press, 1986.

GOLDBERG, S. "Social Competence in Infancy: A Model of Parent-Infant Interaction." *Merrill-Palmer Quarterly* 23 (1977): 163–77.

GREEN, ANDRÉ. "The Analyst, Symbolization and Absence in the Analytic Setting." In *On Private Madness.* New York: International Universities Press, 1986.

———. "Potential Space in Psychoanalysis: The Object in the Setting." In *On Private Madness.* New York: International Universities Press, 1986.

GREENBERG, JAY, AND STEPHEN MITCHELL. *Object Relations in Psychoanalytic Theory.* Cambridge, Mass.: Harvard University Press, 1983.

GUNTRIP, HARRY. *Personality Structure and Human Interaction.* New York: International Universities Press, 1961.

HABERMAS, JÜRGEN. "A Theory of Communicative Competence." In H. P. Dreitzel, ed., *Recent Sociology* no. 2. New York: Macmillan, 1970.

HARRIS, ADRIENNE. "The Rationalization of Infancy." In John Broughton, ed., *Critical Theories of Psychological Development.* New York: Plenum Press, 1987.

HARTMANN, HEINZ. *Ego Psychology and the Problem of Adaptation.* (1939) New York: International Universities Press, 1958.

HEGEL, G. W. F. *Phänomenologie des Geistes.* Hamburg: Felix Meiner Verlag, edition of 1952.

JACOBSON, EDITH. *The Self and the Object World.* New York: International Universities Press, 1964.

KAPLAN, LOUISE. "Symposium on *The Interpersonal World of the Infant.*" In *Contemporary Psychoanalysis* 23 (1987): 27–45.

KELLER, EVELYN. *Reflections on Gender and Science*. New Haven, Conn.: Yale University Press, 1985.

KLEIN, MELANIE. *Envy and Gratitude*. New York: Basic Books, 1957.

KLINNERT, M. D., ET AL. "Emotions as Behavior Regulators: Social Referencing in Infancy." In R. Plutchik and H. Kellerman, eds., *Emotion: Theory, Research, and Experience*, no. 2. New York: Academic Press, 1983.

KOHUT, HEINZ. *The Restoration of the Self*. New York: International Universities Press, 1977.

KUNDERA, MILAN. *The Unbearable Lightness of Being*. New York: Harper and Row, 1984.

LEWIS, M., AND ROSENBLUM, L., EDS. *The Effect of the Infant on Its Caregiver*. New York: John Wiley, 1974.

LICHTENBERG, JOSEPH. *Psychoanalysis and Infant Research*. Hillsdale, N.J.: The Analytic Press, 1983.

LOEWALD, HANS. "The Therapeutic Action of Psychoanalysis." (1960) In *Papers on Psychoanalysis*.

MACFARLANE, J. "Olfaction in the Development of Social Preferences in the Human Neonate." In M. Hofer, ed., *Parent-Infant Interaction*. Amsterdam: Elsevier, 1975.

MAHLER, MARGARET, FRED PINE, AND ANNI BERGMANN. *The Psychological Birth of the Human Infant*. New York: Basic Books, 1975.

MEADE, GEORGE HERBERT. *Mind, Self, and Society*. Chicago: University of Chicago Press, 1955.

MILLER, JEAN BAKER. "What Do We Mean by Relationships?" In *Works in Progress* of the Stone Center, Wellesley, Mass., 1987.

MODELL, ARNOLD. *Object Love and Reality*. New York: International Universities Press, 1968.

PETERFREUND, EMANUEL. "Some Critical Comments on Psychoanalytic Conceptualizations of Infancy." *International Journal of Psycho-analysis* 59 (1978): 427–41.

PIAGET, JEAN. *The Construction of Reality in the Child*. (1937) New York: Basic Books, 1954.

PIAGET, JEAN, AND BARBEL INHELDER. *The Psychology of the Child*. New York: Basic Books, 1969.

PINE, FRED. "In the Beginning: Contributions to a Psychoanalytic Developmental Psychology." *International Review of Psycho-analysis* 8 (1981): 15–33.

SANDER, LOUIS. "Polarity, Paradox, and the Organizing Process in Development." In J. D. Call, E. Galenson, and R. L. Tyson, eds., *Frontiers of Infant Psychiatry*, no. 1. New York: Basic Books, 1983.

SCHACHTEL, ERNST. *Metamorphosis*. New York: Basic Books, 1959.

SCHAFFER, H. R. *The Growth of Sociability*. Harmondsworth, U.K.: Penguin Books, 1971.

STECHLER, G. AND S. KAPLAN. "The Development of the Self: A Psychoanalytic Perspective." *The Psychoanalytic Study of the Child* 35 (1980): 85–106.

STERN, DANIEL. "The Goal and Structure of Mother-Infant Play." *Journal of the American Academy of Child Psychiatry* 13 (1974): 402–21.

———. "A Microanalysis of Mother-Infant Interaction. Behaviors Regulating Social Contact between a Mother and Her Three-and-a-half-month-old Twins." *Journal of the American Academy of Child Psychiatry* 13 (1974): 501–17.

———. "Mother and Infant at Play: The Dyadic Interaction Involving Facial, Vocal and Gaze Behavior." In M. Lewis and L. Rosenblum, eds., *The Effect of the Infant on Its Caregiver*. New York: John Wiley, 1974.

———. *The First Relationship: Infant and Mother*. Cambridge, Mass.: Harvard University Press, 1977.

———. "The Early Development of Schemas of Self, of Other, and of Various Experiences of 'Self with Other.'" In J. Lichtenberg and S. Kaplan, eds., *Reflections on Self Psychology*. Hillsdale, N.J.: The Analytic Press, 1983.

————. *The Interpersonal World of the Infant: A View from Psychoanalysis and Developmental Psychology.* New York: Basic Books, 1985.

STERN, DANIEL, BEATRICE BEEBE, JOSEPH JAFFE, AND STEPHEN BENNETT. "The Infant's Stimulus World During Social Interaction: A Study of Caregiver Behaviors with Particular Reference to Repetition and Timing." In H. R. Schaffer, ed., *Studies in Mother-Infant Interaction.* London: Academic Press, 1977.

SULLIVAN, HARRY STACK. *The Interpersonal Theory of Psychiatry.* New York: Norton, 1953.

TOLPIN, MARIE. "On the Beginnings of the Cohesive Self." *The Psychoanalytic Study of the Child* 34 (1971): 316–52.

TREVARTHEN, COLWYN. "Descriptive Analyses of Infant Communicative Behavior." In H. R. Schaffer, ed., *Studies in Mother-Infant Interaction.* London: Academic Press, 1977.

————. "Communication and Cooperation in Early Infancy: A Description of Primary Intersubjectivity." In M. Bullowa, ed., *Before Speech: The Beginning of Interpersonal Communication.* New York: Cambridge University Press, 1980.

TRONICK, E., H. ALS, AND L. ADAMSON. "Structure of Early Face-to-Face Communicative Interactions." In M. Bullowa, ed., *Before Speech: The Begining of Interpersonal Communication.* New York: Cambridge University Press, 1980.

TRONICK, E., H. ALS, AND T. B. BRAZELTON. "Mutuality in Mother-Infant Interaction." *Journal of Communication* 27 (1977): 74–79.

WATSON, J. S. "Smiling, Cooing, and 'The Game.'" *Merrill-Palmer Quarterly* 18 (1973): 323–39.

WHITE, R. W. "Motivation Reconsidered: The Concept of Competence." *Psychological Review* 66 (1959): 297–333.

WINNICOTT, D. W. "Transitional Objects and Transitional Phenomena." (1951) In *Playing and Reality.* Harmondsworth, U.K.: Penguin Books, 1974.

————. "The Mirror Role of Mother and Family in Child Development." (1967) in *Playing and Reality.*

————. "The Use of an Object and Relating through Identifications." (1971) in *Playing and Reality.*

————. *The Maturational Process and the Facilitating Environment.* New York: International Universities Press, 1965.

————. "The Capacity to Be Alone." (1958) In *The Maturational Process and the Facilitating Environment.*

————. "Ego Distortion in Terms of True and False Self." (1960) In *The Maturational Process and the Facilitating Environment.*

————. *The Child, the Family, and the Outside World.* Harmondsworth, U.K.: Penguin Books, 1964.

————. "Primary Maternal Preoccupation." (1956) In *Through Pediatrics to Psychoanalysis.* London: Hogarth Press, 1978.

daniel n. stern

THE SENSE OF A VERBAL SELF

During the second year of the infant's life language emerges, and in the process the senses of self and other acquire new attributes. Now the self and the other have different and distinct personal world knowledge as well as a new medium of exchange with which to create shared meanings. A new organizing subjective perspective emerges and opens a new domain of relatedness. The possible ways of "being with" another increase enormously. At first glance, language appears to be a straightforward advantage for the augmentation of interpersonal experience. It makes parts of our known experience more shareable with others. In addition, it permits two people to create mutual experiences of meaning that had been unknown before and could never have existed until fashioned by words. It also finally permits the child to begin to construct a narrative of his own life. But in fact language is a double-edged sword. It also makes some parts of our experience less shareable with ourselves and with others. It drives a wedge between two simultaneous forms of interpersonal experience: as it is lived and as it is verbally represented. Experience in the domains of emergent, core- and intersubjective relatedness, which continue irrespective of language, can be embraced only very partially in the domain of verbal relatedness. And to the extent that events in the domain of verbal relatedness are held to be what has really happened, experiences in these other domains suffer an alienation. (They can become the nether domains of experience.) Language, then, causes a split in the experience of the self. It also moves relatedness onto the impersonal, abstract level intrinsic to language and away from the personal, immediate level intrinsic to the other domains of relatedness.

It will be necessary to follow both these lines of development—language as a new form of relatedness and language as a problem for the integration of self-experience and self-with-other experiences. We must somehow take into account these divergent directions that the emergence of a linguistic sense of self has created.

But first, let us see what capacities have developed in the infant that permit a new perspective on the self to emerge and revolutionize the possible ways that the self can be with another and with itself.

From The Interpersonal World of the Infant: A View from Psychoanalysis and Developmental Psychology © *1987 by Basic Books Inc. Reprinted by permission of Basic Books, a division of Harper Collins Publishers Inc*

NEW CAPACITIES AVAILABLE IN THE
SECOND YEAR

Toward the middle of the second year (at around fifteen to eighteen months), children begin to imagine or represent things in their minds in such a way that signs and symbols are now in use. Symbolic play and language now become possible. Children can conceive of and then refer to themselves as external or objective entities. They can communicate about things and persons who are no longer present. (All of these milestones bring Piaget's period of sensorimotor intelligence towards an end.)

These changes in world perspective are best illustrated by Piaget's concept of "deferred imitation" (1954). Deferred imitation captures the essence of the developmental changes needed to lead to the sharing of meanings. At about eighteen months, a child may observe someone perform a behavior that the child has never performed—say dial a telephone, or pretend to bottle-feed a doll, or pour milk into a cup—and later that day, or several days later, imitate the dialing, feeding, or pouring. For infants to be able to perform such simple delayed imitations, several capacities are necessary.

1. They must have developed a capacity to represent accurately things and events done by others that are not yet part of their own action schemas. They must be able to create a mental prototype or representation of what they have witnessed someone else do. Mental representations require some currency or form in which they "exist" or are "laid down" in the mind; visual images and language are the two that first come to mind. (To get around the developmental problem of specifying what form the representation is being processed in, Lichtenberg has called this capacity an "imagining" capacity (1983, p 198). See also Call [1980]; Golinkoff [1983].)

2. They must, of course, already have the physical capacity to perform the action in their repertoires of possible acts.

3. Since the imitation is delayed and being performed when the original model is no longer doing it, perhaps not even around, the representation must be encoded in long-term memory and must be retrieved with a minimum of external cues. The infants must have good recall or evocative memory for the entire representation.

Children have already acquired these three capacities prior to the age of eighteen months. It is the next two capacities that make the difference and truly mark the boundary.

4. To perform delayed imitations, infants must have two versions of the same reality available: the representation of the original act, as performed by the model, and their own actual execution of the act. Furthermore, they must be able to go back and forth between these two versions of reality and make adjustments of one or the other to accomplish a good imitation. This is what Piaget meant by "reversibility" in the coordination of a mental schema and a motor schema. (The infant's capacity for recognizing maternal attunements during intersubjective relatedness falls short of what is now being described. In attunements the infant senses whether two expressions of an internal state are equivalent or not but does not need to make any behavioral adjustments on the basis of these percep-

tions. Moreover, only short-term memory is required for the registration of attunement, since the match is almost immediate.)

5.   Finally, infants must perceive a psychological relationship between themselves and the model who performs the original act, or they would not embark on the delayed imitation to begin with. They must have some way of representing themselves as similar to the model, such that they and the model could be in the same position relative to the act to be imitated (Kagan 1978). This requires some representation of self as an objective entity that can be seen from the outside as well as felt subjectively from the inside. The self has become an objective category as well as a subjective experience (Lewis and Brooks-Gunn 1979; Kagan 1981).

What is most new in this revolution about sense of self is the child's ability to coordinate schemas existing in the mind with operations existing externally in actions or words. The three consequences of this ability that most alter the sense of self and consequently the possibilities for relatedness are the capacity to make the self the object of reflection, the capacity to engage in symbolic action such as play, and the acquisition of language. These consequences, which we will take up in turn, combine to make it possible for the infant to negotiate shared meaning with another about personal knowledge.

THE OBJECTIVE VIEW OF SELF

The evidence that children begin at this age to see themselves objectively is thoroughly argued by Lewis and Brooks-Gunn (1979), Kagan (1981), and Kaye (1982). The most telling points in this argument are infants' behavior in front of a mirror, their use of verbal labels (names and pronouns) to designate self, the establishment of core gender identity (an objective categorization of self), and acts of empathy.

Prior to the age of eighteen months, infants do not seem to know that what they are seeing in a mirror is their own reflection. After eighteen months, they do. This can be shown by surreptitiously marking infants' faces with rouge, so that they are unaware that the mark has been placed. When younger infants see their reflections, they point to the mirror and not to themselves. After the age of eighteen months or so, they touch the rouge on their own faces instead of just pointing to the mirror. They now know that they can be objectified, that is, represented in some form that exists outside of their subjectively felt selves (Amsterdam 1972; Lewis and Brooks-Gunn 1978). Lewis and Brooks-Gunn call this newly objectifiable self the "categorical self," in distinction to the "existential self." It might also be called the "objective self" as against the "subjective self," or the "conceptual self" as against the "experiential self" of the previous levels of relatedness.

In any event, at about the same time infants give many other evidences of being able to objectify self and act as though self were an external category that can be conceptualized. They now begin to use pronouns ("I," "me," "mine") to refer to self, and they sometimes even begin to use proper names.[1] It is also at about this time that gender identity begins to become fixed. Infants recognize that the self as an objective entity can be categorized with other objective entities, either boys or girls.

It is also beginning around this time that empathic acts are seen (Hoffman 1977, 1978; Zahn-Waxler and Radke-Yarrow 1979, 1982). To act empathically the infant must be able to imagine both self as an object who can be experienced by the other and the objectified other's subjective state. Hoffman provides a lovely example of a thirteen-month-old boy who could, at that age, only incompletely sort out whose person (self or other) was to be objectified and whose subjective experience was to be focused upon. The failures in this case are more instructive than the successes. This child characteristically sucked his thumb and pulled on his ear lobe when he was upset. Once he saw his father clearly upset. He went over to his father and pulled the father's ear lobe but sucked on his own thumb. The boy was truly caught halfway between subjective and objective relatedness, but the coming months would see him performing more fully formed acts of empathy.

THE CAPACITY FOR SYMBOLIC PLAY

Lichtenberg (1983) has pointed out how the new capacities for objectifying the self and for coordinating mental and action schemas permit infants to "think" about or "imagine" about their interpersonal life. The clinical work of Herzog that Lichtenberg relies on illustrates this. In a study of eighteen- to twenty-month-old boys whose fathers had recently separated from the family, Herzog (1980) describes the following vignette. An eighteen-month-old boy was miserable because his father had just moved out of the home. During a play session with dolls, the boy doll was sleeping in the same bed as the mother doll. (The mother did, in fact, have the boy sleep in her bed after the father left.) The child got very upset at the dolls' sleeping arrangement. Herzog tried to calm the boy by having the mother doll comfort the boy doll. This did not work. Herzog then brought a daddy doll into the scene. The child first put the daddy doll in bed next to the boy doll. But this solution did not satisfy the child. The child then made the daddy doll put the boy doll in a separate bed and then get into bed with the mother doll. The child then said, "All better now" (Herzog 1980, p. 224). The child had to be juggling three versions of family reality: what he knew to be true at home, what he wished and remembered was once true at home, and what he saw as being enacted in the doll family. Using these three representations, he manipulated the signifying representation (the dolls) to realize the wished-for representation of family life and to repair symbolically the actual situation.

With this new capacity for objectifying the self and coordinating different mental and actional schemas, infants have transcended immediate experience. They now have the psychic mechanisms and operations to share their interpersonal world knowledge and experience, as well as to work on it in imagination or reality. The advance is enormous.

From the point of view of psychodynamic theories, something momentous has happened here. For the first time, the infant can now entertain and maintain a formed wish of how reality ought to be, contrary to fact. Furthermore, this wish can rely on memories and can exist in mental representation buffered in large part from the momentary press of psychophysiological needs. It can carry on an existence like a structure. This is the stuff of dynamic conflict. It reaches far beyond the real or potential distortions in perception due to immaturity or to the influence of "need state" or affect seen at earliest levels of relatedness. Interpersonal interaction can now involve past memories, present realities, and expectations of the future based solely on the past. But when expectations are based on a selective portion of the past, we end up with wishes, as in the case of Herzog's patient.

All these interpersonal goings-on can now take place verbally, or at least they will be reportable to the self and others verbally. The already existing knowledge of interpersonal transactions (real, wished for, and remembered) that involves objectifiable selves and others can be translated into words. When that happens, mutually shared meaning becomes possible and the quantum leap in relatedness occurs.[2]

THE USE OF LANGUAGE

By the time babies start to talk they have already acquired a great deal of world knowledge, not only about how inanimate things work and how their own bodies work but also about how social interactions go. The boy in Herzog's example cannot yet tell us verbally exactly what he wants and doesn't want, but he can enact what he knows and wishes with considerable precision. Similarly, children can point to the rouge on their own noses when they see it in a mirror before they say "me," "mine," or "nose." The point is simply that there is a stretch of time in which rich experiential knowledge "in there" is accumulated, which somehow will later get assembled (although not totally) with a verbal code, language. And at the same time, much new experience will emerge along with the verbalization of the experience.

Such statements seem self-evident, yet until the 1970s most of the work on children's language acquisition was either concerned more with language itself, not experience, or focused on the child's innate mental devices and operations for making sense of language as a formal system, as in the work of Chomsky. There have also been fascinating and invaluable discoveries about the infant's perception of speech sounds, but these are largely outside the scope of this book.

It was mainly the seminal works of Bloom (1973), Brown (1973), Dore (1975, 1979), Greenfield and Smith (1976), and Bruner (1977) that insisted that world knowledge of interpersonal events was the essential key to unlocking the mysteries of language acquisition. As Bruner (1983) put it, a "new functionalism began to temper the formalism of the previous decades" (p. 8). Nonetheless, the words and structures of language have more than a one-to-one relationship to things and events in real experience. Words have an existence, a life of their own that permits language to transcend lived experience and to be generative.

How world knowledge and language are assembled from the beginning of language acquisition remains at the cutting edge of experimental studies of child language in the interpersonal context (Golinkoff 1983; Brunner 1983). This issue has resurfaced simultaneously with a growing interest in the kinds of world knowledge and language structures our theories really look at and the kinds of interactions between experience and language we are imagining take place (Glick 1983). These considerations are necessary to our discussion because the essence of the question is how language may change the sense of self and what the acquisition of language, and all that implies, makes possible between self and others that was not possible before. Since our subject is interpersonal relatedness rather than the equally enormous subject of language acquisition, we will very selectively draw on notions that have particular clinical relevance because they take into account the interpersonal motivational or affective context of language learning.

Michael Holquist (1982) suggests that the problem of different views of understanding language and its acquisition can be approached by asking who "owns" meanings. He defines three major positions. In Personalism, *I* own meaning. This view is deeply rooted in the western humanist tradition of the individual as unique. In contrast, a second view, more likely to be found in departments of comparative literature, holds that *no one* owns meaning. It exists out there in the culture. Neither of these views is very hospitable to our concerns, since it is hard to see how interpersonal events can influence the sharing or joint ownership of meaning in either case. However, Holquist defines a third view, which he calls Dialogism. In this view, *we* own meaning, or "if we do not own it, we may, at least, *rent* meaning" (p. 3). It is this third view that opens the door wide for interpersonal happenings to play a role, and it is from this perspective that the works of several students of language are of such interest.

THE EFFECTS OF LANGUAGE ON SELF-OTHER RELATEDNESS: NEW WAYS OF "BEING-WITH"

Vygotsky (1962) maintained that the problem of understanding language acquisition was, stated oversimply, how do mutually negotiated meanings (*we* meanings) "get in" to the child's mind? As Glick (1983) puts it, "The underlying conceptual problem is the *relationship* that exists between socialized systems of mediation (provided mainly by parents) and the individual's (infant's) reconstruction of these in an interior, and perhaps not fully socialized, way" (p. 16). The problem of language acquisition has become an interpersonal problem. Meaning, in the sense of the linkage between world knowledge (or thought) and words, is no longer a given that is obvious from the beginning. It is something to be negotiated between the parent and child. The exact relationship between thought and word "is not a thing, but a process, a continual movement back and forth from thought to word and from word to thought" (Vygotsky 1962, p. 125). Meaning results from interpersonal negotiations involving what can be agreed upon as shared. And such mutually negotiated meanings (the relation of thought to word) grow, change, develop and are struggled over by two people and thus ultimately owned by *us*.

This view leaves a great deal of room for the emergence of meanings that are unique to the dyad or to the individual.[3] "Good girl," "bad girl," "naughty boy," "happy," "upset," "tired," and a host of other such value and internal-state words will continue (often throughout life) to have the meanings uniquely negotiated between one parent and one child during the early years of assembling world knowledge and language. Only when the child begins to engage in an interpersonal dialectic with other socializing mediators such as peers can these meanings undergo further change. At that stage, new mutually negotiated *we* meanings emerge.

This process of the mutual negotiations of meaning actually applies to all meanings—"dog," "red," "boy," and so on—but it becomes most interesting and less socially constrained with internal state words. (There may be a difference between children in their interest in verbalizing things versus internal states. See Bretherton el al. [1981]; Nelson [1973]; and Clarke-Stewart [1973] for differences between individual styles and sexes.) When daddy says "good girl," the words are assembled with a set of experiences and thoughts that is different from the set assembled with mother's words "good girl." Two meanings, two relations coexist. And, the difference in the two meanings can become a potent source of difficulty in solidifying an identity or self-concept. The two diverse sets of experiences and thoughts are supposed to be congruent because they are claimed by the same words, "good girl." In the learning of language, we act overtly as though meaning lies either inside the self or somewhere out there belonging to anyone and meaning the same to all. This obscures the covert, unique *we* meanings. They become very hard to isolate and rediscover; much of the task of psychotherapy lies in doing so.

Dore has carried the notion of *we* meanings and negotiated shared meanings further in a manner that has implications for interpersonal theories. In the matter of the child's motivation to talk to begin with, Dore believes that infants talk, in part, to re-establish "being-with" experiences (in my terms) or to re-establish the "personal order" (MacMurray 1961). Dore (1985) describes it as follows:

> At this critical period of the child's life (. . . when he begins to walk and talk), his mother . . . reorients him away from the personal order with her, and towards a social order. In other words, whereas their previous interactions were primarily spontaneous, playful, and relatively unorganized for the sake of being together, the mother now begins to require him to organize his action for practical, social purposes: to act on his own (getting his own ball), to fulfill role functions (feeding himself), to behave well by social standards (not throwing his glass), and so on. This induces in the child the fear of having to perform in terms of nonpersonal standards (towards a social order) which orients away from the personal order of infancy. (p. 15)

It is in this context of pressure to maintain the new social order that the infant is motivated by the need and desire to re-establish the personal order with mother (Dore 1985). Dore is quick to point out that motivation alone, of this sort or any other, is not sufficient to explain the appearance of language. From our point of view, however, it adds an interpersonal motive (tenable but unproven) to the interpersonal process already pointed out by Vygotsky.

One of the major imports of this dialogic view of language is that the very process of learning to speak is recast in terms of forming shared experiences, of re-establishing the "personal order," of creating a new type of "being-with" between adult and child. Just as the being-with experiences of intersubjective relatedness required the sense of two subjectivities in alignment—a sharing of inner experience of state—so too, at this new level of verbal relatedness, the infant and mother create a being-with experience using verbal symbols—a sharing of mutually created meanings about personal experience.

The acquisition of language has traditionally been seen as a major step in the achievement of separation and individuation, next only to acquiring locomotion. The present view asserts that the opposite is equally true, that the acquisition of language is potent in the service of union and togetherness. In fact, every word learned is the by-product of uniting two mentalities in a common symbol system, a forging of shared meaning. With each word, children solidify their mental commonality with the parent and later with the other members of the language culture, when they discover that their personal experiential knowledge is part of a larger experience of knowledge, that they are unified with others in a common culture base.

Dore has offered the interesting speculation that language acts in the beginning as a form of "transitional phenomenon." To speak in Winnicott's terms, the word is in a way "discovered" or "created" by the infant, in that the thought or knowledge is already in mind, ready to be linked up with the word. The word is given to the infant from the outside, by mother, but there exists a thought for it to be given to. In this sense the word, as a transitional phenomenon, does not truly belong to the self, nor does it truly belong to the other. It occupies a midway position between the infant's subjectivity and the mother's objectivity. It is "rented" by "us," as Holquist puts it. It is in this deeper sense that language is a union experience, permitting a new level of mental relatedness through shared meaning.

The notion of language as a "transitional object" seems at first glance somewhat fanciful. However, observed evidence makes it seem very real. Katherine Nelson has recorded "crib talk" of a girl before and after her second birthday. Routinely, the infant's father put her to bed. As part of the putting-to-bed ritual, they held a dialogue in which the father went over some of the things that had happened that day and discussed what was planned for the next day. The girl participated actively in this dialogue and at the same time went through many obvious and subtle maneuvers to keep daddy present and talking, to prolong the ritual. She would plead, fuss-cry, insist, cajole, and devise new questions for him, intoned ingenuously. But when he finally said "good night" and left, her voice changed dramatically into a more matter of fact, narrative tone and her monologue began, a soliloquy.

Nelson gathered a small group consisting of herself, Jerome Bruner, John Dore, Carol Feldman, Rita Watson, and me. We met monthly for a year to examine how this child conducted both the dialogue with her father and the monologue after he left. The important features of her monologues were her practice and discovery of word usage. She could be seen to struggle with finding the right linguistic forms to contain her thoughts and knowledge of events. At times, one could see her moving closer and closer, with successive trials, to a more satisfying verbal rendition of her thinking. But even more striking, for the point at hand, is that it was like watching "internalization" happen right before our eyes and ears. After father left, she appeared to be constantly under the threat of feeling alone and distressed. (A younger brother had been born about this time.) To keep herself controlled emotionally, she repeated in her soliloquy topics that had been part of the dialogue with father. Sometimes she seemed to intone in his voice or to recreate something like the previous dialogue with him, in order to reactivate his presence and carry it with her toward the abyss of sleep. This, of course, was not the only purpose that her monologue served (she was also practicing language!), but it certainly felt as though she were also engaged in a "transitional phenomenon," in Winnicott's sense.

Language, then, provides a new way of being related to others (who may be present or absent) by sharing personal world knowledge with them, coming together in the domain of verbal relatedness. These comings-together permit the old and persistent life issues of attachment, autonomy, separation, intimacy, and so on to be reencountered on the previously unavailable plane of relatedness through shared meaning of personal knowledge. But language is not primarily another means for individuation, nor is it primarily another means for creating togetherness. It is rather the means for achieving the next developmental level of relatedness, in which all existential life issues will again be played out.

The advent of language ultimately brings about the ability to narrate one's own life story with all the potential that holds for changing how one views oneself. The making of a narrative is not the same as any other kind of thinking or talking. It appears to involve a different mode of thought from problem solving or pure description. It involves thinking in terms of persons who act as agents with intentions and goals that unfold in some causal sequence with a beginning, middle, and end. (Narrative-making may prove to be a universal human phenomenon reflecting the design of the human mind.) This is a new and exciting area of research in which it is not yet clear how, why or when children construct (or coconstruct with a parent) narratives that begin to form the autobiographical history that ultimately evolves into the life story a patient may first present to a therapist. The domain of verbal relatedness might, in fact, be best subdivided into a sense of a categorical self that objectifies and labels, and of a narrated self that weaves into a story elements from other senses of the self (agency, intentions, causes, goals, and so on).

THE OTHER EDGE OF THE SWORD: THE ALIENATING EFFECT OF LANGUAGE ON SELF-EXPERIENCE AND TOGETHERNESS

This new level of relatedness does not eclipse the levels of core-relatedness and intersubjective relatedness, which continue as ongoing forms of interpersonal experience. It does, however, have the capacity to recast and transform some of the experiences of core- and intersubjective relatedness, so that they lead two lives—their original life as nonverbal experience and a life as the verbalized version of that experience. As Werner and Kaplan (1963) suggest, language grabs hold of a piece of the conglomerate of feeling, sensation, perception, and cognition that constitutes global nonverbal experience. The piece that language takes hold of is transformed by the process of language-making and becomes an experience separate from the original global experience.[4]

Several different relationships can exist between the nonverbal global experience and that part of it that has been transformed into words. At times, the piece that language separates out is quintessential and captures the whole experience beautifully. Language is generally thought to function in this "ideal" way, but in fact it rarely does, and we will have the least to say about this. At other times, the language version and the globally experienced version do not coexist well. The global experience may be fractured or simply poorly represented, in which case it wanders off to lead a misnamed and poorly understood existence. And finally, some global experiences at the level of core- and intersubjective relatedness (such as the very sense of a core self) do not permit language sufficient entry to separate out a piece for linguistic transformation. Such experiences then simply continue underground, nonverbalized, to lead an unnamed (and, to that extent only, unknown) but nonetheless very real existence. (Unusual efforts such as psychoanalysis of poetry or fiction can sometimes claim some of this territory for language, but not in the usual linguistic sense. And this is what gives such power to these processes.)

Specific examples of particular experiences will illustrate this general issue of divergence between world knowledge and words. The notion of divergence, or slippage, between world knowledge and word knowledge is well known as it concerns knowledge of the physical world. Bower (1978) provides an excellent example of it. When a child is shown a lump of clay first rolled long and thin and then made into a fat ball, the child will claim that the ball version of the same amount of clay is heavier. According to the verbal account, the child does not have conservation of volume and weight. One would therefore expect that if the child is handed the two balls, first the thin one and then the fat one, the child's arm would rise up when it received the fat ball, since it was expected to be heavier and the muscles of the arm should be tensed to compensate for the difference. But a high-speed film shows that the arm does not move up. Bower concludes that the child's body, at the sensorimotor level, has already achieved conservation of weight and volume, even though verbally the child seems to have lost or never to have had this capacity. Similar phenomena occur in domains that concern interpersonal world knowledge more directly.

The infant's capacity for amodal perception has loomed large in this overall account. The abilities to sense a core self and other and to sense intersubjective relatedness through attunement have depended in part on amodal capacities. What might happen to the experience of amodal perception when language is applied to it?

Suppose we are considering a child's perception of a patch of yellow sunlight on the wall. The infant will experience the intensity, warmth, shape, brightness, pleasure, and other amodal aspects of the patch. The fact that it is yellow light is not of primary or, for that matter, of any importance. While looking at the patch and feeling-perceiving it (à la Werner) the child is engaged in a global experience resonant with a mix of all the amodal properties, the primary perceptual qualities, of the patch of light—its intensity, warmth, and so on. To maintain this highly flexible and omnidimensional perspective on the patch, the infant must remain blind to those particular properties (secondary and tertiary perceptual qualities, such as color) that specify the sensory channel through which the patch is being experienced. The child must not notice or be made aware that it is a visual experience. Yet that is exactly what language will force the child to do. Someone will enter the room and say, "Oh, *look* at the *yellow* sun*light!*" Words in this case separate out precisely those properties that anchor the experience to a single modality of sensation. By binding it to words, they isolate the experience from the amodal flux in which it was originally experienced. Language can thus fracture amodal global experience. A discontinuity in experience is introduced.

What probably happens in development is that the language version "yellow sunlight" of such perceptual experiences becomes the official version, and the amodal version goes underground and can only resurface when conditions suppress or outweigh the dominance of the linguistic version. Such conditions might include certain contemplative states, certain emotional states, and the perception of certain works of art that are designed to evoke experiences defying verbal categorization. Again, works of the symbolist poets serve as an example of the latter. The paradox that language can evoke experience that transcends words is perhaps the highest tribute to the power of language. But those are words in poetic use. The words in our daily lives more often do the opposite and either fracture amodal global experience or send it underground.

In this area, then, the advent of language is a very mixed blessing to the child. What begins to be lost (or made latent) is enormous; what begins to be gained is also enormous. The infant gains entrance into a wider cultural membership, but at the risk of losing the force and wholeness of original experience.

The verbal rendering of specific instances of life-as-lived presents a similar problem. Recall that in earlier chapters we distinguished *specific episodes* of life-as-lived (for example, "that one time when Mommy put me to bed to go to sleep, but she was distraught and only going through the motions of the bedtime ritual and I was overtired, and she couldn't help me push through that familiar barrier into sleep") and *generalized episodes* ("what happens when Mommy puts me down to sleep"). It is only the generalized ritual that is nameable as "bedtime." No specific instance has a name. Words apply to classes of things ("dog," "tree," "run," and so on). That is where they are most powerful as tools. The generalized episode is some kind of average of similar events. It is a prototype of a class of events-as-lived (generalized interactions [RIGs]): going to bed, eating dinner, bathtime, dressing, walk with Mommy, play with Daddy, peek-a-boo. And words get assembled with experiences of life-as-lived at this generalized level of the prototypic episode. Specific episodes fall through the linguistic sieve and cannot be referenced verbally until the child is very advanced in language, and sometimes never. We see evidence of this all the time in children's frustration at their failures to communicate what seems obvious to them. The child may have to repeat a word several times ("eat!") before the parent figures out what specific instance (which food) of the general class (of edible things) the infant has in mind and expects the adult to produce.

In the clinical literature, such phenomena have often been ascribed to children's belief in or wish for adults' omniscience and omnipotence. In contrast to that view, I suggest that such misunderstandings are not based on the child's notion that the mother knows what is in her child's mind to begin with. They are true misunderstandings about meaning. To the infant who says "eat," that mean a specific edible thing. It requires only understanding, not mind-reading. The mother's misunderstanding serves to teach the child that the child's specific meaning is only a subset of her possible meanings. It is in this way that mutual meanings get negotiated. In such cases, we are observing the infant and mother struggling together with the peculiar nature of language and meaning. We are not observing ruptures and repairs in the infant's sense of an omniscient parent.

The passions, pleasures, and frustrations seem to come more from the success and failure of mental togetherness at the levels of shared meaning, which the infant is motivated toward, not from anxiety at the loss of delegated omnipotence and/or from the good feeling of security when omnipotence is re-established. The misunderstandings simply motivate the infant to learn language better. They do not seriously rupture the child's sense of competence.

There may be more opportunities for such frustrations at the outset of language learning, because at the levels of core- and intersubjective relatedness the mother and infant have had a good deal of time to work out a nonverbal interactive system for relating. Negotiating shared meanings necessarily invokes much failing. To an infant who at prior levels has become accustomed to smoother transactions with mother concerning the import and intent of their mutual behaviors, this may be particularly frustrating.

Our point in demonstrating the many ways that language is inadequate to the task of communicating about specific lived-experience is not to minimize the import of language at all. Rather, it is to identify the forms of slippage between personal world knowledge and official or socialized world knowledge as encoded in language, because the slippage between these two is one of the main ways in which reality and fantasy can begin to diverge. The very nature of language, as a specifier of the sensory modality in use (in contrast to amodal nonspecification) and as a specifier of the generalized episode instead of the specific instance, assures that there will be points of slippage.

There are other points of slippage that should be noted. One of these is in the verbal accounts of internal states. Affect as a form of personal knowledge is very hard to put into words and communicate. Words to label internal states are not among the first to be used by children, even though children have presumably had long familiarity with the internal states (Bretherton el al. 1981). It is easier to label the categories of affective states (happy, sad) than the dimensional features (how happy, how sad). One problem is that the dimensional features of affect are gradient features (a little happy, very happy), while categorical features are not (happy versus not happy). Language is the ideal medium to deal with categorical information—that is partly what naming is all about—but it is at a great disadvantage in dealing with an analogue system, such as fullness of display, in ethological terms, which is geared to express gradient information. And it is the gradient information that may carry the most decisive information in everyday interpersonal communications.

The well-worn joke about the two psychiatrists passing on the sidewalk provides an illustration. They say "hello" and smile as they pass, and then each thinks to himself, "I wonder what he meant by that?" We can untrivialize this story by discussing it in terms of its categorical and gradient information. To begin with, greeting behaviors are conventionalized emotional responses containing elements from the Darwinian categories of surprise and happiness. As soon as one becomes aware that a greeting response will be initiated or responded to, one must tune in to the subtle but inevitable social cues that will be carried in the gradient features of the greeting. A number of factors will influence the gradient features and how each greeter will assess the greeting received: the nature of the relationship between the two greeters, the state of the relationship since their last meeting, the amount of time since they last met, their sexes, their cultural norms, and so on. In accordance with each participant's assessments of these factors, they expect each other to say a "hello" of a roughly specific volume, gusto, and intonational richness and to raise their eyebrows, widen their eyes, and open their smiles to a roughly expected height, width, and duration of display. Any significant variance from these expectations will occasion the question, "I wonder what he meant by that?" Each responder or recipient of the greeting will also be in the active position of gauging exactly how to adjust the delivery of his or her own greeting (Stern et al. 1983).

In this example, the work of interpreting the other person's behavior did not reside in the category of the signal. In fact, it did not even lie, as I have been implying, in the gradient features of the signal as performed. It lay in the discrepancy between the way the gradient features were actually performed and the way they were expected to be performed, given the context. The work of interpretation thus consists of measuring the distance between an imaginary performance (perhaps never before even seen in reality) and an actual performance of gradient features.

There is no reason why the situation should be much different for the child. The infant who hears mother say "Hi, honey" in an unaccustomed way would sense, but would not think to say, "You did not say it right." But the child would be wrong. What mother said, in linguistic fact, is right, but she did not act it (mean it) right. What is said and what is meant have a complicated relationship in the interpersonal domain.

When two messages, usually verbal and nonverbal, clash in the extreme, it has been called a "double-bind message" (Bateson et al. 1956). It is usually the case that the nonverbal message is the one that is meant, and the verbal message is the one of "record." The "on-record" message is the one we are officially accountable for.

Several authors, such as Scherer (1979) and Labov and Fanshel (1977), have pointed out that some of our communications are deniable, while others we are held accountable for. Gradient information is more easily denied. These different signals are going on simultaneously in various communicative channels. Furthermore, for the greatest flexibility and maneuverability of communication it is necessary to have this kind of mix (Garfinkel 1967). Labov and Fanshel (1977) describe this necessity very well in discussing intonational signals; for our purposes, their point applies equally well to other nonverbal behaviors:

> The lack of clarity or discreteness in the intonational signal is not an unfortunate limitation of this channel, but an essential and important aspect of it. Speakers need a form of communication which is deniable. It is advantageous for them to express hostility, challenge the competence of others, or express friendliness and affection in a way that can be denied if they are explicitly held to account for it. If there were not such a deniable channel of communication and intonation contours became so well recognized and explicit that people were accountable for their intonations, then some other mode of deniable communication would indoubtedly develop. (p. 46)

The surest way to keep a channel deniable is to prevent it from becoming a part of the formal language system. In learning a new word, a baby isolates an experience for clear identification and at the same time becomes accountable to mother for that word.

This line of argument suggests that in a multi-channel communicative system there will exist constant environmental or cultural pressure to keep some signals more resistant to explicit accountable encoding than others, so that they will remain deniable. Because language is so good at communicating what, rather than how, something happened, the verbal message invariably becomes the accountable one. A year-old-boy was angry at his mother and in a fit of temper, while not looking at her, yelled, "Aaaaah!" and brought his fist down hard on a puzzle. Mother said, "Don't you yell at your mother." She would have been very unlikely to say, "Don't bring your fist down like that at your mother." Neither message, the verbal one nor the nonverbal one, was more closely directed at her than the other. One is accountable very early for what one says, and this child is being prepared for that by making his vocalization rather than his gestures the accountable act.

One of the consequences of this inevitable division into the accountable and the deniable is that what is deniable to others becomes more and more deniable to oneself. The path into the unconscious (both topographic and potentially dynamic) is being well laid by language. Prior to language, all of one's behaviors have equal status as far as "ownership" is concerned. With the advent of language, some behaviors now have a privileged status with regard to one having to own them. The many messages in many channels are being fragmented by language into a hierarchy of accountability/deniability.

There is another type of slippage between experience and words that deserves mention. Some experiences of self, such as continuity of coherence, the "going on being" of a physically integrated, nonfragmented self, fall into a category something like your heartbeat or regular breathing. Such experiences rarely require the notice needed to be verbally encoded. Yet periodically some transient sense of this experience is revealed, for some inexplicable reason or via psychopathology, with the breathtaking effect of sudden realization that your existential and verbal selves can be light years apart, that the self is unavoidably divided by language.

Many experiences of self-with-other fall into this unverbalized category; mutually gazing into one another's eyes without speaking qualifies. So does the sense of another person's characteristic vitality affects—the individual subtleties of physical style, which are also experienced as the child experiences a patch of sunlight. All such experiences are ineluctable, with the consequence of further distancing personal knowledge as experienced as word or thought. (It is little wonder we need art so badly to bridge these gaps in ourselves.)

A final issue involves the relation between life as experienced and as retold. How much the act of making an autobiographical narrative reflects or necessarily alters the lived experiences that become the personal story is an open question.

Infants' initial interpersonal knowledge is mainly unshareable, amodal, instance-specific, and attuned to nonverbal behaviors in which no one channel of communication has priviledged status with regard to accountability or ownership. Language changes all of that. With its emergence, infants become estranged from direct contact with their own personal experience. Language forces a space between interpersonal experience as lived and as represented. And it is exactly across this space that the connections and associations that constitute neurotic behavior may form. But also with language, infants for the first time can share their personal experience of the world with others, including "being with" others in intimacy, isolation, loneliness, fear, awe, and love.

Finally, with the advent of language and symbolic thinking, children now have the tools to distort and transcend reality. They can create expectations contrary to past experience. They can elaborate a wish contrary to present fact. They can represent someone or something in terms of symbolically associated attributes (for example, bad experiences with mother) that in reality were never experienced all together at any one time but that can be pulled together from isolated episodes into a symbolic representation (the "bad mother" or "incompetent me"). These symbolic condensations finally make possible the distortion of reality and provide the soil for neurotic constructs. Prior to this linguistic ability, infants are confined to reflect the impress of reality. They can now transcend that, for good or ill.

NOTES

1. Pseudo-proper names may appear earlier than semantically controlled pronouns (Dore, personal communication, 1984). There is some question about how much the infant initially sees the name or pronoun as an unencumbered, objectified referent for the self and how much as a referent for a more complex set of situational conditions involving caregiver and self in some activity: "Lucy don't do that!" In any event, the objectification process is well begun.

2. The present description implies that concepts come first and that words are then attached, or that experiences established earlier get translated into words. Much current thinking suggests that felt-experience and words as an expression of felt-experience co-emerge. The present argument does not depend upon this issue, which is crucial to the conception of language development *per se*.

3. An extreme example is the "private speech" of twins.

4. We are not concerned here with the experiences that are created *de novo* by language. Some might claim that all experience rendered linguistically is experience *de novo*, but this position is not being assumed here.

SELECTED BIBLIOGRAPHY

AMSTERDAM, B. K. (1972). Mirror self-image reactions before age two. *Developmental Psychology, 5,* 297–305.

BATESON, G., JACKSON, D., HALEY, J., AND WAKLAND, J. (1956). Toward a theory of schizophrenia. *Behavioral Science, 1,* 251–64.

BLOOM, L. (1973). *One word at a time: The use of single word utterances before syntax.* Hawthorne, N.Y.: Mouton.

BOWER, T. G. R. (1978). The infant's discovery of objects and mother. In E. Thoman (Ed.) *Origins of the infant's social responsiveness.* Hillsdale, N.J.: Erlbaum.

BRETHERTON, I., McNEW, S., AND BEEGHLY-SMITH, M. (1981). Early person knowledge as expressed in gestural and verbal communication: When do infants acquire a "theory of mind"? In M. E. Lamb and L. R. Sherrod (Eds.), *Infant social cognition*. Hillsdale, N.J.: Erlbaum.

BROWN, R. (1973). *A first language: The early stages*. Cambridge, Mass.: Harvard University Press.

BRUNER, J.S. (1977). Early social interaction and language acquisition. In H. R. Schaffer (Ed.), *Studies in mother-infant interaction*. London: Academic Press.

———. (1983). *Child's talk: Learning to use language*. New York: Norton.

CALL, J. D. (1980). Some prelinguistic aspects of language development. *Journal of American Psychoanalytic Association, 28*, 259–90.

CLARKE-STEWART, K. A. (1973). Interactions between mothers and their young children: Characteristics and consequences. *Monographs of the Society of Research in Child Development, 37*(153).

DORE, J. (1975). Holophrases, speech acts and language universals. *Journal of Child Language, 2*, 21–40.

———. (1979). Conversational acts and the acquisition of language. In E. Ochs and B. Schieffelin (Eds.), *Developmental pragmatics*. New York: Academic Press.

———. (1985). Holophrases revisited, dialogically. In M. Barrett (Ed.), *Children's single word speech*. London: Wiley.

GARFINKEL, H. (1967). *Studies in ethnomethodology*. Englewood Cliffs, N.J.: Prentice-Hall.

GLICK, J. (1983, March). *Piaget, Vygotsky and Werner*. Paper presented at the Meeting of the Society for Research in Child Development, Detroit, Mich.

GOLINKOFF, R. (Ed.). (1983). *The transition from pre-linguistic to linguistic communication*. Hillsdale, N.J.: Erlbaum.

GREENFIELD, P., AND SMITH, J. H. (1976). *Language beyond syntax: The development of semantic structure*. New York: Academic Press.

HERZOG, J. (1980). Sleep disturbances and father hunger in 18- to 20-month-old boys: The Erlkoenig-Syndrome. In A. Solnit et al. (Eds.), *The Psychoanalytic Study of the Child, Vol. 35* (pp. 219–36). New Haven, Conn.: Yale University Press.

HOFFMAN, M. L. (1977). Empathy, its development and pre-social implications. *Nebraska Symposium on Motivation, 25*, 169–217.

HOLQUIST, M. (1982). The politics of representation. In S. J. Greenblatt (Ed.), *Allegory and representation*. Baltimore, Md.: Johns Hopkins University Press.

KAGAN, J. (1981). *The second year of life: The emergence of self awareness*. Cambridge, Mass.: Harvard University Press.

———, KEARSLEY, R. B., AND ZELAZO, P. R. (1978). *Infancy: Its place in human development*. Cambridge, Mass.: Harvard University Press.

KAYE, K. (1982). *The mental and social life of babies*. Chicago: University of Chicago Press.

LABOV, W., AND FANSHEL, D. (1977). *Therapeutic discourse*. New York: Academic Press.

LEWIS, M., AND BROOKS-GUNN, J. (1979). *Social cognition and the acquisition of self*. New York: Plenum Press.

LICHTENBERG, J. D. (1983). *Psychoanalysis and infant research*. Hillsdale, N.J.: Analytic Press.

MACMURRAY, J. (1961). *Persons in relation*. London: Faber and Faber.

NELSON, K. (1973). Structure and strategy in learning to talk. *Monographs of the Society for Research in Child Development, 48*(149).

PIAGET, J. (1954). *The construction of reality in the child* (M. Cook, Trans.). New York: Basic Books. (Original work published 1937)

SCHERER, K. (1979). Nonlinguistic vocal indicators of emotion and psychopathology. In C. E. Izard (Ed.), *Emotions in personality and psychopathology*. New York: Plenum Press.

STERN, D. N., BARNETT, R. K., AND SPIEKER, S. (1983). Early transmission of affect: Some research issues. In J. D. Call, F. Galenson, and R. L. Tyson (Eds.), *Frontiers of infant psychiatry*. New York: Basic Books.

VYGOTSKY, L. S. (1962). *Thought and language* (E. Haufmann and G. Vaker, Eds. and Trans.). Cambridge, Mass.: M.I.T. Press.

WERNER, H., AND KAPLAN, B. (1963). *Symbol formation: An organismic-developmental approach to language and expression of thought*. New York: Wiley.

ZAHN-WAXLER, C., RADKE-YARROW, M., AND KING, R. (1979). Child rearing and children's prosocial initiations towards victims of distress. *Child Development, 50*, 319–30.

colwyn trevarthen

COMMUNICATION AND COOPERATION IN EARLY INFANCY

A DESCRIPTION OF PRIMARY INTERSUBJECTIVITY

In film and television recordings of face-to-face interactions of mothers with their infants aged one to three months, my students and I have observed extremely complex behaviours that have led us to accept the idea that human beings are equipped at birth with a mechanism of personality which is sensitive to persons and expresses itself as a person does. Obviously such a mechanism must be formulated largely within the brain before birth without benefit of imitation or training, but the anatomy required seems to be unknown. Beyond question the acts of communication in early infancy are very immature, but they appear powerful enough to take charge of the process by which the cognitive processes of the mind develop. In the first few months, before manipulation is effective in exploring objects, an infant establishes the basis for a deep affectional tie to his mother and other constant companions. He does so by means of this delicate and specifically human system for person-to-person communication.

In this chapter I wish to review this behaviour of young infants to see how far the unspoken part of human communication is present long before the infant can speak and to investigate whether there are rudiments of speech activity as well. Such an inquiry is forced upon us when we admit that language may be part of the larger function of interpersonal communication that grows in the child.

SUBJECTIVITY AND INTERSUBJECTIVITY: DEFINITION OF TERMS

Human beings understand one another intimately and at many levels. To analyse this ability of persons to act together and to share experience in harmony, we have first to view communication in relation to the private activities of conscious, purposeful action. All voluntary actions are performed in such a way that their effects can be anticipated by the actor and then adjusted within the perceived situation to meet the criteria set in advance. Interpersonal communication is controlled by feedback of information, as is all voluntary behaviour. But there is

From Before Speech: The Beginning of Interpersonal Communication, *ed. Margaret Bullowa (Cambridge: Cambridge University Press, 1979), pp. 321–347. Reprinted with the permission of Cambridge University Press.*

an essential difference between a person doing things in relation to the physical world and the control of communication between persons. Two persons can *share* control, each can predict what the other will know and do. Physical objects cannot predict intentions and they have no social relationships.

For infants to share mental control with other persons they must have two skills. First, they must be able to exhibit to others at least the rudiments of individual consciousness and intentionality. This attribute of acting agents I call *subjectivity*. In order to communicate, infants must also be able to adapt or fit this subjective control to the subjectivity of others: they must also demonstrate *intersubjectivity*.[1]

By subjectivity I mean the ability to *show* by coordinated acts that purposes are being consciously regulated. Subjectivity implies that infants master the difficulties of relating objects and situations to themselves and predict consequences, not merely in hidden cognitive processes but in manifest, intelligible actions.

Acts that make subjective processes overt include the following: focussing attention on things, handling and exploring objects with interest in the consequences, orientating or avoiding while anticipating the course of events and meeting or evading them. Acts of these kinds have been found in research with infants that obeys the observational tenets of Piaget in his studies of cognitive development (1936). Of recent work on infant cognition in this tradition, Bower's (1974) is the most comprehensive. Infants one or two months of age may be observed to look at, listen to and touch objects with the beginnings of alertness for the changes in experience that follow what they do. They also perform rudimentary acts of grasping and manipulation, stepping, avoidance or withdrawal which, while ineffectual, have already enough adaptive form to be identified with these purposes (Trevarthen 1974a, 1975). Such patterned and intelligible activity, guided by its effects, shows the subjectivity of infants in their dealings with physical *things*.

Infants also show distinctive behaviours to *persons*. In the second month after birth their reactions to things and persons are so different that we must conclude that these two classes of object are distinct in the infant's awareness (Trevarthen 1975). They seek physical objects as sources of perceptual information or interest, and also as potentially graspable, chewable, kickable, step-on-able or otherwise usable (Trevarthen 1974a, 1975). But persons are communicated with by expressive movements.

It seems at first sight confusing that infants exhibit affective relations to objects over which they are attempting mastery in perception and action. They seem to be trying to communicate feelings to things as well as to people. But is this really what they are doing? This emotional aspect of infant behaviour, which goes beyond either regulation of an internal state of arousal or perception of contingency, has been little studied simply because most psychologists have rejected it out of hand. Nevertheless, pertinent observations have been made. Emotionality in young infants has, for example, been recorded and recognised to be of great importance in relation to learning and cognitive prediction by Papoušek (1967, 1969) and Papoušek & Papoušek (1977). Piaget (1936, 1946) records expressions of 'pleasure in mastery' and 'serious intent' with respect to cognitive tasks, and Wolff (1963, 1969) observed that smiling and cooing or crying of young infants may accompany and signal recognition of a familiar toy.

Facial expressions closely similar to those of adults for the emotions of pleasure, displeasure, fear, surprise, confusion and interest may be distinguished in newborns, or young infants (Charlesworth & Kreutzer 1973; Oster & Ekman 1978). These movements are automatically perceived as 'emotional' by adults. They move other people and strengthen the apparent personality of the infant. Some, such as the smile, are clearly related to events over which the infant has claimed some degree of predictive control. A six-week-old may show pleasure at predicting correctly and displeasure at failure, even if satiated and refusing a physiological 'reward'. The expression of pleasure relates to the cognitive (subjective) prediction itself (Papoušek 1969; Zalazo 1972). In any attempt to understand infants as communicators it must be noted that the effect of the emotional expression can only be interpersonal. Only another person capable of emotion can be influenced by an emotional sign. Like adults, infants act as if they both *know* and *care* about events in their world. Indeed their relationships with other persons would be impossible without the aspects of subjectivity manifested by their prolific but organised emotional expressions.

THE SAMPLE, AND METHODS OF RESEARCH

The following account is focussed on evidence of intersubjective processes between mothers and their infants. This evidence is gleaned from films and video recordings of 165 'staged' encounters with their mothers of thirty-four (fifteen male, nineteen female) infants in their second and third months, some at the Harvard Center for Cognitive Studies but most at the Department of Psychology, University of Edinburgh.[2]

The techniques used have been designed to obtain detailed records of both mother and infant while they are in close communication. The artificial setting does not inhibit rich and close interaction. Mothers visit the laboratory from the time their babies are two to three weeks old. The baby is supported in an infant chair facing, but separate from, the mother. This allows free limb movement. The mother, seated close to her infant, is simply asked to talk to her baby. With the aid of a mirror, both mother and infant behaviours are recorded in near full face on video and film. Combination of video recording including sound with short selections on silent film permits survey of samples of behaviour lasting an hour or more on video and detailed analysis of patterns of action lasting seconds to a few minutes on film. The film is inspected frame by frame on a Perceptoscope projector with variable speed of projection. A back-projection arrangement permits tracing of the film to prepare graphic montages of patterns of action.

The films are of infants with their mothers. A few samples with other females or fathers as partners show that mothers are not absolutely unique, but there are not enough of these to permit comparative statements.

For convenience, expressive and receptive functions of infant and mother will be considered separately. This separation helps start analysis, but it is unnatural both with respect to the way each subject integrates experience with what he or she does and with respect to the intimate cooperation between them. Eventually we will have to put actions and reactions together again to determine how their form depends on their relations within an interplay controlled by both partners.

COMMUNICATIVE EXPRESSIONS OF YOUNG INFANTS

Here I am confining attention to expressions which lead to interpersonal communication, leaving aside well-known feeding, defensive or distress behaviour and signals of physiological state, all of which, while invoking others, are self-regulatory for the infant and disruptive of reciprocal intersubjectivity. The most familiar early expressions, cooing and smiling, are not the only ones pre-adapted to intersubjective exchange. Some of the less familiar expressions seem more important to psychological development. All appear clearly about the end of the first month.

Cooing, also known as pleasure, positive or non-crying vocalisation, is effective as communication only if other persons hear it. Neonates coo weakly, often when alone. When coos become clear and strong in the second month, adults find them pleasing. Coos are easily stimulated by friendly attention and speech, and by toys, such as rattles, if they are moved before the baby's eyes (Wolff 1969). Babies coo when not distressed and especially when distress has been overcome. The appropriate mouth opening and shaping for cooing is often made silently by infants less than two months old. Our films show that mouth movements are patterned separately for speech before the motor coordination of vocal organs with the respiratory apparatus is adequate to produce reliably controlled sound. Vocalised cooing develops in the second month, apparently at least partly in independence of auditory feedback from self or others (Lenneberg et al. 1965). Neither babbling nor laughter develops until after the third month.

Smiling develops parallel to cooing (Washburn 1929; Spitz & Wolf 1946; Ambrose 1961; Wolff 1963). Even premature infants smile and recognisable smiles may occur within minutes of birth (Leboyer 1974). Neonates smile in response to attention, but more weakly and unpredictably than they will a few weeks later. They also smile spontaneously, usually in a fragmentary or ill-formed way, during irregular sleep or drowsiness (Herska 1965; Wolff 1966; Oster & Ekman 1978). In the second month smiling becomes an effective social signal. Even totally blind two-month-olds smile to a voice or tickling, so the infant smile cannot be an imitative response to seeing the smile of others (Freedman 1964; Fraiberg 1968, 1979). Like cooing, it must be based on a motor pattern formed before birth.

Almost all adult facial expressions can be found in photographs and video records of newborns and infants (Darwin 1872; Heska 1965; Ekman 1973; Charlesworth & Kreutzer 1973; Leboyer 1974; Oster & Ekman 1978). Some infant expressions appear different from adult expressions, in correlation with differences in facial structure (Oster & Ekman 1978). Cross-cultural studies of adults and children give evidence for an innate, pan-human facial 'vocabulary' of emotional signs (Ekman 1973; Ekman & Friesen 1971, 1975; Ekman et al. 1972; Eibl-Eibesfeldt 1970).

Our films confirm that emotional expressions can be recognised in infants. They also show facial movements which have little to do with emotion or mood. In relation to language the most significant non-emotional expressions are the lip and tongue movements which I have named 'prespeech'. Like other expressions mentioned, prespeech movements exist at birth, becoming much more distinct by the second and third months when most of our films were made.

By producing prespeech in systematic relation to the signals from a partner in face-to-face communication, infants appear to express a rudiment of intention to speak to that person, although the movements differ from adult speech and are usually not voiced. For example, since young infants lack teeth, there can be no exact matches for the movements for sounds such as /th/, /v/ and /f/. Infant lower jaws are proportionately small, affecting mouth configurations used for vowel sounds and also limiting tongue mobility. Nevertheless, the movements closely resemble lip opening, tightening, pursing and closing the lip and tongue appositions essential to forming adult speech sounds. In photographs these configurations are distinguishable from all other forms of expression. The details of prespeech movements suggest that they are, from their first appearance, already part of a specific mechanism for speech. Furthermore, by directing illumination upward through the open lips during prespeech we have observed that the tongue is exceedingly mobile inside the mouth as well as at the front. Prespeech is emitted in episodes or bursts, often mixed with expressions for happiness, anger, disgust or surprise. But the speech-like movements may occur also when the face is otherwise at rest and quite free from expression of emotion or mood.

All such mouth movements of infants have been explained as being evolved from non-linguistic actions, like kissing or biting, and non-intersubjective acts, like turning to the breast, pushing out food, vomiting and breathing (Eibl-Eibesfeldt 1970; Andrew 1963; Blurton Jones 1971). The tenable hypothesis that these speech-like movements are related to speaking has not been explored.

Posturing of the head, which turns up, down or to the side in many forms of expression, and of the trunk and limbs, seems to be systematically related to particular facial expression. This observation leads to the working hypothesis that total patterns of body expression are present in infants. The most economical theory is that the patterns of expression through posture, which become stereotyped in dance and theatrical mannerisms, are based on innate templates as Darwin (1872) proposed. Study of these patterns requires repeated analysis of videotapes or films or sorting of many photographs. Since it is impossible to attend adequately to several parts of the body in real time, pencil and paper or keyboard encoding from ongoing behaviour are unreliable.

Particular hand movements are closely associated with particular facial expressions, forms of vocalising and prespeech. Some gestures are more often combined with 'big' open-mouthed expressions or calls like those adults make in greeting or attracting attention, or to express excitement, surprise or anger (Darwin 1872; Eibl-Eibesfeldt 1970; Ekman & Friesen 1969). This category includes vigorous hand waving and large open-handed or fisted movements. In contrast, index-finger pointing and finger-thumb closing with the hand held up over the shoulder or near the face are often synchronised with the climaxes of prespeech and the formulation of a new focus for visual attention. The association of lip-pursing or tongue protrusion with index-finger pointing or index-thumb closing, and of open-mouthed calling with wide open hand recalls Peiper's concept of 'spreading' of movements between the eyes, mouth and hand to produce a pattern of simultaneous opening or closing (Peiper 1963). But the combinations are far too numerous and subtle for this to be a satisfactory explanation.

By the second month infants show improved visual focus and their eye movements communicate the changing direction of their visual attention. A two-month-old can elect to look at things of interest and can reject or avoid by looking away. Systematic eye movements to or away from the hand and face of a partner, especially to the eyes or mouth, are important signals in person-to-person interaction (Caron et al. 1973; Maurer & Salapatek 1976). The fact that infants select organs used for expression (eyes, mouth, hands) as foci for attention suggests that looking is a pre-adapted response to particular signal patterns. Eye-to-eye contact has been used as a defining feature of face-to-face communication between young infants and others (Robson 1967; Stern 1974). The development of deliberate well-aimed visual orientating to the mother's eyes when the infant is about six weeks old is the main event of which she is aware at the start of 'strong' communication (Wolff 1963; Robson 1967). At six to eight weeks focussed looking with knitted brows giving way to smiling and prespeech are clearly differentiated in an intelligible and appealing pattern of communicative intent (Rheingold 1961; Stern et al. 1975). Even blind infants orientate to faces. They are well coordinated when they direct their eyes toward voices as well as when they link aiming the eyes with head rotation and attempts to reach and grasp. Blindness easily goes undetected in early infancy because looking movements seem normal (Freedman 1964; Fraiberg 1979).

The whole complex of actions just described seems to imply that the infant has a clear commitment to intentional communication. But do infants adjust their expressions in relation to other people or are their different expressive movements entirely the result of changes in a vague protocommunicative state, one that is pure output stimulated by recognition of a face but is blind and deaf to signals from communicative acts of persons? To answer this question we must examine the sensitivity and responsiveness of infants to signals from people who desire to communicate with them.

INFANTS ADAPT TO EXPRESSIONS OF THE MOTHER

Young infants respond adaptively to a wide range of human signals and these responses demonstrate their elaborate perception of persons.

Infants mimic expressions of adults. Maratos (1973) has shown that infants under one month of age may imitate pitch and duration of sounds, tongue protrusion and mouth opening, but she did not obtain imitation of head rotation, babbling or leg displacement at this age. Meltzoff & Moore (1977) report discriminating imitation of hand gesture, tongue protrusion and jaw drop with open mouth by neonates. I have observed that infants in the second month may imitate hand opening or bringing the two hands together. Piaget (1946), in his careful study of imitation, without the aid of film or video, underestimated the initial imitative competence of infants. When reproducing tongue protrusion or a voice sound even the one-month-old infant shows signs of searching for the right effect, making repeated responses with variations. The search for a desired pattern of movement must be regulated by a process of matching. It does not necessarily depend on body sensations caused by movement of the limbs or face or comparison of seen and felt movements, but some kind of adjustment of the 'image' of a movement to be made to that of a movement seen must be taking place in the brain. In order to imitate, the infant must have a cerebral representation of persons.

Maratos (1975) found that imitation of facial expressions and simple voice sounds declined in the second to fifth months. Deliberate and more accurate reproduction of babbling and crying sounds after thoughtful watching appeared in the fourth and fifth months. Piaget (1946) described similar regulation of imitative accommodation. Observations by Uzgiris (1972) confirm that a more deliberate manner of imitation of expressive movements and vocalisations is characteristic of infants of five months or older. On the basis of my own film data I have called the early form of imitation 'magnetic' and the later 'discretionary' to emphasise the increased deliberation (a more developed self-awareness?) in the second period (Trevarthen 1978).

All movements imitated by infants resemble movements they may formulate on their own. The models offered are themselves imitations of babyish acts (Piaget 1946). Imitation is certainly not passive incorporation of 'new' experiences; it is more a remodelling and integration of components already in spontaneous expression. Therefore, the fact of imitation gives no license to an unqualified empiricist approach to the growth of communicative abilities in man. It merely suggests how the infant may pick up new variants of expressions in collaboration with adults (Trevarthen 1974b).

To imitate, an infant must discriminate the model expression, but more cogent evidence that two- to five-month-olds perceive expressions is the subtle way in which the baby *translates* or *complements* the mother's acts. Even when not imitating, infants in our films show sensitive and specific replies to the communications of their mothers. A smile may elicit a call or a wave. Raised eyebrows may elicit a smile. Frowning may cause the expression of surprise, fear or even sudden crying. The temporal correlations between behaviours in such exchanges have recently been emphasised by authors who describe the 'interactions' of 'rhythmical' and 'cyclical' in a 'communicative network' or 'dyad' (Brazelton et al. 1974; Lewis & Freedle 1973; Schaffer 1977b). Imitation is evidently a special case of intersubjectivity mirroring (Trevarthen 1974b; Sylvester-Bradley & Trevarthen 1978).

The reaction of an infant of three or four weeks to the approach of an adult and to speech and touching is orientation to the face with gaze fixed on eyes or mouth, facial expression of interest or mild surprise (wide open eyes, brow 'knitted,' everted lips, mouth slightly open) and smiling. Experiments with artificial stimuli show that even neonates prefer to look at simplified face-like patterns (Fantz 1963). They seem to explore the configuration of the face, being most attracted to the eyes (Lewis 1969; Carpenter et al. 1970; Wolff 1963, 1969). They are more interested in upright faces (Watson 1972), which adults also see more easily. Experiments show that looking to faces and preference for looking at eyes increases in the second month and is usual thereafter (Caron et al. 1973; Maurer

& Salapatek 1976). Infants discriminate colour, evidently by means of built-in categorisation of wavelength into a code of the primaries: red, yellow, green, blue (Bornstein 1975). Light reflected from the skin of humans of all races is reddish. This may explain the preference infants show for a patch of red in a non-red field, a preference which could aid them in finding a face or hand. Two-month-olds will try to communicate with a televised image of a human face and this permits many experimental manipulations and tests of their understanding of communication behaviour (Papoušek & Papoušek 1974; Murray 1980).

Perception of human sounds is acute in very young infants. Speech is reacted to with particular interest. The pitch characteristics of the voice are preferred to non-voice sounds, and the female voice is preferred to the male (Eisenberg 1975). There is evidence from sucking tests based on operant conditioning that by one month consonant formant transitions[3] in synthetic speech sounds are distinguished (Eimas et al. 1971; Trehub 1973). The mother's individual voice or manner of speaking is recognised and preferred early (Mills & Melhuish 1974).

Finally, the strong response of a newborn to the periodic motion of an object in an otherwise inactive field must contribute to his perception of persons and their communication signals. All voluntary movement is periodic (Bernstein 1967). It has rhythmic coherence, a hierarchical structure of cadences and a strong tendency to synchrony of beats. Movements of different parts of the body demonstrate 'self-synchrony' (Condon 1979). Condon & Sander (1974) have presented evidence that the speech sounds of adults may act as pacemakers for limb movements of listening neonates. It is possible that the neonate becomes locked into adult speech, but much of the periodicity observed in limb movements of neonates is contributed by the infant's own motor pacemakers (Trevarthen 1974a). I believe that they are less passive in their entrainment than has been suggested, and doubt that synchronisation of this kind contributes to the development of language.

We find that close integration of rhythm of mother and baby is one of the clearest features to emerge from microanalysis of happy communications between two-month-olds and their mothers. Coordinated action with synchronisation about a common beat is the framework on which reciprocal exchange of complimentary messages is based (Brazelton et al. 1974). Two-month-olds can stop and start activity, a capacity which is essential for reciprocal exchange. Reply movements by sound making and gesture may extend the same beat as the baby talk of the mother and the head and face movements or touching which accompany her speaking.

When adults are unresponsive, avoiding or aggressive, two-month-olds show tension or distress by facial expressions of fear, yawning, grimacing and frowning, as well as by gaze avoidance, crying, startle movements and threshing or struggling. L. Murray in my laboratory has used an interruption of communication to test the predictions of the infant about communication (Murray 1980). Mothers are asked to stop reacting and to freeze their expressions for one minute in the middle of a happy communicative exchange. The infants give complex emotional responses. They may move as if to shout with sudden waving of the arms and grimaces of excitement while staring at the partner's face. These appear to be acts of appeal or solicitation. Brazelton et al. (1975) report the same results from interruption of exchanges with mothers, and Papoušek & Papoušek

(1975, 1977) have studied the cognitive basis for distress when the infant is confronted with maladapted or artificially distorted maternal signals. These reactions prove that an eight-week-old may respond predictably to unfriendly actions from a familiar person (Tatam 1974; Murray 1980). Signals of distress or protest include self-stimulatory, avoiding and aggressive acts, like those of children who have been chronically isolated from human contact or who are diagnosed as autistic (Clancy & MacBride 1975).

The signs of anxiety and distress when communication is broken show the close integration of subjective emotional states with interpersonal communication. They also show how the infant may move to recover communication if the mother fails to display affection. The infant makes forced, abrupt and large gestures which attract attention, then shows passivity and sadness or grimaces and gestures of distress which stimulate comfort and concern. In a test of the infant's intermodal perception of the mother, Aronson & Rosenbloom (1971) found that one-month-old infants made complex expressions of distress, including crying, when loudspeakers were placed to create an artificial separation between the perceived location of the mother's voice and the location of her face seen through a window. This observation is consistent with what we have seen after disruption of communication.

The infant is clearly equipped to perceive and interpret input from the mother's personality. Indeed, adaptive forms of reply to what the mother does give the infant a considerable control over the communicative exchange from the start. On this base learning will later permit the infant to achieve much more elaborate expressions and more subtle recognition of the mother, adding strength and content to their growing affectional and communicative attachment.

THE MOTHER GENERATES EXPRESSIONS ADAPTED TO HER INFANT'S INTEREST

Our mothers were skilled human communicators. All those who agreed to participate had busy lives. Most were married to men with professional or intermediate classes of occupation and the majority had at least secondary school education and were fluent in spoken language. Our films show that individual mothers differed in the style or range of their expression according to their personalities. Nevertheless, all made the facial expressions and gestures of surprise, amusement, anxiety and so on. Each mother mixed the pan-human language of expressive communication with socially cultivated mannerisms, and with speech that varied widely in content.

There is great richness and variety of structure in adult-to-adult communication, and the infant could conceivably be equipped to respond to some of it at least. However, it is not the adult forms of communication in the other's behaviour to the infant which interest us most, but a special manner which most of the observed mothers developed for capturing the infant's interest (Papoušek & Papoušek 1977; Stern 1974; Snow 1972; Sylvester-Bradley & Trevarthen 1978). Differences in playfulness, sensitive encouragement and contingent pacing of mothers in the home when the baby is three months old are prognostic of the quality of the relationship (security of 'attachment') when the baby is nine months old (Blehar et al. 1977). Clearly there is an optimal adaptation of the mother to the baby.

As soon as a mother begins to talk to the baby her movements become regular and subdued. She speaks more quietly and more gently and becomes highly attentive, spending as much time waiting and watching as speaking. The form of speech is changed in consistent ways towards the regularity, repetition and musical, questioning intonation known as 'baby talk'. Alternatively, the mother may become active and playful, or teasing, making rhythmical and exaggerated movements of her head, trunk and whole body, or reach to touch the infant in emphatic ways. When playing in this way she tends to use nonsense sounds. In visible records of the sounds of baby talk the overall effect is that of repeating patterns as in simple music. Apparently baby talk is regulated to create short dramatic episodes of action, with controlled change of intonation to a short succession of marked climaxes. The same may be said of the mother's playful movements of the head and face, of her touching with the hands and of her singing or nonsense syllables to create voice games. It is probable that baby talk obeys unconscious rules of expression, and that these rules are also applied automatically through the whole range of expressive movements whenever communication is attempted with any being that is conceived to have limited comprehension. The manner of baby talk is close to that sometimes used in speech to animals, foreigners and mentally defective or extremely aged persons. However, I do not believe that simplification is the main purpose of baby talk. A solicitous or caring intent, leading to watchful gentleness, seems more fundamental. It is a specific, assisting form of intersubjectivity, and not simple at all.

In general this automatic adaptation of a mother's behaviour would seem to match infants' perceptions and communicative capacities. Papoušek & Papoušek (1977) consider the mother's baby talk and associated orientating and patterned body movement to be highly adapted to the cognitive, learning and information processing competence of the infant and to give strong support to the initial development of cognition. Most mothers, even when unaware of doing so, tend toward similar patterns of rhythm and repetition. This behaviour of mothers, closely fitted to the baby's needs, makes it possible for the investigator to use baby talk and vocal games to detect infant behaviours which indicate changes in communicative intelligence (Sylvester-Bradley & Trevarthen 1978). It also offers a sensitive way of comparing the communicative styles of mother–infant pairs. This aspect of intersubjectivity with infants, in spite of rules that transcend cultural groups, varies widely in certain details between different individual mothers, and these differences show marked correlations with social class (Blehar et al. 1977; Moss et al. 1969; Lewis & Freedle 1973; Stern 1974).

In a very few of our recording sessions the mother was unable or unwilling to submit to the special requirements of communication with a young infant under laboratory conditions. Then her infant was fretful or avoiding. Individuals less experienced or less involved with an infant than the mother may likewise fail in communication. This is because they fail to support the infant's expressions of pleasure or his prespeech and gestures. It is important to note that our method using staged communicative exchanges in an institutional environment may intimidate the mother, the infant or both and cause a breakdown of intersubjectivity or its change to a distressed form. However, it does not take much observation in homes to determine that 'normal' human communication with infants is very varied in quietness and success. The 'studio' situation does not appear to be outside the range of natural interactions. Even in the home and under optimal conditions the mother has to adapt deliberately to her infant to obtain communication. These observations of failure in communication give strong support to the claim that both infant and mother are sensitive to the quality of each other's expressions.

MOTHERS RESPOND TO THE EXPRESSIONS OF INFANTS

The films show that mothers are captivated and emotionally involved with their infants. As soon as the infants join in communication the behaviour of most mothers quickly becomes subdued and attentive to and dependent on what the infants do. In our films mothers are usually watchful and questioning or show signs or surprise or disbelief. They react as agents who are *subordinate* to acts of babies. Smiling, baby talk, touching and moving the face in and out towards the infants cease, and are succeeded by attentive stillness and orientation to the infants' faces, and by imitation of certain infant expressions.

In the communications we have observed, close imitation of the infants by the mothers is characteristic. The imitated behaviours, often reproduced with playful exaggeration or gentle mockery, include excitement and vigorous calls. Mothers imitate tossing back the head, raising eyebrows in surprise or emphasis, opening the mouth, frowning and laughing. Some mothers include conscious or semiconscious humorous, sometimes teasing or aggressive, reproductions of comical expressions in their imitations, including poking out the tongue or grimacing. But most of the imitation in our sample is unconscious following of the infants' most vigorous or most prominent gestures. The behaviour may be described as mirroring, although, since it is often slightly after the infant in time, 'echo' describes it better. At other times, mothers synchronise with or even slightly anticipate what infants will do. Reflecting excited or melodramatic behaviour evidently plays a role in sustaining communication. This is what Stern et al. (1975) call 'coaction'. It does not form the sole basis for early communication because infants are quite capable from the start of a more subdued dialogue-like alternation of 'utterances' (M.C. Bateson 1979). As a rule, prespeech with gesture is watched and replied to by exclamations of pleasure or surprise like 'Oh, my my!', 'Good heavens!', 'Oh, what a big smile!', 'Ha! That's a big one!' (meaning a story), questioning replies like 'Are you telling me a story?', 'Oh, really?' or even agreement by nodding 'Yes' or saying 'I'm *sure* you're right'. Since mothers reproduce infants' demonstrative acts, it is all the more interesting that they do not usually imitate prespeech and small hand movements such as pointing, but reply to these with baby talk. What they say gives us access to how they perceive infants. The content of baby talk to one two-month-old infant girl, in films taken under the conditions we have standardised, has been analysed by Sylvester-Bradley (Sylvester-Bradley & Trevarthen 1978). He discovered that the mother rarely talked about what needed to be done to attend to the baby's physiological needs. Nearly all the mother's utterances were about how the baby felt, what the baby said and what the baby thought. A mother evidently perceives her baby to be a person like herself. Mothers interpret baby behaviour as not only intended to be communicative, but as verbal and meaningful. They may not remember these complex and elaborate interpretations but this does not detract from the psychological significance of what they do.

In summary: mothers' responses to two-month-old infants are stimulating, attentive, confirmatory, interpretative and highly supportive. They inject meaning into the infants' expressions, but at this stage verbal meaning has no influence on the infants' minds. *What* the mothers say does not tutor infants. Because infants already perceive speech, they are able to assimilate baby talk as a carrier of maternal subjectivity along with changes in maternal appearance and cadence of movement, taking them into their own patterns of communicative expression and deriving organisation from what the mothers do. They take what they require and let the rest go by.

DYADIC COMMUNICATION

The described responses and actions give us the essentials for analysis of intersubjective communication between two- and three-month-old infants and their mothers. The four main functions discussed are as follows:

1. *Infant expressions* include a wide repertoire of indications of subjective mood and of intent to transmit specific contents of experience and purpose, even though these contents themselves are poorly differentiated at this age.

2. *Infant responses* show attention to and imitation of expressions of mothers, including mood and speech.

3. *Maternal expression* tends to a specialised mode of communication adapted to the perceptual capacities of infants.

4. *Maternal responses*, largely unconscious, complement infant expressions and follow them closely.

Putting these together we may create a diagram of mutual interaction. A system like this has many possible states. Most important are states of closely synchronised activity and states of reciprocal or complementary activity. There is no reason to assume that the partners are equally active, and there may be considerable asymmetry of intention. Since one partner is psychologically very immature, asymmetry is likely and must be taken into account. Analysis of filmed exchanges reveals that while the pattern of communication between mother and infant is regulated by *both* partners, it is indeed one-sided and the infant tends to assume control of the course of communication after mother and baby become mutually orientated. I consider the finding that a two-month-old baby may take purposeful initiative in communication as important as the discovery of an innate form of intention to speak with an accompanying code of gestures. The communicative processes of infants are not merely latent precursors of language; they are already functional in directing communication with adults. Thus infants control the social stimulation on which their own development depends.

Evidence for infant control is presented in a diagram of the sequence of events in a communicative exchange.

Stimulated by a simple request to 'talk to' or 'chat with' her baby the mother begins by efforts to attract the infant's attention, principally to obtain eye contact. If the infant is relaxed and alert this is usually achieved in a few seconds. Then the mother smiles and speaks gently, bringing her face close in front of the baby who watches fixedly what she is doing. The first sign of response from the baby is almost always a smile, but he may begin mouth movement or make some other expression.[4] If the mother receives a sign of pleasure or interest from her baby she reacts immediately by imitating his expression or by increasing her solicitations in movement and baby talk or singing etc. But good communication involves reticence on the part of the mother. She must step down as soon as the infant appears ready to make an 'utterance'. Watching, admiring and withdrawing to make way are signs of the mother's willingness to become subordinate to any communicative initiative from the infant. When the infant makes an elaborate gesture, vocalisation or prespeech with gesticulation, the mother reacts with receptive expressions of surprise, pleasure and admiration. We distinguish between the mother's response to more animated and vocal displays of excitement, which she tends to shadow or mirror, and more concentrated unsmiling prespeech which she watches passively and then replies to at the end (cf. Stern et al. 1975).

This accommodative patterning of the mother's response allows the infant to form sequences of activity that take the form of utterances 1–5 seconds long separated by pauses in which the infant watches the mother. Thus phrasing of the exchange results from a cooperative effort. The infant reacts to the mother's attentions, much affected by her shadowing reinforcement of smiling, vocalising, etc., by becoming stimulated to expressive activity before returning to the relaxed state (Bateson 1975; Reingold 1961; Stern et al. 1975).

During prespeech the infant's eye contact and smiling may disappear to give way to an expression of concentration. It seems likely that these indications of withdrawal, with reduction in attention to the mother, are responsible for the mother's deferentially withholding baby talk and other expressions during the infant's utterances. As soon as the infant shows signs of ending his utterance, with reduction in all forms of expression, the mother actively approves and replies. If the infant does not respond, the mother's efforts increase. They are phrased with regular questioning climaxes which may succeed in eliciting immediate responses. Quick, precisely tuned responses of the baby to the mother's climax pauses show that he is following the pattern of the mother's behaviour and that he is particularly sensitive to her more marked signals. If the mother becomes assertive and teasing, the infant at this age may withdraw and cease to communicate. Each partner watches and joins in step with the patterned utterances (or signal displays) of the other. The exact form of the infant's utterances seems mainly determined by his own spontaneous brain processes. Immaturity of comprehension of what the mother does results in his assertiveness which she acknowledges.

The mother finds out what her infant can do as she becomes familiar with him. She creates interpersonal games which become ritual exchanges commenting on or emotionally marking familiar patterns of their companionship. Each mother–infant pair develops conventions of communication. When mothers and infants are interchanged to make pairs of 'strangers' the communication becomes less elaborate and more cautious and seems out of tune. Games and play rituals are characteristic of communication between mothers and their infants older than three months (Trevarthen & Hubley 1978) but the process of personal friendship begins earlier. The restraint in the behaviour of a two- or three-month-old when he is required to communicate with an unfamiliar woman may be due partly to immediate recognition of her different identity, but details of observed behaviour indicate that the process is much more complex. It involves variation in the pattern of response of *both* partners. Women are less confident, less relaxed with a strange infant. Infants often show surprise at an unfamiliar woman's hesitant behaviour. Nevertheless, experienced and confident mother-substitutes can elicit cheerful communicative responses from infants. In these exchanges the communication can be more excited and more playful than the typical exchanges of the infant with his own mother.

We conclude from these observations that the learning by both infant and mother within their communicative interaction is a major factor in the creation of the personal bond between them. Attachment does not appear to be a simple imprinting of the infant to facial appearance or signals from body contact, odour etc. However, I do not wish to conclude on the basis of the artificial exchanges we film that this kind of active communicative practice at two months, enjoyable though it is for infant and mother, is essential to the psychological growth of the infant. Its value to me as an investigator is that it brings out what the infant and mother are capable of and willing to do to achieve communication. What we have seen makes it impossible to ignore the significance of innate intersubjectivity in the mental growth of the infant.

COMMENT

It is often thought that the main cause of development in communication during infancy is the fabrication of structure for the infant by the mother. According to this view the infant's immature acts have rhythm and impulse, but are at the outset exceedingly simple in variety of form. The mother attributes intentions to these seemingly pointless movements, maintaining development by transfer of her intentions and understandings to the infant. This view of the development of communication neglects the regulation of development from within the mind of the child and leaves the child's psychological growth unexplained.

Our findings with infants two to three months of age lead us to conclude that a complex form of mutual understanding develops even at this age. It is both naturally accepted and strongly regulated by the infant. Two-month-olds exhibit many different expressions, some highly emotional, and they make a variety of attempts to gain the lead in an exchange with another person. They also are sensitive to subtle differences in the mother's expression.

The dependent acts of the mother show that she is adapting to the infant, and apparently each pair develops a unique style of communication and a private code. But in primary intersubjectivity there is innovation of meaning by the infant as well as by the mother. Furthermore, inside the earliest communications of man may be observed the embryonic forms of communication by speech itself. In this sense we may cautiously refer to the 'protoconversational' character of these exchanges. The mother, we believe, is right. The infant, though telling her nothing, *is* speaking to her.

Even more important is the precocity of a general interpersonal understanding. In the first functional stage of human communication, before transactions with objects are developed beyond a few simple orientating reactions and thoughtless explorations, the infant recognises the mother and invites her to share a dance of expressions and excitements. The infant needs a partner but knows the principle of the dance well enough, and is not just a puppet to be animated by a miming mother who 'pretends' her baby knows better.

NOTES

1. I use the word 'intersubjectivity' in the sense of Habermas (1970, 1972) when he considers the origins of language from a psychoanalytic viewpoint. It is not a graceful word, but it does specify the linking of subjects who are active in transmitting their understanding to each other. The relating is 'interpersonal', but we need to penetrate the psychological process by which conscious intending subjects relate their mental and emotional processes together. I feel that 'intersubjective' emphasises this.

2. Grateful acknowledgement is given of support from the United States Public Health Service to Professor Jerome Bruner at the Harvard Center for Cognitive Studies, and from the Social Science Research Council of the United Kingdom.

3. When consonants are articulated the flow of air is stopped. Different consonants combined with the same vowels stop the voice for different times. The differences, though of the order of a few thousandths of a second, are perceived by young infants.

4. If the baby has been fretful or sleepy, sight of the attentive mother usually triggers grimaces of sadness, fussiness or crying. We do not persist long in recording this kind of behaviour as our aim is to obtain information about exchanges expressive of complex mental processes of the infant rather than mere physiological or emotional states. An unhappy infant is taken from the chair and left to be attended by the mother.

SELECTED BIBLIOGRAPHY

AARONSON, D. & RIEBER, R. W. (ED.) 1975. *Developmental psycholinguistics and communication disorders*. New York: New York Academy of Sciences.

AMBROSE, A. 1961. The development of the smiling response in early infancy. In Foss 1961, pp. 179–96.

ANDREW, R.J. 1963. Evolution of facial expression. *Science*, 142: 1034–41.

ARONSON, E. & ROSENBLOOM, S. 1971. Space perception in early infancy: perception within a common auditory-visual space. *Science*, 172: 1161–63.

BATESON, M.C. 1975. Mother–infant exchanges: the epigenesis of conversational interaction. In Aaronson & Rieber 1975, pp. 101–13.

———. 1979. *Before speech: the beginning of interpersonal communication*. Cambridge: Cambridge University Press.

BERNSTEIN, N. 1967. *The coordination and regulation of movements*. London: Pergamon.

BLEHAR, M.C., LIEBERMAN, A.F. & AINSWORTH, M.D.S. 1977. Early face-to-face interaction and its relation to later mother–infant attachment. *Child Development*, 48: 182–94.

BLURTON JONES, N. 1971. Criteria for use in describing facial expressions of children. *Human Biology*, 43: 365–413.

BORNSTEIN, M.H. 1975. Qualities of colour vision in infancy. *Journal of Experimental Child Psychology*, 19: 401–19.

BOWER, T.G.R. 1974. *Development in infancy*. San Francisco: W. H. Freeman.

BRAZELTON, T.B., KOSLOWSKI, B. & MAIN, M. 1974. The origins of reciprocity: the early mother–infant interaction. In Lewis & Rosenblum 1974, pp. 49–76.

BRAZELTON, T.B., TRONICK, E., ADAMSON, L., ALS, H. & WISE, S. 1975. Early mother–infant reciprocity. In Ciba 1975, pp. 137–54.

BULLOWA, M. (ED.) 1979. *Before speech: The beginning of interpersonal communication.* Cambridge: Cambridge University Press.

CARON, A. J., CARON, R. F., CALDWELL, R. C. & WEISS, S. J. 1973. Infant perception of the structural properties of the face. *Developmental Psychology,* 9: 385–99.

CARPENTER, G. C., TECCE, J. J., STECHLER, G. & FRIEDMAN, S. 1970. Differential visual behaviour to human and humanoid faces in early infancy. *Merrill-Palmer Quarterly,* 16: 91–108.

CHARLESWORTH, W. R. & KREUTZER, M. A. 1973. Facial expressions of infants and children. In Ekman 1973, pp. 91–168.

CIBA 1975. *Parent–infant interaction.* Ciba Foundation Symposium, n.s. 33. Amsterdam: Elsevier.

CLANCY, H. & McBRIDE, G. 1975. The isolation syndrome in childhood. *Developmental Medicine and Child Neurology,* 17: 198–219.

CONDON, W. S. 1979. *Before speech: the beginning of interpersonal communication.* Cambridge: Cambridge University Press.

CONDON, W. S. & SANDER, L.W. 1974. Neonate movement is synchronized with adult speech: interactional participation and language acquisition. *Science,* 183: 99–101.

DARWIN, C. (1872) 1965. *The expression of the emotions in man and in animals.* Chicago: University of Chicago Press.

EIBL-EIBESFELDT, I. 1970. *Ethology: the biology of behavior.* New York: Holt, Rinehart & Winston. (2nd edn).

———. 1971. *Love and hate.* New York: Holt, Rinehart & Winston.

EIMAS, P.D., SIQUELAND, E.R., JUSCZYK, P. & VIGORITO, J. 1971. Speech perception in infants. *Science,* 171: 303–6. Repr. in Stone et al. 1973, pp. 1180–4.

EISENBERG, R.B. 1975. *Auditory competence in early life: the roots of communicative behavior.* Baltimore: University Park Press.

EKMAN, P. (ED.) 1973. *Darwin and facial expression.* New York: Academic.

EKMAN, P. & FRIESEN, W.V. 1969. The repertoire of nonverbal behavior: categories, origins, usage and coding. *Semiotica,* 1: 49–98.

———. 1971. Constants across cultures in the face and emotion. *Journal of Personality and Social Psychology,* 17: 124–9.

EKMAN, P., FRIESEN, W.V. & ELLSWORTH, P. 1972. *Emotion in the human face: guidelines for research and an integration of findings.* New York: Pergamon.

FANTZ, R.L. 1963. Pattern vision in newborn infants. *Science,* 140: 296–97. Repr. in Stone et al. 1973, pp. 314–16.

FOSS, B.M. 1961, 1963, 1965, 1969. Determinants of infant behaviour, vols. I–IV. London: Methuen.

FRAIBERG, S. 1968. Parallel and divergent patterns in blind and sighted infants. *Psychoanalytic Study of the Child,* vol. XXIII, pp. 264–300. New York: International Universities Press.

———. 1979. *Before speech: the beginning of interpersonal communication.* Cambridge: Cambridge University Press.

FREEDMAN, D.G. 1964. Smiling in blind infants and the issue of innate versus acquired. *Journal of Child Psychology and Psychiatry,* 5: 171–84.

HERSKA, H.S. 1965. *Das Gesicht des Säuglings: Ausdruck und Reifung.* Basle and Stuttgart.

LEBOYER, F. (1974: *Pour une naissance sans violence.* Paris: Editions du Seuil) 1975. *Birth without violence.* London: Wildwood; Repr. London: Fontana, 1977.

LEWIN, R. (ED.) 1975. *Child alive: new insights into the development of young children.* London: Temple Smith; New York: Anchor/Doubleday.

LEWIS, M. 1969. Infants' responses to facial stimuli during the first year of life. *Developmental Psychology*, 1: 75–86. Repr. in Stone et al. 1973, pp. 648–55.

LEWIS, M. & FREEDLE, R. 1973. Mother–infant dyad: the cradle of meaning. In *Communication and affect: language and thought*, ed. P. Pliner et al., pp. 127–55. New York: Academic.

LEWIS, M. & ROSENBLUM, L.A. (ED.) 1974. *The effect of the infant on its caregiver.* New York: Wiley.

LOCK, A. (ED.) 1978. *Action, gesture and symbol: the emergence of language.* New York: Academic.

MARATOS, O. 1973. The origin and development of imitation in the first six months of life. PhD dissertation, University of Geneva.

MARATOS, O. 1975. Trends in the development of imitation in early infancy. In *Proceedings of the OECD Conference on Dips in Learning*, St. Paul de Vence, March 1975, ed. H. Nathan. Paris.

MAURER, D. & SALAPATEK, P. 1976. Developmental changes in the scanning of faces by infants. *Child Development*, 47: 523–27.

MELTZOFF, A.N. & MOORE, M.H. 1977. Imitation of facial and manual gestures by human neonates. *Science*, 198: 75–78.

MILLS, M. & MELHUISH, E. 1974. Recognition of mothers' voice in early infancy. *Nature*, 252: 123–24.

MOSS, H.A., ROBSON, K.S. & PEDERSON, F. 1969. Determinants of maternal stimulation and consequences of treatment for later reaction to strangers. *Developmental Psychology*, 1: 239–47.

MURRAY, L. 1980. The sensitivities and expressive capacities of young infants in communication with their mothers. PhD dissertation, University of Edinburgh.

OSTER, H. & EKMAN, P. 1978. Facial behavior in child development. In *Minnesota symposia on child psychology*, 11, ed. A. Collins. New York: Thomas Y. Cromwell.

PAPOUŠEK, H. 1967. Experimental studies of appetitional behaviour in human newborns and infants. In *Early behaviour*, ed. H.W. Stevenson et al., pp. 249–77. New York: Wiley.

———. 1969. Individual variability in learned responses in human infants. In Robinson 1969, pp. 251–66.

PAPOUŠEK, H. & PAPOUŠEK, M. 1974. Mirror image and self-recognition in young infants. I. A new method of experimental analysis. *Developmental Psychology*, 7: 149–57.

———. 1975. Cognitive aspects of preverbal social interaction between human infants and adults. In Ciba 1975, pp. 241–69.

———. 1977. Mothering and the cognitive head-start: psychobiological considerations. In Schaffer 1977a, pp. 63–85.

PEIPER, A. 1963. *Cerebral function in infancy and childhood.* New York: Consultants Bureau.

PIAGET, J. (1936: *La naissance de l'intelligence chez l'enfant*) 1952. *The origins of intelligence in children.* New York: International Universities Press.

———. (1946: *La formation du symbole chez l'enfant: jeu et rêve image et representation*) 1962. *Play, dreams and imitation in childhood.* New York: Norton.

RHEINGOLD, H.L. 1961. The effect of environmental stimulation upon social and exploratory behaviour in the human infant. In Foss 1961, pp. 143–77. Repr. (abbreviated) in Stone et al. 1973, pp. 789–95.

ROBINSON, R.J. (ED.) 1969. *Brain and early behavior: development in the fetus and infant.* New York: Academic.

ROBSON, K.S. 1967. The role of eye-to-eye contact in maternal–infant attachment. *Journal of Child Psychology and Psychiatry*, 8: 13–25. Repr. in *Annual progress in child psychiatry and child development*, ed. S. Chess & A. Thomas, pp. 92–108. New York: Brunner/Mazel, 1968.

SCHAFFER, H.R. 1977a. *Studies in mother–infant interaction.* Proceedings of the Loch Lomond Symposium, Ross Priory, University of Strathclyde, September 1975. New York: Academic.

———. 1977b. Early interactive development. In Schaffer 1977a, pp. 3–16.

SNOW, C.E. 1972. Mothers' speech to children learning language. *Child Development,* 43: 549–55.

SPITZ, R.A. & WOLF, K.M. 1946. The smiling response. A contribution to the ontogenesis of social relations. *Genetic Psychology Monographs,* 34: 57–125.

STERN, D. 1974. Mother and infant at play: the dyadic interaction involving facial, vocal and gaze behaviors. In Lewis & Rosenblum 1974, pp. 187–213.

———. 1975. Infant regulation of maternal play behavior and/or maternal regulation of infant play behavior. Paper presented to the Society for Research in Child Development, Denver, Colo.

STONE, J.L., SMITH, H.T. & MURPHY, L.B. 1973. *The competent infant.* New York: Basic Books; London: Tavistock, 1974.

SYLVESTER-BRADLEY, B. & TREVARTHEN, C. 1978. Baby-talk as an adaptation to the infant's communication. In Waterson & Snow 1978, pp. 75–92.

TATAM, J. 1974. The effects of an inappropriate partner on infant sociability. MA dissertation, University of Edinburgh.

TREHUB, S.E. 1973. Infants' sensitivity to vowel and tonal contrasts. *Developmental Psychology,* 9: 91–96.

TREVARTHEN, C. 1974a. The psychology of speech development. In *Language and brain: developmental aspects, Neurosciences Research Program Bulletin* (Boston), 12, ed. E.H. Lenneberg, pp. 570–85. Repr. in *Neurosciences research symposium summaries,* 11, ed. F.O. Schmitt et al. Boston, Mass.: Massachusetts Institute of Technology Press, 1975.

———. 1974b. Intersubjectivity and imitation in infants. *Proceedings of the British Psychological Society Annual Convention,* Bangor, p. 33.

———. 1975. Early attempts at speech. In Lewin 1975, pp. 57–74.

———. 1978. Modes of perceiving and modes of acting. In *Modes of perceiving and processing information,* ed. H.L. Pick & E. Saltzman, pp. 99–136. Hillsdale, N.J.: Lawrence Erlbaum.

TREVARTHEN, C. & HUBLEY, P. 1978. Secondary intersubjectivity: confidence, confiding and acts of meaning in the first year. In Lock 1978, pp. 183–229.

UZGIRIS, I.C. 1972. Patterns of vocal and gestural imitation in infants. *Proceedings of the Symposium on Genetic and Social Influences* (International Society for the Study of Behavioural Development, Nijmegen 1971). Basle: Karger. Repr. in Stone et al. 1973, pp. 599–604.

WASHBURN, R.W. 1929. A study of the smiling and laughing of infants in the first year of life. *Genetic Psychology Monographs,* 6: 398–537.

WATERSON, N. & SNOW, C.E. (ED.) 1978. *The development of communication: social and pragmatic factors in language acquisition.* Paper presented at the Third International Child Language Symposium. New York: Wiley.

WATSON, J.S. 1972. Smiling, cooing and 'the game'. *Merrill-Palmer Quarterly,* 18: 323–39.

WOLFF, P.H. 1963. Observations on the early development of smiling. In Foss 1963, pp. 113–38.

———. 1966. *The causes, controls and organization of behavior in the neonate.* Psychological Issues, 5: 1–99 (monograph 17).

———. 1969. The natural history of crying and other vocalizations in early infancy. In Foss 1969, pp. 81–109. Repr. in Stone et al. 1973, pp. 1185–98.

ZALAZO, P.R. 1972. Smiling and vocalizing: a cognitive emphasis. *Merrill-Palmer Quarterly,* 18: 349–65.

john dore

FEELING, FORM, AND INTENTION IN THE BABY'S TRANSITION TO LANGUAGE

In our concern to explain how children learn language, we have invariably assumed one or another source of development as primary. Either the infant's mind
or his environment has dominated inquiry, thus sustaining the infamous nature-
nurture controversy. Investigators have presumed either that the child somehow
invents (creates, etc.) language and then merely adapts to conventional expressions of it; or that the child discovers (induces, etc.) it from the speech of others
and must then somehow make it his own. Though both processes may well be
involved, the locus of their interaction and manner of relationship are, at best,
unclear. Of course, major variations appear in each theoretical camp: Mind theorists argue about whether language is essentially a genetically given faculty versus
a cognitively constructed system (see the Chomsky–Piaget debate in Piattelli-
Palmerini, 1980); social theorists conceive the environment in radically different
ways, ranging from a reinforcement system (Skinner, 1957) to a cultural map to
be progressively internalized (Vygotsky, 1962). And, despite claims by everyone
that both organism and milieu must be attended to, a dichotomy of choice of
primary source still inheres in theories of development.

George Miller (personal communication) compared the failure of behaviorist
explanations to the mystery in nativist ones, concluding that we are caught between "the impossible and the miraculous." Perhaps in response to this theoretical stalemate, and to many years of the dominance of structural models,
psycholinguists have begun to turn to functional theories for frameworks to describe language. We have tried to apply to development notions from the philosophy of language (e.g., Austin, 1962; Searle, 1969; Wittgenstein, 1953), from
the "ethno" sciences (Gumperz & Hymes, 1972), from British functionalism
(Malinowski, 1923) and from literary/psychological/social theorists as diverse
as Burke (1950), Mead (1934), and Goffman (1974). Concerning earliest words,
for example, Bates (1976), Bruner (1975), Cross (1977), Dore (1975), Halliday
(1975), Ochs and Schieffelin (1979), and Snow (1977) have all stressed the social
aspects of language acquisition. This chapter emerges out of this tradition. However, four areas will be stressed which have thus far not been well-developed by
interactional approaches: The personal relationship between mother and infant,
the affective nature of prelinguistic communication, the centrality of dialogue,
and the functional analyses of affective expression.

I propose, as a necessary component of language emergence, the dialogue
between caregiver and infant, as distinct from locating language *in* the mind or *out*
there in speech and social routine. First words will be seen to emerge in the

infant as consequences of dialogical functions of affective expressions across members of an intimate dyad. This treatment is, therefore, not a contribution to a theory of mind, language, or society. Rather, it focuses on the transformation of babbling to words by means of the caregiver's inducement of, first, the anxiety leading to the intention to communicate and, second, the conventional forms of expressions. It argues that, apart from any cognitive invention and social discovery, the origin of words occurs in the immediate context of affective conflict, arising as solutions to maintain and negotiate relationship through dialogue. In short, I plan to describe the affective inputs to intentionality and reference.

Briefly and roughly put, the argument proceeds as follows. Prior to his first words the baby (B) experiences a period that is transitional between words and babbling, usually occurring near the end of the first year. He or she comes to this point with at least these abilities: (1) to act on objects deliberately, to achieve physical goals by means of sensorimotor coordinations; (2) to express affect directly, vocally and/or gesturally, either as an accompaniment to his or her actions (often as though talking to objects), or while gazing at the face of the primary adult caregiver (A), but not alternating gaze with object manipulation; and (3) to attend to A's activity and to respond directly to some of A's vocalizations and gestures directed to him or her (B). These prelinguistic accomplishments are well-documented by numerous investigators (e.g., Bruner, 1978; Stern, 1977; Sugarman-Bell, 1978; and Trevarthen & Hubley, 1979).

I offer here a two stage hypothesis about how mother and infant interact during this period, and suggest that such interaction is a necessary condition for language onset. First, when B expresses affect in a marked way, A *matches* it (for original conception, see Stern, 1982) by either "*analoguing*" to the same affect-state, *complementing* it with a different state, or *imitating* the external form of his behavior. These communicative matches intervene in B's affect-state in the sense that they "analog" it with a differing intensity and often in a different behavioral channel, or they contrast B's affect with an opposing state, or reproduce an observable form of his own affect with an opposing state, or reproduce an observable form of his own affect (recall that initially he expresses spontaneously, so only after A's match can he observe a form for his own affect). On the basis of such behavioral descriptions, I hypothesize that A's interventions in B's affect expressions *transform* them into intents to express those affect-states.

A simple example, from early on in this period, will illustrate this hypothesis. When babies in our culture express delight in any way at some unusual sight, mothers typically clap to express joy along with them. *How can* such a match transform an unmediated expression of delight into an intention to express it? First, B initiates the interaction by his expression; A's clapping provides an analog in an observable form of his own affect. Since B has been observing A all along, and may not have identified with it, he can now observe his own feeling in her behavior. When he claps in response to her clap, he is not merely imitating some form out there in another person. At that moment he discovers a gesture for what he is feeling. Since her form matches his feeling, his clapping expresses his own state, not hers; even though his affect had to "loop through" her to become observable. This may be the original moment of "cognizing" a connection between internal state and external sign for it. The behavioral form can then be reproduced when feeling the same affect, thereby allowing both B and A together to "*re*-cognize" and share the same affect state. Perhaps without her analog of his state in another form, he could not become aware of his own state—there would be nothing to observe. This awareness may be the origin of intention—the moment when the motivation for an expression finds an observable form that can be focussed upon and then reproduced.

But this does not explain *why* a B *would* change from expressing to intending. For this we must postulate that the B is motivated to maintain some intimate state of communion with A. He needs to adapt to her ways of doing and expressing in order to achieve, maintain, repair, and later renegotiate their relationship. So, by clapping, for example, he can invoke in her and himself a pleasurable affect state to share, and therefore to ensure solidarity. This is a familiar enough assumption in psychodynamic theories, but it does not go far enough. It is the negative case, with its conflict of affect, that better accounts for the emergence of intention.

Conflict arises when A's communicative match *contravenes* B's affect-state. For example, when the baby we describe tries to mouth an object, his mother prohibits it; this occasions B's affect expression of a "protest" with an abrupt, high-pitched, vowel-like utterance accompanied by arm-flapping in apparent anger; A then reprimands B with an obviously angry, intense "Don't you yell at your mother!"; to which B responds with a still higher pitched, indeed violent, "protest." B here again initiates interaction with the positive affect action of mouthing. A blocks that affect, in a sense knowing his pleasure but contravening it. B of course can not "cognize" her behavior as a form for his affect. However, his protest is provoked by her prohibition, thereby providing a potential link between his affect and her *complement;* that is, his protest is an unmediated expression of negative affect which analogs her negative act of prohibition. Moreover, the hypothesis that *A induces intentions in B* is seen more clearly in the subsequent round of this interaction. After matching intense prohibitions and protests, A shifts her tone to a lower pitch with a repeated "I said 'no'" while pulling the piece away from him again; at this he protests most violently, looking at her. It seems as though at this moment he has become aware, through her contravention, of his own negative affect, and can begin to *intend to express* it for the first time. Thus, what began as a complement of her prohibition of his pleasure, concludes as a double, crossmodal "analoguing" of the same affect: her pulling the piece away matched by his reaching and pulling it back, her intense reprimand matched by his intense protest. Out of such conflicts his marked motivated expressions become transformed into intentions to express.

But, again, *why?* If B's affect is breached by prohibition, rather than attuned to, the conflict threatens communion. Anxiety arises. Being able to express his state intentionally allows B to invite a match of positive affect and to deny negative matches. It allows him *to test the state of their relationship.* The intent to express becomes the first cognitive tool for communicating about their relative states in their dialogue with one another. Because the same affect can be differentiated into two forms and communicated cross-modally, partnership in dialogue emerges. But *the analog of affect is the foundation of dialogue.*

The second part of this two stage hypothesis is that *A induces in B conventional forms* for expressing shared affect-states. Given that B can already intend to express his state, the question arises: How does A intervene in B's expressions to change their form? But we are not concerned with the mere echoing of forms, so much as the shared meaningfulness of expressions for the dyad. Now, some degree of meaningfulness must already inhere in B's intentions to express a shared state, some minimal awareness that a form somehow matches an internal state. Although this requires some cognitive processing, the content of what B is aware of is not yet a cognitive category; it is an affective match. The problem is then not, as in cognitive approaches, to identify the overlap in semantic features of the B's first words and his caregiver's. Rather, it is to identify the procedures they use to effect "meaningful" exchanges (i.e., effective, consequential, motivating, interactions) and to specify the processes by which word meanings emerge from expressions intended and interpreted as shared affect states.

One possibility here, adumbrated by Vygotsky's (1978) dictum that intrapsychic events first occur on an interpsychic level, would be that *their* conversational procedures become *his* psycholinguistic processes: That her ways of staging scenes, indicating objects, searching for words to fit them, contrasting meanings, and so on, in their affectively meaningful and shared interactions become his ways of, say, sorting information into distinctive semantic sets. In this way A would at least highly constrain possible interpretations of their shared affect. The central problem would then become the means whereby affectively meaningful communicative actions *between* A and B are transformed into personal meanings-for-words *in* B. This shifts emphasis away from asking what biological and cognitive categories B brings to the task of language learning toward asking how categories emerge from interpersonally shared affect states and the behavioral forms in which they are expressed. Thus, we assume that word meanings are consequences in B of what AB feel and do. The dialogue they engage in is the interface between his functional intents and her formal requirements for interpretation. Though A cannot give B his needs, motives and intents, she does supply him with the forms necessary to express them.

When B intends to express affect to A, A matches B's expression with a conventional form. This intervenes in B's expressive form, transforming it toward conventional recognizability. A either *analogs* B's expression with a more specific form, or *complements* it with a contrasting one, or *imitates* his form closely without marked affect. *Formal analogs*, even when they are not affective attunements as well, nevertheless serve to replace B's idiosyncratic forms for expressing himself. That is, assuming that they already share affect and that B initially expresses it idiosyncratically, A's imposition of conventional form merely supplies a close substitute for what B is already expressing. A's utterance gives form to B's intent. And this may well be the moment that B first realizes that his form expresses some content, and the moment when he originally cognizes some connection between his own content and his mother's form for expressing it.

When the mother of the 12-month-old girl in our second example below asks "Wanna play with the castle?", the B turns to gaze at her. A then points to the pile of "castle" blocks and says "This!", emphatically stressing both her vocalization and her pointing gesture. B replies with an unintelligible utterance, low in pitch, volume, intensity, and duration, resembling an aspirated stop followed by a back vowel (roughly /hkyə/). A responds with a high-pitched, rising "No?" in a pleasant tone of surprise. At this B repeats "No!" with an intense, abrupt tone and emphatic head nod. However, contrary to the expected semantically negative "answer", B proceeds to knock over some of the blocks.

Describing this complex communicative match, it is clear that B intentionally expresses her response to A, behaviorally manifested by her body orientation to A and the blocks, her gazing toward A and her vocalizing to her. A interprets B's unintelligible utterance as negative, but she is either unsure, surprised, or both; so A produces what might have been the B's "answer." But this is no mere imitation. A marks her semantically negative content with positive affect; simultaneously giving B's utterance conventional form and soliciting clarification. Further, for B's part, when she repeats "No!" it is not with A's surprise tone, but with an emphatic one, perhaps analoguing A's emphasis on "This!" earlier. Here we see a conversion from B's initial intent to "answer" vocally but unintelligibly to her accommodation to A's form of answering. Again, like clapping for gleeful affect, here A *trans-forms* B's expression to conventional status!

However, in this case there is no direct affect attunement. Rather, a more complex interplay of affect and form takes place. B apparently takes the form of A's negative content, but omits the pleasant tone of surprise on that form, and assimilates the emphatic marking of A's prior "This!" to her own "No!" Moreover, this reply constitutes a move in a conflict of the agendas they are negotiating for B's behavior: B has been playing with a phone while A is recommending block play. (In fact, A's behavior may be an elaborate distraction from B's playing with the real phone, not unlike in principle from our first mother's prohibitions.) Thus, we have a degree of tension, if not anxiety, in their agenda clash, motivating B's apparent rejection. Finally, however, B's "no" has not acquired word status since she does go to the blocks, and during this same time period she does not contrast "yes and no" in a semantically consistent way.

We can ask the same two questions of this word-*like* emergence that we asked of the origin of the intention to express: How can a B do it and why would he? The first has been the concern of most approaches to acquisition; most recently cognitive theories have dominated the market. And, indeed, some degree of cognitive processing must occur if a B is to, say, contrast positive and negative semantic features in the form of "yeses" and "nos." Moreover, the infant must be able to adapt and produce linguistically contrastive sounds. Both cognitive and phonological contrastivity are necessary inputs to language. Here I suggest that the interpersonal matching of affect is also necessary, and the three together may be sufficient to "cause" language.

The salience of motivation in this account leads to the conclusion that the dialogical basis of language occurs when the dyadic partners match, analog, complement, imitate, and mismatch each other's affect, but express themselves in different forms. Adaptation to each other's affect and form constitutes the dyad's very identity (from which B derives his identify; see Mead, 1934). In Piagetian terms, A accommodates to B's affect and assimilates it to her forms; B accommodates to A's forms and assimilates them to his affect and cognition. Tension always exists from the disequilibrium of their matches, at all levels. Mismatches of both kind and intensity abound in every dyad. After intentionality emerges the only solution to mutual comprehension in dialogue is a shared system of linguistic symbols.

Again, to be in communion, to be understood, to be effective in conveying intent and content, B must adapt to A's forms. Not only uncertainty and ambiguity, but also anxiety is reduced by being able to express states, needs, desires for objects, and so on by unequivocal symbols; that is, words that disambiguate among items desired at the right moment. Words reconstitute the dyad's inter-subjectivity. Trevarthen and Hubley (1979) describe a "secondary intersub-jectivity" evident at 9 months of age in the form of interactional synchronies between dyadic partners across several behavioral modalities. Words transform this into a symbolic intersubjectivity that allows for convenient reproducibility of form and interchangeability of speaker. This contributes directly to the emergence of both ego identity and social competence (see Erikson, 1968).

INDEXICALITY, INTENTIONALITY, AND ACCOUNTABILITY

In order to clarify earlier hypotheses, fuller analyses of our two examples will be necessary. But, first, a few related notions must be mentioned which will help with the data analyses. These include the status of the baby's vocalizations at this period, changes in his intentionality, and the social nature of the mother's motivation and behavior at this time. This section will be an attempt to show how the baby's "indexical forms" and intentional expressions change under the influence of the adult's pervasively "accountable" behavior.

Investigators agree, almost unanimously, that between babbling and the first genuinely referential words the child progresses through an intermediate phase of word-like productions. Piaget (1952) called these "symbols" (tied to sensori-motor schemata) as distinct from linguistic "signs" and Halliday (1975) described this period as "proto-language." In Dore (1975) I called them "primitive speech acts,"; Dore, Franklin, Miller, and Ramer (1976) described them as "phoneti-cally consistent forms,"; and here I refer to them as "indexical expressions."

Unlike babbling, "indexicals" have a well delimited shape, bounded by pause and often directed at objects. They include expressions of affect (early in this phase especially forms like squeals of joy and cries of frustration) as well as syllable-like sequences, often combining phoneme-like sounds with marked af-fect. They occur repeatedly, though in variable phonetic form, in a child's rep-ertoire of sounds, and can be loosely correlated with recurring internal and environmental conditions. In fact, indexicals do not appear to be detachable from the child's affect state at first; that is, not appearing to be mediated by intention to express to another initially. Nor are they displaced, in the sense that words are, in time and place from their moment of articulation. Although they function systematically from the point of view of the adult's interpretation, they are not organized into contrastive sets in semantic domains the way first words are. Dore et al. (1976) grouped these forms into four categories: *affect expressions*, such as /ei::/ for pleasure; *instrumentals*, such as /ʌʔ/ while reaching for some-thing; *indicating expressions* to take note of or point out some aspect of the envi-ronment, often accompanied by pointing; and *groupings* that appear to reflect an interaction between subjective state and attention to objective properties, such as when two different groups of sounds are used with the same group of objects but differ in the affect they express.

Thus far in our analyses of the data from this project there seem to be two types and two phases of development of indexical expressions. The first, *affect indexicals*, seem to emerge from early crying and delight sounds, at the beginning of the transitional phase being exemplified primarily by grunts of protest or squeals of glee. They are occasionally directed to someone via gaze, and are dominated by gestures, facial expressions, and tones typical of aroused affect states; an example is the B's protest described earlier. In such behavior the affect is more salient than the form is conventional, and it tends to be replaced by forms like "stop" and "no" later in development. The second type, *formal indexicals*, exhibit less affect-indicating behaviors, and increasingly approximate the surface forms of adult speech. They are better-defined syllabically, phonemically more stable, and more varied prosodically than the affective type. For example, the B in the same prohibition episode above produced /i::⌐ᴧ/ in a tone which, although it manifested some mild pleasure, was marked by much lower pitch, less intensity, slower and less abrupt features than the protest. This type ranges from such conventional seeming "vowels" through B's imitations of A's words to apparent word-forms.

A majority of investigators currently consider such forms to be "widely over-generalized word uses" (Bowerman, 1978), as though they *refer* in a linguistic sense. Here I suggest that, although they do indicate empirical complexes, they lack the semantically discrete, contrastive, displaced, referential features of genuine words. In Dore (1978a), for example, a boy as late as 15 months used the term "bee" to index such diverse occurrences as falling leaves, crawling ants, spots on a wall, bleeps on a T.V. screen, and his father slapping a table. It is difficult to see the commonality in such extensions, and the indexical did not contrast with others in a set for movement terms. Assuming that such an indexical expression does intend something prior to becoming a word proper, the question here is: What occurs between infant and interlocutor that transforms the indexical to a word?

A direct answer requires an adequate characterization of adult behavior, but first I want to specify two phases within the indexical period in terms of intentionality. The difference between the affective and formal *type* of indexical corresponds roughly to the *time* of their emergence; in general, indexicals marked heavily with affect eventually give way to more formally marked indexicals, though an affective stratum of word use continues. Recall that we are discussing a period between two other kinds of intentionality: the intent to achieve a physical goal and the intention to convey a word meaning. In the first the infant is aware of a practical end and can institute various means to achieve it, largely by sensorimotor actions on objects, best described in terms of Piaget's (1952) middle stages of sensorimotor intelligence. The baby, typically crawling, moves to, grasps, manipulates, and otherwise explores the properties of objects, including his own body and the face of his caregiver. A prototypical example is the mouthing of objects which, however elementary, satisfies most investigators' criteria for inferring an *intent-to-act*. This type has been widely described as a cognitive acquisition. It is used here as input to the transitional phase in that such actions are what mothers typically react to, comment on, match and otherwise intervene in.

At the other end of development we have the much discussed *intention-to-convey* lexical content. This is what is acquired by the end of the transitional period. The intention-to-convey presupposes the development of recognizable words whose intensional meaning features partly overlap the adult's. Their forms are phonemically stable and largely conventional; their use is displaced in time and space, detached from the immediate context and well established in memory; the choice of one over another routinely exhibits a semantic contrast among a limited set of items (like "yes-no" or "ball-baby" from a set of responses or toys); and toward the end of the single-word utterance period, the term chosen will function as a predicate (e.g., B will point to a cookie and say "eat." See Bloom 1973; Dore 1978a; Greenfield & Smith, 1976; deLaguna, 1927/1963 for details). Moreover, in addition to semantic information, word conveyances also function to communicate expectations. With them B induces in A the recognition that: (1) B is referring to some particular conceptual domain; (2) he intends to communicate some illocutionary function like requesting or answering; (3) B expects A to recognize both his intent and content; and (4) he expects A to do something about it, like complying or at least acknowledging him (see Dore 1978b).

Between the intent-to-act on objects and the intention-to-convey word meaning, there occurs a transitional phase of intentionality, coinciding with what we have formally described as the period of indexical expressions. Intentional expressions of this sort are more than physical actions, but less than intended word meanings. This is the period that requires closer empirical scrutiny and clearer theoretical formulation than has been available in previous explanations of language acquisition. From our preliminary analyses it appears that, for many children at least, this period itself can be subdivided into two phases: an "intending-*in*-expressing" and "intending-*to* express" (to distinguish these from the intent-to-act and the intention-to-convey, where forms of the word-root "intend" are meant to mimic development). The empirical difference between the two subtypes of intentional expression should be apparent from the earlier discussion of how mothers induce intentionality from motivation in their children. Recall that our 9-month-old addresses (i::/ to the doll he is about to mouth and /æ ↗/ in protest, swinging at his mother's arm. Although these differ in form type (formal and affective, respectively), they both exemplify "intending-*in*-expressing."

Such vocalizations are closer to the intent-to-act insofar as they accompany actions and are not addressed directly to people. They express some state, but are not *intended* to express a specific state. They are not mediated, premeditated, or planned, but rather immediate, spontaneous, and reflexive. Philosophers like Langer (1972) call them "presentational" intentions: automatic ways of reacting to a particular event, as opposed to a choice of possible responses from among a set of known, appropriate, alternative ones. Empirically, intendings-*in*-expressing incorporate two behavioral modalities: vocal plus gesture or gaze-at-object, but not both. Vocalizations are either accompaniments to actions, or, when addressed in the direction of another, are not intoned, with onset and pause, to solicit responses, even though they may receive routine responses from an attentive adult.

In contrast, "intending-*to*-express" is closer to the intention to convey words. It does not merely add more of the same to an action, but rather supplement if with an amplifying concern, usually involving something to be done or said about the object. They are directly addressed to someone, with sharp focus of personal gaze to indicate the other's status as addressee. They are premeditated expressions, evidenced by the time delay between onset of personal gaze and onset of vocalization. Thus they seem to be cognitively mediated. They are "representational" intentions to the extent that some kind of deliberation takes place, some rudimentary cognitive content is executed. The empirical evidence for such a characterization consists in the integration of three modalities, synchronized across persons, movements, and objects. That is, the infant can alternate rapidly between acting on an object and vocalizing to someone about it, the behaviors therefore ensembled within a single theme. A typical example is the "no" by the 12-month-old girl previously described. While it does echo the A's preceding phonemes, its prosody expresses a quite different internal state from A's. Yet it is not quite a word insofar as it does not actually contrast with "yes," but rather fulfills the general function of responding to solicitations. (Recall that B went on to act as if she said "yes" and that the two words were not semantically productive for her at this time.) The phenomena described here as two kinds of intentional expressions before words have been reported widely in the diary literature on language development, but have not been isolated for study, nor related to affect development and interaction in the dyad. Whether they occur in the chronological order we found in our babies is a matter for further, quantitative research. We turn now to A's contribution in order to explain how her behavior interacts with B's development of indexical forms and intentional expressions as described earlier.

In principle, the dialogue between A and B can be construed as the influence of A's culture on B's mind, of A's socialized forms on B's motivated actions; but also as the influence of B's needs on A's responses. What are the properties of A's socialized responses and how do they interface with B's motives and intents? We must assume that A is herself highly motivated to socialize her baby successfully, not only to consciously provide her B with words (the hallmark of normalcy and intelligence in our society); but, more pervasively, as a thoroughly socialized agent she can not help but act in culturally appropriate and pragmatically effective ways. All her behavior is meaningful and *accountable in form*. Not only are all words and almost all actions of A's conventional in form; they constitute the totality of what is acceptable behavior for the child.

Garfinkel (1967) describes "everyday activities as members' methods for making these same activities visibly-rational-and-reportable-for-all-practical-purposes [p. vii]." These methods are *accountable* in that they are "situated practices of looking and telling . . . which consist of an endless, ongoing, contingent accomplishment [p. 1]." To talk "accountably" then, is to display mutually recognizable rules of usage for a situation at hand. The two primary properties of accountable talk, according to Garfinkel, are *indexicality*, the displaying of a part of a circumstance, making it sharable; and *reflexivity*, that indexical expressions constitute the very accomplishment of the circumstance. See Dore and McDermott (1982) for an example of how talk both creates and is determined by its contexts.

Five other properties of accountability, which Garfinkel adapted from Schutz (1962) are the following: (1) accountable practices function against a background of assumed *relevancies;* that is, taken-for-granted, known-in-common, sensible expectancies of acting in term of "what everyone knows," which operate tacitly until they are breached; (2) The *"et-cetera-ness"* of such relevancies consists in there existing "more than one can say at the moment," but which nevertheless functions as an expectancy that is an unspecified part of our agreement in behaving accountably; our agreement, whatever it turns out to be specifically, is therefore inherently incomplete and subject to upcoming contingencies, and thus always subject to further revision; (3) conversation is a *situated* accomplishment of a mutual context of interaction consisting of mutually sensible displays of concerted efforts toward consensus; (4) such situated displays must be temporally *sequenced* vis-a-vis each other, and aligned so as to be recognizably sensible (i.e., accountable); and (5) because of these features of relevant expectancies, et-cetera-ness, situatedness, and sequentiality, conversation must be interpreted procedurally in terms of a *prospective-retrospective* analysis; that is, members must await future developments in order to "locate" past displays, which themselves "project" prospects for future clarification.

Garfinkel (1967) argued that a "common understanding consists of an inner-temporal course of interpretive work [p. 25]"; that shared agreement derives from "social methods for accomplishing the member's recognition that something was said-according-to-a-rule and not the demonstrable matching of substantive matters [p. 30]"; and that common understanding consists in "the enforceable character of actions in compliance with the expectancies of everyday life as a morality [p. 53]." He continues, "The features of the real society are produced by persons' motivated compliance with these background expectancies [p. 53]." When such expectancies are breached, the member "should have no alternative but to try to normalize the resultant incongruities." Such breaches lead to bewilderment, a "specifically senseless environment" and ultimately to "internal conflict, psychosocial isolation, acute and nameless anxiety along with various symptoms of acute depersonalization [p. 55]."

Regarding language acquisition, first words can be construed as the acquisition of accountable objects, as well as the more traditional intentional objects. In this view the word acquired is not merely the symbolic consequence of intentional development. It is, specifically, the consequence of *interpreted* intentions; and, still more specifically, B's intending expressions are interpreted *accountably* by A. The crux of development is, thus, how B's intentions become accountable. Insofar as words exhibit the aforementioned features, words are accountable objects par excellence.

We have already discussed how express*ings* are indexical, but early AB utterances are reflexive as well in that they constitute part of their accomplishment *in* talking. That is, the talk not only indexes their mutual attention to context, but it *performs* it in that such talk *is* the doing of "what we are now doing is playing, eating, etc."; and it displays how "we are together" or not on this. In analoguing B's affect, A gives form to *their* feeling. This form integrates B's state with an accountable form for expressing it. And A's form also *is* their most immediate context; the external, accountable, mutually recognizable form of their shared affect.

Since word uses must always function against a background of relevancies, A must know both more than she can say and more than B could know. Her word uses relative to B's intendings-in (to)-express will foreground only a small part of a word's meaning, and only that part relevant to the circumstances at hand. Future uses of the "same word" will be applied to different circumstances (i.e., objects, events) and thus will contingently exhibit different meanings. Her work at expanding B's form uses *in any way* must constitute a revision of meaning for his form. To that extent the mother must pervasively *breach* any expectancies of relevant meaning that B has begun to acquire for a form.

The "et-cetera" clause for any word's meaning, and of course any minimal meanings B may have for a form, entails that its application will be subject to contingencies not-knowable-in-advance. While a schema, although open to change, is entirely contained cognitively at any given moment, a word, being an accountable object as well, can never be entirely stabilized in that way. So, when A revises B's word use, she is in effect not only breaching what he may have thought they agreed to as that word's meaning, but she also conveys to him something like "that's what it meant all along, from the start." This may of course be quite disorienting for the child. It certainly must compete with any tendency to cognitively fix discrete meanings. And, of course, such change-from-without is quite distinct from creation-from-within. Such competition and conflict may motivate B's need to learn more language.

Since A in a sense operates "inside of" B's affect, her interventions into his indexical expressions can introject into them three dimensions of meaning. Her words have a distinctness and specificity and effectiveness relative to the circumstances A and B have jointly focussed upon; they have a discreteness and contrastiveness relative to other words in a semantic system; and, most deeply, her words inherently reflect the *moral* status of something like "that's the only *right* way to say this here." If B is motivated to adapt to A's forms and their uses, these dimensions of meaning automatically accrue to his accommodation to her forms. He has many hundreds of opportunities to realize their meanings, especially since she routinely interprets his forms as meaningful before he can intend them as such.

However, at the same time we have seen how A pervasively breaches and unconsciously revises any degree of meaningfulness B may have constructed for his affective experience expressed by her forms. B's acquisition of meanings progresses from his first attempts to act with and "index with" word-like forms, to A's breaches of such attempts, to his bind of being "overthrown again," to his learning more about the word's accountable meaning so as to stabilize his linguistic cognition as a *defense* against the pervasive incursion of her breaches. In other words, the disequilibrium between her communicative matches and his affective state and cognitive awareness becomes a motivational (even moral) crisis for him if his personal identity with her as partners in communion (now communication) is threatened by too many mismatches or failures on her part to "uptake" his affect or intent to express.

The emergence of word meaning must also depend upon the situatedness of word uses. It is perhaps this that prompted Wittgenstein (1953) to view the meaning of a word as its collection of uses. In developmental studies, the emphasis on cognitive processes and products has obscured the importance of use preceding meaning. When meanings are treated as calculable and computable intensional features of words, the influence of accountable uses is devalued. In that case, too, the extensions of words to newer circumstances, the dyad's methods for establishing meanings and the very motivation for their emergence are neglected as well. Ultimately, with the neglect of such rich inputs, it is tempting to postulate innate linguistic knowledge, but here we are recommending that we should first explore fully how prelinguistic intentional expressions become accountable in form. By "use-preceding-meaning" here I mean B's indexical expressions before they are transformed into accountable word forms. Indexicals become increasingly specified for meaningfulness because of their situated uses, A's revisions and B's cognitive readjustments. Innateness in the above case would not be epistemological (as Chomsky, 1965, argued), but would involve B's natural expression of affect and A's innate tendency to attune to it *cross-modally* (see Stern, 1982).

This accountable viewpoint of the social situatedness of early word usage sheds new light on the well-known "here-and-now-ness" of early language. Situatedness includes more than the "action bases" for concepts that words refer to (cf. Piaget). More crucially, earliest acquisition seems to be *inter*actionally situated. Not only does B's form increasingly approximate A's, but, since some forms continue to function as indexical expressions, they are idiosyncratic rather than accountably conventional. These are "projections" or prospects that B tries out; the indexical uses of "bee" mentioned earlier. In such cases A often adapts to B's usage temporarily; but she eventually orients *automatically* to its more accountable uses. Thus, such *un*accountable functions disappear.

Also, sequentiality allows for the method of interpretation Garfinkel calls prospective—retrospective analysis. For word learning, we suggest this works in the following way. For some affect-state or intent-to-express B produces some indexical form associated with it. This serves to project a potential connection between the two, which is both imitated from the A and recognized by her as a communicative attempt on B's part. In a sense the projected sound has "prospects" for meaning which the B cannot know beforehand. It is the A's investiture of the sound with situated meaningfulness that retrospectively supplies the B's prospect with meaning. Similarly, across many usages B retrospectively recognizes what he meant by previously projected prospects of word meanings.

In this way the AB dyad co-constructs his lexicon. They create word meanings together such that: (1) B gets to know more about what A knows, thereby increasing his "communing" power with her; (2) A knows what B knows, thereby allowing her to socialize him properly, to know what to work on next; and (3) to create a domain between them in which B can creatively "play" with meanings and change them around, while for accountable purposes they both have tools with which to negotiate concerted activity, including more word learning. In Garfinkel's terms, all of this *is* the origin of a *reciprocity of perspective* whereby the world known in common can be objectively expressed.

ILLUSTRATIVE ANALYSES OF INTERACTIONS DURING THE TRANSITIONAL PERIOD

The analyses here attempt to demonstrate the sequencing and alignment, as well as the ambiguity, of A's forms with B's functions. Several levels of interaction are referred to, ranging from the agenda being negotiated to the multiple functions of the behavioral bits. The examples are excerpts from transcripts of interactions from a corpus of 10 mother–infant pairs who were videotaped for one hour in a playroom at New York Hospital in a study conducted by Dr. Daniel Stern. The scenes involved changes in personnel and props (e.g., mother–baby alone, stranger with mother, mother absent, new toy attraction, etc.) and were repeated at intervals of 4, 6, 9, 12, 18, 24, and 36 months. The study was originally concerned with such issues as infant individuation, changes in interactional patterns, and infant's responses to mothers' prosodies. Thus far it is clear that, before speech production, babies orient systematically to their mothers' vocal tones. The babies' exact responses to changes in mothers' voice qualities (along dimensions of pitch, intensity, etc.) are now being studied, but for our purpose here it is sufficient to refer to tones impressionistically. Finally, the two examples here were chosen because they illustrated differences in sex, age, level of development, the "mood" of the scene, and two styles of AB interaction in general.

The examples analyzed here are organized around the notion of a communicative match (derived from Stern's notion of affective attunement, 1982). A match occurs whenever some *marked motivated behavior*, as an affect expression by B is directly responded to by A. Thus, on the one hand the notion of an AB affect match is a theoretical postulate, on the other such matches are identifiable in a fairly rigorous empirical way. These occur in sequences of at least two moves in a round: the B's initiation, A's response, with optional moves related to these first two which do not initiate another round. Here three types of match are scored: analogs are matches of affect wherein a partner responds to another's affect expression in the same dimension (i.e., positive or negative); complements are contrastive matches, manifested in the opposite dimension of the initiation; and imitations are non-affect matches of external form, with no apparent marked affect.

The data here are also described at the levels of agenda and of *specific communicative function*. "Agenda" is defined as a verbal and/or gestural focus on a topic or activity; play routines, "word-work," and prohibition agendas. These are executed in rounds by specific functions, such as playfully intoned indexical and acknowledgement, invitation-answer, or prohibitable-prohibitive rounds. Each example here exhibits a different kind of agenda conflict which locally motivates the communicative functions and more generally motivates the infant's acquisition of language. In Table 1 a prohibition-and-protest sequence, a mother and her 9-month-old boy negotiate a conflict between playing with a puzzle board (her explicitly recommended agenda) and mouthing a piece of the puzzle (his repeatedly "behaved agenda"). But apart from the superordinate puzzle-play agenda, A alternates between two subagendas of prohibiting him from mouthing and interpreting his vocalizations as words. These are referred to as play, prohibition, and "word-work," respectively.

A sets B up for her puzzle-play agenda by arranging him physically next to the board, telling him where to put the leaf. B's /i::/ initiates a round of behavior insofar as it is a marked motivated behavior. This indexical expression combines a vowel-like form with mild positive affect; for descriptive purposes it is more of a formal indexical than an affective one. It may be echoing A's "leaf," but there is no evidence that it (nor any of B's forms at this time) approach word status. Perhaps because of the dual form-affect properties of /i::/, A replies in a correspondingly double way: Her word "eat" expands his form into an accountable one (which incorporates his mouthing action also); and her intonation is "play-

Table 1
A Prohibition Episode Negotiated between a Mother and Her Nine-Month-Old Boy

#	Match type	Adult behaviors	Baby behaviors	Communicative functions
		Put the leaf in there.	(holding a piece of a puzzle in hands)	directive
		That's a part of a puzzle.		comment
1			/ i::: ↲ / (raising piece to mouth; hesitates, then looks around to A)	"pleasure" indexical
				preventable
	IMI	No. It's not to eat. (playful		preventive
	ANA	tone; shaking head)		
			(puts piece in his mouth)	prohibitable
2	IMI	That's a *leaf*.		
	COM	No / :: ↲ / (pulling piece away with her finger)		prohibitive
	ANA		/ŋ:ʔʌ̄/ (flapping arms angrily)	protest-1
	ANA	Don't you yell at your mother (moving piece away from B)		reprimand
3			/ m::m ↲ / (reaching for piece)	elicitive
	COM	I said *NO!* (high, intense, abrupt, angry tone; but she gives the piece back to him)		denial
				compliance
4			(puts piece in his mouth)	prohibitable
	COM	(pulls piece out of mouth)		prohibitive
	ANA		/æ ↗ / (high-pitched; arm flapping)	protest-2
	COM	I said no. (low, lax; pulling piece away)		warning
	COM		/æ ↗ / (highest pitch; examining piece)	protest-3
5			(puts piece in mouth) / m::m /	"pleasure" indexical
	COM	Does that taste good? (rocking head up and down)		accusation
			(takes it out; examines it)	compliance
		It's only cardboard.		comment
6			(puts it back in mouth)	prohibitable
	COM	Huh? Does that taste good? Let's put it back! (taking it out of his mouth)		accusation
				directive
				prohibitive
	ANA		(flaps arm weakly) / ʌ? /	protest-4

ful" relative to what preceded and followed it, thus, analoguing his pleasure. His raising the piece toward his mouth is scored as a "preventable" functionally, not yet a prohibitable, while her utterance functions as a preventive. Round 2 begins with his mouthing, prohibitable action. First she expands to another /i/-word, "leaf," but her "no" shifts to a tense, elongated, slow rising-falling tone which, together with her pulling the piece away, constitutes a prohibitive. Round 2 continues because B immediately protests her prohibitive with an "angry" vocalization and arm flaps. She responds by reprimanding him and pulling the piece away again.

Regarding communicative matches in round 2, A's "leaf" imitates B's /i/ from round 1 (though this time she labels the object involved rather than the action "eat"). But her tone shift on "no" and accompanying act complement his mouthing because of the contrast between his presumed pleasure and her clear displeasure. Then we see *B* analoguing her displeasure in his angry protest. Still more negative affect is displayed by her reprimand. Thus, the conflict between their preferred agendas mounts, as displayed both by communicative match and function type. Regarding the accountability work, A interprets the vocalization in his protest as a "yell," and moving the piece away from him confirms that she is attempting to hold him accountable *not* to mouth. Further, while A's initial complement induces him to protest the first time, her moving the piece away occasions his next act of trying to retrieve it.

Round 3 is initiated by his elongated nasal and reaching. This is scored as an *elicitive* function, as distinct from a *solicit*, because it is an "intending-in-express-ing" or "presentational act" and not an intent to express *to* A that he wants the piece; that is, not a representational and illocutionary act of soliciting it, as might be manifested by personal gaze that *references* A as well as the object. A treats the elicitive *as if* B might be soliciting the piece from her. (Such *as-if* interpretations intervene in B's state, and his subsequent observation of them provides the beginning of the transformation of them from presentational to representational intentions, e.g., from elicitive to solicitive; initial solicitives in our data are often manifested behaviorally in the following sequence—onset of personal gaze, onset of vocalization, offset of vocalization, offset or alternation of gaze with object manipulation.) Additionally, while A's angry vocalization here complements B's affect by blocking his desire, her giving him back the puzzle piece at the same time complies with his desire. This ambiguous double signal of denying vocally what she complies with gesturally must bind B, perhaps inducing further anxiety and leading to the violent protests to come. Her giving and taking of the piece may even induce the change from elicitive to protest.

After A complements his pleasure in mouthing at round 4, it is then B who analogs A's negative affect with his second, more emphatic protest. A's tone then shifts downward, as though to contrast with his anger. But she retains the same words—"I said no," and pulls the piece away again! This occasions his most aggressive protest which, relative to her lowering of tone, complements her state with a much more negative one. This is their climax. He triumphs temporarily. Then, in round 5, she complements his pleasure indexical with an ironically intoned accusation, continuing the commentary as he examines the piece. In round 6, he performs the prohibitable mouthing again; she again complements it with an accusation. But this time she takes the piece away permanently, to which he weakly protests, and ultimately loses the skirmish. A's agenda of not-mouthing holds sway over his mouthing.

Table 2 involves a 12-month-old girl engaged in her "behaved agenda" of telephone play-and-talk in contrast to her mother's mildly recommended "castle-block" play for her. Moreover, the example is critical for showing how A's forms complete B's speech functions. We offer a brief analysis of this example primarily as a contrast with the "prohibition" scene. This mother can not be characterized as "prohibitive" in any sense, since she rarely blocks her baby from doing what she wants. However, she is "interventional" in our sense in that she does try to distract her B's attention away from prohibitable actions (or, conversely, attract B to hers). An example from the same session as our excerpt was when the B knocked the phone handle off its cradle; A, having failed with mild (playfully intoned) pleas like "Okay, let's hang it up now," waits until B goes to another toy before rearranging the phone herself. Even when B is handling the electric outlet, A merely tries to distract her. A almost always matches B's play efforts with a playful or encouraging tone.

B initiates this example with a characteristic, continuous, babble-like "cackle" while reaching for the phone. But, after a pause, B's final syllable terminates with a rise. Because personal gaze follows her terminal rise, almost immediately and *before* A's response, B's utterance is scored as a solicitive. A's acknowledgement of it analogs her daughter's positive state. Then A "imitates" B by carving out of her cackle three syllables, labeling the object of attention, "telephone." This is an orientation to external form, rather than internal state. B then imitates the prosody of A's "telephone," almost perfectly, but she continues to use her own idiosyncratic segmental phone types and terminates again with a rise. Because of the absence of personal gaze this time, the utterance is scored as an elicitive. A analogs it with an acknowledgement. B then turns to face A and initiates round 3 by producing a solicitive with a rising terminal contour. Again A analogs it with an acknowledgement. B walks away, vocalizing, this time without a rise, communicatively functioning as an accompaniment.

The episode shifts to a mild agenda conflict when in round 3 A invites B to play "castle" with the blocks on the floor between them. After getting B's attention, A nods, emphatically points to the blocks and prosodically stresses her invitation with a second part, "this!" B's first attempt at an ostensible "answer" is phonetically uninterpretable for content. It is a complement on the match level because of the stark contrast behaviorally between A's excited offer and B's apparently negative attitude. Then A in turn complements B's response with a more excited, surprised "no?" This functions as a clarification question, and apparently influences B's more conventionally formed answer. Here again, A's form intervenes in B's prior "quasi-function," transforming its response status into an accountable form. More interestingly, B's "no" not only adapts to A's segmental phonemes but also utilizes the emphatic stress and head nod from A's earlier "this." While in round 2, B adapted to the prosody of "telephone," here she *re-envoices* A's prosody, phonemes, and gestures to give full conventional form to what earlier was a "quasi-answer" at best. In other words, in both cases B is becoming accountable to the appropriate forms for expressing her intents.

Yet, despite its form, B's "no" is apparently not semantically contrastive, since she proceeds to violate the putative truth value of "her" answer by playing with

Table 2
A Play-with-Competitive-Agenda Episode between
Mother and 12-Month-Old Girl

#	Match types	Adult behaviors	Baby behaviors	Communicative functions
		Boy, there's so much to do.		comment
1			/ dikədæ . . . / pause / dæ ↗ / (while reaching toward telephone; then turns to A)	solicitive
	ANA	Yea! (high-pitch, elongated slow rising, playful tone)		acknowledgement
			(turns to phone)	
	IMI	Telephone. / ↲ / (slow rising and falling contour)		label
2	IMI		dætəkæ ↗ / (same prosody as A's "telephone," with rising terminal contour)	elicitive
3	ANA	Aha.	(turns to A)	acknowledgement
			/ dɪkæ ↑ / (emphatic stress)	solicitive
	ANA	Yea. / /		acknowledgement
			(walking toward corner) / dəkɪdæ /	accompaniment
		Wanna play with the castle?		invitation
			(turns to A)	
		This! (emphatic stress and emphatic pointing)		
4	COM		/ hkyɔ / (very low pitch, intensity)	"answer"
	COM	NO? (high-pitch, "surprise")		clarification
	IMI		NO! (high, abrupt tone; emphatic head nod)	answer
	COM	Okay.		acknowledgement
5			(walks to A; hesitates; then knocks some blocks over) / dəkæ ↗ / ("joyful," emphatic stress; glances at A)	solicitive
	ANA	Yea. (breathy, laughed) Knocked it over, didn't ya? Let's see. Whata ya gonna do with the rest of the castle?		acknowledgement
				"questionings"
			(turns to phone)	"ignore"
		Nothing! ("ironic" tone)		self-answer

the blocks. At this point the answer is only negligibly hers, and more of a ventriloquating of A's answer for her. A gives conventional form to B's functional capacity to answer, but she cannot give her semantic contrastivity itself. The main point here is that As show Bs how to answer before they can comprehend the forms they use. Also, apart from the semantic mismatch, B's going to the blocks here signals solidarity with A, just as A's tones do with her.

However, B's hesitation before knocking the block down suggests (as did our "prohibition" baby's hesitation) that she is becoming aware of the clash in agenda between her and A, and perhaps beginning to reflect upon her choice of game. Here this A accepts her B's choice to forego the "castle" game. Although A mildly prefers block-play for B in her subsequent questioning, she ultimately accepts B's reorientation to the phone (unlike the mother in Example). A's final remark of "nothing" (like the above mother's "it's just cardboard") seems to be addressed to someone other than the child—some adult audience or herself or perhaps such ironies are played to the camera. At any rate, utterances of this sort remind us of the multiple "voices" we all perform from the dialogical point of view. Just as B's "no" is more "their" word than hers, "nothing" is less their word (or even A's word) than it is the word of some wider social grouping.

CONCLUSION

The approach to language proposed here is obviously attempting to integrate and extend the social-interactional (Mead, Vygotsky, Bruner, etc.) and the affective (Langer, Erikson, Stern, etc.) traditions. I assume that, while affect is the primary dimension of early communication, it is the cross-personal dialogue of affect that is most crucial for language emergence. Cognition is secondary in two senses: (1) it operates to construct meaning systems already begun by connections between affective states and socialized forms of expressions; and (2) intentionality itself emerges out of the more fundamental motivation toward persons and the objective world. The difference between this approach and current cognitive, linguistic, and social ones is best reflected in the nature of dialogue. This "dia-" logic of the dyad is different in kind, chronologically prior, and theoretically more fundamental than the "mono-" logics assumed by most philosophies of science. Instead of, for example, the logic that A is only A and not B, *Adult* and *Baby* here are one, irreducible unit. Thus, the problem of language emergence is reversed: It is not how A communicates to a separate B, so much as how AB become differentiated into distinct language-using ego entities.

A final note regarding the definition of "word." In the psycholinguistic (and dominant) definition, contrastive, semantic, intensional features of words are "known" (computed, chosen, etc.) somehow by the child. To explain their origin one must appeal to innate linguistic knowledge or some specific cognitive function. But, defined pragmatically, the word is the symbolic consequence of intended and interpreted affect form complexes, used first as indexical expressions of personal (social, objective, etc.) contexts to express one's self and to commune with others, only secondarily accruing to a system of displaced meanings.

I do not claim to have fully explained word emergence here. However, I hope that I have at least pointed to a possible type of explanation that neither appeals to innate linguistic knowledge nor to the primacy of cognition, but rather to an interpersonal dialogue of affect expression as the (possibly innate) basis of symbolic consciousness.

ACKNOWLEDGMENTS

The data for this paper came from a project conducted by Dr. Daniel Stern of the New York Hospital. Without these data and his insights into the attunement of affect between mothers and babies, this paper could not exist. I thank him and Helen Marwick of Edinburgh University for their description of the prohibition segment reported herein. I am deeply indebted to Lois Bloom for her close reading and helpful recommendations for revision of a prior draft. I also thank our editor, co-contributor and conference organizer, Roberta Golinkoff, for her patience, the challenging ideas of her paper which so closely relates to mine, and her helpful comments on mine. Finally, I thank Catherine Snow and Bambi Schieffelin for their constant encouragement, and Ray McDermott for his constant criticism, and their feedback during the long writing of this paper. None of the above of course agrees with my account completely. That is the beauty of our dialogue.

SELECTED BIBLIOGRAPHY

AUSTIN, J. *How to do things with words*. New York: Oxford University Press, 1962.

BATES, E. *Language and context: The acquisition of pragmatics*. New York: Academic Press, 1976.

BLOOM, L. *One word at a time: The use of single word utterances before syntax*. The Hague: Mouton, 1973.

BOWERMAN, M. Systematizing semantic knowledge: Changes over time in the child's organization of word meaning. *Child Development*, 1978, *49*, 977–987.

BRUNER, J. The ontogenesis of speech acts. *Journal of Child Language*, 1975, 2, 1–20.

———. From communication to language: A psychological perspective. In I. Markova (Ed.), *The social context of language*. London: Wiley, 1978.

BURKE, K. *A rhetoric of motives*. Englewood Cliffs, N.J.: Prentice-Hall, 1950.

CHOMSKY, N. *Aspects of the theory of syntax*. Cambridge, Mass.: M.I.T. Press, 1965.

CROSS, T. Mothers' speech adjustment: The Contribution of selected child listener variables. In C. Snow & C. Ferguson (Eds.), *Talking to children: Language input and acquisition*. Cambridge, Mass.: Cambridge University Press, 1977.

DORE, J. Holophrases, speech acts, and language universals. *Journal of Child Language*, 1975, 2, 21–39.

———. Concepts, communicative acts, and the language acquisition device. Invited address to the Boston Child Language Conference, September, 1978a.

———. Conditions for the acquisition of speech acts. In I. Markova (Ed.), *The social context of language*. London: Wiley, 1978b.

DORE, J., FRANKLIN, M., MILLER, R., & RAMER, A. Transitional phenomena in early language acquisition. *Journal of Child Language*, 1976, *3*, 13–28.

DORE, J., & MCDERMOTT, R. Linguistic indeterminacy and social context in utterance interpretation. *Language*, 1982, *58*, 374–398.

ERIKSON, E. *Identity: Youth and crisis*. New York: Norton, 1968.

GARFINKEL, H. *Studies in ethnomethodology*. Englewood Cliffs, N.J.: Prentice-Hall, 1967.

GOFFMAN, E. *Frame analysis*. New York: Harper, 1974.

GREENFIELD, P., & SMITH, J. *The structure of communication in early language development*. New York: Academic Press, 1976.

GUMPERZ, J., & HYMES, D. *Directions is sociolingusitics: The ethnography of communication.* New York: Holt, Rinehart & Winston, 1972.

HALLIDAY, M. *Learning how to mean.* London: Edward Arnold, 1975.

DELAGUNA, G. *Speech: Its function and development.* Bloomington, Ind: Indiana University Press, 1963. (Originally published 1927.)

LANGER, S. *Mind: An essay on human feeling.* Baltimore, Md.: The Johns Hoopkins University Press, 1972.

MALINOWSKI, B. The problem of meaning in primitive languages. In C. Ogden, & I. Richards, *The meaning of meaning.* New York: Harcourt, Brace, & World, 1923.

MEAD, G. *Mind, self, and society.* Chicago, Ill.: Chicago University Press, 1934.

MILLER, G. Personal communication, 1979.

OCHS, E., & SCHIEFFELIN, B. *Developmental pragmatics.* New York: Academic Press, 1979.

PIATTELLI-PALMARINI, M. (Ed.), *Language and learning: The debate between Jean Piaget and Noam Chomsky.* Cambridge, Mass.: Harvard University Press, 1980.

PIAGET, J. *The origins of intelligence in children.* New York: International Universities Press, 1952.

SHUTZ, A. *Collected papers II: Studies in social theory.* The Hague: Nijhoff, 1962.

SEARLE, J. *Speech acts.* Cambridge, Mass.: Cambridge University Press, 1969.

SKINNER, B. *Verbal behavior.* New York: Appleton-Century-Crofts, 1957.

SNOW, C. The development of conversation between mothers and babies. *Journal of Child Language,* 1977, *4*, 1–22.

STERN, D. *The first relationship.* Cambridge, Mass.: Harvard University Press, 1977.

———. "Attunement of internal states by way of 'inter-modal fluency'". Paper delivered at International Conference of Infancy Studies. Austin, Texas, March 1982.

SUGARMAN-BELL, S. Some organizational aspects of pre-verbal communication. In I. Markova (Ed.), *The social context of language.* London: Wiley, 1978.

TREVARTHEN, G., & HUBLEY, P. Secondary intersubjectivity: Confidence, confiding, and acts of meaning in the first year. In A. Lock (Ed.), *Action, gesture and symbol.* London: Academic Press, 1979.

VYGOTSKY, L. *Thought and language.* Cambridge, Mass.: M.I.T. Press, 1962.

———. *Mind in society.* (Edited and translated by M. Cole, V. John-Steiner, S. Scribner, & E. Souberman). Cambridge, Mass.: Harvard University Press, 1978.

WITTGENSTEIN, L. *Philosophical investigations.* New York: Macmillan, 1953.

jean berko gleason

SEX DIFFERENCES IN
PARENT—CHILD INTERACTION

Since by now it is well documented that there are differences in the ways grown men and women speak, it seems reasonable at this point to ask where those differences originate. There are, of course, a number of plausible explanations of the origins of sex differences in language: They can arise either from inborn differences or as a result of environmental forces, or perhaps as a result of an interaction between the two. In this chapter, the emphasis will be on environmental forces, especially the role mothers and fathers play in shaping the language of their daughters and sons. This is not an attempt, however, to say that there are no inborn differences. The work of McKeever (1987) Witelson and Pallie (1973), and many others has shown that it is entirely likely that the language areas of the brains of males and females are not identical: Specialization for language appears to develop earlier in the brains of females, and males appear to be more vulnerable to every kind of insult that affects language development and retention at every age from early childhood through advanced old age.

Even if there were no differences in the neuroanatomical bases of language in males and females, there would be other obvious differences that, though not themselves linguistic, could have a differential effect on language development. Young males, for instance, are more physically aggressive than females in all cultures that have been studied (Maccoby and Jacklin, 1974). It should not surprise us, therefore, to find adults uttering more negative statements and more prohibitions to boys than to girls, and that is exactly what Cherry and Lewis (1976) found. Adults spent more time trying to control young boys, and adult language, of course, reflected those efforts. If children's language development is affected by the kinds of language they hear when interacting with adults, girls and boys may develop different kinds of language because they are spoken to differently. Thus, males and females may produce and elicit different kinds of language because of their different neurological and behavioral dispositions; and these possibly inborn differences may be amplified by society.

There are also powerful environmental forces that shape the way individuals speak and that lead to stylistic variation: Males and females speak differently as a reflection of their gender roles. The use of certain lexical items, syntactic forms, and intonation patterns cannot be reasonably tied to either neurological or inborn behavioral differences, since they are culturally constrained. The use of the adjective "darling" in English, for instance, or a special set of pronouns in Japanese, may be limited to women, but not for any intrinsic reason.

From Language, Gender, and Sex in Comparative Perspective, *ed. Susan U. Philips, Susan Steele, and Christine Tanz (Cambridge: Cambridge University Press, 1987), pp. 189–199. Reprinted with the permission of Cambridge University Press.*

There is general agreement that, for whatever reason, men and women speak differently as adults. Presumably, these differences began to emerge at some point in childhood, and the most likely context of their development lies in the arena of parent-child interaction.

INPUT LANGUAGE

We may well ask the questions, When do little boys and girls first begin to sound like males and females? and What role do parents have in the development of whatever differences there are? But questions of this sort are very recent indeed. The ontogenesis of sex differences in language has hardly been explored, and only very recently have we had any information at all about the possible differences in the speech directed to girls and boys by their mothers and fathers.

One major reason for the dearth of information on what is obviously an interesting and important topic lies in the nature of the theories that have dominated the study of children's language development in the years since Chomsky first published *Syntactic Structures* (1957). The models of child language acquisition that dominated the field in the 1950s and 1960s were child-centered and did not consider the role of adults, except insofar as they were thought to provide a rather degenerate sample of language that the young language-learning child could feed into her or his Language Acquisition Device. It was generally assumed that differences in the language the child heard (and this language was called Input Language) did not matter, since the child's Language Acquisition Device was equipped with suitable filters for processing out those elements that were not of use at a given time. The search was for universals, with an emphasis on the acquisition of syntax. The burden of acquisition lay on the child, and the role of adults in the child's environment was minimized; it was assumed that all the child needed to set the Language Acquisition Device in motion was to overhear a sufficiently large sample of the target language.

In the late 1960s this picture began to change for a variety of reasons. Among other things, a number of researchers (for instance, Gleason, 1973; Remick, 1971; Snow, 1972) began to wonder if it was really true that young children had to learn the rules of language from listening to a complex and degenerate corpus of adult speech. This led investigators to study the language of mothers of young language-learning children. The results of those studies are well known: Mothers' speech to young children is much less complex than their speech to other adults and appears to contain design features that may make the learning of language easier. The language of mothers to their 2-year-olds is slow, redundant, simple, and, above all, grammatical. This special speech may or may not make the acquisition of syntax simpler: There is still a raging controversy in the field on this subject, with some (e.g., Moerk, 1975) claiming that mothers' speech contains all of the elements necessary to teach children grammatical language, and others (e.g. Gleitman, Newport, and Gleitman, 1984) claiming that what appears to be simple in mothers' speech is not and that mothers' speech at best can have only a superficial influence on children's acquisition of language.

No one contests, however, that mothers' speech has the particular form that has been described by so many researchers, and it is that very special kind of speech that is now referred to as *input language*. (Those who think it is unimportant and uninteresting tend to call it "Motherese," but for a number of reasons that will soon become apparent, this is a misnomer.) Another name for input language is Child Directed Speech (CDS), which is a bit more accurate, since the special features of this speech are necessitated by the child who is being addressed rather than by the person, who may or may not be a mother, who produces it.

Once it became clear that mothers have a special way of speaking to young children, a number of questions arose in addition to those that center on the acquisition of syntax. These questions have to do with stylistic (or registral) variation: Input language, or CDS, is clearly a separate style, or register. It appears in the speech of women who are not mothers, in the speech of fathers, and, indeed, in the speech of all speakers, child and adult, who are addressing young children. Shatz and Gelman (1973) showed that even 4-year-olds make some modifications in their usual speech when they speak to 2-year-olds. Other researchers (Giattino and Hogan, 1975; Golinkoff and Ames, 1979) showed that fathers' speech also contained the simplifying and clarifying modifications that had been noted in mothers' speech. Thus, input language (CDS) containing some special features is produced by all speakers addressing young children. Bohannon and Marquis (1977) suggest that it is children themselves who cause these modifications, because it can be demonstrated that speakers adjust the complexity of their utterances in accordance with the signals of comprehension or noncomprehension produced by their addressees. While this can be shown experimentally, it is also true that speakers have preconceived notions of how to talk to young children: Adults simplify and clarify their speech when they only think they are talking on the phone to 2-year-olds (Snow, 1972), and young children in preschool produce typical "baby talk" when playing with dolls (Sachs and Devin, 1976; Andersen, 1977). Some of the features of CDS are undoubtedly tied to communication pressure (for instance, clear enunciation) but others are part of a conventionalized speech register (for instance, calling a rabbit a "bunny"). Young children acquire this register as part of their developing communicative competence, and adults use this register in speaking to young children.

Input language is not a unitary phenomenon, however. It changes over time and becomes more complex as children's ability to comprehend it changes. By the time children are 4 or 5, adults speak to them in a "language of socialization" that emphasizes not so much syntactic clarity, or the rules of language, as the rules of society. Speech to a 2-year-old contains many phrases like "See the bunny. It's a nice bunny. Pat the bunny," while speech to a 5-year-old contains many phrases like "Look both ways before you cross the street," "Say thank you to Mrs. Williams," and "Sit up at the table."

CDS thus occurs in different forms, depending on the *age* of the child being addressed. There may be some argument about the relation between the syntax used by adults in their CDS and the acquisition of syntax by children, but there is general agreement that adults explicitly teach children social conventions and that the adult language is the medium of that education.

What remains to be determined is whether the *sex* of the child as well as the age of the child has an effect on the CDS, and, additionally, whether CDS varies according to the *sex of the speaker*. Unless girls and boys are exposed to different adult models or are spoken to differently, we are hard pressed to provide an environmental explanation for how sex differences in their own language might possibly originate. In the rest of this chapter, a number of studies originating in our own laboratory will be discussed. The questions to be considered involve: (1) differences between mothers' and fathers' speech to children, regardless of the child's sex, (2) differences in parents' speech to boys and to girls, and (3) emerging sex-associated differences in the speech of children.

RESEARCH SETTINGS

The research was carried out in both naturalistic and laboratory settings. Initially, we obtained a small sample of families whom we visited in their homes, making audiorecordings of family interaction. At the same time, for comparison, we made recordings of male and female teachers in a day-care setting (Gleason, 1975). We then obtained funding to conduct a laboratory and home study of a much larger sample of families. Twenty-four families participated in this study. Each family had a child between the ages of 2 and 5; the mothers were the primary caretakers, and the fathers worked outside the home in professional occupations. Twelve of the child subjects were girls and twelve were boys, about evenly matched for age.

METHODS

In the laboratory portion of the study, each child was seen and videotaped twice, once with the father and once with the mother, in a counterbalanced design. Recording sessions lasted a half hour, which was divided among three activities: "reading" a picture book that had no words (Mercer-Mayer's *The Great Cat Chase*); taking apart (and attempting to put back together) a toy Playskool car; and playing store with a number of grocery items, paper bags, and a toy cash register. Toward the end of the session a research assistant entered the laboratory playroom with a gift for the child. This assistant followed a script, designed to maximize the likelihood that the parent and child would say, "Hi," "Thanks," and "Goodbye" (see our article of that name; Greif and Gleason, 1980). This was accomplished by, for instance, holding out the gift; saying, "Here's a little gift just for you"; and then waiting expectantly. Obviously, the pressure on a parent under the circumstances is to tell the child to say "Thanks" or personally to say "Thanks." In this way we were able to look at sex differences in politeness behavior in fathers, mothers, girls, and boys.

The laboratory videotapes were transcribed and analyzed in all of the standard ways (e.g., for mean length of utterance and sentence type), as well as for features thought to be differentially represented in the speech of females and males. We looked for tag questions, for instance, as in "It's hot in here, *isn't it?*," a construction often claimed to be used more by women than by men.

The home and day-care studies relied only on audiotapes, since we felt that taking a videocamera into subjects' dining rooms was too intrusive; the same held true in the day-care center. Since these studies have been reported in detail elsewhere, the major findings, along with their implications for the study of sex differences in language, will be reported here rather than the means and standard deviations associated with their statistical analyses. The interested reader is referred to Bellinger and Gleason, 1982; Gleason, 1973, 1975, 1980; Gleason and Greif, 1983; Gleason and Weintraub, 1976; and Masur and Gleason, 1980. These report on both the laboratory and home studies. It should be added here that the twenty-four families who participated in the laboratory study were also seen at home: A recording of a family dinner where both parents and the child were present was made in each family. Our current work centers on these dinner transcripts (Gleason, Perlmann, and Greif, 1984).

DIFFERENCES IN THE SPEECH OF MOTHERS AND FATHERS TO GIRLS AND BOYS

HOME STUDIES

Our first study was of several families at home. Like other researchers, we found that there were very few substantive differences in the speech of the mothers and fathers; but there were some notable exceptions. It should be noted here that in this first home study a male research assistant participated and remained with the family while the recording was made. This may have led to some exaggerated "macho" behavior on the part of the fathers. In our later home study, where we recorded the dinner interactions of our twenty-four families, we learned to leave a small cassette player with them, with the instruction to turn it on when they were about to have dinner. This much less intrusive method resulted in what seemed to be a more natural interaction.

In the first study (with the male assistant in attendance) we found that the syntactic measures of males and females were roughly equivalent. The only real syntactic difference was that the mean length of utterance of the fathers was less closely related to the child they were addressing than the mothers' MLU was to the child they were addressing. This seemed to reflect two things. The first is that the mothers appeared to be more "in tune" with their child than the fathers. Other evidence for this lies in the fact that in our study and others (see Stein, 1976) mothers were better able to understand what their child was saying than fathers were, and misunderstood less often than fathers did. The second thing that the disparity between father and mother MLU reflects is the fact that in the home sample fathers, especially when they talked to their sons, used many more imperatives than mothers did. Since an imperative lacks a subject (e.g., "Stop that"), the MLU is quite short. The fathers used many more direct imperatives than the mothers did, especially when talking to their sons, and so had disproportionately short MLUs when talking to boys. In one family, which had two children, the father had a longer MLU when talking with his 3-year-old daughter than with his 5-year-old son. Needless to say, he used many imperatives with his son.

In these home samples, the fathers produced approximately twice as many direct imperatives as the mothers—in fact, 38 percent of the fathers' utterances were in this form. Mothers were more likely to couch their imperative intentions in conventionalized polite forms (e.g., "Would you take your plate off the table, sweetie?"). It should be noted that this tendency to give orders is somewhat mitigated in the laboratory, where the differences in imperatives were slight, since, apparently, public behavior is a good deal more polite than private behavior at home.

The other major differences we found, which appear to be robust, were in choice of lexical items: Fathers used rarer vocabulary than mothers. Again, this finding has been replicated elsewhere, including in our own laboratory, where a father talking to his very young son referred, for instance, to a "construction site." The fathers at home also used a number of rather disparaging terms of address with their sons: One father called his son "dingaling"; another referred to his preschooler as "nutcake" and "Magoo." Again, we observed similar nomenclature in the laboratory, where one father called his son "wise guy." The fathers at home also had a tendency to threaten their sons, e.g., "Don't go in there again or I'll break your head." We did not see threats in the laboratory. Thus, rare lexemes, direct imperatives, threats, and rather pejorative names marked the fathers' speech at home. All of these features except the rare vocabulary were more likely to be found in speech to boys than to girls.

Unfortunately, these results have been neither replicated nor disconfirmed by others, since home studies are rare. Each of the features mentioned is a good candidate for emerging differences in the speech of boys and girls; but, with the exception of imperatives, which will be discussed shortly, these features have not been found (or sought) in the language of young children. If fathers serve as models for their sons, we would expect young boys, when compared with girls, to use more threats, more imperatives, more "funny" names. The research remains to be done, however, and if early sex differences of this type are found, they cannot all be attributed to the influence of parents, since children also find models among their peers and in society's stereotypical representation of the sexes.

LABORATORY STUDIES

A number of our own studies in the laboratory revealed sex differences in parents' speech, some of them also confirming earlier home findings. In addition to those already discussed, several might be mentioned here.

Lexical Differences

In this study (Masur and Gleason, 1980) we looked at the speech of mothers and fathers to their children in the laboratory situation where they played with an automobile that could be disassembled. The auto, of course, is not a neutral toy; most observers would agree that it is male-oriented. In their conversations with their children in this situation there were several differences between mothers and fathers but few in the way boys and girls were addressed. Basically, the fathers were more likely than the mothers to provide the actual names of the car parts and to ask their children to produce them. The fathers were more cognitively demanding, expecting their children to display their knowledge by naming the car parts and tools and explaining their function. Thus, in this laboratory situation, fathers modeled different behavior from mothers while treating boys and girls in roughly equivalent fashion.

The mothers, rather than name the car parts or associated tools, said things like "That's the turn thing" rather than "wrench," and they frequently referred to nuts as bolts and vice versa. If children follow the models of their same-sex parent, we might expect to find among the emerging differences in children's language a greater specificity and demandingness among boys, at least when dealing with topics perceived as in their domain, such as sports and tools, and more lexical vagueness among girls, perhaps reflected in the use of more general vocabulary—more use of words like "thing" and "whatsis."

Politeness

In this study, we looked at politeness behavior in the laboratory situation described above, where the child was given a gift (Greif and Gleason, 1980). We did not find differences in the ways boys and girls were treated: Both sexes were encouraged (actually urged) to say thank you when given a gift and, to a lesser degree, to say "Hi" and "Good-bye" as well. There were large differences in the mothers' and fathers' own politeness behavior, however: The mothers were much more likely to say thank you to the assistant when their child was given a gift than the fathers were. There were also some differences in the children's own spontaneous behavior; Boys were more likely to say "Hi" than girls were. If parents provide models for their same-sex children, we would, therefore, expect to see in the emerging language of the little girls more conventional expressions of politeness than in the speech of boys. The greater percentage of greetings in the speech of boys is quite interesting, since it may reflect either less shyness on the part of boys, which itself may be related to sex-role expectations, or it may be more directly related to the fact that there is more emphasis on greeting behavior among males than among females in our society—adult males are obliged, for instance, to rise and offer their hands, whereas females have a great deal more latitude in what is permissible. It is impossible to discuss differential modeling of greeting behavior by parents, since virtually all of the parents said hello when the assistant said hello to them.

Interruptions

This study (Greif, 1980) examined the frequency of interruptions in the speech of parents and children across the three laboratory situations (playing store, reading a book, taking apart the toy auto). Greif looked at both simultaneous speech, where the speakers overlap, and outright interruptions, where one speaker wrests the floor from another. Here she found differences in the amount of interruption experienced by girls and boys, as well as differences in the amount of interruption experienced by girls and boys, as well as differences in the number of interruptions produced by mothers and fathers. Fathers interrupted their children more than mothers did, and both fathers and mothers interrupted little girls more than they interrupted little boys. Children interrupted their parents less frequently than parents interrupted their children, despite a cultural belief that it is children who often interrupt. Given the large number of interruptions produced by parents, it seems likely that the cultural strictures against interruptions are more related to status considerations involving who may interrupt whom than to a belief that interrupting per se is unacceptable behavior. Interruptions are therefore another area where we might look for emerging sex differences in the language of girls and boys, but they might be expected to be found only in certain permissible contexts, as, for instance, among peers.

Directives

A competent speaker can produce many different surface structures in order to express a directive intent. We looked at the production of directives in the situation where parent and child were playing with the toy car (Bellinger and Gleason, 1982). Three forms of directives in particular were examined: direct imperatives, conventionalized polite imperatives that occur in question form, and implied indirect imperatives. Examples are:

> *Direct imperative:* "Turn the bolt with the wrench."
> *Conventionalized polite imperative:* "Could you turn the bolt with the wrench?"
> *Implied indirect imperative:* "The wheel is going to fall off."

In this study we found that mothers were more likely to use the question forms and that fathers' speech had a higher proportion than mothers' speech of both the direct imperatives and the implied indirect forms. If children follow the model of their same-sex parent, we would expect little girls to use the polite question forms more and little boys to begin to use the direct imperatives and the implied forms more than the girls. As they get older, we would expect, for instance, that females would say, "Would you move your car, please?" to a person who had double-parked next to them, whereas males would be more likely to say, "You car is blocking mine." Looking at the speech of the young children in our laboratory situation (for purposes of this study ten families were used, five with boys and five with girls), we found that by the age of 4 these young children were indeed producing the same forms of directives as their same-sex parent: Boys produced more direct imperatives and more implied forms than girls, and girls produced more polite question forms than boys.

SEX DIFFERENCES IN THE LANGUAGE OF CHILDREN

As this paper has tried to indicate, very little work has been done on the emergence of sex differences in the language of children. Yet we know that since men and women speak differently, those differences must begin to emerge at some point in time. The research cited here has described differences in parents' speech to children in the use of jocular names, threats, directives, complex vocabulary, politeness, and interruptions. For directives, we were able to show that preschoolers were already stylistically similar to their same-sex parent. Some researchers (e.g., Lakoff, 1973) have suggested that all children speak "women's language" until the age of 5 or 6, but this is probably a reflection less of the facts than of our lack of sophisticated methods of analysis and good hypotheses about what to look for when seeking differences: Differences can be found in the speech of even very young children when we have precise features to investigate.

This observation is provocative: Developmental psychologists representing various theoretical schools (Freudian, cognitive, social learning) have suggested that children do not have a firm sex-role identity until about the age of 5. Others (e.g., Money and Erhardt, 1972) have pointed out, however, that after the age of 18 months it is very difficult to reannounce the sex of a child if there has been an initial misidentification; that is, a child who was thought to be of one sex cannot after this point easily make the transition to the other sex, even when the chromosomes say it must be so. Perhaps one of the reasons for this is that the child has already begun to absorb sex-role related behaviors at some level. These may include specific linguistic features.

This chapter has attempted to suggest some areas for further research. More careful research on the language of parents and other adults is certainly in order, but it is also time to turn our attention to the emerging language of children in order to find the earliest evidences of linguistic sexual dimorphism.

In doing this research it will be important to examine children's language in a variety of context that allow us to separate out age, sex-role, and status considerations. Since, for instance, status factors militate against children's using imperatives with their parents and with older people, one area to look for these differences is in peer language. The speech children use when talking with one another is, of course, a separate register itself, and one that has hardly been studied. Some of the features of peer language must surely be learned from other children or other models: Male parents rarely make noises like dive-bombers or machine guns; yet these sound effects are common in the speech of young boys and not in that of young girls. By the same token, male and female teenagers undoubtedly use different features in their speech. Since communicative competence requires appropriate linguistic use even before adulthood, all of these populations are worth studying in order to understand the nature of sex differences in language. Transitory phenomena should be noted, along with those enduring features that ultimately mark as distinct the language of grown women and men.

SELECTED BIBLIOGRAPHY

ANDERSEN, E. S. 1977. Learning to speak with style: a study of the socio-linguistic skills of children. Doctoral dissertation, Stanford University.

BELLINGER, D., AND J. B. GLEASON. 1982. Sex differences in parental directives to young children. Sex Roles 8:1123–1139.

CHERRY, L., AND M. LEWIS. 1976. Mothers and two-year-olds: a study of sex differentiated aspects of verbal interaction. *Developmental Psychology* 12:278–282.

CHOMSKY, N. 1957. *Syntactic structures.* The Hague: Mouton.

GIATTINO, J., AND J. G. HOGAN. 1975. Analysis of a father's speech to his language-learning child. *Journal of Speech and Hearing Disorders* 40:524–537.

GLEASON, J. B. 1973. Code switching in children's language. In *Development and the acquisition of language,* ed. T. E. Moore, pp. 159–167. New York: Academic Press.

———. 1975. Fathers and other strangers: men's speech to young children. In *Georgetown University round table on language and linguistics,* ed. D. P. Dato, pp. 289–297. Washington, D.C.: Georgetown University Press, 1981.

———. 1980. The acquisition of social speech: routines and politeness formulas. In *Lan-*

guage: social psychological perspectives, ed. H. Giles, W. P. Robinson, and P. N. Smith, pp. 21–27. Oxford: Pergamon Press.

GLEASON, J. B., AND E. B. GREIF. 1983. Men's speech to young children. In *Language, gender and society*, ed. C. Kramarae and N. Henley. Rowley, Mass.: Newbury House.

GLEASON, J. B., R. Y. PERLMANN, AND E. B. GREIF. 1984. What's the magic word: learning language through politeness routines. *Discourse Processes* 7:493–502.

GLEASON, J. B., AND S. WEINTRAUB. 1976. The acquisition of routines in child language. *Language in Society* 5:129–136.

GLEITMAN, L. R., E. L. NEWPORT, AND H. GLEITMAN. 1984. The current status of the motherese hypothesis. *Journal of Child Language* 143–79.

GOLINKOFF, R., AND G. AMES. 1979. A comparison of fathers' and mothers' speech with their young children. *Child Development* 50:28–32.

GREIF, E. B., AND J. B. GLEASON. Hi, thanks and goodbye: more routine information. *Language in Society* 9:159–166.

LAKOFF, R. 1973. Language and women's place. *Language in Society* 2:45–80.

MACCOBY, E., AND C. JACKLIN. 1974. *The psychology of sex differences*. Stanford, Calif.: Stanford University Press.

MASUR, E., AND J. B. GLEASON. 1980. Parent–child interaction and the acquisition of lexical information during play. *Developmental Psychology* 16:404–409.

MOERK, E. L. 1975. Verbal interactions between children and their mothers during the preschool years. *Developmental Psychology* 11:788–794.

MONEY, J., AND A. A. ERHARDT. 1972. *Man and woman, boy and girl*. Baltimore: Johns Hopkins University Press.

REMICK, L. 1971. The maternal environment of linguistic development. Doctoral dissertation, University of California at Davis.

SACHS, J., AND J. DEVIN. 1976. Young children's use of age-appropriate speech styles in social interaction and role playing. *Journal of Child Language* 3:81–98.

SHATZ, M., AND R. GELMAN. 1973. The development of communication skills: modifications in the speech of young children as function of the listener. *Monographs of the Society for Research in Child Development* 38(152):1–27.

SNOW, C. 1972. Mother's speech to children learning language. *Child Development* 43:549–565.

WITELSON, S. F., AND W. PALLIE. 1973. Left hemisphere specialization for language in the newborn. *Brain* 96:641–646.

part three

WHO SAYS WHAT TO WHOM?

Empirical Studies of Language and Gender

W hereas most of the authors included in the first two sections of this book are psychoanalysts, philosophers, or developmental psychologists by training, the material in this section stems from the fields of linguistics, experimental psychology, anthropology, and sociology and is rarely cited either by the authors of the essays of the previous two sections or by literary critics and theorists interested in questions of language and gender. These studies are empirical both in their approach to language use and in their observations on gender. As determinedly empirical work, they employ different basic assumptions and vocabularies—in fact a different epistemology—from most of the essays of Parts One and Two. Premier among those different assumptions is that it is ultimately impossible to come to any conclusion about how women or men produce and comprehend language without finding out with as much precision as possible how individuals actually speak. Moreover, empirical research has demonstrated that people do not speak the same way all the time and in every context. One must qualify generalizations that women speak one way and men another, or that all women speak in the same ways: for example, one might find that black schoolgirls speaking to boys their own age may follow quite different tendencies in speech patterns from when they are talking with their parents or with other girls, and these patterns may differ radically in various parts of the country or world, and according to the economic background of the speakers. Similarly, white women speaking to other white women in the United States may adopt different patterns of speech than when talking to men or to women of another race, although the contrast may be greater in the rural South than in the urban North, and greater in the home or some other private context than in public areas. Scholars conducting empirical research on gender and language are more interested in questions about the actual use and comprehension of particular parts of speech, idioms, or interactive patterns than in those about whether one can argue that language is inherently associated with a maternal or paternal absence or presence, during what stage of psychological development language learning may occur, or how symbolic elements influence semiotic study.

This is not to say that empirical work contains no theoretical grounding or that it promotes no theoretical development. On the contrary, much of the most interesting work produced by empirical researchers demonstrates a clear understanding of the symbolic and cultural issues raised by theorists and discusses the data of particular studies in light of broad theoretical concerns. Cheris Kramarae's *Women and Men Speaking: Frameworks for Analysis*, for example, uses the frameworks of Lacan, Irigaray, and other theorists to broaden and critique the implications of particular directions and conclusions of empirical research as well as using empirical observations to question earlier theorizing. Kramarae's excellent and sophisticated analysis of current empirical and theoretical work on language brings several hypotheses about language study into convergence. Taking a different approach, Dennis Baron's historical study *Grammar and Gender* analyzes the material of rhetorics, grammar books, and dictionaries. Although neither empirical nor theoretical in a strict sense, Baron's meticulous historical research provides a useful grounding for both approaches to language study. Yet even when dealing closely with theoretical or historical issues, empirical studies focus on what can be known rather than on the construction of universal or otherwise generalizable frameworks for conceiving of language; it is this primary focus that characterizes empirical study.

Before describing the types of empirical research currently dominating the field of gender study, it may be useful to glance briefly at more specific differences in interest and approach assumed by empirical and theoretical approaches to such study. For this purpose, perhaps the most useful point of focus is the kind of study perceived as typifying empirical research by both its critics—who have trivialized such study widely in the popular press—and its supporters, namely studies investigating the use of prescriptive ("generic") masculine terms. Empirical researchers in this area follow up the very specific question of what effects the use of prescriptive language may have both on speakers and on their audience. In her 1975 study "Cro-Magnon Woman—In Eclipse," for example, Linda Harrison shows that five hundred junior high school students were overwhelmingly inclined to respond to generic masculine anthropological language (cavemen, Cro-magnon man, early man) with masculine images only, as though cave women did not exist—in other words, they "misinterpreted" the prescriptive use of "man." Early studies by Wendy Martyna indicate that males are significantly more likely than females to use masculine pronouns as though they are generic yet to interpret intended generic uses as sex-specific, that is, as referring to males only ("Beyond the He/Man Approach" in 1980; "What Does 'He' Mean?" in 1978; and "The Psychology of the Generic Masculine" in 1980). Again, historical research illuminates empirical studies. In *Language and the Sexes* (1983), Francine Frank and Frank Anshen trace the historical roots of prescriptive pronoun use, from the truly general Old English equivalent for "man" (as opposed to the sex-specific terms "wif" for woman and "wer" or "carl" for man), through an 1850 law of the British Parliament declaring that "in all acts words importing the masculine gender shall be deemed and taken to include females," up to current ambiguous and misleading usage (Frank and Anshen, 72–73). Dale Spender's 1980 *Man Made Language* similarly stresses the relatively recent and deliberate historical construction of the practice that masculine terms serve to represent both sexes. Spender cites a Mr. Wilson in 1553 as apparently the first to insist "that it was more *natural* to place the man *before* the woman, as for example in male and female, husband and wife." By 1646, she continues, a grammarian had taken the concept of natural precedence to the point of arguing that men should "take 'pride of place'" both because it was "proper" and because "the male gender was the *worthier* gender" (147). And in 1746, John Kirkby formulated as one of his "Eighty Eight Grammatical Rules" that "the male gender was *more comprehensive* than the female" (148) thus laying the groundwork for the nineteenth century's act of Parliament.

Even these early studies on prescriptive pronoun use, however, were not simply empirical or historical in their focus; many framed the assumptions of their research in theoretical terms, although not in the symbolic, developmental, or semiotic terms of psychoanalytic and philosophical theory. Most—like much feminist work on gender and language—take the influential and much debated hypothesis that language determines thought developed by Edward Sapir and his student Benjamin Lee Whorf as a starting point. In her 1980 "Beyond the He/Man Approach" essay, for example, Martyna modifies this hypothesis to argue that "language may influence, rather than determine, thought and behavior patterns," concluding that "the issue" in studies of pronoun use "is not what *can* be said about the sexes" in some ideal world in which thought is transparently revealed in language, "but what can be *most easily* and *most clearly* said, given the constraints of the [prescriptive] *he/man* approach and other forms of sexist language." In 1983, in "Prescriptive Grammar and the Pronoun Problem," Donald G. MacKay reviews the Sapir-Whorf hypothesis, concluding that while it is not true that language influences all thought, *evaluative* thought is more likely to be influenced by language than is *descriptive* thought, and that "prescriptive *he does influence* . . . subjective or personal judgments concerning the *value* of concepts or events." In an earlier essay, "Language, Thought and Social Attitudes" (1980), MacKay tested students for several factors after each read a passage written using either prescriptive "he" or neutral language. Here MacKay found that use of prescriptive "he" influences a readers' comprehension of the passage, judgment of its personal relevance, and hypothesis as to the gender of the supposed author. For example, males perceive greater self relevance and have superior comprehension of paragraphs containing prescriptive "he" than females do, while females are more likely to judge that such prose is written by a man.

The point of the research briefly summarized here and other such specifically focused work is to provide distinct and clear rebuttal to common ideological and cultural assumptions about gender and language use. The tenacity of such assumptions about language is revealed not just in the responses of individuals in test situations but in public media response to the very existence of such research and the concerns it expresses. Altogether typical of such response in the 1970s is the columnist Edmund Shimberg's ridicule of the suggestion that prescriptive pronouns and words including the marker "man" (for example, "Chairman") be replaced with non-sexist usage ("Chairperson"); Shimberg alters utterly neutral words containing the letters "man" ("mangled," "manipulate") as though the nonsense of such transformation proves that no words contain significantly prescriptive content: "'It was interesting to see how a group with obviously personsongled egos were able to personipulate an organization the size of ours into looking like a pack of fools. 'Chairperson' indeed!'" (cited in Kramarae's *Women and Men Speaking* 1981, 113). Martyna begins "Beyond the He/Man Approach" (1980) with a brief response to such press: "*Time* calls it 'Ms-guided' (Kanfer, 1972), a syndicated columnist, 'linguistic lunacy' (Van Horne, 1976). *T.V. Guide* (1971) wonders what the 'women's lib redhots' with 'the nutty pronouns' are doing. The media still haven't gotten the message: The case against sexist language was not constructed as comic relief for critics of women's liberation." Empirical research has demonstrated that use of prescriptive masculine language is ambiguous and misleading and can lead to significant false conclusions—for example, that women should not apply for jobs advertised in prescriptive language, or that women are not included in primary philosophical statements of Western thought.

Evidence of the significance of such research, despite continuing ridicule, appears in the recent publication of several guides to non-sexist language usage, such as those authorized by the American Society of Public Administration and by the National Council of Teachers of English, or such as independently produced studies like Val Dumond's *The Elements of Nonsexist Usage: A Guide to Inclusive Spoken and Written English* (1990) and Rosalie Maggio's *The Dictionary of Bias-Free Usage: A Guide to Nondiscriminatory Language* (1991). Alleen Pace Nilsen provides an interesting history of the production of such guides in her 1987 "Guidelines Against Sexist Language: A Case History." Francine Wattman Frank and Paula A. Treichler provide an excellent bibliography of handbooks and guidelines as well as important essays on the topic of sexism in language in their 1989 collection *Language, Gender, and Professional Writing: Theoretical Approaches and Guidelines for Nonsexist Usage.* Also useful is Felicia Mitchell's bibliography to "College English Handbooks and Pronominal Usage Guidelines: Mixed Reactions to Nonsexist Language" in the fall 1992 volume of *Women and Language;* this journal frequently publishes bibliographies on both guides to non-sexist usage and research on gender and language, as well as publishing brief original studies and essays.

Although women's proper language use has been a repeated topic of behavior manuals and etiquette books for centuries, it was not until the turn of the twentieth century with the publications of Danish linguist Otto Jespersen that language and gender studies received much attention in linguistic scholarship. In 1922, Jespersen published his philosophy of language, along with a short survey of the "history of the science of language in order to show how [*these*] problems have been previously treated" (9) in the influential *Language: Its Nature, Development, and Origins.* The third section of this volume, "The Individual and the World," contains a chapter called "The Woman." International in scope and focusing on speech characteristics from taboo words to phonetics and grammar to sentence structure and vocabulary, Jespersen compiles and gives "scientific" authority to many of the stereotypes of women's speech that continue to prevail at the end of the twentieth century. Although some of Jespersen's information is taken from anthropological or linguistic studies of language, more comes from sources that are more likely to carry the weight of cultural presupposition than the precision of science—namely, the characterizations of women in the theatre and in novels, and the observations of world travelers. Jespersen also gives authority to the then widely held popular assumption that men's speech is normative, hence that women's different speech is deviant: to study language, one attends to men's speech, while to study women's speech is primarily to study women.

Within the field of linguistics, no alternate hypotheses about language norms or about the identification of gender with women arose for nearly half a century. Early feminist cultural critics, however, were responding to popular and literary assumptions which hold male behavior to be the standard and norm even before Jespersen's authorizing 1922 publication of *Language.* Most notably, in her 1914 *The Man-Made World, or Our Androcentric Culture,* Charlotte Perkins Gilman propounds with brilliant irony the "Gynaecocentric Theory" as opposed to the "Androcentric Theory of Life"—the former holding "that the female is the race type, and the male, originally but a sex type, reaching a later equality with the female" (n.p.). In her preface, Gilman reminds her readers, "Men have written copiously about women, treating them always as females, with an offensiveness and falsity patent to modern minds." Her book reverses this tendency by treating "men as males in contradistinction to their qualities as human beings," looking, for example, to rams, roosters, and peacocks for observations about the characteristics of the male. In the chapter on literature (as close as Gilman comes to addressing the issue of language directly), she argues that as an effect of "men having been accepted as humanity, [and] women but a side-issue," we have a "masculized literature": "We can readily see, that if women had always written the books, no men either writing or reading them, that would have surely 'feminized' our literature; but we have not in our minds the concept, much less the word, for an over-masculized influence" (88–89). While clearly in part a spoof of those studies which ascribe all characteristics of women to their sex rather than to cultural, educational, and intellectual factors that would mark them as individual agents responsible for their behavioral choices, Gilman's *The Man-Made World* also seriously criticizes the patriarchal structure of international social and economic systems. Yet as neither her work nor that of other writers—for example, Virginia Woolf, who wrote generally about language and gender in *A Room of One's Own*—had any direct linguistic applications it played no role in the study of gender and language. It was not until Robin Lakoff's far less radical but linguistically specific *Language and Woman's Place* appeared in 1975 that research turned notably to a reexamination of both the differences between men's and women's language use and the continued assumption that men's language constituted the norm (Lakoff, this volume).

Lakoff, like Jespersen, describes women's speech as weaker than or inferior to men's in several basic ways. Similarly, she uses literary texts, casual conversation, and personal observation more than empirical work as the basis for her observations (although this can be explained in part by the dearth of studies on women's language use available before 1975). Unlike Jespersen, however, Lakoff proceeds from a perspective sympathetic to women, and she ascribes even women's speech deficiencies, as she sees them, to incidental factors of education and access rather than to inherent difference. Morevoer, Lakoff suggests albeit tentatively that a differential in men's and women's power may account in part for their different verbal strategies and skills. The combination of her sympathetic description of women's language as she perceives it and provocative conclusions about the sexism embedded in the structure and idioms of the English language galvanized empirical research in this area. *Language and Woman's Place* has probably stimulated more empirical work on women's language than any other single study. Attempting as often to prove Lakoff wrong as to support her claims, linguists, psychologists, and anthropologists began to study women's actual language and to question simple notions of gender-marked linguistic difference and a male-identified language norm.

An example of both a specific response to Lakoff and the growing interest in language and gender issues, Francine Frank and Frank Anshen's 1983 *Language and the Sexes* provides an excellent introductory summary to empirical research in all areas of language and gender study. Not presenting original work itself, the book summarizes important findings in the field and provides a useful bibliography for further reading, at a linguistic level accessible to undergraduate students and lay readers. Frank and Anshen also importantly move beyond Lakoff in their discussion of patterns of speech in and among various ethnic and racial communities in the United States and gay and lesbian communities. These emphases mark a crucial shift that occurs in empirical work on language during the 1980s. As suggested in the Introduction, the focus and conception of the field began to move from that of "women's language" to the broader and more evenhanded "gender" and language—a shift that displaces male speakers from the linguistic norm and that acknowledges multiple constructions of gender, hence of differences in various men's and women's language(s). This shift is also marked by the title of Frank and Anshen's book: *Language and the Sexes* gives us an altogether different sense of the field than Lakoff's earlier titular reference to "Woman's Place."

Despite and because of this shift, some researchers continue to focus their attention specifically on women's speech patterns, primarily as women interact with other women. Studies in this area of empirical research have contributed to some of the most exciting departures from the field's early focus on either middle-class white women's language use or women's language patterns perceived as an offshoot of broader anthropological research. Majorie Harness Goodwin has been among the most important researchers in this area with her linguistic studies of the language patterns of African American girls and boys. Goodwin's 1990 *He-Said-She-Said: Talk as Social Organization among Black Children* focuses on a part of the English-speaking population seldom studied in this way, providing extensive new information about her subjects' uses of English, a rich resource for later crosscultural and developmental studies, and significant implications for ethnographic reliance on narratives or reports as primary data sources. The chapter reprinted in this volume, "Instigating," focuses on girls' deliberate use of a particular kind of storytelling to generate conflict between people. Resembling the more broadly studied black speech event called "signifying" as well as general features of storytelling, "instigating" both shares characteristics with boys' storytelling dispute processes and contains specific gender markers of its own, just as it both manipulates and expands what are considered typical narrative processes. Goodwin concludes broadly that "anthropologists, rather than accepting reports as instances of the events they describe, must seriously investigate the process of reporting itself" (279).

The following essay, Penelope Brown's "Gender, Politeness, and Confrontation in Tenejapa," similarly focuses on conversational interaction between women and on dispute processes, but she turns her attention to the women of a community of peasant Mayan Indians in Tenejapa, Mexico, who speak a language called Tzeltal. Examining dispute settlement in a Tzeltal court case, Brown observes how gender meanings can become transformed in different contexts. In particular, the politeness that characterizes Tenejapan women's speech in ordinary social interactions continues to characterize their speech in a court dispute, but in the latter context those same speech markers are used to convey the opposite affects—namely, hostility and contradiction. As Brown concludes, a speech marker must be seen contextually in order to be understood: politeness forms do not always indicate positive affect. Brown suggests that Japanese women may in particular circumstances engage in a similar manipulation of cooperative or agreement language strategies to emphasize disagreement.

These studies by Goodwin and Brown are significant in their descriptions of particular populations of speakers and in their particular lines of analysis, but also in their important challenging of biases or shortcomings in studies of language and gender based on the assumption that white or Anglo middle-class language practice is representative of female (or male) speech. As Nancy M. Henley states in her 1992 review essay "Ethnicity and Gender Issues in Language," these and several other "investigations by and/or of women and men of color" have corrected the misperception that all "women's language" is "weak, uncertain, trivial, 'hypercorrect,' linguistically conservative, overpolite, and highly differentiated from men's," on the one hand, and the misperception on the other that only African American males, for example, are skilled performers of ritual insult in African American culture or other ideas based on studies of community language use that are focused solely on males. Attending to both sex bias in language and sex difference in language use, Henley's essay reviews the history of research in this field. She briefly summarizes early and mid-twentieth-century anthropological treatises on "women's language" in societies distant and distinct from the United States as well as linguistic studies in English. The review also summarizes recent studies of links between race/ethnicity and sex bias in the English language, innovation in language use, and bilingual or code-switching behavior and abilities as well as the effects of race/ethnicity on various aspects of conversational interaction. This review is hortatory as well as descriptive; Henley concludes by reminding readers that racism, ethnocentrism, classism, and sexism may interfere with research as well as affecting language patterns. Yet at the same time, "The study of ethnicity, language, and gender, properly done, may help to lead us closer to [an equal world]" for all speakers (11).

As mentioned previously, the prescriptive use of masculine pronouns was among the earliest linguistic problems studied when empirical research began to focus on particular aspects of language use as they interact with and are affected by social constructions of gender. Mykol C. Hamilton, Barbara Hunter, and Shannon Stuart-Smith's "Jury Instructions Worded in the Masculine Generic: Can a Woman Claim Self-Defense When 'He' Is Threatened?" (this volume) provides an excellent example of continued work in this area. Arguing not just that the use of ostensibly generic rather than sex-specific language markers carries connotative and often unconscious force for both the speaker and the listeners, Hamilton, Hunter, and Stuart-Smith show further that important real consequences may follow from such misrepresentation—in this case, life and death consequences. Juries may not fully understand a female defendant's situation if she is always referred to as "the defendant, *he.*" Similarly in an earlier publication, "Masculine Generic Terms and Misperception of AIDS Risk" (1988), Hamilton argues that the use of terms that can be understood as either generic or sex-specific ("homosexuals," "gays," and "bisexuals") in AIDS education material has created the widespread misperception that lesbians are as responsible for the spread of AIDS as are gay men. Through these two differently focused studies, Hamilton contends that generic pronoun use may be equally misleading and harmful in blocking women from seeming to be agents in their own right and in assigning them full responsibility, if not blame, that is more appropriately directed at men: in other words, one may misunderstand a prescriptive masculine pronoun to mean that women are not included or to mean that they are—and both assumptions may carry harmful consequences for women.

Marianne LaFrance and Eugene Hahn's new essay "The Disappearing Agent:

Gender Stereotypes, Interpersonal Verbs, and Implicit Causality" (this volume) represents another area of empirical research focused on the use of a particular linguistic element, but this time on an aspect of language that ostensibly has nothing to do with gender. Interpersonal verbs are those that describe interactions between people: "Mary likes Sue" or "Sue criticizes John." Although perhaps unconsciously to the speaker, the structure of these verb clauses carries distinct implications of causality: research has shown that when the verb describes an interpersonal *action* (John compliments Tim), people are likely to believe that it has to do with the subject of the action (John likes to compliment everyone). In contrast, when the verb describes an emotional state (Mary likes Sue), people tend to think it has more to do with Sue's attributes, or with the object of the verb (everyone likes her). Using such studies, LaFrance and Hahn ask the additional cognitive question of how gender-based preconceptions interact with linguistic structures when individuals assign causality to women or to men. Again, their interest lies in suggesting what may be the social or psychological consequences of a persistent language pattern—here what they call the "disappearance" of the female "agent"—as much as in establishing that such a pattern exists. The data of their studies show that in the use of interpersonal verbs, gender-based preconceptions about male and female subjects and objects affect causality to make the female recede "from causal view if the person she is acting on or has feelings about is male," even when linguistic theory predicts that she should be seen as the causal agent. In other words, this aspect of language renders women invisible just as the use of prescriptive "he" does.

Similarly, research that focuses on male/female interaction has found that women are "disappearing" partners in mixed-sex conversation or group discussion. In a 1975 study of interruptions in cross-sex conversations, "Sex Roles, Interruptions and Silences in Conversation," Candace West and Don H. Zimmerman found that women are interrupted more than men, that they are interrupted sooner in their conversational turn (that is, given less opportunity to speak before interruption), and that men do more of the interrupting. Other studies have shown that men also tend to talk longer per turn and to take more turns at talking than women in cross-sex conversations (for example, Barbara Eakins and Gene Eakins's 1976 "Verbal Turn-Taking and Exchanges in Faculty Dialogue," and Michael Argyle, Mansur Lalljee, and Mark Cook's 1968 "The Effects of Visibility on Interaction in a Dyad"). More recently, Franca Pizzini's 1991 study of family health clinics in Italy, "Communication Hierarchies in Humour; Gender Differences in the Obstetrical/Gynaecological Setting," examines the ways in which humor reinforces existing power relationships in conversations between patients and doctors in the obstetrical/gynaecological setting, concluding that there is a "markedly higher use of humorous remarks by male [than female] gynaecologists in order to stop patients from talking" (486).

Pamela Fishman published a ground-breaking study in this field in 1983—"Interaction: The Work Women Do"—showing that women tend to perform more than men of what could be called the conversational "housework" of encouraging and promoting conversational exchange while men, through silence or delayed minimal responses, tend to dominate the choice of topic and direction of conversation that may be pursued. In a more specifically focused study using a broader research base and included in this section, Candace West follows up

Fishman's earlier work: West's essay "Rethinking 'Sex Differences' in Conversational Topics: It's Not What They Say but How They Say It" critiques earlier studies on conversational interaction between women and men and on topic production in conversation which have focused on content analysis, instead of proposing that such research shift to an analysis of "the specific mechanisms involved in producing topicality" or in structuring conversation. The salient features for this analysis are why and how a particular topic succeeds in producing conversation and in what context, rather than just who initiates the topic and what it is. West concludes, in fact, that "topical 'choices' do not necessarily reflect individual interests in conversations between women and men" (38). Consequently, " 'sex differences' in conversational topics may result not so much from the distinctive interests women and men bring to conversation as they do from their differential opportunities to express whatever interests they have and very different propensities for doing certain kinds of conversational work" (39).

The final three essays included in this section reflect an important new direction in language and gender research—namely, a self-critical analysis of where this field is going and how it may best accomplish what seem to be its general aims. Representing a range of interdisciplinary perspectives, these essays show the depth of analysis characterizing the best empirical work as well as the breadth of the field. Nancy M. Henley and Cheris Kramarae in their 1991 "Gender, Power, and Miscommunication" address the popular and recently popularized field of miscommunication between the sexes (for example, Tannen 1990) as a starting point for their more critical positioning of empirical language and gender study in the wider realm of the social sciences' study of behavior. Calling attention to the flaws in the "female deficit" theory and to any simple understanding of "two culture" or "psychological difference" theories, Henley and Kramarae instead include social and anthropological studies of cultures, contexts, and power relationships as well as psychological and linguistic studies in their conceptualization of male/female miscommunication. Such an analytical survey shows not only the range of work being done specifically in the field of cross-gender misunderstanding but the challenges and rewards of combining disparate types of research in interpreting particular instances or patterns of linguistic behavior. Notably, Henley and Kramarae also discuss the "interaction of race/ ethnicity, gender, and class" and "same-sex and gay-straight issues" in miscommunication as central to their discussion.

Susan Gal's 1991 "Between Speech and Silence: The Problematics of Research on Language and Gender" takes a cross-cultural approach to argue that the research from many traditions of language use must be conceptually integrated through an analysis of power relations. As she states, although the symbolic side of conversational interaction is frequently neglected in empirical study, "the notions of symbolic domination through patterns of language use and of gender as both structure and practice are essential to [conceptual integration of multi- and cross-cultural research]." Echoing Henley and Kramarae's insistence on complex combinations of disparate types of research, Gal calls for research on the precise forms and conventions of women's everyday and expressive language uses within the contexts of the institutions and cultural constructions that frame their lives. The goal is not to show simply that power defines social reality but to reveal subtle ways in which very different aspects of women's speech may constitute a variety of strategic responses to dominant, hegemonic cultural forms. Moreover, Gal insistently places both elements of such research in an international context responsible to several linguistic and cultural traditions. Only through such inclusiveness can one begin to understand the variety of manipulations particular uses of language may undergo. As she puts it, "strong protest can appear in silent gestures . . . or [as] verbal yet veiled . . . or [as] explicit and public" gestures; there is no single kind of "powerful" or "resistant" manipulation of language.

Penelope Eckert's and Sally McConnell-Ginet's 1992 "Think Practically and Look Locally: Language and Gender as Community-Based Practice" also organizes its discussion around notions of both difference and power, or male dominance in gender relations. As do the authors of the two preceding essays, Eckert and McConnell-Ginet seek to reveal "the concrete complexities of language as used by real people engaged in social practice." Their particular contribution to the development of research in gender and language lies in their stress that the interaction of gender and language is rooted "in the everyday social practices of particular local communities," defining community so as to indicate that all individuals exist within several overlapping or exclusive communities simultaneously (for example, a speaker's communities may include her "Philadelphia neighborhood of working class African American families," her "'scholastic-track' class in an integrated school outside the neighborhood," and so on). Language practice differs for each of these community contexts and therefore must be analyzed in specific contextual terms. "Janus-like, power in language wears two faces," Eckert and McConnell-Ginet argue: it is situated by and responds to individual agency in face-to-face interactions or other concrete activities involving language (watching movies, reading, etc.), and "it is historically constituted and responsive to the community's coordinated endeavors." As Kramarae and Henley and Gal also argue, in other words, taking only one approach to the study of any single aspect of women's and men's language use cannot suffice; significant advances in language and gender theory from now on "can come only through the intensive collaboration of people in a variety of fields, and working in a variety of communities" (Eckert and McConnell-Ginet, this volume).

The field of language and gender study is widely varied in its choices of topical focus and in its methodological approaches. To encourage ease of comparison with the work in the earlier sections and among the studies reprinted here themselves and because far more work has been done in this area than in any other, I have chosen to include primarily work about speakers of English living in the United States. As the last three essays summarized contend, however, the field of language and gender study is moving strongly in the direction of increasingly crosscultural and multicultural as well as interdisciplinary research. The conclusions of these essays also place important constraints on the universalizing tendencies of psychoanalytic theories about language production and symbolic value, as being bound by specific cultural assumptions not always acknowledged by their authors or as part of their analysis. The contribution of empirical work to the area of language and gender study lies precisely in its repeated reminder of (and increasingly sophisticated information about) such constraints. Nonetheless, as is obvious from the familiarity of the researchers whose work is included in this section with the appropriate theoretical work as well as with other empirical research conducted from a broad range of perspectives, the authors of these essays seek not to constrain but to contribute to the richness and vitality of the continuing language and gender "debate."

Cristanne Miller

SELECTED BIBLIOGRAPHY

ABEL, ELIZABETH. *Writing and Sexual Difference.* Special Issue of *Critical Inquiry* 8, 2 (Winter 1981).

ARGYLE, MICHAEL, MANSUR LALLJEE, AND MARK COOK. "The Effects of Visibility on Interaction in a Dyad." *Human Relations* 21 (1968): 3–17.

BARON, DENNIS. *Grammar and Gender.* New Haven: Yale University Press, 1986.

CAMERON, DEBORAH. *Feminism and Linguistic Theory.* New York: St. Martin's Press, 1985.

COATES, JENNIFER. *Women, Men, and Language: A Sociolinguistic Account of Sex Differences in Language.* London & New York: Longman, 1986.

———— AND DEBORAH CAMERON, EDS. *Women in their Speech Communities: New Perspectives on Language and Sex.* London & New York: Longman, 1988.

DUBOIS, BETTY LOU AND ISABEL CROUCH. *The Sociology of the Languages of American Women.* San Antonio, Texas: Trinity University, 1976.

DUMOND, VAL. *The Elements of Nonsexist Usage: A Guide to Inclusive Spoken and Written English.* New York: Prentice-Hall 1990.

EAKINS, BARBARA AND GENE EAKINS. "Verbal Turn-Taking and Exchanges in Faculty Dialogue." In *The Sociology of the Languages of American Women.* Eds. Betty Lou Dubois and Isabel Crouch. San Antonio, Texas: Trinity University, 1976. Pages 53–62.

FISHMAN, PAMELA. "Interaction: The Work Women Do." In *Language, Gender and Society.* Eds. Barrie Thorne, Cheris Kramarae, and Nancy Henley. Rowley, Mass: Newbury House Pubs., 1983. Pages 89–101.

FRANK, FRANCINE AND FRANK ANSHEN. *Language and the Sexes.* Albany, New York: State University of New York Press, 1983.

FRANK, FRANCINE WATTMAN AND PAULA TREICHLER, EDS. *Language, Gender, and Professional Writing: Theoretical Approaches and Guidelines for Nonsexist Usage.* New York: The Modern Language Association of America, 1989.

GILMAN, CHARLOTTE PERKINS. *The Man-Made World, or Our Androcentric Culture.* New York: Charlton Company, 1914.

GOODWIN, MARJORIE HARNESS. *He-Said-She-Said: Talk as Social Organization Among Black Children.* Bloomington, Indiana University Press, 1990.

HARRISON, LINDA. "Cro-Magnon Woman—In Eclipse." *The Science Teacher.* (April 1975): 8–11.

HAMILTON, MYKOL C. "Masculine Generic Terms and Misperception of AIDS Risk." *Journal of Applied Social Psychology.* 18, 14 (1988): 1222–1240.

HENLEY, NANCY. *Body Politics: Power, Sex and Nonverbal Communication.* Englewood Cliffs, N.J.: Prentice-Hall, Spectrum, 1977.

————. "Ethnicity and Gender Issues in Language." In *Handbook of Cultural*

Diversity in Feminist Psychology. Ed. H. Landrine. Washington, D.C.: American Psychological Association, 1992.

HOUSTON, MARSHA AND CHERIS KRAMARAE, EDS. *Women Speaking from Silence*. Special issue of *Discourse & Society*. 2, 4 (1991).

JESPERSEN, OTTO. *Language: Its Native Development and Origins*. London: Allen and Unwin, 1922.

KRAMARAE, CHERIS, ED. *Technology and Women's Voices: Keeping in Touch*. London: Routledge & Kegan Paul, 1988.

———. *Women and Men Speaking: Frameworks for Analysis*. Rowley, Mass.: Newbury House Publishers, 1981.

LAKOFF, ROBIN. *Language and Women's Place*. New York: Harper and Row, 1975.

LAKOFF, ROBIN TOLMACH. *Talking Power: The Politics of Language in Our Lives*. New York: Basic Books, 1990.

LANDRINE, H. ED. *Handbook of Cultural Diversity in Feminist Psychology*. Washington, D.C.: American Psychological Association, 1992.

MACKAY, DONALD G. "Language, Thought and Social Attitudes." In *Language: Social Psychological Perspectives*. Eds. Howard Giles, W. Peter Robinson, and Philip M. Smith. New York: Pergamon Press, 1980. Pages 89–96.

———. "Prescriptive Grammar and the Pronoun Problem." In *Language, Gender and Society*. Eds. Barrie Thorne, Cheris Kramarae, and Nancy Henley. Rowley, Mass: Newbury House Publishers, 1983. Pages 38–53.

MAGGIO, ROSALIE. *The Dictionary of Bias-Free Usage: A Guide to Nondiscriminatory Language*. Phoenix: Oryx Press, 1991.

MARTYNA, WENDY. "Beyond the He/Man Approach: The Case for Nonsexist Language," 1980. In *Language, Gender and Society*. Eds. Barrie Thorne, Cheris Kramarae, and Nancy Henley. Rowley, Mass: Newbury House Publishers, 1983. Pages 25–37.

———. "What Does 'He' Mean?" *Journal of Communication* 28 (Winter 1978): 131–138.

———. "The Psychology of the Generic Masculine." In *Women and Language in Literature and Society*. Eds. Sally McConnell-Ginet, Ruth Borker and Nelly Furman. New York: Praeger, 1980. Pages 69–78.

MCCONNELL-GINET, SALLY, RUTH BORKER AND NELLY FURMAN, EDS. *Women and Language in Literature and Society*. New York: Praeger, 1980.

MILLER, CASEY AND KATE SWIFT. *Words and Women: New Language in New Times*. New York: Harper Collins Publishers, 1976, updated 1991.

———. *The Handbook of Nonsexist Writing for Writers, Editors and Speakers*. New York: Lippincott & Crowell, Publishers, 1980.

MITCHELL, FELICIA. "College English Handbooks and Pronominal Usage Guidelines: Mixed Reactions to Nonsexist Language." *Women and Language* XV, 2 (1992): 37–41.

NILSEN, ALLEEN PACE. "Guidelines Against Sexist Language: A Case History." In *Women and Language in Transition*. Joyce Penfield, Ed. Albany, New York: State University of New York Press, 1987.

PENELOPE, JULIA. *Speaking Freely: Unlearning the Lies of The Fathers' Tongues*. New York: Pergamon Press, 1990.

PENFIELD, JOYCE, ED. *Women and Language in Transition*. Albany: State University of New York Press, 1987.

PHILIPS, SUSAN R., SUSAN STEELE AND CHRISTINE TANZ, EDS. *Language, Gender and Sex in Comparative Perspective.* Cambridge: Cambridge University Press, 1987.

PIZZINI, FRANCA. "Communication Hierarchies in Humour: Gender Differences in the Obstetrical/Gynaecological Setting." *Discourse & Society,* special issue *Women Speaking from Silence.* Eds., Marsha Houston and Cheris Kramarae. 2, 4 (1991): 477–488.

POYNTON, CATE. *Language and Gender: Making the Difference.* Oxford and New York: Oxford University Press, 1989.

SMITH, PHILIP M. *Language, The Sexes and Society.* Oxford and New York: Basil Blackwell, 1985.

SPENDER, DALE. *Man Made Language.* London: Routledge & Kegan Paul, 1980.

TANNEN, DEBORAH. *Talking Voices: Repetition, Dialogue, and Imagery in Conversational Discourse.* Cambridge: Cambridge University Press, 1989.

———. *You Just Don't Understand: Women and Men in Conversation.* New York: Morrow, 1990.

THORNE, BARRIE AND NANCY HENLEY, EDS. *Language and Sex: Difference and Dominance.* Rowley, Mass.: Newbury House Publishers, 1975.

——— CHERIS KRAMARAE AND NANCY HENLEY, EDS. *Language, Gender and Society.* Rowley, Mass: Newbury House Publishers, 1983.

VETTERLING-BRAGGIN, MARY, ED. *Sexist Language: A Modern Philosophical Analysis.* Totowa, N.J.: Littlefield, Adams and Co., 1981.

WOOLF, VIRGINIA. *A Room of One's Own.* San Diego: Harcourt, Brace, Jovanovich, 1929; reissued 1981.

ZIMMERMAN, DONALD H. AND CANDACE WEST. "Sex Roles, Interruptions and Silences in Conversation." In *Language and Sex: Difference and Dominance.* Eds. Barrie Thorne and Nancy Henley. Rowley, Mass: Newbury House Publishers, 1975. Pages 105–129.

robin lakoff

LANGUAGE AND WOMAN'S PLACE

Language uses us as much as we use language. As much as our choice of forms of expression is guided by the thoughts we want to express, to the same extent the way we feel about the things in the real world governs the way we express ourselves about these things. Two words can be synonymous in their denotative sense, but one will be used in case a speaker feels favorably toward the object the word denotes, the other if he is unfavorably disposed. Similar situations are legion, involving unexpectedness, interest, and other emotional reactions on the part of the speaker to what he is talking about. Thus, while two speakers may be talking about the same thing or real-world situation, their descriptions may end up sounding utterly unrelated. The following well-known paradigm will be illustrative.

(1) *(a)* I am strong-minded.
   (b) You are obstinate.
   (c) He is pigheaded.

If it is indeed true that our feelings about the world color our expression of our thoughts, then we can use our linguistic behavior as a diagnostic of our hidden feelings about things. For often—as anyone with even a nodding acquaintance with modern psychoanalytic writing knows too well—we can interpret our overt actions, or our perceptions, in accordance with our desires, distorting them as we see fit. But the linguistic data are there, in black and white, or on tape, unambiguous and unavoidable. Hence, while in the ideal world other kinds of evidence for sociological phenomena would be desirable along with, or in addition to, linguistic evidence, sometimes at least the latter is all we can get with certainty. This is especially likely in emotionally charged areas like that of sexism and other forms of discriminatory behavior. This book, then, is an attempt to provide diagnostic evidence from language use for one type of inequity that has been claimed to exist in our society: that between the roles of men and women. I will attempt to discover what language use can tell us about the nature and extent of any inequity; and finally to ask whether anything can be done, from the linguistic end of the problem: does one correct a social inequity by changing linguistic disparities? We will find, I think, that women experience linguistic discrimination in two ways: in the way they are taught to use language, and in the way general language use treats them. Both tend, as we shall see, to relegate women to certain subservient functions: that of sex object, or servant; and there-

From "Language and Woman's Place," Language and Society, *2 (1973): 45–80. Reprinted with the permission of Cambridge University Press.*

fore certain lexical items mean one thing applied to men, another to women, a difference that cannot be predicted except with reference to the different roles the sexes play in society.

The data on which I am basing my claims have been gathered mainly by introspection: I have examined my own speech and that of my acquaintances, and have used my own intuitions in analyzing it. I have also made use of the media: in some ways, the speech heard, for example, in commercials or situation comedies on television mirrors the speech of the television-watching community: if it did not (not necessarily as an exact replica, but perhaps as a reflection of how the audience sees itself or wishes it were), it would not succeed. The sociologist, anthropologist or ethnomethodologist familiar with what seem to him more error-proof data-gathering techniques, such as the recording of random conversation, may object that these introspective methods may produce dubious results. But first, it should be noted that *any* procedure is at some point introspective: the gatherer must analyze his data, after all. Then, one necessarily selects a subgroup of the population to work with: is the educated, white, middle-class group that the writer of the book identifies with less worthy of study than any other? And finally, there is the purely pragmatic issue: random conversation must go on for quite some time, and the recorder must be exceedingly lucky anyway, in order to produce evidence of any particular hypothesis, for example, that there is sexism in language, that there is not sexism in language. If we are to have a good sample of data to analyze, this will have to be elicited artificially from someone; I submit I am as good an artificial source of data as anyone.

These defenses are not meant to suggest that either the methodology or the results are final, or perfect. I mean to suggest one possible approach to the problem, one set of facts. I do feel that the majority of the claims I make will hold for the majority of speakers of English; that, in fact, much may, *mutatis mutandis*, be universal. But granting that this study does in itself represent the speech of only a small subpart of the community, it is still of use in indicating directions for further research in this area: in providing a basis for comparison, a taking-off point for further studies, a means of discovering what is universal in the data and what is not, and why. That is to say, I present what follows less as the final word on the subject of sexism in language—anything but that!—than as a goad to further research.

If a little girl "talks rough" like a boy, she will normally be ostracized, scolded, or made fun of. In this way society, in the form of a child's parents and friends, keeps her in line, in her place. This socializing process is, in most of its aspects, harmless and often necessary, but in this particular instance—the teaching of special linguistic uses to little girls—it raises serious problems, though the teachers may well be unaware of this. If the little girl learns her lesson well, she is not rewarded with unquestioned acceptance on the part of society; rather, the acquisition of this special style of speech will later be an excuse others use to keep her in a demeaning position, to refuse to take her seriously as a human being. Because of the way she speaks, the little girl—now grown to womanhood—will be accused of being unable to speak precisely or to express herself forcefully.

I am sure that the preceding paragraph contains an oversimplified description of the language-learning process in American society. Rather than saying that little boys and little girls, from the very start, learn two different ways of speaking, I think, from observation and reports by others, that the process is more complicated. Since the mother and other women are the dominant influences in the lives of most children under the age of five, probably both boys and girls first learn "women's language" as their first language. (I am told that in Japanese, children of both sexes use the particles proper for women until the age of five or so; then the little boy starts to be ridiculed if he uses them, and so soon learns to desist.) As they grow older, boys especially go through a stage of rough talk, as described by Spock and others; this is probably discouraged in little girls more strongly than in little boys, in whom parents may often find it more amusing than shocking. By the time children are ten or so, and split up into same-sex peer groups, the two languages are already present, according to my recollections and observations. But it seems that what has happened is that the boys have unlearned their original form of expression, and adopted new forms of expression, while the girls retain their old ways of speech. (One wonders whether this is related in any way to the often-noticed fact that little boys innovate, in their play, much more than little girls.) The ultimate result is the same, of course, whatever the interpretation.

So a girl is damned if she does, damned if she doesn't. If she refuses to talk like a lady, she is ridiculed and subjected to criticism as unfeminine; if she does learn, she is ridiculed as unable to think clearly, unable to take part in a serious discussion: in some sense, as less than fully human. These two choices which a woman has—to be less than a woman or less than a person—are highly painful.

An objection may be raised here that I am overstating the case against women's language, since most women who get as far as college learn to switch from women's to neutral language under appropriate situations (in class, talking to professors, at job interviews, and such). But I think this objection overlooks a number of problems. First, if a girl must learn two dialects, she becomes in effect a bilingual. Like many bilinguals, she may never really be master of either language, though her command of both is adequate enough for most purposes, she may never feel really comfortable using either, and never be certain that she is using the right one in the right place to the right person. Shifting from one language to another requires special awareness to the nuances of social situations, special alertness to possible disapproval. It may be that the extra energy that must be (subconsciously or otherwise) expended in this game is energy sapped from more creative work, and hinders women from expressing themselves as well, as fully, or as freely as they might otherwise. Thus, if a girl knows that a professor will be receptive to comments that sound scholarly, objective, unemotional, she will of course be tempted to use neutral language in class or in conference. But if she knows that, as a man, he will respond more approvingly to her at other levels if she uses women's language, and sounds frilly and feminine, won't she be confused as well as sorely tempted in two directions at once? It is often noticed that women participate less in class discussion than men—perhaps this linguistic indecisiveness is one reason why. (Incidentally, I don't find this true in my classes.)

It will be found that the overall effect of "women's language"—meaning both language restricted in use to women and language descriptive of women alone—

is this: it submerges a woman's personal identity, by denying her the means of expressing herself strongly, on the one hand, and encouraging expressions that suggest triviality in subject matter and uncertainty about it; and, when a woman is being discussed, by treating her as an object—sexual or otherwise—but never a serious person with individual views. Of course, other forms of behavior in this society have the same purpose; but the phenomena seem especially clear linguistically.

The ultimate effect of these discrepancies is that women are systematically denied access to power, on the grounds that they are not capable of holding it as demonstrated by their linguistic behavior along with other aspects of their behavior; and the irony here is that women are made to feel that they deserve such treatment, because of inadequacies in their own intelligence and/or education. But in fact it is precisely because women have learned their lessons so well that they later suffer such discrimination. (This situation is of course true to some extent for all disadvantaged groups: white males of Anglo-Saxon descent set the standards and seem to expect other groups to be respectful of them but not to adopt them—they are to "keep in their place.")

I should like now to talk at length about some specific examples of linguistic phenomena I have described in general terms above. I want to talk first about the ways in which women's speech differs from men's speech; and then, to discuss a number of cases in which it seems clear that women are discriminated against (usually unconsciously) by the language everyone uses. I think it will become evident from this discussion that both types of phenomena reflect a deep bias on the part of our culture (and, indeed, of every culture I have ever heard of) against women being accorded full status as rational creatures and individuals in their own right; and finally, I would like to talk briefly about what might be done, and perhaps what should not be done, to remedy things.

TALKING LIKE A LADY

"Women's language" shows up in all levels of the grammar of English. We find differences in the choice and frequency of lexical items; in the situations in which certain syntactic rules are performed; in intonational and other supersegmental patterns. As an example of lexical differences, imagine a man and a woman both looking at the same wall, painted a pinkish shade of purple. The woman may say (2):

(2)   The wall is mauve,

with no one consequently forming any special impression of her as a result of the words alone; but if the man should say (2), one might well conclude he was imitating a woman sarcastically or was a homosexual or an interior decorator. Women, then, make far more precise discriminations in naming colors than do men; words like *beige, ecru, aquamarine, lavender,* and so on are unremarkable in a woman's active vocabulary, but absent from that of most men. I have seen a man helpless with suppressed laughter at a discussion between two other people as to whether a book jacket was to be described as "lavender" or "mauve." Men find such discussion amusing because they consider such a question trivial, irrelevant to the real world.

We might ask why fine discrimination of color is relevant for women, but not for men. A clue is contained in the way many men in our society view other "unworldly" topics, such as high culture and the Church, as outside the world of men's work, relegated to women and men whose masculinity is not unquestionable. Men tend to relegate to women things that are not of concern to them, or do not involve their egos. Among these are problems of fine color discrimination. We might rephrase this point by saying that since women are not expected to make decisions on important matters, such as what kind of job to hold, they are relegated the noncrucial decisions as a sop. Deciding whether to name a color "lavender" or "mauve" is one such sop.

If it is agreed that this lexical disparity reflects a social inequity in the position of women, one may ask how to remedy it. Obviously, no one could seriously recommend legislating against the use of the terms "mauve" and "lavender" by women, or forcing men to learn to use them. All we can do is give women the opportunity to participate in the real decisions of life.

Aside from specific lexical items like color names, we find differences between the speech of women and that of men in the use of particles that grammarians often describe as "meaningless." There may be no referent for them, but they are far from meaningless: they define the social context of an utterance, indicate the relationship the speaker feels between himself and his addressee, between himself and what he is talking about.

As an experiment, one might present native speakers of standard American English with pairs of sentences, identical syntactically and in terms of referential lexical items, and differing merely in the choice of "meaningless" particle, and ask them which was spoken by a man, which a woman. Consider:

(3) *(a)*   Oh dear, you've put the peanut butter in the refrigerator again.
    (b)   Shit, you've put the peanut butter in the refrigerator again.

It is safe to predict that people would classify the first sentence as part of "women's language," the second as "men's language." It is true that many self-respecting women are becoming able to use sentences like (3) *(b)* publicly without flinching, but this is a relatively recent development, and while perhaps the majority of Middle America might condone the use of *(b)* for men, they would still disapprove of its use by women. (It is of interest, by the way, to note that men's language is increasingly being used by women, but women's language is not being adopted by men, apart from those who reject the American masculine image [for example, homosexuals]. This is analogous to the fact that men's jobs are being sought by women, but few men are rushing to become housewives or secretaries. The language of the favored group, the group that holds the power, along with its nonlinguistic behavior, is generally adopted by the other group, not vice versa. In any event, it is a truism to state that the "stronger" expletives are reserved for men, and the "weaker" ones for women.)

Now we may ask what we mean by "stronger" and "weaker" expletives. (If these particles were indeed meaningless, none would be stronger than any other.) The difference between using "shit" (or "damn," or one of many others) as opposed to "oh dear," or "goodness," or "oh fudge" lies in how forcefully one says how one feels—perhaps, one might say, choice of particle is a function of how strongly one allows oneself to feel about something, so that the strength of an emotion conveyed in a sentence corresponds to the strength of the particle. Hence in a really serious situation, the use of "trivializing" (that is, "women's") particles constitutes a joke, or at any rate, is highly inappropriate. (In conformity with current linguistic practice, throughout this work an asterisk (*) will be used to mark a sentence that is inappropriate in some sense, either because it is syntactically deviant or used in the wrong social context.)

(4) *(a)* *Oh fudge, my hair is on fire.
   (b) *Dear me, did he kidnap the baby?

As children, women are encouraged to be "little ladies." Little ladies don't scream as vociferously as little boys, and they are chastised more severely for throwing tantrums or showing temper: "high spirits" are expected and therefore tolerated in little boys; docility and resignation are the corresponding traits expected of little girls. Now, we tend to excuse a show of temper by a man where we would not excuse an identical tirade from a woman: women are allowed to fuss and complain, but only a man can bellow in rage. It is sometimes claimed that there is a biological basis for this behavior difference, though I don't believe conclusive evidence exists that the early differences in behavior that have been observed are not the results of very different treatment of babies of the two sexes from the beginning; but surely the use of different particles by men and women is a learned trait, merely mirroring nonlinguistic differences again, and again pointing out an inequity that exists between the treatment of men, and society's expectations of them, and the treatment of women. Allowing men stronger means of expression than are open to women further reinforces men's position of strength in the real world: for surely we listen with more attention the more strongly and forcefully someone expresses opinions, and a speaker unable—for whatever reason—to be forceful in stating his views is much less likely to be taken seriously. Ability to use strong particles like "shit" and "hell" is, of course, only incidental to the inequity that exists rather than its cause. But once again, apparently accidental linguistic usage suggests that women are denied equality partially for linguistic reasons, and that an examination of language points up precisely an area in which inequity exists. Further, if someone is allowed to show emotions, and consequently does, others may well be able to view him as a real individual in his own right, as they could not if he never showed emotion. Here again, then, the behavior a woman learns as "correct" prevents her from being taken seriously as an individual, and further is considered "correct" and necessary for a woman precisely because society does *not* consider her seriously as an individual.

Similar sorts of disparities exist elsewhere in the vocabulary. There is, for instance, a group of adjectives which have, besides their specific and literal meanings, another use, that of indicating the speaker's approbation or admiration for something. Some of these adjectives are neutral as to sex of speaker: either men or women may use them. But another set seems, in its figurative use, to be largely confined to women's speech. Representative lists of both types are below:

neutral	*women only*
great	adorable
terrific	charming
cool	sweet
neat	lovely
	divine

As with the color words and swear words already discussed, for a man to stray into the "women's" column is apt to be damaging to his reputation, though here a woman may freely use the neutral words. But it should not be inferred from this that a woman's use of the "women's" words is without its risks. Where a woman has a choice between the neutral words and the women's words, as a man has not, she may be suggesting very different things about her own personality and her view of the subject matter by her choice of words of the first set or words of the second.

(5) *(a)*   What a terrific idea!
    (b)   What a divine idea!

It seems to me that *(a)* might be used under any appropriate conditions by a female speaker. But *(b)* is more restricted. Probably it is used appropriately (even by the sort of speaker for whom it was normal) only in case the speaker feels the idea referred to to be essentially frivolous, trivial, or unimportant to the world at large—only an amusement for the speaker herself. Consider, then, a woman advertising executive at an advertising conference. However feminine an advertising executive she is, she is much more likely to express her approval with (5) *(a)* than with *(b)*, which might cause raised eyebrows, and the reaction: "That's what we get for putting a woman in charge of this company."

On the other hand, suppose a friend suggests to the same woman that she should dye her French poodles to match her cigarette lighter. In this case, the suggestion really concerns only her, and the impression she will make on people. In this case, she may use *(b)*, from the "woman's language." So the choice is not really free: words restricted to "women's language" suggest that concepts to which they are applied are not relevant to the real world of (male) influence and power.

One may ask whether there really are not analogous terms that are available to men—terms that denote approval of the trivial, the personal; that express approbation in terms of one's own personal emotional reaction, rather than by gauging the likely general reaction. There does in fact seem to be one such word: it is the hippie invention "groovy," which seems to have most of the connotations that separate "lovely" and "divine" from "great" and "terrific" excepting only that it does not mark the speaker as feminine or effeminate.

(6) *(a)*   What a terrific steel mill!
    (b)   *What a lovely steel mill! (male speaking)
    (c)   What a groovey steel mill!

I think it is significant that this word was introduced by the hippies, and, when used seriously rather than sarcastically, used principally by people who have accepted the hippies' values. Principal among these is the denial of the Protestant work ethic: to a hippie, something can be worth thinking about even if it isn't influential in the power structure, or moneymaking. Hippies are separated from the activities of the real world just as women are—though in the former case it is due to a decision on their parts, while this is not uncontroversially true in the case of women. For both these groups, it is possible to express approval of things in a personal way—though one does so at the risk of losing one's credibility with members of the power structure. It is also true, according to some speakers, that upper-class British men may use the words listed in the "women's" column, as well as the specific color words and others we have categorized as specifically feminine, without raising doubts as to their masculinity among other speakers of the same dialect. (This is not true for lower-class Britons, however.) The reason may be that commitment to the work ethic need not necessarily be displayed: one may be or appear to be a gentleman of leisure, interested in various pursuits, but not involved in mundane (business or political) affairs, in such a culture, without incurring disgrace. This is rather analogous to the position of a woman in American middle-class society, so we should not be surprised if these special lexical items are usable by both groups. This fact points indeed to a more general conclusion. These words aren't, basically, "feminine"; rather, they signal "uninvolved," or "out of power." Any group in a society to which these labels are applicable may presumably use these words; they are often considered "feminine," "unmasculine," because women are the "uninvolved," "out of power" group *par excellence*.

Another group that has, ostensibly at least, taken itself out of the search for power and money is that of academic men. They are frequently viewed by other groups as analogous in some ways to women—they don't really work, they are supported in their frivolous pursuits by others, what they do doesn't really count in the real world, and so on. The suburban home finds its counterpart in the ivory tower: one is supposedly shielded from harsh realities in both. Therefore it is not too surprising that many academic men (especially those who emulate British norms) may violate many of these sacrosanct rules I have just laid down: they often use "women's language." Among themselves, this does not occasion ridicule. But to a truck driver, a professor saying, "What a lovely hat!" is undoubtedly laughable, all the more so as it reinforces his stereotype of professors as effete snobs.

When we leave the lexicon and venture into syntax,, we find that syntactically too women's speech is peculiar. To my knowledge, there is no syntactic rule in English that only women may use. But there is at least one rule that a woman will use in more conversational situations than a man. (This fact indicates, of course, that the applicability of syntactic rules is governed partly by social context—the positions in society of the speaker and addressee, with respect to each other, and the impression one seeks to make on the other.) This is the rule of tag-question formation.[1]

A tag, in its usage as well as its syntactic shape (in English) is midway between an outright statement and a yes-no question: it is less assertive than the former, but more confident than the latter. Therefore it is usable under certain contextual situations: not those in which a statement would be appropriate, nor those in which a yes-no question is generally used, but in situations intermediate between these.

One makes a statement when one has confidence in his knowledge and is pretty certain that his statement will be believed; one asks a question when one lacks knowledge on some point and has reason to believe that this gap can and will be remedied by an answer by the addressee. A tag question, being intermediate between these, is used when the speaker is stating a claim, but lacks full confidence in the truth of that claim. So if I say

(7)   Is John here?

I will probably not be surprised if my respondent answers "no"; but if I say

(8)   John is here, isn't he?

instead, chances are I am already biased in favor of a positive answer, wanting only confirmation by the addressee. I still want a response from him, as I do with a yes-no question; but I have enough knowledge (or think I have) to predict that response, much as with a declarative statement. A tag question, then, might be thought of as a declarative statement without the assumption that the statement is to be believed by the addressee: one has an out, as with a question. A tag gives the addressee leeway, not forcing him to go along with the views of the speaker.

There are situations in which a tag is legitimate, in fact the only legitimate sentence form. So, for example, if I have seen something only indistinctly, and have reason to believe my addressee had a better view, I can say:

(9)   I had my glasses off. He was out at third, wasn't he?

Sometimes we find a tag question used in cases in which the speaker knows as well as the addressee what the answer must be, and doesn't need confirmation. One such situation is when the speaker is making "small talk," trying to elicit conversation from the addressee:

(10)   Sure is hot here, isn't it?

In discussing personal feelings or opinions, only the speaker normally has any way of knowing the correct answer. Strictly speaking, questioning one's own opinions is futile. Sentences like (11) are usually ridiculous.

(11)   *I have a headache, don't I?

But similar cases do, apparently, exist, in which it is the speaker's opinions, rather than perceptions, for which corroboration is sought, as in (12):

(12)   The way prices are rising is horrendous, isn't it?

While there are of course other possible interpretations of a sentence like this, one possibility is that the speaker has a particular answer in mind—"yes" or "no"—but is reluctant to state it baldly. It is my impression, though I do not have precise statistical evidence, that this sort of tag question is much more apt to be used by women than by men. If this is indeed true, why is it true?

These sentence types provide a means whereby a speaker can avoid committing himself, and thereby avoid coming into conflict with the addressee. The problem is that, by so doing, a speaker may also give the impression of not being really sure of himself, of looking to the addressee for confirmation, even of having no views of his own. This last criticism is, of course, one often leveled at women. One wonders how much of it reflects a use of language that has been imposed on women from their earliest years.

Related to this special use of a syntactic rule is a widespread difference perceptible in women's intonational patterns.[2] There is a peculiar sentence intonation pattern, found in English as far as I know only among women, which has the form of a declarative answer to a question, and is used as such, but has the rising inflection typical of a yes-no question, as well as being especially hesitant. The effect is as though one were seeking confirmation, though at the same time the speaker may be the only one who has the requisite information.

(13) *(a)*   When will dinner be ready?
     (b)   Oh . . . around six o'clock . . . ?

It is as though *(b)* were saying, "Six o'clock, if that's OK with you, if you agree." *(a)* is put in the position of having to provide confirmation, and *(b)* sounds unsure. Here we find unwillingness to assert an opinion carried to an extreme. One likely consequence is that these sorts of speech patterns are taken to reflect something real about character and play a part in not taking a woman seriously or trusting her with any real responsibilities, since "she can't make up her mind" and "isn't sure of herself." And here again we see that people form judgments about other people on the basis of superficial linguistic behavior that may have nothing to do with inner character, but has been imposed upon the speaker, on pain of worse punishment than not being taken seriously.

Such features are probably part of the general fact that women's speech sounds much more "polite" than men's. One aspect of politeness is as we have just described: leaving a decision open, not imposing your mind, or views, or claims on anyone else. Thus a tag question is a kind of polite statement, in that it does not force agreement or belief on the addressee. A request may be in the same sense a polite command, in that it does not overtly require obedience, but rather suggests something be done as a favor to the speaker. An overt order (as in an imperative) expresses the (often impolite) assumption of the speaker's superior position to the addressee, carrying with it the right to enforce compliance, whereas with a request the decision on the face of it is left up to the addressee. (The same is true of suggestions: here, the implication is not that the addressee is in danger if he does not comply—merely that he will be glad if he does. Once again, the decision is up to the addressee, and a suggestion therefore is politer than an order.) The more particles in a sentence that reinforce the notion that it is a request, rather than an order, the politer the result. The sentences of (14) illustrate these points: (14) *(a)* is a direct order, *(b)* and *(c)* simple requests, and *(d)* and *(e)* compound requests.[3]

(14)*(a)*   Close the door.
  (b)   Please close the door.
  (c)   Will you close the door?
  (d)   Will you please close the door?
  (e)   Won't you close the door?

Let me first explain why *(e)* has been classified as a compound request. (A sentence like *Won't you please close the door* would then count as a doubly compound request.) A sentence like (14) *(c)* is close in sense to "Are you willing to close the door?" According to the normal rules of polite conversation, to agree that you are willing is to agree to do the thing asked of you. Hence this apparent inquiry functions as a request, leaving the decision up to the willingness of the addressee. Phrasing it as a positive question makes the (implicit) assumption that a "yes" answer will be forthcoming. Sentence (14) *(d)* is more polite than *(b)* or *(c)* because it combines them: *please* indicating that to accede will be to do something for the speaker, and *will you*, as noted, suggesting that the addressee has the final decision. If, now, the question is phrased with a negative, as in (14) *(e)*, the speaker seems to suggest the stronger likelihood of a negative response from the addressee. Since the assumption is then that the addressee is that much freer to refuse, (14) *(e)* acts as a more polite request than (14) *(c)* or *(d)*: *(c)* and *(d)* put the burden of refusal on the addressee, as *(e)* does not.

Given these facts, one can see the connection between tag questions and tag orders and other requests. In all these cases, the speaker is not committed as with a simple declarative or affirmative. And the more one compounds a request, the more characteristic it is of women's speech, the less of men's. A sentence that begins *Won't you please* (without special emphasis on *please*) seems to me at least to have a distinctly unmasculine sound. Little girls are indeed taught to talk like little ladies, in that their speech is in many ways more polite than that of boys or men, and the reason for this is that politeness involves an absence of a strong statement, and women's speech is devised to prevent the expression of strong statements.

NOTES

1. Within the lexicon itself, there seems to be a parallel phenomenon to tag-question usage, which I refrain from discussing in the body of the text because the facts are controversial and I do not understand them fully. The intensive *so*, used where purists would insist upon an absolute superlative, heavily stressed, seems more characteristic of women's language than of men's, though it is found in the latter, particularly in the speech of male academics. Consider, for instance, the following sentences:

(a) I feel *so* unhappy!
(b) That movie made me *so* sick!

Men seem to have the least difficulty using this construction when the sentence is unemotional, or nonsubjective—without reference to the speaker himself:

(c) That sunset is *so* beautiful!

(d) Fred is *so* dumb!

Substituting an equative like *so* for absolute superlatives (like *very, really, utterly*) seems to be a way of backing out of committing oneself strongly to an opinion, rather like tag questions (cf. discussion below, in the text). One might hedge in this way with perfect right in making aesthetic judgments, as in *(c)*, or intellectual judgments, as in *(d)*. But it is somewhat odd to hedge in describing one's own mental or emotional state: who, after all, is qualified to contradict one on this? To hedge in this situation is to seek to avoid making any strong statement: a characteristic, as we have noted already and shall note further, of women's speech.

2. For analogues outside of English to these uses of tag questions and special intonation patterns, ct. my discussion of Japanese particles in "Language in Context," *Language*, 48 (1972), 907–27. It is to be expected that similar cases will be found in many other languages as well. See, for example, M. R. Haas's very interesting discussion of differences between men's and women's speech (mostly involving lexical dissimilarities) in many languages, in D. Hymes, ed., *Language in Culture and Society* (New York: Harper & Row, 1964).

3. For more detailed discussion of these problems, see Lakoff, "Language in Context."

marjorie harness goodwin

INSTIGATING

Unlike the boys, girls do not generally utilize direct methods in evaluating one another. They seldom give each other bald commands or insults, and making explicit statements about one's achievements or possessions is avoided. Such actions are felt to indicate someone who "thinks she cute" or above another, thus violating the comparatively egalitarian ethos of the girls. These different cultural perceptions lead to different ways in which stories which are part of dispute processes are built by the teller, and involve others in the process of storytelling. Rather than directly confronting one another with complaints about the actions of a girl in the play group, girls characteristically discuss their grievances about other girls in their absence. Through an elaborated storytelling procedure called "instigating," girls learn that absent parties have been talking about them behind their backs, and commit themselves to future confrontations with such individuals.

The activity of reporting to a recipient what was said about her in her absence constitutes an important stage preliminary to the confrontation event. It is the point at which such an event becomes socially recognizable as an actionable offense. The party talked about may then confront the party who was reportedly talking about her "behind her back." Such informing typically is accomplished through use of stories by a girl who will stand as neither accuser nor defendant. This type of storytelling is called "instigating" by the children. Girls talk about the activity of deliberately presenting the facts in such a way as to create conflict between people in the following way: [1]

(1) Martha: Everytime she- we do somp'm she don't like
              she go and tell somebody a lie.
              She make up somp'm and then she always
              go away.

The instigator may initiate a sequence of events which leads to conflict as part of a process of sanctioning the behavior of a girl who steps outside the bounds of appropriate behavior or as a way of demonstrating her ability to orchestrate such events.

Instigating possesses features of the black speech event analyzed as "signifying" by Kochman (1970) and Mitchell-Kernan (1971, 1972). According to

Mitchell-Kernan (1972:165, 166), signifying refers to "a way of encoding messages or meanings in natural conversations which involves, in most cases, an element of indirection" either with reference to "(1) the meaning or message the speaker is adjudged as intending to convey; (2) the addressee—the person or persons to whom the message is directed; (3) the goal orientation or intent of the speaker." In discussing signifying, Kochman (1970:157) has stated that "the signifier reports or repeats what someone else has said about the listener; the 'report' is couched in plausible language designed to compel belief and arouse feelings of anger and hostility."

The sequence of events which occurs as a result of stories' being told about what was said in a story recipient's absence is parallel to the sequencing of events resulting from the "signifying" which occurs in one of the most popular of black folklore forms, "The Signifying Monkey" (Abrahams 1964:147–157; Dorson 1967:98–99). In that tale's "toast" form, the monkey provokes a dispute between the lion and the elephant by telling the lion that the elephant was insulting him behind his back. The lion then confronts the elephant:

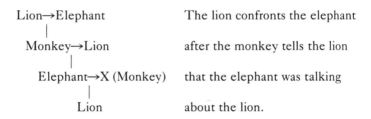

Lion→Elephant	The lion confronts the elephant
Monkey→Lion	after the monkey tells the lion
Elephant→X (Monkey)	that the elephant was talking
Lion	about the lion.

In the girls' he-said-she-said event, a parallel series of events occurs when an intermediary party (like the monkey) reports to someone what was said about her in her absence.

In both the he-said-she-said and "The Signifying Monkey," past events are reported in such a way as to lead to confrontation; however, the offenses at issue in the folktale are not the more general activity of having talked about someone in her absence but rather personal insults. The folklore form of "The Signifying Monkey" crystalizes what in everyday life is a recognizable event configuration in black culture; however, the positions in the he-said-she-said drama are transformed into animal figures,[2] and thus involvement in the story is not contingent on personal involvement with its characters.

The larger framework of the he-said-she-said dispute provides organization for the storytelling process in several ways:

1. It provides structure for the cited characters and their activities within the story.
2. It influences the types of analysis recipients must engage in to appropriately understand the story.
3. It makes relevant specific types of next moves by recipients: for example, evaluations of the offending party's actions during the story, pledges to future courses of action near the story's ending, and rehearsals of future events at story completion and upon subsequent retellings.

STRUCTURE IN TELLING AND LISTENING TO "INSTIGATING" STORIES

Bringing about a future confrontation has direct bearing upon the way speaker structures her instigating story and recipients respond to it. Through dramatic character development, speaker skillfully guides her recipients to interpret the events she is relating in the way she wants them to, and attempts to coimplicate hearers in forms of future activity. Recipients' responses to instigating stories are differentiated, depending upon the identity relationship of listeners to figures in the story. Much of Goffman's (1974) work on "the frame analysis of talk" and animation of characters (ibid.: 516–544) will be relevant here.

COMPLICATING LISTENERS

The complete transcripts of two separate stories which will be analyzed here appear at the end of the chapter. Briefly, the first story is told to both Julia and Barbara. In it Bea recounts what Kerry has been saying about Julia behind her back. Julia then leaves, and Bea starts a new set of stories in which she tells Barbara what Kerry said about *her* (Barbara).

The description of the past is organized so as to demonstrate that the events being recounted constitute *offenses*. Moreover, the presentation of past events is carefully managed so as to elicit from its recipient, now positioned by the story as an *offended party*, pejorative comments about the party who offended her, without this appearing as the direct intent of the speaker's story.

We will start by examining the initiation of Bea's first story, recounting what Kerry said about Julia:

(2)

11	Bea:	*How- how-* h- um, uh h- h- how about me
12		and *Julia,* *h and all them um, and
13		*Ke*rry, *h⌐and all them-
14	Julia:	⌊*Isn't Kerry mad* at
15		*me* or *s:om*p'm,
16		(0.4)
17	Bea:	*I'on'* kn//ow.
18	Barbara:	Kerry~*a*lways~mad~at somebody.
19		°*I*⌐'on' care.
20	Julia:	⌊Cuz- cuz cuz I wouldn't, cu:z she
21		ain't put my *n*ame on that *p*aper.
22	Bea:	*I* know cuz OH yeah. *Oh* yeah.

This story beginning has the form of a reminiscence. Bea requests that others remember with her a particular event: "*How- how-* h- um, uh h- h- how about me and *Julia,* *h and all of them um, and *Ke*rry." The numerous hesitations in her speech contribute to the highly charged framing of this talk. The proposed story concerns negative attributes of Kerry. The telling of derogatory stories, especially in the context of the he-said-she-said, poses particular problems for participants. That is, such stories constitute instances of talking behind someone's back, the very action at issue in a he-said-she-said.

Among Maple Street girls, responding to another's pejorative statement about an absent party is viewed in a particular way: it is seen as "getting involved." Participants themselves display an orientation toward the structured possibility of there being a "slot" (Sacks 1972:341–342) for an evaluative comment following a pejorative statement of a prior speaker. Consider the following:

(3)   Kerry: You know I was gonna have Jimmy-
                           I was have a Hallow-
                           I'm havin' a Halloween party? = So I said um,
                           so I said uh: Martha-
                           All Julia wanna do is *dance* at the party.
                           Tch! She don't wanna play no games or nothin'.
→ Bea: I ain't gonna say *n*othin'
                           cuz I don't wanna be involved.
→ Martha: Me neither. I don't wanna say nothin'
                           about nobody else business.

A party who tells about another runs a particular risk: current recipient might tell the absent party that current speaker is talking about her behind her back.[3] The activity of righteously informing someone of an offense against her can itself be taken and cast as an offense. Are there ways in which a party telling such a story can protect herself against such risk? One way might be to implicate her recipient in a similar telling so that both are equally guilty and equally vulnerable. However, this still poses problems; specifically, it would be most advantageous for each party if the other would implicate herself first. This can lead to a delicate negotiation at the beginning of the story: in #2, lines 11–13, when Bea brings up Kerry's offenses toward Julia, she requests the opinion of others, while refusing to state her own position. In response, Julia asks a question that describes her relationship to Kerry in a particular way: "*Is*n't *Kerry mad* at *me* or s:*om*p'm" (lines 14–15). If Bea in fact provides a story at this point demonstrating how Kerry is mad at Julia, Bea will have talked negatively about Kerry before Julia has coimplicated herself in a similar position. Bea subsequently passes up the opportunity to tell such a story by saying "*I 'on'* know" (line 17). Then Julia provides an answer to her own question: "Cuz- cuz cuz I wouldn't, cu:z she ain't put my *n*ame on that *p*aper" (lines 20–21). Only after Julia implicates herself does Bea begin to join in the telling (line 22).

CITED CHARACTERS AND CURRENT PARTICIPANTS

Instigating stories concern others within one's play group who are judged to have behaved in an inappropriate fashion. Such stories share certain features in common:

1.   The principal character in the story is a party who is not present.
2.   The nonpresent party performs actions directed toward some other party.
3.   These actions can be seen as offenses.

Although much of girls' gossip concerns negative evaluations of female age-mates' activities, such conversation need not necessarily lead to a confrontation if the activities of the absent party were not in the past directed toward the present recipient of the teller's talk. Thus the feature of instigating stories which distinguishes them from other types of stories used in dispute processes (such as those of the boys discussed earlier) is that:

4.   The target of the offense is the present hearer.

The placement of present recipient within the story as a principal figure provides for her involvement in it and, consequently, for the story's rather enduring life-span by comparison with other recountings.

Some evidence is available that the teller takes into account the four features listed above in the construction of her instigating stories. In the data being examined, Bea's initial stories (#2) involve offenses Kerry committed toward Julia. These include having said that Julia was acting "stupid" and inappropriately when girls were telling jokes, and having intentionally excluded Julia's name from a hall bathroom pass. During these stories, both Julia and Barbara are present. However, Julia then departs, leaving only Barbara as audience to Bea. Bea now starts a new series of stories (#4) in which Barbara is the target of a different set of offenses by Kerry. There involve Kerry's having said something about Barbara in her absence (that she had nothing to do with writing on the sidewalk and street about her) and having reported to Bea that "Barbara need to *go* somewhere." Thus when one hearer (Julia) leaves (prior to the beginning of #4), the speaker modifies her stories. In both sets of stories, the absent party who commits the offenses, Kerry, remains constant. However, the recipient of her actions is changed so that the target of the offense remains the present hearer. Through such changes, the speaker maintains the relevance of her story for its immediate recipient. What happens here demonstrates the importance of not restricting analysis of stories to isolated texts or performances by speakers, but rather including the story's recipients within the scope of analysis, since they can indeed be quite consequential for its organization.

Stories may also be locally organized with respect to the figure selected as the offender. The fact that Kerry is reportedly the agent of offensive talk in the story to Julia may well be why she is selected as a similar agent in the stories to Barbara several minutes later. When the confrontation is played out, it is discovered that it was actually Julia, rather than Kerry, who said something about Barbara in the past. Bea is found to have misrepresented the person who performed the offensive actions in order to create conflict between Barbara and Kerry.

Larger political processes within the girls' group might also be relevant to the selection of Kerry as offender in these stories. Gluckman (1963:308) has noted that gossip can be used "to control aspiring individuals." In the present data, Kerry is the same age as the other girls but has skipped a year in school, and they are annoyed at her for previewing everything that will happen to them in junior high. The structure of the immediate reporting situation, as well as larger social processes within the girls' group, is thus relevant to how past events are organized within these stories, and the way in which particular members of the girls' group become cited figures (Goffman 1974:529–532) within the stories.

In replaying past events, the teller animates (Goffman 1974) the cited figures within her stories in ways that are relevant to the larger social projects within which the stories are embedded.[4] In a variety of ways, the absent party's actions toward the current hearer are portrayed as offensive. Thus, in describing what Kerry said about Julia, Bea (lines 26–31) reports that Kerry had characterized Julia as having acted stupid:

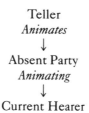

(2)

26	Bea:	*She* said, *She* said that um, (0.6)
27		that (0.8) if that *girl* wasn't
28		there = *You* know that girl that always
29		makes those funny jokes, *h Sh'aid if
30		that *girl* wasn't there *you* wouldn't be
31		*ac*tin', (0.4) a:ll *stu*pid like that.

Continuing on, Bea (lines 34–35) animates Kerry's voice as she reports that Kerry had said that Julia had been cursing:

(2)

35	Bea:	And she said that *you* sai:d, that,
36		"*Ah:* go tuh-" (0.5) somp'm like tha:t.

As Bea further elaborates her story about Kerry, she relates how Kerry had attempted to exclude Julia's name from a permission slip to go to the bathroom, or "hall pass." At the same time that she describes Kerry's actions as offensive, she portrays Julia as someone whose actions were appropriate and exemplary (lines 64–66) and herself as someone who took up for Julia (lines 68–69):

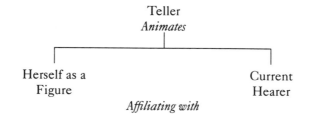

(2)

64	Bea	An' j- And Julia w'just sittin'
65		up there actin' - actin':, ac- ac- actin'
66		sensible. An' she up- and she up there
67		talking 'bout, and she- *I* said, I s'd I
68		s'd I s'd "This is how I'm- I'm gonna

69   put Julia *na*:me down here." Cu- m- m-
70   Cuz she had made a pa:ss you know. *h
71   She had made a *pa*:ss.

Bea's stuttering adds to the dramatic quality of her talk as she expresses excitement about what she is relating. As Bea animates Kerry's voice, she colors her talk with a whiny, high-pitched, defensive tone, enacting Kerry's distaste for having to include Julia's name. Immediately following, however, Bea again portrays herself as someone who *defended* the position of her present hearer against the offender:

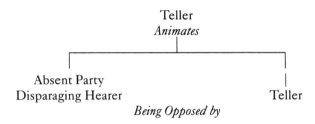

Teller
Animates

Absent Party
Disparaging Hearer   Teller
Being Opposed by

(2)
77   Bea: I s'd- I s'd "*How: co*:me you
78   ain't put Julia name down here." *h So
79   she said, she said ((*whiny, defensive tone*))
80   "That other girl called 'er so,
81   she no:t *wi*:th *u*:s, so,"
82   That's what she said too. (0.2) So *I*
83   said, s- so I snatched the paper
84   wi'her. I said wh- when we were playin'
85   wi'that paper?

(2)
93   Bea: But she ain't even put your *na*me down
94   there. *I* just put it *down* there. Me
95   and Martha put it down. =An' I said, and
96   she said "*Gi*mme-that-paper. =I don't
97   wanna have her *na*me *d*own here." I s- I
98   s- I s- I said "She woulda allowed *you*
99   name."

Quite different forms of affect and alignment toward Julia's perspective are conveyed by Bea's animation of Kerry and of herself. While Bea portrays Kerry as having willfully excluded Julia from the group going to the bathroom, Bea describes herself as having actively defended Julia against Kerry. She talked back to Kerry, arguing that Julia would certainly not have conducted herself as Kerry had, and even snatched the bathroom pass from Kerry to write down Julia's name so that she would be included. Bea structures her stories so that her characters take up contrasting stances with reference to the issues at stake, and they thus stand in sharp relief.

Speaker not only carefully crafts her own description of events; she also acts upon any indication by recipient of her alignment toward the absent party. For example, when Julia makes an evaluative comment— "OO: r'mind me a-you old b:aldheaded Kerry" (lines 108–109)—at the close of the story about Kerry's actions toward Julia, Bea states, "*I* should say it in fronta her *face*. (0.8) Bal': head" (lines 110–111). Bea presents a model of how she herself would confront the offending party and invites recipient to see the action in question as she herself does: as an action deserving in return an aggravated response, such as a personal insult.

Suggestions for how to act toward the absent party may also take the form of stories in which *speaker* rather than recipient appears as principal character reacting to actions of the offending party. Briefly, the speaker makes her suggestions by telling her present recipient the kinds of actions that *she herself* takes against the offender, these actions being appropriate next moves to the offenses described in the informing stories:

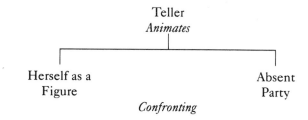

```
Teller
Animates

Herself as a                          Absent
  Figure                              Party
        Confronting
```

(4)

58	Bea:	Oh yea, oh yeah. = *She* was, *she*- w's
59		*she* was in Rochele: house you know, and
60		she said that um, that- I heard her
61		say um, (0.4) um um uh uh "*Jul*ia said
62		y'all been talking behind my back." =I
63 →		said I'm a- I'm a say "H:oney, I'm gl*a*:d.
64		that *you* know I'm talkin' be*hind your*
65		*back.* Because *I*- because *I meant*
66		for you to know *any*way." An' she said,
67		I- said "I don't have to talk behind
68		your back. =I can talk in front of your
69		*face too.*"

(4)

142	Bea:	*h And she was leanin'
143		against- I- I said, I s'd I s'd I s'd I
144		said, "*Hey* girl don't lean against that
145		thing cuz it's *weak* e*nough*." *h And
146		she said and she said *h she- she did
147		like that. =She say, "Tch!" ((*rolling*
148		*eyes*)) / / like that. I s'd- I said "You
149		c'd *roll* your eyes all you *want* to.

150	Barbara:	Yeah if somebody do that to her-
151		And if ⌐you know what?
152	Bea:	└Cuz I'm *t*ellin' you. (0.5)
153		*T*ellin' - I'm not *ask*in' you." (0.4) An' I
154		ain't say no *plea*:se *ei*ther.

In these stories Bea tells how she confronted Kerry with aggravated insults. Specifically, she describes how she told Kerry to her face that she had talked about her behind her back (lines 63–66). In addition, Bea describes having performed insulting actions directly to Kerry's face, issuing a direct command to her. "Cuz I'm *t*ellin' you. (0.5) *T*ellin' - I'm not *ask*in' you" (lines 152–153). The bald on-record nature of the command is highlighted by placing it in contrast to a more mitigated form which was not said: "An' I ain't say no *plea*:se *ei*ther" (lines 153–154).

Providing evaluation through descriptions of past activities is quite consequential for the process of eliciting from recipient a promise to confront the offender in the future. On the one hand, objectionable actions performed by the absent party can be interpreted as explicit offenses against current recipient. On the other hand, speaker's description of her own actions in response to such offenses, i.e., confronting the offender, can provide recipient with a guide for how she should act toward that party. Thus Julia's statement that she will confront Kerry occurs right after Bea has described how she confronted Kerry about having excluded Julia's name from the bathroom pass.

(2)

| 86 | Julia: | I'm a I'm a *t*ell about herself. |

Reports of actions in the past can thus lead to commitments to perform relevant answers to them in the future.

Thus through a variety of activities—passing up the opportunity to align herself with a definitive position before hearer does at story beginning, presenting herself as having defended the offended party in the past, and portraying how she boldly confronted the offending party—speaker carefully works to coimplicate her present recipient in a next course of action. Features of indirection are evident in the reporting in several ways. In accordance with Kochman's (1970: 157) definition of indirection, the teller presents a believable picture of past events involving what was said about the recipient which arouses feelings of anger and hostility. In keeping with Mitchell-Kernan's (1972: 166) analysis of indirection, the goal orientation of speaker in presenting her stories is obscured. Although the report is supposedly a narrative account of past events involving teller and offending party, and speaker's alignment of righteous indignation toward these acts, it may also function to suggest future courses of action for present recipient.

DIFFERENTIATED RECIPIENTS' RESPONSES

As we have seen, the stories used in instigating contain extensive reported speech (Vološinov 1973) as speakers animate the characters in their talk. The recipients of the present reports, in accord with Goffman's (1974: 503) idealization of listener response, display that they "have been stirred" by the events the narrator describes. A current participant who was absent when the things said about her were reported to have been said can now answer those charges. In addition, in that these recountings are embedded within a larger realm of action, one which provides for the dynamic involvement of coparticipants and is not restricted to the present encounter, recipients are invited by the narrator to be moved to action. The report of offenses in the he-said-she-said event is specifically constructed to inform someone that she has (from the teller's perspective) been offended and thereby to invite her to take action against the offender. This prospect of future involvement may provide for recipients' participation and engrossment in the present in more active roles than generally occur in response to stories.

In responding to talk, participants pay close attention to the differential access they have to the events being talked about. Listeners as well as speakers occupy multiple identities vis-à-vis both the teller in the present and the cited figures in the reported story. They thus differ with respect to their involvement or engrossment in the events being recounted. Parties who were present when the action described occurred and are figures in the story not only may respond to the story but also may participate in its telling, as Julia does in response to Bea's first instigating story:

(2)
47	Julia:	So: *she* wouldn' be *a*ctin' *li*ke *that*
48		wi' that *oth*er girl. = *She* the one picked
49		*me* to *sit* wi'them. = *h She said ⌈"Julia you
50	Bea:	⌊Y:ahp.
51	Julia:	sit with her, *h and I'll sit with her,
52		*h an Bea an'-an' Bea an'-
53		an' an' Martha sit together."

(2)
101	Julia:	I said Kerry, "°How come you ain't put my
102		name."
103	Barbara:	Here go B/ /ea, "uh uh uh well-"
104	Julia:	"You put that *oth*er girl (name down)
105		didn't you. I thought *you* was gonna
106		have- owl: a hall pass with that *oth*er
107		girl." That's °what Kerry said. I said
108		(What's~her~problem.)

Such a collaborative telling is dependent upon knowledge of the event and generally utilizes past tense.

Implicated recipients are not restricted to making comments about events that they directly experienced. A listener who has had attacks made upon her may respond to these attacks in the present, despite the fact that her attacker is not present but exists only as a cited figure in another's story. One form of counter is a challenge to the truth of statements concerning her. For example, when Bea reports that Kerry had accused Julia of swearing, she quickly denies the charge:

(2)
```
  35    Bea:        She- and she said that you sai:d, that,
  36                "Ah: go tuh-" (0.5) somp'm like ⌈tha:t.
  37 →  Julia:                                 ⌊°No I
  38                didn't.
```

A dialogue between events and participants who are separated from each other by both space and time thus occurs, as a present participant addresses actions performed against her in the past by someone who is now absent. Moreover, as will be seen shortly, such events can have consequences for the future as well.

Bea's report that Kerry characterized Julia's actions in the past as "acting stupid" (lines 28–30) is likewise countered by Julia, who says in an aggravated tone:

(2)
```
  33    Julia:      But was I actin' stupid with them?
```

Such a response not only answers charges in the past but also solicits an alliance with the current teller against the offender. A second form of counter to a reported statement which denigrates the current recipient may be a return pejorative statement about the cited figure:

(2)
```
  45    Bea:        She said, hh that you wouldn't be actin'
  46                like that aroun' - around people.
  47 →  Julia:      So: she wouldn' be actin' like that
  48                wi'that other girl.
```

When Barbara is told that Kerry has said that she didn't have anything to do with the writing that is the subject of another dispute, she answers that past action with a current challenge. Even though the events at issue would seem to be positive ones from Barbara's perspective—not being found guilty for having written pejorative things about Kerry—the fact that Kerry *said* something about Barbara in her absence makes relevant a response from her. The identity of the offended party is thus a position which is collaboratively brought into existence through both teller's description of a third party's past activities and recipient's orientation toward absent party's past actions as offenses.[5]

(4)
```
  32    Barbara:    If I wro:te somp'm then I wrote
  33                it. = Then I got somp'm to do with
  34                it. = W'then I wrote it.
```

(4)
```
  48    Barbara:    WELL IF I WROTE SOME'EN I HAD SOMP'M
  49                T'DO with it.
```

The present encounter encompasses a dialogue not only between participants and events in the present, but also between participants and events from previous encounters. As seen above, a present participant may answer charges made by someone absent from the present interaction who currently exists only as a cited figure in the talk of another speaker. Parties denied the opportunity to counter offensive statements about them in the past when the offenses were committed may deal with them in their retelling. In this way the offended party may also discover the present speaker's alignment toward the cited speaker's statements by observing her next utterances to the counter.

All of the responses examined so far were made by current recipients who were figures in the cited story. The offense committed against them in the past warranted their indignant responses to the charges made against them. However, responses of this type, denials for example, are not available to a current listener who is not mentioned in the story and has not been maligned. How can a party in such a position respond to the telling? During the first set of narratives about how Kerry acted toward Julia, Barbara is in precisely this position. She is not a character in the recounting and has not been offended. When her actions are examined, it is found she provides general comments on the offender's character, referring to ongoing attributes of her in the present progressive tense. For example:

(2)
| 18 | Barbara: | Kerry~*al*ways~mad~at somebody. |
| 19 | | °*I* 'on' care. |

(2)
40	Barbara:	Kerry *al*ways say somp'm. = When you
42		*jump* in her *face* she gonna de*ny*
43		it.

In the first story (#2), Barbara's evaluations provide a structural alternative to the way in which Julia, a figure in the event recounted, participates in it. While Julia has access to the events being talked about, Barbara does not. Julia can therefore answer Kerry's charges with her own version of the incidents at issue. The events recounted thus have a differential relevance to the current situation of each participant; while Julia's character has been called into question, Barbara's has not. Julia, unlike Barbara, has both motivation and standing to answer the charges raised by Kerry.

The structures used by Barbara provide a creative solution to the problem of talking about the event that is currently on the floor. Despite the fact that this event does not involve her in the way that it does the others present, Barbara helps to constitute it. In brief, the talk of the moment creates a field of relevance that implicates those present to it in a variety of different ways, and this has consequences for the detailed organization of the action that each party produces.

PREPLAYINGS: FUTURE STORIES IN RESPONSE TO INSTIGATING STORIES

By telling stories, instigators portray how they treated an absent party in the past, as a way of suggesting how their current addressee should treat that party in the future

future. Through their descriptions, instigators report events which can be seen as offensive and provide recipients the opportunity to assume the identity of offended party. However, the mere reporting of offenses is not itself sufficient to bring about a future confrontation; rather, a recipient must publicly analyze the event in question as an offense against her and state that she will seek redress by confronting her offender:

(2)
86	Julia:	I'm a I'm a *t*ell her about herself
87		to*day*.

Actions such as these constitute far stronger evaluations than mere complaints about the prior actions of offending party. In essence, current recipient commits herself to taking action in the future against the party who offended her.

In comparing the kinds of evaluative responses Julia and Barbara give to the stories Bea tells, Barbara in #4 takes a much stronger stance vis-à-vis Kerry's reported actions than Julia. In response to instigating stories, offended party (Barbara) produces a series of future stories in which she projects what she will do when she confronts her offender (Kerry):

(4)
6	Barbara:	Well you *t*ell her to *c*ome say it in
7		front of my fa:ce. (0.6) And *I*'ll *p*ut
8		*her* somewhere.

(4)
22	Barbara:	So, she got anything t'say she
23		come say it in front of my face. (1.0)
24		I better not *see Ke*rry today. (2.5) I
25		*ain*'t gonna say- I'm~a~say "Kerry *what*
26		*you say* about me."

(4)
101	Barbara:	I better not see Kerry to*day*. I'm a
102		say "Kerry *I* heard *y*ou was talkin' 'bout
103		me."

(4)
157	Barbara:	W'll I'm tellin' ya
158		*I* better not catch *K*erry to*day*. Cuz if
159		I catch her I'm gonna give *her* a wor:d
160		from my *mou*th.

Bea's stories about past events in which Barbara was offended permit Barbara to describe future scenes that are the contingent outcome of events emerging in the present. To provide strong demonstrations of her understanding of Bea's stories, Barbara makes herself a character who confronts Kerry, just as Bea had in the past. These stories not only give Barbara the opportunity to seriously answer Bea's suggestions, they also permit her to construct a future scene in which she carries out a confrontation with Kerry. In these scenes Barbara is the accuser and Kerry is the defendant. These enacted sequences have certain regular features: (1) an evaluation of the offending party's actions, (2) an accusation, and (3) a response to the accusation.

Barbara evaluates Bea's stories by making statements about how the offender should have acted:

(4)

22	Barbara:	So, she got anything t'say she
23		come say it in front of my face.

Her evaluations also include warnings for Kerry:

(4)

118	Barbara:	I better not catch you t'day. = I'm a
119		*tell her butt o*:ff.

(4)

157	Barbara:	W'll I'm tellin' ya
158		*I* better not catch *K*erry to*day.* Cuz if
159		I catch her I'm gonna give *her* a wor:d
160		from my *mou*th.

Combined with the warning may be a statement of how she will confront Kerry with a formal complaint:

(4)

101	Barbara:	I better not see Kerry to*day.* I'm a
102		say "Kerry *I* heard *y*ou was talkin' 'bout
103		me."

(4)

24	Barbara:	I better not *see K*erry today. (2.5) I
25		*ain*'t gonna say- I'm~a~say "Kerry *what*
26		*you say* about me."

Following the offended's enactment of her own future action as an accuser, she projects how the defending party will respond with denials, actions that are expected following opening accusations:

(4)

26	Barbara:	She gonna say
28		"I ain't *say* nuttin'."

(2)

105	Barbara:	Then she gonna say "I ain't-
106		*What I* say about you."

At the close of the future stories, Barbara enacts additional parts of the drama, which are contingent on Kerry's response to Barbara:

(4)

> 121   Barbara: An if she get *bad* at me:*e*: I'm a,
> 122   punch her in the eye.

(4)

> 160   Barbara: An' if she *j*ump in
> 161   my *f*ace I'm a punch her in her *fa*:ce.

Note that these projected accusations differ from actual he-said-she-said accusations in that Barbara does not include reference to Bea, the party who told her about the offenses. The lack of specificity concerning the reporter is adaptive to the immediate interaction. The party who informed the accuser of an offense is someone within the present interaction. Were the accusation to contain a reference to a specific person who informed on the offending party, this would call attention to the fact that at the next stage of the event the party in the present interaction who had reported the offense could be identified as someone who talked about the defendant in her absence.

Offended parties' responses which constitute plans to confront the offending party are made in the presence of witnesses; they thus provide displays of someone's intentions to seek redress for the offenses perpetrated against her. Failure to follow through with a commitment statement such as "I'm a *t*ell her about herself to*day*" can be remarked on as demonstrating inconsistencies in a person's talk and actions, thus reflecting negatively on her character. Indeed, when Julia later fails to confront Kerry, others use her actions in the present exchange to talk about the way in which she had promised to tell Kerry off but then did nothing:

(5)

> Bea: Yeah and Julia all the time talking
>   'bout she was gonna tell whats-her-name
>   off. And *she* ain't do it.

Alignments taken up in the midst of an exchange such as this can thus be interpreted as commitments to undertake future action for which parties may be held responsible by others. People who refuse to confront once they have reported their intentions are said to "swag," "mole," or "back down" from a future confrontation and may be ridiculed in statements such as "You molin' out." The fact that a statement about future intentions can be treated as a relevantly absent event at a future time provides some demonstration of how responses to instigating stories are geared into larger social projects.

These enactments of possible worlds (Lakoff 1968) in which Barbara is confronting Kerry not only provide strong displays of her commitment to carry out a confrontation with Kerry but also enable her to rehearse future lines in that encounter.[6] Such enactments might be viewed as idealized versions (Werner and Fenton 1973:538–539) of the sequence of activity in the actual confronting.

That is, a minimal he-said-she-said sequence would, given this model, contain an accusation, a defense, and a warning or evaluation of offender's actions.

Typically anthropologists, and ethnoscientists in particular, employ *elicited informants' accounts* to substantiate their statements about the "ideational order." Quite frequently such accounts occur as the product of interaction between informants and researchers (Briggs 1986; Jordan and Suchman 1987; Mishler 1986) fitted to the expectations participants have for such encounters. Alternatively, anthropologists might make use of talk between members of the group being studied. As these stories show, participants in their talk to one another provide rather precise images of confrontation encounters, specifying minimal sequences of appropriate utterance types.

STORIES RETOLD BY INSTIGATOR TO PERIPHERAL PARTIES

He-said-she-said confrontations are dramatic events that the whole street looks forward to with eager anticipation. Between the instigating and the confrontation stages, selective reporting of prior talk occurs when the instigator meets someone who is not a principal to the dispute but will act as audience to it. After the storyteller secures recipient's commitment to confront the offending party, an instigator may tell a friend not involved in the conflict about what happened. This occurs as Bea (instigator) meets Martha (peripheral party) and relates what had just occurred with Barbara (offended party). As argued earlier, narrative generally is told from the perspective of teller about her own past actions. However, in the stories related to peripheral figures, instigator emphasizes offended party's past statements which are important to the future confrontation but eliminates her own work in soliciting such statements. In her retelling, Bea omits entirely the stories she told to Julia. She downplays her own role in the past stories, summarizing her participation with a single statement—"I had told Barbara what um, what Kerry said about her?" (lines 1–3)—and then launches into her story about the offended party's promise to confront the offending party. Informing Barbara of these events had in fact involved the major portion of the informing process. However, this is reported succinctly and in indirect speech. By way of contrast, Bea reports in direct speech Barbara's response to her informings (lines 4–11):

1	Bea:	Hey you- you n- you know- you know I-
2		I- I had told *Ba*rbara, what um,
3		what Kerry said about her? And I-
4		and she said "I *be*tter *no*t see um,
5		um *Ke*rry, b'cause" she said she said
6		"Well I'm comin' around Maple
7		and I *just be*tter not *see* her
8		b'cause I'm- b'cause I'm gonna tell her
9		behind her- in front of her *fa*ce
10		and *no*t be*hi*nd her-
11		I mean in front of/ /her face."

12	Martha:	She call her baldheaded and all that?
13	Bea:	Yep. And she said- she said- she said
14		I'm gonna-

In the initial storytelling session, the crucial events at issue were the actions of the offending party (Kerry). Such events were important in that they constructed a portrait of the absent party as an offender. When a story is retold to someone who may be a future witness to the confrontation, a detailed chronology of past events is not key to the activity of involving a listener in some future stage of the he-said-she-said events. The crucial aspect of the past story is, rather, responses of the offended party to the report: in particular, whether or not she will seek a confrontation. Indeed, it is this latter action that brings into existence the drama that will engross the spectator. As Martha, after hearing Bea's report (and anticipating the future confrontation), states:

(7)	Martha:	Can't wait t'see this
		A::Ctio:*n*. Mm*fh*. Mm*ffh*.

In that offended party's responses projected a future confrontation, they are relevant to the peripheral figure's future participation. Bea marks the importance of these responses not only by placing them very early in the story, but also through their elaboration.

FUTURE HYPOTHETICAL STORIES TOLD BY INSTIGATOR AND PERIPHERAL PARTY

In response to Bea's replaying of her informing to Barbara, both Bea and Martha collaborate in constructing a future story. They elaborate hypothetical events occurring when offended meets offending party; however, their projections, which include admissions of guilt and personal insults, do not, in fact, occur in confrontation sequences.

1	Martha:	Can't wait t'see this
2		A::Ctio:*n*. Mm*fh*. MM*fh*.
3	Bea:	But if *Bar*bara say / / she
4	Martha:	I laugh- I laugh I laugh if Kerry say-
5		Bea s- I laugh if Barbara say,
6		"*I wrote* it
7		so what you gonna *do* about it."
8	Bea:	*She* say, she- and- and- and she
9		and she probably gonna back out.
10	Martha:	I know.
11	Bea:	*Boouh* *b*oouh / / boouh
12	Martha:	And then she gonna say "You didn't
13		*ha*ve to *write* that about me Barbara."
14		She might call her Barbara *fat* somp'm.
15		= Barbara say "Least I don't have no long:

16		bumpy legs and bumpy neck. *S*pot legs,
17		*h Least I don't gonna fluff my hair up
18		to make me look like / / I hadda bush."
19	Bea:	Y'know *she's*- she-
20		least she *fa*tter than her.
21	Martha:	Yeah an' "*L*east I got bones. =
22		At least I got *shape*."
23		That's what she could say. (0.6)
24		Barbara *is* cuter than her though.
25	Bea:	Yah:p. And Barbara got *shape* too.

In this sequence the party who was a nonparticipant in the informing stories but is present at the replaying of such stories, Martha, projects herself as a spectator to an upcoming confrontation (lines 5–7): "I laugh if Barbara say, '*I wrote* it so what you gonna *do* about it.'" The enactment of the future event, however, is made up of forms of utterances which contrast with those which are actually enacted in a confrontation. Martha notes that it would be an event which would evoke an unusual response, laughter, were Barbara actually to admit the offense. In dramatizing what Kerry and Barbara would say to each other, Martha and Bea use personal insults (lines 15–22), actions which among girls rarely occur in someone's presence.

The informing about a past meeting with an offended party serves to recruit potential spectators to the event. It provides for forms of enactments about possible future events for those not occupying the identity of offended or offending party in the confrontation, in much the same way that informing about offenses to an offended party provides for enactments by that party.[7] License in building dialogue in future stories occurs in part because girls are talking about absent parties rather than involving themselves in providing an accurate depiction of an event. In addition, the reporting is a way of recruiting potential spectators to the event, in that it provides for their involvement at a future time.

The way in which Bea presents her description of past events to Martha differs from her informings to Julia and Barbara. Although in the stories Bea told to Julia and Barbara (#2 and #4) she took precautions to elicit responses from them with regard to their alignment toward the offending party, building in opportunities for them to do so before indicating her own orientation toward Kerry, with Martha (#6 and #8) she launches into her story in an unguarded fashion. While Julia and Barbara appear as cited characters in the stories Bea tells, Martha does not. Moreover, in that Martha and Bea are best friends who complain to one another about both Kerry and Barbara, Bea can expect Martha to side with her on most issues. In fact, as seen earlier when this he-said-she-said is played out, after Kerry confronts Bea for having talked about her, both Martha and Bea provide denials. The friendship alignments between girls are thus important in the structuring of gossip stories.

Stories tied to the he-said-she-said event thus take a variety of forms; they include (1) initial instigating stories between instigator and offended party, (2) future stories of offended party in response to instigating stories, (3) retold stories about the instigating session between instigator and offended, and (4) hypothetical stories between instigator and peripheral parties. In delivering her stories, instigator carefully shapes them to elicit from her listeners responses which will promote involvement in a future confrontation. She embellishes past dialogue which will evoke recipient response and downplays talk of her own which could be viewed in an objectionable way. Offended party for her part, too, carefully omits the role of instigating party in evoking a future stage. Finally, hypothetical future stories provide a way for instigator and peripheral party to talk about absent parties and play with speech actions which are generally taboo in female interaction.

The form of listener analysis and participation examined here demonstrates the competence of listeners to interpret events in culturally appropriate terms. Questions and enactments of future scenes display to the teller that the listener is performing at each point in the story an ongoing analysis of events. In order to demonstrate understanding in a relevant way and to have this understanding ratified, listeners make use of procedures for projecting future stages in the he-said-she-said.

A COMPARISON OF BOYS' AND GIRLS' DISPUTE STORIES

We may now compare the forms of participation which are made available in boys' and girls' dispute stories. Within dispute processes, girls' and boys' stories share several features in common: (1) the principal topic is offenses of another, and (2) one of the characters in the story is a *present participant*. In the case of boys' stories, cited offenses deal with wrongdoings of a present participant. Among girls, however, offenses concern *reported deeds of absent parties*. Although both girls and boys oppose the reported descriptions, such structural differences lead them to make alternative types of responses. While boys who are offended parties direct counters to *principal storyteller*, girls direct their counters to *cited figures* who offended them in the past. In that the offending party is absent from the instigating event, girls, in contrast to boys, cannot resolve their disagreements in the present interaction.

A second point of contrast in boys' and girls' dispute stories is that *principal hearer* is portrayed in different ways. While in Chopper's story Tony has performed objectionable actions in the past as a coward, in girls' instigating stories the present hearers (Julia and Barbara) have performed exemplary actions in the past, which sharply contrast with the objectionable actions of an absent party (Kerry). The portrayal of characters and events within dispute stories has consequences for the form and timing of interaction which ensues. Thus, while boys' dispute stories engender disagreements which permit negotiation in the *immediate setting*, girls' stories engender alignments of "two against one" against an absent third party who will be confronted *at some future time*. Offended party reacts to the story by stating not only that she disapproves of the offending party's actions toward her in the past but that she is prepared to confront her offender. Although boys' stories have little motive power beyond the present situation, girls' instigating stories are embedded within a larger social process. They constitute a preliminary stage in a larger procedure of sanctioning inappropriate behavior which may extend over several weeks and provide for the involvement of participants in multiple phases of activity.

In both girls' and boys' stories, recipient response from parties other than those who are principal figures in the story aids in the teller's depiction of the offending party; nonfocal participants provide comments on the offender's character. In the boys' stories, this is accomplished largely through laughter, requests for elaboration, and repetition of quoted refrains of the principal character's speech in a past event. Girls' comments or evaluations likewise blatantly display that the story instances inappropriate behavior of an offending party. Among the girls, nonfocal participants make their commentary principally by referring to ongoing objectionable attributes of the offender.

The girls' and boys' stories investigated here tell of future and imaginary events as well as past occurrences. In boys' stories, the party cast as the offender may initiate hypothetical stories; in an attempt to counter pejorative descriptions made about him, offended party may portray storyteller in imaginary events in which he appears cowardly. With respect to girls' instigating stories, the primary organization of the descriptions in them as well as responses to them is to be found not in properties of the past events being described but rather in the structure of the present interaction, which includes an anticipated future. That anticipation is possible because of the embeddedness of this entire process, including the constructing and understanding of the stories, within a larger cultural event, the he-said-she-said. Such stories therefore differ from the forms of those most frequently dealt with by students of stories. Although Goffman (1974:505) has noted the possibility of "preplays," most researchers have a narrower vision of what constitutes a narrative; generally narrative is considered "a method of recapitulating past experience by matching a verbal sequence of clauses to the sequence of clauses which (it is inferred) actually occurred" (Labov 1972a: 359–360).[8] Given this orientation toward the structuring of stories, it is not surprising that researchers of narratives make use of role-played data or elicited texts, assuming that narratives can be analyzed in isolation from the course of events in which they are embedded. While accounts informants give anthropologists can perhaps best be depicted as social constructions (Bruner 1986:141), they are most frequently portrayed as context-free renderings of experience.

Anthropologists frequently rely on reports as primary data sources, and one of their central concerns has been how accurately the report corresponds to the initial events which it describes (Bilmes 1975).[9] By way of contrast, Sacks (1963, 1972:331–332) argues that the central issue is not the correspondence between the report and the event it describes but rather the organization of the description as a situated cultural object in its own right. In the present investigation I have been concerned not with how accurately a story reflects the initial event it describes, but rather with the problem of how the description of the past is constructed in the first place[10] such that it is a recognizable cultural object appropriate to the ongoing social project of the moment. Indeed, I wish to argue, as does Vološinov (1971), that the context of reporting itself provides the description with its primary organization. Such an argument concerning the nature of reports is important for the enterprise of ethnography. Anthropologists, rather than accepting reports as instances of the events they describe, must seriously investigate the process of reporting itself.

GIRLS' INSTIGATING STORIES

(2)   *Bea, Barbara, and Julia are sitting on*
                                       Julia's steps discussing substitute teachers
                                       during a teachers' strike.

1	Barb:	*Teach* us some little *six*th-grade work.
2		(0.4) *That's* how these volun*teers* doin'
3		now. A little um, *h *Ad*din' 'n' all
4		that.
5	Bea:	*Y*ahp. *Y*ahp. // *Y*ahp. An' when
6		we was in the-
7	Barb:	Twenny and twenny is // forty an' all
8		that.
9	Bea:	*H*ow 'bout when we was in-
10	Barb:	Oo I *hate* that junk.
11	Bea:	*H*ow- *how*- h- um, uh h- h- how about me
12		and *Jul*ia, *h and all them um, and
13		*K*erry, *h ⌐and all them-
14	Julia:	⌊*Is*n't Kerry *mad* at
15		*me* or *s:om*p'm,
16		(0.4)
17	Bea:	*I'on'* kn// ow.
18	Barb:	Kerry~*al*ways~mad~at somebody.
19		°*I* ⌐'on' care.
20	Julia:	⌊Cuz- cuz cuz I wouldn't, cu:z she
21		ain't put my *n*ame on that *p*aper.
22	Bea:	*I* know cuz ⌐OH yeah. *Oh* yeah.
23	Barb:	⌊An' next she,
24		(0.3)
25	Barb:	⌐talk~'bout~*peo*ple.
26	Bea:	⌊*She* said, *She* said that um, (0.6)
27		that (0.8) if that *girl* wasn't
28		there = *You* know that girl that always
29		makes those funny jokes, *h Sh'aid if
30		that *girl* wasn't there *you* wouldn't be
31		*ac*tin' (0.4) a:ll *stu*pid like that.
32		°Sh-
33	Julia:	⌊But *was* I actin' stupid w⌐ith them
34	Bea:	⌊Nope, no, =And
35		she- and she said that *you* sai:d, that,
36		"*Ah*: go tuh-" (0.5) somp'm like⌐tha:t.
37	Julia:	⌊°No I
38		didn't.
39	Bea:	She's- an' uh- somp'm like *that*. She's-

40	Barb:	Ke⌐rry *al*ways say somp'm. = When you =
41	Bea:	└She-
42	Barb:	=*jump* in her *face* she gonna de*ny*
43		it.
44	Bea:	Yah:p Y⌐ahp. = An' she said, *h An'- and
45	Julia:	└°Right on.
46	Bea:	she said, hh that *you* wouldn't be *ac*tin'
47		*li*ke *that* aroun'- around *peo*ple.
48	Julia:	So: *she* wouldn' be *ac*tin' *li*ke *that*
49		wi'that *oth*er girl. = *She* the one picked
50		*me* to *sit* wi'them. = *h She said ⌐"Julia you
51	Bea:	└Y:ahp.
52	Julia:	sit with her, *h and I'll sit with her,
53		*h an' Bea an'- an' Bea an'-
54		an' an' ⌐Martha sit together."
55	Barb:	└SHE TELLIN' Y'ALL WHERE TA SIT
56		AT?
57		(0.2)
58	Bea:	An' so *we* sat together, An' s- and s- and
59		so Julia was ju:st s:ittin' right
60		there. = An' the girl, an'- an'- the girl:
61		next to her? *h and the girl kept on
62		getting back up. *h Ask the teacher
63		can she go t'the bathroom. An' Julia
64		say she don' *wa*nna go t'the bathroom
65		w'her. An j- And Julia w'just sittin'
66		up there actin'- actin':, ac- ac- actin'
67		sensible. An she up- and she up there
68		talking 'bout, and she- *I* said, I s'd I
69		s'd I s'd "This is how I'm- I'm gonna
70		put Julia *na*:me down here." Cu- m- m-
71		Cuz she had made a pa:ss you know. *h
72		She had made a *pa*:ss.
73		(0.2)
74	Bea:	⌐For all us to go down to the bathroom.
75	Barb:	└Y'all go down t'the bathroom?
76	Bea:	For ALLA- yeah. Yeah. For u:m, (0.4)
77		for- for alla us- t'go to the
78		bathroom. = I s'd- I s'd "*How*:*co*:me you
79		ain't put Julia name down here." *h So
80		she said, she said ((*whiny, defensive tone*))
81		"That other girl called 'er so,
82		she no:t *wi*:th *u*:s, so,"
83		That's what she said too. (0.2) So *I*
84		said, s- so I snatched the paper
85		wi'her. I said wh- when we were playin'
86		wi'that paper?
87	Julia:	I'm a I'm a *t*ell her about herself

88		to*da*ͺy. Well,
89	Bea:	[Huh? huh remember when we're
90		snatchin' that ͺpaper.
91	Barb:	[An' she gonna tell you
92		another story any*way*. / / (Are you gonna
93		talk to her today?)
94	Bea:	But she ain't even put your *na*me down
95		there. *I* just put it *down* there. Me
96		and Martha put it down. = An I said, and
97		she said "*Gi*mme-that-paper. = I don't
98		wanna have her *na*me *d*own here." I s- I
99		s- I s- I said "She woulda allowed *you*
100		name (if you started)."
101		(1.0)
102	Julia:	I said Kerry "°How come you ain't put my
103		name."
104	Barb:	Here go B / / ea, "uh uh uh well-"
105	Julia:	"You put that *o*ther girl (name down)
106		didn't you. I thought *you* was gonna
107		have- owl: a hall pass with that *o*ther
108		girl." That's °what Kerry said. I said
109		(What's~her~problem.) OO: r'mind me a-
110		you old b:aldheaded Kerry.
111	Bea:	*I* should say it in fronta her *f*ace.
112		(0.8) Bal': head.
113	Barb:	Hey 'member when what we did th(h)e
114		o(h)ther ti(*h*)me.

(3)		*The following occurs 45 seconds later*
		after Julia has gone inside.
1	Bea:	She shouldn't be *w*ritin' things, about
2		me. (0.5) An' so- An' so- so she said
3		*Bar*bara, Barbara need ta *go*
4		somewhere.
5		(1.0)
6	Barb:	Well you *t*ell her to *c*ome say it in
7		front of my fa:ce (0.6) And *I*'ll *p*ut
8		*her* somewhere. (3.8) An' Barbara
9		ain't got nuttin t'do with *w*hat.
10	Bea:	*Write*- um doin' um, ͺthat- that thing.
11	Barb:	[What do y'*all*
12		got ta do with it.
13	Bea:	Because because um, *I* don't know what
14		we got to do with it. Buͺt she said-
15	Barb:	[W'll *she*
16		don't know what *she* tal*k*in' 'bout.
17	Bea:	But- but she- but we *di:d* have somp'm

18		to do because we was *ma:d* at *her.*
19		Because we didn't *like* her no more.
20		(0.6) And *that's* why, (0.6) Somebody
21		the one ⌐that use-
22	Barb:	⌊So, she got anything t'say she
23		come say it in front of my face. (1.0)
24		I better not *see Ke*rry today. (2.5) I
25		*ain*'t gonna say- I'm∼a∼say "Kerry *what*
26		*you say* about m⌐e." She gonna say
27	Bea:	⌊*((whiny))* (Nyang)
28	Barb:	"I ain't *say* nuttin'."
29	Bea:	(behind her face) she meant - sh'ent You
30		know you- you know what. She-she
31		chan⌐gin it.
32	Barb:	⌊If I *wro:*te somp'm then I *wrote*
33		it. =Then I got somp'm to do with
34		it. =W'then I *wrote* it.
35		(0.5)
36	Bea:	And *she* said, an'- an'- she u:m ah
37		whah. (I'm sorry oh.) I'm a walk you
38		home. *She* said that um,
39	Barb:	She get on my *ne*rves.
40	Bea:	She said that um, =
41	Barb:	=*Now*n I got somp'm ta write about her
42		*now*::.
43		(0.5)
44	Bea:	Oh yea. =She sai:d tha:t, (0.4) that
45		um, you wouldn't have nuttin ta do with
46		it, and every*thing*, and *plus*, (0.5)
47	Bea:	⌐um,
48	Barb:	⌊WELL IF I WROTE SOME 'EN *I* HAD SOMP'M
49		T'*DO* with it.
50	Bea:	An she said, *I* wanna see what I was
51		gettin' ready ta say, (2.0) °And um,
52	Barb:	She gonna de*ny* every *word.* =Now *watch.*
53		I c'n put more up there for her the:n.
54		(2.0)
55	Bea:	⌐*What,*
56	Barb:	⌊An' in magic marker °so there.
57		(0.6)
58	Bea:	Oh yea, oh yea. =*She* was, she- w's
59		*she* was in Rochele: house you know, and
60		she said that um, that- I heard her
61		say um, (0.4) um um uh uh "*Jul*ia said
62		y'all been talking behind my back." =I
63		said I'm a- I'm a say "H:oney, I'm gla:d.
64		that *you* know I'm *t*alkin' be*hind your*

65		*back.* Because *I-* because *I meant*
66		for you to know *any*way." An' she said,
67		I- said "I don't have to talk behind
68		your back. = I can talk in front of your
69		*face too.*" / / And she said-
70	Barb:	That's all I write. I didn't
71		write that. *I* wrote *that.*
72		(1.2)
73	Bea:	Over here. *I* write *this-* I cleared it
74		*off.* Because *Lan*da *wrote*
75		and I- *h ⌐and *I* made it *big*ger.
76	Barb:	└Mmm,
77		(0.2)
78	Bea:	So she said, ⌐That first-
79	Barb:	└And the other I did with
80		my finger on the cars ⌐and all that.
81	Bea:	└An'- so- *I* said,
82		an'- an' so we were playin *sch*ool you
83		know at Rochele's house? And *boy we*
84		*t*ore her *all-* we said, I got
85		uh y'know ⌐I was doin' some signs?
86	Barb:	└I better *not* go around an
87		catch Kerry.
88	Bea:	And Ro*chele* called her *bald* headed
89		right∼in∼fronta∼her face. She said "You
90		*bald* headed *thing.*" Because she was
91		messin' with Rochele. = I said, and so she
92		said, you know we were playin' around
93		with her? And she said "You *bald* headed
94		thing." = She said, "Rochele YOU DON'T
95		LIKE IT?" I said I said ⌐that's why-
96	Barb:	└Yeah she gonna
97		base in some little kid's ⌐face.
98	Bea:	└Yeah. And
99		she said, / /I said AND I SAID = I said I
100		said "What are ya doin' to her."
101	Barb:	I better not see Kerry to*day.* I'm a
102		say "Kerry *I* heard *y*ou was talkin'
103		'bout me."
104	Bea:	I a s⌐ay-
105	Barb:	└Then she gonna say "I ain't- *What*
106		*I* say about you." I say "Ain't none
107		yer *bus*iness what you said. = You come
108		say it in front a my *f*ace since what =
109		you been tell everybody *el*se." (0.4)
110		*((falsetto))* OO;, And I can put more
111		and I'm a put some- some °bad words in

```
112            to day.
113            (0.5)
114   Bea:     She said, and she was saying,
115             ⌈she said-
116             ⌊Now I got somp'm to write ⌈about.
117   Bea:                                 ⌊I said,
118   Barb:    I better not catch you t'day. = I'm a
119            tell her butt o:ff.
120            (0.4)
121   Barb:    An' if she // get bad at me:e: I'm a,
122            punch her in the eye.
123   Bea:     I said, I s- I said, said, Hey
124            Barbara I said, "Why don't you" um, I
125            s- I- I- I- and "Why don' you stop.
126            messing with her." And she said she
127            said "She called me baldheaded."
128             = I said,
129   Barb:    That's right.
130   Bea:     =⌈An' so-
131   Barb:     ⌊That's her name so call her name back.
132   Bea:     Guess what. Guess what. Uh- we- w-
133            an' we was up finger waving? = And I said,
134            I said, I said I said ((does motion))
135            like that. = I did.
136            hh An' ⌈just like that. = *h and I said =
137   Barb:          ⌊OO::,
138   Bea:     an' I an' I was doin' all those sig:ns in
139            her face and everything? (0.5) *h And
140            she said that um, (1.0) And then she-
141            an you- and she s- °She- roll her eye
142            like that. *h And she was leanin'
143            against- I- I said, I s'd I s'd Is'd I
144            said, "Hey girl don't lean against that
145            thing cuz it's weak enough." *h And
146            she said and she said *h she- she did
147            like that. = She say, "Tch!" ((rolling
148            eyes)) // like that. I s'd- I said "You
149            c'd roll your eyes all you want to.
150   Barb:    Yeah if somebody do that to her-
151            And if ⌈you know what?
152   Bea:            ⌊Cuz I'm tellin' you. (0.5)
153            Tellin' - I'm not askin' you." (0.4) An' I
154            ain't say no plea:se either.
155   Barb:    mm hmm.
156   Bea:     ((chews fingers))
157   Barb:    Don't do that. (1.5) W'll I'm tellin' ya
158            I better not catch Kerry today. Cuz if
```

159		I catch her I'm gonna give *her* a wor:d
160		from my *mouth*. (0.6) An' if she *j*ump in
161		my *f*ace I'm a punch her in her *fa*:ce.
162		(1.5) And she can talk behind my ba:ck
163		she better say somp'm in front of my
164		face.
165		(1.5)
166		*((Boy walks down the street.))*
167	Barb:	OO: there go the *Tack*. *h *hh *hh Eh
168		That's your na(h)me.
169		(1.5)
170		*((Barbara starts down the street.))*
171	Barb:	°h See y'all.
172	Bea:	*See* you.

TRANSCRIPTION

The stories discussed in this chapter draw on a collection of transcripts of over two hundred hours of conversation. Texts of actual instances of the phenomenon discussed are provided so that others might inspect the records which form the basis for my analysis.

Data are transcribed according to the system developed by Jefferson and described in Sacks, Schegloff, and Jefferson (1974: 731–733). The following are the features most relevant to the present analysis:

EXAMPLE
NUMBER

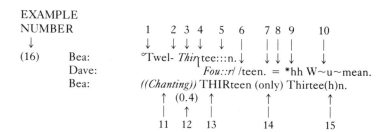

1. Low Volume: A degree sign indicates that talk it precedes is low in volume.
2. Cut-off: A dash marks a sudden cut-off of the current sound. Here, instead of bringing the word "twelve" to completion, Bea interrupts it in mid-course.
3. Italics: Italics indicate some form of emphasis, which may be signaled by changes in pitch and/or amplitude.
4. Overlap Bracket: A left bracket marks the point at which the current talk is overlapped by other talk. Thus Dave's "*Thir*teen" begins during the last syllable of Bea's "*Four*teen." Two speakers beginning to speak simultaneously are shown by a left bracket at the beginning of a line.
5. Lengthening: Colons indicate that the sound immediately preceding has been noticeably lengthened.
6. Overlap Slashes: Double slashes provide an alternative method of marking over-

lap. When they are used the overlapping talk is not indented to the point of overlap. Here Bea's last line begins just after the "*Four*" in Dave's "*Four*teen."

7.   Intonation: Punctuation symbols are used to mark intonation changes rather than as grammatical symbols:

- A period indicates a falling contour.
- A question mark indicates a rising contour.
- A comma indicates a falling-rising contour.

8.   Latching: The equal signs indicate "latching"; there is no interval between the end of a prior turn and the start of a next piece of talk.
9.   Inbreath: A series of *h*'s preceded by an asterisk marks an inbreath. Without the asterisk the *h*'s mark an outbreath.
10.   Rapid Speech: Tildes indicate that speech is slurred together because it is spoken rapidly.
11.   Comments: Double parentheses enclose material that is not part of the talk being transcribed, for example, a comment by the transcriber if the talk was spoken in some special way.
12.   Silence: Numbers in parentheses mark silences in seconds and tenths of seconds.
13.   Increased Volume: Capitals indicate increased volume.
14.   Problematic Hearing: Material in parentheses indicates a hearing that the transcriber was uncertain about.
15.   Breathiness, Laughter: An *h* in parentheses indicates plosive aspiration, which could result from events such as breathiness, laughter, or crying.

NOTES

1. Katriel (1985:480), discussing Israeli children's conflict, describes the role of "troublemaker" as a party who is said to "exaggerate in the direction of bad things."

2. See Sacks (1978:262) for a consideration of the motive power of preformulated talk.

3. Parsons (1966:386–478) describes how in the Oaxacan town of Mitla there is hesitancy in repeating stories to others acquainted with the target of the story because of the fear of initiating a dispute and hostility.

4. Rose (1987:176) discusses the performance features of gossip about another among black adults, arguing that in such talk "one could literally, for the moment, wear the persona and speech of another."

5. In addition, the alignments offended parties maintain with the offending party may also account for different types of responses. Julia is a close friend of Kerry's, while Barbara rarely plays with her or anyone on the older girls' street. Thus Barbara, in contrast to Julia, has little to lose by confronting Kerry.

6. Labov (1972:395–396) in describing structural complexity in narratives states that the ability of a narrator to move "back and forth from real to imaginary events" is more generally characteristic of adults than of children. In these sequences, however, girls move with little effort from past to future and possible events.

7. The intent and function of audience participation in public litigations of black adults are discussed in Rose (1987:220–221).

8. A reformulation of this definition appears in Labov (1982).

9. A similar concern is expressed by folklorists studying *memorates*. The investigator must attempt to make clear how authentically a memorate reflects original supernormal experience (Honko 1964: 11).

10. See Bateson (1947: 650).

SELECTED BIBLIOGRAPHY

ABRAHAMS, ROGER D. (1963). Some Jump Rope Rhymes from South Philadelphia. *Keystone Folklore Quarterly* 8: 3–5.

———. (1964). *Deep Down in the Jungle: Negro Narrative Folklore from the Streets of Philadelphia.* Hatboro: Pennsylvania Folklore Associates.

BATESON, GREGORY. (1947). Sex and Culture. *Annals New York Academy of Sciences* 47: 603–663.

BILMES, JACK. (1975). Misinformation in Verbal Accounts: Some Fundamental Considerations. *Man* 10: 60–71.

BRIGGS, CHARLES. (1985). Treasure Tales and Pedagogical Discourse in Mexicano New Mexico, *Journal of American Folklore* 98: 287—314.

———. (1986). *Learning How to Ask: A Sociolinguistic Appraisal of the Role of the Interview in Social Science Research.* Cambridge: Cambridge University Press.

BRUNER, EDWARD M. (1986). Ethnography as Narrative. In *The Anthropology of Experience.* Victor Turner and Edward M. Bruner, eds. Pp. 139–155. Urbana: University of Illinois Press.

DORSON, RICHARD M. (1967). *American Negro Folktales.* Greenwich, Conn.: Fawcett Publications.

GLUCKMAN, MAX. (1955). *The Judicial Process among the Barotse of Northern Rhodesia.* Glencoe: The Free Press.

———. (1963). Gossip and Scandal. *Current Anthropology* 4: 307–315.

GOFFMAN, ERVING. (1974). *Frame Analysis: An Essay on the Organization of Experience.* New York: Harper and Row.

GOODWIN, MARJORIE HARNESS AND CHARLES GOODWIN. (1990). *He-Said-She-Said.* Pp. 259–279, 299–305. Bloomington: Indiana University Press.

HONKO, LAURI. (1964). Memorates and the Study of Folk Beliefs. *Journal of the Folklore Institute* 1: 5–19.

JORDAN, BRIGITTE AND LUCY SUCHMAN. (1987). Interactional Troubles in Survey Interviews. Paper presented in the session Cognitive Aspects of Surveys, 1987 American Statistical Association Meetings, August 19, 1987, San Francisco.

KATRIEL, TAMAR. (1985). *Brogez:* Ritual and Strategy in Israeli Children's Conflicts. *Language in Society* 14: 467–490.

KOCHMAN, THOMAS. (1970). Toward an Ethnography of Black American Speech Behavior. In *Afro-American Anthropology.* Norman E. Whitten, Jr., and John F. Szwed, eds. Pp. 145–162. New York: Free Press.

LABOV, WILLIAM. (1970). *The Study of Nonstandard English.* Champaign, Ill.: National Council of Teachers.

———. (1972). *Language in the Inner City: Studies in the Black English Vernacular.* Philadelphia: University of Pennsylvania Press.

LAKOFF, GEORGE. (1968). *Counterparts, or the Problem of Reference in Transformational Grammar.* Bloomington: Indiana University, Linguistics Club.

MISHLER, ELLIOT G. (1986). *Research Interviewing: Context and Narrative.* Cambridge, Mass.: Harvard University Press.

MITCHELL-KERNAN, CLAUDIA. (1971). Language Behavior in a Black Urban Community.

Monographs of the Language Behavior Laboratory, No. 2, University of California, Berkeley.

———. (1972). Signifying and Marking: Two Afro-American Speech Acts. In *Directions in Sociolinguistics: The Ethnography of Communication*. John J. Gumperz and Dell Hymes, eds. Pp. 161–179. New York: Holt, Rinehart and Winston.

PARSONS, E. C. (1966). *Mitla, Town of the Souls*. Chicago: University of Chicago Press.

ROSE, DAN. (1987). *Black American Street Life: South Philadelphia, 1969–1971*. Philadelphia: University of Pennsylvania Press.

SACKS, HARVEY. (1963). Sociological Description. *Berkeley Journal of Sociology* 8: 1–16.

———. 1972 On the Analyzability of Stories by Children. In *Directions in Sociolinguistics: The Ethnography of Communication*. John J. Gumperz and Dell Hymes, eds. Pp. 325–345. New York: Holt, Rinehart and Winston.

———. (1978). Some Technical Considerations of a Dirty Joke. In *Studies in the Organization of Conversational Interaction*. Jim Schenkein, ed. Pp. 249–269. New York: Academic Press.

SACKS, HARVEY, EMANUEL A. SCHEGLOFF, AND GAIL JEFFERSON. (1974). A Simplest Systematics for the Organization of Turn-Taking for Conversation. *Language* 50: 696–735.

VOLOŠINOV, V. N. (1971). Reported Speech. In *Readings in Russian Poetics: Formalist and Structuralist Views*. Ladislav Matejka and Krystyna Pomorska, eds. Pp. 149–175. Cambridge, Mass.: MIT Press.

———. (1973). *Marxism and the Philosophy of Language*. Translated by Ladislav Matejka and I. R. Titunik. New York: Seminar Press. (First Published 1929 and 1930).

WERNER, OSWALD AND JOANN FENTON. (1973). Method and Theory in Ethnoscience or Ethnoepistemology. In *A Handbook of Method in Cultural Anthropology*. Raoul Naroll and Ronald Cohen, eds. Pp. 537–578. New York: Columbia University Press.

penelope brown

GENDER, POLITENESS, AND
CONFRONTATION IN TENEJAPA

This paper examines some interactional details of a court case that took place in the Mexican community of Tenejapa, a community of peasant Mayan Indians who speak a language called Tzeltal, and compares it with Tzeltal verbal interaction in other contexts. In particular, I want to contrast women's speaking style in amicable cooperative 'ordinary' Tzeltal conversation with their speech in angry confrontation in a Tzeltal court case, the *only* context in this society in which face-to-face angry confrontation is authorized for women.

The purpose of this study is to explore how relations between language and gender are context dependent, with respect to both the kind of discourse—in this case cooperative versus confrontational interaction—and the speech event and the particular norms governing talk within it. Yet, despite this context dependency, women's characteristic concerns, and the ways of speaking characteristic of women in this society that derive from those concerns, put their stamp on interactions with radically different interactional goals, so that gender is, in some senses, a 'master status' transcending contexts in this society.

Specifically, what I want to claim is that, in many ways, the interactional conduct of a Tzeltal court case, a formal arena for face-to-face confrontation with the aim of settling disputes between people, is the *inverse* of interactional conduct in ordinary conversation in Tenejapan society. That is, ordinary conversational structures and interactional norms are systematically violated in a public display of indignation and anger. Nevertheless, in this context, certain features pervasive in women's speech in ordinary amicable conversation—features used to convey positive affect, empathy, agreement, sympathetic understanding—are here carried over but are used to convey the *opposite:* negative affect, hostility, contradiction.

In short, even when women *aren't* being polite—emphatically the opposite—their characteristically female 'ways of putting things' indirectly, using irony and rhetorical questions for positive politeness, carry over but with inverted functions: to emphatically contradict or disagree.

In what follows I first give a brief indication of some current issues in language and gender research to which this study is oriented. Second, I describe conversational structures employed in ordinary Tzeltal conversation, as well as the norms governing Tzeltal interaction in general and women's normal public demeanor in particular. Third, I describe the organization of Tzeltal court cases and show how interaction in the courtroom flouts certain of these norms systematically. Finally, I draw some conclusions about (1) the nature of dispute settle-

From Discourse Processes: A Multicultural Journal. *Reprinted by permission of Ablex Publishing Corp.*

ment in Tenejapa, (2) how gender meanings can get transformed in different contexts, and (3) implications for language and gender research in other contexts and societies.

CURRENT THEMES IN LANGUAGE AND GENDER RESEARCH

Out of the past 15 years of cross-linguistic and cross-cultural research into aspects of the relationship between language and gender has gradually emerged the perspective into which I want to place the data discussed in this paper. This perspective, which has been promoted in my own work (Brown, 1979, 1980; Brown & Levinson, 1979, 1987) and more recently cogently argued for in, for example, McConnell-Ginet (1988), Philips, Steele, and Tanz (1987), and Ochs (1992), has several basic tenets:

1.   Although gender-based differences in language are, for most languages examined to date, fairly minimal in language structure, they are pervasive in language use, especially in clusters of linguistic features that differentiate male and female *communicative styles*.
2.   For the most part, gender is not marked directly, but gender indexing is *indirect*, via other connections between gender and habitual uses of language (speech acts, speech events, social activities, interactional goals, and strategies).
3.   Gender indexing is *context dependent* in very interesting, patterned, ways.

In this view, the study of language and gender is part of the more general study of relations between language and social meaning (Ochs, 1992). We have to think in terms of a complex web of social meanings being conveyed when individuals speak, gender being only one, and not necessarily always a relevant one, of these social meanings.

What is needed is a much better understanding of both gender, as a social attribute, and how social meanings like gender are expressed in speech. What kind of a thing is gender? Is it a master status, omni-relevant in all situations? How is it related to social roles, to activities and speech events? To what extent do gender norms constrain people's behavior even in situations in which gender should be irrelevant? How do different social meanings (for example, professional identity versus gender identity) interact with each other? How do these reflect speakers' perceptions of their social relationships?

The study reported here is oriented to these sorts of questions; it aims to illustrate with an example from my own work in southern Mexico what I think is a profitable approach to the problem of trying to understand the ways in which gender influences language use and is reflected in that use. To the extent that gender influences the social meanings that people express when they speak, these can be discovered by conversation-analytic techniques applied to interactions in different social contexts, when language is being used to achieve different purposes.

This paper takes up this banner in one particular domain, comparing gender influences on language usage in casual cooperative conversation with those in angry confrontation. The Tzeltal case exemplifies the approach originally promoted by

Garfinkel (1967): If you want to understand social norms, look at how they are breached and how the management of breaches reinstates the norms.[1]

ETHNOGRAPHIC BACKGROUND

Tenejapa is a peasant Mayan community in the Chiapas highlands of southern Mexico, about 20 miles from the town of San Cristóbal de la Casas. It is a corporate community of Tzeltal-speaking Indians, in a populous rural area where there are many other Indian communities of Tzeltal or Tzotzil speakers, each of which maintains a strong ethnic identity distinguishing it from the others and from the dominant Ladino (Mexican national) culture.

As a corporate community, Tenejapa has its own hierarchy of civil–religious officials who run the local political system with a large degree of autonomy, although it is subject to the Mexican laws and policies in some arenas (schooling and health, principally). In law, Tenejapa can settle its own disputes, except for very serious ones such as murder, which go to the Mexican court in San Cristóbal.

The community consists of dispersed hamlets, connected by a dense network of foot trails, and a ceremonial center, where local political and religious ceremonies are based and where people holding political or religious offices live during their tenure. Here there is a large church, the locus of the community's religious ceremonies, and a town hall (Cabildo), which is the locus of political activities; it is here that our court case takes place.

NORMS OF INTERACTION

My 1972–1973 fieldwork in Tenejapa focussed on gender differentiation in this community, in particular male–female styles of interaction (Brown 1979, 1980). In this work it became clear that, on many indices, women can be seen to be 'more polite' than men; men are more direct and straightforward in their speech. Thus, compared with men, women are more positively polite to intimates and familiars, expending more interactional effort in reassuring their interlocutors of their interest in, and appreciation of, their conversational contributions. They are also more negatively polite in public, where they are normally self-annihilating kinesically and operate under very stringent interactional constraints including strong inhibitions against public displays of emotion or public confrontation, which do not apply to nearly such an extent for men. Self-control and self-humbling are crucial aspects of a woman's public presentation of self; sanctions against behaving otherwise include ridicule by one's peers and potential physical punishment by fathers, elder brothers, or husbands.

Women's demeanor in public is highly constrained; eye contact tends to be avoided, and deference to or social distance from unfamiliars is indicated by using a very high-pitched register. Among familiars, 'positive politeness' imbues most interaction with elaborated expression of sympathy, approval, and interest. Rhetorical questions and ironies are a conventionalized mode of expression among women. They are used to stress shared understandings and values, emphatic empathy and agreement, as in these two examples taken from normal conversation in relaxed situations.[2]

1   A: . . . mak ma wan sc'ahubotik ta stamel ʔin c'i
                 . . . perhaps it's not possible that we get tired from bend-
                 ing over to pick (coffee, that has fallen to the ground)
                 then! (conveys sympathetic understanding: of course, it's
                 tiring!)
     B: mak bi yuʔuni ma sc'ahub.
                 Perhaps why don't (we) get tired. (conveys: We sure do!)
     A: yak mak.
                 Yes, perhaps. (We do!)
2   A: mak ban yaʔwil ʔaʔba
                 Perhaps where do we see each other?
                 (conveys: Nowhere, we never get a chance to see one
                 another.)
     B: huʔu
                 No (agrees with implicature: No, nowhere.)

Women use this form of expression notably more than men do; indeed, it seems
to be a highly conventionalized form of feminine positive politeness in this society (see Brown 1979, chap. 4, for more details).

CASUAL CONVERSATIONAL STYLE

Tzeltal conversation is archetypally two-party, with speaker and respondent roles
distinguished. Turn-taking rules apply quite rigidly; overlap is relatively rare and
covers relatively short segments of the utterance at speaker-transition points.
The floor is passed back and forth at regular short intervals, and interruptions
are relatively few. Even during the telling of a story or anecdote (where one
interlocutor has all the information and is trying to impart it to the other), the
respondent takes up each point with a response indicating interest, understanding, an appropriate emotional reaction, or simply the Tzeltal equivalent of 'yeah,
I hear you, go on.' These, essentially backchannel, comments occupy a full turn;
they normally do not overlap with the storyteller's running speech as they often
do in English conversations. Smiles, nods, or other nonverbal attempts to respond might accompany, but cannot supplant, a verbal response.

   These responses often take the form of repeating part of the prior speaker's
utterance, elaborated with appropriate prosodic indications of surprise, interest,
or agreement. These repetitions structure Tzeltal conversations into neat little
sequences of utterance, plus repeat-response, plus optional repeat of the repeat
or part of it), and so on, resulting in interchanges like the following, which illustrates this highly characteristic structure of Tzeltal conversation:

3   (from a conversation between an elderly woman (GM) and her visiting
           granddaughter (GD), who is explaining how it is that she has come vis-
           iting so late in the day)
           GD: haʔte haʔ ye z'in ʔa kaʔyix tal haʔal hoʔotike
                        But so it was, we-excl. got rained on (on the way here)

GM:	eh! la?wa?yix tal z'in
	Oh! you got (rained on) then
	[
GD:	la!
	(we) did!
GM:	la ha? in sab i
	That was this morning.
GD:	ha?
	It was.
GM:	ha?
	It was.
GD:	ha?
	It was.
GM:	ha?te hic suhtat nix tal ?a z'in
	But so thus you've just returned (from hot country) then.
GD:	suht nix z'in
	So (we) have just returned.
GM:	suht
	Returned.
GD:	suht
	Returned.

The conversational uses of such repeats as responses to an utterance have been reported for other languages and societies (see, for example, Tannen 1987, 1989, for English; Haverkate 1989, p. 402, for Spanish), but in Tzeltal these are conventionalized as the normal way to respond to an interlocutor's narrating or explaining something. Men in Tenejapa do this too, in casual speech, but their repeat cycles tend in general to be shorter and less affectively positively polite.

ARENAS FOR CONFLICT

Women in daily interaction tend to suppress conflict. It is veiled, even in private, and, between nonintimate women, angry confrontation rarely, if ever, occurs. Interaction is simply avoided, and gossip, mockery, and backbiting against the object of one's anger are expressed to sympathetic intimates.

Anger between women who are intimates (for example, members of one's own household, family, or neighbors) is normally expressed through controlled 'leakage', in which silence, nonresponsiveness, or terse replies (clipped pronunciation and abrupt timing) to proffered utterances can indicate restrained anger. There might also be kinesic distancing, avoidance of smiling, of eye contact, and of physical contact, which contrast with normal relaxed behavior to suggest anger. It is common to declare stiffly, if questioned, that one is not angry, to insist that nothing is wrong, and, if pressed, to launch into a tirade of self-abuse, saying, in effect, 'I'm a terrible person, a no-good, a bum'. In this context it is overwhelmingly obvious that the person is angry, but there are strong constraints on overtly admitting it to the object of one's anger.[3]

Men, in contrast, can and do express conflict overtly in relatively private contexts; both verbal and physical abuse from husband to wife are routine in many households. In public arenas, men are likely to express open conflict only if drunk.

Procedures for dispute settlement operate at various levels. They might be worked out through family mediation or taken up in front of a local hamlet arbitrator, in informal meetings with the two sides both presenting their points of view; the arbitrator (a schoolmaster or church leader, for example) has, however, no authority to impose a settlement.

The forum of last resort for irresolvable conflicts is the Tenejapan court; this is resisted by most, as here private quarrels (and their embarrassing or humiliating details) are exposed to public view. That is what happened in the case we're going to examine here.

A TENEJAPAN COURT CASE

FORMAT AND PROCEDURES

The format of a typical court case at this community level is a hearing in the Cabildo, presided over by the Tenejapan president or judge, either of whom can act as judge for the case. The 'plaintiff' (the person who originated the case with a complaint to the judge) and the 'defendant' (the accused party, who has been summoned to the court) appear, and each is given a chance to present his or her case.[4] This is done in a special named speech style, (*col k'op*, 'explaining speech'), which is a sequential presentation of argument (with features similar to those of narrative in casual conversation) laying out the source and details of the dispute from the speaker's point of view.[5] A number of Tenejapan officials who have an interest in the case, or who have nothing else to do, may be present as audience to the transaction, though they rarely participate. The judge presides, listens, asks questions, and eventually decides what ruling to make. This ruling is discussed, and may be modified, until all participants agree to it. Then it is typed up by the Ladino secretary in an official document (an *acta*), which is signed by all three; copies are retained by each participant and a copy goes into the court record.

This process is set in motion by a complaint, when the plaintiff comes to the president or the judge, or to one of the officials representing the plaintiff's local hamlet, and asks for the defendant to be summoned to court. The officials representing the defendant's hamlet go to his or her house and fetch the defendant to the town, where a hearing takes place in the Cabildo (or at the president's house). People who are afraid or ashamed to appear may get someone to appear for them—a representative who is deemed good at speaking in public. Friends of the court, family supporters, witnesses, and casual bystanders may all be present, may wander in and out, and may contribute to the discussion. Normally the defendant pays the fee exacted by the officials for the summons; in addition, fines or jail or a period of community service (for example, work on church repairs) might be imposed. In cases involving moral breaches, a lecture might be given to the wrongdoer by the judge. The procedure ends with the signing of the *acta* by all three parties.

The majority of issues tried in this forum are domestic quarrels, including adultery, physical violence such as wife-beating and drunken attacks, child support, divorce and property settlement. They can also involve land disputes and inheritance disagreements, debts, property damage or (rarely) theft, interactional hostilities (drunken insults, character assassination), and witchcraft.[6]

The procedure, then, is straightforward: When the opponent is not present in the courtroom (because he or she couldn't be found or is already in jail, for example), the plaintiff 'explains' his or her complaint in a long narrative detailing the cause and conduct of the dispute. The judge asks questions, then makes a ruling. The tone of the court cases we observed with no opponent present was generally earnest, calm, and self-righteous. When the opponent is present, however, as is normally the case, blatant interactional confrontation can occur between the two, in which the interaction violates, point by point, the interactional norms of cooperative discourse, resulting in a display of confrontation for rhetorical (and perhaps cathartic) ends.

THE CASE OF THE RUNAWAY DAUGHTER-IN-LAW

In the case we are considering here, a woman, the principal plaintiff, complains that her former daughter-in-law owes her a lot of money. The background of this complaint is as follows: The daughter-in-law married her son after a normal Tenejapan courtship, stayed with him in his parents' household for 5 months, then ran away and married another Tenejapan man without any divorce proceedings first. This breach of social relations, outrageous by Tenejapan standards, is not the subject of this case, however; in fact it only comes up obliquely in the 40 minutes of the proceedings. The complaint is that the daughter-in-law, while living with her first husband's family, received a number of gifts from her husband and his parents. These gifts were things normally (but not obligatorily) given to new brides and included a corn-grinding machine, a skirt, a red belt, a white belt, some meat, and some thread for weaving. The plaintiff has no (official) complaint against this girl for leaving her husband, but she claims that she should be paid for all these items that were given to the bride, in good faith, as a new daughter-in-law.

The defendant pleading here isn't the wife who remarried, but her *mother*. The daughter doesn't appear in court (she was too ashamed, due to her 'bad' behavior, it was said). The claims are against her natal family, represented here by her mother.

The case takes place in the Cabildo, around a large central table. The judge is seated at one side, the litigants take up standing positions at the end near the door. The Ladino secretary is typing business letters (unrelated to this case) at the far end of the room. Around the table on benches against the wall are seated about 10 Tenejapan officials and litigants from preceding cases, as well as a number of bystanders (plus the two ethnographers, filming and taping the event). The case begins when the judge addresses the plaintiff and asks her to explain her complaint (she has previously entered, greeted the judge, and stood waiting at the end of the table while another case was presented). The plaintiff presents her claims, and the defendant (the runaway wife's mother) vociferously argues against these claims. There is a lot of disagreement, simultaneous speech between the defendant and the plaintiff, and overt expression of hostility, anger, and contempt—quite extraordinary by Tenejapan standards. The interaction alternates between sections in which the judge poses questions and the plaintiff or the defendant replies, in an orderly fashion, and those in which they take off in mutually oriented antagonistic tirades while the judge quietly listens. Eventually the judge succeeds in getting them to agree that the defendant will pay the plaintiff 900 pesos for the gifts and that she will bring the money to court the following Sunday. This solution represents a compromise between the amount of money the plaintiff claimed (totalling some 1,200 pesos) and the amount the defendant concedes is due (somewhat less than 900p), as well as in the amount of time she is given to come up with the money. The local official is paid for his summons by the defendant, and the case ends (to be followed immediately by another one) when the two women leave the courtroom.

INTERACTION IN THE COURTROOM CONTEXT

Here I focus on specific contrasts between courtroom behavior and ordinary interaction.

Speech Event Demarcation

There are no clear boundaries to the event. Minimal greetings are given by the plaintiff, none by the defendant, and no farewells at all. And, although the case is started by the judge's saying to the plaintiff: "So I'll listen to your speech now ma'am", it is readily interrupted when he is called to attend to other business, and, although the two parties may carry on their presentation, the judge isn't listening.[7]

Participants

There are three main participants (plaintiff, defendant, and judge), with a large audience of about 10 officials and several litigants from other cases, including a number of men from the neighboring Indian community of Chamula. With this 'audience' (or, more strictly, 'copresent bystanders,' not necessarily attending) under other circumstances the behavior of Tenejapan women would be extremely circumspect. Members of the audience frequently engage in background conversation not addressed to the case at hand. Periodically the judge is drawn into this background conversation, especially when required to say ritual greetings or farewells to men who are entering or leaving the courtroom, but the litigants in our case ignore this entirely.[8]

Roles of speaker and addressee are fluid and rapidly switched, and the large degree of overlapping speech means that both the plaintiff and the defendant can be both speaker and addressee simultaneously. The judge's institutional role as adjudicator is operated with restraint; he does not heavy-handedly push the parties toward a resolution but allows them to work toward one themselves with minimal interference. And his role as listener is not rigidly upheld; although some of the time he does conscientiously display his attentiveness with hms, uhuhs, and the like, at several points he turns to other business. The audience takes no part in the argument or discussion of the case.

Although the judge is the monitor of the proceedings, except at the beginning when he invites the plaintiff to begin and asks her some questions, he rarely exercises his right to choose the next speaker. Generally, turn taking operates as a local management system, as in ordinary casual conversation.

Turn-Taking Structure

The most interesting features of the interaction are in the management of turn taking, which has two distinctive characteristics:

1. An overall dyadic structure is imposed on what is, in principle, a three-party interaction.
2. Periodically the normal turn-taking rules are suspended in interaction between the two women, and they speak simultaneously.

First, despite the fact that there are three main participants, the interaction overwhelmingly displays a dyadic structure, with two of the three participants addressing one another (in an A-B-A-B-A-B sequential structure). The third party frequently tries to gain the floor and participate in the dialogue but either fails entirely (is ignored by the two) or succeeds in gaining only one addressee, and the dyadic structure is retained with different members constituting the dyad. Thus, over the entire event, speech alternates among the judge-plaintiff dyad, the plaintiff-defendant dyad, and the judge-defendant dyad.

Speech in ordinary conversation also shows a marked tendency toward dyadic exchanges, but the clearly demarcated roles of speaker and respondent, with the respondent replying with encouraging repetitions of the speaker's utterances, is almost entirely absent in the courtroom.

The most surprising feature of this interaction, compared with speech in other contexts, is the simultaneous speech of the plaintiff and the defendant for extended periods. As a result of persistent attempts to gain the floor by the party not included in the dyad of the moment, there are frequent interruptions and a great deal of overlap, which in extreme instances consists of the plaintiff and the defendant speaking simultaneously *at* one another for as much as half a minute. Sometimes their utterances, though heavily overlapping, are responding to one another's remarks and challenges; at other times they are apparently totally independent tirades.

Thus, the basic dyadic structure of the interaction is continually being challenged by the party left out at any moment, but the successful challenge only succeeds in shifting the constitution of the dyad. Interactional orderliness is also maintained to some degree by the judge exercising his monitoring role; periodically he interjects questions to break up a dyadic interchange and redirect the topic. Frequently, however, his attempts fail.

4   Judge's attempts to monitor
     (D = defendant   P = plaintiff   J = Judge)
     (P is in the middle of her explanation to J about the background to her claims against D)

302   P: ha? ye z'i (. . .) waxakeb to k'al ?a kuc'tik te pox
So it was for 8 days we drank the booze together
[   ]   [   ]

303 → J: bweno
Ok,

304   J: ha? nax bal ?a z'i bi   =
That was how it was, eh?

305   (J)   = yu? me ya?-
because if you -
[   ]

306   D: ehhh cuhkilal =
(to P)   Eh, the belt -

307   (D)   peru bi yu?un ha? nax ya?toy ?a?ba
but why is it you just pride yourself
= [   ]

308   P: ha? (.) waxakeb k'al ?a kuc' ho?tik ?a poxe (.)
(to D)   It is so. For 8 days we drank the booze that time,

309   (P)   (ba kuzi) k'amal ba ya slekot z'in te =
?   where it was made good then, at
[[   ]

        J: ((laughs))

311   D (to P)   ehhh:

312   (P):   = pask'ue
Easter
[   ]

313 → J: yu? nax z'i ha? nax bal z'i ya stikun te -
Just because, so is it just that he sent -
[   ]

314   D: mac'a lah: (.)
Who, was it said

315   (D)   mac'a xkucoh ?ocel (teklum) (.)
who had carried (it) entering town?

316   (D)   tatik ya- ?a scelbet ?a?ba mac'a ?a skucoh (. . .)
the man, he ?-ed for you, the one who had carried
[ ]   [   ]

317   P: hoo
Huh.

318   P: mak ha? z'i kerem ku?un
Perhaps it was my boy, eh

319   (D):   = pepsi c'e =
the Pepsis, eh?!
[ ]

320   J: hoo
Huh.

321   P: = ha? bal z'i kerem ku?uni =
(to D)   Was it my own boy then?

322 → J: = ya   na   wan z'i stolik   ?in te   pox c'e
They perhaps paid for this booze then, eh?!
[   ]

323	D (to P);	xk'otok (cikin) bi mak
		His (ear?) returned perhaps, eh?
324	P (to J);	hai?
		What?
325	J:	ya wan ʔa (st- kurik na)
		Perhaps he (?)
		[ ]
326	P:	ma niwan sʔos stikun bel ʔa huc stukel
		Perhaps he didn't send away (for it)
327	(P)	yaʔwaʔy z'in pox yan z'in te haʔ nax kalat . . . .
		you see then, the booze, or it's just as I tell you,
		[ ]
328	J:	hoo
		Yeah

(P continues her explanation to J)

This refusal to yield the floor is extremely marked behavior by two women to a male official; he, however, treats the interchanges as a normal and expected part of the proceedings, not as an extraordinary breakdown.

The simultaneous speech of the women and their refusal to yield the floor are important vehicles for their expression of antagonism. The mood of dynamic confrontation that permeates this interaction is also carried more explicitly by their aggressive kinetics, direct eye contact, and aggressive gestures that suggest contempt or disgust. Occasionally there are overt insults and abusive words, but prosodic indication of anger and emphasis is rampant throughout.

In short, interactional antagonism is carried to a large extent in breakdowns and manipulations of the turn-taking rules: in interruptions, overlaps, and speech that is simultaneous and nonresponding. In contrast, the plaintiff's and defendant's interchanges with the judge are much more orderly and slower, with fewer overlaps and interruptions. Both the plaintiff and the defendant occasionally use the Tzeltal 'respect voice' (very high pitch) to the judge, though never to each other.

A final realm for the display of antagonism is in the very noticeable absence of preference for agreement; indeed, in direct contradictions of one another's claims, especially via an exploitation of women's typical positive politeness agreement strategy—rhetorical questions and ironies—which are here done sarcastically, as challenges. Let's look at some of these in detail.

5		Irony and rhetorical questions as confrontation
		(P has been listing her claims; J has just said 'wait a minute' and be-
		gun to write them down, one by one).
231	J:	te: um =
		the, um
232	P:	= hm
		umhm
233		(1.5)

234	J:	zekel z'i
		(for the) skirt, then
235	P:	hm (.) ox-cehp z'in zekele (1.5) ca?cehp cuhkilal
		Hm, three hundred then for the skirt, two hundred for
		the belt.
236 →	D:	bi yu?un ma ha?uk z'in mak yu? ma ho?winikuk (sti) =
		Why wasn't it then, perhaps it wasn't one hundred or so
		(ironic: conveys: it *was* only worth 100 pesos)
237	(D)	= mak bit'il ta? ya stoytik yu? mak ha? te sle bi xan ? ae
		how is it that they overstate (the price of the belt)
		because perhaps it's that she (P) is looking for
		something else
238		(1)
239	(D)	(. . . . .) hobe (. . . .) =
		[ ]
240	P:	ya stak xa?leben (.)
		You can look for (it - the belt) for me,
241	(P)	ya stak xa?leben shol teme hice
		you can look for a replacement for it if that's the way it is
		(i.e., if you think that was a cheap belt, get a better one!)
		[ ]
242 →	D:	= ha? yu? wan ha? z'i baz'il szozil z'i mak ma
		ha? =
		It's that, perhaps it's that it's real wool then per-
		haps! (Conveys: It *wasn't* of real wool; i.e., it
		was cheap!)
243	(D)	= (tay z'in men)
		(perhaps it's not then)
		[ ]
244 →	P:	mancuk ?a z'in mak yu? ma toyoluk k'uxel
		z'i =
		So what about that then, perhaps
		it's not
		that it was expensive then
		(conveys: It *was* expensive!)
245 →	D:	= toyol nanix stukel ?a z'i bi mak
		Really expensive, (it is) itself then, perhaps, eh?
		(conveys sarcasm: It was *really* cheap!)

The effectiveness of this ironic phrasing of agreement, sarcastic agreement, to convey disagreement relies on the conventional use of irony to agree, and the disagreement is thereby made more poignant, more dramatic, taking place as it does against the background of feminine positive politeness. By the same token, the occasional sarcastic use of normally respectful address forms underlines the women's hostile intent.

CONCLUSION

This Tzeltal court case is a paradigm example of verbal interaction in one social context (a court case) being played out in opposition to the norms for verbal interaction in another social context (everyday public interaction), in order (partially) to reinforce those first-context norms (appropriate gender behavior) and, as I now argue, where face is threatened, in order to restore face. For the case under discussion is indeed partly about money but largely about face, and personal reputation. In the buildup to this confrontation, appropriate female role behavior and affinal-behaviour have been grossly transgressed: Both parties have been publicly shamed. The conduct of the court case is, to a large extent, oriented toward reinstating them in the community.

Two distinct things are at issue in this court case:

1.   A dispute about financial outlays, requiring a monetary settlement
2.   Face, as implicated in female roles, especially in the female in-law relationships

In aid of 1 is the content of the argument in court, which is overtly about the rights and wrongs of financial outlays: whether they occurred, whether they legitimately were part of the marriage ceremonies or part of subsequent in-law relationship obligations, and, therefore, whether they should be reimbursed due to the breakdown of the in-law relationship. In aid of 2 is the whole style of the courtroom proceedings: the plaintiff's portrayal of innocent outrage, indicating a generalized message to the effect that 'this person has so rent the social fabric that I'm justified in breaking the norms of propriety governing female behavior' (specifically, nonconfrontation). By successfully displaying her outrage, she (1) reestablishes her face, (2) influences the financial outcome of the case, and (3) gets cathartic release from long-term pent-up anger. The defendant, by responding with a display of innocent outrage, casts doubt on the authenticity of the plaintiff's outrage and gains certain concessions in the financial outcome.

In Tenejapa, then, despite the strong constraints against public displays of anger, there is an institutionalized context (and mode) for confrontation: a dramatized outrage played against the backdrop of appropriate norms for female behavior. The very excessiveness of the hostility expressed suggests that, in Tenejapa, litigation involves a form of *drama* in which the litigants are given scope to dramatize their antagonism, to display their anger and outrage in direct face-to-face confrontation, in ways almost unheard of in other contexts. The forum of the courtroom provides a frame for this display that makes it interactionally manageable; such open display of anger outside the courtroom would be, for women, unthinkably dangerous, provoking accusations of witchcraft. The protagonists here are breaking the norms (in a controlled manner), in order to affirm the norms of appropriate female behavior.

I do not mean to suggest that all women in Tenejapan court cases behave in this confrontational manner, nor that men never do, but only that in court such behavior is not only sanctioned but actually necessary to reestablish one's besmirched reputation.

The courtroom solution results in a compromise, negotiated between the two protagonists, that reinstates both in the community with some face left. Gossip-ers can now have a field day with the details of the dispute; nonetheless, by going through the court procedure the plaintiff reestablishes herself as 'not exploited and shamed,' and the defendant reestablishes herself as having paid for her daughter's flouting of social norms.

But here we find the paradox at the heart of Tzeltal litigation. If the display and revelation in the courtroom interaction accomplishes the working out of anger and the reinstatement of public 'face', at the same time it works against one of the most cherished Tenejapan values: self-protection through emphatic insistence on privacy. Privacy is an overwhelming concern in Tenejapan social life; in this small, gossip-ridden community people are extremely sensitive to what others know about them, as well as to what they can learn, and infer, about others from their behavior. Hiding the details of one's personal effects and social relations from prying eyes is a dominant concern in interpersonal conduct.[9] In this context it is astonishing that cases are ever brought to court at all, and indeed, public exposure of one's private affairs in court is much feared. Litigation is a form of mutual punishment, at least potentially, through which the air is cleared. Face is saved by face being thrown to the winds.

That in a small-scale, face-to-face, nonhierarchical peasant society where privacy is a dominant concern, disputes are settled in a confrontational display is perhaps not too surprising. And that they are likely not to remain settled is perhaps an obvious consequence of their agonistic display.

What can we conclude from all this about gender and language in Tenejapa? The norms of gender-appropriate behaviour are clear: Politeness, restraint, and circumspection are enjoined. Nonetheless, in one kind of social context, litigation, whether at the local level or in the official Tenejapa court, where a woman's reputation is on the line, inverted behavior occurs: Women are given license to excel in public demonstrations of anger and outrage. Indeed, such a display seems part of the very process of, and essential to, reestablishing one's stained reputation, one's public face.[10]

This provides clear evidence, for Tenejapan society, that gender is not a unified one-dimensional feature of one's social identity; one's gender has different applicability (and different effects) in different kinds of situations. We do find (in Tenejapan society, at any rate) gender-characteristic patterns of speaking across contexts—even contexts as contrastive as those we've been considering—that indicate that gender-specific 'ways of putting things' can operate across contexts, and this is perhaps especially so when one's face *qua* woman (or man) is implicated in the different contexts.

In a recent paper, Elinor Ochs (1992) puts forward an analysis of how gender is indexed that can help us understand what is happening in Tenejapa. Ochs argues that the relation of gender is not a straightforward mapping of linguistic form onto the social meaning of gender but is constituted and mediated at least partly by the relation of language to what she calls *stances:* general interactional poses having to do with how one presents oneself to others; for example, hesitation/aggression, or coarseness/delicacy, or accommodation versus nonaccommodation to the addressee. I think that the ironies and rhetorical questions that proliferate in Tenejapan women's speech are manifesting a characteristic female stance, emphasizing in-group solidarity expressed through ironic agreement and displays of shared values; women's joking and humor in Tenejapa also often take the form of irony. In amicable interactions, women's positively polite ironic phraseology assumes and stresses shared values and norms, cooperation, mutual sympathy and understanding. In the courtroom confrontation this stance is evoked, but from a distance, ironically, in the sarcastic politeness of hostile pseudo-agreement.

As Ochs (1992) puts it,

> the relation between language and gender is mediated and constituted through a web of socially organized pragmatic meanings. Knowledge of how language relates to gender is not a catalogue of correlations between particular linguistic forms and sex of speakers, referents, addressees and the like. Rather, such knowledge entails tacit understanding of 1) how particular linguistic forms can be used to perform particular pragmatic work (such as conveying stance and social action) and 2) norms, preferences and expectations regarding the distribution of this work vis à vis particular social identities of speakers, referents, addressees.

She goes on to argue that we need to understand, then, (1) how particular linguistic forms can be used to perform particular pragmatic work, and (2) what are the norms, expectations, and preferences about the distribution of this work across gender categories. Continuity in women's verbal practices across diverse situations is due to habitual gender differences in things like stance and social action (for example, confirmation checks), which carry over from situation to situation.

The Tenejapan case is a beautiful example of this, for it is the exception that proves the rule: Even when women are *not* being polite, characteristic female strategies of indirectness and politeness are manifested in their speech.

This suggests that, for a deeper understanding of language and gender, we need to take very detailed looks at gender behavior in different situations. One situation casts light on others, especially if one (like confrontation) is defined in opposition to the other (ordinary courteous interaction). By looking at how gender meanings get transformed in contexts of confrontation, we can explore the complex situational variability in what speakers, male or female, are aiming at when they speak. For example, is it cooperation, harmony, the 'we' code that is being evoked, or is the interaction one of conflict or self-defense, in the idiom of 'I versus you'?

Most significantly, the Tenejapa case suggests how we might try to make sense of the widespread finding in language and gender research that women interact more cooperatively than men do, at least on the surface; that a patina of agreement is put over women's interactions in many contexts and in different societies. With the Tenejapan women, this cooperative ethos spills over into their noncooperative discourse. The result is sarcastic cooperation and sarcastic indirectness: exploiting mutual knowledge and shared agreement strategies to emphasize disagreement. In Tenejapa (and in Japan, it has been suggested)[11] this particular stance is a woman's forte, and it makes the criticism/disagreement all the more painful, as the superficial amicability in which it is couched adds an additional barbed element to the contrast.

One would hope that close attention to these situation-specific kinds of speech events will improve our understanding of how and when gender is implicated in interaction and, when it is, just how it affects women's and men's ways of speaking. Only then will we be in a position to address the more general comparative sorts of questions posed by Ochs (1992): What kinds of meanings (social, pragmatic) are women and men likely to index in their speech in different kinds of societies, and how do such gender meanings relate to the positions and the images of men and women in society?

NOTES

In previous incarnations, this paper was given at the Australian Anthropological Society meetings in August, 1981, and at seminars at the Australian National University; at Sussex University, England, in 1983; at the University of Colorado, Boulder, and at the Max Planck Institute for Psycholinguistics in Nijmegen, Holland, in 1988. I am grateful for the many comments that improved my thinking about the issues herein addressed. The fieldwork on which this paper is based was conducted by Stephen Levinson and me in July–August 1980, when four court cases in addition to the one analysed here were taped-recorded and filmed with Super-8 equipment, in a project funded by the Department of Anthropology, Research School of Pacific Studies, The Australian National University.

1. This study is pertinent not only as an exploration of language and gender, the emphasis in the paper presented here, but also as a contribution to the literature on the organization of courtroom speech, as contrasted with speech in other contexts (see, for example, Atkinson & Drew, 1979; Lakoff, 1989), and to the recently burgeoning interest in how face-to-face confrontation is managed (for example, Goodwin & Goodwin, 1987; Haviland, 1989).

2. The Tzeltal data cited here come from films and/or tape recordings of natural interactions in Tenejapa. Transcription conventions: Square brackets [] indicate overlapping speech; = indicates speech tied to that on the next line with no pause; dots in parentheses (. . .) indicate material omitted; a single dot in parentheses (.) indicates a micropause; numbers in parentheses, for example (1.5), indicate approximate pauses in seconds; words in parentheses () indicate sections where transcription is uncertain; an arrow→ draws attention to a line of transcript under discussion. The Tzeltal transcription is roughly phonemic: *c* represents the sound spelled in English *ch*, *x* corresponds to English *sh*, *z* represents English *ts*, ? indicates a glottal stop, and ' indicates that the preceding consonant is glottalized. Speakers' initials are in parentheses when the line following is a continuation of a turn begun on a prior line. Question mark? in translation indicates translation uncertain.

3. There are, of course, personality differences among individuals. I am describing a general cultural constraint on the mode of expression of anger, which individuals may differentially bow to.

4. I use the labels *plaintiff* and *defendant* in these restricted senses here, although these are very unsatisfactory terms insofar as they carry all the connotations of western legal practice, which are inapplicable in the Tenejapan case. The summons-initiator, who lodges the original complaint, and the summons-recipient, who is the object of the complaint, might well switch complainer–complainee roles in the course of the proceedings: Plaintiff might become the accused and defendent the accuser, and indeed, the original plaintiff might be the one who is hauled off to jail.

5. Despite this named style, Tzeltal speakers themselves do not categorize speech in the courtroom as different in kind from that taking place in other contexts. Conversation in Tzeltal is a form of *?ac k'op*, 'new speech', covering all the secular and modern genres of speech (joking, conversing, word play, speechmaking), as distinct from the special

genres of *poko k'op*, 'ancient speech', which cover the sacred and ritual uses of words and music. The speech in a court case is a kind of *ʔac k'op*, with structural features similar in most respects to those of casual conversation (*ʔayanel*); it is not a specialized genre (see Stross, 1974), and 'explaining speech' in other contexts is also called *col k'op*.

6. Serious crimes under Ladino law, especially murder, are not tried in the Tenejapan court but are sent to a Ladino court in San Cristóbal. Major crimes (murder, by violence or witchcraft, and major theft) often do not come to court at all. The culprit flees and lies low for awhile, possibly for years; then he may return and all may be, if not forgotten, ignored.

7. It should be noted that Tenejapan cases differ in this respect from the case reported by Nash (1970) for the nearby Tzeltal community of Amatenango, which was much more formally structured and bounded. See also Collier's (1973) description of Tzotzil courts in Zinacantan.

8. They also completely ignore the camera, two tape recorders, and the two foreign ethnographers in the room. At no point do their eyes meet the camera, and they appear oblivious to it. (This was not the case during our filming of casual interaction.)

9. This is even more true in the neighboring community of Zinacantan (Haviland & Haviland 1983). There women are apparently much more circumspect about entering into court cases at all (Devereaux 1988).

10. This is particularly clear in cases where the charge is an assault on a girl's sexual reputation. In one hearing I observed at the hamlet level, a girl who had been publicly accused by a woman of 'wanting to marry the woman's son', produced an hour-long tirade violently protesting her innocence, outrage, and humiliation at the unjust slander. Her reputation as a 'good' girl was thereby publicly reinstated, a matter of some importance in a society where the sullying of an unmarried girl's reputation, whether justified or not, can provoke beatings from her father and/or brother.

11. The connection between Japanese women and ironic politeness as rudeness was suggested to me by a Japanese student at one of the seminars in which this material was presented. In Brown (1979) I illustrated Tenejapan women's ironic stance in much more detail and made the suggestion that an ironic stance is perhaps especially the ploy of the downtrodden or underprivileged.

SELECTED BIBLIOGRAPHY

ATKINSON, J. MAXWELL, & DREW, PAUL. (1979). *Order in court: The organisation of verbal interaction in judicial settings.* London: Macmillan.

BROWN, PENELOPE. (1979). *Language, interaction and sex roles in a Mayan community: A study of politeness and the position of women.* Unpublished doctoral dissertation, University of California, Berkeley.

————. (1980). How and why are women more polite: Some evidence from a Mayan community. In Sally McConnell-Ginet, Ruth Borker, & Nelly Furman (Eds.), *Women and language in literature and society* (pp. 111–149). New York: Praeger.

BROWN, PENELOPE, & LEVINSON, STEPHEN C. (1979). Social structure, groups, and interaction. In Klaus Scherer & Howard Giles (Eds.), *Social markers in speech* (pp. 291–341). Cambridge: Cambridge University Press.

————. (1987). *Politeness: some universals in language usage.* Cambridge: Cambridge University Press.

COLLIER, JANE F. (1973). *Law and social change in Zinacantan.* Stanford, CA: Stanford University Press.

DEVEREAUX, LESLIE. (1988). Gender difference in Zinacantan. In Marilyn Strathern

(Ed.), *Dealing with inequality: Analysing gender relations in Melanesia and beyond* (pp. 89–111). Cambridge: Cambridge University Press.

GARFINKEL, HAROLD. (1967). *Studies in ethnomethodology.* Englewood Cliffs, NJ: Prentice-Hall.

GOODWIN, MARJORIE HARNESS, & GOODWIN, CHARLES. (1987). Children's arguing. In Susan Phillips, Susan Steele, & Christine Tanz (Eds.), *Language, gender and sex in comparative perspective* (pp. 200–248). Cambridge: Cambridge University Press.

HAVERKATE, HENK. (1988). Towards a typology of politeness strategy in communicative interaction. *Multilingua, 7* (4), 385–409.

HAVILAND, JOHN B. (1989). Sure, sure: Evidence and affect. In Elinor Ochs & Bambi Schieffelin (Eds.), *Discourse and affect,* Special issue of *Text, 9* (1), 27–68.

HAVILAND, LESLIE K., & HAVILAND, JOHN B. (1983). Privacy in a Mexican village. In S. I. Benn & G. F. Gauss (Eds.), *Public and private in social life* (341–361). London: Croom Helm.

LAKOFF, ROBIN TOLMACH. (1975). *Language and woman's place.* New York: Harper & Row.

———. (1989). The limits of politeness: Therapeutic and courtroom discourse. In Sachiko Ide (Ed.), *Linguistic politeness II, Multilingua, 8,* 2–3.

McCONNELL-GINET, SALLY. (1988). Language and gender. In Frederick J. Newmeyer (Ed.), *Cambridge Survey of Linguistics:* Vol. 4, 75–99. Cambridge: Cambridge University Press.

MILLER, BARBARA D., Ed. *Sex and gender hierarchies.* Cambridge: Cambridge University Press.

NASH, JUNE. (1970). Rhetoric of a Maya Indian court. *Estudios de Cultura Maya: Vol. VIII.*

OCHS, ELINOR. (1992). Indexing gender. In Barbara Miller (Ed.), *Gender hierarchies.*

PHILIPS, SUSAN U., STEELE, SUSAN, & TANZ, CHRISTINE. (1987). *Language, gender and sex in comparative perspective.* Cambridge: Cambridge University Press.

STRECKER, IVO. (1988). *The social practice of symbolization: An anthropological analysis.* London: Athlone.

STROSS, BRIAN. (1974). Speaking of speaking: Tenejapan Tzeltal metalinguistics. In Richard Bauman & Joel Sherzer (Eds.), *Exploration in the ethnography of speaking* (pp. 213–239). Cambridge: Cambridge University Press.

TANNEN, DEBORAH. (1987). Repetition in conversation: Toward a poetics of talk. *Language, 63*(3), 574–605.

———. (1989). *Talking voices: Repetition, dialogue, and imagery in conversational discourse.* Cambridge: University Press.

mykol c. hamilton, barbara hunter, and shannon stuart-smith

JURY INSTRUCTIONS WORDED IN THE MASCULINE GENERIC

Can a Woman Claim Self-Defense When "He" Is Threatened?

Masculine generic terms, or the use of such words as "man" and "he" to refer to both sexes, have come under fire for their inherent male bias. Psychologists, linguists, and sociologists have gathered empirical evidence indicting masculine generics; lawyers, editors, and others have put forward cogent arguments against the use of masculine generics in their respective fields. The predominant theme has been that masculine generics exclude women, promoting an androcentric point of view, ignoring women individually and collectively.

The empirical evidence for cognitive exclusion of women is strong. Masculine generics lead to male-biased mental imagery in both the communicator (Hamilton, 1988a) and the audience (Hamilton & Henley, 1982; Martyna, 1978, Experiments 1 & 2). People who are asked to create or select drawings to illustrate titles or stories written in the masculine generic (e.g., "Urban Man") tend to produce exclusively male drawings (Harrison & Passero, 1975; Schneider & Hacker, 1973). Several studies have found that subjects are likely to believe a woman does not "fit" in a sentence worded in the masculine generic (Martyna, 1978, Experiments 3 & 4; MacKay & Fulkerson, 1979; Silveira, 1980).

The complaints go even deeper than cognitive exclusion, and research has also demonstrated behavioral implications. For example, job advertisements worded in the masculine generic have a negative effect on women's job interest (Bem & Bem, 1973; Stericker, 1981) and a study by Henley, Gruber, and Lerner (1984) indicates that alternatives to the masculine generic may positively affect the self-esteem of young girls. Hamilton (1988b) found that use of another male-biased term ("homosexual") in media reports leads some people to believe that lesbian sexual behaviors are as likely to put one at risk for contracting AIDS as are heterosexual or gay male sexual behaviors. Another study (Hamilton, 1989) showed that a proposed (and now adopted) nonsexist version of Maine's constitution affected young women's beliefs, attitudes, and self-assessments positively, when compared with the original male-biased version.

A chief complaint of legal scholars from the United States, Great Britain, Australia, and Canada has been that statutes worded in the masculine generic are subject to extremely inconsistent interpretation (Cox & Ray, 1986; Conveyancer's Notebook, 1985). For example, despite the fact that sections (rules) guiding interpretation state that words such as "man" and "he" should always be seen as including women as well as men, statutes written in the masculine generic have been used to exclude women from male-dominated professions. For example, in an 1875 case, Lavinia Goodell was denied admission to the bar because the statute regulating bar admission referred to attorneys as "he." Her petition to the court asserted that the statute should be interpreted in accordance with the earlier section stating that "every word importing the masculine gender only may extend and be applied to females as well as to males" (cited in Cox & Ray, 1986, p. 23). The court denied her petition, asserting that "the language of the statute, of itself, confessedly applied to males only" (p. 23). Several writers (Baron, 1986; Conveyancer's Notebook, 1985; Kanowitz, 1973; Ritchie, 1975; Scott, 1985) have noted that the selective application of rules governing linguistic interpretation is still quite common. As Scott (1985, p. 164) states: "Where a statute imposed duties or penalties on persons, where the masculine form was used it was asserted that women were included. . . . Yet where a statute imposed privileges or benefits upon persons, the opposite was the case: courts held that women were not intended to be included within the terms of the legislation. . . . To deprive women of rights, privileges, or benefits, the judiciary manipulated the law." Selective interpretation has had, then, concrete negative effects on women's lives.

Recently the possible impact of masculine generics in another legal context has been spotlighted. Attorney Elizabeth Schneider successfully argued to the Supreme Court of the state of Washington (*Washington, State of, v. Yvonne Wanrow*, 1977) that the jury in a 1973 murder case may have been unable to consider adequately the female defendant's plea of self-defense, due in part to the masculine generic wording of the judge's instructions concerning the self-defense decision. The jury was instructed, for example, to consider whether "he [the person who is claiming self-defense] has a right to stand his ground," and Schneider claimed that such wording may have prevented the jury from putting themselves in defendant Yvonne Wanrow's shoes, assessing risk of death or bodily harm from *her* personal point of view.

Schneider's claim, while intuitively plausible, could only be speculative. The present study is a direct laboratory test of the hypothesis that a decision about the reasonableness of a woman's self-defense claim is affected by the pronouns used in jury instructions. We tested the hypothesis by giving college students the facts of the Wanrow case in writing, then asking them to read the original (masculine pronouns) or modified (non-male-biased pronouns) jury instructions concerning the issue of self-defense, and finally soliciting their opinions about whether Ms. Wanrow had acted in self-defense, what crime she had committed, and what her punishment should be.[1]

METHOD

SUBJECTS

Seventy-two introductory psychology students from the University of Kentucky participated in the experiment for course credit; 37 were males, 33 were females, and 2 subjects did not indicate their sex. Ages ranged from 17 to 27 years of age, with a mean age of 19.35. Subjects were approximately evenly distributed by sex across the three conditions.

PROCEDURE

Subjects were told they were participating in a study on jury decision making and that they were to imagine that they were members of an actual jury while completing the experimental tasks. They were given a brief written description of the facts of the Wanrow case, which they read silently as the female experimenter read it aloud to them, then they spent four minutes studying the description individually. The case involved a confrontation between Ms. Wanrow and Mr. Wesler, a man she suspected had tried to molest her young son. Under a rather ambiguous set of circumstances,[2] she ultimately shot Mr. Wesler at close range, killing him. The defense claimed Wanrow shot Wesler in self-defense. There is considerable question as to whether this claim was warranted, and the written description given to subjects reflected the ambiguity of the facts. For example, subjects were told that there were other people nearby when the shooting took place, implying that Ms. Wanrow should perhaps have solicited aid rather than shooting Wesler. On the other hand, subjects learned that Ms. Wanrow was rather small, had a broken leg, and was using a crutch, all of which could have increased her fear of bodily harm from a threatening individual.

After the four minutes, the descriptions were collected and subjects were given a written transcript of the actual jury instructions defining self-defense. They were told to read the instructions carefully to themselves twice. One third of the subjects received jury instructions worded in the original masculine generic, another third read instructions using "he or she" constructions in place of the "he" constructions, and the last third read instructions containing "she" constructions throughout. The following is a transcript of the jury instructions in their original form (boldface ours; not presented in boldface to subjects):

> when there is no reasonable ground for the person attacked to believe that **his** person is in imminent danger of death or great bodily harm, and it appears to **him** that only an ordinary battery is intended and is all that **he** has reasonable grounds to fear from **his** assailant, **he** has a right to stand **his** ground and repel such an assault. But **he** has *no right* to repel a threatened assault by the use of bare hands or a deadly weapon, unless **he** believes, and has reasonable grounds to believe, that **he** is in imminent danger of death or great bodily harm.

Subjects were next asked to respond to opinion questions concerning the case. The first question was "Do you think the defendant acted in self-defense?" Subjects marked "yes" or "no." We hypothesized that subjects who read the original "he" version would be less likely to believe Wanrow had acted in self-defense than subjects in the other two groups. The use of two different non-male-biased versions was exploratory.

The second question concerned the severity of the crime: "If the jury decided that the defendant did not act in self-defense, what crime do you think she should be convicted of?" Subjects had four choices, presented in decreasing order of severity—first degree murder, second degree murder, manslaughter, or negligent manslaughter. Definitions were given for each of these crimes. Subjects were then asked: "If the defendant is found guilty, what punishment do you think the judge should decide on?" Subjects were to check one of seven recommendations for punishment, ranging from the most severe punishment—the death penalty—to the least severe punishment—less than a year of incarceration. On the last page of the questionnaire, subjects were asked to indicate their age, sex, and any guesses they might have as to the hypotheses of the experiment.

HYPOTHESES

The central hypothesis was that subjects in the "he" condition, due to their relative inability to take the defendant's point of view, would be less likely to believe Wanrow had acted in self-defense than would subjects in either of the other two conditions. We also hypothesized that those in the "he" condition would attribute a worse crime to Wanrow (when asked to assume her guilt) than would subjects in the other two conditions, and would recommend harsher punishment. Our reasoning here was that since subjects in the nonsexist language conditions would more likely believe Wanrow had acted in self-defense (first hypothesis), they would have difficulty assuming she was guilty, and would therefore be more lenient in ascribing a crime and recommending punishment.

We also hypothesized some sex-related differences. Calhoun, Selby, & Warring (1976) found that women tend to identify with rape victims more than men do, and research by Towson and Zanna (1983) demonstrated that women make more lenient legal judgments than men concerning retaliation of a rape by the victim or her fiancé, as well as viewing a retaliatory act as more justified. Though Wanrow was not a victim of sexual assault nor the fiancée of a victim, she believed her son had narrowly missed being sexually assaulted by Wesler; thus her point of view may have been analogous to that of an assault victim's fiancé. We hypothesized that female subjects in our study might identify more than male subjects with Wanrow and thus be more likely to believe she had acted in self-defense, and to make more lenient judgments concerning punishment and the crime committed.

RESULTS

None of the subjects' guesses about the hypotheses came near the truth. The few who ventured a guess believed we were studying moral reasoning or attitudes toward crime. Thus demand characteristics were probably not high.

As predicted, opinion as to whether Yvonne Wanrow had acted in self-defense differed significantly depending on pronoun condition, $\chi^2_{(2)} = 10.24$, $p < .01$.

Table 1
Number of "Yes" and "No" Responses to the
Self-Defense Question: Pronoun Condition

Response	Pronoun condition		
	He	*He or She*	*She*
Yes	5	16	11
No	19	8	13
Total	24	24	24

Table 2
Number of "Yes" and "No" Responses to the
Self-Defense Question: Subject Sex

Response	Subject sex	
	Male	*Female*
Yes	15	16
No	22	17
Total	37	33

(See Table 1 for frequencies of "yes" and "no" responses on the self-defense question.) Further, in a series of pairwise planned comparisons, we found the following. Subjects in the "he" condition were significantly less likely than subjects in the "he or she" condition to believe Wanrow had acted in self-defense (5 out of 24 vs. 16 out of 24, respectively), $\chi^2_{(1)} = 10.24$, $p < .005$. More subjects marked "yes" for self-defense in the "she" condition (11 of 24) than in the "he" condition (5 of 24), though this difference did not reach significance, $\chi^2_{(1)} = 3.38$, $p < .06$. There was no significant difference between the two non-male-biased conditions (16/24 vs. 11/24 "yes" responses).

The second hypothesis concerning self-defense, that more female than male subjects would believe Wanrow had acted in self-defense, was also tested by chi square. Results of this test were not significant. (See Table 2.)

Next we analyzed subjects' ratings of the severity of the crime (Crime Severity) using a two-way analysis of variance with pronoun condition and subject sex as independent variables. (See Table 3.) The predicted main effect for pronoun condition was not significant. There was, however, a significant effect for subject sex in the predicted direction, with male subjects viewing the crime as more severe than female subjects ($MM = 2.82$ vs. $FM = 3.31$, respectively, on the 4-point scale; smaller numbers indicate a more serious crime), $F_{(1,68)} = 4.26$ $p < .02$. The interaction effect was not significant, as expected.

Next we looked at what punishment subjects felt the defendant should receive (Punishment Severity), assuming the jury found her guilty. A two-way analysis of variance revealed that neither pronoun condition nor subject sex had a significant effect on Punishment. An interaction effect had not been predicted and was not found.

Table 3
Number of Male and Female Subjects Choosing Each Crime Severity Rating

	Pronoun condition					
	He		*He/She*		*She*	
Crime severity	*Males*	*Females*	*Males*	*Females*	*Males*	*Females*
First degree murder	2	0	1	0	3	0
Second degree murder	0	0	0	3	2	0
Manslaughter	8	7	7	4	7	6
Negligent manslaughter	2	5	3	4	2	4

DISCUSSION

Our central hypothesis was confirmed—for our "jurors," masculine generic wording of jury instructions concerning self-defense gave Yvonne Wanrow less chance of winning her claim of self-defense than did the two non-male-biased versions, with significance obtained for one non-male-biased pronoun, a trend toward significance for the other. We had not hypothesized a difference between the effects of the two non-male-biased pronouns, "he or she" and "she." As it turned out, only "he or she" produced a significantly different result from "he" on Self-defense, with the "she" condition producing a nearly significant difference. Nevertheless, because the two non-male-biased pronouns did not behave significantly differently from each other, it seems likely that the two non-male-biased pronouns in fact function in the same way. We believe that our results indicate that such an effect could have been operating in the actual trial, as Elizabeth Schneider argued in the appeal, and could operate in other legal situations where a woman's behavior is measured against a male standard.

The effect of pronoun was not strong enough to cause a difference on subjects' responses about the severity of Wanrow's possible crime or their recommendations for her punishment. We had hypothesized that if the male pronoun led to fewer decisions of self-defense, this would in turn cause subjects in the male pronoun condition to give more severe ratings on Crime Severity and on Punishment Severity. A look at the frequencies of the four possible responses to the crime question reveals that the nonsignificant pronoun effect could be due to the lack of variation in responses. Eighty-four percent of the respondents believed the crime Wanrow committed, assuming she was found guilty, was either manslaughter or negligent manslaughter. Perhaps the details given about the possible crime were sufficiently clear that they overrode any possible pronoun effect. There was considerably more variation on the punishment question, so a similar explanation for the nonsignificant pronoun effect is not suggested.

We had hypothesized a main effect of subject sex on Self-defense, Crime Severity, and Punishment Severity, believing that female subjects would be more lenient toward Wanrow in each decision than would male subjects. The hypothesis was confirmed for Crime Severity but not for Punishment Severity or Self-defense. The finding for Crime Severity corroborates Towson & Zanna's (1983) finding that female subjects are more lenient in their legal judgments than male subjects about those who retaliate against their own sexual assault or that of someone close to them; the findings for Punishment Severity and Self-defense do not.

CONCLUSIONS

The results of the present study indicate that the most important decision before the jury in many murder trials, the decision concerning self-defense, might potentially be affected by the pronoun used in jury instructions. In exploring this particular use of the masculine generic, however, we looked at only one very specific instance in which masculine pronouns are used in a legal setting. There are many other areas in which male-biased language is used in the law, and it seems reasonable to speculate that there would be similarly serious effects in such instances. For example, in deciding a standard of conduct in negligence, jurors have traditionally been instructed to apply the "reasonable man" standard—would the reasonable man have behaved as the defendant did under like circumstances? The reasonable man has been defined as someone of reasonable prudence, someone who would exercise reasonable caution; one definition describes him as follows: "He is an ideal, a standard . . . one who never drives his ball until those in front of him have definitely vacated the putting-green which is his own objective; who never from one year's end to another makes an excessive demand upon his wife, his neighbors, his servants . . ." (Herbert, cited in Prosser, Wade, & Schwartz, 1982). In recent years the standard applied is often that of the "reasonable person," but this has not completely replaced the "reasonable man" standard. The results of the present study, in combination with all else we now know about the masculine generic noun and pronoun, tell us that the days of the reasonable man standard and of other uses of a "generic" masculine should be over. As any number of studies have shown (Hamilton & Henley, 1982; Martyna, 1978) using "he" and "man" leads people to think about males rather than about both females and males (or some average of the two), and as we have seen in the present study, because of physical differences between women and men, it is not always sensible to ask people to judge the reasonableness of a woman's behavior on the basis of what a man would have done.

Further studies could be done to determine, one by one, the potential effects of using the words "man" and "he" and their variants in different legal settings. But the authors would argue that this should not be necessary. The verdict is in.

NOTES

1. Subjects also rated Wanrow on a series of adjective traits, in an exploratory analysis. No significant differences were found for condition or sex of subject; therefore this measure will not be discussed in the paper.

2. The description given to subjects was a shortened version of the case summary in *Criminal law and its processes: Cases and materials* (Kadish, Schulhofer, and Paulsen, 1983). Facts presented were faithful to the summary, with the exception that in order to indicate Wanrow's feeling of being threatened in relatively few words, we stated that Wesler's hand was raised over his head as he approached her.

SELECTED BIBLIOGRAPHY

BARON, D. (1986). *Grammar and gender.* New Haven: Yale University Press.

BEM, S. L., & BEM, D. J. (1973). Does sex-biased job advertising "aid and abet" sex discrimination? *Journal of Applied Social Psychology, 3*(1), 6–18.

CALHOUN, L. G., SELBY, J. W., & WARRING, L. J. (1976). Social perception of the victim's causal role in rape: An exploratory examination of four factors. *Human Relations, 29,* 517–526.

CONVEYANCER'S NOTEBOOK. (1985, May–June). *The Conveyancer and Property Lawyer,* 157–236.

COX, B. J. & RAY, M. B. (1986, June). Avoiding gender-biased language in legal writing. *Wisconsin Bar Bulletin, 59,* 23–25.

HAMILTON, M. C. (1988a). Using masculine generics: Does generic 'he' increase male bias in the user's imagery? *Sex Roles, 19,* 785–799.

HAMILTON, M. C. (1988b). Masculine generic terms and misperception of AIDS risk. *Journal of Applied Social Psychology, 18,* 122–124.

HAMILTON, M. C. (1989, March). *Does male-biased language in a state constitution really hurt?* Paper presented at the meeting of the Association for Women in Psychology, Newport, RI.

HAMILTON, M. C., & HENLEY, N. M. (1982, April). *Detrimental consequences of generic masculine usage.* Paper presented at the meeting of the Western Psychological Association, Sacramento, CA.

HARRISON, L. & PASSERO, R. N. (1975). Sexism in the language of elementary school textbooks. *Science and Children, 12*(4), 22–25.

HENLEY, N. M., GRUBER, B., & LERNER, L. (1984, October). *Effects of sex-biased language on attitudes and self-esteem.* Paper presented at the Southern California Language and Gender Interest Group.

KADISH, S. H., SCHULHOFER, S. J., & AND PAULSEN, M. G. (1983). *Criminal law and its processes: Cases and materials* (4th ed.). Boston: Little, Brown.

KANOWITZ, L. (1973). *Sex roles in law and society.* Albuquerque: University of New Mexico Press.

MACKAY, D. G., & FULKERSON, D. C. (1979). On the comprehension and production of pronouns. *Journal of Verbal Learning and Verbal Behavior, 18,* 661–673.

MARTYNA, W. (1978). Using and understanding the generic masculine: A social psychological approach to language and the sexes. *Dissertation Abstracts International, 39,* 3050B.

PROSSER, W. L., WADE, J. W., & SCHWARTZ, V. E. (1982). *Torts: Cases and materials* (7th ed.). Mineola, NY: Foundation Press.

RITCHIE, M. (1975, Winter). Alice through the statutes. *McGill Law Journal, 21,* 685–707.

SCHNEIDER, J., & HACKER, S. (1973). Sex role imagery and the use of the generic "man" in introductory texts. *American Sociologist, 8,* 12–18.

SCOTT, J. A. (1985, March). Sexism in legal language. *Australian Law Journal, 59,* 163–173.

SILVEIRA, J. (1980). Generic masculine words and thinking. In C. Kramarae (Ed.). *The voices and words of women and men* (pp. 165–178). Oxford: Pergamon Press.

STERICKER, A. (1981). Does this "he or she" business really make a difference? The effect of masculine pronouns as generics on job attitudes. *Sex Roles, 7,* 637–641.

TOWSON, S. M. J., & ZANNA, M. P. (1983). Retaliation against sexual assault: Self-defense or public duty? *Psychology of Women Quarterly, 8,* 89–99.

Washington, State of, v. Yvonne Wanrow. (1977). Supreme Court of Washington (559 Pacific Report, 2d series), 548–559.

marianne lafrance and eugene hahn

THE DISAPPEARING AGENT

Gender Stereotypes, Interpersonal Verbs, and Implicit Causality

In daily life, we are often intrigued by why people do what they do. Did person X get angry because someone else provoked him or her or because person X is prone to angry outbursts? Social psychologists frame this question in terms of causal attribution, that is, whether an event is perceived to be caused by something external to the person (e.g., the situation was provocative) or internal to the person (e.g., a personality disposition to be angry). The resulting attribution either to the situation or to the person is not trivial. For having decided that a display of anger was caused by something outside rather than inside the person is likely to lead to very different ideas about whether a person is seen as acting on his or her own or whether a person's actions are believed to have been driven by forces outside the person's control.

How do people figure out who is responsible for interpersonal events, especially since details are frequently incomplete or unclear? Attribution theory is the term given to research exploring how ordinary people explain ordinary as well as extraordinary interpersonal events. It appears that people are reluctant to believe that things just happen and instead make use of whatever information is available. Recent research suggests that gender stereotypes and linguistic carriers of implicit causality constitute two important sources of information that people use in helping them decide.

With respect to the role of stereotypic preconceptions, studies have explored for example whether people explain the same outcomes by women and men the same way. Deaux (1976) concluded that causal explanations for successful performance differ depending on the gender of the person experiencing the success. She found that men's success is more often attributed to skill or natural talent, while women's success is more likely attributed to luck or hard work. Thus, accomplishments by men are seen to be caused more by inherent qualities, while those by women are attributed more to elements outside her command or to transient factors. The present chapter extends work in the area of attribution of causality by exploring who people see as causal in interpersonal events involving women and men. That is, are women and men seen as equivalently causal when they act on and feel things toward each other?

The endeavor to understand how people make attributions has taken an interesting twist lately as researchers have begun also to pay close attention to the role that language plays in the social attribution process. Since people's actions vis-à-vis each other are often verbally described rather than observed directly, verbal description is an important avenue for investigating how implicit causality is conveyed. Word selection, specifically verb choice, can slant interpretation in one direction over another, even in the absence of an explicit formulation as to why someone did something to someone else. In what follows, we describe a program of research designed to study a number of issues concerning how verb choice and gender preconceptions combine to affect people's attributions of causality. The domain to be explained consists of simple, interpersonal events involving actions and feelings. Specifically, people are asked to explain short sentences of the kind "S likes O" or "S criticizes O" in which either a male or female sentence-subject is described as feeling something about or doing something to either a male or female sentence-object. The key question has to do with how verb selection and target gender separately and together affect the perception of who is seen to be driving the action in interpersonal events involving women or men or women and men.

VERB TYPE AND IMPLICIT CAUSALITY

There can be no doubt that words carry a great deal of implicit information (Miller & Johnson-Laird, 1976) and psychologists studying language have long been interested in how information conveyed by the main verb of a sentence contributes to the sentence's grammatical structure (Healy & Miller, 1971). More recently, their attention has focused on the particular issue of implicit causality of verbs. Results show that different verb types are regularly associated with different kinds of causal inference (Abelson & Kanouse, 1966; Au, 1986; Brown & Fish, 1983; Cunningham, Starr & Kanouse, 1979; Fiedler & Semin, 1988; Garvey & Caramazza, 1974; Hoffman & Tchir, 1990; McArthur, 1972; Van Kleeck, Hillger, & Brown, 1988).

Consider the following two simple sentences: "Paul compliments Jim" and "Paul likes Jim." Both sentences describe positive interpersonal occurrences yet research shows that they tend to elicit different causal inferences about why the event occurred. When the verb describes an interpersonal *action*, it tends to imply causation by the sentence-subject. Why does Paul compliment Jim? People are likely to believe that it has something to do with Paul. In contrast, where the verb describes an emotional state, as in "Paul likes Jim," the tendency is to see the sentence-object as causal. Why does Paul like Jim? People think that it has more to do with the kind of person Jim is. In other words, people infer that the sentence-subject is causal when the interpersonal event involves an action verb but that they infer that the object of the sentence is causal when the event entails one person's feeling something about another. Thus, the act "John criticizes Tim" leads to the attribution that John is the causal agent, but the state "Sara abhors Jen" leads people to infer that Jen is the locus of causality (Brown & Fish, 1983).

The implicit causality carried by verb type has caught the attention of both linguistically oriented psychologists and social psychologists. Garvey and Caramazza (1974) coined the term "implicit causality" to describe a property of transitive verbs that relates two nouns referencing human or animate beings in such a way that "one or the other of the noun phrases is implicated as the assumed locus of the underlying cause of the action or attitude" (p. 460). Garvey and Caramazza argued that implicit causality is part of the semantics of the verb root: Some verbs, such as "confess" and "approach" assign the cause of the event to the subject noun phrase, while others, such as "fear" and "admire," assign the cause to the object noun phrase. By examining subjects' completion of sentence frames, such as "The teacher approached the student because he . . . ," these researchers established that, when asked to do so, English speakers reliably attribute causality to subject noun phrases for some verbs and to object noun phrases for other verbs.

Garvey and Caramazza (1974) identified the "locus of the underlying cause" as the relevant factor in determining a verb's implicit causality, but they stopped short of a full explanation of why that factor is critical and how one determines this locus. Brown & Fish (1983) followed by proposing that verbs steer causality through one of two routes. In the first route, verbs direct causality through associated morphology. Specifically, the assumption of where causality lies is predicted by the nature of the dispositional adjectives derived from the verb in question. Nearly every verb has an associated adjective; the adjectives associated with the verbs "to hate" and "to love" are, respectively, "hateful" and "lovable," while the adjectives associated with the verbs "to criticize" and "to help" are, respectively, "critical" and "helpful."

Brown and Fish (1983) showed that adjectives derived from action verbs mostly refer to the sentence-subject while adjectives derived from state verbs refer mostly to the sentence object, thus accounting for the different attributions. The action verb "to compliment" is associated with the adjective "complimentary" rather than "complimentable," which refers to the sentence-subject in the sentence "Paul compliments Jim." In contrast, the adjective derived from the state verb "to like" is "likable," which refers to the sentence object in the sentence "Paul likes Jim." Why does Paul compliment Jim and why does Paul like Jim? Because Paul is complimentary and Jim is likable. Despite the fact that Brown & Fish (1983) believed that morphology alone was insufficient to explain resulting inferences, a more recent investigation has provided strong supporting data (Hoffman & Tchir, 1990).

Brown & Fish's alternative explanation suggests more cognitive involvement on the part of the perceiver. They assert that the two verb types (action and state) are associated, respectively, with two naturally occurring cognitive schema or frameworks: an agent-patient schema and a stimulus-experience schema. *Agent* is the role of performing an action; *Patient* is the role of being acted upon. *Stimulus* is the role of giving rise to a certain mental or emotional state; *Experiencer* is the role of experiencing a given state. Action verbs draw on an "agent-patient schema" and state verbs call on an "experiencer-stimulus schema." In action verbs, the agent (the sentence-subject) is perceived to possess more causal weight than the patient (the sentence-object) because actions lead one to locate causality in aspects in the agent which are viewed as potentially enacted toward a whole range of patients. Said another way, the category of persons who can act is presumed to be restricted in size, thus being a unique case, while the category of persons who can be acted on includes just about everyone. The person belonging to the more restricted category is regarded as more causal.

In state verbs, the stimulus for the feeling state, that is, the sentence-object, has more causal weight than the person experiencing the state because causality is argued to reside in aspects in the stimulus conceived to generalize across experiencers. Analogous to that of action verbs, the condition of being able to stimulate an experience in others is present less often than the condition of being able to experience a state, which presumably can happen to anyone. In sum, the category of persons who can be the recipient of an action or who can experience a state includes practically everyone and thus is a general case. The argument is that verbs provide more information about the special case person than the general case person. In action verbs, the special case person is the agent (sentence-subject), and in state verbs, the special case person is the stimulus (sentence-object), with the consequence that both are seen to be more causal in their respective contexts. Hilton & Slugoski (1986) have also argued that causality is attributed to that which is considered unusual.

More recently, Fiedler and Semin (1988) suggested that the schemas advanced by Brown and Fish (1983) were necessary but not sufficient to understand implicit causality. They advanced the argument that different attributions result from the fact that different verb types implicitly supply different before and after contexts. In their studies, subjects respond to simple target sentences by supplying the context, namely sentences that could have plausibly preceded and followed the target sentences. These supplied sentences are then coded as to whether the original sentence-subject or the original sentence-object is the sentence-subject. Results support the idea that action verbs locate causality in sentence-subject because the supplied context had the direction of causality flowing from the sentence-subject (in the antecedent sentence) to the sentence-object (in the consequent sentence), whereas state verbs imply a reverse direction of causality, such that the action was seen to flow from the sentence-object to the sentence-subject.

Despite the fact that there is continuing controversy over what constitutes the best interpretation of the different patterns of causality as a function of verb type as well as some new debate concerning the appropriate number and classification of verb types (Au, 1986; Brown & Fish, 1983; Corrigan, 1988; Levin, 1992; Semin & Fieldler, 1991), the attributional bias associated with action and state verbs appears fairly robust, occurring in several languages (Van Kleeck, Hillger & Brown, 1988) and even in children's speech (Au, 1986). Nevertheless, there are indications that implicit causality does not spring from verb type alone; verbs are but one variable in a larger sentence framework that helps people fill in necessary gaps. Corrigan (1988), for example, has found that causality implicit in verbs can vary as a function of other implied factors such as the "animacy" of the sentence-subject and sentence-object. Related to animacy is the gender of the sentence participants. The someone who does something to or feels something about someone else has to have a sex. The present investigation began with the assumption that preconceptions about gender would interact with verb type to affect resulting patterns of causality. In other words, it seemed likely that patterns of causality might change depending on which sex was doing what to

which other sex. What follows is a brief description of how gender-based preconceptions affect perceptions and attributions.

GENDER-BASED PRECONCEPTIONS

Stereotypes are cognitive preconceptions. Stereotypes occur when target individuals are classified by others as having something in common because they are
perceived to be members of a particular group. Stereotypes are often associated
with salient physical characteristics such as ethnicity, age, physical attractiveness, and of course, gender. Gender stereotypes are "structured sets of beliefs
about the personal attributes of men and women" (Ashmore & Del Boca, 1979,
p. 222). Once a person's sex is identified, all kinds of beliefs concerning his or
her presumed characteristics may be tapped. Research by Broverman (Broverman et al., 1972; Rosenkrantz et al., 1968) and Spence (e.g., Spence, Helmreich
& Stapp, 1974) suggests that there are two groups of traits that are generally held
to differentiate men from women. The first group are related to one's propensity
to act: Men are typically viewed as more active, independent, and instrumental,
while women are seen as more passive, dependent, and ineffective. The second
group of traits are related to expressiveness and emotionality. Men are perceived
as being less likely to express their emotions, while women are described as
being more warm, tender, and expressive. Gender stereotypes supply information about a person's tendency to act in certain ways, and this information may
thus contribute to inferences about who has been causal in an interpersonal
event.

It may even be the case that gender stereotypes are especially likely to be
activated when one is hearing or reading about an event rather than encountering
an individual in person. As noted earlier, Deaux (1976) found that causal explanations for achievement behavior differ as a function of gender. Four causes of
success and failure have been studied extensively from an attributional perspective: ability, effort, luck, and task difficulty (Weiner et al., 1971). Each of these
causes has two dimensions: the source controlling the outcome (internal versus
external) and the temporal stability of the factor influencing the outcome (stable
versus temporary). Ability is described as internal and stable while effort is described as internal and unstable (Weiner et al., 1971). Data on perceived differences in causal attributions about men and women in terms of the Weiner
taxonomy suggest that the explanations differ markedly (Cash et al., 1977;
Deaux & Emswiller, 1974; Etaugh & Brown, 1975; Feather & Simon, 1975;
Haccoun & Stacey, 1980). Men's successful performance is more likely to be
attributed to ability, whereas women's identical performance is attributed to effort or luck.

If one were to focus instead not on a single person's performance outcome but
on an interpersonal event involving two people, how might people account for
it? Existing work indicates that action verbs lead one to believe that the act
originated in the person who acted and state verbs lead one to believe that the
act originated in the person who generated the feeling. But does this pattern
hold when the gender of the sentence participants changes?

Even though there now exists a considerable literature relating gender to language and some literature relating gender to thought (cf. Carli, 1990; Dabbs &

Ruback, 1984; Kimble, Yoshikawa & Zehr, 1981; Mulac, Lundell & Bradac, 1986; Steckler & Rosenthal, 1985; Thorne, Kramarae & Henley, 1983), the literature on the causality implied by verb type has rarely considered the possible impact of targets' gender on causal inferences. In fact, most research on implicit causality generated by verb type has adopted male names. For example, in their classic study, Brown and Fish (1983) used either male names or no names, for example, "A likes B" in the target sentences. A few studies have varied gender of sentence participants but have provided no data as to its effect. For example, both Au (1986) and Corrigan (1988) employed some gender combinations, but neither reported results bearing on this factor. Two recent studies conducted in Italian (Franco & Arcuri, 1990; Mannetti & De Grada, 1991) reported no significant effects for gender combination, but the lack of a gender effect may be attributable in the Franco and Arcuri study to the fact that they used only same-sex pairs and attributable in the Mannetti & De Grada study to the fact that they analyzed gender only as one of four dyadic combinations rather than considering separate effects due to sex of sentence-subject and sex of object. Consequently, it is not possible to conclude that gender had no effect on attributed causality since a single variable may mask separate gender of subject and object effects.

We aimed to rectify this neglect by designing a study in which the gender of both targets would be incorporated into the design. We expected that gender would make a difference but were initially of two minds as to the effect it might have. On the one hand, sex of sentence-subject might affect causality by interacting with verb type. Since social stereotypes suggest that males act while females react (Ruble, 1983), or as Berger (1972) put it, that men *act* and women *appear*, action verbs might be more strongly associated with male behavior, whereas state verbs might be more strongly associated with female behavior. Thus, sentences presenting action verbs with males as agents might attribute more causality to the agent than if males were described as feeling something about someone. Conversely, sentences presenting state verbs with females as sentence-subjects might attribute more causality to females but less if they were described as taking some action since females are supposed to be more emotional rather than proactive.

But it also seemed possible that target sex might affect attributions through another path. Perhaps male agents or male stimuli are seen as more causal than female agents or stimuli regardless of verb type simply because they are ascribed more agency and power than females. He is significant; she is inconsequential. For example, a recent study found that when everything else was held constant, males were listened to more, recalled better, and assigned more causality than females saying exactly the same thing (Robinson & McArthur, 1982). Consequently, when presented with descriptions of males acting or being the stimuli to others' states, perceivers might assume that the behavior originated with them but when females act or are the stimulus to someone's state, the more likely assumption may be that the cause lies elsewhere.

VERB VALENCE AND IMPLICIT CAUSALITY

In addition to verb type, the valence of the verb likely also affects attributions. Most verbs have an evaluative cast to them, being either positive or negative.

For example, verbs such as "to help" or "to love" are inherently more positive than verbs like "to harass" or "to loathe." The question concerns whether negative verbs and positive verbs tend to push attributions of causality in different ways. Other research in social perception indicates that people's judgments tend to be strongly affected by evaluative negative content (Skowronski & Carlston, 1989). It may be that verb valence simply exaggerates attributional patterns due to verb type, but it seems possible that verb valence may interact with target gender in distinct ways.

In sum, the research reported in this chapter joins the gender-language debate by exploring how people explain interpersonal events involving women and men. Two key dimensions are proposed to influence how people assign causality. The first is linguistic, namely verb type and verb valence and the second is cognitive, namely gender-based preconceptions.

ASSESSING CAUSALITY

As noted earlier, most of the research assessing the effects of gender on causal attributions has focused on performance outcomes by single individuals (success or failure) and has utilized Weiner's taxonomy to measure how much the outcome is perceived to have been due to particular factors (ability, effort, luck, task difficulty). In contrast, the focus here is on interpersonal events involving two people, and the issue is measuring how much perceivers believe that the action or feeling originates in the person who acts or feels or that it springs from the person who is acted on or felt about. There are several ways this might be done (Brown & Fish, 1983). One could for example provide simple sentences such as "Paul likes Jim" and simply ask people to indicate whether that condition is due more to Paul or Jim. Or one could have perceivers rate the degree to which they believe each person is responsible and then compare the assessments. Another more complicated approach would be to try to assess the degree to which perceivers believe the action or feeling is unique, that is, whether the act or feeling would likely be done by others and to others. Does Paul like other people besides Jim and is Jim liked by people other than Paul? If Paul likes few other people and Jim is liked by people other than Paul, the strong suggestion is that something about Jim causes Paul to like him. Kelley (1967) labeled these two dimensions of uniqueness *consensus* and *distinctiveness*. Measuring consensus and distinctiveness is the strategy adopted here as a way to get at perceivers' underlying beliefs about people's capacities to act. If others don't behave the same way toward a particular other and if the person behaves the same way toward other people, then we are more likely to see that person as the cause of the action. Conversely, if everyone behaves the same way toward this particular person and if the behaving person acts this way only toward this particular other, then we are more likely to see that recipient as the cause of the behavior.

TAKING CONSENSUS INTO ACCOUNT

Consider the sentence "Dave helps Ann." In abstract form, the argument is "<sentence-subject> <verb> <sentence-object>." The sentence-subject (Dave) is the person doing something or feeling something in the sentence; the sentence-object (Ann) is the recipient of the action or the stimulus for the feeling of the sentence-subject. Finally, the verb describes the action or feeling: in this case, helping. We now show how beliefs about consensus and distinctiveness enable people to assign causality.

Consensus is the extent to which sentence-subjects other than the one specifically mentioned are perceived also to engage in that behavior vis-à-vis the sentence-object. When there is high consensus, it means that other sentence-subjects are thought to act or feel the same way toward the sentence-object. High consensus means many people in addition to Dave help Ann. When there is low consensus, few other sentence-subjects besides the one described act or feel the same way toward the sentence-object. In other words, low consensus means that practically no one except Dave helps Ann. When there is high consensus, the sentence-object appears to be causal in that this person acts as a magnet for this kind of action or feeling from others; when there is low consensus, the attention shifts away from the sentence-object to the sentence-subject since the sentence-object does not elicit this behavior from others.

TAKING DISTINCTIVENESS INTO ACCOUNT

Distinctiveness, on the other hand, is the extent to which the sentence-subject is perceived as acting or feeling the same way toward others. High distinctiveness means that the sentence-subject is seen as acting or feeling this way toward few others. The act or feeling is distinct to this particular other. That is, high distinctiveness indicates the sentence-subject treats this sentence-object differently than he or she treats other sentence-objects. In our earlier example, high distinctiveness would mean that Dave helps only Ann. When there is low distinctiveness, the sentence-subject is perceived as acting or feeling this way toward many others. Thus, low distinctiveness means that Dave is perceived as helping just about everyone, including Ann. So another way to think of distinctiveness is the degree to which the person engaging in the named behavior also behaves likewise in other contexts. When there is high distinctiveness, a sentence-subject acts or feels this way only in relation to this person. When there is low distinctiveness, the sentence-subject acts or feels this way toward others.

Kelley's (1967) attribution model predicts that actors are perceived as the cause of the event when both consensus and distinctiveness are low. In our example, if only Dave and no one else helps Ann (low consensus), and if Dave helps everyone who crosses his path (low distinctiveness), then it appears that something about Dave rather than Ann caused the helping. In contrast, the model predicts and finds that the sentence-object is perceived to be the cause when both consensus and distinctiveness are high. Thus, if just about everyone helps Ann (high consensus), and Dave helps almost no one except Ann (high distinctiveness), then it is likely that Ann and not Dave will be seen as having brought about the helping. Recall that the data indicate that helping is an action verb and hence is associated more with low consensus and low distinctiveness.

QUANTIFYING CONSENSUS AND DISTINCTIVENESS

In sum, the combined ratings of perceived consensus and distinctiveness not only provide information on who is perceived to be primarily responsible for an interpersonal event but also give indications of how much perceivers believe that a person's actions are unique. For example, if observers assume that there is higher consensus and higher distinctiveness when female agents act than when male agents act, the implication is that females are seen to be less causal and less unique as individuals.

MEASURING CONSENSUS AND DISTINCTIVENESS

These two dimensions were assessed quantitatively in our research. Research participants were presented with sixty simple sentences. After each, they were asked to make two ratings, each on a nine-point scale. The first, which was designed to tap consensus, was done by asking subjects to respond to the following general format:

Probably (many . . . . few) other people <verb> <sentence-object>.

Accordingly, if the sentence to be rated was "Dave helps Ann," research participants were asked to indicate a mark somewhere between "many" and "few" on the following:

Probably (many . . . . few) other people help Ann.

The second rating assessed perception of distinctiveness. This was done by asking subjects to use the following format to make a rating:

Probably <sentence-subject> <verb> (many . . . . few) other people.

Thus, to the sentence "Dave helps Ann," subjects would be asked to mark an X on the following:

Probably Dave helps (many . . . . few) other people.

Ratings were converted into numbers from 1 to 9 corresponding to where subjects placed their two Xs. Low consensus and low distinctiveness reflected the perception that the sentence-subject was causal; high consensus and high distinctiveness reflected the perception that the sentence-object was causal.

Eighty research subjects were given a form on which were printed sixty sentences, each of which was followed by two scales on which they were to make their ratings. All sentences took the form <sentence-subject> <verb> <sentence-object>. For each sentence, two names such as Dave or Ann were inserted into the sentence-subject and sentence-object positions, and a verb, such as "likes" or "helps," was inserted into the verb position. We varied the gender of the sentence-subject and the sentence-object by inserting male and female first names in four different versions of the questionnaire. Thus, one-quarter of the research participants read sentences with males as both sentence-subjects and sentence-objects; a second quarter read sentences with females as both sentence-subjects and sentence-objects; a third quarter read sentences with males as sentence-subjects and females as sentence-objects; and a final quarter read sentences with females as sentence-subjects and males as sentence-objects.

The verbs themselves varied along two dimensions. The first was verb type, with thirty verbs describing actions, such as "help" and "threaten," and thirty verbs describing emotional or cognitive states, such as "hate" or "forget." The second varied verb aspect was verb valence, such that of the thirty action verbs, half were positive, such as "encourage" and "protect," while the other half were negative, such as "harass" and "criticize"; half the state verbs were positive, such as "trust" and "respect," and half were negative, such as "despise" and "fear." In sum, each research subject had examples of both verb types and verb valences but only one gender combination even though different names were used. The ratings on consensus and distinctiveness were statistically analyzed to determine the effects of four factors on the attribution of who was causal: verb type, verb valence, sex of sentence-subject, and sex of sentence-object.

EFFECT OF VERB TYPE

The findings substantiated our general framework, namely that both linguistic and cognitive preconceptions regarding gender contribute to assessments of who was perceived to be causal in interpersonal events involving men and women. To begin with, the results replicated prior work by others which showed that action verbs tended to throw the causal light on the sentence-subject while state verbs tended to highlight the centrality of the sentence-object in causing the behavior.

EFFECT OF TARGET GENDER

The critical question for our purposes, however, involved looking at how gender affected these attributional patterns. On this count, several findings were of note, including some surprising ones. Our early speculation had been that female agents might be seen as less causal than male agents as a result of sex-stereotypes which assign them less agency than males. That was, in fact, not the case. Consensus and distinctiveness ratings did not differ significantly when there were female *sentence-subjects* as opposed to male sentence-subjects. But gender did affect ratings both directly and in combination with verb type and verb valence.

Regarding the direct effect, our findings showed that the gender of the *sentence-object* had a statistically significant effect showing that the sentence-subject received more attention when the sentence-object was female than when the sentence-object was male. When a single measure of causality is formed by subtracting scores on consensus from scores on distinctiveness, the result is that the sentence-subject is perceived to be more causal when he or she acts toward a female than toward a male. In other words, when a male is on the receiving end of others' actions or feelings he draws attention away from the actor, whereas the actor maintains central stage when a female is on the receiving end. Keep in mind also that this effect was significant across both positive and negative action verbs and feeling verbs, although the effect was especially noteworthy in the case of state verbs. The usual pattern is for state verbs to throw casual light on the sentence-object. That pattern held when males were the sentence-objects (stimuli) in state verb sentences. However, when a female was the person about whom someone felt something, instead of her being seen as the cause of the feeling, the person experiencing the feeling received the attention.

The tendency for women to be discounted was especially pronounced in mixed-sex pairs when a female behaved toward a male. Distinctiveness was higher for women who acted or felt toward men than for any other gender pairing. This means that women's actions and states toward men are judged not to be a statement about women but rather about men. In other words, the finding of high distinctiveness in this pair compared with that in other gender pairings means that it is the male recipient who is perceived to call forth the women's behavior rather than an activity that originates within her. Observers perceived that women act or feel toward men because men elicit the act or feeling. When a woman acts or feels toward a man, it is perceived as being brought about because of something about him. In contrast, the other gender combinations had significantly lower distinctiveness ratings, indicating that the causal locus was more in the person who acted or felt than the person acted on or felt about. Such a perception is consistent with the stereotype that views women as more reactive than proactive in male-female interactions.

These results also indicate that attributions of causality depend on simultaneously taking into account both the sex of the doer/feeler and the sex of the recipient of the act or feeling. Observers of interpersonal events appear to weigh the capacity-to-act of the sentence-subject against that of the sentence-object to draw the act. When the sentence-object is a female, the sentence-subject of either sex seems more instrumental. She appears to be the occasion for others' actions. But when the sentence-object is a male, who is presumed to be more agentic, causality of the sentence-subject is diminished, especially when the sentence-subject is female. Thus, our data suggest that observers consider there to be something special about male-female interactions in that when she acts on him, he is the one that is noticed.

EFFECT OF VERB VALENCE

Verb valence caused more attention to be drawn to the person who did or felt the negative thing. Negatively valenced verbs led perceivers to locate more causality in the negative doer/feeler than did positively valenced verbs. In other words, sentence-subjects are more singular when their actions or feelings are negative.

But valence was also found to vary with the gender of sentence-object in a way not predicted by previous work on language and gender. Tests showed that for negatively valenced verbs as opposed to positively valenced verbs, sentence-subjects seem even more focal when the sentence-object is female than when the sentence-object is male. These findings suggest the following interpretation: Someone who acts negatively toward or feels negatively about a woman stands out more than someone who does or feels the same toward a man. Future work will have to sort out why the agent comes more into view when a female rather than a male is the recipient of negative behavior.

Finally, female sentence-subjects were seen to be more causal than male sentence-subjects for positive actions or feelings, while male sentence-subjects were seen as more causal than female sentence-subjects for negative actions or feelings. Such a finding is consistent with both Broverman's (Broverman et al., 1972; Rosenkrantz et al., 1968) and Spence's (Spence et al., 1974) work, which found that women were considered to be warmer and kinder than men. Thus, women seem more causal than men for positive actions because they seem kinder than the average sentence-subject (low consensus), and this kindness is part of their personality, which they show to many others (low distinctiveness).

CONCLUSIONS

Our research confirms that verbs carry implicit presumptions about who is more causal when someone acts or feels but that the particular character of these presumptions clearly depends on the gender of the people involved. We had begun by thinking that male agents might be seen as more causal than female agents. Actually the more critical main effect turned out to be not the sex of the sentence-subject but the sex of the sentence-object. When a female was on the receiving end of another's actions or feelings, then the person who acted or felt became significantly more salient. Her role appeared to be more foil than main player.

From the research, we also saw that gender composition affects assigned causality. Regardless of verb type, when the interacting pair consisted of a female sentence-subject and a male sentence-object, there were fewer attributions to her than in any other gender combination. In other words, a female recedes from causal view if the person she is acting on or has feelings about is male, an effect that we have labeled the *disappearing agent effect*. She also disappears when theory would predict she should be present. Specifically, research focusing on state verbs has consistently shown that the stimulus person is seen to be more causal than the experiencer. For male stimuli in state verb sentences, this holds up; for female stimuli that are sentence-objects, however, the evidence suggests no such partiality. Both consensus and distinctiveness ratings are nearly equal and in the middle of the scale when a female is the stimulus for someone else's affective state.

Using a different measure of causality, a more recent study in our laboratory confirmed that gender combination affects who is seen to have it within her or him to act. When a female acts in relation to a male, participants rated her as less likely to be the kind of person who does this sort of thing than when a male acts in relation to a female. Another variation of this disappearing act is evident in the findings focusing on causality attributed to the object of the sentence. When a female is presented as acting on a male or as feeling something about him, more inferences are drawn about him than about her than when she is acted upon by him.

In all, the findings show that language affects thought but that existing thoughts about women and men constrain what it is possible to think. The results indicate that people think not only that females are less causal when their partner is male but that their role as recipient is to make the person who is acting or feeling more central. In describing women's invisibility in the literary arena eighty years ago, Virginia Woolf noted that "anonymous was a woman." She will remain anonymous as long as our thoughts conspire with our verbs to make her so.

SELECTED BIBLIOGRAPHY

ABELSON, R. P., & KANOUSE, D. E. (1966). Subjective acceptance of verbal generalizations. In S. Feldman (Ed.) *Cognitive consistency: Motivational antecedents and behavioral
consequents* (pp. 171–197). Academic Press.

ASHMORE, R. D. & DEL BOCA, F. K. (1979). Sex stereotypes and implicit personality
theory: Toward a cognitive-social psychological conceptualization. *Sex Roles*, 5,
219–248.

AU, T. K.-F. (1986). A verb is worth a thousand words: The causes and consequences of
interpersonal events implicit in language. *Journal of Memory and Language*, 25,
104–122.

BERGER, J. (1972). *Ways of seeing.* Baltimore, MD: Penguin Books.

BROVERMAN, I. K., VOGEL, S. R., BROVERMAN, D. M., CLARKSON, F. E., & ROSEN-
KRANTZ, P. S. (1972). Sex-role stereotypes: A current appraisal. *Journal of Social
Issues*, 28, 59–78.

BROWN, R., & FISH, D. (1983). The psychological causality implicit in language. *Cognition*, 14, 233–274.

CARLI, L. (1990). Gender, language, and influence. *Journal of Personality and Social Psychology*, 59, 941–951.

CASH, T. F., GILLEN, B., BURNS, D. S. (1977). Sexism and "beautyism" in personnel
consultant decision-making. *Journal of Applied Psychology*, 62, 301–310.

CORRIGAN, R. (1988). Who dun it? The influence of actor-patient animacy and type of
verb in the making of causal attributions. *Journal of Memory and Language*, 27,
447–465.

CUNNINGHAM, J. D., STARR, P. A., & KANOUSE, D. E. (1979). Self as actor, active observer, and passive observer: Implications for causal attributions. *Journal of Personality and Social Psychology*, 37, 1146–1152.

DABBS, J. M., & RUBACK, R. B. (1984). Vocal patterns in male and female groups. *Personality and Social Psychology Bulletin*, 10, 518–525.

DEAUX, K. (1976). Sex: A perspective on the attribution process. In Harvey, J. H., Ickes,
W. J., & Kidd, R. F. (Eds.) *New Directions in Attribution Research*. Hillsdale, NJ:
Lawrence Erlbaum Associates.

DEAUX, K., & EMSWILLER, T. (1974). Explanations of successful performance on sex-
linked tasks: What is skill for the male is luck for the female. *Journal of Personality
and Social Psychology*, 29, 80–85.

DUNCAN, B. L. (1976). Differential social perception and attribution of intergroup violence: Testing the lower limits of stereotyping of Blacks. *Journal of Personality and
Social Psychology*, 34, 590–598.

ETAUGH, C., & BROWN, B. (1975). Perceiving the causes of success and failure of male
and female performers. *Developmental Psychology*, 11, 103.

FEATHER, N. T., & SIMON, J. G. (1975). Reactions to male and female success and failure
in sex-linked occupations: Impressions of personality, causal attribution and perceived likelihood of differential consequences. *Journal of Personality and Social Psychology*, 31, 20–31.

FIEDLER, K., & SEMIN, G. R. (1988). On the causal information conveyed by different
interpersonal verbs: The role of implicit sentence context. *Social Cognition*, 6, 21–39.

FRANCO, F., & ARCURI, L. (1990). The effect of semantic valence on implicit causality of
verbs. *British Journal of Social Psychology*, 29, 161–170.

GARVEY, C., & CARAMAZZA, A. (1974). Implicit causality in verbs. *Linguistic Inquiry*, 5,
459–464.

HACCOUN, D. M., & STACY, S. (1980). Perceptions of male and female success or failure in relation to spouse encouragement and sex-association of occupation. *Sex Roles*, 6, 819–831.

HEALY, A. F., & MILLER, G. A. (1971). The relative contribution of nouns and verbs to sentence acceptability and comprehensibility. *Psychonomic Science*, 21, 94–96.

HILTON, D., & SLUGOSKI, B. (1986). Knowledge-based causal attribution: The abnormal condition focus model. *Psychological Review*, 93, 75–88.

HOFFMAN, C., & TCHIR, M. A. (1990). Interpersonal verbs and dispositional adjectives: The psychology of causality embodied in language. *Journal of Personality and Social Psychology*, 58, 765–778.

JONES, E. E. (1990). *Interpersonal perception*. New York: W. H. Freeman and Company.

KANOUSE, D. E., & HANSON, R. L. (1972). Negativity in evaluations. In E. E. Jones, D. E. Kanouse, H. H. Kelley, R. E. Nisbett, S. Valins, & B. Weiner (Eds.) *Attribution: Perceiving the causes of behavior* (pp. 47–62). Morristown, NJ: General Learning Press.

KELLEY, H. H. (1967). Attribution theory in social psychology. In D. Levine (Ed.), *Nebraska Symposium on Motivation* (Vol. 15, pp. 192–238). Lincoln: University of Nebraska Press.

KIMBLE, C. E., YOSHIKAWA, J. C., & ZEHR, H. D. (1981). Vocal and verbal assertiveness in same-sex and mixed-sex groups. *Journal of Personality and Social Psychology*, 40, 1047–1054.

LEVIN, B. (1992). *English verb classes and alternations: A preliminary investigation*. Cambridge, MA: MIT Press.

MANNETTI, L., & DE GRADA, E. (1991). Interpersonal verbs: Implicit causality of action verbs and contextual factors. *European Journal of Social Psychology*, 21, 429–443.

MCARTHUR, L. (1972). The how and what of why: Some determinants and consequents of causal attribution. *Journal of Personality and Social Psychology*, 22, 171–193.

MILLER, G. A., & JOHNSON-LAIRD, P. (1976). *Language and perception*. Cambridge, MA: Harvard University Press.

MULAC, A., LUNDELL, R. L., & BRADAC, J. J. (1986). Male/female language differences and attributional consequences in a public speaking situation: Toward an explanation of the gender-linked language effect. *Communication Monographs*, 53, 115–129.

ROBINSON, J., & MCARTHUR, L. Z. (1982). Impact of salient vocal qualities on causal attribution for a speaker's behavior. *Journal of Personality and Social Psychology*, 43, 236–247.

ROSENKRANTZ, P. S., VOGEL, S. R., BEE, H., BROVERMAN, I. K., & BROVERMAN, D. M. (1968). Sex-role stereotypes and self-concepts in college students. *Journal of Consulting and Clinical Psychology*, 32, 287–295.

RUBLE, T. L. (1983). Sex stereotypes: Issues of change in the 1970's. *Sex Roles*, 9, 397–402.

SAGAR, H. A., & SCHOFIELD, J. W. (1980). Racial and behavioral cues in Black and White children's perceptions of ambiguously aggressive acts. *Journal of Personality and Social Psychology*, 39, 590–598.

SCHNEIDER, D. J., & BLANKMEYER, B. L. (1983). Prototype salience and implicit personality theories. *Journal of Personality and Social Psychology*, 44, 712–722.

SEMIN, G. R., & FIEDLER, K. (1991). The linguistic category model, its bases, applications and range. *European Review of Social Psychology*, 2, 1–30.

SKOWRONSKI, J. J., & CARLSTON, D. E. (1989). Negativity and extremity biases in impression formation: A review of explanations. *Psychological Bulletin*, 105, 131–142.

SNYDER, M., TANKE, E. D., & BERSCHIED, E. (1977). Social perception and interpersonal behavior: On the self-fulfilling nature of social stereotypes. *Journal of Personality and Social Psychology*, 35, 656–666.

SPENCE, J. T., HELMREICH, R., & STAPP, J. (1974). The personal attributes questionnaire:

A measure of sex role stereotypes and masculinity-femininity. *Catalog of Selected Documents in Psychology*, 4, 43–44.

STECKLER, N. A., & ROSENTHAL, R., (1985). Sex differences in nonverbal and verbal communication with bosses, peers, and subordinates. *Journal of Applied Psychology*, 70, 157–163.

THORNE, B., KRAMARAE, C., & HENLEY, M. (Eds.) (1983). *Language, gender and society.* Rowley, MA: Newbury House Publisher.

VAN KLEECK, M. H., HILLGER, L. A., & BROWN, R. (1988). Pitting verbal schemas against information variables in attribution. *Social Cognition*, 6, 89–106.

WEINER, B., FRIEZE, I. H., KUKLA, A., REED, L., REST, S., & ROSENBAUM, R. M. (1971). *Perceiving the cause of success and failure.* Morristown, NJ: General Learning Press.

candace west

RETHINKING "SEX DIFFERENCES" IN CONVERSATIONAL TOPICS

It's Not What They Say but How They Say It

Over the past 70 years, empirical evidence from a variety of studies has suggested that women and men talk about decidedly different things. For example, field researchers who relied on eavesdropping in public places during the 1920s and 1930s found that men spoke most often about business and money, while women spoke most often about clothes, men, and themselves (Carlson, Cook, and Stromberg 1936; Landis 1927; Landis and Burtt 1924; Moore 1922). Investigators who used questionnaires to study self-disclosure during the 1950s and 1960s found that women revealed more about themselves than men did, to their parents as well as to their friends (Dimond and Munz 1967; Himelstein and Lubin 1965; Jourard and Landsman 1960; Jourard and Lasakow 1958; Jourard and Richman 1963; Pederson and Breglio 1968; Pederson and Higbee 1968). Experimenters studying small groups in the 1970s and early 1980s also found that women talked more to one another about their homes and their feelings than men did (Aries 1976; Ayres 1980). The apparent consistency of these findings, produced through multiple methods of measurement, led many researchers to attribute them to fundamental sex differences. As Henry Moore (1922, p. 214) concluded in one of the earliest studies in this genre: "After making every possible allowance for differences in convention and personal experience, it is hard to escape the conviction that the original nature here depicted is of two fundamentally different sorts, and that the two types could hardly be permanently adapted to identical interests."

To be sure, Moore (1922) put the case more starkly than most researchers who followed him. For example, some (Carlson et al. 1936; Landis and Burtt 1924) subsequently observed that women's and men's conversational topics varied with the settings in which they conversed: talk about symphony artists and other amusements was more common at concerts, whereas talk about clothes and decoration increased in front of store window displays. Other researchers (Stoke and West 1931; Watson, Breed and Posman 1948) later noted that the magnitude of the differences between what women and men talked about was smaller among college students and among persons in the same age group and social class more generally. Still others showed that differences in women's and men's conversational topics corresponded with differences in their

From Advances in Group Processes *9 (1992): 131–162. Copyright © 1992 by JAI Press, Inc. All rights of reproduction in any form reserved.*

primary activities. Where work was divided into separate "men's" and "women's" spheres—for example, in a small Spanish village (Harding 1975), in an English coal mining town (Klein 1971), and in an American working-class community (Komarovsky 1967)—so too was what got talked about. As Bischoping (1993) observes, these variations on the general pattern led a number of scholars to reconceptualize "sex differences" in conversational topics as the products of sex roles within larger societies.

Despite this reconceptualization, and despite numerous changes in the primary activities of women and men in U.S. society, most contemporary studies continue to report that women and men talk about decidedly different things, among themselves as well as to one another. Research on self-disclosure in the 1980s indicates that adolescent and adult women friends converse more often about themselves and their close relationships (Aries and Johnson 1983; Johnson and Aries 1983), although men disclose more to their women friends than they do to other men (Hacker 1981). Ethnographic research in the work place in the same decade (Kipers 1987) suggests that women workers speak more of their homes and families, while men speak more of work-related concerns. And a contemporary replication of Moore's (1922) study using college students (Bischoping 1993) reports that while women and men have become more similar in their topical "choices," men still talk more about work and leisure, and women still talk more about men and appearances.

One interpretation of the seeming robustness of these findings might be that Moore's (1922, p. 214) initial hypothesis was correct, namely, "that there are very considerable and ineradicable differences in the original capacities of the two sexes for certain types of enthusiasm." Another interpretation might be that sex roles have not really changed that much in the seven decades these findings have accumulated and that, hence, women still talk of interests related to their primary role responsibilities, while men still talk of interests related to theirs (Kipers 1987, pp. 549–550). However, these interpretations rest on two hitherto unexamined assumptions: (1) that the study of what women and men talk about is best pursued by some form of content analysis (cf. Maynard 1980, p. 263) and (2) that observed differences in women's and men's topical "choices" afford an undistorted reflection of their distinctive interests (see especially Moore 1922; Landis 1927; Landis and Burtt 1924).

In this paper, I advance a critical examination of these assumptions. I begin by reviewing research by conversation analysts, which indicates that topical talk is as much the product of *how* speakers introduce, develop, and shift between potential "mentionables" as it is the product of what they actually say (Button 1985, 1987, 1991; Button and Casey 1984, 1985; Maynard 1980; Maynard and Zimmerman 1984; Sacks 1967, 1971; Schegloff and Sacks 1973). This research indicates that we must move beyond analyses focused on content and consider the specific mechanisms involved in producing *topicality*, that is, an achievement, the product of organized practices and systematic efforts by parties to talk (Maynard 1980). Conceiving of the problem this way shifts us from a preoccupation with conversational content to a focus on conversational structure. And as I will later demonstrate, it also allows us access to very different information about "sex differences" in topical talk than has heretofore been available or possible to appreciate.

PRODUCING TOPICALITY

One of the primary mechanisms involved in productions of topicality is the organization of turn-taking in conversation. This mechanism systematically generates speakers' ongoing obligations to produce turns at talk that exhibit their understanding of prior turns at talk (Sacks, Schegloff, and Jefferson, 1974, pp. 728–729; Maynard 1980, p. 263). Demonstrations of prior turn understanding provide speakers with a way for ensuring that they are heard (and heard correctly), but they also provide an analytical resource, namely a "proof procedure" for establishing what a prior turn was addressed to. For example, Button and Casey (1984) show that speakers often use expressions like "Really?", "Oh yeah?" and "Oh really?" to *generate* topicality in conjunction with some bit of news delivery (see also Schegloff 1982). These expressions are used in a three-part sequence of talk (see utterances with arrows below), including: (1) a query that "solicits" the announcement of news, (2) the announcement of the news itself, and (3) the "topicalizing" utterance that provides a warrant for its further development (Button and Casey 1984, p. 168):[1]

→ Nancy:	Anything else to re*port*,
	(0.3)
Hyla:	*Uh*:::::::m:::,
	(0.4)
→ Hyla:	Getting my *h*air cut tihmorrow =
→ Nancy:	= Oh Rilly?
	((continues on topic))

Through these specific procedures, recipients of "news" show their appreciation of newsworthy reports issued in prior turns and provide for next turns that further address those reports.

To be sure, all prior turns do not feature items that are newsworthy (i.e., reports that merit such extravagant displays of appreciation as "Oh *r*illy?"). More commonly, speakers demonstrate simple understanding of prior turns through acknowledgment tokens ("Um-hmm", "Hm", "Mm") that show their attention and comprehension. While topical talk is produced collaboratively, Maynard (1980, pp. 269–270) notes that it often involves a division of labor in which one party takes on the responsibilities of topical speaker and the other provides ongoing displays of hearing and understanding.

Speakers can also demonstrate their understanding of prior turns through *substitution practices* that tie the intelligibility of some current turn to antecedents produced in a prior turn. For example, a speaker can use various substitute expressions (such as "it," "them," "this," "that," "here," "there") that link their current utterance to some item that appeared in a prior turn at talk (Goffman 1983; Sacks 1967):

DYAD 15:92–94

Craig:	So what do you THI::NK about the bicycles on campus?
→ Marta:	I think they're terrible.
→ Craig:	Sure is about a MIL:LION of 'em.

A speaker can also show understanding of a prior turn through deletions that render an utterance intelligible only in a context of that prior turn (Goffman 1983):

<pre>
     Steve: I: am jus' kind of taking whatever I'm interested in.
                   I- I- enJOY going to school. So.
                   (0.4)
→ Carla: That's ⎡ me: too.   ⎤
→ Steve: ⎣ Jus'- learnin ⎦ g
</pre>

Using such substitutions and deletions is both a right and an obligation of speakers involved in talk-on-topic, for, as Goffman observes, speakers' failures to make use of these means of succinctness can lead others to question their motives. The speaker who iterates what would routinely be deleted may be heard as "[U]nserious, emphatic, sarcastic, ironic, distancing, overly polite and the like . . . Each utterance proposes, and contributes to the presuppositions of, a jointly inhabitable mental world, and even though such worlds last only as long as there is a warrant for a common focus of attention, one should not think one can go around failing to sustain them" (Goffman 1983, p. 26). Hence, the use of substitutions and deletions facilitates speakers' production of topically coherent talk in particular conversational contexts.

The turn-taking organization of conversation thus provides speakers specific procedures for achieving topicality and, in turn, our sense of talk as being "about" something. Speakers' obligations to display prior turn understandaing are what generate the possibilities involved in the use of topicalizing utterances, monitoring responses, and the various substitution and deletion practices here described. However, this description raises a further question, namely, the conditions under which a current topic can be terminated and a new topic posed.

TOPIC TERMINATION

Since topical talk develops on a turn-by-turn basis, many conversational topics appear to be "flowing of themselves" (Moore 1922, p. 211), with no clearly delineated beginnings or ends (Sacks 1971; see also Jefferson 1984). But others exhibit observable boundaries, created through speakers' collaborative activities (Button 1985, 1987, 1991; Button and Casey 1984; Schegloff and Sacks 1973). One way that conversationalists can formally move to terminate a topic is through the exchange of objects such as "We-ell," "Okay," and "Alright" (Schegloff and Sacks 1973, p. 306). These objects can be used to "pass" turns at talk by filling a turnspace without producing a topically coherent utterance or commencing the initiation of a new topic. Speakers establish the warrant for termination and an opportunity to shift to a new topic of talk through an exchange in which they collaboratively suspend the relevance of the next turn on the topic-in-progress.

Another way that speakers can provide for the possibility of topic change is by exchanges that collaboratively summarize a topic-in-progress (Button 1991). For example, an *aphoristic conclusion* may be drawn through one party's description of a "lesson" or "moral" of the talk-so-far and another party's affirmation of it (Schegloff and Sacks 1973; see also Button 1991):

DYAD 19:202–208

```
    Andy:          YEAH, they never DID come through with any presents
                   either.
                   ((five lines deleted on lack of presents))
→   Andy:          Well there's ALways Christmas, hh-hh-heh-heh
                   °heh ⌈ heh heh ⌉ .h
→   Beth:               ⌊ Ye:ah  ⌋
```

Alternatively, one speaker may *formulate part of the prior talk* in summary form
and another, affirm that formulation (Button 1991):

DYAD 21:09–15

```
    Jeff:   I wanned to do an experiment. My sister did an experiment
            when she wen' here. An: I wanned to try something. You know?
            I've never done anything like⌈ this befo::re.         ⌉
    Liz:                                 ⌊ I've really never ⌋ been a statistic
            or anyth ⌈ ing like that eh-huh-huh-huh-huh-huh-.h-.h ⌉
→   Jeff:            ⌊ THAT's ri:ght, I wanned to be a           ⌋
            statistic I wanned to learn how I fit in with the (norm or)
            something I gues:s =
→   Liz:   = Um hmm
```

Or, one party may provide a summarizing *assessment* of some prior talk and another, agree with that assessment (Button 1991). Pomerantz (1984) observes that
agreement is the preferred response to first assessments (except first assessments
that consist of speakers' self-deprecations):

DYAD 21 : 204–209

```
    Jeff:          I was lucky though, I got nice people in my hall.
                   (0.4)
    Liz:           Is that right?
                   (0.2)
    Jeff:          Ye:ah.
                   (0.3)
→   Liz:           'At MAKEs a big diff'rence.
                   (0.8)
→   Jeff:          Uh hu:h =
```

In each of the cases here presented, the speaker who initiates the summary also
furnishes the possibility of concluding talk on the topic-so-far. And in each case,
the speaker who affirms, acknowledges, or agrees with the summary thereby
demonstrates their orientation to the topic as possibly terminated (Button 1991).

Any of these "closing implicative" activities may be *held over* in speakers' next
turns at talk (Button 1991). For example, in the excerpt just above, Liz, with

whose assessment Jeff has just agreed, still reaffirms this assessment in her next turn:

DYAD 21:208–210

Liz:	At MAKEs a big diff'rence.
	(0.8)
Jeff:	Uh hu:h =
→ Liz:	= Really does.

Nonetheless, speakers whose next turns preserve components of concluding exchanges are not elaborating further on the topic, nor are they furnishing one another with further resources for such elaboration. Thus, they are still orienting to talk on the topic-in-progress as possibly concluded and still preserving a warrant for topic change.

Speakers may also provide for the possibility of topic change by *making arrangements*, for instance, to meet someone at some time in the future or to do something at some date in the future (Button 1985, 1987, 1991; Schegloff and Sacks 1973).[2] While discussing those arrangements, the speaker who proposes a future plan of action may furnish a possible resolution of how things can be arranged (e.g., "I'll see you there at five, then"), and thereby provide a warrant for treating talk about arrangements as possibly concluded. A next speaker's agreement with the plan of action (e.g., "okay") thereby concurs with that possibility. Button (1991, p. 260) observes that these activities furnish speakers with systematic procedures for organizing the very trajectories of topics-in-progress, allowing them collaboratively to display talk on a topic as "capped-off" and through these means, collaboratively to organize topic closure.

Of course, talk on a topic-in-progress may also be terminated through conversationalists' *lack* of verbal activity. Maynard (1980, p. 265) observes that topic changes often occur where a series of silences ensues, "indicating the failure of a prior topic to yield successful transfer of speakership." Moreover, Zimmerman and I (Zimmerman and West 1975) found that when acknowledgment tokens ("Um-hmm," "Mm") are preceded by substantial delays (e.g., silences of a second or more), they may discourage speakers' continuation of talk on some topic-in-progress and thereby provide a warrant for topic change:

DYAD 24:218–225

Tina:	my boyfrien's taking (Physics) Six 'n tch so .hh like they 'ave experimen's, they walk in 'n they uh .hh say well- DO everything you wanna do with a spring an' find out how it works .h h- 'r some-h-thing .h! Yuh kn:ow, NOTHing- it's no:t .h like- Chemistry 'r something like thAT where you- .h yuh know you go down .h 'n do this
Mike:	Yeah
Tina:	'n this 'n th a:t.
	(1.0)

Mike:	Hm.
	(1.8)
Tina:	°(Whew, it's) rilly we:ird. (0.6) Not so goo:d.
	(3.9)
Mike:	h-h-h-h
	(6.0)
Tina:	Hmmm:

Here, for example, talk about a topic-in-progress might better be described as having "died" than having been collaboratively concluded. Mike's minimal contributions, coupled with the substantial and progressively longer silences between speaker transitions, suggest a pattern of extinction (Zimmerman and West 1975). However, like topic closure, topic "extinction" also suspends the relevance of any next turn on the prior talk, and thereby provides a warrant for topic change.

It is important to note that, even though topic extinction and topic closure afford the possibility of topic change, neither guarantees *that* a change will occur, determines *when* it will occur, or establishes *who* will initiate it. Previously unmentioned mentionables may be introduced in the turnspace following a closing implicative exchange, in the turnspace following held-over components of that exchange, or not at all (Button 1987, 1991). And in the wake of a possible instance of topic closure, any conversationalist may launch a new line of talk, irrespective of who initiated the concluding sequence. To identify cases of actual topic transition, one must also be able to identify a *topic change*.

TOPIC CHANGE

Maynard (1980, pp. 263–264) characterizes a topic change as an utterance that is unrelated to the talk in preceding turns in that it uses new referents, thereby providing the warrant for a series of utterances constituting a different line of talk. This analytical description grounds commonsensical understandings of topic change in speakers' systematic procedures for its production. Maynard offers the means of identifying points of topical transition in actual conversation by specifying those features that distinguish topic changes from ongoing on-topic talk.

Consider the example just below:

DYAD 19:53–58

01	Andy:	So I have to run all the way over here. (.6) .h
02		Make sure I wouldn't be late. How- how long have you
03		been here anyway?
		(0.3)
04	Beth:	Oh just a few minutes. (0.7) 'Bout ten minutes.
05	Andy:	Oh! Jus' ten minutes! °heh-heh-heh Oh.
06	Beth:	I ⌈ t does ⌉ n' ⌈ matter. ⌉
07	Andy:	⌊ Well. ⌋ ⌊ So I didn't ⌋ blo::w it too long.
		(1.7)
08	Andy:	Where do you cOME from.

Note that Andy's and Beth's utterances in lines 01 through 05 provide a turn-by-turn display of prior turn understanding and relatedness, through specific conversational procedures. Answers ("Oh just a few minutes.") follow questions, displays of appreciation ("Oh! Jus' ten minutes! heh-heh-heh Oh.") follow news deliveries, and the entire sequence is peppered with various substitution and deletion practices ("So I have to run all the way over here," "Make sure I wouldn' be late," "'Bout ten minutes"). In contrast, the question on line 08 (after the topic-closing exchange on lines 06 and 07) shows no evident sequential or referential relationship to prior turns. Rather, its lack of relation to prior talk and use of new referents afford the possibility of a new line of talk:

DYAD 19:58–60

08	Andy:	Where do you cOME from.
		(0.7)
09	Beth:	Ventura. Not too fa:r from home.
		(0.3)
→ 10	Andy:	No not at all you go home every weekend? . . .

Following the topic-closing exchanges presented earlier, we noted similar transitions. In every instance, the speaker's initiation of a possible topic change proposed its referential and sequential independence from prior turns at talk.

To be sure, not all prior turns at talk are addressed to some topic-in-progress because not all prior talk is "topical." For example, unacquainted persons rely heavily on "pre-topical" question-answer pairs to generate talk, and such exchanges (e.g., "What year are you?", "Sophomore.") do not always generate conversational topics (Maynard and Zimmerman 1984, p. 306). Therefore, turns that appear in the wake of these activities—even when clearly independent in referential and sequential terms—cannot constitute "changes" from some topic-at-hand. In order to identify "a topic change," one must be able to demonstrate a prior orientation to some topic-in-progress (from which a change can be observed).

Thus, the detailed examination of conversationalists' procedures for "capping-off" talk on a prior topic and initiating a new line of talk offers an alternative to analyses focused primarily on content. It provides a means of analyzing topical transitions as achievements, things that are "organized and made observable in patterned ways that can be described" (Maynard 1980, p. 263). One can thereby ground a structural analysis of topical transitions in the close inspection of speakers' procedures for introducing, developing and shifting between potential mentionables. One can also examine these procedures to see how "sex differences" in conversational topics are constructed.

CONVERSATIONAL SHIFT WORK

Recently, Garcia and I undertook an examination of speakers' procedures for shifting between potential mentionables in five dyadic encounters between women and men who were meeting for the first time (West and Garcia 1988). Participants in these encounters were white first-year and second-year university students (five women and five men) between 18 and 21 years old. They were randomly paired with one another (women with men), introduced in a laboratory setting, and asked to "relax and get to know one another" prior to discussing and resolving a problem (bicycle safety on campus). Our analysis focused on the twelve-minute conversations they generated while getting to know one another, which were tape recorded and transcribed in their entirety (for further description of our methods of data collection, see West and Garcia 1988, pp. 558–559).

To analyze these encounters, we first identified all cases of possible topic change, that is, turns at talk that displayed neither a sequential nor referential relationship to prior turns. Since topic transitions are produced on a turn-by-turn basis, we could treat these as independent events. We excluded those sequentially and referentially independent turns that followed exchanges of greetings, introductions, and pretopical queries and replies, because they do not constitute conversational "topics."

Next, we examined the series of turns that preceded each possible topic change to determine *how* speakers arrived at these points of transition. We classified those cases that were preceded by a series of silences (two or more pauses of more than a second between speaker turns) and/or a series of unsuccessful attempts to produce topical talk (two or more minimal responses to another's contributions to some topic-in-progress) as *topic extinctions*. We classified those cases of possible topic change that were preceded by collaborative topic-bounding activities (drawing aphoristic conclusions, formulating prior talk, offering assessments, holding over components of prior concluding exchanges, making arrangements, and formally closing a topic down through a preclosing exchange) as *topic closings*. In the course of these classifications, we discovered still a third category of topic transitions, namely, shifts on the part of one party to talk, in the absence of any evident collaboration by the other (see the section on unilateral topic transitions below).

Of course, our strategy provided a conservative estimate of the total amount of work devoted to topic closure. By limiting our focus to closure techniques that were used in actual cases of topic transition, we did not include the full range of possible topic closings (such as those in which preclosings were followed by further on-topic talk). Moreover, the fact that we were analyzing topic transitions between unacquainted persons means our analysis may have yielded more cases of possible topic change than might occur between acquainted persons. However, our concern was not merely how *much* work was involved, but how the work was allocated between women and men.

COLLABORATIVE TRANSITIONS

In these encounters, we found 33 instances of possible topic change, that is, turns at talk that were neither sequentially nor referentially related to prior turns (Maynard 1980). We observed a mean number of 6.6 changes per conversation, with a range of 3 to 10 changes across the 5 conversations we analyzed. Of the 33 instances of possible topic change, 42 percent (14) followed collaborative topic-bounding exchanges by parties to talk. For example, speakers initiated possible topic changes following jointly produced assessments:

DYAD 24: 162–168, simplified version

      Tina: I was thinking of going in for social: SociOLogy 'n .h an'
                    research 'n stuff but GAW:d it looks so- .h hh so uh .h-henh-
                    henh ⌈ like rATs in ⌉ henh-henh ma:zes henh an' stuff
      Mike: ⌊ Compl'cated? ⌋
→ Tina: like th- .hh-.hh.h Rill:y. °tch Not very PERson-h-al = hunh-
                    hunh-hunh .hh
→ Mike: 'S *de*personalizing hh
→ Tina: Uh = ye:ah, rilly. Who:'s (y') Sosh One professor this quarter.

Following aphoristic conclusions:

DYAD 19: 257–266, simplified version

      Beth: He goes- he told this friend one time 'e wuz with us 'n
                    he goes Oh! Ye::ah they were both in my class an KARin
                    deSERVed her A. I'm not so su:re about
                    Carolyn. ⌈ But he ⌉ gave her an
      Andy: ⌊ hh-heh ⌋
      Beth: A anyway:. Think it wuz 'ee only ⌈ one ⌉ she go:t. =
      Andy: ⌊ .h ⌋   = heh-hunh
                    HH HEH-HEH! °heh-hh-hh-hh ⌈ .hh ⌉
→ Beth: ⌊ HE'S ⌋ really fu:nny though.
                    He's like that.
→ Andy: O:h
→ Beth: .h hhhh Wonder if it's been te- I'm SU:RE it's been ten minutes.

And following arrangements:

DYAD 22: 31–36, simplified version

      Carla: °What er we sposed ta do: (talk about bicycles anyhow)
      Steve: Ah. I 'ave a feeling that we're going to be talking about
                    bicycles.
      Carla: °heh-eh! =
      Steve: = hh-hh! =
→ Carla: = You get to re:ad it:
                    ((here, "it" refers to the contents of an envelope sitting
                    between them—a statement of the problem they will be
                    asked to discuss))
→ Steve: °Okay What- What's yer MAjor?

Of the 14 topic changes that were provided for by these activities, 6 were initiated by women and 8 were initiated by men. Put another way, women initiated nearly as many changes as men did *when those changes were warranted* by collaboratively produced junctures in topics-so-far.

In another 10 cases of topic change (representing 30% of the total cases we observed), apparent extinction of a prior topic-in-progress preceded the change, for example:

DYAD 4: 206–213

01	Tina:	seems like- (.) .h ev'rybody's alot more ser:ious this
02		year. (1.5) Rilly. =
03	Mike:	=tch It's fi:ne with ME:
		(0.5)
04	Tina:	eh-hunh-hunh-hunh Prob'ly keeps my gra:des goin' up. .hh
05		The CUR::VE high-henh-henh-henh-henh .hh
		(0.2)
06	Mike:	Oh ye:ah? hh-hh
		(3.5)
07	Tina:	Yeah. 'F ev'rybody ELse is studying, then you 'afta study
08		tWIce as hard to keep up -h. *he:ad* of 'em hunh-hunh .hh
		(2.8)
09	Mike:	Ye:ah. That's true:.
		(7.1)
10	Mike:	hhhh-hhhh
		(0.8)
11	Tina:	So, 'r you taking Che:m?

Here, a series of substantial silences between speaker turns culminates in a dramatic 7.1 second lapse (following Mike's delayed recipient response on line 09). Of the 10 cases of topic change following prior topic extinction, 6 were initiated by women and 4 were initiated by men. Thus, women were as likely as men were to initiate topic changes *when those changes were warranted* by the extinction of prior topics of talk.

In short, the majority (72%) of topic transitions in our collection was produced through women's and men's joint activity (topic-bounding exchanges) or inactivity (lapses in talk and failures to achieve speaker transitions). Twelve of them involved possible topic changes by women and twelve involved possible topic changes by men. Thus, those topic changes that were warranted by speakers' collaborative activity or silence were equally divided between women and men.

But in the remaining 27 percent (9), we could find no evidence of collaborative topic closure nor any indications of topical extinction. Rather, these transitions seemed to result from *unilateral shifts* on the part of a single party to talk.

UNILATERAL TOPIC TRANSITIONS

Men initiated all nine of the apparently unilateral changes we observed (West and Garcia 1988). In two cases, they initiated topic changes in the wake of women's "passed turns":

DYAD 24: 155–156

	Tina:	He doesn't do anything with the
		(2.0)

Tina:	the hh (0.8) (Na:cima).
	(1.6)
Tina:	So henh-henh-henh .eh-.eh =
Mike:	= When does this thing get started.

For example, here, Tina employs "So" to fill a turnspace without producing a topically coherent utterance or initiating a new topic, and Mike attaches his possible topic change to the laughter that comes with it. One might argue that Tina provides a warrant for topic change by taking a passing turn in the first instance, thereby displaying her orientation to the prior talk as possibly concluded. Mike does not, however, affirm that possibility by acknowledging it or agreeing with it, thus completing a preclosing exchange (Schegloff and Sacks 1973, p. 306). On the contrary, he shifts immediately to a new line of talk.

We found other seemingly unilateral topic changes that actually intervened in the course of topics-in-progress:

DYAD 19:9–19

```
Andy:    I:'m in Sosh. Sosh On:e, but I find it's so much
         Be ⌈ e Es ⌉ that- (tch) (0.2) .h ⌈ I'm    ⌉
Beth:       ⌊ Oh:: ⌋                       ⌊ We:ll, ⌋  this is my ma::jor
Andy:    °Oh!
         (0.3)
Beth:    hunh-hunh- ⌈ hunh-hunh, unh-huh ⌉
Andy:               ⌊ My goo:dness!      ⌋ h-hh =
Beth:    = But I'm not gonna do it, like I wanna go to law school.
Andy:    Oh I follow.
         (1.0)
Beth:    So it's a good ⌈ major for that ⌉
Andy:                   ⌊ Did ju         ⌋ take this fer- did you sign
         up for this test to impress?
```

Just above, Andy's initiation of a change interrupts Beth's possible "summing up" ("So it's a good major for that"). Not only does he fail to acknowledge Beth's possible summary, but her lack of completion intonation indicates that it might not have ended as it did if the interruption had not occurred (see also Maynard and Zimmerman 1984, pp. 310–312).

But the most interesting cases of apparently unilateral topic change were those that were initiated in the wake of potential tellables, that is, things about which more *could* have been said *if only they had been pursued*. In the excerpt just below, for example, Beth broaches a complaint while she explains her decision to transfer to another university:

DYAD 19:60–67

Andy:	you go home every weekend?
	(0.2)

Beth:	No
	(0.3)
Andy:	No?
Beth:	= I'm gonna- try (an') go to Berkeley next year. I didn'
	wanna go here. Really. It's too close to home.
	(0.6)
Andy:	What's up at Berkeley.
	(0.9)
Andy:	Is ⎡ the::re ⎤ ⎡ (a-) ⎤
Beth:	⎣ En:: ⎦ uthing. Just an in ⎣ teres ⎦ ting school.
	(2.0)
Andy:	You a soph:omore.

First, Beth states her decision ("I'm gonna- try (an') go to Berkeley, next year.")
Then, she ventures her complaint ("I didn' wanna go here. Really. It's too close
to home.") But Andy's next turn ("What's up at Berkeley?" does not display his
focus on her immediately prior complaint. Instead, it recasts the object of the
topic-in-progress as Berkeley per se (Maynard 1980, pp. 274–275). In the process, he glosses over Beth's complaint about being "too close to home" and when
Beth cuts off Andy's further question about Berkeley ("En: :uthing. Just an
interesting school."), he initiates a possible topic change.

Of course, Beth's response to Andy's question might itself be described as
unilateral, suggesting that there is nothing more to be said on the subject. Yet
as other analyses have shown (Button and Casey 1984, 1985; Jefferson 1980),
whether there *is* anything further to be said after "nothing" is determined in the
course of conversation. Button and Casey (1984, pp. 179–187) observe that
negative responses such as "E::nuthing" are often followed by next speakers'
further queries about a presumed "something" that has yet to be told. In the
case at hand, Garcia and I (1988, p. 565) argued that the *lack* of such followup
warranted our characterization of Beth's original complaint as broaching a tellable
that was not pursued.

To demonstrate fully the lack of pursuit involved in such shifts from potential
tellables, Garcia and I contrasted the excerpts above with others from the same
conversations (West and Garcia 1988, p. 566), for example:

DYAD 21:81–97

01	Jeff:	. . . Berkeley's gotten so DIFficult ta get into this year.
		(0.2)
02	Liz:	Is 'at ri::ght.
		(0.3)
03	Jeff:	Aw:, it was UNbelievable! I had three-point six:: (0.3) in
04		high school 'r three-point-six-two 'r somethin' =
05	Liz:	Um ⎡ hm:: ⎤
06	Jeff:	⎣ AND: ⎦ um:
		(0.3)⌐
07	Jeff:	I wasn' t acCEPted. I know a girl with a three-point-seven-
08		FOUR wasn't accepted, .hh =

09	Liz:	= What were your tES' scores, did you do okay (on them)?
10	Jeff:	I did oka:: h y, I got u:m a five-sixty in Math and a se-
11		no:, a five-sixty in ENG:lish, and a seven-ten in Math.
		(0.2)
12	Liz:	An' you didn' get acCEPted-? Yer
13		KIDD hh ing hh me = heh- ⎡ heh! ⎤
14	Jeff:	⎣ No::. ⎦
15		(.)
16	Liz:	Ga::wd!
		(0.3)
17	Jeff:	They were rea::lly tough.
		(.)
18	Liz:	That's rEAlly amAZing.

Here, Jeff is the prospective "troubles teller" (cf. Jefferson 1980), and he provides an initial intimation of that fact on line 01 ("Berkeley's gotton so DIFficult ta get into this year.") But in this excerpt, Liz offers ongoing acknowledgment tokens ("Um-hmm") and displays of astonishment ("Yer KIDD hh ing me!", "Gawd!") that are sometimes inserted virtually between breaths in Jeff's progressive unfolding of his trouble (cf. Fishman 1978).

And, consider the example just below:

DYAD 19: 152–158

01	Andy:	There's discuss::ion: an':: short- .h There's ya' know,
02		written an' oral exams frequently. Er (.) once in awhile
03		at least.
04	Beth:	Yeah, I'd like to take uh- ⎡ something like ⎤ Hist'ry (of)
05	Andy:	⎣ .hhh-hh-hh-hh ⎦
06	Beth:	Philosophy 'r something where you don' afta do any of that
07		kinda-
		(1.0)
08	Beth:	I don't thINK that way,
		(0.6)
09	Beth:	I'm not that logical.
		(0.4)
10	Beth:	Yuh know they go step by step.
		(1.2)
11	Beth:	'N I just- (0.5) I'm REally an irRAtional person sometimes.
12		(.) So
		(0.6)
13	Andy:	Where do you li:ve in Eye Vee?

Preceding this exchange, Beth and Andy had been discussing philosophy classes in which there were no examinations and students' grades were determined by their exposition of a "single question that they have been thinking about." On lines 08 and 09, Beth describes herself as the kind of person for whom such requirements would be problematic ("I don't think that way, I'm not that logical."). After a 0.4 second pause, she expands on this point ("Yuh know they go step by step"), and after a 1.2 second pause, she puts her initial self-description in still stronger terms ("I'm REally an irRAtional person sometimes.").

One could focus on the topic-in-progress in this sequence as one that is in the process of being "extinguished," noting, for example, the failure of Beth's prior utterances to generate talk from Andy at transition relevance places (cf. Maynard 1980, pp. 270–271). However, Garcia and I argue that there is something further going on in this exchange, something that allows us to pinpoint responsibility for the silences that ensue (West and Garcia 1988, pp. 567–568). Note that in the context of its occurrence, Beth's description of herself as "not that logical" and ← not the sort of person who "think[s] that way" is not a neutral description, but a negative self-assessment. As Pomerantz (1984, pp. 77–90) has demonstrated, the general preference for agreement with assessments in next turns (and thus, the closing implicative basis for those activities) does not operate in the case of negative self-assessments: to the contrary, agreements with negative self-assessments are *dispreferred*, and the turn following such an assessment is where the recipient's agreement is relevant. To the extent that Beth's negative self-assessments *invite* Andy's disagreement (and thereby, invite him to avoid criticism of his co-participant), Beth may be orienting to his failure to speak as an agreement in the course of production, that is, as unstated agreement with her negative self-assessment.

Of course, the fact that Beth and Andy are meeting for the first time might lead a devil's advocate to dispute our interpretation, suggesting that Andy has little information with which to disagree with Beth's assessment (perhaps she really *is* "an irrational person"—how would he know?).[3] But prior acquaintanceship is not a prerequisite for using the various forms of disagreement that are available to next speakers, for example, reformulating the negative quality as one that is widely shared ("Yeah, most people aren't made that way") or denying the relevance of the grounds for the other's negative self-assessment ("Well, that's not a good measure of what anyone's learned"; see Pomerantz 1984, pp. 83–90). Hence, Andy's silence in the wake of Beth's (increasingly) negative self-assessments cannot be dismissed as a function of the fact that they are meeting for the first time. What that fact makes even more salient is his seemingly unilateral topic change.

WHAT THEY SAY AND HOW THEY SAY IT

To pursue this point further, Garcia and I drew on Elgin's (1984, p. 29) description of a form of inactivity for which there is no word in the English language: "To refrain from asking . . . especially when it's clear that someone badly wants you to ask—for example, when someone wants to be asked about their state of mind or health and clearly wants to talk about it." This description provided us an initial means of characterizing a familiar phenomenon: refraining from asking when there are grounds for asking or when someone "clearly wants to talk about it."

We found that, through unilateral topic changes, conversationalists achieved a then-and-there determination of activities that would not be pursued and tellables that would not be told. In the process of such determinations, they provided an in situ enactment of their "essential natures" as women or men. As Zimmerman and I have suggested (West and Zimmerman 1987, p. 143), "Whenever people face issues of allocation—who is to do what, get what, plan or execute action, direct or be directed, incumbency in significant social categories such as "female" and "male" seems to become pointedly relevant. How such issues are resolved conditions the exhibition, dramatization, or celebration of one's "essential nature" as a woman or a man."

Following this suggestion, Garcia and I observed that if the resolution of issues of allocation sets the stage for the enactment of our "essential natures" as women or men, the determination of what tellables will and will not be told affords a fine vehicle for this production. A person engaged in this activity may be held accountable for their performance of the activity *as a woman* or *a man* "and their incumbency in one or the other sex category can be used to legitimate or discredit their other activities" (West and Zimmerman 1987, p. 136). Thus, explanation of the relationship between a woman's major and her plans for law school (perhaps an unwomanly aspiration) was aborted midstream, discussion of a woman's sentiments about being "too close" to family members (perhaps an unmanly course of talk) never took place; and a woman's assessment of herself as "really an irrational person sometimes" met with no disagreement.

The point of our analysis was not merely that women pursued certain courses of conversational activity (such as descriptions of their feelings) that men preferred to eschew (West and Garcia 1988, pp. 570–571). Rather, we argued that women's pursuit of these activities—and men's curtailment of them—both drew on and exhibited what it was to be a woman—or a man—in these contexts (see West and Zimmerman 1987, p. 144). Hence, evidence of women's "essential" supportiveness could be found in their collaborative efforts to introduce and develop potential mentionables, and evidence of men's "essential" control could be found in their unilateral shifts from one set of mentionables to another.

The moral of our story, then, was not that men always (or even typically) changed topics unilaterally: this was not the case in the conversations we analyzed. Instead, the moral was that, *when* unilateral changes occurred, they were initiated by men, and initiated in ways that cut short the development of women's activities and tellables. The exercise of control over topics-in-progress *was* the demonstration of "essential manly nature" in these conversational contexts (West and Garcia 1988, p. 571).

CONCLUSIONS

Our results show that topical "choices" do not necessarily reflect individual interests in conversations between women and men. Where men initiated unilateral shifts, we found women's tellables that did not get told *because* men did not pursue them. These included what others might categorize as "self-revelations" (such as feelings about home and family) but they also included "less personal" mentionables (such as plans for law school). This does not imply that women and men talk in concert about what men want to talk about or what men are "really" interested in. Conversely, it implies that *what* women and men are interested in is co-determined turn by turn, in and through their conversational practices. It also implies that "sex differences" in conversational topics may result not so much from the distinctive interests women and men bring to conversation as they do from their differential opportunities to express whatever interests they have and very different propensities for doing certain kinds of conversational work (West and Garcia 1988, p. 571).

TRANSCRIBING CONVENTIONS

The transcribing conventions used in these data are based on those devised by Gail Jefferson in the course of research undertaken with Harvey Sacks (Sacks, Schegloff, ed. Jefferson 1974, pp. 731–733).

A: When I was youn ⌈ ger ⌉
B: ⌊ I ⌋ do

Brackets around portions of utterances indicate that the portions bracketed overlap one another. Segments to the left and right of these denote talk in the clear.

B: 'S what I said =
A: = But you didn't

An equal sign is used to indicate that no time elapsed between the objects "latched" by the marks.

?!,."

Punctuation marks are used for intonation, not grammar.

LOUDLY

Capital letters are used to mark speech that is much louder than surrounding talk.

°softly

Degree signs are used to mark speech that is much quieter than surrounding talk.

((sniff))

Double parentheses designate descriptions, rather than transcriptions.

(0.5)

Parentheses around a number mark silences in seconds and tenths of seconds.

We:::ll

Colons indicate that the immediately prior syllable is prolonged.

But-

A hyphen marks an abrupt cut-off point in the production of the immediately prior syllable.

(word)

Single parentheses with words in them offer candidate hearings of unintelligible items.

( )

Empty parentheses encase untimed pauses.

(#)

Parentheses around a score sign designate a pause of about one second.

(.)

Parentheses around a period indicate a pause of one-tenth of one second.

hh, hh eh-heh, .engh-henh

These are breathing and laughter indicators. A period followed by "hh's" marks an inhalation. The "hh's" alone stand for exhalation. The "eh-heh" and ".engh-henh" are laughter syllables (inhaled when preceded by a period).

ACKNOWLEDGMENT

For their helpful comments on an earlier draft of this paper, I thank Renee Anspach, Carol Brooks Gardner, Aída Hurtado, the editors of this volume, and, especially, Douglas Maynard.

NOTES

1. Unless otherwise designated, all excerpts are taken from the conversations analyzed in West and Garcia (1988), identified by dyad and line number. The names used to represent speakers are pseudonyms.

2. Further topic-closing techniques consist of activities such as "announcing closure" (e.g., "Hey, I gotta go.") and "reiterating a reason for the call" (e.g., "Well, I just wanted to phone and make sure you were okay."). These alternatives were not available to the speakers whose conversations Garcia and I analyzed (West and Garcia 1988), so I do not discuss them here (see Button 1985, 1987, 1991; and Schegloff and Sacks 1973).

3. A devil's advocate also might contend that Beth's pattern of repeated self-denigration is difficult to handle interpersonally, insofar as it is difficult to be put in the position of bolstering someone's ego, and increasingly so, as the self-denigrations pile up. However, from a conversation analytic point of view, the question is whether this "pattern" would have emerged if Andy had voiced a response to begin with. Since agreement with negative self-assessments is dispreferred, and since responses to such assessments are relevant in the turns following them, Beth's repeated (and escalating) negative self-assessments may constitute responses to Andy's successive failures to speak.

SELECTED BIBLIOGRAPHY

ARIES, E. 1976. "Interaction Patterns and Themes of Male, Female and Mixed Groups." *Small Group Behavior* 7:7–18.

ARIES, E. J. AND F. L. JOHNSON. 1983. "Close Friendship in Adulthood: Conversational Content between Same-Sex Friends." *Sex Roles* 9:1183–1196.

AYRES, J. 1980. "Relationship Stages and Sex as Factors in Topic Dwell Time." *Western Journal of Speech Communication* 44:253–260.

BISCHOPING, K. 1993. "Gender Differences in Conversation Topics: 1922–1990." *Sex Roles* 28:1–18.

BUTTON, G. 1985. "End of an Awkward Report: The Social Organization of Topic Closure in Naturally Occurring Conversation." G00230092, London: Economic and Social Research Council.

———. 1987. "Moving Out of Closings." In *Talk and Social Organisation*, edited by G. Button and J. R. E. Lee. Clevedon, England: Multilingual Matters.

———. 1991. "Conversation in a Series." In *Talk and Social Structure*, edited by D. Boden and D. H. Zimmerman, Cambridge, MA: Polity Press.

BUTTON, G. AND N. CASEY. 1984. "Generating Topic: The Use of Topic Initial Elicitors." In *Structures of Social Action: Studies in Conversation Analysis*, edited by J. M. Atkinson and J. Heritage. Cambridge, MA: Cambridge University Press.

———. 1985. "Topic Nomination and Topic Pursuit." *Human Studies* 8:3–55.

CARLSON, J. S., S. W. COOK, AND E. L. STROMBERG. 1936. "Sex Differences in Conversation." *Journal of Applied Psychology* 20:727–735.

DIMOND, R. E. AND D. C. MUNZ. 1967. "Ordinal Position of Birth and Self-Disclosure in High School Students." *Psychological Reports* 21:829–833.

ELGIN, S. H. 1984. *Native Tongue.* New York: Daw Books.

FISHMAN, P. 1978. "Interaction: The Work Women Do." *Social Problems* 25:397–406.

GOFFMAN, E. 1983. "Felicity's Condition." *American Journal of Sociology* 89:1–53.

HACKER, H. M. 1981. "Blabber-Mouths and Clams: Sex Differences in Self-Disclosure in Same-Sex and Cross-Sex Friendship Dyads." *Psychology of Women Quarterly* 5:385–401.

HARDING, S. 1975. "Women and Words in a Spanish Village." In *Towards an Anthropology of Women*, edited by R. Reiter. New York: Monthly Review Press.

HIMELSTEIN, P. AND B. LUBIN. 1965. "Attempted Validation of the Self-Disclosure Inventory by the Peer Nomination Technique," *Journal of Psychology* 61:13–16.

JEFFERSON, G. 1980. "On Trouble-Premonitory Response to Inquiry." *Sociological Inquiry* 50:153–185.

———. 1984. "On Stepwise Transition from Talk About a Trouble to Inappropriately Next-Positioned Matters." In *Structures of Social Action: Studies in Conversation Analysis*, edited by J. M. Atkinson and J. Heritage. Cambridge, MA: Cambridge University Press.

JOHNSON, F. L. AND E. J. ARIES. 1983. "Conversational Patterns Among Same-Sex Pairs of Late-Adolescent Close Friends." *Journal of Genetic Psychology* 142:225–238.

JOURARD, S. M. AND M. J. LANDSMAN. 1960. "Cognition, Cathexis, and the 'Dyadic Effect' in Men's Self-Disclosing Behavior." *Merrill-Palmer Quarterly* 6:178–186.

JOURARD, S. M. AND P. LASAKOW. 1958. "Some Factors in Self-Disclosure." *Journal of Abnormal and Social Psychology* 56:91–98.

JOURARD, S. M. AND P. RICHMAN. 1963. "Factors in the Self-Disclosure Inputs of College Students." *Merrill-Palmer Quarterly* 9:141–148.

KIPERS, P. S. 1987. "Gender and Topic." *Language and Society* 16:543–557.

KLEIN, J. 1971. "The Family in 'Traditional' Working-Class England." In *Sociology of the Family*, edited by M. Anderson, Baltimore, MD: Penguin.

KOMAROVSKY, M. 1967. *Blue Collar Marriage.* New York: Vintage.

LANDIS, C. 1927. "National Differences in Conversation." *Journal of Abnormal and Social Psychology* 21:354–357.

LANDIS, M. H. AND H. E. BURTT. 1924. "A Study of Conversations." *Journal of Comparative Psychology* 4:81–89.

MAYNARD, D. W. 1980. "Placement of Topic Changes in Conversation." *Semiotica* 30:263–290.

MAYNARD, D. W. AND D. H. ZIMMERMAN. 1984. "Topical Talk, Ritual and the Social Organization of Relationships." *Social Psychology Quarterly* 47:301–316.

MOORE, H. T. 1922. "Further Data Concerning Sex Differences." *Journal of Abnormal and Social Psychology* 17:210–214.

PEDERSON, D. M. AND V. J. BREGLIO. 1968. "The Correlation of Two Self-Disclosure Inventories with Actual Self-Disclosure: A Validity Study." *Journal of Psychology* 68:291–298.

PEDERSON, D. M. AND K. L. HIGBEE. 1968. "An Evaluation of the Equivalence and Construct Validity of Various Measures of Self-Disclosure." *Educational and Psychological Measurement* 28:511–523.

POMERANTZ, A. 1984. "Agreeing with Assessments: Some Features of Preferred/Dispreferred Turn Shapes." In *Structures of Social Action: Studies in Conversation Analysis*, edited by J. M. Atkinson and J. Heritage. Cambridge, MA: Cambridge University Press.

Sacks, H. 1967. Unpublished lecture, transcribed by Gail Jefferson. University of California, Irvine, March 9.

———. 1971. Unpublished lecture, transcribed by Gail Jefferson. University of California, Irvine, April 26.

Sacks, H., E. A. Schegloff, and G. Jefferson. 1974. "A Simplest Systematics for the Organization of Turn-Taking for Conversation." *Language* 50 : 696–735.

Schegloff, E. A. 1982. "Discourse as an Interactional Achievement: Some Uses of 'Uh huh' and Other Things that Come between Sentences." In *Analyzing Discourse: Text and Talk*. Georgetown University Roundtable on Language and Linguistics, March, 1981, edited by D. Tannen. Washington, DC: Georgetown University Press.

Schegloff, E. A. and H. Sacks. 1973. "Opening Up Closings." *Semiotics* 8 : 289–327.

Stoke, S. M. and E. D. West. 1931. "Sex Differences in Conversational Interests." *Journal of Social Psychology,* 2 : 120–126.

Watson, J., W. Breed, and H. Posman. 1948. "A Study of Urban Conversation: Sample of 1,001 Remarks Overheard in Manhattan." *Journal of Social Psychology* 28 : 121–133.

West, C. and A. Garcia. 1988. "Conversational Shift Work: A Study of Topical Transitions Between Women and Men." *Social Problems* 35 : 551–575.

West, C. and D. H. Zimmerman. 1987. "Doing Gender." *Gender & Society* 1 : 125–151.

Zimmerman, D. H. and C. West. 1975. "Sex Roles, Interruptions and Silences in Conversation." In *Language and Sex: Difference and Dominance*, edited by B. Thorne and N. Henley. Rowley, MA: Newbury House.

nancy m. henley and cheris kramarae

GENDER, POWER, AND MISCOMMUNICATION

Females and males seem to have frequent problems of miscommunication, most notably in adult heterosexual interaction. Many magazines and books, in fact, offer to teach one sex,[1] usually women, how to interpret the other. Women's reactions to men's "street talk" is another example that what is ostensibly meant by one sex may not be what is understood by the other (Gardner, 1980). An extreme form of miscommunication is sometimes said to occur in cases of date, acquaintance, and marital rape, when a frequently offered explanation is that a male has interpreted a female's "no" as part of sexual play. Problematic heterosexual communication takes place not only in verbal, but in nonverbal interaction also, as facial expressions, gestures, and other bodily expressions may be intended as one kind of signal but received as another.

Nonsexual interaction also provides the circumstances of miscommunication. Patterns of sex difference in speech interaction may lead to difficulties in communication, as evidenced in such behaviors as interruption, overlap, and "backchanneling," or in hedging and apologizing. There are also sex-related differences in lexical usage which may lead to miscommunication: for example, the different meanings in the terms used by women and men to evaluate, or the different understandings they may have of masculine forms used generically (e.g., *mankind*). Space limitations prevent us from offering a complete summary of these differences; however, examples appear throughout the chapter, along with their miscommunicative consequences. For those who wish further background on this topic, summaries and reviews of sex differences in language and communication are widely available, for example in Key (1975), Kramarae (1981), McConnell-Ginet, Borker, and Furman (1980), Thorne and Henley (1975), Thorne, Kramarae, and Henley (1983) and others. All miscommunication does not necessarily lead to immediate disruption and repair of the conversation: It may be unnoted or unacknowledged at the time by the interactants, only to come up, or be discovered, later when the different understandings lead to unexpected different outcomes, such as one voicing support and the other nonsupport for a proposal, or dressing up versus dressing down for a social event.

Female-male miscommunication has been interpreted in a number of ways, most notably as an innocent by-product of different socialization patterns and different gender cultures, occurring in interaction between speakers who are ostensibly social equals (Maltz & Borker, 1982). We wish to examine cross-sex miscommunication and the explanations surrounding it with special attention to

From Miscommunication and Problematic Talk, *ed. N. Coupland, H. Giles, and J. M. Wiemann, pp. 18–43. Newbury Park, California: Reprinted by Permission of Sage Publications, 1991.*

the context of sexual inequality. This context creates the gender-polarized conditions that give different interpretations and different evaluations of women's and men's language usage; suggest that men and women have distinctive languages which demand interpretation to one another, and tend to create denial and reinterpretation of women's negations in the sexual realm. It is our belief that, viewed in the context of male power and female subordination, the explanation that miscommunication is the unfortunate but innocent by-product of cultural difference collapses.

This pattern of polarization, differential evaluation, denial, and reinterpretation is the same as that between different ethnic, racial, religious, age, and class groups (for example), when there is social inequality based on these differences: although cultural differences between groups are undeniable and may lead undeniably to miscommunication, that is not the end of the story. Hierarchies determine whose version of the communication situation will prevail; whose speech style will be seen as normal; who will be required to learn the communication style, and interpret the meaning, of the other; whose language style will be seen as deviant, irrational, and inferior; and who will be required to imitate the other's style in order to fit into the society. Yet the situation of sex difference is not totally parallel: sex status intercuts and sometimes contrasts with other statuses; and no other two social groups are so closely interwoven as men and women.

THEORIES OF FEMALE/MALE MISCOMMUNICATION

Explanatory theories of cross-sex miscommunication are based on expositions of gender differences in language usage, so it is to these we must first turn. The most influential theories have been *female deficit* theory and *two cultures* theory. We begin with them and present them in most detail. Then we look more briefly at other explanations that stress social power, psychological difference, language system-based problems, and cross-sex "pseudocommunication." We have found all of these explanations for miscommunication helpful and all of them limited. We next discuss some broad issues that must be addressed in an adequate theory of cross-sex miscommunication, and in the last section of the essay propose an alternative theory, which we call a multi-determined social context approach.

FEMALE DEFICIT

Despite women's supposed bilingualism in knowing both men's and women's language forms (Lakoff, 1973, 1975) and often-cited superior female language abilities (e.g., Garai & Scheinfeld, 1968; Maccoby & Jacklin, 1974), women's communication is often evaluated as handicapped, maladaptive, and needing remediation. To a notion of deviancy from a masculine norm are added assumptions and statements of the inferiority of "women's language." For example, the linguist Otto Jespersen (1922), in a widely cited book chapter, wrote that women have a less extensive vocabulary than men, have less complex sentence constructions, and speak with little prior thought and hence often leave their sentences incomplete (pp. 237–254).

Although more sympathetic to women than is Jespersen's chapter, Robin Lakoff's (1975) influential exploratory essay about the ways women's speech differs from men's still suggests that women are disadvantaged relative to men by a basically inferior, less forceful "women's language" which they learn through socialization. Lakoff emphasizes various female forms and styles conveying weakness, uncertainty, and unimportance. Her analysis of women's language clearly identifies it as inferior to "neutral" or men's language, and as contributing to women's inferior status; for example she suggests that women who use women's language" are "systematically denied access to power" (p. 7); she names the recognition of women as experts in making fine color distinctions linguistically "a sop," given in place of decision-making power (p. 9); and writes that women's lexicon and syntax are "peculiar" (p. 14). (Note that Lakoff's theory, besides being one of deficit, is also characterized as psychological; see that section below).

Earlier female deficit theories, like Jespersen's, seem to have been based in an unquestioned biological causation, women having naturally inferior reasoning capacity to that of men, for example, or having essential difference from men in interests, assertiveness, and so on. The more recent sociobiological theory (Tiger & Fox, 1971; Wilson, 1975) would attribute sex difference in speech to behaviors that display and exaggerate sex difference in order to help select superior mates, as a means to ensure survival of offspring.

Other recent deficit theories, such as Lakoff's, stress environmental rather than biological causation, either through women's socialization to speak "women's language" or through women's isolation from the cultural mainstream, leading to different life experiences from men's, and therefore deviant perceptions and values.

Consequences and Implications of Female Deficit Theory

Theories of female deficit, along with those of cultural difference (see below), have probably had the most consequence in our daily lives. A primary consequence of female deficit theory is the expansion of notions of male normativeness. By this we mean a view that sees female/male difference as female deviation from what is often called "the" norm, but is actually the male cultural form. The male normativeness is manifested in several ways.

1. *There is a focus on female forms and female "difference."* This is obvious in the many recent writings on language and gender that emphasize female speech, such as *Language and Woman's Place* (Lakoff, 1975), *The Way Women Write* (Hiatt, 1977), *Women's Language and Style* (Butturff & Epstein, 1978), and "How and Why Are Women More Polite" (Brown, 1980). Although most writing about language and speech is tacitly based on men's actions, very little is written on men's language and speech forms per se, which should merit as much attention as female ones, as distinctive cultural forms. This focus on the female is found not only in recent writings, but has earlier origins in, for example, the chapter on "The Woman" in Jespersen's *Language: Its Nature, Development and Origin* (1922), and the early writings of anthropologists who observed in faraway cultures what they often

called "women's languages" (e.g., Blood, 1962; Chamberlain, 1912). The focus on female difference of course emphasizes the underlying assumption that the female is a deviant (Schur, 1983) while the male is "normal" and speaks "the language." The ultimate conclusion of this view defines women as puzzling or unknowable, remaining for linguists "one of the mysteries of the universe" (Shuy, 1970, cited in Nichols, 1983).

2.   *There is pressure on women to use "men's" language.* Lakoff takes for granted that women will want to use men's language, though she does not always call it that:

> most women who get as far as college learn to switch from women's to neutral language under appropriate situations (in class, talking to professors, at job interviews, and such) . . . if a girl knows that a professor will be receptive to comments that sound scholarly, objective, unemotional, she will of course be tempted to use neutral language in class or in conference. (1975, pp. 6–7)

In the late 1970s and early 1980s, the general problem with communication between women and men was presented as women's hesitancy in stating their interests and wishes. The basic solution presented by many "experts" was (especially in the U.S.) assertiveness training, which was to help women change their behavior and be more assertive (e.g., Baer, 1976; Butler, 1976). That is, both the blame and the potential solution were located within the woman experiencing trouble in making others understand her (Henley, 1979, 1980).

3.   *There is an expectation that females should (re-)interpret male expressions.* Lakoff suggests that girls and women have to be bilingual, to speak both women's and men's languages. But there is no suggestion that boys or men have to be bilingual, even though she claims that young boys learn women's language as their first language, and have to unlearn it by around the age of 10 (Lakoff, 1975, pp. 6–7). Why are not men already bilingual, or why are they not too required to become bilingual?

Evaluation of Female Deficit Theory

This requirement of bilingualism, or bidialectalism, if it is true (we know of no empirical research directly on the question), would be more invidious than it might at first appear. We believe there is an implicit deficit theory underlying dominant U.S. culture, which requires (and teaches, through popular magazines) female, not males, to learn to read the silence, lack of emotional expression, or brutality of the other sex as not only other than, but more benign than, it appears. From a young girl's re-framing of a boy's insults and hits as signs that he likes her, to a woman's re-framing of her husband's battering as a perverse demonstration of caring, females are encouraged to use their greater knowledge of males' communication to interpret men's assaultive behavior, to make it in an almost magical way "not so" (Baughman, 1988).

Women, on the other hand, are not reinterpreted by men. They are in fact often characterized as uninterpretable and unfathomable by men. Yet many theorists and researchers have written about the ways that dominant groups of a social hierarchy (e.g., men) largely determine the dominant communication system of the society, and about the ways subordinate groups (e.g., women) are silenced and made inarticulate in the language (E. Ardener, 1975; S. Ardener,

1975; Kramarae, 1981). This *muted group* theory argues that women's voices are less heard than men's in part because they are trying to express women's experiences that are rarely given attention and they are trying to express them in a language system not designed for their interests and concerns; hence their language may at times seem unfathomable to men.

Although Jespersen's (1922) romp through examples of female deficit had many hearings in bibliographies, his statements and evidence are no longer given official credence. Nevertheless, the new theories have had strong effect; a belief in women's "inferior talk" is undoubtedly still the basis for many stereotypes affecting women's lives. Lakoff's suggestions and recommendations have led to many written papers that treat her hypotheses as fact or as the most important communication factors to study; this legacy persists in advice books that caution women to, for example, avoid "weak, feminine" tag questions. These simplistic critiques too often ignore context and within-gender variation, and treat women's expressions as feeble deviations from men's stronger expressions.

We reject much in the theories of female deficit because of their biased evaluation of female and male speech styles, and we reject biologically based theories as ignoring the large and complex contributions of culture and psychology to speech differences. However, the point made by Lakoff that society differentially evaluates women's and men's speech is largely true and must be taken into account in any theory of difference and miscommunication.

TWO CULTURES

Daniel Maltz and Ruth Borker, in their influential 1982 paper "A Cultural Approach to Male-Female Miscommunication," apply Gumperz's (1982a) approach to the study of difficulties in cross-ethnic communication to those in cross-sex miscommunication. This was one of the first papers on sex-related differences and similarities to discuss systems of talk rather than collections of variables. Because of this, their work has served as a valuable basis for further discussion about relations between women's and men's speech.

Rejecting social power-based and psychological explanations of female/male difference (explained below), Maltz and Borker prefer to think of both cross-sex and cross-ethnic communication problems as examples of the larger phenomenon of cultural difference and miscommunication. They put forward what they consider a preferable alternative explanation, that American men and women come from different sociolinguistic subcultures which have different conceptions of friendly conversation, different rules for engaging in it, and different rules for interpreting it. Even when women and men are attempting to interact as equals, the cultural differences lead to miscommunication. Another proponent of this two-cultures view is Deborah Tannen (1987), who writes:

> Women and men have different past experiences. . . . Boys and girls grow up in different worlds. . . . And as adults they travel in different worlds, reinforcing patterns established in childhood. These cultural differences include different expectations about the role of talk in relationships and how it fulfills that role. (p. 125)

When styles differ, misunderstandings are always rife. (p. 127)

Maltz and Borker (1982) compare the situation in cross-sex communication with that in interethnic communication, in which communication problems are understood as personality clashes or interpreted through ethnic stereotypes. Gumperz's framework offers a better interpretation, they emphasize, because "it does not assume that problems are the result of bad faith, but rather sees them as the result of individuals wrongly interpreting cues according to their own rules" (p. 201). (Note that this is what Fishman's "Social power (b)" explanation, below, does too.)

Maltz and Borker see the sources of the different cultures to lie in the peer groups of middle childhood: The rules for friendly interaction and conversation are being learned at a time when peer groups are primarily of a single sex, and the two styles are quite different. The world of girls, they assert (based on their own experience and on published studies of child play), is one of cooperation and equality of power; but because of heavy emotional investment in pair friendships, girls must learn to read relationships and situations sensitively. The world of boys, on the other hand, is said to be heirarchical; dominance is primary, and words are used to attain and maintain it, also to gain and keep an audience and to assert identity. The adult extension of these group differences in speech situations is that women's speech is interactional: It engages the other and explicitly builds on the other's contributions, and there is a progressive development to the overall conversation; while men's speech is characterized by storytelling, arguing, and verbal posturing (verbal aggressiveness). They discuss six areas "in which men and women probably possess different conversational rules, so that miscommunication is likely to occur" (Maltz & Borker, 1982, pp. 212–213).

1. *Minimal response.* As a prime example of different rules based on gender subcultures leading to misinterpretation, they cite the finding of gender-differential use of minimal responses (Fishman, 1978/1983; Hirschman, 1973: West & Zimmerman, 1977; Zimmerman & West, 1975). (A minimal response is something like "uh-huh" or "mm-hmm," given in response to another's talk.) Women's meaning by the positive minimal response (PMR) is said to be something like "continue, I'm listening," while men's is said to be something like "I agree, I follow you." These two different meanings of the expression and interpretation of PMRs can explain, Maltz and Borker claim, several of the sex-related differences and miscommunication findings: (a) women's more frequent use of PMRs than men's; (b) men's confusion when women give PMRs to their (men's) speech, then later are found not to agree; and (c) women's complaint that men are not listening enough when they (women) talk.

    (For the other rule differences they cite [pp. 212–213], Maltz and Borker do not make direct links to research evidence. However, their reviews of boys' and girls', women's and men's conversational interaction patterns in the previous pages of their paper contain many references, and we include some pertinent ones in the following brief summaries.)

2. *The meaning of questions.* Women use questions for conversational maintenance; men tend to use them as requests for information (Fishman, 1978/1983; Hirschman, 1973).

3. *The linking of one's utterance to the previous utterance.* Women tend to make this link explicitly, but for men no such rule seems to exist, or they explicitly ignore it (Hirschman, 1973; Kalčik, 1975).
4. *The interpretation of verbal aggressiveness.* Women see verbal aggressiveness as personally directed and as negative. For men, it helps to organize conversational flow (Faris, 1966; Goodwin, 1980).
5. *Topic flow and shift.* In women's conversations, topics are developed and expanded, and topic shifts are gradual. But men tend to stay on a topic as narrowly defined, and then to make an abrupt topic shift (Hirschman, 1973; Kalčik, 1975).
6. *Problem sharing and advice giving.* Women tend to discuss and share their problems, to reassure one another and listen mutually. Men, however, interpret the introduction of a problem as a request for a solution, and they tend to act as experts and offer advice rather than sympathize or share their own problems (Kalčik, 1975; Maltz & Borker also cite anecdotal and informant information in their footnote 4, p. 216).

All of these differences which they claim in conversational rules are, according to Maltz and Borker, potential sources of misunderstanding between the sexes, as other sex-related differences in language usage may be.

Consequences and Implications of Two Cultures Theory

Although earlier "women's" problem with language was seen as nonassertiveness, more recently the basic problem has been named *miscommunication*, and the general solution advocated by many lay and professional researchers is to help everyone recognize that women and men have different cultures, different needs and experiences, which lead to different ways of understanding and relating to one another. Colette Bouchez (1987) summarizes the evidence from academic and popular media for these "different worlds." She writes that often men and women have "enormously different interpretations of some of the key emotional words," that adults in the same culture often speak "very different and often conflicting languages," and that some of the "latest psychological research" tells us that the "misguided signals" between the sexes "may in fact be the underlying problem in such serious contemporary issues as sexual harrassment, some forms of job discrimination, and may also have an effect on the rising statistics of divorce and so-called 'date rape'" (p. 4).

One consequence of the cultural difference approach is this explanation of date and marital rape and other such forms of sexual aggression as extreme examples of miscommunication, in which males and females had different interpretations of their own and each others' behavior, and communication breakdown resulted. Sexual communication is an often difficult matter in western societies, complex in its layers of subtlety, indecision, game-playing, sex-specific prescription, and choices to understand or not understand. Muehlenhard and Hollabaugh (1988), though finding that over 60% of some 600 undergraduate women they questioned reported *never* saying "no" when they meant "yes," found 39% to report they had used token resistance at least once, primarily for practical reasons. To the extent that women communicate imprecisely the distinction between determined and token resistance, and/or men fail to understand the distinction, sexual miscommunication may result. Accuracy in encoding and decoding may be quite consequential here: as MacKinnon (1987) points out, men's understanding is part of the legal definition of rape. A man must both understand a woman does not want intercourse and force her to engage in it anyway, to be convicted of rape.

But is rape in such a circumstance truly a matter only of "missed" communication? No; in actuality, power tracks its dirty feet across this stage. Greater social power gives men the right to pay less attention to, or discount, women's protests, the right to be less adept at interpreting their communications than women are of men's, the right to believe women are inscrutable. Greater social power gives men the privilege of defining the situation—at the time, telling women that they "really wanted it," or later, in a court.

And greater social power gives men the ability to turn definitions of the situation into physical violation. If the problem really were cultural difference alone, would we have such scenarios? In purely cultural difference, the male's and the female's understanding of the situation would each prevail about equally. The outcome might be arguments in which either part's definition would prevail and the "losing" party would go home angry; or the couple might have sullen evenings of unexpressed expectations and disappointments; or when a man's definition of the situation won out, the woman would only be forced to agree that her interpretation of their interaction was wrong—but she would not be raped as a consequence.

Evaluation of Two Cultures Theory

We have presented two cultures theory in such detail because it is both prominent and seductive as an explanation for between-gender miscommunication (see, e.g., Aries, 1987; Tannen, 1987, 1990). For the same reasons, it is advisable to present a detailed critique of the theory. We note at the outset that authors before us have expressed dissatisfaction with this theory, though their criticisms have been brief (Coates, 1986, p. 154; DeFranciso, 1989, pp. 185–186; Graddol & Swann, 1989, pp. 89–91; Thorne, 1986, p. 168; Treichler & Kramarae, 1983, p. 120; Whalen & Whalen, 1986, p. 48ff.).

The first point to be made about the claim of cultural difference is that there is truth in it: Clearly there are differences in communication style between men and women, exacerbated by sex segregation in different situations, which surely are implicated in misunderstandings. As we have been among those cataloguing these differences, we would be among the last to deny them and their potential effect. Our point here is that cultural difference alone cannot adequately explain the full pattern of language difference and miscommunication; and that in fact such an explanation badly misrepresents these phenomena.

REINTERPRETING DIFFERENCES—CULTURE OR POWER?

We begin with the six female-male differences that Maltz and Borker cite as innocently underlying miscommunication, and argue that those differences may be interpreted in another light when the context of cultural *dominance* as well as that of cultural *difference* is taken into account.

1. *Positive minimal response.* First, Maltz and Borker's interpretation of positive minimal responses suggests that if, for example, women *did not* give frequent PMRs in listening to men, but instead used them only sparingly, as men do, that men would be satisfied and find women easy to understand in this regard. However, men respond to women's—and to other men's—PMRs as reinforcement—that is, they keep talking. PMRs are the basis of what is called *verbal reinforcement* (Verplanck, 1955); there is an extensive psychological literature showing that people tend to speak more, and more of any particular speech form, when reinforced with PMRs. (The question of sex-differential response to PMRs is subject to empirical test: When asked, would men say women who were giving customary PMRs were agreeing? What would be their response if women did not give PMRs?)

   But beyond this, Maltz and Borker completely ignore the political use of minimal responses. Zimmerman and West (1975) found men to use *delayed* minimal response (leaving a silence before giving a minimal response) with women more than vice versa. Fishman (1978/1983) similarly reports that "male usages of the minimal response displayed lack of interest" (1983, p. 95). Such behavior can discourage interaction and lead to the failure of topics initiated by women to become joint topics of the conversation (Fishman, 1978/1983), or even extinguish a speaker's conversation (Zimmerman & West, 1975). This seemingly innocent cultural difference, then, has the effect of supporting male dominance of conversation.

2. *The meaning of questions.* Males' understanding of questions as requests for information rather than as conversational maintenance devices may alternatively be heard as taking to themselves the voice of authority.

3. *The linking of one's utterance to the previous utterance.* Men's not having, or ignoring, a rule that demands that their utterance link to and thus recognize another's contribution (Sacks, Schegloff, & Jefferson, 1974) may be seen as exercising a common prerogative of power. Those with lesser power do not have the option to ignore the other's rules, or common rules.

4. *The interpretation of verbal aggressiveness.* Men's overt use of aggressiveness against an interlocutor in organizing conversational flow may also be seen as a prerogative of power. In situations of inequality, the one of lesser power dare not show aggressiveness to the other, especially unilaterally.

5. *Topic flow and shift.* Men's tendency to make abrupt topic shifts, that is, to ignore basic conversational rules, like their tendency not to link to the previous utterance (even when on the same topic), may likewise be seen as a prerogative of power, the power to define and control a situation.

6. *Problem sharing and advice giving.* Men's tendency to take the mention of a problem as an opportunity to act as experts and offer advice rather than sympathize or share their own problems is, like the tendency to treat questions solely as requests for information, again the prerogative of authority.

In sum, the characteristics that Maltz and Borker cite for females' speech are the ones appropriate to "friendly conversation," while the ones cited for males' speech are not neutral but indicate very uncooperative, disruptive sorts of conversational interaction (e.g., see Sacks, Schegloff, & Jefferson, 1974). In addition, they tend to be self-centered, also consistent with the stance of the powerful. [For further evidence of men's greater conversational rule-violating behavior than women's (in political debate), see Edelsky & Adams, 1990.]

If gender speech differences were *simply* cultural differences, there would be no pattern to them implicating dominance and power. In fact, Maltz and Borker remark that psychological differences or power differentials "may make some contribution" (p. 199). Indeed, two indications point to the *predominance* of power/dominance factors in female-male miscommunication:

a.   First, as illustrated above, there is a clear pattern for language style associated
        with men to be that of power and dominance, and that associated with women
        to be that of powerlessness and submissiveness (see also, for example, Lakoff,
        1973; Kramarae, Schlutz, & O'Barr, 1984; Thorne & Henley, 1975).
b.   Tannen (1982) states that in systematic study of couples, "certain types of
        communications were *particularly given to misinterpretation*—requests, excuses,
        explanation; in short, *verbalizations associated with getting one's way*" (p. 220; em-
        phasis added). "Getting one's way" is a denatured term for "exercising power."

Thus the overall pattern of miscommunication is not random, but rather founded in, and we would add, expressive of, the inequality of women and men. If power differentials simply provided an overlay, as Maltz and Borker imply, they would not be the *predominant* context factor in miscommunication, but a minor one among many. Clearly, the place of power must be recognized in miscommunication problems between women and men, as it must between any two cultural groups differing in power.

Maltz and Borker's elaborate explanations of girls' and boys' worlds as the biasing factors in creating two cultures of friendly conversational speech seem to require the startling assumption that the gender-differentiated behaviors came first, alinguistically, and the speech came later, and was shaped to fit the behaviors. Rather, it stands to reason that the speech and behavior patterns developed together. This point is important because Maltz and Borker imply that they have settled the question of "why these features and not others" by the explanation of childhood single-sex groups. As the explanation only points to childhood gender cultures to explain the existence of particular forms, it cannot answer the question of why certain language features, as opposed to others, are associated with girls and women, or boys and men. The links to power and dominance made above, however, do give a rational explanation for the source of particular features.

SOCIAL POWER

Two social power-based explanations that have been offered for differences in women's and men's speech in cross-sex conversation are cited by Maltz and Borker (1982):

Social power (a): This explanation states that men's conversation dominance parallels their social/political dominance, men's speech being a vehicle for male displays of power—"a power based in the larger social order but reinforced and expressed in face-to-face interaction with women" (Maltz & Borker, 1982, pp. 198–199). The chief proponent of this point of view is identified as sociologist Candace West (West, 1979; West & Zimmerman, 1977, 1987; Zimmerman & West, 1975).

Social power (b): According to this explanation, gender inequality enters conversation through the mechanism of gender role training, which serves to obscure the issue of power; the use of power by men is an unconscious consequence of gender role prescriptions. The identified proponent of this view is sociologist Pamela Fishman (1978/1983).

Evaluation of Social Power Theories

Arguments based on social power are crucial to an understanding of female/male communication and its problems—both social power (a) regarding dominance display correlating with sex hierarchy, and social power (b) regarding dominance differences in communication styles to which the genders are differently socialized. Contrary to Maltz and Borker's claim, it is the examination of dominance that tells why certain forms and not others are used by the different genders. Our evaluation of two cultures theory (above) explores the advantages of social power analysis in more detail.

Social power does not in itself tell the full story, however, if it ignores psychological difference and intercultural misunderstanding which arise from differential social power and differential socialization. A theory that integrates these different sources of gender-differentiated styles will offer fuller explanation and understanding of cross-gender miscommunication.

PSYCHOLOGICAL DIFFERENCE

One psychological explanation, that of Lakoff (1973), also reviewed by Maltz and Borker, states that socialization to speak and act in feminine ways makes women "as unassertive and insecure as they have been made to sound" (Maltz & Borker, 1982, p. 199); the incompatibility of adulthood and femininity saps women's confidence and strength until their speech is not just designed to meet gender role requirements, but fits the actual personalities developed as a consequence of such requirements.

A rather different psychological theory is put forward by French structuralist/feminist psychoanalysts Luce Irigaray (1980) and Hélène Cixous (1976), who stress language as the medium that places humans in culture. These theorists argue the importance of women's different biology and sexual pleasure, distinctive sexual differences that create a different unconscious from that of men, and the potential source of new female discourses to resist conventional androcentric culture and language. These approaches focus on commonalities of psychosexual differences rather than on historical and material factors of women's lives. With this psychological approach, many of women's experiences are considered repressed or distorted when women are required to use the linguistic processes created by men in a phallocentric culture. Although the essentialist nature of these approaches has been frequently and usefully criticized, it should be noted that not only this, but most of the theoretical approaches available pay little attention to the issues of difference and dominance (e.g., in race, class, age, ethnicity, nationality) within the category called *women*.

Evaluation of Psychological Difference Theories

The psychological effects of socialization, sexuality, subordination, and societal constraints should not be ignored in any examination of sex differences in communication and cross-sex miscommunication. Psychological difference can at the least underlie contrasting meanings attached to the same utterance; at the most, if the French theorists are correct, women and men create different psyches altogether. However, as with previous explanations, a theory based solely on psychological difference is limited: Communicative interaction does not take place within a single psyche, but between individuals (with psyches) in social contexts. An important task for social scientists, including communication researchers and theorists, is the delineation of the interaction of the psychological and the societal.

FAULTY LINGUISTIC SYSTEMS

Other approaches as well as that of Irigaray (1980) and Cixous (1976) (described above) suggest that as long as the language systems we use are created and governed by men, women will not be able to speak themselves clearly—to men or women.

AMBIGUOUS SIGNALS

Using an analysis that calls attention to our inherited linguistic systems, Deakins (1987) argues that English and other languages set the stage for ambiguity in that the same linguistic signs can be (and are) used to code both power and solidarity (see also Brown & Gilman, 1960; Henley, 1977). For example, a boss may intend to code for solidarity by saying "Good morning, Mary" and touching his secretary, but she can interpret it either as solidarity or power, especially if she is not likely to say "Good morning, Bill," but rather will use "Good morning, Mr. Jones," which may be understood as either lack of power or distance.

The indeterminacy of language systems which use the same linguistic signals for different communication function is surely a factor in many misunderstandings; however, often the ways ambiguous terms are used and understood can be explained by discussions of dominance issues.

DOMINANT METAPHORS

Although partly a corollary of the two cultures argument, and partly corollary to the *faulty linguistic system* approach, the *dominant metaphors* perspective has a distinct life of its own. For some years many articles, talks, and books about women in corporate management positions have stressed the ways managerial competence has been defined through metaphors derived from military and team-sports models (see, e.g., Harragan, 1977; Hennig & Jardim, 1977; Wheeless & Berryman-Fink, 1985). Some of the problems between women and men in management comes, it is argued, from women's not understanding, not appreciating, or not being able to use these metaphors to describe interactions.

For example, the manager who declares that "What this outfit needs is fewer tight ends and more wide receivers" may alienate employees who find the metaphor inappropriate, and confuse others who are unfamiliar with football. Ritchie (1987) believes that the use of such male-oriented, simplistic metaphors from boyhood games and dreams is decreasing. He reports hearing in specialized workplaces more use of music metaphors, with the symphony conductor coordinating the work of men and women expert at playing only one or two instruments.

Whether or not Ritchie is right about the decreased use of male-oriented metaphors, it is clear that the study of metaphors in organizations is increasing. In his book *Women, Fire, and Dangerous Things*, about what the categories we use reveal about our understandings, George Lakoff (1987) suggests that male-female interaction is governed in part by the metaphors we have for talking about lust—none of which are about a "healthy mutual lust" but instead are categories of hunger, animals, heat, insanity, machines, games, war, and physical forces.

In related work Julia Penelope (1986) argues that the "heteropatriarchal" metaphor of *control* ("being in control," "taking control") is the underlying concept that holds the sex/love/power/violence alliance together (pp. 89–90).

In her study of metaphors of conflict used in feminist organizations, Loren Blewett (1988) stresses the unchallenged ease with which metaphorical constructs are passed on within organizations, and the abundance of metaphors that encourage viewing conflict as war and violence. In focusing on women's uses of metaphors, including those that come from organizations and activities run by men, Blewett encourages discussion of problems that occur when the terminology we use undermines our desire for "non-destructive" interaction.

All of these useful discussions of metaphors recommend that we pay attention to the metaphorical concepts that often encourage violence and promote divisions.

CROSS-SEX "PSEUDOCOMMUNICATION"

Cahill (1981) adopts Habermas's (1970) term *pseudocommunication* to apply to the situation in which

> Variously categorized members of a society, because they share a common language and many common experiences, are likely to mistakenly assume that a consensus exists among them concerning the meaning of communicative behaviors. This mistaken assumption "produces a system of reciprocal misunderstandings, which are not recognized as such" or pseudocommunication. (Cahill, 1981, p. 77, quoting Habermas, 1970)

Reviewing reported verbal and nonverbal communication differences between the sexes like the ones cited here, Cahill notes that pseudocommunication is especially likely to occur in this intergroup relationship. He describes the intentions and interpretations underlying two examples of probable misunderstandings of gender displays.

In one example, a *dominance misunderstanding,* a male and female who are casually acquainted meet at an informal social gathering. He "pulls up into full posture and protrudes his chest"; she "cants her head and gives a sidelong glance" (p. 80). After a short conversation, he cups her elbow in his hand and announces the presence of a friend he wishes her to meet. She says she wants to attend to other friends, but he attempts to guide her across the room by the elbow hold. She frees her arm and protests; they have a minor dispute and separate. According to Cahill's pseudo communication interpretation, the male understands (perhaps unconsciously) his nonverbal display at their meeting as one of dominance, and her responding display as one of submission. But the female had understood their displays as those of courting or quasi-courting (Scheflen, 1965). Thus when she did not submit to his request to meet his friend, "the male's understanding of the situated dominance alignment was violated" (p. 80). And when he attempted to enforce that alignment, the female's understanding of the terms of the contact, courting/quasi-courting, was violated. Pseudocommunication—both believing they had understood the other's signals—had occurred, a form of miscommunication—and both felt their implied agreed-upon understanding of the situation had been betrayed.

Intimacy misunderstanding may occur because of, for example, a female's greater amount of interactional gaze than a male's, which he may misinterpret as indicating intimacy. He may thus reciprocate with behavior indicating intimacy, which she may consider sexually aggressive. Her seeming forwardness followed by seeming withdrawal will likely be seen by him as the actions of sexual tease. In another scenario, such female behavior directed at another male may provoke a proprietary male to a jealous response which she would consider unreasonable and overly possessive.

Although such description seems very much in the realm of the cultural difference approach, Cahill differentiates his pseudocommunication explanation by relating it clearly to trans-situational male dominance and privilege. The concept of cross-sex pseudocommunication provides a link between macro and micro levels of analysis (e.g., between explaining the prevalence of male violence against women societally and structurally and explaining a concrete instance of male violence biographically and situationally). It provides such a link because cross-sex pseudocommunication and trans-situational sexual inequality, he states, are reflexively interrelated:

> Trans-situational male dominance rests on the exclusion of women from culturally valued social activities. . . . This very sexual division of social activities results in cross-sex pseudocommunication. Cross-sex pseudocommunication, in turn, serves to perpetuate the segregation of the sexes. . . . Because it causes stressful communication, cross-sex pseudocommunication promotes preferences for same-sexed co-workers and, therefore, perpetuates occupational sex segregation. . . . Cross-sex pseudocommunication also promotes trans-situational male dominance more directly. By reminding women of their physical vulnerability when in the presence of males, cross-sex pseudocommunication promotes women's apparent submission to situated assertions of male dominance. (pp. 84–85)

Cahill's (1981) perspective is broader than the others in both proposing the mechanism by which cross-sex miscommunications are engendered and placing the mechanism in the specific context of cultural male dominance; and by linking micro and macro levels of analysis. However, the basic mechanism remains that of distinct female and male cultures arising from different experiences, thus it too suffers from some of the limitations of the two cultures perspective.

SOME CONSIDERATIONS FOR A BETTER THEORY OF FEMALE-MALE MISCOMMUNICATION

In working toward a more comprehensive theory of cross-sex miscommunication, we suggest the following broad considerations:

- Theories of female-male miscommunication have been put forward primarily by white theorists (which we are too) and are based largely on explanations of the actions of whites; to this extent their generalizability within the English-speaking, or any broader, community may be limited. (See the more extensive discussion in the next section.)
- As with all interactions, we need to recognize talk as an active process in a context that often involves speakers who may have different and changing concerns and who do not always have the conveying of information, politeness, rapport, clarity, agreement, understanding, and accommodation as primary goals. Discussions of miscommunication seldom, for example, talk about *anger* and *frustration* as emotions and expressions present *during* the conversation, not only as results of miscommunication. Women's anger in particular has frequently been denied or interpreted in terms of misunderstanding, inarticulation, and confusion.
- We might usefully consider the contemporary focus on miscommunication between women and men as a device that has encouraged thinking about oppositional spheres, as if women and men have innately quite separate interests and concerns. Attention to miscommunication is often a way to stress *difference* while ignoring *hierarchy*. Usually these discussions of miscommunication ignore the links between problems heard in female-male conversations and the inequities women experience through family policies, property laws, salary scales, and other repressive/discriminatory practices.
- We can recognize that boys and girls, women and men, belong, or are assigned by others, to particular age, sexual orientation, class, and race groups. Media attention to miscommunication pays little attention to this fact, assuming that only *gender variants* are involved. This is probably due in part to the fact that talk about "the battle of the sexes" is still often done flippantly, and casually. (In Western countries talk about the battle of the sexes still sounds much less serious and threatening than, for example, talk about the "battle of blacks and whites.") One way to trivialize the topic of female-male interaction is to simplify it, ignoring the interaction of race, class, age, sexual orientation, and sex group.
- Women and men need to be asked about what they experience as communication problems. The popular media have found it easy to talk about "mis-

communication" which seems to mean primarily women and men talking past each other by unwittingly using terms or concepts not understood by the other. Blame is often equally assigned to women and men in this (popular for the mass media) battle of the sexes.

- We need to consider further the definition of *miscommunication*. Is it an interpretive error experienced by at least one of the interactants? A mismatch between the speaker's intention and the hearer's interpretation? A response by one that indicates that she or he hasn't understood? How do we know when "misunderstandings" are intentional?
- We can recognize that all confusing talk does not involve "confusion" onthe part of one or both interactants. For example, a speaker might deliberately obfuscate. Further, a speaker who says something unintelligible to another may be little interested in hearing a clarifying question; repair of misunderstandings or confusions usually requires work on the part of both speakers. *Not* acknowledging communication problems is a common strategy for speakers who try to avoid confrontation in order to avoid another's anger and laws.

The Interaction of Race/Ethnicity, Gender, and Class in Miscommunication

The types of problematic talk experienced might be quite different for white/ Anglo women and women of color; and for women of different classes. In the case of race/ethnicity,[2] for example, many black women in English-speaking countries have not grown up in patriarchal, nuclear families but in matrifocal or extended families; the same is true for many Native American women. They may experience a lot of interracial "miscommunication" in talks with both white women and white men (Kochman, 1981; Stanback, 1987).

Class differences, which are well known to affect language use and values, must also interact with gender factors in creating, and affecting the nature of, miscommunication. Ethnicity, class, and gender may work either independently or interactively. The fact that race/ethnicity and class are largely confounded in multiracial societies puts special communicative strain on women of color, whose ideas, opinions, and interpretations are often not taken seriously.[3] In addition, the confounding of race/ethnicity and class sometimes causes class differences to be seen as racial ones; and the assumption of male speech as the norm may lead to taking it as an expression of a culture, rather than that of males of the culture, and ignoring females' speech, especially that of women of color.

White/Anglo middle- and upper-class cultural dominance is shown not only in the pressures on other races and classes to adapt to the dominant culture, and in the experience of those races' and classes' being wrongly interpreted, but also in the paucity of studies investigating communication within nondominant groups and between classes, races, and ethnicities. But distorting what information there is is the fact that too often observations and studies (the few that exist) of cross-ethnic and cross-class talk ignore issues of power and dominance related to gender, race, and class (e.g., Kochman, 1981).

A basic question we need to pursue here is: Do studies of interracial/interethnic miscommunication apply equally to women and men? Is there an interaction of race/ethnicity and gender such that different races/ethnic groups have different gender differences and different gender power relations, and consequently different loci of misunderstanding? Future studies need to account for the inter-related influences of culture, class, age, and gender—and of racism, classism, ageism, sexism and so on. As Stanback (1987) writes, a systemic, feminist perspective should be concerned "with exposing and altering the underlying values of the society, values which support racist, sexist, and classist institutions and behaviors, including communication behaviors."

SAME-SEX AND GAY-STRAIGHT ISSUES IN MISCOMMUNICATION

Left untouched in this discussion, built as it is on a literature focused on cross-sex communication, is the question of how *same*-sex communication might be detrimentally affected by issues of male dominance. Fasteau (1974), for example, discusses obstacles to communication among men based on macho role-playing that precludes expression of feelings. A parallel might be found in talk among women based on expressions of closeness; might truthful communication be buried under obligatory expressions (feminine role-playing) of closeness?

Same-sex miscommunication may also originate from gay-straight differences and stereotypes. Many gay males and lesbians, for example, report the experience of a straight same-sex friend or acquaintance reacting oversensitively to a touch or other expression of warmth, obviously misunderstanding it as a sexual advance. Cahill (1981) notes that males' typical aversion to the touch of other males may be explained by a combination of homophobia and the equation of intimacy with sexual desire (found in the research of Nguyen, Heslin, & Nguyen, 1975): "The touch of a male would produce a homophobic reaction in another male only if it was interpreted as indicating sexual desire. Notably, females do not exhibit a similar aversion to the touch of other females" (p. 82). Here, too is the potential for miscommunication based on cultural difference and dominance—that between homosexual and heterosexual cultures. This topic certainly deserves further exploration.

POLARIZING AND REIFYING GENDER NOTIONS

A prominent danger in examining sex differences is that of exaggerating them and ignoring sex similarity. A more insidious danger is that of accepting sex as an unproblematic category (Thorne, 1990). Similarities between the sexes are downplayed and differences exaggerated, as a general rule in Western societies, as is well evidenced by the elaboration of his-and-hers products, from pink and blue baby outfits and gender-typed children's toys to sex-customized razors, deodorants, and household tools for adults. Added to the cultural tendency to exaggerate difference is that contributed by the scholarly literature on sex difference, which has often focused uncritically on difference rather than on its underpinnings.

The exaggeration of sex difference gets much impetus from school settings, where the assumption of essential differences seems virtually institutionalized. Here children are treated as separate social categories by their teachers (e.g.,

made to line up in separate-sex lines, pitted as girls versus boys in many com-
petitions such as spelling bees or undeclared races to complete group tasks like
cleaning up), and addressed as separate categories even when treated as a single
one ("Listen, boys and girls . . .")

Despite the cultural emphasis on group difference, similarities of behavior
between females and males, in language as in other areas, are far greater than
differences, as many feminist scholars have pointed out. Maccoby and Jacklin
(1974), for example, in their extensive survey of studies of sex difference, found
only four out of hundreds of sex differences reported in the literature to be what
they considered "fairly well established." Kramarae (1977, 1981) has demonstrated that gender stereotypes of speech are much stronger than actual speech
differences. Sattel (1983) and DeFrancisco (1989), among others, make the point
that males' and females' speech forms reflect strategies for usage, not restricted
repertories. Thorne (1990) points out that "Gender separation among children is
not as total as the 'separate worlds' rendering suggests, and the amount of separation varies by situation" (p. 103). She notes, for instance, that many children
are more segregated by gender when playing on school playgrounds than when
in their neighborhoods, but most observational studies of children are conducted
at schools.

A subtler, and therefore worse, problem is the simplistic and unthinking conception of sex and gender to be found in most writing, scholarly and popular.
Thorne (1986) writes:

> Statistical findings of difference are often portrayed as dichotomous, neglect-
> ing the considerable individual variation that exists. . . . The sex difference
> approach tends to abstract gender from its social context, to assume that
> males and females are qualitatively and permanently different (with differ-
> ences perhaps unfolding through separate developmental lines). These as-
> sumptions mask the possibility that gender arrangements and patterns of
> similarity and difference may vary by situation, race, social class, region, or
> subculture. (p. 168)

Thorne emphasizes the complexity of the notion of gender, and strongly criticizes the tendency to rigidify and polarize gender categories in writing on sex
difference: "Gender should be conceptualized as a system of relationship rather
than as an immutable and dichotomous given" (p. 168).

A MULTI-DETERMINED SOCIAL CONTEXT APPROACH TO FEMALE/MALE MISCOMMUNICATION

We envision a comprehensive approach that does not have to choose *between* the
different explanations offered, but rather that recognizes the important factors of
each of these as forces. The difference in feminine and masculine cultures is
real, but it is not the only fact of existence for men and women in our society;
differences due to race, ethnicity, class, age, sexual preference, and so on may
compound and interact with gender differences; and cultural commonality exists
too. Most importantly, cultural difference does not exist within a political

vacuum; rather, the strength of difference, the types of difference, the values applied to different forms, the dominance of certain forms—all are shaped by the context of male supremacy and female subordination.

Furthermore, cultural segregation and hierarchy may combine to produce psychological effects in both women and men that independently engender and consolidate language forms which express superior and subordinate status. Both macrolevel power (a), based on structural male dominance, and micro-level power (b), based on individual socialization, exist and influence language use and therefore miscommunication. Structural male dominance favors the growth of faulty linguistic systems, including dominant metaphors, which express primarily male experience and further add to making women a muted group— leading to further problems in communication. At the same time, the general assumption that men's and women's words and behaviors mean the same leads to the problem of pseudocommunication, the false belief that we have understood each other, and misunderstandings may compound.

The differences and misunderstandings created by these factors are not equally engaged in all contexts: gender (like dominance) varies in meaning and prominence in different contexts. And this may be so for the different explanatory factors as well. For example, it may be that different speech cultures, to the extent that they exist, come primarily into play with marital/partner communication, as when wives/women say they want husbands/partners to engage in more emotionally sharing communication (Rubin, 1976; Tannen, 1987). Cross-sex pseudocommunication may occur especially in (hetero)sexual or potentially sexual situations. Social power may be said to enter broadly with all these factors, but may most specifically structure conversational interaction patterns. Rather than debating the merits of one factor over another, we would do well to turn our attention to ascertaining the contexts in which different factors enter to make cross-sex communication problematic.

In addition, this social context model assumes that men's as well as women's communicative behaviors are to be explained, to be studied as "caused"; that neither's speech is understood as either norm or deviant; that not only women's, but also men's psychology is seen as developing from their situation in the social structure, and as affecting their language style; that patterns of cross-sex misunderstanding may differ between racial, ethnic, age, and sexual preference groups, and the pattern in the dominant white/Anglo and straight culture cannot be taken as indicative of all. The model sees communication within the context of gender hierarchy as well as of gender segregation and socialization and assumes that not only the more noticeable (and often superficial) gender differences in speech are seen as underlying cross-sex miscommunication, but that also to be considered are deeper concerns of women's exclusion from the linguistic structuring of experience.

CONCLUSION

The patterns of miscommunication we have discussed occur within the cultural context of male power and female subordination: The accepted interpretation of an interaction (e.g., refusal versus teasing, seduction versus rape, difference versus inequality) is generally that of the more powerful person, therefore that of the male tends to prevail. The *metastructure* of interpretation—not what the interpretation is, but *whose interpretation is accepted*—is one of inequality. Females are required to develop special sensitivity to interpret males' silence, lack of emotional expression, or brutality, and to help men express themselves, while men often seem to be trained deliberately to misinterpret much of women's meaning. Yet it is women's communication style that is often labeled as inadequate and maladaptive, requiring remediation in which white-collar masculine norms are generally imposed.

As we have seen, miscommunication may be used to stigmatize: less powerful individuals (because of their ethnicity, class, sex, etc.) may be defined as deviant communicators, incapable of expressing themselves adequately. "Problems of communication" are often diagnosed in difficult interaction to obscure problems that arise from unequal power rather than from communication. The explanation of "separate but equal cultures" has been a means of avoiding reference to power and to racial and ethnic domination, and should be recognized for its implicit denial of sex domination as well. The complex patterns described above fit into the larger structure of female-male myths and power relations. One may in fact ask how well male dominance could be maintained if we had open and equally-valued communication between women and men. The construction of miscommunication between the sexes emerges as a powerful tool, maybe even a necessity, to maintain the structure of male supremacy.

ACKNOWLEDGMENT

A much-condensed version of this chapter was presented at the annual meeting of the National Women's Studies Association, June 1988, in Minneapolis, Minnesota. The authors wish to thank Barrie Thorne, Candace West, Vickie Mays, and Gail Wyatt for their helpful suggestions and contributions to their thinking. Nancy Henley wishes to thank members of the Southern California Language and Gender Interest Group; members of the University of California, Santa Cruz 1987–1988 Language and Gender Organized Research Activity; members of her spring 1988 graduate seminar on "Theories and Controversies in Gender and Communication"; audiences at the University of Southern California Annenberg School of Communication and Bard College; and research assistants Jennifer Murphy and Jennifer Stadler, for their discussions and sharing of ideas on these topics. Cheris Kramarae wishes to thank members of her Women and Language class at the University of Illinois and her class on Language, Gender and Social Control at the University of Oregon for their thoughtful suggestions and stimulation.

NOTES

1. In this chapter we have tried (except when quoting others) to use *sex* to refer to the two groups designated by women/girls/females and men/boys/males, and *gender* when referring to the general social structure of characteristics and relationships of those two groups. This may seem a backtracking from an earlier feminist position in which, since about the mid-1970s, many feminists have advocated reserving the term *sex* for biological distinctions and using *gender* for the more commonly referenced social ones. There are two reasons for our choice: (1) In recent years the recognition has grown that what had

been seen as biological is itself so tied up with social categorization as to make the distinction problematic; and (2) at the same time, the term *gender* has been used so frequently and ambiguously that it has lost its earlier significance, and now seems often to be used to *avoid* any reference to social constructs and hierarchical relationships. This problem with terminology requires more attention than we can give it here, but we have tried, in an admittedly imperfect way, to restore some recognition of these social/political concerns.

2. We use both terms *race* and *ethnicity* here to refer to concepts associated with persons of color. *Race* and *ethnicity* are somewhat parallel to *sex* and *gender* in their associations with biological versus social distinctions, respectively; however, it has long been acknowledged that race is a social, not a biological, concept, and we intend its use in that way only. Nevertheless, the two terms are not co-extensive, and we use *ethnicity* as well to remind us that there are various ethnicities within races. *Ethnicity* is not used alone, however, because its singular usage often tends to obliterate issues of color.

3. Etter-Lewis (1987) suggests that black women often use indirect confrontation— "fussin' and cussin' people out under their breath"—as a response to racist and sexist interaction. (See Stanback, 1987, 1988, for discussion of the research on black women and communication.)

SELECTED BIBLIOGRAPHY

ARDENER, E. (1975). The "problem" revisited. In S. Ardener (Ed.), *Perceiving women*. London: Malaby Press.

ARDENER, S. (Ed.). (1975). *Perceiving women*. London: Malaby Press.

ARIES, E. (1987). Gender and communication. In P. Shaver & C. Hendrick (Eds.), *Sex and gender*. Newbury Park, CA: Sage.

BAER, J. (1976). *How to be an assertive (not aggressive) woman in life, in love, and on the job: A total guide to self-assertiveness*. New York: New American Library.

BAUGHMAN, L. (1988). Graduate paper, Department of Speech Communication, University of Illinois, Urbana-Champaign.

BLEWITT, L. (1988). Metaphor and conflict in feminist organizations. *Women and Language, 11*(1), 40–43.

BLOOD, D. (1962). Women's speech characteristics in Cham. *Asian Culture, 3*, 139–43.

BOUCHEZ, C. (1987, October 7). Male vs. female. *Chicago Tribune*, sec. 2, p. 4.

BROWN, P. (1980). How and why are women more polite: Some evidence from a Mayan community. In S. McConnell-Ginet, R. Borker, & N. Furman (Eds.), *Women and language in literature and society* (pp. 111–136). New York: Praeger.

BROWN, R., & Gilman, A. (1960). The pronouns of power and solidarity. In T.A. Sebeok (Ed.), *Style in language*. Cambridge: M.I.T. Press.

BUTLER, P.E. (1976). *Self-assertion for women: A guide to becoming androgynous*. New York: Canfield.

BUTTURFF, D., & Epstein, E. (Eds.). (1978). *Women's language and style*. Akron, OH: L&S Books.

CAHILL, S. E. (1981). Cross-sex pseudocommunication. *Berkeley Journal of Sociology, 26*, 75–88.

CHAMBERLAIN, A. (1912). Women's language. *American Anthropologist, 14*, 579–581.

CIXOUS, H. (1976). The laugh of the Medusa (K. Cohen & P. Cohen, Trans.). *Signs, 1*, 875–893.

COATES, J. (1986). *Women, men and language*. London: Longman.

DEAKINS, A. (1987, October). The *tu/vous* dilemma: Gender, power and solidarity. Paper presented at the conference on Communication, Language, and Gender, Milwaukee, WI.

DeFrancisco, V.L. (1989). *Marital communication: A Feminist qualitative analysis.* Unpublished doctoral dissertation. University of Illinois at Urbana-Champaign.

Edelsky, C., & Adams, K. (1990). Creating inequality: Breaking the rules in debates. *Journal of Language and Social Psychology.*

Etter-Lewis, G. (1987, June). *Fussin'.* Paper presented at the National Women's Studies Association, Atlanta, GA.

Faris, J. C. (1966). The dynamics of verbal exchange: A Newfoundland example. *Anthropologica, 8*(2), 235–248.

Fasteau, M. F. (1974). *The male machine.* New York: McGraw-Hill.

Fishman, P. M. (1983). Interaction: The work women do. In B. Thorne, C. Kramarae, & N. Henley (Eds.), *Language, gender and society.* Rowley, MA: Newbury House. (Reprinted from *Social Problems,* 1977, 25, pp. 397–406)

Garai, J.E., & Scheinfeld, A. (1968). Sex differences in mental and behavioral traits. *Genetic Psychology Monographs, 77,* 169–299.

Gardner, C. B. (1980). Passing by: Street remarks, address rights, and the urban female. *Sociological Quarterly, 50*(3–4), 328–356.

Goodwin, M. (1980). Directive-response speech sequences in girls' and boys' task activities. In S. McConnell-Ginet, R. Borker, & N. Furman (Eds), *Women and language in literature and society* (pp. 157–173). New York: Praeger.

Graddol, D., & Swann, J. (1989). *Gender voice.* Oxford, UK: Basil Blackwell.

Gumperz, J. J. (1982a). *Discourse strategies.* Cambridge, UK: Cambridge University Press.

Habermas, J. (1970). Toward a theory of communicative competence. In H. P. Dreutzek (Ed.), *Recent sociology no. 2: Patterns of communicative behavior* (pp. 115–148). New York: Macmillan.

Harragan, B. L. (1977). *Games mother never taught you.* New York: Rawson Associates.

Henley, N. M. (1977). *Body politics: Power, sex, and nonverbal communication.* Englewood Cliffs, NJ: Prentice-Hall.

Henley, N. M. (1980). Assertiveness training in the social context. *Assert, 30,* 1–2.

Henning, M., & Jardim, A. (1977). *The managerial woman.* Garden City, NY: Doubleday.

Hiatt, M. (1977). *The way women write.* New York: Teachers College Press.

Hirschman, L. (1973, December). *Female-male differences in conversational interaction.* Paper presented at the meeting of the Linguistic Society of America, San Diego, CA.

Irigaray, L. (1980). When our lips speak together (C. Burke, Trans.) *Signs, 6,* 66–79.

Jespersen, O. (1922). The woman. In *Language: Its nature, development and origins.* London: Allen and Unwin.

Kalcik, S. (1975). " . . . Like Anne's gynecologist or the time I was almost raped": Personal narratives in women's rap groups. In C. R. Farrer (Ed.), *Women and folklore.* Austin: University of Texas Press.

Key, M. R. (1975). *Male/female language.* Metuchen, NJ: Scarecrow Press.

Kochman, T. (1981). *Black and white styles in conflict.* Chicago: University of Chicago Press.

Kramarae, C. (1977). Perceptions of female and male speech. *Language and Speech, 20,* 151–161.

Kramarae, C. (1981). *Women and men speaking.* Rowley, MA: Newbury House.

Kramarae, C., Schulz, M., & O'Barr, W. (Eds.). (1984). *Language and power.* Beverly Hills, CA: Sage.

Lakoff, G. (1987). *Women, fire, and dangerous things: What categories reveal about the mind.* Chicago: University of Chicago Press.

Lakoff, R. (1973). Language and woman's place. *Language in Society 2,* 45–79.

Lakoff, R. (1975). *Language and woman's place.* New York: Harper & Row.

Maccoby, E. E. & Jacklin, C. B. (1974). *The psychology of sex differences.* Stanford, CA: Stanford University Press.

MacKinnon, C. (1987). Feminism, Marxism, method, and the state: Toward feminist jurisprudence. In S. Harding (Ed.), *Feminism and methodology* (pp. 135–136). Bloomington: Indiana University Press.

MALTZ, D. N., & Borker, R. A. (1982). A cultural approach to male-female miscommunication. In J. J. Gumperz (Ed.), *Language and social identity* (pp. 195–216). Cambridge, UK: Cambridge University Press.

MCCONNELL-GINET, S., Borker, R., & Furman, N. (1980). *Women and language in literature and society.* New York: Praeger.

MUEHLENHARD, C. L., & Hollabaugh, L. C. (1988). Do women sometimes say no when they mean yes? The prevalence and correlates of women's token resistance to sex. *Journal of Personality and Social Psychology, 54,* 872–879.

NGUYEN, T., HESLIN, R., & Nguyen, M. L. (1975). The meanings of touch: Sex differences. *Journal of Communication, 25,* 92–103.

NICHOLS, P. C. (1983). Linguistic options and choices for black women in the rural south. In B. Thorne, C. Kramarae, & N. Henley (Eds.), *Language, gender and society* (pp. 54–68). Rowley, MA: Newbury House.

PENELOPE, J. (1986). Heteropatriarchal semantics: Just two kinds of people in the world. *Lesbian Ethics, 2,* 58–80.

RITCHIE, J. B. (1987, June 7). Metaphors in harmony. *Baltimore Sun.* Perspective, 5B.

RUBIN, L. B. (1976). *Worlds of pain: Life in the working-class family.* New York: Basic Books.

SACKS, H., Schegloff, E. A., & Jefferson, G. (1974). A simplest systematics for the organization of turn-taking for conversation. *Language, 50,* 696–735.

SATTEL, J. (1983). Men, inexpressiveness, and power. In B. Thorne, C. Kramarae, & N. Henley (Eds.), *Language, gender, and society* (pp. 118–124). Rowley, MA: Newbury House.

SCHEFLEN, A. (1965). Quasi-courtship behavior in psychotherapy. *Psychiatry, 28,* 245–257.

SHUY, R. (1970). Sociolinguistic research at the Center for Applied Linguistics: The correlation of language and sex. *Industrial Days of Sociolinguistics.* Rome: Istituto Luigi Sturzo.

STANBACK, M. H. (1987, November). *Claiming our space; finding our voice: Feminist theory and black women's talk.* Paper presented at the Black and Women's Caucuses, Speech Communication Association, Boston, MA.

STANBACK, M. H. (1988). What makes scholarship about black women and communication feminist communication scholarship? *Women's Studies in Communication, 11,* 28–31.

TANNEN, D. (1982). Ethnic style in male-female conversation. In J. J. Gumperz (Ed.), *Language and social identity* (pp. 217–231). Cambridge, UK: Cambridge University Press.

TANNEN, D. (1987). *That's not what I meant! How conversational style makes or breaks relationships.* New York: Ballantine.

TANNEN, D. (1990). *You just don't understand: Women and men in conversation.* New York: Morrow.

THORNE, B. (1986). Girls and boys together. . . . But mostly apart: Gender arrangements in elementary schools. In W. W. Hartup & Z. Rubin (Eds.), *Relationships and development.* Hillsdale, NJ: Lawrence Erlbaum.

THORNE, B. (1990). Children and gender: Constructions of difference. In D. Rhode (Ed.), *Theoretical perspectives on sexual difference.* New Haven, CT: Yale University Press.

THORNE, B., & Henley, N. (1975). Difference and dominance: An overview of language, gender, and society. In B. Thorne & N. Henley (Eds.), *Language and sex: Difference and dominance* (pp. 5–42). Rowley, MA: Newbury House.

THORNE, B., Kramarae, C., & Henley, N. (Eds.). (1983). *Language, gender and society.* Rowley, MA: Newbury House.

TIGER, L., & Fox, R. (1971). *The imperial animal.* New York: Holt, Rinehart & Winston.

TREICHLER, P., & Kramarae, C. (1983). Women's talk in the ivory tower. *Communication Quarterly, 31,* 118–132.

VERPLANCK, W. (1955). The control of the content of conversation: Reinforcement of statements of opinion. *Journal of Abnormal and Social Psychology, 51,* 668–676.

WEST, C. (1979). Against our will: Male interruptions of females in cross-sex conversations. In J. Orasanu, M. K. Slater, & L. L. Adler (Eds.), *Language, sex and gender: Does la différence make a difference?* New York: New York Academy of Sciences.

WEST, C., & Zimmerman, D. (1977). Women's place in everyday talk: Reflections on parent-child interaction. *Social Problems, 14,* 521–529.

WEST, C., & Zimmerman, D. (1987). Doing gender. *Gender & Society, 1,* 125–151.

WHALEN, J., & Whalen, M. (1986). *"Doing gender" and children's natural language practices.* Working paper No. 23. Eugene: University of Oregon, Center for the Study of Women in Society.

WHEELESS, V. E., & Berryman-Fink, C. (1985). Perceptions of women managers and their communicator competencies. *Communication Quarterly, 33,* 137–148.

WILSON, E. (1975). *Sociobiology: The new synthesis.* Cambridge, MA: Harvard University Press.

ZIMMERMAN, D. H., & West, C. (1975). Sex roles, interruptions, and silences in conversations. In B. Thorne & N. Henley (Eds.), *Language and sex: Difference and dominance* (pp. 105–129). Rowley, MA: Newbury House.

susan gal

BETWEEN SPEECH AND SILENCE

The Problematics of Research on Language and Gender

The historic silence of women in public life, and women's attempts to gain a voice in politics and literature, have been major themes of recent feminist scholarship. It has become clear that gender relations are created not only by a sexual division of labor and a set of symbolic images, but also through contrasting possibilities of expression for men and women. Feminists have explicitly written about scholarship's responsibility to "hear women's words" and have rightly argued the theoretical importance of "rediscover[ing] women's voices" (Smith-Rosenberg 1985: 11, 26).

In these writings, silence is generally deplored, because it is taken to be a result and a symbol of passivity and powerlessness: those who are denied speech cannot make their experience known and thus cannot influence the course of their lives or of history.[1] In a telling contrast, other scholars have emphasized the paradoxical power of silence, especially in certain institutional settings. In religious confession, modern psychotherapy, bureaucratic interviews, and in police interrogation, the relations of coercion are reversed: where self-exposure is required, it is the silent listener who judges, and who thereby exerts power over the one who speaks (Foucault 1978: 61–62). Similarly, silence in American households is often a weapon of masculine power (Sattel 1983). But silence can also be a strategic defense against the powerful, as when Western Apache men use it to baffle, disconcert, and exclude white outsiders (Basso 1979). And this does not exhaust the meanings of silence. For the English Quakers of the seventeenth century, both men and women, the refusal to speak when others expected them to marked an ideological commitment. It was the opposite of passivity, indeed a form of political protest (Bauman 1983).[2]

The juxtaposition of these different constructions of silence highlights the three issues I would like to raise in this chapter. First, and most generally, the example of silence suggests a close link between gender, the use of speech (or silence), and the exercise of power. But it also shows that the link is not direct. On the contrary, it appears that silence, like any linguistic form, gains different meanings and has different material effects within specific institutional and cultural contexts. Silence and inarticulateness are not, in themselves, necessarily signs of powerlessness. Indeed, my first goal is to draw on a cultural analysis to show how the links between linguistic practices, power, and gender are themselves culturally constructed.

Yet these cultural constructions are not always stable, nor passively accepted and reproduced by speakers. The examples of silence as subversive defense and even political protest suggest that linguistic forms, even the most apparently quiescent, are strategic actions, created as responses to cultural and institutional contexts (Gumperz 1982). Although sociolinguistic studies have long noted differences between men's and women's everyday linguistic forms, much early research considered talk to be simply an index of identity: merely one of the many behaviors learned through socialization which formed part of men's and women's different social roles. Recent reconceptualizations of gender reject this implicit role theory and promise a deeper understanding of the genesis and persistence of gender differences in speech. They argue that gender is better seen as a system of culturally constructed relations of power, produced and reproduced in interaction between and among men and women.[3] I draw on sociolinguistic studies of everyday talk to provide evidence that it is in part through verbal practices in social interaction that the structural relations of gender and dominance are perpetuated and sometimes subverted: in social institutions such as schools, courts, and political assemblies, talk is often used to judge, define, and legitimate speakers. Thus, small interactional skirmishes have striking material consequences. My second goal is to show how verbal interaction, whatever else it accomplishes, is often the site of struggle about gender definitions and power; it concerns who can speak where about what.

Finally, such struggles about gaining a voice, and my earlier example of women's silence in public life, draw attention to a currently widespread and influential metaphor in both feminist and nonfeminist social science. Terms such as "women's language," "voice," or "words" are routinely used not only to designate everyday talk but also, much more broadly, to denote the public expression of a particular perspective on self and social life, the effort to represent one's own experience, rather than accepting the representations of more powerful others. And similarly, "silence" and "muteness" (E. Ardener 1975) are used not only in their ordinary senses of an inability or reluctance to create utterances in conversational exchange, but as references as well to the failure to produce one's own separate, socially significant discourse. It is in this broader sense that feminist historians have rediscovered women's words. Here, "word" becomes a synecdoche for "consciousness."

Yet, despite this metaphorical link, everyday talk and the broader notion of a gendered consciousness have only rarely been investigated together, or by the same scholars. Studies of gender differences in everyday talk have tended to focus on the formal properties of speech—intonational, phonological, syntactic, and pragmatic differences between men and women, and the institutional and interactional contexts in which they occur. In contrast, studies of "women's voice" have focused more on values and beliefs: whether or not women have cultural conceptions or symbolic systems concerning self, morality, or social reality, different from those of the dominant discourse.[4] That the two are inextricably linked becomes evident when we view both kinds of research as studies of symbolic domination.

As my discussion of the culturally defined links between speech and power will show, some linguistic strategies and genres are more highly valued and carry more authority than others. In a classic case of symbolic domination, even those who do not control these authoritative forms consider them more credible or persuasive (Bourdieu 1977b). Archetypal examples include standard languages and ritual speech. But these respected linguistic practices are not simply forms; they deliver characteristic cultural definitions of social life that, embodied in divisions of labor and the structure of institutions, serve the interests of some groups better than others. Indeed, it is in part through such linguistic practices that speakers within institutions impose on others their group's definition of events, people, and actions. This ability to make others accept and enact one's representation of the world is another aspect of symbolic domination. But such cultural power rarely goes uncontested. Resistance to a dominant cultural order occurs when devalued linguistic strategies and genres are practiced and celebrated despite widespread denigration; it occurs as well when these devalued practices propose or embody alternate models of the social world.

Several influential social theories that differ importantly in other respects have in one way or another articulated this insight. Whether we use Gramsci's term "cultural hegemony," or symbolic domination (Bourdieu 1977a); oppositional, emergent, and residual cultures (Williams 1973); or subjugated knowledges (Foucault 1980), the central notion remains: the control of discourse or of representations of reality occurs in social interaction, located in institutions, and is a source of social power; it may be, therefore, the occasion for coercion, conflict, or complicity.[5] Missing from these theories is a concept of gender as a structure of social relations (separate from class or ethnicity), reproduced but also challenged in everyday practice. These theories neither notice nor explain the subtlety, subversion, and opposition to dominant definitions which feminists have discovered in many women's genres, and sometimes embedded in women's everyday talk. Indeed, even the authority of some (male) linguistic forms and their dominance of social institutions such as medicine or the political process remain mysterious without a theory of gender.

This interaction of gender and discourse has been explored by recent feminist analyses in literature and anthropology; some have suggested that women's "voices" often differ significantly in form as well as content from dominant discourse.[6] The importance of integrating the study of everyday talk with the study of "women's voice" becomes apparent: the attention to the details of linguistic form and context typical of research into everyday talk is indispensable in order to gain access to women's often veiled genres and muted "words." And both kinds of studies must attend not only to words but to the interactional practices and the broader political and economic context of communication in order to understand the process by which women's voices—in both senses—are routinely suppressed or manage to emerge. My final aim is to show that, if we understand women's everyday talk and linguistic genres as forms of resistance, we hear, in any culture, not so much a clear and heretofore neglected "woman's voice," or separate culture, but rather linguistic practices that are more ambiguous, often contradictory, differing among women of different classes and ethnic groups and ranging from accommodation to opposition, subversion, rejection, or autonomous reconstruction of reigning cultural definitions.

Thus, my theme is the link between gender, speech, and power, and the ways this can be conceptualized on the basis of recent empirical research. I will first explore what counts, cross-culturally, as powerful speech; then show the differential power of men's and women's linguistic strategies in social institutions; and finally reinterpret women's strategies and linguistic genres as forms of resistance to symbolic domination.

CULTURAL CONSTRUCTIONS

Many cultures posit a close connection between the use of language and the emergence of the self. This is well illustrated by the Laymi Indians of Highland Bolivia, a group of settled peasants engaged in subsistence agriculture. They represent a newborn individual's progression to a fully socialized human in terms of the child's relation to language: a baby becomes a child when it starts to say words; the passage from childhood to young adulthood is said to occur when the individual can speak and understand fully (Harris 1980: 72). Some cultural conceptions that link person and language appear not to be focused on gender at all. For instance, the metalinguistic discourse of the Kaluli in New Guinea classifies speakers largely on the basis of clan or village origin (Schieffelin 1987). Similarly, in Samoa rank seems much more important in ideas about speech than gender (Ochs 1987). Nevertheless, there are many cases in which not just personhood, but gender as well are conceptualized in terms of language. Such conceptualizations define the symbolic significance of men's and women's speech features: what is powerful and weak, beautiful or execrable, masculine and feminine, in the realm of talk. Men's and women's linguistic practices are profoundly shaped by such cultural images.[7]

Perhaps the best example is Keenan's (1974) study of the Malagasy of Madagascar, who explicitly associate different styles of talk with men and women. According to the Malagasy, men characteristically use an indirect, ornate and respectful style that avoids confrontation and disagreement with others; women use a direct style of speaking associated with excitableness and anger, that is seen as a source of conflict and threat in interpersonal relations. Women are excluded from the major formal genre of oratory that is required for participation in political events. And men avoid a series of speech activities that women engage in, such as accusations, market haggling and gossip. Importantly, these differences are linked to notions about power. First, both men and women consider men's speech far superior. Second, it is women's directness, defined as inept, that is said to bar them from political authority and from speaking at political meetings where the egalitarian social system requires that the existence of conflict be skillfully hidden.

Yet, cross-cultural evidence indicates that indirectness is not always associated with masculinity, nor confrontation with women. The case of American gender stereotypes provides an informative contrast. The cultural evaluation of American middle-class speech is revealed in studies of Midwestern teenagers who think of men's speech as "aggressive," "forceful," "blunt," and "authoritarian," whereas women's speech is considered "gentle," "trivial," "correct," and "polite." Only careful empirical research can document the subtle differences that actually exist between American men's and women's speech, but these stereotypes provide the expectations and ideals against which speakers are routinely judged (Kramarae 1980). Indeed, there is an entire literature of advice books, etiquette manuals, and philological and linguistic tracts published in the United States and Western Europe which have for several centuries constructed, without benefit of evidence, images of male and female "natures" linked to their supposed speech patterns (Kramarae 1980: 91).[8] From the example of the Malagasy and American stereotypes it might appear that, whether blunt or indirect, verbal skills of some kind are associated with authority and power. A contrast to both is provided by Irvine's (1979) description of the Wolof of Senegal, who are organized into a stratified caste system. High caste nobles derive their power from an inherited quality manifested as a sense of reserve in all activities. Diffidence and inarticulateness are so much a part of noble demeanor that elite men often hire low-status professional orators to speak for them in order to avoid showing verbal fluency in public. Thus, cultural conceptions demand that ordinary men and women be more articulate than men with high status.

Although inarticulateness is a trait that is a sign of a Wolof man's elite identity, it is exactly inarticulateness that is represented as women's defining and debilitating condition in rural Greece. The image of women is not unitary in Greece: they are seen as both garrulous and silent. But in both modes women are conceptualized as incapable of controlling themselves and therefore of achieving the articulate and swaggering self-display that constitutes the culturally constructed image of powerful men (Herzfeld 1985).

These examples from disparate groups provide a useful demonstration that the links between gender, power, and linguistic practices are not "natural" and can be constructed in quite different ways. But these examples are static and seem to imply that speakers passively follow abstract cultural dictates. A historical case is helpful then, because it charts *changes* in conceptualizations and shows how ideals come to restrict women's possibilities of expression. Outram (1987) considers the dilemma of elite women during the French Revolution. The discourse of the French Revolution, glorifying male *vertu*, identified the influence of women with the system of patronage, sexual favors, and corruption of power under the Old Regime, in which elite women had actively participated. The discourse of the Revolution, in deliberate contrast, was committed to an antifeminine logic: political revolution could only take place if women and their corrupting influence were excluded from public speaking and from the exercise of power. Outram argues that, in part as a result of this new conceptualization, the famous and powerful political participation of upper-class women in the Old Regime was replaced, in the era of the Revolution, with vigorous attacks on female political activists. By the new logic, elite women's public speech and activities brought their sexual virtue into question. For a woman, to be political was to be corrupt; the revolutionary discourse of universal equality applied only to men. Women who wanted to be both respectable and political had very few choices: one of the best-known figures of the Revolution, who was later imprisoned for her participation, provides a telling example. Mme. Jeanne Roland's political activity included providing a forum in which men debated the issues of the day. Her memoirs and letters reveal that it demanded a painful compromise: this well-informed woman retained respect by listening to the men's political discussions but remained herself utterly silent.

The historical dimension in Outram's study allows us not only to chart the effect of changing discourse but to specify the social source of the cultural constructions in a way not possible in the more static descriptions of non-Western cases. These particular cultural definitions were not simply the product of some age-old and monolithic male dominance but emerged articulately in the ideas of revolutionary theorists and Enlightenment philosophers. Perhaps other patterns of ideas about gender differences in speech could be traced to similarly specific times and social contexts. For example, it is a recurrent and unexplained finding of recent sociolinguistic surveys that in North American, British, and some other industrialized cities, middle- and working-class men more frequently use pronunciations characteristic of the working class than do their female counterparts. And all men evaluate working-class features more positively than do women (e.g. Labov 1974; Trudgill 1983). Clearly the phonological symbolizations of gender and of social class are inextricably linked. The universalizing explanations offered so far credit women in general with greater sensitivity to language and prestige. But these theories founder on counter-examples from other societies. Instead, I suggest these findings gain meaning within a broader cultural pattern. The linguistic evidence links manliness with "tough" working-class culture and femaleness with "respectability," "gentility," and "high culture" as part of a general symbolic structure that, many analyses suggest, emerged on both sides of the Atlantic in the nineteenth century and continues to be one component of current gender images.[9]

In short, the culturally constructed link between types of verbal skill, gender identity, and power not only is variable but is dependent on an entire web of related conceptions and, as the final examples hint, on historical and political economic processes as well.

POWER IN EVERYDAY TALK

Jeanne Roland's silence was neither natural nor an automatic acquiescence to Revolutionary cultural conceptions. Instead, her letters and memoirs allow us to understand the forums she created and her public silence as strategic responses to a cultural double-bind that offered her either speech or respect, but not both. Neither wholly determined by cultural images and changing social structures, nor entirely a matter of her own agency, Mme. Roland's speech and interaction are excellent examples of *practices* that reproduce gender images and relations or, as later examples will show, sometimes tacitly criticize and resist them.

Interactional sociolinguistics provides the tools for analyzing speech strategies as practices actively constructed by speakers in response to cultural and structural constraints. If speech enacts a discourse strategy and is not simply a reflex or signal of social identity, then attention must be paid not only to the gender identity of the speaker but also to the gender of the audience and the varying cultural salience of gender in different social contexts. Male-female differences in speech have been found in every society studied; but the nature of the contrasts is staggeringly diverse, occurring in varying parts of the linguistic system: phonology, pragmatics, syntax, morphology, and lexicon (see Philips 1987). Here I will pay special attention to co-occurring features of speech that form patterns, called styles, genres, or ways of speaking, which are linked, in some way, to gender.[10]

Unlike the earliest studies that noted only obligatory linguistic differences between men and women, current research distinguishes cases where a speech form is normatively *required* for men or women from cases where it is a favored strategy for one gender because it enacts, consciously or not, men's and women's contrasting values or interactional goals (McConnell-Ginet 1988). Such differences in values and goals emerge with force when the division of labor creates largely separate worlds for men and women, so that "members of each sex learn to be proficient in different linguistic skills and to do different things with words" (Borker 1980: 31). Indeed, considerable ethnographic evidence suggests that differences in verbal genres between men and women are widespread, especially where men's and women's activities are distinctly defined (Sherzer 1987).

For example, among the Kuna Indians of Lowland Panama, speech genres emerge from the division of labor. Genres associated with public political meetings and ritualized attempts to cure illness are largely restricted to men, whereas the more privately performed genres of lullabies and tuneful mourning are restricted to women (Sherzer 1987). Similarly, among the Kaluli, living in the Southern Highlands of Papua New Guinea, it is the men who tell several types of stories, recite magical formulae for hunting, and perform songs and dances in major political and ceremonial contexts. Women compose more limited ceremonial songs and engage in expressive public weeping on occasions of profound loss (Schieffelin 1987). Among the Laymi Indians of Bolivia, women control and create genres of publicly performed song and music that are essential to courting and to the ritual cycle; men control speaking in the local political assembly and speaking directed to the spirits in curing rituals (Harris 1980).

These studies underline the fact that in many societies women actively create and perform major expressive activities, often in public, a point also emphasized by feminist folklorists (Jordan and deCaro 1986). Such evidence effectively counters the persistent but erroneous image of women as universally silent in public or restricted to domestic activities. It highlights as well one function of speech in a gender system: genre differences create the kind of pervasive behavioral contrast that transforms gradients of human difference into culturally salient dichotomies of masculinity and femininity. But, a simple catalogue of "his-and-hers" genres obscures the important insight that women's special verbal skills are often strategic *responses*—more or less successful—to positions of relative powerlessness.

For example, in a Hungarian-German bilingual town in Austria, women use German more than men do. Women's use of German corresponds to their general rejection of the peasant way of life associated with the Hungarian language and their acceptance of the wage labor symbolized by speaking German. It is, in part, women's relative powerlessness in the peasant social order that makes the escape to worker status so attractive for them and, thus, explains the verbal strategies they use (Gal 1978).[11]

Strategies are not always directed toward change. In a Tenejapan village of southern Mexico, women are more polite than men in two ways. They use many more linguistic particles that emphasize solidarity with their interactional partner and also use more of a contrasting set of particles that avoid imposition and stress the listener's separateness and autonomy. Indeed, women's intent to impose by requesting, commanding, or criticizing is often couched in irony. Because irony requires the listener to infer the speaker's intent, irony allows the speaker to disclaim the intent if it results in challenge or threat. Men use less irony and fewer particles of either kind, showing considerably less sensitivity to the details of social relationships and context. Women's usage is an interactional strategy, an accommodation arising from their social and even physical vulnerability to men, and the consequent necessity to show deference to men, on the one hand, and maintain strong networks of solidarity with women, on the other hand. This suggests that levels and types of politeness strategies used by women to men and to other women may well be a sensitive measure of women's structural power in many societies (Brown 1980).

But women's responses to powerlessness, although they may also be attempts to subvert male authority, may only end by reproducing it. A striking example is Harding's (1975) analysis of a peasant village in Spain. Women and men characteristically occupy different physical spaces (the house and shops versus the plaza and the fields); have different work and concerns (family and neighbors versus land, politics, economics); and different speech genres. Whereas men argue in public, as a form of verbal play requiring an appreciative audience; women talk in small, closed groups of kin, often practicing "gossip"—the gathering and evaluating of information about people—as their only means of social control. Harding argues that it is women's subordinate position to men, and not simply separation, that leads women to develop special "manipulative" verbal skills such as teasing out information, carefully watching others so as to anticipate their needs, and using irony or self-effacing methods of persuasion. Gossip itself is women's most powerful verbal tool, but it is two-edged. It tends to subvert male authority, by judging people in terms of values the male-dominant system rejects. But partly as a result of this subversion it is condemned and decried by the dominant culture. Moreover, it is seen by all as a negative form of power that makes or breaks reputations, causes conflict, and disrupts relationships. It is negative in another sense too. As Harding reveals, women develop this genre for lack of other forms of power, but they are trapped by it themselves: "Th[e] sense, if not fact, of being under constant verbal surveillance restricts the behavior of women and helps keep them in their place" (1975: 103).

Although there is no parallel separation of the sexes in the United States, American men and women also seem to use somewhat different verbal strategies in conversation. In a provocative synthesis of recent research findings, Maltz and Borker (1982) argue that sex-segregated children's play groups, common in American society, create gender-specific verbal cultures whose practices speakers retain into adulthood. But the gender differences are so subtle people are aware only of their result: frequent miscommunication between men and women who otherwise claim to be friends and status equals. Maltz and Borker rely in part on Goodwin's careful studies of children's play groups in an urban black neighborhood, but information on white children and adults of various classes and ethnic groups also seems to support their generalizations about men's and women's strategies.

For instance, boys and men organize into relatively large hierarchical groups, using direct commands and vying with one another for leadership positions by holding forth in competitive verbal display. Side comments and challenges are the proper responses by those who do not have the floor. Girls, by contrast, play in smaller groups, forming exclusive coalitions. There is plenty of conflict in all-girl groups, but their verbal interactions implicitly deny conflict and hierarchy, phrasing commands as proposals for future activity (Goodwin 1980). Girls and women carefully link their utterances to the previous speaker's contribution and develop one another's topics, asking questions for conversational maintenance rather than for information or challenge. But these differences are not as innocent as Maltz and Borker's image of parallel, mutually miscomprehending gender-cultures would suggest.

One way of interpreting the female strategies is as a set of practices that, whatever the actual power relations within the girls' or women's group, nevertheless enact values of support and solidarity that directly oppose and implicitly criticize the boys' and men's practices of heroic individuality, competition, and the celebration of hierarchy. In this sense the two "cultures" are not separate at all, but define each other, enacting in speech forms several familiar cultural oppositions in American discourse about gender.

They are also not equal in power. Goodwin and Goodwin's most recent reports (1987) indicate that when boys and girls argue together, the boys' strategy is employed by all. This suggests that the boys' strategy is dominant in two senses: the girls but not the boys must learn both, and the boys seem to be able to impose theirs on the girls in cross-sex interaction. This kind of dominance is also suggested by a series of studies on patterns of interruption in cross-sex interactions among status equals. Between pairs of speakers who knew each other well, as well as between those who were strangers, men interrupted women more than either sex interrupted in same-sex interactions. Moreover, the assumption that interruption is a gesture of dominance is supported by the finding that adults interrupt children more than the reverse (West and Zimmerman 1983).[12] A study of naturally occurring conversation by young American married couples in their homes is also suggestive in this regard. Although the women raised almost twice as many topics of conversation as the men, the topics raised by men were the ones that were accepted and elaborated in the conversation by both men and women. Yet it was the women who provided most of the interactional "work," the questions and minimal responses ("uh-huh") that kept the conversation going (Fishman 1978). More systematic evidence is needed, especially about the effects of social context on the details of such everyday talk. And we need replications across classes and ethnic groups of studies relying on very small samples of white middle-class speakers. Nevertheless, in cross-gender talk, as in the cross-ethnic miscommunication on which Maltz and Borker model their analysis (Gumperz 1982), it seems clear that the differences in strategies provide an opportunity for the more powerful group to enact and reinforce its dominance through the microprocesses of verbal interaction.

But a major flaw in many of the studies of linguistic strategy I have discussed so far is their assumption that speech and gender are best investigated in informal conversations, often in one-to-one or small-group relationships in the family or neighborhood. This creates the illusion that gendered talk is mainly a personal characteristic or limited to the institution of the family. Yet, as much feminist research has demonstrated, gender as a structural principle also organizes other social institutions: workplaces, schools, courts, political assemblies, and the state show characteristic patterns in the recruitment, allocation, treatment, and mobility of men as opposed to women. These are inscribed in the organization of the institution. Patterns of talk and interaction play an important role in maintaining, legitimating, and often hiding the gendered aspect of these institutional arrangements. The role of men's and women's linguistic strategies within institutions deserve considerably more attention than it has so far received. I will discuss only a few suggestive examples from schools and bureaucracies in the United States, and from political assemblies in several small-scale societies.

Within institutions, such settings as interviews, meetings, and other characteristic verbal encounters are often crucial for decision making. On the basis of talk some individuals are hired, chosen to participate, receive resources or promotions and authority, while others are denied. In complex, capitalist societies the class and ethnic background of speakers is crucial in such gate-keeping encounters (Erickson and Schultz 1982). And gender routinely interacts with class and ethnicity. For instance, in a study of speech in American courts, the testimony of witnesses using the linguistic forms characteristic of women with no courtroom experience and of low-status men was judged by experimental subjects to be less credible, less convincing, and less trustworthy than testimony delivered in a style characteristic of speakers with high status (O'Barr and Atkins 1980). It appears that courts reinforce the authority of forms associated with high-status speakers, who tend to be men.

The "meeting" is a speech event ubiquitous in American bureaucratic, corporate, and academic life. In a study of faculty meetings, Edelsky (1981) approached the university as a workplace and not as an educational institution. In meetings with equal numbers of male and female participants of equal occupation status, she asked whether women were as successful as men in "getting the floor," that is, in winning the opportunity to talk and thereby contribute to the decisions. But a direct comparison of men's and women's participation was not possible. Who spoke and how often depended on the implicit rules by which speakers participated. And there were at least two sets of rules, two kinds of "floors." In episodes characterized by the first kind of "floor," speakers took longer and fewer turns, fewer speakers participated overall, they did not overlap much, there were many false starts and hesitations, and speakers used their turns for reporting and voicing opinions. The other kind of "floor" occurred at the same meetings but during different episodes. It was characterized by much overlap and simultaneous talk but little hesitation in speaking, and by more general participation by many speakers who collaboratively constructed a group picture of "what's-going-on." Several speakers performed the same communicative functions such as suggesting an idea, arguing, or agreeing; joking, teasing and wisecracking were more frequent.

It is evident that the interactional strategies of American men and women, as outlined by Maltz and Borker, are differently suited to the two kinds of "floor." It was men who monopolized the first kind of floor, by taking *longer* turns, holding forth and dominating the construction of the floor through the time they took talking. In the second kind of floor, where everyone took shorter turns, men and women took turns of about equal length, and all speakers participated as equals in the communicative functions performed (1981: 416). Importantly, the first, more formal kind of floor, in which women participated less, occurred vastly *more* frequently, at least in this institutional setting. Explicit and tacit struggles between speakers about how meetings are to be conducted are conflicts about the control of institutional power. Even among status equals and in mixed-sex groups, the interactional constraints of institutional events such as meetings are not gender neutral but weighted in favor of male interactional strategies. Although organization of the meeting *masks* the fact that speakers are excluded on the basis of gender, it simultaneously *accomplishes* that very exclusion.

Perhaps more pervasively than any other institution, schools judge, define, and categorize their charges on the basis of linguistic performance. The different strategies of boys and girls can also affect their access to linguistic resources, such as literacy, that schooling offers. A single example will suffice to suggest how ethnic differences interact with gender in this process. In her fine comparison of language acquisition and training for literacy in three Southern communities in the United States, Heath (1983) carefully describes the complex and artful linguistic practices of a black working-class community. Children must master "analogy" questions posed by their elders, in which they are encouraged to see the parallels and connections among disparate events and tell about them cleverly, without spelling out explicitly what the links are. Such descriptions differ from school requirements that match middle-class patterns. And what is expected of black girls at home differs considerably from the more extensive verbal skills demanded of boys. Working-class black girls, in contrast to boys of their own group, are neither expected nor encouraged to practice a wide range of story-telling tactics in competitive "onstage" public arenas where community adults as well as children watch and judge (1983: 95–98, 105–112).

The results of these differences emerge in a parallel study of teacher-student interaction in a first-grade classroom with both black and white students (Michaels 1981). When the white teachers—all women—instituted a "sharing time" ("show and tell") activity, they had the explicit goal of bridging the gap between the oral discourse the children already knew and the literate discourse strategies they would eventually have to use in written communication. They asked the children to tell about a specific object or give a narrative account about some important past event. For the white boys and girls this worked quite well. They told topic-focused stories that the teachers understood; and the teachers' questions and comments helped the students make their stories more explicit and develop the more complex structures of standard literacy. The working-class black girls, however, organized their stories to resemble children's responses to "analogy" questions. They noted abstract parallels between disparate situations and events and relied on the listener to infer the implicit links. Although the white teachers were of the same gender as the black girls and had excellent intentions, they failed to understand this principle and thus were unable to collaborate with the black girls in producing more elaborate, structurally complex stories. The black girls felt frustrated; their stories were rarely even completed before the teachers cut them off. As a result, they could not benefit from the steps toward literate, standard discourse that the classroom activity apparently accomplished for the white children. The teachers were also frustrated. To them it appeared that the girls could not "stick to the point" nor discern what was "important." On the basis of many such interactions the black girls would be judged intellectually inadequate.

This ability of social institutions to create gendered definitions of speakers through talk is equally illustrated by political assemblies in small-scale societies where adult men consider each other equals. In many such societies, as among the Malagasy and the Laymi Indians described above, only men talk at public, political meetings. Ethnographers have repeatedly described men's talk in this context as allusive and indirect, making use of images, parables, and metaphors to hide, veil, or render ambiguous the referential message, thereby denying conflict (Brenneis and Myers 1984). Women are excluded on the grounds that they lack the necessary verbal subtlety. This seems to suggest that speech differences are powerful indeed, since they seem to directly limit women's access to the political process. However, ethnographers also report that the meetings are not the main site of decision making, and indirect speech is not primarily a means of persuasion or coercion. Usually decisions are made and consensus reached before and after the meeting in informal discussions that employ a more direct style and in which women participate actively, thereby having considerable effect on decisions (Harris 1980: 73; Keenan, 1974; Lederman 1984). What, then, is the meaning and effect of women's exclusion from speaking at meetings?

The linguistic form of political meetings defines not how decision making actually occurs, but rather what can be shown "onstage"; what can be focused on as the legitimate reality. Comparative evidence suggests that meetings at which orders are given or announced by leaders ratify an ideology of hierarchy, regardless of the way decisions were originally reached. Meetings in which indirectness creates a lack of coercion and hierarchy between participants ratify an ideology of egalitarian relations, at least in societies where there are few other institutionalized political structures (Irvine 1979). If men's indirect oratory constructs the social reality of an egalitarian male polity, then the exclusion of women creates the reality and legitimates the ideology of women's subordination to that polity. As Lederman (1984) points out about the Mendi of New Guinea, for the women listening in silence at such a meeting, this reality is all the harder to challenge since it is formally acted out but never explicitly articulated.

In sum, societal institutions are not neutral contexts for talk. They are organized to define, demonstrate, and enforce the legitimacy and authority of linguistic strategies used by one gender—or men of one class or ethnic group— while denying the power of others.[13] Forms that diverge are devalued by the dominant ideologies. "Floors" with many participants, black girls' stories, women's gossip in Spain, Mendi women's directness, all attempt to contest the hegemony of the dominant forms. But it is not the "floor" that is judged inauspicious, rather women are seen as timid or unable to express themselves; it is not that the black girls have different story-telling experiences than white children and less training than black boys, but that they cannot think properly. Despite the resistance demonstrated in women's linguistic practices, Bourdieu's (1977b) remark about the effects of this kind of linguistic domination applies: by authorizing some linguistic practices and not others, the institution appears to demonstrate the inferiority of those who use unauthorized forms and often inculcates in them feelings of worthlessness.

But notice that the Mendi meeting, the forums of Mme. Roland, and single-speaker "floors" also illustrate another sort of symbolic power I mentioned at the start of this chapter: they are interactional and linguistic forms, but they also attempt to impose and legitimate certain definitions of women, men, and society. I now turn to a fuller discussion of this second aspect of symbolic domination and the way women's voices are sometimes raised against it.

GENRES OF RESISTANCE

Despite the long-standing Western emphasis on language as primarily a means of representing an already existing reality, anthropologists have long been aware of the ways in which the metaphors, literary genres, and interactional arrangements readily available in a community actively shape the way speakers define the social world. In short, conventional language and its conventional usage are not neutral media for describing social life. Some formulations about social life, when inscribed in a division of labor or other organizational form, serve one group's interests better than that of others. A hegemonic discourse, in this broad sense, is a form of power, and it is sometimes resisted or contested.

This important and quite general notion of a dynamic between dominant and subordinate discourses or practices has been discussed, in many forms and with many terminologies, by a variety of social theorists. However, feminist scholars have been strongly influenced by a limited version of this insight, explicitly applied to women. E. Ardener (1975) and S. Ardener (1975) argue that women, due to their structural positions, have models of reality that differ from the male-dominated societal model. The form of women's models is often nonverbal, inarticulate, or veiled, while the discourse of men is more verbal and explicit, and thereby more congruent with the usual discourse of Western social science. Being unable to express their structurally generated views in the dominant and masculine discourse, women are neither understood nor heeded, and become inarticulate, "muted," or even silent. In such cases women may talk a lot, but they do not express their own, different social reality.[14]

The "muted-group" thesis usefully draws attention to the importance of the symbolic language, the form, of dominant and subordinate discourse. However, as I will demonstrate with a series of examples, the Ardeners' formulation is flawed in several respects. First, it assumes that "mutedness" is a static reflex of women's structural position. In contrast, when viewed in terms of broader theories of gender and symbolic domination, "mutedness" becomes only one of many theoretically possible outcomes of gender relations. A much wider array of women's verbal strategies and genres become visible, some considerably more articulate and more actively oppositional to dominant models than the "mutedness" thesis allows. Second, if domination and resistance are matters of interactional practice as well as structure, as I have been arguing, then we must focus not on "mutedness" as a structural product but on the processes by which women are rendered "mute" or manage to construct dissenting genres and resisting discourses. Finally, as Warren and Bourque suggest: ". . . understanding dominance and muting [as processes] requires a broader analysis of the political, economic and institutional contexts in which reality is negotiated" (1985: 261).

Ethnography itself is such a context, for ethnographic reports are deeply implicated in the process of representing self and others, creating images of social reality through language. Keenly aware of this, feminist critics of anthropology have charged that women in the societies studied were ignored or perceived as inert because androcentric ethnographers dismissed women and their concerns, making them appear passive and silent. Feminists challenged the authority and credibility of these male-biased accounts. But the Ardeners' thesis suggests that the problem is more complex. It claims that women rarely "speak" in social anthropological reports because social science investigators of both sexes demand the kind of articulate models provided by men, not by muted women. And indeed, some women anthropologists have also complained of the inarticulateness of women informants in some contexts. It seems there is a need to reexamine how ethnographies are created. Currently, just such a reexamination is also the project of anthropologists who are similarly challenging the authority of ethnographic writing, but on different grounds. Following postmodernist trends in philosophy, they assert that traditional ethnographies mask the actual practice of fieldwork and writing (Clifford and Marcus 1986). By claiming to accurately represent the facts about an exotic culture, the naive realist conventions of ethnographic writing implicitly deny that ethnographic facts are selected, indeed constructed, in the encounter between the anthropologist and the "other" who is her/his subject. In order to reflect the process of ethnographic knowledge, these critics suggest experimentation with literary forms so that writing may be a "polyvocal" and dialogic production in which the ethnographer lets the people speak and ethnographic facts are shown to be jointly produced by ethnographer and informant.

What has received too little attention in all these critiques is the unavoidable power-charged verbal encounter in which anthropologists and native speakers, with different interests, goals, and deeply unequal positions, meet and attempt to talk. Keesing (1985) provides a fine example of the ethnographic interview as a linguistic practice. in order to record women's versions of native life (kastom) among the Kwaio, a tenaciously traditional group living in the Solomon Islands of the South Pacific, Keesing had to analyze what he calls the "micropolitics" of talk. In response to Keesing's requests, the men created and told life histories eagerly and artfully, even though the Kwaio lack such a genre as well as a tradition of self-revelation and self-explanation on which the Western literary form of the autobiography is based. In contrast, Keesing recounts that he could not elicit autobiographical narratives from women, not even those who were old, knowledgeable, and influential. They spoke to him in a fragmented, inarticulate and joking way, especially in front of elder men who urged them to cooperate. They appeared distressed with what was requested of them: "mute." A subsequent fieldtrip, eight years later, this time with a woman ethnographer, brought quite different results. In sessions with *both* ethnographers, Kwaio women took control of the encounters, even bringing female friends as audience to the recording sessions. But, unlike the men, who had provided societal rules and personal life narratives, the women rejected the ethnographers' personal questions and instead created moral texts about the virtues of womanhood, inserting personal experiences only to illustrate women's possible paths through life. Through their texts, Kwaio women were reformulating and embellishing a long-standing strategy of Kwaio men: to enlist the (at first) unknowing anthropologist in their efforts to codify and authorize Kwaio custom. By legitimating their own customs in an anthropologized form the Kwaio men were able to use it to resist the demands of state regulations, thereby attempting, through vigorous neo-traditionalism, to maintain their political autonomy in the face of colonial and neo-colonial incursions.

A deeper understanding of Kwaio women's talk requires a revisions of all three critiques of anthropological fieldwork. Clearly Kwaio women were not so much structurally mute and inarticulate as responsive to the immediate interactional context, especially relations of gender inequality within their own society and in the ethnographic interview. Pragmatic analyses of the interview as a speech event suggest it is the ethnographer's task to discover the conditions under which informants can talk. Similarly, it is not enough to insist, as the postmodernist critics do, that the ethnographic encounter and the genres that emerge from it are jointly produced. Although important and accurate, this observation by itself ignores the importance of gender and other forms of inequality. It omits the several levels of unequal power and privilege that characterize the ethnographic encounter and which also determine who is able to talk and what it is possible or strategic to say. The women's inarticulateness and subsequent "voice," as much as the men's systematization of their culture, were responses to wide fields of force that assure that some texts or genres are more powerful than others, making a simple coproduction of ethnographic texts impossible (Asad 1986; Polier and Roseberry 1988: 15). Finally, feminists would have confidently predicted the changes produced by the presence of a woman anthropologist and would have understood that the genre of autobiography is problematic, not only because it is culturally specific to the West, but also because it has been shaped by Western gender ideology that assumes a male subject.[15] Yet the case of Kwaio women suggests revisions and expansions for gender theories as well: a female ethnographer may be only part of the answer. In this case, the presence of the male anthropologist was also important, for the women were attuned to his established role as mediator between the Kwaio and the outside world. Thus, attention must be paid to relations of power that connect Kwaio society to a world system in which, as the Kwaio are aware, anthropologists, as wielders of Western discourse, have authority that Kwaio women, perhaps differently than men, can try to channel to their own ends through the ethnographic interview.

Ethnography is only one of the many contexts in which we can observe the processes that make women seem "mute." Another example is provided by an elite intellectual study group, the Men's and Women's Club of 1880s London, and their discussions of sexuality (Walkowitz 1986). Club rules asserted men's and women's equality, but rule number seventeen, which was accepted by all, stipulated that discussion must stay within a Darwinian, scientific framework. This proviso both assured and hid men's dominance. For women members respected, but lacked, such scientific knowledge. This is at once an instance of linguistic domination and an attempt at imposition of a social reality: women's private letters reveal that many found the terms of such a science inadequate to express "complex thought and feeling" about the difficulties of their sexual lives. Minutes of the meetings suggest that face-to-face with men, women were often silenced by this dilemma. But other data show various attempts to formulate opposition: transforming or adapting men's scientific arguments in papers written for the club, writing private letters of complaint to one another, and even attempting to create a different idiom for talking about sexuality by drawing on public events of the time.

If women are not always silent or inarticulate, then the task of anthropology is to seek out and understand the genres and discourses women produce. Especially revealing are genres created by speakers themselves, to reflect on their own experience, that are not primarily a product of the ethnographic interview. As I have already shown, students of everyday talk have identified men's and women's often different verbal genres; students of oral literature have catalogued their forms and the rules for their performance (e.g., Sherzer 1987). But these are not simply "ways of speaking"; the differences in content or perspective that they often construct deserve equal attention. Indeed, it is in the conjunction of form, content, and context of performance that women's consciousness emerges. First, my examples will demonstrate the great range of articulateness evident in women's genres. Second, although women's genres often diverge from men's, and are sometimes autonomous constructions, the evidence does not support a thesis of separate women's cultures. On the contrary, women's genres can best be read as commentary that shows a range of response—acceptance, resistance, subversion, and opposition—to dominant, often male discourse.

Women sometimes produce a cultural commentary of gesture and ritual that may be called inarticulate because it rejects words altogether. An important instance occurred in the Nigerian Women's War of 1929. During the massive protests against proposed taxation of women's property by the colonial government, women reformulated on a large scale a locally practiced custom of obscene dancing, called "sitting on a man," that traditionally occurred at the houses of men who had overstepped social mores upheld by women. Contemporary witnesses of the Women's War report that women's protests included marching nude, lying on the ground kicking their legs in the air, and making obscene gestures. As Ifeka-Moller (1975) explains, these gestures were mysterious and alarming to European observers but, for the women and men involved, they constituted an eloquent protest against the male political control and government taxation that women saw as a violation of their rights.

A similarly gestural but much more contradictory and acquiescent practice is American women's consumption of popular romantic novels. If we analyze only the texts themselves, romance readers appear as passive consumers of a hegemonic popular culture that demeans them by presenting images of women as illogical and magnetized by male brutality. But Radway (1984) examines not just the content but the social event of reading. She shows that for many romance readers, reading itself, often done in stolen moments of privacy, is a combative act, contesting the usual self-abnegation of their lives. Yet, although revealing a real tension in dominant gender ideology, this is a limited and self-defeating protest: reading allows temporary escape from limited lives, but the texts make those limited lives seem more desirable.

A more verbally explicit and subversive, yet veiled and ambiguous genre, is the oral lyric poetry (ghinnawas) performed among intimates by the Bedouin of Egypt's Western Desert. In describing these delicate, brief, and artfully improvised performances, Abu-Lughod (1986) stresses that the dominant ideology, the "public language" of the Bedouin, is one of honor, autonomy, self-mastery, personal strength, and sexual modesty. The poems directly violate this code of honor and implicitly criticize it by expressing the feelings of dependency, emotional vulnerability, and romantic longing condemned by the official view.

The poetry constitutes what Abu-Lughod calls a "dissident or subversive discourse . . . most closely associated with youths and women, the disadvantaged dependents who least embody the ideals of Bedouin society and have least to gain in the system as structured. . . . Poetry is the discourse of opposition to the system and of defiance of those who represent it" (1986: 251). But the poetry is anything but a spontaneous outpouring of feeling. Indeed, its formal properties and context of performance enhance its ability to subtly carry messages counter to official ideals. It is formulaic, thereby disguising the identities of poet, addressee, and subject. It is fleeting and ambiguous, performed by women and youths among trusted intimates who can decipher it exactly because they already know the reciter well. Yet, this poetry of subversion and defiance is not only tolerated; it is culturally elaborated and admired because of the paradoxical intertwining of official and dissident discourse. The oral poetry reveals a fundamental tension of Bedouin social and political life which, while valuing and demanding autonomy and equality between lineages, demands inequality between the genders and generations within lineages and families. "A discourse of defiance by those slighted in the system, [poetry] is exalted because a refusal to be dominated is key to Bedouin political life, and it is avoided by [male] elders because it threatens to expose the illegitimacy of their authority" (Abu-Lughod 1986: 254). Thus, the verbal genre of women and youths reveals the contradictions of the ruling ideology.

My final example is a poetic genre more verbally explicit, more directly critical of social and political relations, and much less accepted by official ideologies. Though limited to a much smaller segment of the female population, it is equally revealing of contradictions in dominant discourses. Migrant laborers, moving between the mines of South Africa and their native Lesotho, compose a genre of poetic songs called *lifela*, performed competitively by "men of eloquence," often for a fee, usually at social gatherings in border towns. They sing of poverty and forced migration; their songs reinforce a rootedness in the rural village, despite migration, and a longing for traditional gerontocratic and patriarchal social relations. However, there are also some women who sing lifela. But their circumstances, as well as the content of their poetry, are significantly different.

In the current migrant system, women's position is in many ways even worse than men's. Women are forbidden to migrate by the legal system, but left alone in the village they must make decisions without being granted the autonomy to do so. "The South African government, the Lesotho government and male Basotho attitudes have openly conspired to prevent female migration, which threatens the divided-family system on which both the migratory labor system and male domestic power are based" (Coplan 1987: 424). Female poets are among those who have managed to escape these constraints and have migrated illegally. Although for men South Africa is unequivocally a land of wage slavery, for these migrant women it represents relative choice, opportunity and autonomy. Women have borrowed the men's genre but have transformed it, providing a considerably more radical social critique. Rather than identifying with rural life, the women's poetry sharply and explicitly criticizes men, proclaims traditional marriage unworkable, but recognizes as well the physical dangers and insecurity of life as an illegal migrant. The women's opposition is palpable not only in the content of the poetry, but also during the performance of the poems/songs in the tavern:

"Male . . . patrons, stung by the critical barbs of female performers routinely rise to sing spontaneous retorts . . . [but] are shouted down or even pushed aside by [female poets] determined to hold the floor" (Coplan 1987: 429).

Such attempts to silence the protest songs of migrant women in Lesotho return us to the *process* by which women are either rendered "mute" or are able to construct an alternate discourse, resisting attempts to suppress it. I have attempted one approach to this question, examining women's genres as practices, analyzing ethnographic interviews or Bedouin poetry very much as I did earlier examples of "ways of speaking" such as collaborative "floors" and gossip: focusing on the immediate interactional context of the genre—the participant structure of the interview, the intimacy of Bedouin confidantes, the liminality of border taverns—for clues to the forces that allow it to be performed. More broadly, however, the issue of when and how women's subversion or opposition to hegemonic culture emerges is as much a question about the structure of gender systems and political economy as about linguistic practices, genres, and counter-discourses. Comparative work, such as Warren and Bourque's (1985) study of women's public speaking in two quite differently organized Peruvian communities, or study of the social identities of women who sing lifela, can start to illuminate this issue, as can historical research into changing images of sex and gender (Steedman et al. 1985; Walkowitz 1986). Another research tactic is to compare women of different classes and ethnic groups, using linguistic practices to raise the classic issue of the relationship between consciousness and social position.

A study of this kind is Martin's investigation of American women's discourse about their own reproductive processes, as compared to the dominant discourse on this subject, which is medical science. Martin (1987) used the same linguistic metric to compare medical textbooks and women's folk models: the system of metaphors through which reality is made comprehensible and meaningful in each. She demonstrates that medical texts construct the body as a model of industrial society, with cells as factories having systems of management and control. The physical events of menstruation are constructed by science as failed production and an alarming breakdown of authority in the body.

Comparing this system of metaphors to women's ways of talking about menstruation in interviews, Martin found that middle-class women acquiesce to the medical model. They explain menstruation in medical terms, dwelling on internal organs and processes, worrying about the "correct" color of the blood. But working-class women, both black and white, shared "an absolute reluctance to give the medical view of menstruation" (1987: 109), in spite of exposure to it at school and the interviewers' many efforts to elicit it. Instead, working-class women described menstruation in phenomenological terms untouched by the medical model: what it feels like, looks like, smells like in immediate experience. Martin concludes that "middle class women appear much more 'mystified' by the general cultural models than working class women. They have bought the . . . medical accounts" (1987: 111). Perhaps this is due to their favorable opportunities for satisfying employment and thus positive attitudes toward both the image of production and schooling as a source of information. Once again, gender and class are intertwined. This is certainly a start toward understanding the processes by which some women but not others develop divergent and resistant consciousness; or why subordinate men sometimes share women's practices.[16]

These diverse examples of women's genres, drawn from many parts of the world and many kinds of sociopolitical formations, were chosen in part to highlight the observation that women's resistance or criticism is sometimes couched in implicit forms such as ambiguity and irony but is, in other cases, much more directly expressed. Indeed, the examples illustrate a range of linguistic explicitness (gestural; brief and ambiguous; extended and explicit); diverse social contexts (public demonstration, closed meeting, intimate conversation, paid performance); and several levels of subversion or opposition to dominant discourses (from self-defeating complicity, to resistance, to open criticism). Interestingly, it seems that these three parameters do not correlate in any simple way. Strong protest can appear in silent gestures, as in the women's war; or in the explicit public performances of critical poetry. Resistance may be knowing yet silent, as in American working-class women's refusal of some medical metaphors, verbal yet veiled as in Bedouin poetry, verbal but privately expressed, as in the Men's and Women's Club, or explicit and public, as in bilingual Austrian women's use of German. But in each case, women's linguistic practices made visible a crack, a fault line in the dominant male discourse of gender and power, revealing it to be not monolithic but contradictory and thus vulnerable.

CONCLUSIONS

I have argued that gender relations are constructed, in part, through different possibilities of expression for men and women. Tools from several scholarly traditions are needed in order to unravel how linguistic practices, gender, and power are intertwined. The research and analyses from several traditions, which I have brought together here to clarify and inform one another, deserve to be conceptually integrated. The notions of symbolic domination through patterns of language use and of gender as both structure and practice are essential to that endeavor.

Cultural constructions of language, gender, and power shape men's and women's ideas and ideals about their own linguistic practices. Students of everyday talk have often neglected this symbolic side of interaction. For instance, even such seemingly small details as the systematic differences between American boys' and girls' turn-taking in single-sex play groups fit and reinforce the broad cultural logic of gender symbolism in the United States. However, women's acquiescence to such cultural expectations is neither passive nor automatic. Indeed, as students of everyday talk have shown, women actively construct linguistic strategies in response to these cultural conceptions and to the relations of gender inequality they encode. Although women's practices sometimes bring change in established structures, often, as in the case of Spanish women's gossip, the strategy may aim to resist male dominance but ends by reproducing and legitimating it. This is in part because men and women interact not as individuals but in institutions such as workplaces, families, schools, and political forums, where much decision making about resources and social selection for mobility occurs through talk. And institutions are far from neutral arenas: they are structured along gender lines, to lend authority not only to reigning classes and ethnic groups but specifically to men's linguistic practices.

But power is more than an authoritative voice in decision making; its strongest form may well be the ability to define social reality, to impose visions of the world. Such visions are inscribed in language and enacted in interaction. Although women's everyday talk and women's "voice" or consciousness as evidenced in expressive genres have been studied quite separately, I have argued that both can be understood as strategic responses, often of resistance, to dominant, hegemonic cultural forms. Thus, attention to linguistic detail, context of performance, and the nature of the dominant forms is essential to both endeavors. The precise form of questions and turn-taking is crucial in understanding the construction of different "floors" in American meetings (everyday talk); the exact, formal conventions of intimate Bedouin poetry (expressive genre) is indispensable to understanding how it is suited to the expression of vulnerability and dependence. Although the linguistic materials are quite different, both collaborative "floors" and intimate poetry locate a contradiction in dominant discourse and subvert it through rival practices. One undermines the hierarchical form and ideology of meetings that favor men's expertise in competitive talk; the other is seen as the opposite of ordinary talk and undermines the cultural rule of honor, threatening to reveal the illegitimacy of elder men's authority. This returns us to the cultural constructions we started with, now revealed not only as ideas that differentiate the genders but as discourses that are sources of power, which are enacted, and sometimes contested, in talk.

ACKNOWLEDGMENTS

I would like to thank Micaela di Leonardo, Judith Gerson, Suzanne Lebsock, Michael Moffatt, Kit Woolard, and Viviana Zelizer for careful readings and encouragement, and Bambi Schieffelin for her bibliographic suggestions. This paper is dedicated to the memory of Ruth Borker.

NOTES

1. The question of "silence" in feminist scholarship is twofold. On the one hand, the titles of some recent books suffice to illustrate a concern with obstacles to women's self-expression: *Silences* (Olsen), *On lies, secrets and silence* (Rich), *Stealing the language* (Ostriker), *Man made language* (Spender). On the other hand, the fact that social science has neglected women makes women of the past and other cultures *seem* silent, when in fact the silence is that of current western scholarship. I return to this issue late in the essay. Even everyday usage, such as the generic "he" for persons of unspecified sex, has the effect of making women appear silent.

2. There is a growing literature on the meanings of silence, which is usefully reviewed in D. Tannen and M. Saville-Troike (1984). The relationship of silence to women's speech is mentioned in Thorne, Kramarae, and Henley (1983; 16–17). S. Smith (1987: 49) highlights the irony of Foucault's assertions, when applied to women's writing; Moi (1985) discusses femininity and silence from the perspective of literary criticism.

3. Some of the influential works that have developed and argued for this conception are: Rubin 1975, Kelly-Gadol 1976, Gerson and Peiss 1985, Connell 1987.

4. Among such works, perhaps the best-known evocation of "women's voice" is Gil-

ligan (1982) and the literature inspired by it. Also relevant here are historians' discussions of women's culture which stress the content of beliefs and values (e.g., Smith-Rosenberg 1985; see debate in Feminist Studies 1980).

5. Lears (1985) provides an excellent discussion of Gramsci's contribution and the analytical uses of "cultural hegemony"; see also Lukes (1974). I have pointed to a very general and fundamental concern that these theorists share, ignoring for my purposes their many differences, e.g. the relative importance of history and human agency as opposed to structure, or how to conceptualize the relationship between material and ideational forces.

6. Feminist literary critics have provided diverse analyses of this relationship; see Furman (1980) and Moi's (1985) critical review. Recent western feminist practice itself provides a handy example in consciousness raising, which is a new *form* of linguistic practice as well as a challenge to dominant definitions about gender. Sec. 4 discusses the anthropological evidence.

7. Borker (1980) makes this point and provides many examples, some of which are also cited here. Hymes (e.g. 1974) has long argued for the analysis of speakers' ideas about speaking and its relation to social categories. Silverstein (1985) provides a detailed discussion of the way such conceptions, along with culturally constructed notions about how language works, that is, linguistic ideology, mediate between social change and changes in the internal workings of language, e.g. phonology, address systems, morphology.

8. For a fine example of linguistic advice to eighteenth-century American women, see Lebsock (1987: 42). Linguistic theory itself has been more deeply involved with definitions of gender than is generally recognized. Cameron (1985) provides a useful discussion of the way notions of gender originally drawn from definitions of men and women were used to define grammatical gender, then later recycled from language to social life and used to justify gender arrangements.

9. Such a gender/class link is suggested, in passing, in a number of works. For example, the relationship between working-class culture and masculinity is described for British adolescents by Willis (1977) and extended to adults by Connell (1987: 109). The connection between images of femininity and middle-class gentility in nineteenth-century America is suggested by Halttunen (1982) and Douglas (1977). Smith-Rosenberg (1985) discusses Davy Crockett as the poor, tough, "uncultured" archetype of American masculinity, along with other, contrasting images of gender in the nineteenth century.

10. I will not be discussing a range of important, related issues that are critically reviewed by McConnell-Ginet (1988), e.g., the process by which speech strategies become part of *language* as a form of cognitive competence, and the semantic coding of gender inequality in the lexicon, among others. An early and influential essay that offered hypotheses about men's and women's styles in middle-class America was Lakoff (1975).

11. Such strategic language choices, associated with the differential life circumstances of men and women in bilingual communities, have been reported by several researchers. The choices of women vary according to the specific historical and political economic circumstances of the community, so that women are sometimes conservers of ethnic languages and sometimes leaders in the shift away from them.

12. The generality of these patterns of interruption has been questioned by some researchers and deserves more study. Other studies of parent-child interaction provide interesting and contrasting evidence of power asymmetry in speech and how it supports American cultural conceptions about gender. Ochs (1992) compared Samoan and middle-class American patterns of childrearing and found that American mothers accommodate much more to children, both verbally and nonverbally; indeed, the middle-class image of the "good mother" requires this. For instance, American mothers routinely reinterpret speech and action that are joint activities of mother and child as the praiseworthy accomplishment of the child alone. This has important consequences for children's view of women. It not only constructs the child as more competent than he or she really is but also

serves to deny or veil the contribution and greater knowledge of the female caregiver. For both male and female children, American devaluations of women are reproduced through such interaction.

13. Interactions in many other institutions deserve more attention in these terms. For a recent attempt to understand interactions between women patients and doctors in American clinics see Fisher (1988). For a discussion of educational reform based on similar ideas, see Treichler and Kramarae (1983), and the very different approach of Walkerdine (1985).

14. The Ardeners' thesis is more complex, but the parts I have summarized have had strong influence not only on the Ardener's own circle (see articles in Ardener 1975) but also on other feminist writers such as Showalter, Kramarae, Spender, and Warren and Bourque (1985).

15. Many scholars argue that the Western genre of autobiography arose in the late Middle Ages, in the midst of profoundly reformulated notions of individualism and its relation to the movement of history (Olney 1980; Stanton 1984). Because these notions of the new "Man" assumed a male subject, women's autobiographies in the West have often been perceived as illegitimate and suspect (Smith 1987: 43). Kwaio women's refusal to recite the personal narratives and societal rules characteristic of men's responses to similar ethnographic questions, their insistence instead on moral justifications of womanhood, evoke a parallel strategy in western women's autobiographies, in which a recurring figure of divided consciousness can be read as the authors' awareness that they are being read as *women* and thus judged differently in their self-constructions (Smith 1987).

16. The evidence about class is more ambiguous when birth metaphors are also considered. Women of all classes (as well as some doctors) have invented new metaphors for birth that reject the analogy between the production of goods and the production of babies. Such new metaphors, essential for *re*-organizing experience, have been embodied in the varied new institutions of birth clinics, at-home births and other women's health movements in the United States and Europe. As Martin (1987) argues, linguistic practices are not only reflexes of existing structural categories of speakers, but are also newly created, forming the conditions necessary to build new institutional structures.

SELECTED BIBLIOGRAPHY

ABU-LUGHOD, I. 1986. *Veiled sentiments.* Berkeley, Los Angeles, London: University of California Press.

ARDENER, E. 1975. Belief and the problem of women. In *Perceiving women.* S. Ardener, ed. London: Malaby.

ARDENER, S. 1975. Introduction. In *Perceiving women.* S. Ardener, ed. London: Malaby.

ASAD, T. 1986. The concept of cultural translation in British social anthropology. In *Writing culture.* J. Clifford and G. Marcus, eds. Berkeley, Los Angeles, London: University of California Press.

BASSO, K. 1979. *Portraits of the whiteman.* New York: Cambridge University Press.

BAUMAN, R. 1983. *Let your words be few.* New York: Cambridge University Press.

BORKER, R. 1980. Anthropology. In *Language and women in literature and society.* S. McConnell-Ginet, R. Borker, and N. Furman, eds. New York: Praeger.

BOURDIEU, P. 1977a. *Outline of a theory of practice.* New York: Cambridge University Press.

———. 1977b. The economics of linguistic exchanges. *Social Science Information* 16 (6): 645–668.

BRENNEIS, D. L., AND F. MYERS. 1984. *Dangerous words.* New York: New York University Press.

BROWN, P. 1980. How and why are women more polite: Some evidence from a Mayan community. In *Women and language in literature and society*. S. McConnell-Ginet, R. Borker, and N. Furman, eds. New York: Praeger.

CAMERON, D. 1985. *Feminism and linguistic theory*. New York: St. Martin's Press.

CLIFFORD, J. AND G. MARCUS, EDS. 1986. *Writing culture*. Berkeley, Los Angeles, London: University of California Press.

CONNELL, R. W. 1987. *Gender and power*. Stanford: Stanford University Press.

COPLAN, D. B. 1987. Eloquent knowledge: Lesotho migrants' songs and the anthropology of experience. *American Ethnologist* 14 (3): 413–433.

DOUGLAS, ANN. 1977. *The feminization of American culture*. New York: Alfred A. Knopf.

EDELSKY, C. 1981. Whose got the floor? *Language in Society* 10 (3): 383–422.

ERICKSON, F., AND J. SCHULTZ. 1982. *The counselor as gatekeeper*. New York: Academic Press.

FISHER, S. 1988. *In the patient's best interest*. New Brunswick, N.J.: Rutgers University Press.

FISHMAN, P. 1978. Interaction: The work women do. *Social Problems* 25 (4): 397–406.

FOUCAULT, M. 1978. *The history of sexuality*. Vol. 1. New York: Pantheon.

———. 1980. *Power/knowledge: Selected interviews and other writings*. Colin Gordon, ed. New York: Pantheon.

FURMAN, N. 1980. Textual feminism. In *Women and language in literature and society*. S. McConnell-Ginet, R. Borker, and N. Furman, eds. New York: Praeger.

GAL, S. 1978. Peasant men can't get wives: Language and sex roles in a bilingual community. *Language in Society* 7 (1): 1–17.

GERSON, J., AND K. PEISS. 1985. Boundaries, negotiation, consciousness: Reconceptualizing gender relations. *Social Problems* 32 (4): 317–331.

GILLIGAN, C. 1982. *In a different voice*. Cambridge, Mass.: Harvard University Press.

GOODWIN, M. 1980. Directive-response speech sequences in girls' and boys' task activities. In *Women and language in literature and society*. S. McConnell-Ginet, R. Borker, and N. Furman, eds. New York: Praeger.

GOODWIN, M., AND C. GOODWIN. 1987. Children's arguing. In *Language, gender and sex in comparative perspective*. S. Philips, S. Steele, and C. Tanz, eds. New York: Cambridge University Press.

GUMPERZ, J. 1982. *Discourse strategies*. New York: Cambridge University Press.

HARDING, S. 1975. Women and words in a Spanish village. In *Toward an anthropology of women*. R. Reiter, ed. New York: Monthly Review.

HARRIS, O. 1980. The power of signs: Gender, culture and the wild in the Bolivian Andes. In *Nature, culture and gender*. C. MacCormack and M. Strathern, eds. New York: Cambridge University Press.

HALTUNNEN, K. 1982. *Confidence men and painted women*. New Haven: Yale University Press.

HEATH, S. 1983. *Ways with words*. New York: Cambridge University Press.

HERZFELD, M. 1985. *The poetics of manhood*. Princeton University Press.

HYMES, D. 1974. *Foundations in sociolinguistics*. Philadelphia: University of Pennsylvania Press.

IFEKA-MOLLER, C. 1975. Female militancy and colonial revolt: The Women's War of 1929, eastern Nigeria. In *Perceiving women*. S. Ardener, ed. London: Malaby.

IRVINE, J. 1979. Formality and informality in communicative events. *American Anthropologist* 81: 779–790.

JORDAN, R. A., AND F. A. DECARO. 1986. Women and the study of folklore. *Signs* 11 (3): 500–518.

KEENAN, E. 1974. Norm-makers and norm-breakers: Uses of speech by men and women in a Malagasy community. In *Explorations in the ethnography of speaking*. R. Bauman and J. Sherzer, eds. New York: Cambridge University Press.

KEESING, R. 1985. Kwaio women speak: The micropolitics of autobiography in a Solomon Island society. *American Anthropologist* 87 (1): 27–39.

KELLY-GADOL, J. 1976. The social relation of the sexes: Methodological implications of women's history. *Signs* I: 809–824.

KRAMARAE, C. 1980. Gender: How she speaks. In *Attitudes towards language variation*. E. B. Ryan and H. Giles, eds. London: Edward Arnold.

LABOV, W. 1974. *Sociolinguistic patterns*. Philadelphia: University of Pennsylvania Press.

LAKOFF, R. 1975. *Language and women's place*. New York.

LEARS, J. 1985. The concept of cultural hegemony: Problems and possibilities. *American Historical Review* 90: 567–593.

LEBSOCK, S. 1987. *"A share of honor"*: *Virginia women 1600–1945*. Richmond: Virginia State Library.

LEDERMAN, R. 1984. Who speaks here: Formality and the politics of gender in Mendi, Highland Papua New Guinea. In *Dangerous words*. D. Brenneis and F. Myers, eds. New York: NYU Press.

LUKES, S. 1974. *Power: A radical view*. London: Macmillan.

MALTZ, D., AND R. BORKER. 1982. A cultural approach to male-female miscommunication. In *Language and social identity*, J. Gumperz, ed. New York: Cambridge University Press.

MARTIN, E. 1987. *The woman in the body*. Boston: Beacon.

MCCONNELL-GINET, S. 1988. Language and gender. In *Linguistics: The Cambridge survey*. F. Newmeyer, ed. New York: Cambridge University Press.

MICHAELS, S. 1981. "Sharing time": Children's narrative styles and differential access to literacy. *Language in Society* 10 (3): 423–442.

MOI, T. 1985. *Sexual/textual politics*. London: Methuen.

O'BARR, W. M. AND B. K. ATKINS. 1980. "Women's language" or "powerless language"? In *Women and language in literature and society*. S. McConnell-Ginet et al., eds. New York: Praeger.

OCHS, E. 1987. The impact of stratification and socialization on men's and women's speech in Western Samoa. In *Language, gender and sex in comparative perspective*. S. Philips et al., eds. New York: Cambridge University Press.

———. 1992. Indexing gender. In *Sex and gender hierarchies*. Barbara Miller, ed. Cambridge: Cambridge University Press.

OLNEY, J. 1980. Autobiography and the cultural moment. In *Autobiography*: *Essays theoretical and critical*. J. Olney, ed. Princeton: Princeton University Press.

OUTRAM, D. 1987. Le langage male de la vertu: Women and the discourse of the French Revolution. In *The social history of language*. P. Burke and R. Porter, eds. New York: Cambridge University Press.

PHILIPS, S. 1987. Introduction. In *Language, gender and sex in comparative perspective*. S. Philips et al., eds. New York: Cambridge University Press.

POLIER, N., AND W. ROSEBERRY. 1988. Tristes tropes. MS. New York: New School for Social Research.

RADWAY, J. 1984. *Reading the romance*. Chapel Hill: University of North Carolina Press.

RUBIN, G. 1975. The traffic in women: Notes on the "political economy" of sex. In *Toward an anthropology of women*. R. Reiter, ed. New York: Monthly Review.

SATTEL, J. W. 1983. Men, inexpressiveness and power. In *Language, gender and society*. B. Thorne, C. Kramarae, and N. Henley, eds. Rowley, Mass.: Newbury House.

SCHIEFFELIN, B. 1987. Do different worlds mean different words?: An example from Papua New Guinea. In *Language, gender and sex in comparative perspective*. S. Philips et al., eds. New York: Cambridge University Press.

SHERZER, J. 1987. A diversity of voices: Men's and women's speech in ethnographic perspective. In *Language, gender and sex in comparative perspective*. S. Philips et al., eds. New York: Cambridge University Press.

SILVERSTEIN, M. 1985. Language and the culture of gender: At the intersection of structure, usage and ideology. In *Signs in society*. E. Mertz and R. Permentier, eds. New York: Academic.

SMITH, S. 1987. *A poetics of women's autobiography*. Bloomington: University of Indiana Press.

SMITH-ROSENBERG, C. 1985. *Disorderly conduct: Visions of gender in Victorian America*. New York: Oxford.

STANTON, D. 1984. Autogynography: Is the subject different? In *The female autograph*. D. Stanton, ed. Chicago: University of Chicago Press.

STEEDMAN, C., C. UNWIN, AND V. WALKERDINE, EDS. 1985. *Language, gender and childhood*. London: Routledge & Kegan Paul.

TANNEN, D., AND M. SAVILLE-TROIKE, EDS. 1984. *Perspectives on silence*. Washington, D.C.: Georgetown University Press.

THORNE, B., C. KRAMARAE, AND N. HENLEY. 1983. Language, gender and society: Opening a second decade of research. In *Language, gender and society*. B. Thorne et al., eds. Rowley, Mass.: Newbury House.

TREICHLER, P. A., AND C. KRAMARAE. 1983. Women's talk in the ivory tower. *Communication Quarterly* 31 (2): 118–132.

TRUDGILL, P. 1983. Sex and covert prestige: Linguistic change in an urban dialect of Norwich. In *Language in use*. J. Baugh and J. Sherzer, eds. Englewood Cliffs, N.J.: Prentice-Hall.

WALKERDINE, V. 1985. On the regulation of speaking and silence. In Carolyn Steedman, Cathy Unwin and Valerie Walkerdine, eds. *Language, gender and childhood*. London: Routledge and Kegan Paul.

WALKOWITZ, J. 1986. Science, feminism and romance: The Men's and Women's Club 1885–1889. *History Workshop Journal* (Spring): 37–59.

WARREN, K., AND S. BOURQUE. 1985. Gender, power and communication: Responses to political muting in the Andes. In *Women living change*. S. Bourque and D. R. Divine, eds. Philadelphia: Temple University Press.

WEST, C. AND D. ZIMMERMAN. 1983. Small insults: A study of interruptions in cross-sex conversations between unacquainted persons. In *Language, gender and society*. B. Thorne et al., eds. Rowley, Mass.: Newbury House.

WILLIAMS, R. 1973. Base and superstructure in Marxist cultural theory. *New Left Review* 82: 3–16.

WILLIS, P. 1977. *Learning to labor*. Westmead, England: Saxon House.

penelope eckert and
sally mcconnell-ginet

THINK PRACTICALLY AND LOOK LOCALLY

Language and Gender as Community-Based Practice

How do gender and language interact? For the past 20 years or so, linguists, anthropologists, psychologists, sociologists, and feminist thinkers have explored many aspects of this question. There are now dozens of books and hundreds of course offerings on gender and language (14, 20, 41, 60, 67, 92, 98, 99), specialized articles are found in many journals and collections (15, 21, 59, 78, 87, 90, 109, 110, 115), and review articles continue to appear (8, 32, 47, 74, 76, 89). Topics treated include sexist, heterosexist, and racist language; interruptions; graffiti and street remarks; names and forms of address; politeness; tag questions; directives; motherese; children's talk during play; schoolroom discourse; bilingualism and language contact; metaphors; shifts in word meanings; the language of science, religion, and war; silence and volubility; intonation; emotional expressiveness; religious and political rhetoric; sociolinguistic variation; and language change. This list is far from comprehensive but its scatter suggests an absence of theoretical coherence in language and gender studies.

Partial integration of the range of linguistic phenomena that seem sensitive to gender is sometimes attempted by trying to explain them all in terms of a general feature of gender identities or relations. The most influential frameworks in which this has been attempted can be thought of as emphasizing either gender difference or (men's) dominance. Thorne & Henley (108) highlighted these two modes of explanation in their early anthology, *Language and Sex: Difference and Dominance,* although they were ahead of their time in proposing that difference and dominance would probably both enter into explaining gender-language interactions.

We have organized much of our discussion around difference on the one hand (especially as a component of gender identities) and power on the other (especially male dominance as a component of gender relations). However, we have tried to shift attention away from an opposition of the two and toward the processes through which each feeds the other to produce the concrete complexities of language as used by real people engaged in social practice. In our second section, we discuss the separation between the sexes (allegedly producing distinctive female and male communicative cultures); there we also critically discuss sex as a determinant of social address and the resulting orientation toward linguistic variation and change. In our third section, we look at accounts of male power in language and the subordination of women at personal and at institutional levels; we briefly consider other kinds of hierarchical relations, such as those across class and racial boundaries; and we examine larger issues about language and power. But in both the second and third sections we note some of the ways that gender difference helps create hierarchical and other kinds of gender relations; and we indicate how those power relations in turn help construct "women", "men", and their language. Not only are difference and dominance both involved in gender, but they are also jointly constructed and prove ultimately inseparable. These constructions are different at different times and places, and the constructors are people, not faceless abstractions like "society." It is the mutual engagement of human agents in a wide range of activities that creates, sustains, challenges, and sometimes changes society and its institutions, including gender and language.

We aim here to encourage a view of the interaction of gender and language that roots each in the everyday social practices of particular local communities and sees them as jointly constructed in those practices. Thus we use our critical reviews of others' research primarily to hang flesh on the bones of a community-based practice orientation, within which we propose to think about language, about gender, and about their interaction as living social practices in local communities. To think practically and look locally is to abandon several assumptions common in gender and language studies: that gender can be isolated from other aspects of social identity and relations, that gender has the same meaning across communities, and that the linguistic manifestations of that meaning are also the same across communities.

To think practically about gender is to focus on the historical processes of constructing gender categories and power relations: "Gender" becomes a dynamic verb. We speak of practices (and traits and activities and values) as "gendered" where they enter in some important way into "gendering" people and their relations. That is, gendered practices construct members of a community "as" women or "as" men (or members of other gender categories), and this construction crucially also involves constructing relations between and within each sex. Looking locally, we see that the same community practices that help constitute a particular person as a woman may, for example, also help constitute her as "African-American" and "middle-class" and "a mother" and "a sister" and "a neighbor" and so on. We often speak of "women" and of "men" (or sometimes of "female" and "male"), referring to those so constituted in their own communities. But in talking globally, we do not want to suggest that gendered identities and relations have any common core "fixed" by their (initial classificatory) link to reproductive biology. Dichotomous sex-based categories often (not always!) provide an easily applicable way to sort an entire community into two non-overlapping groups. But the content of those categories (including the social relations within and between the groups) is constantly being constituted and in various ways transformed as the members of that community engage with one another in various practices. There is no guarantee that "women" (or "men") in a particular community will in fact constitute themselves as a coherent social group with distinctive common interests. Even practices closely tied to reproductive biology (e.g. those revolving around menstruation and the "disease" of PMS) are connected in complex ways to other social practices (e.g. class-related employment possibilities; see 71), thus making it problematic to speak of "women's" position or interest without reference to other factors.

It used to be fashionable to draw a sharp distinction between sex (biology and what it supposedly "determines"—i.e. femaleness or maleness) and gender (cultural beliefs and norms linked to sex, often more specifically a normative conception of individual attributes associated with sex—i.e. femininity or masculinity). Practice-theoretic approaches to gender make it clear, however, that this dichotomy cannot be maintained (e.g. 22). What looks like laudable terminological clarity in the service of workable analytical distinctions turns out to mask intellectual confusion. Bodies and biological processes are inextricably part of cultural histories, affected by human inventions ranging from the purely symbolic to the technological. It isn't that cultures simply "interpret" or assign "significance" as a cultural overlay to basically biological distinctions connected to sex; rather, social practices constitute in historically specific and changing ways not only gender (and sexual) relations but also such basic gender (and sexual) categories as "woman" and "man" and related categories such as "girl" or "lesbian" or "transsexual" or "lady" or "bitch." "Female" and "male" label distinctions in potential sexual reproductive roles: All cultures known to us sort people at birth into two groups on the basis of anatomical distinctions potentially relevant to those roles. Crucially, however, what is made of those categories and how they link to other sex-related categories and relations emerges only in the historical play of social practices, including their link to such phenomena as medical and technological changes in reproductive possibilities. "Defining" these various terms is not preliminary to but an ongoing component of developing a scholarly practice centered on questions of gender.

Language enters into the social practices that gender people and their activities and ideas in many different ways, developing and using category labels like "woman" and "man" being only a small part of the story. To understand precisely how language interacts with gender (and with other symbolic and social phenomena) requires that we look locally, closely observing linguistic and gender practices in the context of a particular community's social practices. Gumperz (42) defines a speech community as a group of speakers who share rules and norms for the use of a language. This definition suggests the importance of practice in delineating sociolinguistically significant groupings, but it does not directly address social relations and differentiation among members of a single community (though implicitly treating differentiation as revealing "sub-" communities). Nor does it make fully explicit the role of practice in mediating the relation between language and society.

To explore in detail how social practice and individual "place" in the community interconnect, sociolinguists need a conception of a community that articulates place with practice. We therefore adopt Lave & Wenger's notion of the "community of practice" (69, 116). A community of practice is an aggregate of people who come together around mutual engagement in an endeavor. Ways of doing things, ways of talking, beliefs, values, power relations—in short, practices—emerge in the course of this mutual endeavor. As a social construct, a community of practice is different from the traditional community, primarily because it is defined simultaneously by its membership and by the practice in which that membership engages. (This does not mean that communities of practice are necessarily egalitarian or consensual—simply that their membership and practices grow out of mutual engagement.) In addition, relations between and among communities of practice, and relations between communities of practice and institutions, are important: Individuals typically negotiate multiple memberships (in families, or teams, in workplaces, etc), many of them important for understanding the gender-language interaction. A focus on language and gender as practice within communities of practice can, we think, provide a deeper understanding of how gender and language may interact and how those interactions may matter.

DIFFERENCE: GENDER IDENTITIES

In thinking about gender, many start by looking at sex differences. We discuss two strands of sociolinguistic research that have emphasized differences among speakers. One strand starts with a view of gender differences as arising in female and male subcultures, each of which is characterized by gender values and modes of interaction. These studies focus on an array of discourse phenomena as implementations of those values and interactional modes, analyzing cross-sex communicative problems as stemming from gender/cultural differences in norms of appropriate discourse. Language is of interest simply as part of communicative interaction: The larger inquiry is sociocultural, and so language is considered together with such nonverbal phenomena as gaze direction and posture.

The other strand comprises more extensive research from a wider range of research projects. It offers, however, no fully articulated conception of gender and focuses on linguistic phenomena at a structural level: Sex is seen as one of several attributes determining social address or "place" in a community (theoretically on a par with class, race, age) and also determining a distinctive relation to linguistic variation (e.g. pronunciation patterns or orientation toward standard grammar). Gender is of interest just because sex seems in many instances to correlate significantly with linguistic variation, often interacting with class and other components of social address: The starting point is linguistic variation within a population and its relation to social address and to structural linguistic change.

SEX AS THE BASIS OF SEPARATE (BUT EQUAL) SUBCULTURES

As we shall see in the section on power, below, many have argued that differences in women's and men's relations to language—both in systemic matters, such as how vowels are pronounced, and in the dynamics of conversational interaction—are produced by, and themselves help reproduce, male power. At least some analysts, however, have thought of individual cross-sex interactions as plagued by misunderstandings that cannot be explained adequately in terms of the man's control or the woman's submission. According to these researchers, such misunderstandings seem rather to reflect prevalent gender differences in preferred communicative styles and interactional strategies.

Gumperz and colleagues (43) have explained certain problematic interactions and social tension in encounters between members of different social groups as arising from unrecognized differences in the communication patterns those social groups favor. Originally applied to different ethnic, national, and regional groups, this model was extended to tensions between women and men by Maltz & Borker (70), who proposed that norms of friendly peer conversation are learned mainly in single-sex preadolescent peer groups, and that these norms are radically different for females and males, yet essentially the same within each sex across many different local communities. Adult women and men, then, may unwittingly bring different norms to their interactions, each assuming that the other is flouting established norms rather than adhering to a different but equally valid set: She assumes he means what she would mean by making (or not making) a particular conversational move, whereas his intended import is different; and he likewise misjudges her contributions to their exchange. The intended analogue is the young American woman responding with indignation to the British hotel clerk's "shall I knock you up in the morning," hearing a sexual proposition where wake-up service is being offered. Although this model does not account for why boys and girls develop different cultures along the same lines in distinct local communities, it implies that gender practices in the wider society (e.g. the United States) are the key.

Tannen (105) elaborates the Maltz-Borker picture, expanding considerably on the cultural models of male and female conversational practice. Although the general two-culture model does not in itself dictate a particular "essentialist" conception of how female interactional norms might differ from male, the model has in fact been coupled with a currently popular view of "women's" and "men's" ways of thinking and behaving (5, 35). The claim is that women emphasize connection with others, avoiding overt confrontations and direct disagreement, seeking empathy and understanding rather than guidance from their conversational partners, offering intimacy, suggesting or asking rather than directing or telling, preferring the tête-à-tête to talk in larger groups; boys continue boyish patterns of self-assertion into manhood, competing with one another to establish their individual claims to hierarchical status, proferring instruction rather than tea or sympathy, displaying their own ideas and claims for others to confirm but also engaging with relish in defending them against expected attacks of the sort they themselves frequently launch, seeking large audiences and avoiding showing themselves as vulnerable. Neither male nor female is culpable for misunderstandings and disappointments in cross-sex interaction, since each is simply continuing in the track established in the innocence of childhood. Where much work on language and gender ignores male behavior by treating it as a neutral norm from which women deviate, this work has the great merit of trying to account for men's behavior as well as women's. It also has the merit of recognizing that women are not defined simply in terms of their relation to men and that women may actively espouse values and pursue goals not set for them by men. The stereotypes are familiar, but they paint a much more positive view of the "female" subculture and sometimes a less flattering view of the "male" than may have been traditional.

What has seemed to many the most interesting consequence of the dual-culture model—namely, that cross-sex communicative problems derive from inadequate knowledge of interactional norms in the "other" culture—seems to suppose that people ignore all but the interactional possibilities predominant in their own gender-specific subcultures and make no real interactional choices, simply acting as passive sponges who soak up gendered identities. We do not deny that sex separation in childhood may result in gendering some adult interests, strategies, and social values, that such gender differentiation may go unnoticed, or that ignorance of it may cause misunderstandings. But the emphasis on separation and resulting ignorance misses people's active engagement in the reproduction of or resistance to gender arrangements in their communities. For example, indirect requests are a familiar interactional resource in many communities of practice. Every English speaker knows that an interrogative such as "do you think you can finish this by tomorrow?" can function as a polite request or a sugar-coated command, as well as a genuine information-seeking question. The misinterpretation of requests-masquerading-as-questions is likewise available to all speakers as a strategy of resistance: The child's "Not really, mom" in response to her "Would you like to set the table?" tries to read mom's directive literally, thus forcing her to display openly her actual coercive authority. When a man reads a woman's "no" as "yes" he actively exploits his "understanding" of the female style as different from his own—as being indirect rather than straightforward. His reading is possible not because his subculture taught *him* to encourage and welcome sexual advances by feigning their rejection; rather, he tells himself that such coyness is part of "femininity," a mode of being he views as significantly different from his own. The dual-culture approach posits the speakers' mistaken belief in shared norms and symbols. Gender relations in many actual communities of practice familiar to us, however, are often founded on (possibly mistaken) presuppositions not of sameness but of difference ("woman—the eternal mystery"). By taking separation as given, theorists ignore the place of this separation in the practice of the wider community. In fact, both real differences and the belief in differences serve as interactional resources in the reproduction of gender arrangements, of oppression, and of more positive liaisons.

The commonest criticism of the dual-culture model is that it ignores power (41, 48, 97). Where interpretations are disputed, whose cultural norms prevail? Dominance relations between cultures have indeed received little attention in Gumperz-style analyses of communicative conflict. But the dual-culture theory can certainly accommodate power asymmetries. The theory might well predict that those in the subordinated culture would be more likely to "understand" the interactive dialect of their oppressors than vice versa, on the direct analogy to the position of those who speak stigmatized vernaculars or minority languages (Black English Vernacular or Spanish in New York City, for example). But the appeal of the theory is that it minimizes blame for cross-cultural tensions for both the dominating and the dominated group: There is no more agency (and hence no more responsibility) in becoming an interrupter rather than a "good listener" than there is in becoming a speaker of Quechua rather than English. To deny agency and assume interactional difficulties arise simply from insufficient knowledge of differences is to preclude the possibility that people sometimes use differences (and beliefs about differences) strategically in constructing their social relations. In other words, dual-culture theory cannot recognize, let alone explain, strategic appeals to (real or perceived) differences. Yet strategic appeals to difference in constructing gender relations are apparent from even casual observation of social practice: Careful examination of unsatisfactory social relations in cases where cultural separation is more pervasive (e.g. different racial groups) may well also show uses of difference (or beliefs about it) in constructing dominance and other relations. The dual-culture theorists are right in insisting on the importance of interactional devices in gender relations, but their "no-fault" analysis makes it virtually impossible to see how gender differences in interactional strategies are constructed and how interactional strategies (more precisely, strategists) construct gender relations from a repertoire of similarities and differences and ideas about them.

SEX AS SOCIAL ADDRESS

Sociolinguists working in the quantitative paradigm pioneered by Labov have found significant correlations within geographic communities between linguistic variables and speakers' demographic characteristics—socioeconomic class, race, age, and sex (65, 114). The most striking findings concern phonological variation. Variationists have garnered empirical data that describe the spread of patterned sound shifts through and between communities. Regular, systematic sound change appears to enter communities through the speech of the locally oriented working- and lower-middle-class population, and then to move upwards through the socioeconomic hierarchy. People tend to develop and regulate their linguistic repertoire through contact with language used by those they speak with regularly. Thus the partial separation between classes, racial groups, and generations—the relatively infrequent contact across these social boundaries—seems to affect linguistic change much as physical and political divisions do. Social addresses, however, are not all equal. In a sense, variationists consider gender precisely because sex differences in variation emerge even in communities where the sexes are not systematically separated the way socioeconomic or racial groups are. Some such differences may result from different kinds of contact outside the home community—contacts that might significantly affect exposure to standard dialects or to vernacular varieties not heard at home (9, 62). Because most gender differences in variation cannot be explained in this way, however, sociolinguists have reasoned thus about gender identity: If it isn't separation that differentiates the sexes in their linguistic behavior then it must be some aspect of the distinctive content of their gendered personalities or social positions. Differences in the use of linguistic variables, then, reflect sex-based differences in social practice.

Variation studies have used correlations to determine the role of linguistic variables in social practice. Sociolinguistic variables are seen as passive "markers" of the speaker's place in the social grid (particularly in the socioeconomic hierarchy). Correlation of a linguistic variable (or a certain frequency of its use) with a demographic category gives a rudimentary social meaning to that variable within the community: The variable "means" membership in the demographic group correlated with its use. Speakers are seen as making strategic use of sociolinguistic markers in order to affirm membership in their own social group, or to claim membership in other groups to which they aspire. According to this idea working-class speakers use local vernacular variables to claim the local goods and services due authentically local people (64); the hypercorrect patterns in the formal speech of the lower middle class assert membership in the middle class (66). Variables that women use more than men throughout different strata of a community signal female identity in that community (49), and men who rarely use those variables thereby signal their male identity (45, 62). In all these cases, identity, interpreted in terms of place in the social grid, is seen as given, and manipulation of the linguistic repertoire is seen as making claims about these given identities.

Analysts have, however, recognized linguistic variation as doing more than just marking group membership. The fact that the middle class is more resistant to phonological change than the working class has been attributed to the nature of class-based participation in the marketplace (93), and class differences in variation have been attributed to class-based differences in social network structure (80). A variety of patterns of variation have been associated with social network and local orientation (63, 66, 106). Nichols (83) found linguistic behavior among women differentiated by whether or not they had access to the marketplace (in the sense of opportunities for paid work); the different forms of women's and men's participation in the marketplace accounted for language differences across gender boundaries (teaching school requires greater adherence to standard language norms than construction work, for example). Milroy (80) has found complex relations between linguistic differences among women and market-related differences in their social network structure (whether, for example, coworkers are also neighbors or kin).

Although explanations of language variation are becoming more sophisticated as ethnographic studies provide more richly textured data and analyses, the relations between variation and social practice, and between variation and gender, require further elucidation. Finding practice-based explanations of sex correlations will require a significant leap beyond the correlational and class-based modes of explanation used so far. Explanations that do recognize the contributions of practice to variation have typically tried to infer psychological dynamics from correlations rather than from observations of gender dynamics in the communities from which the correlations have been extracted. Speakers who use language patterns that mark (i.e. that are statistically associated with) the social stratum above their own are characterized as upwardly mobile, prestige oriented, and/or insecure. Such correlational interpretation of linguistic variables involves a certain circularity. For example, a number of studies find that women make greater use than men of historically conservative variants. These variants have been interpreted as prestige markers, and women's greater use of them has been said to reflect status consciousness or prestige orientation. But no independent evidence is offered that the patterns in question have (only) the social meaning analysts have assigned on a correlational basis. How they figure in the social practice of the women and men using them has not been examined in detail. When other correlations have emerged in which women have made greater use of historically innovative variants than men, these innovative variants have also been interpreted as prestige markers, maintaining the characterization of women as prestige oriented (62, 113). What is at issue is not whether women in a particular community are or are not upwardly mobile or status conscious. Our methodological point is rather that the social meanings of linguistic variables cannot be ascertained merely on the basis of the social address of those who use them most frequently. Nor are linguistic variables unambiguous (13, 16). A variable acquires multiple meanings through the uses made of it in communities of practice. In this respect it is like other informationally rich symbols (cf the discussion of indirect requests above, p. 437, and of tag questions and rising intonations on declaratives below, p. 447).

A COMMUNITY-BASED PRACTICE VIEW OF DIFFERENCE

What many of the studies cited above have found are *tendencies* toward gender-differentiated practice that have implications for language. It is important to remember that statements like "women emphasize connection in their talk whereas men seek status" are statistical generalizations. We must take care not to infer from such unmodified claims about "women" and "men" that individuals who don't fit the generalization are deviants from some "normative" gender model. This is especially true when women and men are characterized as "different" from one another on a particular dimension. If gender resides in difference, what explains the tremendous variability we see in actual behavior *within* sex categories? Is this variability statistical noise in a basically dichotomous gender system? Or are differences among men and among women also important aspects of gender? Tomboys and goody-goodies, homemakers and career women, body builders and fashion models, secretaries and executives, basketball coaches and French teachers, professors and students, mothers and daughters—these are all categories of girls and women whose mutual differences are part of their construction of themselves and each other as gendered beings. When femaleness and maleness are differentiated in terms of such attributes as power, ambition, physical coordination, rebelliousness, caring, or docility, the role of these attributes in creating and texturing important differences among very female identities and very male identities tends to become invisible. Analysts all too often slide from statistical generalizations to quasi-definitional or prototypical characterizations of "women" and of "men," thus inaccurately homogenizing both categories and marginalizing those who do not match the prototypes.

The point here is not that statistical generalizations about the females and the males in a particular community are automatically suspect. But to stop with such generalizations or to see finding such "differences" as the major goal of investigations of gender and language is problematic. Correlations simply indicate areas where further investigation might shed light on the linguistic and other practices that enter into gender dynamics in a community. An emphasis on difference as constitutive of gender draws attention away from a more serious investigation of the relations among language, gender, and other components of social identity. Gender can be thought of as a sex-based way of experiencing other social attributes such as class, ethnicity, or age (and also less obviously social qualities like ambition, athleticism, musicality, and the like). To examine gender independently as if it were just "added on" to such other aspects of identity is to miss its significance and force. Certainly to interpret broad sex patterns in language use without considering other aspects of social identity and relations is to paint with one eye closed. Speakers are not assembled out of independent modules:

part European American, part female, part middle-aged, part feminist, part intellectual.

Abstracting gender from other aspects of social identity also leads to premature generalization even about "normative" conceptions of femaleness and maleness. While neither of the two strands of research discussed above is theoretically committed to a "universalizing" conception of women or of men, research in both has tended to take gender identity as given, at least in broad strokes, at a global level. Although many of the most audible voices in both the dual-culture and the social-address traditions have indicated clearly that the particular context of gender identities is variable cross-culturally, they have nonetheless spoken of "women" and of "men" in ways that underplay not only cross-cultural differences but also the variability within each gender class for a given culture, much of which is highly structured socially. The strong temptation (one we have sometimes succumbed to ourselves) is to apply theoretical accounts of gender difference globally to women and men.

The portrayal of women as self-effacing, indirect, and particularly concerned with connection derives from research on the American white middle class. Drawing on contrasts with Samoa, Ochs (85) suggests that this "mainstream" American stereotype of women's speech owes much to child-centered mothering practices. Tannen's research on interactions between ethnicity and preference for directness (102) casts doubt on a simple relation between gender and indirection, and African American women have also protested unwarranted assumptions that directness contradicts universal norms of womanhood (81). One might still maintain that most women are less direct than most men in each of these local communities, but research in Madagascar showing most women as direct and most men as indirect (56) contradicts even this weak version of the generalization. Lakoff (68) proposes that women's linguistic patterns, whatever they may be, will be seen as somehow improper; but this is a generalization about evaluation, not linguistic behavior. Once we raise the question of just who might "see" women's language as deficient, a question that Lakoff ignores by using agentless passives and faceless abstractions like "the culture," it becomes apparent that in few communities will evaluations of women's (or of men's) speech be completely uniform. Not only may people recognize diversity among women and among men in their ways of speaking; one person may celebrate the very same gendered stereotype another deprecates. There may be statistically significant correlations between sex and preferred interactional styles and norms that hold across different communities of practice, related to one another via their orientation to common structures and institutions (e.g. to a national state, mass media, educational systems). Some correlations may even hold globally (though only a wide range of detailed local studies could establish these). But such observations would not demonstrate that gender can be isolated from other dimensions of social life, as having some "essence" to be abstracted from the varied sociohistorical circumstances in which people become "women" and "men."

Rather than try to abstract gender from social practice, we need to focus on gender in its full complexity: how gender is constructed in social practice, and how this construction intertwines with that of other components of identity and difference, and of language. This requires studying how people negotiate meanings in and among the specific communities of practice to which they belong.

What, then, is the relation between gender differences and communities of practice? People's access and exposure to, need for, and interest in different communities of practice are related to such things as their class, age, and ethnicity, as well as to their sex. Working-class people are more likely than middle-class people to be members of unions, bowling teams, and close-knit neighborhoods. Upper-middle-class people are more likely than working-class people to be members of tennis clubs, orchestras, and professional organizations. Men are more likely than women to be members of football teams, armies, and boards of directors. Women are more likely to be members of secretarial pools, aerobics classes, and consciousness raising groups. These aspects of membership combine in complex ways. For example, associated with differences in age, class, and ethnicity are differences in the extent to which the sexes belong to different communities of practice. And different people—for a variety of reasons—will articulate their multiple memberships differently. A female executive living in a male-dominated household will have difficulty articulating her membership in her domestic and professional communities of practice; a male executive "head of household" will likely have no such trouble. A lesbian lawyer "closeted" within the legal community may also belong to a"women's" community whose membership defines itself in opposition to the larger heterosexual world. The woman who scrubs toilets in the households of these two women may be a respected lay leader in her local church, facing still another set of tensions in negotiating multiple memberships. Gender is also reproduced in differential forms of participation in particular communities of practice. Women tend to be subordinate to men in the workplace; women in the military do not engage in combat; and in the academy, most theoretical disciplines are overwhelmingly male, with women concentrated in descriptive and applied work that "supports" theorizing. Women and men may also participate differently in single-sex communities of practice. For example, if all-women's groups do in fact tend to be more egalitarian than all-men's groups, as some current literature claims, then women's and men's forms of participation in such groups will differ. Relations within same-sex groups will, of course, be related in turn to the place of such groups in the larger society. Only recently, for example, have women's sports begun to receive significant recognition, and men's sports continue to involve far greater visibility, power, and authority. This articulation with power outside the team in turn translates into different possibilities for relations within. Further, the relations among communities of practice when they come together in overarching communities of practice also reproduce gender arrangements. For example, the relation between male varsity sports teams and cheerleading squads illustrates a more general pattern of men's organizations and women's auxiliaries. Umbrella communities of this kind do not offer all members the same status. When several families get together for a meal and the women team up to do the serving and cleaning up while the men watch football, gender differentiation (including differentiation in language use) is being reproduced within the family on an institutional level.

The individual's development of gender identity within a community of practice (e.g. the Philadelphia neighborhood of working class African American families Goodwin [38, 39, 40] describes) is inseparable from the continual construction of gender within that community of practice, and from the ongoing construction of class, race, and local identities. Nor can it be isolated from that same individual's participation and construction of gender identity in other communities of practice (e.g. her "scholastic-track" class in an integrated school outside the neighborhood). Speakers develop linguistic patterns as they act in their various communities. Sociolinguistics have tended to see this process as one of acquisition of something relatively "fixed." Like social identity, the symbolic value of a linguistic form is taken as given, and the speaker simply learns it and uses it either mechanically or strategically. But in practice, social meaning, social identity, community membership, and the symbolic value of linguistic form are constantly and mutually constructed. (Indeed the variationists' circular construction of the social meaning of variables can be seen as part of this process.) And the relation between gender and language resides in the modes of participation available to various individuals within various communities of practice as a direct or indirect function of gender. These modes of participation determine not only the development of particular strategies of performance and interpretation, but more generally access to meaning and to meaning-making rights.

People use the attribution of difference to construct social hierarchies. In hierarchies, dominant community members attribute deviance only to subordinates; their own distinctive properties they consider unremarkable—the norm. Even if subordinate members are not seen explicitly as deficient, they are disadvantaged by this process of nonreciprocal difference attribution because social practices and institutions favor the interests of "normal" participants (6). Many of the studies reviewed here offer evidence elucidating the power dynamics of gender differences in language use. Not all of the authors cited note this aspect of the phenomena they discuss, but recasting their work within such a framework gives us a rich picture of the dynamics of linguistic power.

POWER: GENDER RELATIONS

Power is not all that connects gender identities to gender relations (consider, for example, intimacy and desire). Differences between and within gender groups can support collaborative efforts in community endeavors, dividing labor and drawing on multiple talents (72), and can function in structuring desire (and not only heterosexual desire; see 61). But interest in power has been the engine driving most research on language and gender, motivated partly by the desire to understand male dominance and partly by the desire to dismantle it (sometimes along with other social inequalities).

Janus-like, power in language wears two faces. First, it is situated in and fed by individual agency; situated power resides primarily in face-to-face interactions but also in other concrete activities like reading or going to the movies. Second, it is historically constituted and responsive to the community's coordinated endeavors; social historical power resides in the relation of situated interaction to other situations, social activities, and institutionalized social and linguistic practices. This duality of power in language derives directly from the duality of social practice: Individual agents plan and interpret situated actions and activities, but their planning and interpretation rely on a social history of negotiating coordinated interpretations and normative expectations (and in turn feed into that history). And the duality of social practice is directly linked to the duality of meaning. What speakers "mean" in their situated utterances and how their interlocutors interpret them is the situated face of meaning; its historical community face involves the linguistic system(s) with conventionalized meanings and usage norms to which utterance meanings are oriented. The real power of language, its social and intellectual value, is found in the interplay between these two aspects of meaning and in the room for development afforded by the adaptability of conventions (e.g. indirection, irony, metaphor, pervasive vagueness, and ambiguity).

The overwhelming tendency in language and gender research has been to emphasize either speakers and their social relations (e.g. women's disadvantages in conversation) or the meanings and norms encoded in the linguistic systems and practices historically available to them (such sexist patterns as conflating generic human with masculine in forms like "he" or "man"). But linguistic forms have no power except as given in people's mouths and ears (or via other media); talk about meaning that leaves out the people who mean is at best limited. We begin by looking at power in situated interactions, then expand the discussion to include more explicit considerations of the community's attempted coordination of symbolic practices (and control of their potential power). We emphasize the existence of alternatives to androcentric world views and practices, moving finally to consideration of power and gender dynamics and change in communities of practice.

INTERACTIONAL REPRODUCTION OF GENDER AND MALE POWER

Lakoff blazed new ground some 20 years ago by hypothesizing that gender difference in the use of English among mainstream white middle-class Americans helped maintain male dominance (67). She followed a long tradition in characterizing "women's language" as different from the standard set by men in being polite, tentative, indirect, imprecise, noncommital, deferential, closer to norms of grammatical "correctness" and less colloquial, emotionally expressive but euphemistic, and so on. However, she departed radically from the misogynistic tradition that gave rise to such stereotypes by arguing that this sort of speech was forced on girls and women as the price of social approval for being appropriately "feminine." At the same time, she saw women's language as keeping them from becoming effective communicators in positions where they might act as independent and nonsubordinate agents. Although challenges have been mounted to many of Lakoff's proposed formal characterizations of "women's language" and to the functions (and hence "meanings") she assigns to those forms, her ideas have been important in suggesting that genderized language use might figure in reproducing men's advantage over women at both personal and institutional levels.

Lakoff's early work prompted analysts to consider how language might connect to men's dominance in the professions and public life. She argued that norms of conversational interaction operative in mainstream American middle-class communities put a woman speaker in a double bind. Behavior that satisfies what is expected of her as a woman disqualifies her in the marketplace: To speak "as a woman" is to speak "as an underling"; and authoritative speech is, according to Lakoff, incompatible with cultural norms of femininity. Lakoff also proposed that linguistic conventions put women at an expressive disadvantage by encoding an androcentric (more specifically a misogynistic) perspective on women themselves. Lakoff not only noted explicitly insulting terms for referring to and addressing women, but also used linguistic techniques to highlight the problematic assumptions that underlie the widespread use of such apparently innocent words as "lady" and "girl."

Impressed by the suggestion that institutionalized male power might be instantiated in everyday linguistic exchanges, investigators began in the mid-1970s to look at such exchanges as potential arenas of sexual politics. A variety of approaches were taken to investigating institutionalized male power in interactions. One was to test gender stereotypes—particularly to assess the empirical evidence on the portrayals of gendered speech in the scholarly literature on language and gender (23, 25). Another kind of study granted (provisionally) the accuracy of stereotypical characterizations of the form of gendered speech but then reanalyzed the functions of those forms, seeing "women's" interactional moves in cross-sex contexts as resisting or coping with the dominance embodied in "men's" moves and as sometimes having other functions as well (29, 73). These studies, too, sought to efface the misogynist underpinnings of many prevalent beliefs about gender differences in language. A different but related strategy has been to examine interaction in single-sex groups, often in order to explore the possible dimensions of gender-specific verbal cultures (55; a study by Goodwin [38] has been widely cited as evidence for separate cultures but is not understood as such by its author). The emphasis of all these efforts has been on women's language, since an important motivation of the work was to attack casual (and often demeaning) female stereotypes. Of course, these scholars also wanted to compensate for the fact that much sociolingistic investigation had ignored women's language use.

One stereotype to come under empirical scrutiny early was that of the talkative woman. Swacker (100) showed that, given the task of describing a picture, the college men in her study talked far longer than the women and tended also to make more positive (if incorrect) statements; women were more tentative in the face of insufficient information. These intriguing results raise questions about how the men and women interpreted their obligations and rights in the context of the task. There are clearly situations in which men are expected and licensed to talk more, and others in which women are; and men and women have differential rights and obligations to talk about particular topics. There is not likely to be a simple relation between amount of talk and gender, or for that matter between amount of talk and power. There are enormous cultural differences in the relationship between power/authority and verbosity (1, 8, 95).

Swacker's speakers were performing solo, doing what was asked of them without threat of competition or benefit of cooperation. Conversational interactions offer other complications, interruptions being one important focus for exploring gender and power in language use. Early studies found that men interrupt more than women (in same-sex and in cross-sex interactions) and that women get interrupted more than men (36, 117, 118, 120); similar patterns of dominant interrupters seemed to emerge in asymmetries of parent-child and doctor-patient interaction. Recent reviews of research on sex differences in amount of speech and on interruptions and overlapping speech show, however, that matters are considerably more complicated (53, 54, 101, 104) than such observations might suggest. First of all, identification of interruptions that usurp others' speaking rights creates serious analytical problems; overlaps and speaker changes interpreted as disruptive interruptions are formally no different from those that function as supportive devices in conversation. Furthermore, conversational turn-taking norms and behavior are not the same in all regional or ethnic groups or situations, and investigation in a variety of settings does not give a clear picture of connections between gender and interruptions even for middle-class whites. Edelsky (28) and Coates (19) found women in certain informal situations regularly overlapping their speech, and Kalčik's study of women's rap groups (55) notes continual collaboration in topic development as supported by overlaps and mutual sentence completion.

In addition, control is not always a matter of monopolizing "air-time" or of other forms of overt bullying. Control can be exercised through refusing to talk (29, 51, 58) or through making someone else talk (17). An individual's conversational contribution is evaluated in retrospect, and inasmuch as silence can signal the inappropriateness or unsatisfactoriness of the preceding turn, it can be a powerful tool for devaluing contributions. In the same way, an individual may continue to provide talk in order to fill in the threatening silence offered by the interlocutor. Such talk may then be evaluated—by both parties—as idle chatter. The potential for devaluation of women's contributions (by both men and women) under these circumstances is tremendous. This interactional construction of the worth of what is said, of the weightiness of different speakers' words for ongoing community-wide purposes, contributes to the development and maintenance of a community history. Such a history tends to reproduce androcentric values in its ongoing conventions and norms—in familiar messages and in the unexamined assumptions that hide in the historically constituted backgrounds against which discourses unfold within the community. A contributor not accorded attention and respect will find her capacity reduced for full participation in the social elaboration of thought, meaning, and community values. The cycle may be vicious in even subtler ways. Strategies undertaken in recognition of situational disadvantage often additionally convey recognition (and at least apparent acceptance) of subordination. Faced with less than energetic participation from the interlocutor, for example, a person may well employ compensatory linguistic strategies to establish the right to talk. Fishman's (29) study of several graduate student couples showed women having considerable difficulty introducing topics and starting conversations with their male partners. They fell back on such strategies as the opening questions that children use to get the floor—"Do you know what?" Announcing perceived lack of entitlement in this way ultimately confirms both partners in their views of the locus of control. As O'Barr & Atkins (84) noted, powerless strategies reproduce powerlessness, signaling the lack of authority (and presumptive value in the community) of their users.

Pointing to the fact that devaluation and limited authority tend to reproduce themselves must not be seen as "blaming the victim" for interactional failures but as showing how dominance can be exercised in the absence of overt coercion. The cycle for a woman may start with social devaluation of her speech, and that devaluation may handicap her capacity for effective speech even where interlocutors might be disposed to treat her as a valued colleague in common enterprises. (Such dispositions are hardly commonplace.) Women and men may utter the same linguistic form but not be able to accomplish the same things by doing so because both men and women presume the lesser value of women's contributions to community endeavors. The power lies not in the forms themselves but in the complex web that connects those forms to those who utter and interpret them and their kinds of membership in the community of practice in which the utterance occurs. Two linguistic forms have been highlighted as evidence of women's interactive insecurity—tag questions ("We should leave, shouldn't we?") and rising "question" intonation in declarative sentences ("My name is Lee?"). It was early recognized that the tag form could carry an intonation that seemed more nearly coercive than insecure or deferential; early quantitative studies of tag questions (23, 25) did not directly examine whether the forms they counted encoded tentativeness and insecurity, however, but concentrated on whether or not they characterized women's speech "in general," finding different sex correlations in quite different situations. However, it has been pointed out (17) that, even keeping intonation constant, tag questions can be heard in exactly the same conversational setting as either deferential or threatening, depending on relations among the participants and the activities in which they are engaged. Similar comments have been made about interpretation of rising intonations in contexts of assertion. Guy et al (45) provide quantitative evidence that Australian women use more rising intonations than men do overall, and suggest that this is a result of women's tentativeness. In an ethnographic study, McLemore (79) showed that rising intonation could be a powerful strategy within a Texas sorority; one speaker reported, however, that she would never use such an intonation in a male-dominated situation, because there it would sound "weak." Even within the sorority, the power of the rise correlated with its user's social position (pledges, for example, sounded "weak" when using repeated rises). This leads us to the more general observation that speech strategies are evaluated in the context of the identities of the participants and their status in specific interactions. The same language may be interpreted differently, for example, depending on whether it is used by a man or a woman. As Lakoff has pointed out, a woman using the same powerful language strategies as a man might well be evaluated as more aggressive than the man. Conversely, language strategies that are heard as powerful when used by a man (e.g. slow, measured delivery) may well not be heard as such when employed by a woman.

ALTERNATIVE AND CHANGING NORMS AND CONVENTIONS

It can be discouraging to survey the ways women's linguistic "differences" from men can disadvantage women as agents reshaping the linguistic norms of their communities. However, we have many indications that this situation can be challenged successfully. Male "control" in situated interactions and in the course of shaping evolving community norms is at best partial and certainly not monolithic. Both women and men have complex arrays of "interests" to further through their actions and have ambivalent connections to community endeavors.

Some of the studies cited above emphasize women's agency, their active participation in interactions. In addition, a number of researchers (re)examining women's participation in linguistic practices find this active agency important not just for the individual agents but for developing socially viable countercurrents and giving alternative meanings to linguistic strategies and forms. Although some "coping" practices ultimately help maintain existing inequities (simply making them more "bearable" for the oppressed), other countercurrents have more potential for transforming communities.

Politeness, for example, is often associated with women's language use. Researchers have tended to see politeness as either passive enforced deference (e.g. 67) or willful "prissy" avoidance of real social engagement (for an early critique of this view see 2). As noted above in the discussion of variation and adherence to "standard language" norms, women's alleged "correctness" can also be viewed as evidence that they are repressed prigs (the "schoolmarm" image) or timid and unimaginative shrinking violets. Alternative functional characterizations may be somewhat more positive, linking women's politeness and correctness to their nurturing roles and to the educative and "civilizing" functions they often serve.

Quite different interpretations have seen these same "women's" linguistic features arising as (partial) strategic solutions to the problems posed for women by their social oppression. Trudgill (113) proposed that women's relative phonological conservatism in Norwich England reflects a symbolic compensation for a lack of access to the marketplace. Eckert (26, 27) has expanded on this view, arguing that women are constrained in a variety of ways to accumulate symbolic capital more generally. Deuchar (24) has argued, furthermore, that where women's language is more standard than men's it may serve to defend them against accusations of stupidity or ignorance, thus increasing the likelihood that they will be recognized as agents, capable not only of communicating but also of creating meanings, as not only consumers but also producers of symbols. Speculations like these gain support from observations of such "women's language" features as politeness and "correctness" in the context of community practice.

Community-based studies show clearly, for example, that politeness is not simply a matter of arbitrary conventional norms constraining individuals ("Ask Kim nicely!") but of intricate and connected strategies to foster social connections and potential alliances and to subvert institutionalized status advantages (see 12 for a general account). Brown (11) examines language use in a Mayan community where in-marrying women are structurally subordinated in many ways, including being subjected to physical violence from husbands and mothers-in-law. Although they do defer to men, they accord respect to other women and foster positive affiliative ties both with other women and with men. In general, they fine-tune their politeness strategies to enhance their individual positions, even using the forms of respect ironically as weapons in such rare (and socially problematic) activities as direct confrontation in the courtroom (10). Lack of other resources having forced these women to develop such nuanced linguistic skills, they actively use them to lessen their social disadvantage and increase their social power (albeit only in limited ways).

A number of community studies detail other concrete ways women refuse to accept passively certain problematic features of their participation in community practices, often reevaluating those practices from alternative perspectives. Radway (92), for example, found that a number of women who were avid readers of "bodice-ripping" romances exercised considerable selectivity in their reading

and were not, as some critics argued, simply feeding a perverse masochism produced by a misogynistic culture. They actively sought visions of capable women
and (at least eventually) admiring and respecting men; they saw their own reading activities as having educational value and as asserting their own self-worth
and entitlement to pleasure. They recognized, however, that others did not share
their assessment. Furthermore, as Radway points out, reading romances may
have prevented their issuing more fundamental challenges to the unsatisfactory
state of gender relations in their communities of practice, including in their
marriages.

Studies that emphasize access as a determining factor in the "acquisition" of
language varieties have an underlying functionalist flavor. Specific language varieties are associated with specific situations; speakers are then cast both as passive users of whatever language varieties they happen to come into contact with
and as passive participants in whatever situations they happen to find themselves
in. But language choice can be an important strategy for gaining control over
one's exposure to people, situations, and opportunities. Gal's study (33) of language shift in a Hungarian-speaking agricultural community in Austria shows
young women emerging as leaders in social change and language shift as part of
a move to gain greater control over their own lives—and young men holding back
in order to maintain control over theirs. In this male-dominated peasant community, women see their interests as conflicting with those of local men. By
rejecting Hungarian for German, they reject the roles and identity of a peasant
wife in a male-dominated agricultural community, in favor of greater access to
jobs and marriage partners in the emerging local industrial economy. Their local
male peers' retention of Hungarian, on the other hand, is consonant with the
greater attractiveness for men of the traditional agricultural life.

Harding's (46) description of women's verbal behavior in a Spanish village
might seem to support either Tannen's generalized claim that women seek connection or less flattering views of women as "gossips." But Harding's rich ethnographic observations show that this behavior plays a different role in overall
practice. Though formal authority and political power in the village are vested
in men, the men depend on their wives for information (obtained through talk
with other women); this information is offered to husbands in forms designed to
influence their evaluation of affairs and their subsequent decisions. Thus the
women gain considerable influence over many important matters in the community, though that influence is exercised only with the cooperation of men and
only within the general parameters of existing practices and relations.

Misogyny in evaluating women's speech (e.g. trivializing it as "gossip") has
certainly been prevalent, and sexist patterns of language use are now well documented. Baron (3) provides a useful historical perspective, and Frank & Treichler (31) offer a superb summary of the field accompanied by excellent
annotated bibliographies. Much of this work has focused on American English
(and on heterosexual white middle-class speakers thereof; but see 47, 119); but
the project of documenting male dominance in speech evaluation, and that of
documenting misogyny and heterosexism in widespread usage patterns and rhetorical practices, have recently become international (50, 52, 86, 112). Scholars
have also begun to study linguistic androcentrism in such enterprises as science
and philosophy (30, 82).

Women do not always accept views excluding them from active participation in shaping the community's endeavors and practices. Visible and effective resistance has characterized the (mainly white and middle-class) feminist movement, ranging from new publications like *Ms.*, to consciousness-raising groups, to assertiveness training, to nonsexist language guidelines (see 31; for Canada's bilingual situation, see 57). Just as striking though less visible in the mainstream are the many refusals to accept wholeheartedly women's relegation to inferior status. Martin's (71) compelling ethnographic study of ways of talking about women's reproductive experiences shows that although authoritative (mainly male) voices in the community (e.g. the medical establishment) do sometimes enforce views of women as under these authorities' control ("managing childbirth"), women can see themselves as active agents. Class privilege may make resistance to predominant views of gender less likely. For example, middle-class women tend to accept the medical model of menstruation, childbirth, and menopause far more readily than do working-class women. Why? Perhaps because the middle-class women far more often depend directly for their personal and economic well-being on men much like those in the medical establishment: Doctors' wives or daughters or sisters have a general interest in doctors' continued authority, and some middle-class women (indeed increasingly many these days) aspire to be accepted as members of that medical establishment themselves.

Some feminists have spoken of men's "control" of language: Men set norms that limit and devalue "women's language" and they appropriate meaning-making for themselves. Male-controlled meaning leads not only to what is called sexist language but also to exclusion of women's contributions from the wide range of cultural values and from what counts as knowledge. Language has been described as "man made" (99) and, more recently, as shaped in and serving the interests of a "patriarchal universe of discourse" (87). The claim is that men (sometimes "modified": e.g. elite white heterosexual men) derogate women and their language and impose on women definitions of reality that serve men's interests at the expense of women's, suppressing or at least ignoring women's meanings. There are subtle as well as simplistic versions of the view that men have shaped language as an instrument for their own sexual, social, political, and intellectual ends. Even the subtlest versions fail to show how norms and conventions might confer or sustain privilege without overt coercion or conscious direction. Nor have their proponents investigated the complex ways linguistic power relates to gendered individuals, including resistant practices like those mentioned above.

Ultimately the view that males have made language an instrument of their own purposes also misses the real potency of language by assuming its meanings float in the ether, unattached to social and linguistic practices. McConnell-Ginet (75, 77) explains semantic change as possible precisely because linguistic forms do not come permanently glued to meanings but are endowed with meanings in the course of social practice. The history of linguistic and social practice constrains but does not determine what a speaker can mean. Male domination in conversation, then—be it subtle or overt—can impose male-oriented meanings on linguistic forms and reinforce them; but meanings are never uniform, nor can they be completely controlled. There is always room for resistance, challenge, and alternatives. Male-centered perspectives can seem to infect "the language" itself, but protection afforded them by existing linguistic conventions of meaning is never complete: Such conventions (and thus "the language") must be continuously sustained in ongoing interactions. Thus we cannot separate so-called "semantic" issues from the kinds of interactive dynamics we have discussed above; on the contrary, it is through these dynamics (including the ways individual interactions connect to wider community practices and institutions) that "the language" and conventions for using it are constituted.

The fact that in most societies familiar to us there are more stereotypes of female language than of male indicates the pervasiveness of the view that women and their relation to language are deviant or "other." Ironically, however, the cumulative effect of a new research focus on women has been to perpetuate this view of men as "normal" and women as needing to be studied. For example, many still refer to the study of language and gender as the study of "women's language." Just as racial privilege maintains the illusion that racial difference resides in people of color, and as heterosexual privilege sustains the illusion that differences in sexuality reside in lesbians and gay males, male privilege sustains the myth that male talk and male meaning-making are not gendered. Such privilege affects the interpretation of speech differences; it also affects how people use language to represent and direct their own and others' thought and action. "Women's words" have too often been interpreted by analysts from male-centered perspectives that ignore multiple possibilities of meaning: To mount any real challenge to women's linguistic disadvantage, we must shift scholarly attention to "men's words" and to language more generally. Black & Coward suggest (7) that men's linguistic advantage over women, in our own and other Western cultures, may derive primarily from the fact that in many communities of practice there exist familiar ways of talking and thinking—roughly what they and other theorists call "discourses"—that constitute men as ungendered autonomous beings and women as gendered and dependent on men. Such discourses involve more than use of such so-called masculine generic forms as "he" or "man," extending to a more general presumption that maleness is a norm while femaleness is a special condition—a presumption that supports a wide range of linguistic and other social practices. One need not believe the presumption to fall into its trap. Even someone attacking the privilege of "white, male heterosexuals" can slip and imply that "most Americans" are in that category, and feminists can eloquently defend the rights of "women and other (!) minorities." The "majority" here is quite clearly not a literal one, yet we have almost certainly ourselves lapsed into such profoundly problematic misstatements (though not, we hope, in this review).

COMMUNITY PRACTICES AND LINGUISTIC POWER

As we have seen, sexual asymmetries in culturally sanctioned power can be both deeper and more subtly connected to language than is suggested by accounts of enforced female deference or male tyranny in local speech activities. Language is a key symbolic and communicative resource, central to developing the ways of thinking and doing that give communities of practice their character. As the preceding sections show, dominance relations among individuals or groups cannot be assessed simply by surveying who says what to whom. Relations of equality or dominance are partly produced in and through what is said (and through histories of similar utterances and their interpretations), as are the speaker and the auditor. The utterance "How about some more coffee, hon?" must be understood in light of two quite different practices when spoken, on the one hand, by a wife holding her empty cup up to her husband and, on the other, by a young male airline passenger to the middle-aged woman pushing the refreshment cart. A marriage creates a persistent community of practice typically involving a rich array of couple-specific practices. The airplane is a very short-lived community involving limited and routine practices common to many similar communities. In both cases power relations derive in part from such conversational exchanges and their place in community practice.

Dominance is sustained by privileging in community practice a particular perspective on language, obscuring its status as one among many perspectives, and naturalizing it as neutral or "unmarked." The privileged can assume their own positions to be norms toward which everyone else orients; they can judge other positions while supposing their own to be invulnerable to less privileged assessment. This privileged relation to a symbolic system, which we shall call symbolic privilege, carries with it interpretive and evaluative authority that requires no explanation or justification.

Symbolic privilege is not, of course, absolute; it is a matter of degree. Nor is a person's rank in symbolic privilege fixed. A woman might have considerable symbolic privilege in her neighborhood but rank low in her office; she might exercise considerable authority in talk about nutrition but not in discussion of finance. Symbolic privilege in some communities of practice may extend far beyond local settings, perhaps through institutions and practices associated with them. Treichler (111) recounts the lovely story of a woman collecting citations for the *Oxford English Dictionary* who used in, and then collected from, her own published writings words and meanings she wanted "authorized" by dictionary inclusion. Symbolic privilege is seldom so obvious or so self-consciously wielded.

Symbolic resources do, of course, mediate access to material resources, but they are ultimately more difficult to monopolize and control. The function and meaning of linguistic forms must be created by situated use if language is to serve the changing needs of communities. A language that cannot grow or change is a defective social and cognitive instrument. Growth and change may threaten established linguistic privilege.

EPILOG

Despite the studies of language and gender discussed above we do not yet have a coherent view of the interaction of gender and language. Existing theories have tended to draw on popular conceptions of gender—e.g. as a set of sex-determined attributes of individuals (a kind of "femininity" or "masculinity," often associated with a particular division of social activities such as childcare or making war), or as a relation of oppression of females by males. As we have emphasized, gender cannot be understood simply as a matter of individual attributes: Femininity connects to masculinity, femininities and masculinities connect to one another, and all connect to other dimensions of social categorization. Nor is gender reducible to a relation between "women" and "men" as undifferentiated groups. Rather, gender is constructed in a complex array of social practices within communities, practices that in many cases connect to personal attributes and to power relations but that do so in varied, subtle, and changing ways.

Although a number of scholars have attempted to understand language as rooted in social practice, relatively little progress has been made in explaining how social practices within communities, practices that in many cases connect to personal attributes and to power relations but that do so in varied, subtle, and changing ways.

Although a number of scholars have attempted to understand language as rooted in social practice, relatively little progress has been made in explaining how social practices relate to linguistic structures and systems. With only a few exceptions (e.g. 7, 32), linguists have ignored recent work in social theory that might eventually deepen our understanding of the social dimensions of cognition (and of the cognitive dimensions of social practice). Even less attention has been paid to the social (including the linguistic) construction of gender categories: The notions of "women" and "men" are typically taken for granted in sociolinguistics. Nor has much attention been given to the variety of ways gender relations and privilege are constructed. Dominance is often seen as either a matter of deference and/or coercion; other aspects of gender relations—e.g. sexual attraction—are typically ignored. Theoretical work in gender studies (e.g. 6, 22, 96, 107) is still not well known among theorists of society and culture (but see 37 as an interesting contribution), and sociolinguistic studies have only rarely taken advantage of recent developments in understanding gender (but see e.g. 39).

Sociolinguists working on questions of language and gender need to build bridges to other communities of scholarly practice whose endeavors focus more centrally on gender. Many linguists talk about gender only because sex has seemed to emerge as a significant variable in their study of phenomena like variation, intonation, or the use of indirection in discourse. They try to elucidate particular aspects of language use or linguistic structure; they seldom hold themselves accountable to gender theory, or even to linguistic theory beyond their own area of specialization. Others who talk about language do so from an interest not in language itself but in gender (not always an analytical or intellectual interest); such scholars may miss insights into the detailed workings of language that linguistics can provide. No community of intellectual practice yet centers on the interactions of gender and language. It is therefore impossible at this point to share approaches to the important questions or evaluations of interim answers.

Investigators have not neglected to look at others' observations before proposing accounts of gender and language interactions. Citations abound in support of claims that women's language reflects conservatism, prestige consciousness, upward mobility, insecurity, deference, nurturance, emotivity, connectedness, sensitivity to others, and solidarity; and that men's language reflects toughness, lack of affect, competitiveness, and independence. But the observations on which such claims are based have all been made at different times and in different circumstances with different populations. One seldom finds good evidence from social practice for the gender characterizations made (evidence of the kind provided by Brown for her claim [11] that the Mayan women in the Mexican village of Tenejapa are politer than their male peers), and it is rarer still to find evidence from social practice of the comparability of observations made in distinct local communities.

It seems clear that the content of gender categories and their connections to linguistic behavior can only be determined by ethnographic study. Such study will likely demonstrate that gender categories intertwine with other social classifications (e.g. class, age, race) within communities of practice; the categories' content and their connections with linguistic behavior will likely work differently in distinct communities of practice. But, as we have noted, there are also deeper difficulties than those posed by premature generalization across communities about gender-language correlations. First, such generalizations tend to forestall close examination of how features like vernacular use (variously interpreted as discussed above, pp. 439, 448) might enter into the social practices of the community. Which activities and situations promote use of the vernacular by those who "tend" to avoid it and for those who "tend" to favor it?

Second, to ask how "women" (or "men") behave "as a group" is to focus on gender conformity and ignore intragender differences (especially challenges to gender hegemony). Suppose in a particular community a given woman uses more (or a given man less) vernacular than other female and male community members, respectively. Are there patterns of exception to community-wide generalizations that can be explained by a deeper understanding of the community's social practices? Can looking at these patterned exceptions yield insight into mechanisms of social and linguistic change?

Third, focus on gender content diverts attention from what may ultimately prove the far more interesting question: How does social practice "use" gender differences (seen as central to gender "content") in constructing gender relations and other social relations (and vice versa). What role does language play in this reciprocal construction of gender difference and gender relations? The diversity of gender differences and relations across and within communities should help us better understand the possible parameters of interaction between language and gender (and, more generally, among language, thought, and society).

Every informed and detailed study of a single language contributes to our understanding of linguistic universals, and every informed and detailed study of a social group contributes to our understanding of social and cultural universals. Both linguists (e.g. 18) and anthropologists (e.g. 34) have argued, however, that such universals are more formal than substantive. Linguists and anthropologists generally agree that comparative studies are essential to getting a grip on the ranges of human language, thought, and social life. We have nothing so grandiose in mind as a detailed theory of the general principles and parameters of gender and language interactions. We certainly are not recommending linguistic theory as a model for thinking about those interactions. What we do want to stress, however, is the great variability both in the factors that constitute gender—the character of gender differences and beliefs about them—and in relations between genders. The latter include not only sex-linked power asymmetries but also other aspects of social ties and social relations (including connections to other social hierarchies and to what Connell [22] dubs the "cathexis" complex of desire, liking, and aversion). We still have little idea of what general principles may be at play in the joint construction of gender differences and gender relations.

Significant further advances in the study of language and gender must involve unprecedented integration. Such integration can come only through the intensive collaboration of people working in a variety of fields and a variety of communities. Language and gender studies, in fact, require an interdisciplinary community of scholarly practice. Isolated individuals who try to straddle two fields can often offer insights, but progress depends on getting people from a variety of fields to collaborate closely in building a common and broad-based understanding. Collaboration is needed among people in different fields and among people doing similar work in more than one community. A collaborative effort among ethnographers in many different communities might arrive at a view of gender dynamics across communities rich enough to begin to permit generalizations about the relation to language of those dynamics. These would not simply be studies of women or of men. These studies would explore how "women" and "men" are constructed as social categories. They would also explore how these constructions link to relations among those constructed as "women" and among those constructed as "men" (including those constructed as atypical or deviant members of their categories) as well as to relations between those assigned to different categories. These studies would be studies not of language in isolation from other social practices but of the linguistic dimensions of social practice (and, more generally, the complex social and cognitive character of so-called [socio]linguistic competence"). By approaching both gender and language as constructed in communities of practice, we may be able to strengthen claims about the social and cognitive importance of their interaction. We may likewise succeed in enriching our view of social conflict and change, thus deepening our understanding of the profoundly historical character of gender, of language, and of their connections.

ACKNOWLEDGMENTS

The authors thank the many colleagues from whom we have learned about language, gender, and their interaction, including especially the participants in our 1991 Linguistic Society of America Summer Institute course. We also owe a lot to the others who have worked on these topics, including many scholars whose work we have not happened to cite. Special thanks to Carl Ginet and Sandra Bem for helpful comments and encouragement at critical stages; to Nancy Henley, Cheris Kramarae, and Barrie Thorne for suggested references; to Etienne Wenger for a useful evening of talk about communities of practice; to the computer folks who tried to make our e-mail connections work; and to Karen Powell for assembling the bibliography. Each of us thanks the other for intellectual and other kinds of companionship, and we agree to share authorial responsibility completely. Our names appear in alphabetical order.

SELECTED BIBLIOGRAPHY

1. ALBERT, E. M. 1972. Culture patterning of speech behavior in Burundi. See Ref. 44, pp. 72–105
2. ANGLE, J., HESSE, S. 1976. *Hoity-Toity Talk and Women*. Work. Pap. 131. Cent. Res. Soc. Organ., Univ. Mich.

3. BARON, D. 1986. *Grammar and Gender.* New Haven: Yale Univ. Press.
4. BAUMAN, R., SHERZER, J., EDS. 1974. *Explorations in the Ethnography of Speaking.* Cambridge: Cambridge Univ. Press
5. BELENKY, M. F., GOLDBERG, N. R., TARULE, J. M. 1986. *Women's Ways of Knowing.* New York: Basic Books
6. BEM, S. L. 1993. *The Lenses of Gender: Transforming the Debate on Sexual Inequality.* New Haven: Yale Univ. Press.
7. BLACK, M., COWARD, R. 1990. Linguistic, social and sexual relations. See Ref. 15, pp. 111–33
8. BORKER, R., MALTZ, D. 1989. Anthropological perspectives on gender and language. In *Gender and Anthropology: Critical Reviews for Research in Teaching,* ed. S. Morgen, pp. 411–37. Washington, DC: Am. Anthropol. Assoc.
9. BORTONI-RICARDO, S. M. 1985. *The Urbanization of Rural Dialect Speakers.* Cambridge: Cambridge Univ. Press
10. BROWN, P. 1990. Gender, politeness, and confrontation in Tenejapa. *Discourse Process.* 13:123–41
11. BROWN, P. 1980. How and why are women more polite: Some evidence from a Mayan community. See Ref. 78, pp. 111–36
12. BROWN, P., LEVINSON, S. 1987. *Politeness: Some Universals in Language Use.* Cambridge: Cambridge Univ. Press
13. BROWN, P., LEVINSON, S. 1979. Social structure, groups and interaction. In *Social Markers in Speech,* ed. K. R. Scherer, H. Giles, pp. 291–342. Cambridge: Cambridge Univ. Press
14. CAMERON, D. 1985. *Feminism and Linguistic Theory.* London: Macmillan
15. CAMERON, D. 1990. *The Feminist Critique of Language: A Reader.* London/New York: Routledge
16. CAMERON, D., COATES, J. 1988. Some problems in the sociolinguistic explanation of sex differences. See Ref. 21, pp. 13–26
17. CAMERON, D., McALINDEN, F., O'LEARY, K. 1988. Lakoff in context: The social and linguistic function of tag questions. See Ref. 21, pp. 74–93
18. CHOMSKY, N. 1986. *Knowledge of Language: Its Nature, Origin and Use.* New York: Praeger
19. COATES, J. 1988. Gossip revisited: Language in all-female groups. See Ref. 21, pp. 94–122
20. COATES, J. 1986. *Women, Men and Language.* London: Longman
21. COATES, J., CAMERON, D., EDS. 1988. *Women in Their Speech Communities: New Perspectives on Language and Sex.* London/New York: Longman
22. CONNELL, R. W. 1987. *Gender and Power.* Stanford, CA: Stanford Univ. Press
23. CROSBY, F., NYQUIST, L. 1977. The female register: An empirical study of Lakoff's hypothesis. *Lang. Soc.* 6:313–22
24. DEUCHAR, M. 1988. A pragmatic account of women's use of standard speech. See Ref. 21, pp. 27–32
25. DUBOIS, B. L., CROUCH, I. 1975. The question of tag questions in women's speech: They don't really use more of them, do they? *Lang. Soc.* 4:289–94
26. ECKERT, P. 1990. Cooperative competition in adolescent girl talk. *Discourse Process.* 13:92–122
27. ECKERT, P. 1990. The whole woman: Sex and gender differences in variation. *Lang. Variation Change* 1:245–67
28. EDELSKY, C. 1981. Who's got the floor? *Lang. Soc.* 10:383–421
29. FISHMAN, P. M. 1983. Interaction: The work women do. See Ref. 109, pp. 89–102
30. FOX KELLER, E. 1987. The gender/science system: Or is sex to gender as nature is to science? *Hypatia 2*

31. FRANK, F. W., TREICHLER, P. A. 1989. *Language, Gender, and Professional Writing: Theoretical Approaches and Guidelines for Nonsexist Usage.* New York: Modern Language Assoc.

32. GAL, S. 1991. Between speech and silence: The problematics of research on language and gender. In *Gender at the Crossroads of Knowledge: Feminist Anthropology in the Postmodern Era,* ed. M. DiLeonardo, pp. 175–203. Berkeley: Univ. Calif. Press

33. GAL, S. 1978. Peasant men can't get wives: Language change and sex roles in a bilingual community. *Lang. Soc.* 7:1–16

34. GEERTZ, C. 1973. *The Interpretation of Cultures.* New York: Basic Books

35. GILLIGAN, C. 1982. *In a Different Voice.* Cambridge: Harvard Univ. Press

36. GLEASON, J. B., GREIF, E. B. 1983. Men's speech to young children. See Ref. 109, pp. 140–50

37. GOFFMAN, E. 1977. The arrangement between the sexes. *Theory Soc.* 4:301–32

38. GOODWIN, M. H. 1980. Directive-response speech sequences in girls' and boys' task activities. See Ref. 78, pp. 157–73

39. GOODWIN, M. H. 1991. *He-Said-She-Said.* Bloomington: Indiana Univ. Press

40. GOODWIN, M. H. 1990. Tactical uses of stories: Participation frameworks within girls' and boys' disputes. *Discourse Process.* 13:33–72

41. GRADDOL, D., SWANN, J. 1989. *Gender Voices.* Oxford: Basil Blackwell

42. GUMPERZ, J. J. 1972. Introduction. See Ref. 44, pp. 1–25

43. GUMPERZ, J. J., ED. 1982. *Language and Social Identity.* Cambridge: Cambridge Univ. Press

44. GUMPERZ, J. J., HYMES, D., EDS. 1972. *Directions in Sociolinguistics.* New York: Holt, Rinehart & Winston

45. GUY, G., HORVATH, B., VONWILLER, J., DAISLEY, E., ROGERS, I. 1986. An intonational change in progress in Australian English. *Lang. Soc.* 15:23–52

46. HARDING, S. 1975. Women and words in a Spanish village. In *Toward an Anthropology of Women,* ed. R. R. Reiter, pp. 283–308. New York: Monthly Review Press

47. HENLEY, N. M. 1992. Ethnicity and gender issues in language. In *Handbook of Cultural Diversity in Feminist Psychology,* ed. H. Landrine. Washington DC: Am. Technol. Assoc.

48. HENLEY, N., KRAMARAE, C. 1991. Gender, power, and miscommunication. In *Problem Talk and Problem Contexts,* ed. N. Coupland, H. Giles, J. Wiemann, pp. 18–43. Newbury Park, CA: Sage

49. HINDLE, D. 1979. *The social and situational conditioning of phonetic variation.* Dissertation. Univ. Penn.

50. HIRAGA, M. K. 1991. Metaphors Japanese women live by. *Work, Pap. Lang., Gender, Sexism* 1:38–57

51. HOUSTON, M., KRAMARAE, C. 1991. Speaking from silence: Methods of silencing and resistance. *Discourse Soc.* 2:387–99

52. IDE, S., MCGLOIN, N. H., EDS. 1990. *Aspects of Japanese Women's Language.* Tokyo: Kurosio

53. JAMES, D., CLARKE, S. 1992. Women, men and interruptions: A critical review. See Ref. 103.

54. JAMES, D., DRAKICH, J. 1992. Understanding gender differences in amount of talk: A critical review of research. See Ref. 103.

55. KALČIK, S. 1975. ". . . like Ann's gynecologist or the time I was almost raped": Personal narratives in women's rap groups." *J. Am. Folklore* 88:3–11

56. KEENAN, E. 1974. Norm-makers, norm-breakers: Uses of speech by men and women in a Malagasy community. See Ref. 4, pp. 125–43

57. KING, R. 1991. *Talking Gender: A Guide to Nonsexist Communication.* Toronto: Copp Clark Pitman/Longman

58. KOMAROVSKY, M. 1962. *Blue-Collar Marriage*. New Haven/London: Yale Univ. Press
59. KRAMARAE, C. 1988. *Technology and Women's Voices: Keeping in Touch*. New York/London: Routledge & Kegan Paul
60. KRAMARAE, C. 1981. *Women and Men Speaking: Frameworks for Analysis*. Rowley, MA: Newbury House
61. KRIEGER, S. 1983. *The Mirror Dance: Identity in a Women's Community*. Philadelphia: Temple Univ. Press
62. LABOV, W. 1991. The intersection of sex and social class in the course of linguistic change. *Lang. Variation Change* 2 : 205–51
63. LABOV, W. 1972. The linguistic consequences of being a lame. In *Language in the Inner City*, ed. W. Labov, pp. 255–92. Philadelphia: Univ. Penn. Press
64. LABOV, W. 1980. The social origins of sound change. In *Locating Language in Time and Space*, ed. W. Labov, pp. 251–65. New York: Academic
65. LABOV, W. 1966. *The Social Stratification of English in New York City*. Washington, DC: Cent. Appl. Linguist.
66. LABOV, W. 1972. *Sociolinguistic Patterns*. Philadelphia: Univ. Penn. Press
67. LAKOFF, R. 1975. *Language and Woman's Place*. New York: Harper & Row
68. LAKOFF, R. T. 1990. *Talking Power: The Politics of Language in Our Lives*. New York: Basic Books
69. LAVE, J., WENGER, E. 1991. *Situated Learning: Legitimate Peripheral Participation*. Cambridge: Cambridge Univ. Press
70. MALTZ, D. N., BORKER, R. A. 1982. A cultural approach to male-female miscommunication. See Ref. 43, pp. 196–216
71. MARTIN, E. 1987. *The Woman in the Body: A Cultural Analysis of Reproduction*. Boston: Beacon Press
72. MCCONNELL-GINET, S. 1980. Difference and language: A linguist's perspective. In *The Future of Difference*, ed. H. Eisenstein, pp. 157–66. Boston: G. K. Hall
73. MCCONNELL-GINET, S. 1983. Intonation in a man's world. See Ref. 109, pp. 69–88
74. MCCONNELL-GINET, S. 1988. Language and gender. In *Linguistics: The Cambridge Survey*, ed. F. J. Newmeyer, pp. 75–99. Cambridge: Cambridge Univ. Press.
75. MCCONNELL-GINET, S. 1984. The origins of sexist language in discourse. In *Discourses in Reading and Linguistics*, ed. S. J. White, V. Teller, pp. 123–35. Ann. NY Acad. Sci.
76. MCCONNELL-GINET, S. 1983. Review article. *Language* 59 : 373–91
77. MCCONNELL-GINET, S. 1989. The sexual (re)production of meaning: A discourse based theory. See Ref. 31, pp. 35–50
78. MCCONNELL-GINET, S., BORKER, R. A., FURMAN, N., EDS. 1980. *Women and Language in Literature and Society*. New York: Praeger
79. MCLEMORE, C. 1991. The interpretation of L*H in English. In *Linguistic Forum 32*, ed. C. McLemore, pp. 175–96. Austin: Univ. Texas Dep. Linguist & Cent. Cogn. Sci.
80. MILROY, L. 1980. *Language and Social Networks*. Oxford: Blackwell
81. MORGAN, M. 1991. Indirectness and Interpretation in African American Women's Discourse. *Pragmatics* 1 : 421–52.
82. MOULTON, J. 1983. The adversary paradigm in philosophy. In *Discovering Reality*, ed. S. Harding, M. B. Hintikka. Boston/Dordrecht: Reidel
83. NICHOLS, P. C. 1983. Linguistic options and choices for black women in the rural south. See Ref. 109, pp. 54–68
84. O'BARR, W. M., ATKINS, B. K. 1980. "Women's language" or "powerless language"? See Ref. 78, pp. 93–110
85. OCHS, E. 1991. Indexing gender. In *Rethinking Context*, ed. A. Duranti, C. Goodwin. Cambridge: Cambridge Univ. Press

86. PAUWELS, A., ED. 1987. *Women and Language in Australian and New Zealand Society.* Mosman, NSW: Aust. Professional Publ.
87. PENELOPE, J. 1990. *Speaking Freely: Unlearning the Lies of the Fathers' Tongues.* New York: Pergamon
88. PENFIELD, J. 1987. *Women and Language in Transition.* Albany, NY: SUNY Press
89. PHILIPS, S. U. 1980. Sex differences and language. *Annu. Rev. Anthropol.* 9:523–44
90. PHILIPS, S. U., STEELE, S., TANZ, C., EDS. 1987. *Language, Gender, and Sex in Comparative Perspective.* Cambridge: Cambridge Univ. Press
91. POYNTON, C. 1989. *Language and Gender.* Oxford: Oxford Univ. Press
92. RADWAY, J. A. 1984. *Reading the Romance: Women, Patriarchy, and Popular Literature.* Chapel Hill, NC: Univ. NC Press
93. SANKOFF, D., LABERGE, S. 1978. The linguistic market and the statistical explanation of variability. In *Linguistic Variation: Models and Methods,* ed. D. Sankoff, pp. 239–50. New York: Academic
94. SATTEL, J. 1983. Men, inexpressiveness and power. See Ref. 109, pp. 119–24
95. SCOLLON, R., SCOLLON, S. B. K. 1980. *Athabaskan-English Interethnic Communication.* Fairbanks: Cent. Cross-cultural Stud., Univ. Alaska
96. SEGAL, L. 1990. *Slow Motion: Changing Masculinities, Changing Men.* New Brunswick, NJ: Rutgers Univ. Press
97. SINGH, R., LELE, J. K. 1990. Language, power and cross-sex communication in Hindi and Indian English revisited. *Lang. Soc.* 19:541–46
98. SMITH, P. M. 1985. *Language, the Sexes and Society.* Oxford: Blackwell
99. SPENDER, D. 1980. *Man Made Language.* London: Routledge & Kegan Paul
100. SWACKER, M. 1975. The sex of speaker as a sociolinguistic variable. See Ref. 108, pp. 76–83
101. SWANN, J. 1988. Talk control: An illustration from the classroom of problems in analysing male dominance of conversation. See Ref. 21, pp. 123–40
102. TANNEN, D. 1982. Ethnic style in male-female communication. See Ref. 43, pp. 217–31
103. TANNEN, D., ED. 1992. *Gender and Conversational Interaction.* Oxford: Oxford Univ. Press
104. TANNEN, D. 1989. Interpreting interruption in conversation. *Pap. 25th Annu. Meet. Chicago Linguist. Soc., Part 2: Parasession on Language and Context.* Chicago: Univ. Chicago Press
105. TANNEN, D. 1990. *You Just Don't Understand: Women and Men in Conversation.* New York: Morrow
106. THOMAS, B. 1988. Differences of sex and sects: linguistic variation and social networks on a Welsh mining village. See Ref. 21, pp. 51–60
107. THORNE, B. 1990. Children and gender: Constructions of difference. In *Theoretical Perspectives on Sexual Difference,* ed. D. Rhode, pp. 100–12. New Haven: Yale Univ. Press
108. THORNE, B., HENLEY, N., EDS. 1975. *Language and Sex: Difference and Dominance.* Rowley, MA: Newbury House
109. THORNE, B., KRAMARAE, C., HENLEY, N., EDS. 1983. *Language, Gender and Society.* Rowley, MA: Newbury House
110. TODD, A. D., FISHER, S. 1988. *Gender and Discourse: The Power of Talk.* Norwood, NJ: Ablex
111. TREICHLER, P. A. 1989. From discourse to dictionary: How sexist meanings are authorized. See Ref. 31, pp. 51–79
112. TRÖMMEL-PLÖTZ, S. 1982. *Frauensprache-Sprache der Veränderung.* Frankfurt-am-Main: Fischer

113. TRUDGILL, P. 1972. Sex, covert prestige and linguistic change in the urban British English of Norwich. *Lang. Soc.* 1:179–95

114. TRUDGILL, P. 1974. *The Social Differentiation of English in Norwich*. Cambridge: Cambridge Univ. Press

115. VETTERLING-BRAGGIN, M., ED. 1981. *Sexist Language; A Modern Philosophical Analysis*. Totowa, NJ: Littlefield, Adams & Co.

116. WENGER, E. 1993. *Communities of Practice*. New York: Cambridge Univ. Press. In press

117. WEST, C., ZIMMERMAN, D. H. 1983. Small insults: A study of interruptions in cross-sex conversations between unacquainted persons. See Ref. 109, pp. 102–17

118. WEST, C., ZIMMERMAN, D. H. 1977. Women's place in everyday talk: Reflections on parent-child interaction. *Soc. Probl.* 24:521–29

119. WOLFE, S. J. 1988. The rhetoric of heterosexism. In *Gender and Discourse: The Power of Talk*, ed. A. D. Todd, S. Fisher, pp. 199–244. Norwood, NJ: Ablex

120. ZIMMERMAN, D., WEST, C. 1975. Sex roles, interruptions and silences in conversation. See Ref. 108, pp. 105–29

INDEX

ABOUT THE AUTHORS

JESSICA BENJAMIN is affiliated with the Postdoctoral Program in Psychotherapy and Psychoanalysis at New York University. She has written extensively on psychoanalysis and psychology and is the author of *The Bonds of Love: Psychoanalysis, Feminism, and the Problem of Domination*.

PENELOPE BROWN conducts crosscultural anthropological research on women and politeness. In addition to authoring essays on the subject, she has published collaborative work with Steven Levinson, including *Politeness: Some Universals in Language Use*.

HÉLÈNE CIXOUS is the Head of the Centre d'Etudes Féminines and Professor of English at the Université de Paris VIII—Vincennes. She is the author of *The Exile of James Joyce, The Book of Promethea, Writing Differences*, and *'Coming to Writing' & Other Essays*. She is coauthor with Catherine Clément of *The Newly Born Woman*.

NANCY J. CHODOROW is Professor of Sociology at the University of California, Berkeley, and a psychoanalyst in private practice. She is the author of *The Reproduction of Mothering: Psychoanalysis and the Sociology of Gender, Feminism and Psychoanalytic Theory*, and the forthcoming *Femininities, Masculinities, Sexualities: Some Psychoanalytic Constructions*.

JOHN DORE is Professor of Psychology at Baruch College and the Graduate School, City University of New York. He has written primarily on the psychology of language and children's discourse.

PENELOPE ECKERT is Senior Research Scientist, Institute for Research on Learning, and Consulting Associate Professor, Department of Linguistics, Stanford University. She writes extensively on gender and language. Her recent work includes "Communities of Practice: Where Language, Gender, and Power All Live," "The Whole Woman: Sex and Gender Differences in Variation," and "Cooperative Competition in Adolescent Girl Talk."

SIGMUND FREUD was a practicing psychoanalyst based primarily in Vienna, Austria. He is well known for developing the field of psychoanalysis and is the author of numerous texts and essays, including *On Sexuality, Introductory Lectures on Psychoanalysis, The Interpretation of Dreams, Civilization and Its Discontents, The Case of Dora, Beyond the Pleasure Principle, Moses and Monotheism,* and *Totem and Taboo.*

SUSAN GAL is Professor of Anthropology at Rutgers University. She has published essays on gender and language use among bilinguals and has an essay in press on East European Politics and Societies entitled "Women and the Transition from State-Socialism: The Abortion Debate in Hungary." She is currently engaged in a large comparative research project entitled "The Politics of Reproduction after Socialism."

JEAN BERKO GLEASON is Professor of Psychology at Boston University. She is author and editor of *The Development of Language* and coeditor of *Psycholinguistics*. She has written primarily on language development in children and developmental sociolinguistics, especially on gender differences in parent-child conversational interaction.

MARJORIE HARNESS GOODWIN is Professor of Anthropology at the University of South Carolina, Columbia. She is well known for her studies of language patterns of African-American girls and boys. She is the author of *He-Said-She-Said: Talk as Social Organization among Black Children.*

EUGENE HAHN is a graduate student at the University of Texas, Austin. His work-in-progress includes a study of sex-role attitude change over the last twenty years and an examination of how sex-role attitudes can be changed by exposure to sentences describing male/female interactions.

MYKOL C. HAMILTON is Assistant Professor of Psychology at Centre College. She has published several studies on male-biased language, including "Masculine Bias in the Attribution of Personhood: People = Male, Male = People," "Masculine Generic Terms and Misperception of AIDS Risk," and "Using Masculine Generics: Does Generic 'He' Increase Male Bias in the User's Imagery?"

NANCY M. HENLEY, Professor of Psychology at the University of California, Los Angeles, writes extensively on language and gender. With Barrie Thorne, she is coeditor of *Language and Sex: Difference and Dominance;* and with Thorne and Cheris Kramarae, coeditor of *Language, Gender, and Society.* Her major works in progress include studies of masculine generics and the use of passive voice to describe violence against women.

BARBARA HUNTER is a doctoral candidate, ABD, at Pennsylvania State University in Social Psychology with a minor in Women's Studies. She works on the development of modern sexism: interracial dating, homosexuality, the impact of attitudes toward women on jury decision-making, husbands' responses to their wives' menstrual cycles, and women's and men's token resistance and compliance to sexual intercourse.

LUCE IRIGARAY is affiliated with École des Hautes Études en Sciences Sociales in Paris and is a psychoanalyst. She has published widely on the relationship between language, psychology, and gender. Three of her best-known studies are *Speculum of the Other Woman, This Sex Which Is Not One,* and *Sexes and Genealogies.*

JUDITH V. JORDAN is affiliated with the Stone Center for Developmental Services and Studies, Wellesley College. She has written extensively on women's growth and has published *Women's Growth in Connection: Writings from the Stone Center.*

SUZANNE JUHASZ is Professor of English at the University of Colorado, Boulder, and Editor of *The Emily Dickinson Journal.* Her books include *The Undiscovered Continent: Emily Dickinson and the Space of the Mind; Feminist Critics Read Emily Dickinson; Naked and Fiery Forms: Modern American Poetry by Women; Metaphor and the Poetry of Williams, Pound, and Stevens;* and with Cristanne Miller and Martha Nell Smith, *Comic Power in Emily Dickinson. Reading from the Heart: Women Readers, Women Writers, and the Story of True Love* is forthcoming.

CHERIS KRAMARAE is Professor of Speech Communication, Linguistics, and Sociology, and coordinator of Women's Studies at the University of Illinois at Urbana-Champaign. She is the author, editor, or coeditor of many articles and eight books on women and language, including *Women and Men Speaking: Language, Gender, and Society; Amazons, Blue-stockings, and Crones: A Feminist Dictionary; Technology and Women's Voices;* and *Women, Information Technology, and Scholarship.*

JULIA KRISTÉVA is Professor at the Université de Paris VII as well as a psychoanalyst. Among her most prominent publications are *Desire in Language: A Semiotic Approach to Literature and Art; Tales of Love, Powers of Horror: An Essay on Abjection; Revolution in Poetic Language; About Chinese Women;* and *In the Beginning Was Love.*

JACQUES LACAN was a theorist and practicing psychoanalyst based primarily in Paris. He is well known for his book-length studies *Language of the Self, Écrits, Feminine Sexuality,* and *The Four Fundamental Concepts of Psycho-Analysis,* as well as numerous essays.

MARIANNE LaFRANCE is Professor of Psychology at Boston College. Her recent work includes "Gender and Interruption: Individual Infraction or Violation of the Social Order," a coauthored essay with M. Banaji, "Towards a Reconsideration of the Gender-Emotion Relationship," and a coauthored essay with Nancy Henley, "On Oppressing Hypotheses or Sex Differences in Nonverbal Sensitivity Revisited," in *Power and Gender.*

ROBIN LAKOFF is Professor of Linguistics at the University of California, Berkeley. She is the author of *Language and Woman's Place, Face Value, the Politics of Beauty,* and *Talking Power: The Politics of Language in Our Lives.*

SALLY MCCONNELL-GINET is Professor of Linguistics and Director of Women's Studies at Cornell University. Among her publications are *Women and Language in Literature and Society,* coedited with Nelly Furman and the late Ruth Borker; "Intonation in a Man's World," *Signs;* "Gender and Language" in *Linguistics: The Cambridge Survey;* and "The Sexual (Re)Production of Meaning" with Penelope Eckert in *Language, Gender, and Professional Writing.*

CRISTANNE MILLER is Associate Professor of English at Pomona College. On the subject of language and gender, she has published "Who Talks Like a Women's Magazine? Language and Gender in Popular Women's and Men's Magazines," *Journal of American Culture;* and a second essay, "M. Nourbese Philip and the Poetics and Politics of Silence," is forthcoming in *Semantics of Silence in Linguistics and Literature.* Her most recent books are *Comic Power in Emily Dickinson,* coauthored with Suzanne Juhasz and Martha Nell Smith and the forthcoming *Feminist Measures: Soundings in Poetry and Theory,* coedited with Lynn Keller. She is now completing *Questions of Authority: The Example of Marianne Moore.* She has published extensively on Emily Dickinson and other women poets.

CAMILLE ROMAN is Assistant Professor of English at Washington State University, Pullman. She writes on gender in twentieth-century culture and literature. Her most recent essays include "D. H. Lawrence's (Pre)Oedipal Poetics and Postmoderns Sylvia Plath and Frank O'Hara," and she is currently working on a book-length study entitled *Postmodern Homemaking: Figuring the Family in Recent American Poetry.*

HORTENSE J. SPILLERS is Professor of English and Women's Studies at Emory University. She is the author of *Conjuring: Black Women, Fiction, and Literary Tradition* and *Comparative American Identities: Race, Sex, and Nationality.*

GAYATRI CHAKRAVORTY SPIVAK is Professor of English at Columbia University. She has published widely in postcolonial criticism and theory. Among her best-known studies are *The Post-Colonial Critic: Interviews, Strategies, Dialogues; Selected Subaltern Studies;* and *In Other Worlds: Essays in Cultural Politics.*

DANIEL N. STERN, M.D., is currently Professor of Psychology, University of Geneva; Adjunct Professor of Psychiatry, Cornell University Medical College; and Instructor, Columbia University Center for Psychoanalytic Training and Research. He is the author of three books on the socio-affective development of the infant and the infant-parent relationship, *The First Relationship: Infant and Mother*, *The Interpersonal World of the Infant*, and *The Diary of a Baby*.

SHANNON STUART-SMITH holds degrees in philosophy and law. She collaborates with Mykol Hamilton on language study, and one of their coauthored essays, "Sociobiology Revisited: Natural Selection and Dominance of the Human Female Over the Human Male," is forthcoming in the second edition of Sheila Ruth's *Issues in Feminism*.

COLWYN TREVARTHEN is Professor of Psychology at the University of Edinburgh, Scotland, and director of the Edinburgh Centre for Research in Child Development. He has published widely on brain development and the development of communication in infancy. Currently he is primarily studying communicating underlying language and music and the role of emotions in psychological growth and education.

CANDACE WEST is Professor of Sociology at the University of California, Santa Cruz. Her recent articles include "Reconceptualizing Gender in Physician-Patient Relationships," *Social Science and Medicine;* "Power, Inequality and the Accomplishment of Gender" (with Sarah Fenstermaker) in *Theory on Gender/Feminism in Theory*, edited by Paula England; and "Accounting for Cosmetic Surgery" (with Diana Dull) in *Social Problems*.

DONALD WOODS WINNICOTT was a practicing pediatrician and a psychoanalyst. Among his best-known works are *Collected Papers: Through Pediatrics to Psycho-Analysis*, *The Maturational Processes and the Facilitating Environment*, *The Family and Individual Development*, and *Playing and Reality*.